The Master's Chair

By

Mackenzie Morgan

Cover by John Ward

ISBN-13: 978-1481211338

ISBN-10: 1481211331

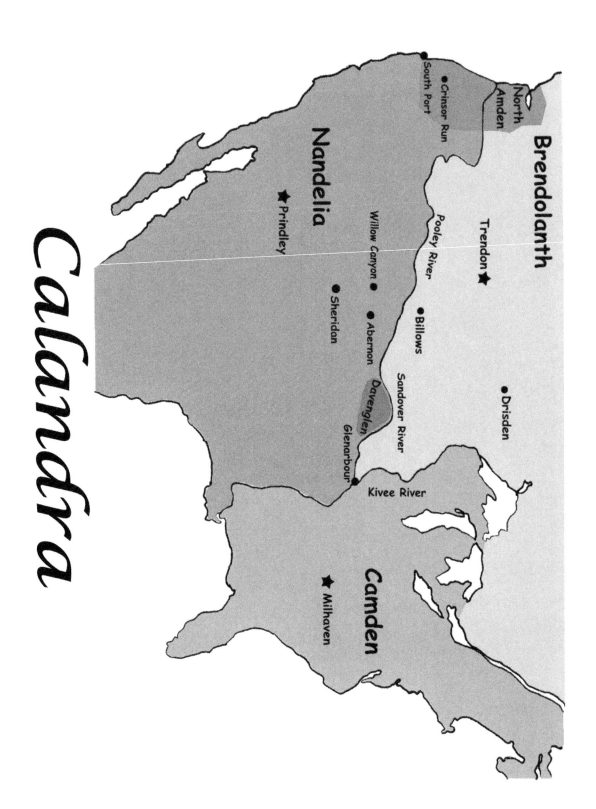

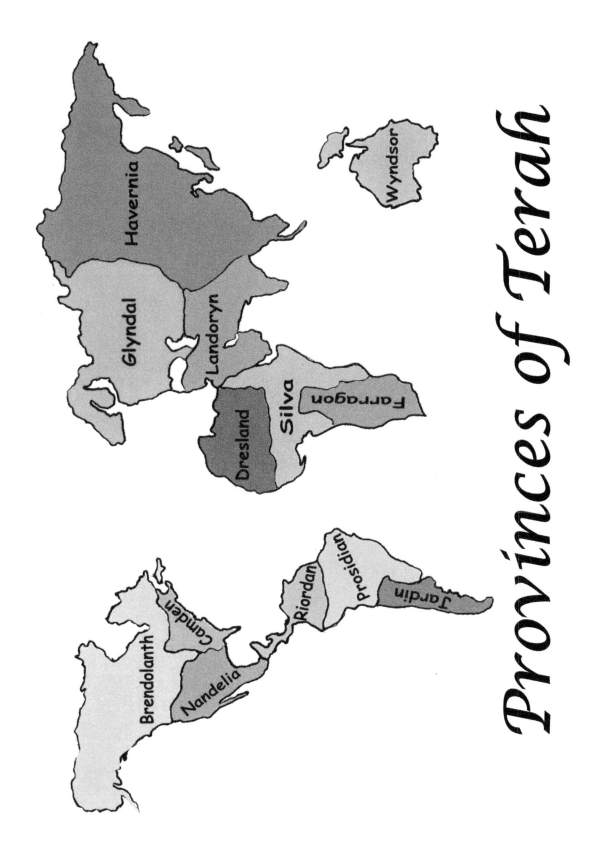

Provinces of Terah

Chapter 1

August, 24 Years Ago

Milhaven, Camden

He had never heard of Charles Dickens but Badec would have agreed with him. It was the best of times; it was the worst of times.

Earlier that evening, his wife, Yvonne, had told him that she'd had a vision. She had seen herself giving birth to their son. She had smiled as she'd told him that she had suspected she might be pregnant, but now she was sure, and since she'd seen blooms on the camellia bushes in her vision, it was her guess that their baby was due sometime around the middle of March.

Badec had been thrilled. They were going to have a child. In only seven short months, their son would draw his first breath. The only time in his life that he'd been happier was the day Yvonne had promised to marry him.

Then, after they had planned the announcement party, made a list of people to invite, and picked out a name for their son, she had quietly told him about the rest of her vision. Yvonne had also seen her own death, less than a week after the birth of their son.

The bottom fell out Badec's world and the despair that swept through him was darker than any he'd ever known.

After Yvonne fell asleep, Badec slipped out onto the balcony and stared through the moonless night. He could just make out the mountains to the east, but the river that ran behind his castle was completely lost in the darkness. The only night sounds were the gentle footsteps of the guards as they patrolled the roof and grounds.

Nothing he had ever experienced could compare to the desolation he felt. He had always known that, barring accidents or assassination, he would outlive Yvonne. The elven blood that had come from his grandmother would extend his lifespan by more than a hundred years, so he had expected to be the one left alone, but it shouldn't have come so soon. They should have had at least another fifty years together. She should have lived long enough to see her son grow up, to see him become a man.

As Badec thought of his son, his heartbeat quickened and a ray of warmth flickered through the deep cold that had settled over his spirit. His first child. His son. His heir.

A sudden chill ran through him. If Yvonne was right, if she did die, this child would be his only child, the one and only heir to the Master's Chair, the most powerful position on all of Terah. His son would be a target for every sorcerer who wanted to take the seat away from the House of Nordin. How was he going to protect him? Where could he send him? Who could raise him? Questions swirled through his mind as the stars slowly made their way across the heavens.

Gradually, as the night wore on, he came to terms with everything Yvonne had told him, and as the pale light of dawn crept over the mountains, Badec turned and left the balcony. He still had no idea how he was going to live without his wife, but at least he had figured out how he was going to protect his son.

~ ~ ~ ~

When Badec reached the office that morning, he greeted his pages, picked up his messages, and headed towards his private office as usual. As he passed Laryn's desk, he asked her to join him for a few minutes.

Laryn picked up some paper and a quill pen and followed her brother into his office. She and Badec were close, closer than most brothers and sisters, closer than the best of friends. She was his confidante, his advisor, his right hand.

Laryn was the only one of the brothers and sisters who had been born without the gift of magic, but what had seemed like a weakness at the time had turned out to be her strength. Instead of spending her childhood with non-magical foster parents like her siblings, she had lived at the castle with their parents. During those years she had watched, and she had learned.

When Badec reached his twenty-fifth birthday and began his training as a sorcerer, he asked her to be his assistant. She quickly agreed and was at his side everyday, encouraging, bullying, cajoling, always driving him to be better, stronger, quicker. When their father died and Badec assumed his role as the Seated Sorcerer of Camden and the Master Sorcerer of Terah, he asked her to be his second, his second-in-command. She didn't even hesitate.

Laryn was also one of the few people in the world who could tell when something was bothering her brother, and before she even closed the door to his office, she knew something was wrong, very wrong.

Badec was already at his desk, thumbing through his messages absent-mindedly, when Laryn sat down at the small desk across the room from him. Without looking up he said, "I need to send some messages. The first one goes to Duane. As far as I know he's in Crinsor Run, but if he isn't, they'll know how to reach him. Ask him if he and Xantha can be here Saturday afternoon. I need to meet with them."

Laryn frowned. "Do you want me to send it or take it?"

"Send it," Badec answered, looking up. "Why?"

"Today's Thursday. If we send it, the earliest he could get it is late tomorrow afternoon. I guess they could probably leave immediately, but even so, it's a long way from Crinsor Run to Milhaven. Xantha's fast, but a pegasus can only fly so far in one day."

Badec hesitated and then nodded. "You're right. Make it for next Saturday, the sixteenth. One week won't really make any difference and it'll give us a little more time to get everything else set up."

Laryn looked up and raised her eyebrows. "Get what set up?"

"I want as few people around here that day as possible. I'd like none, but I have a feeling that's not going to happen."

Laryn agreed. "The guard's not going anywhere."

"I know, but I want to get rid of as many of them as possible. And I want the staff out of here too, the kitchen staff, the groundskeepers, the grooms, the pages, everyone."

"All right," Laryn said slowly. "Have you come up with a cover story or do you want me to?"

"Tell them that we're having a big party the next weekend, on the twenty-third. Yvonne and I made out the guest list last night. We'll get the pages started on the invitations as soon as we get done in here."

Layrn nodded as she made notes.

"Tell the staff that the preparations are going to take a lot of work and I want everyone well-rested before we begin, so everyone is to take two days off before it all starts. Half the staff can take Friday and Saturday and other half can take Saturday and Sunday. We can fend for ourselves for one day." Then, after a moment he added, "With luck, no one will notice the overlap. Some of the grooms might, but if they do, tell them that we'll tend to the horses on Saturday. And as for the ones who live here, tell them to find somewhere else to be that day. They can visit some of their friends or relatives, go to Milhaven, or just go for a walk."

Laryn cut her eyes up to her brother without raising her head. "And I'm supposed to tell them all of this without making them suspicious?"

"You can do it."

"Right," Laryn mumbled. Then she cleared her throat and said, "You do realize that some of the staff feel like we can't survive even one day without them and they'll come in to check on us no matter what you say."

"I know," Badec said with a sigh. "Just do the best you can. We'll plan to meet around 2:00. That will give them time to check us out and see that we're still alive and well. With luck we'll be able to get everyone out of here by lunch." He paused and thought for a minute. "I know you won't be able to get all of the guards to go, but try to have as few here as possible, and only the most closemouthed and loyal."

Laryn frowned. "If you're that concerned about privacy, why not hold the meeting somewhere else?"

Badec shook his head. "I considered that, but I really want to hold it here."

"Is there anyone else you want at this meeting?"

"Kalen, the dwarf."

"The Gate Keeper?"

Badec nodded. "And Pallor, but I'll take care of notifying him. Oh, and tell Kalen that I'm going to ask Pallor to go by the Gate House to pick him up."

"All right. How long should I ask them to be prepared to stay?"

"An hour or so. The meeting won't take long. Of course Duane and Xantha are welcome to stay the night, or longer it they want to, before they head back."

Laryn grinned. "That'll make Shelandra happy."

"Shelandra?"

"You know, the elf who's been helping out in the kitchen so that she can learn more about how humans prepare their food. She and our cooks have been exchanging recipes for months. Anyway, she has a bit of a thing for Duane, and I'm sure I saw his eyes light up when she brought him a mug of scog the last time he was here."

"Are you sure it wasn't the scog that put that light in his eyes?"

Laryn rolled her eyes in answer.

"Then why hasn't he done something about it?"

"He's too shy, but if he hangs around here very much, she'll take care of it."

"Poor boy," Badec said, shaking his head.

Laryn chuckled. "Anything else?"

"Not as far as the meeting is concerned, but I'd like for you to personally send the party invitations to the family. I'd like for them to be here by Friday afternoon and stay through Monday if they can. Tell them we'll pick them up if they want us to."

Laryn nodded.

Then Badec handed her the list he and Yvonne had made the night before. "Here's the rest of the guest list. I've put stars by the ones who'll probably need some place to stay. After the invitations have been sent, have the pages get to work on the housing, and send one of the pages into town to hang up signs inviting everyone in the area to the feast that Saturday."

Laryn nodded and gathered her notes.

"Oh, and one more thing. Send a message to Glendymere. I'd like to talk to him about something when he has a free morning."

Laryn stood up to go but hesitated before opening the door. She turned back to her brother and asked, "Is everything all right?"

Badec waffled his hand. "I'll fill you in later. For now, just get those messages off."

~ ~ ~ ~

After lunch on the sixteenth, Laryn carried a pitcher of scog back to the office to wait for Duane, Pallor, and Kalen to arrive. The castle was so empty it felt spooky. She had never heard it so quiet. Even in the dead of night you could hear footsteps as the guards walked their patrols, but today there were only two guards on duty, and they were both outside.

Duane and Xantha had flown in on Thursday, but the August heat was too much for the elf, so, much to Shelandra's dismay, he and Xantha had flown up to one of the nearby mountaintops and set up camp.

Duane had promised Laryn that they would get back before two, and at half past one, he walked through the office door. "I don't see why in the world Badec doesn't move his castle to the top of a mountain somewhere, some place where you can breathe. This heat's stifling."

Laryn smiled and asked, "Would you like some scog?"

Before Duane could answer, the air shimmered and Pallor and Kalen materialized. They made an odd looking pair. Pallor was almost a carbon copy of his cousin Duane: over six feet tall, thin as a rail, with pointed ears and diamond shaped eyes. Kalen, on the other hand, didn't quite come up to Pallor's waist and he was about half as wide as he was tall. Like all dwarves, he was incredibly strong, but not very agile.

After Laryn greeted Pallor and Kalen, she stepped back behind her desk, out of the way. The three men had been friends longer than she'd been alive, and she knew she wouldn't get a word in edgewise for the next few minutes. While she was waiting for things to settle down, she poured three mugs of scog and handed them out.

When her guests had finished their scog and caught each other up-to-date, Kalen turned towards her and asked, "What's this all about, Laryn?

"I don't know," she answered with a slight shrug. "He told me to ask you to come, but he didn't tell me why. I imagine we'll all find out in a few minutes." Then she turned towards Duane and asked, "Where's Xantha? Badec wants him to be at this meeting, too."

Duane's eyebrows twitched, but he shrugged and said, "I left him out at the stable, with his head in a bucket of oats. I assume he's still out there somewhere."

"Well, I guess it's time," Laryn said. "Badec and Yvonne are waiting for us in the garden." She led her guests out of the office, through the castle, and out the back.

Laryn was so nervous that her palms were damp. Badec had never kept anything from her before. Over the past week, she had given him several openings, but her brother hadn't told her what was wrong, and she knew that something was, something major.

When they reached the stable, Xantha was standing near the water trough. *"Are you sure he wants me at the meeting? I'll be more than happy to wait out here,"* he asked telepathically, as his eyes slid away from Laryn and over to the half-empty bucket of oats.

"I'm sure," Laryn said with a weak smile. She reached up and scratched Xantha between his ears. "Come on. I'll get you some more oats after we find out what Badec wants."

With a longing look at the bucket, Xantha fell in behind the others.

As Laryn led them toward the garden gate, the two guards who were on duty that afternoon stepped to the side to let them pass and then resumed their positions blocking the entrance.

In the middle of the garden was a small circular clearing bordered by four benches and backed by a wall about three feet high. Yvonne was seated on one of the benches and Badec was standing behind her, with his hands on her shoulders. After everyone was settled in the clearing, the wall began to glow and electrical sparks danced along the top. The air above the wall shimmered and a dome of bright light formed over their heads. Then Badec nodded to all of them, sat down beside Yvonne, and took her hand.

Laryn looked closely at her brother and his wife. He was a solidly built man, about forty years old, handsome in a rugged sort of way, with intense, dark eyes. She was slim, in her mid-thirties, with a delicate beauty and large, soft brown eyes. Usually there was a happy glow about them whenever they were together but now they both looked tense, and whatever was causing the strain had added years to their faces. The knot of apprehension tightened in the pit of Laryn's stomach.

"A little more than a week ago, Yvonne had a vision," Badec began, and then he paused, not sure what to say next.

"I saw our son's birth," Yvonne said, picking up the thread of conversation. "It should be in about seven months, sometime around the middle of March."

"Congratulations!" Duane said with a big grin. "It's about time you had an heir, Badec."

"That's wonderful news, but why all the secrecy?" Pallor asked as he waved his hand towards the sparkling dome.

"I don't think that's all she has to tell us," Kalen cautioned quietly.

"Kalen's right," Yvonne said matter-of-factly. "My son's birth wasn't all I saw in that vision. I also saw my own death a few days later."

The silence was complete. Badec sighed, took Yvonne's hand, raised it to his lips, and gently kissed it.

Laryn felt like her insides were collapsing and she had trouble getting her breath. Tears began to well in her eyes and a thick knot formed in the back of her throat. It couldn't be true. Not Yvonne. Not yet. He wasn't ready. None of them were.

"Are you sure?" Duane asked. "I mean, do your visions always ...?"

Yvonne nodded. "Yes, at least they've always come true in the past."

"I don't know what to say," Kalen whispered.

Yvonne held up her hand, palm out. "Please," she whispered. Then she cleared her throat again and said, "We're not here to talk about my death. I'm not afraid to die, although as I'm sure you can imagine, I'd rather it weren't going to be quite so soon. But the reason we asked you here is to make arrangements for my son's future. I need to know that he'll be all right, that everything is ready for him."

Badec slipped his arm around Yvonne's waist. "Since he'll be my only child, we need to find a foster home where he'll be safe from my enemies for the next twenty-five years."

Kalen glanced around the group, his gaze settling on Pallor. "You want to hide him on Earth, don't you?"

Badec hesitated a moment and then nodded. "There's no place on Terah where he'd really be safe. As he begins to grow up, if he resembles either one of us ... " Badec shook his head. "We're too well known. Someone would figure it out."

"Not to mention that if he's half as powerful as you are magically ... ," Duane began.

Badec nodded and finished for him. "Any sorcerer anywhere nearby would figure it out before he was six years old."

Pallor cleared his throat and asked, "But who's going to raise him? Do you have someone in mind? Do you know someone on Earth?"

Badec shook his head no. "That's where you come in. You're the only one who's lived on Earth lately. I was hoping you might have some thoughts along that line."

"Right off hand, I have absolutely no idea where to start, but let me think about it," Pallor said.

"Are you or Laryn planning to visit him on Earth and let him know who he really is?" Duane asked.

"We can't. It would be too risky," Badec answered, looking at Laryn.

"No one could follow you to Earth," Pallor pointed out.

"I feel sure you're right about that, but that's not the problem," Badec answered. "No one from Earth knows that Terah exists. We want to keep it that way. I don't know what might happen if my son found out he was from another world, much less that his father is a sorcerer."

"Then he's not going to know who he is until he returns to Terah?" Kalen asked hesitantly.

Badec shook his head.

"Won't that cause a lot of problems when it's time for him to return?" Pallor asked. "What if he's not willing to leave?"

"He won't have any choice," Yvonne said quietly. "It would be best if my son grows up thinking that his foster parents are his real parents, but even if they tell him that he's not theirs, he can't know anything about us until he returns to Terah." Yvonne paused, took a deep breath, and said, "I know what I'm going to say will sound harsh, but even though his foster parents must care enough about him to provide for him and protect him, there needs to be a distance, almost a coldness between them, so that he doesn't feel torn when the time comes to leave them behind." She looked directly at Pallor. "You know the kind of man he needs to be as well as we do, and I'm afraid that the burden of making sure he's ready to handle whatever he has to is going to fall primarily on your shoulders. I know it's a lot to ask, but you're the only one who can do it."

Pallor stared at her for a full minute and then slowly nodded.

"Xantha," Badec said in his mind, and waited for the pegasus to answer.

"I know. A mind link," Xantha answered Badec privately.

"Please."

Xantha nodded, but Badec was the only one who noticed.

Then Badec stood up and said, "I trust the five of you to work out the details for fostering my son. Guard him well. The future of Terah will rest on his shoulders."

The air over the wall cleared as Badec put his arm around his wife's shoulders and led her out of the garden.

After they were out of sight, Duane quietly asked, "What do we do now? We can't very well discuss this out here in the open."

"Badec probably doesn't want it discussed around here at all," Kalen answered.

Laryn swallowed hard. "Maybe we should meet at the Gate House."

Pallor shook his head. "I need to go back to Earth first. I've got a lot of research to do before we can make any plans." Then he took a four inch silver key out of his pocket and looked at Kalen. "Are you ready to go? I'll drop you off at the Gate House before I head back to Earth."

"Wait a minute," Duane said, putting his hand on Pallor's arm. "When are we going to meet? How long do you need? A week?"

Pallor shook his head. "I don't know, but let's plan to meet in a month. How about four weeks from today? By then I should at least have a better idea what we're up against." He held his arm out to Kalen and Kalen put his hand on Pallor's arm.

Duane and Laryn nodded as the air shimmered and Pallor and Kalen vanished.

Chapter 2

Pallor Investigates

Within minutes Pallor was in his office in his house back on Earth. He supported himself by writing fantasy and mystery novels under the name of Paul Stewart. It wasn't his first pseudonym, and it probably wouldn't be his last, but he figured he had another twenty or thirty years before he had to come up with a new identity and break into writing all over again.

One of the advantages of being an author was that he could live anywhere he wanted to, which for the past ten years had been about fifteen miles from Seattle. It also provided a perfect excuse for him to ask questions, and he'd cultivated contacts all over the United States, all in the name of research.

Even with all the research he'd done in the past, Pallor had no idea how to go about arranging for an adoption, it had never come up before, so he started pacing and thinking. Surely, among all the people he knew, there was someone who could point him in the right direction.

After a few minutes he paused. He'd call Mike.

Mike Kirkpatrick was a lawyer. He represented Pallor with publishing companies and was the closest thing to a friend that Pallor had ever had on Earth. Mike would know where to begin.

Pallor sat down at his desk and picked up the phone. He tried the office number first, even though it was Saturday afternoon. After the fifth ring, the answering service picked up. He hung up and dialed Mike's home phone. On the third ring, a familiar voice said, "Hello, you've reached the Kirkpatrick residence. Top dog speaking."

Pallor chuckled. "You're in a good mood."

"Yeah, I am," Mike admitted. "I've got a steak thawing, a nice bottle of wine, and there's a baseball game on television. Life can't get much better than that. What're you up to?"

"I've got a slight problem, and I wanted to talk to you about it."

"Work?"

"Not really. Personal."

"Okay, why don't you come on over. Katie's out buying school stuff with the kids this afternoon. Then she's going to take them for a pizza and a movie, so we'll have the house to ourselves for a while. I'll pull another steak out of the freezer."

"Fine. Be there in half an hour."

~ ~ ~ ~

During the baseball game, Pallor thought about several different ways he could present his problem to Mike. He finally decided to use the "my friend has a problem" approach, which had the added advantage of being true.

While they were outside grilling the steaks, he said, "Mike, I have a friend who's pregnant and wants to put her baby up for adoption."

"That won't be a problem. There are a lot of people out there who want to adopt an infant. All she'd have to do is get in touch with an adoption agency and they'd handle all the details. I can get you a list of the top agencies if you want me to."

"I don't think that's going to work."

"Why not?"

"She wants me to pick out the parents and keep an eye on things until her son is grown."

Mike frowned and slowly shook his head. "The birth mother gives up all rights once the adoption is final."

"She's not willing to do that."

Mike concentrated on the steaks and didn't say anything for a few minutes. Finally he sighed and said, "It's possible that you might be able to find someone through a private adoption who would agree to your terms, but I doubt it. How much money does your friend want for her baby?"

Pallor shook his head vigorously. "No, it's not like that, Mike. She doesn't want any money."

"Are you sure? Most birth mothers get quite a bit for their babies in private adoptions."

"I'm positive. No money. She'll pay her lawyer's fees and the adoptive parents can pay the agency or lawyer they deal with, but no money comes to her."

"Well, if they don't have to pay her, it may be a little easier to find someone who'd agree to her conditions. Let me make a couple of phone calls Monday and see what I can come up with. When do you want to get started on the search?"

"The baby's not due until March, but she wants this settled. I'd like to be able to have everything set up within a month if possible."

Mike nodded and then gave Pallor a long, searching look. "Let me ask one question, and remember, I'm your lawyer. Nothing you tell me goes any farther."

Pallor nodded.

"Are you the baby's father?"

Pallor's mouth dropped open. It hadn't crossed his mind that someone might think that, but it was a logical conclusion. "No. Honest. She's just a friend. Not a girlfriend."

"And you're willing to go through the hassle of meeting with lawyers, interviewing prospective parents, setting up the adoption, and keeping tabs on her child for the next eighteen or twenty years for 'just a friend'?"

"She's a very good friend."

Mike looked at Pallor sideways and mumbled, "She must be."

~ ~ ~ ~

Monday morning Pallor was seated at his desk trying to concentrate on the plot to a new book when the phone rang. It was Mike.

"I've got a lawyer lined up for you. I think you'll like him, and he's good."

"Great. When can I see him?"

"How about 1:30 this afternoon?"

Pallor grabbed a notepad and jotted down the time. "What's his name?"

"Charles Blalock," Mike answered. Then he gave Pallor directions to Blalock's office.

"How much did you tell him?"

"That you had a friend who needed to put her baby up for adoption, that she wanted to pick the parents, and that you were going to be keeping an eye on the child until he's grown."

"What was his reaction to that?"

"He said it would make it a little harder for you to find the right couple, but not impossible." Pallor could hear papers rustling in the background. Then Mike said, "Look, I've got a client waiting, I've got to go. But one more thing. Take a few minutes this morning and get exactly what you're looking for and what stipulations you want on the adoption contract outlined in your head. The more information you can give him up front, the better."

"Got it," Pallor said. "And thanks. I owe you."

"Next time you bring the steaks and the wine," Mike said as he hung up the phone.

~ ~ ~ ~

At 1:00, Pallor parked in the small parking area at the rear of one of the old homes in Seattle that had been transformed into offices. According to Mike, Mr. Blalock's office was on the second floor, so Pallor got out of his car and made his way around to the front of the house and up to the second floor. When he opened the door to Mr. Blalock's office, the receptionist looked up from her computer, took off her glasses, and asked, "May I help you?"

"I'm here to see Mr. Charles Blalock."

"And your name?" she asked as she opened a thick appointment book.

"Paul Stewart."

"I'm sorry, but I don't have a Paul Stewart listed for today, sir, and Mr. Blalock is quite busy. Would you like to schedule an appointment?" she asked as she put her glasses back on and picked up a pen.

Pallor frowned. "If you don't mind, would you check with him? I'm sure he said 1:30 today."

She grumbled, but she picked up the phone and said, "Mr. Blalock? There's a man out here who says he has a 1:30 appointment with you. I don't have his name on the schedule." A few seconds later she put her hand over the mouthpiece and asked, "What did you say your name was?"

"Paul Stewart."

"A Mr. Paul Stewart." Another pause. "Oh, I see." She covered the mouthpiece again, smiled at Pallor, and pointed towards one of the doors. "You may go in now, Mr. Stewart."

"Thank you."

As Pallor walked toward the door, he heard her say, "Mr. Blalock, I've asked you not to do that. When you make appointments, you never write them down out here, and then I end up scheduling someone else in that same time slot and before you know it, we have an office full of unhappy people."

Pallor grinned to himself and gently knocked on the door. When he heard a muffled "Come in," he opened the door and walked inside.

Mr. Blalock motioned Pallor to a seat while he was still holding the phone to his ear. He rolled his eyes and said, "Yes, Marcy. I see your point. We'll have to talk about it later. Mr. Stewart is here for his appointment." Mr. Blalock hung up the phone and turned towards Pallor. "Sometimes I wonder who's the boss around here. Well, what can I do for you? Mr. Kirkpatrick said something about an adoption problem?"

Pallor nodded. "I need to find an adoptive home for a boy who will be born next spring, probably mid-March."

Mr. Blalock pulled out a legal pad and began making notes. "All right. What can you tell me about the family you're looking for?"

Pallor frowned. He wasn't sure what Mr. Blalock meant.

"Do you want the child to have siblings, or would you rather he be an only child?"

"No siblings."

"What race?"

"White. Both of his parents are white."

Mr. Blalock kept writing as he asked, "What about religious preference?"

"Protestant."

"Financial status?"

"Well, they have to be financially secure."

"What area of the country are you interested in? Around here? I understand you'll be keeping a check on the child."

"It really doesn't matter. I don't need to live in the same area, just check in on him a couple of times a year."

Mr. Blalock nodded. "Now, what else can you tell me about them?"

Pallor had put some thought into this, but he still wasn't sure what to say. "Well, the mother wants him to be well-cared for, but not smothered, so it would probably be better if he were not the center of their lives. She wants him to grow up to be independent and to think for himself, but at the same time to respect other people and their ideas, so they can't be domineering or intolerant."

"Are you planning to interview the prospective parents yourself?"

"Yes."

"Good, because I doubt if any of these things are going to show up in background checks or financial statements, but when I hire the private investigator, I'll clue him in on what to look out for."

Pallor nodded.

"Does she have any feelings one way or the other about the schools he attends? Would public school be okay? Or is she going to want him to go to private schools?"

"Based on his parents, he should be quite intelligent and she does want to make sure he's challenged intellectually. It sort of depends on where he's living and what the schools are like around there, but if he needs private schools, she'll be happy to pay for them. And she'll pick up the tab for college."

Mr. Blalock held out his hand, palm out, as he continued writing. "I'd leave that out for now. Let's just say that you'll need access to all medical and school records. Then, later, if you think he needs to go to a private school, you can make arrangements with the adoptive parents. You don't want to mention that the birth mother would be willing to pay for it up front, or they'll go on a shopping spree for the most expensive schools they can find, starting with daycare. And if I were you, I'd wait until the child is ready to start applying to colleges before you decide how you want to handle that. You may want to pay the school directly and let him attend on a scholarship-type deal, especially if you have a particular school in mind that you want him to go to."

Pallor nodded.

"What else?"

"I don't know how to word this, but it has to be in the contract somewhere that if I think he's being abused, neglected, or harmed in any way, I'm going to pull him out of that home."

Mr. Blalock lifted his eyebrows, but he kept on writing. "All right. That may limit your choices a bit, but I'll see what I can do. Anything else?"

"She doesn't want him in any kind of spotlight, so no celebrities, no one who's going to go into politics, or anything like that, and of course, no criminal records."

Mr. Blalock nodded as he continued making notes. When he finished writing, he looked up at Pallor expectantly.

Pallor shook his head and said, "Something else may come up once I start interviewing, but that's all I can think of right now."

"Okay. Now, about my retainer. Who's going to be paying that?"

"She's going to pay it, but you'll get it from me. She doesn't want anything that'll lead back to her."

"She'll have to sign the adoption papers."

Pallor shook his head.

"All right. I'll see what I can work out." Then he picked up his phone, punched a button, and said, "Marcy, Mr. Stewart is leaving now. Please set up a follow-up appointment for two weeks from today." After he hung up the phone he said, "I should be able to have some names for you by then. I understand you want to have this settled in about a month?"

"I want to be able to present her with some options in a month. She'll make the final decision."

"Of course. Are you going to handle setting up the interviews?"

"Yes. I want to see them in their homes. I want to get a feel for what it would be like if he were to live there."

Mr. Blalock nodded. "I'm going to make a suggestion. You can take it or not. When you get ready to interview the prospective parents, tell them when you'll be there rather than ask them when it would be convenient. You want to set yourself up as the dominant one in this arrangement from the beginning. It's a little thing, but…"

"Thank you. That's a good suggestion," Pallor said as he took out his checkbook. "Now, if you'll tell me how much you need up front…"

~ ~ ~ ~

Two weeks later, on Tuesday, September 2, Pallor walked back into Mr. Blalock's office. Marcy was typing away, but this time when she looked up at him, she smiled and nodded. "Good afternoon, Mr. Stewart. He's expecting you in the conference room," she said as she stood up and led the way to a different door.

When the door opened, Pallor saw Mr. Blalock seated at the head of a large table with a stack of folders in front of him.

"Would you like something to drink?" Marcy asked.

"No, thank you."

Mr. Blalock motioned for Pallor to have a seat as Marcy quietly left and shut the door. "I've found six couples who meet your requirements and who are willing to agree to the stipulations that you want included in the contract. I won't pretend that they're all the cream of the crop as far as parents go though."

"I understand. I'm just glad you were able to find so many who would agree to the terms."

Mr. Blalock nodded and pointed to the folders. "Do you want to go over the files here, or do you want to take them with you?"

"What's in them?"

"Mainly background checks and financial statements. Each of these couples has approached a lawyer who handles private adoptions. That's how I got their names. Some said they were tired of waiting for a child; some said they didn't want the hassle of dealing with an adoption agency. Truthfully, most of them have probably been turned down for one reason or another. Anyway, their lawyers provided us with some basic information based on their interviews with their clients. I have to tell you, it's going to take you some time to go through all this."

"Then I'd rather take them with me. Do you have a box or something?"

Mr. Blalock got up to get one. "I know you're planning to go to their homes to interview them, so I had their lawyers provide directions. I hope they're accurate, but I wouldn't guarantee it."

"Thanks."

Mr. Blalock packed the folders in a box, handed it to Pallor, and opened the door for him. "Let me know what you want me to do next. If she's happy with one of these, we'll get started on the paperwork. If not, we'll go back and search some more, although I can't promise that we'll find anyone she'll like any better."

~ ~ ~ ~

As soon as Pallor got home, he went through the six sets of folders to find the addresses. He jotted down the names of the towns, picked up the phone, and called his travel agent. When he got her on the line, he said, "Cynthia, I've got a challenging problem for you. If you can get it all worked out, I'll take you out to dinner, anywhere you want to go."

"Right. I'll just add that to the list of what you already owe me," she said with a chuckle. Then she got serious. "Okay. Where are you off to now?"

"Los Angeles, Key Biscayne, New York City, Memphis, Aspen, and Ottumwa, Iowa."

"What are you doing? A book tour?"

"No, interviews. Look, I don't care what order I go in, but I've got to get in and out of all these cities and be back here by Friday, September 12. Oh, and if you can arrange it, I'd like to be in New York at some point over the weekend."

"When can you leave?"

"Tomorrow."

"Okay. Since you're doing interviews, you'll need at least twenty-four hours in each of the cities, right?"

"Yes, and a rental car."

"And a hotel room. Got it. I'll call you back in a couple of hours. Wish me luck!"

But before he could do that, she'd hung up the phone.

Chapter 3

The Search Begins

By lunchtime on Wednesday, Pallor was flying towards Aspen, Colorado. Once again, Cynthia had come through. He was booked into a hotel less than a mile from the airport and a rental car was supposed to be waiting for him when he landed.

After he had picked up his itinerary Tuesday afternoon, he'd called Mr. and Mrs. Haverston and made an appointment for Wednesday evening at 7:00 at their condo. He figured he'd get back to the hotel sometime around 10:00, which would give him plenty of time to get a good night's sleep. His flight out of Aspen wasn't until Thursday afternoon.

While he was in flight, Pallor went back over the background and financial statements on the Haverstons. The background checks listed Marvin Haverston's age as thirty-eight and Clarissa's as thirty-five, and although he had attended Dartmouth, there was no record that he'd graduated, and there was no indication that she'd even graduated from high school. They had been married for ten years, but had been engaged for more than three years before they got married, and had been seeing each other for a couple of years before that. There was a note from the private investigator that it seemed to be common knowledge that the reason they'd had such a long engagement was that his mother disapproved of her and had threatened to cut her son off if he married her. Although his mother eventually relented, she still felt that her son had married beneath him.

According to the investigator, their only income was a monthly allowance from his mother. The title to the condo was in her name, as were the titles to the cars registered to that address, and she was the one who paid the maid, cook, and chauffeur.

Pallor checked into the hotel, ate dinner, and drove out to their condo. As he approached the area, he could tell the price of real estate was going up. The housing developments were farther and farther from the main road, and when he reached theirs, he found a manned security gate. After he had shown his ID and the guard had called the Haverstons to verify that they were expecting him, the guard gave him explicit directions as to where to park and then opened the gate to let him through.

A woman in her early twenties opened the door when he rang the bell and asked him to follow her. She was dressed in a dark gray maid's uniform and led him down an entrance hall lined with expensive paintings. The floor was covered with various-sized oriental rugs, and although she walked on them as if they were nothing, he felt guilty stepping on them. They were of museum quality. When they reached an arched opening, she stepped to the side and waved him through.

The room he entered was done completely in white: white furniture, white walls, white carpet, white curtains, and white throw pillows. The only color was provided by the ornate collection of blown glass that was scattered about on every flat surface in the room.

Clarissa Haverston was draped over one of the long white couches in a flimsy dressing gown that was probably advertised as a hostess gown and sold for hundreds of dollars. She was smoking a cigarette in an eight-inch holder and drinking champagne out of a flute. Marvin Haverston stood next to the fireplace in a red velvet smoking jacket, complete with ascot. He had a pipe in one hand and a shot glass with an amber liquid in it in the other.

As Pallor entered, Mr. Haverston raised his glass in greeting and said, "Would you care for a shot of thirty-year-old Laphroaig? Sorry I can't offer you anything older, but the last time we were in London, they were out of the forty-year-old."

Pallor shook his head and said, "No, thank you. I'm driving, and I'm not familiar with the area, but I do appreciate the offer." He had an incredible urge to laugh. The whole thing looked so staged. Surely these people didn't live like this. No one did.

Mr. Haverston waved with his pipe towards one of the chairs. "Have a seat, my good man. Are you sure there's nothing we can get you?"

"No, really, I'm fine," Pallor said as he sat on the edge of the chair Mr. Haverston had indicated. "If you don't mind, I'm a little pressed for time. I just arrived in Aspen a couple of hours ago, and I have to catch a plane out of here tomorrow, and I do have a few questions that I'd like to ask."

"Anything," Mrs. Haverston said, "and please, call me Clarissa."

Pallor thanked her and said, " It's obvious that you're well off, and I feel sure that you would qualify for a child with the regular adoption agencies. Could you tell me why you're interested in a private adoption?"

Clarissa fluttered her eyes and said, "I have a feeling we can trust Mr. Stewart. Don't you, dear?"

Mr. Haverston grunted. "I guess so, but we can't take any chances that anything we tell you will get back to Mummy."

Pallor had the urge to laugh again, but he stifled it and nodded. "Anything you tell me will be kept in strictest confidence."

Clarissa and her husband looked at each other for a moment, and then he nodded, so she said, "When I was younger, about seventeen, I made a little boo-boo and had to have it taken care of. Only the doctor wasn't that good a doctor, and I ended up unable to have babies."

When Pallor didn't say anything, Haverston cleared his throat and added, "You see, Mummy considers it my duty to provide her with a grandchild, preferably a grandson, to carry on the family name. She's been after us to get pregnant ever since the wedding, and lately she's started threatening to cut us off if we don't. Only Clarissa can't and we can't tell her why. If Mummy knew about Clarissa's past, she'd have our marriage annulled."

Clarissa nodded. "We'll have to pretend that I'm pregnant and tell her that the child is ours. She can't ever know that it's adopted."

"You do understand that if you were to adopt my friend's son, I'll have to have free access to everything, don't you?" Pallor asked.

"Certainly. That's no problem," Mr. Haverston said. "We just have to insist that Mummy never find out that he's not ours. She'd cut me off in a heartbeat, and then where would we be?"

Where indeed? Pallor thought. "Where would you raise your son? Here, in Aspen?"

"Sometimes," Clarissa said. "We have this condo, a house in Boston, the condo in Palm Springs, and a house in Bermuda. We find that things go better if we stay wherever my husband's mother isn't."

"I see," Pallor said. "What about school?"

Mr. Haverston spoke up. "When the time comes for school, you can help us pick out a good boarding school, maybe something overseas."

Pallor nodded and stood up. "Well, I guess that about covers everything I had. Do you have any questions?"

Clarissa nodded. "Just a couple. Is the mother all right? And do you know anything about the father? I mean, we don't want a child who's going to be handicapped or crazy or anything."

How about a sorcerer? Or a seer? Pallor thought. "I assure you, she's intelligent, sane, and healthy, and so is he. She just can't keep the child. She has a career that's very important to her and it takes all of her time."

"Well, not quite all of her time," Clarissa giggled.

"When will you be bringing us the child?" Mr. Haverston asked.

Pallor hesitated and then said, "I'm afraid there might have been a miscommunication. I'm interviewing several couples for the mother. She has the final say. I'll get back with you in about a month, one way or the other. And if she decides that she'd like for you to raise her son, we'll sort out all the details then."

"Well, should I go ahead and announce my pregnancy?" Clarissa asked.

"No, not yet," Pallor said, thinking never, if it were up to him. "The baby isn't due until mid-March. There'll be plenty of time to make announcements later." Then Pallor thanked them for their time and left.

~ ~ ~ ~

His flight from Aspen to Des Moines didn't leave until 4:00 Thursday afternoon, so Thursday morning, before checking out of his hotel, he reviewed the folder on the Peters. They were both in their early forties and had grown up on adjoining farms. After they married, their parents had sold them both of the farms for nominal amounts, so while on paper they were worth quite a bit, as far as working capital was concerned, they were living season to season. A bad year would pretty much wipe them out. Their only fallback was a couple hundred acres of woodlands that could either be sold outright or cut for lumber. They had used lumber from a few of the acres to pay the initial fees with their lawyer. Neither of them had gone to college, but both had finished high school, and Mr. Peters had taken several extension courses through a local community college.

By the time he had arrived in Des Moines, picked up his rental car, grabbed a bite to eat, and driven to Ottumwa, he was bushed. All he wanted was a shower and a bed.

After he checked into his motel, he pulled out the directions to the Peters's farm and compared them to the area map that had been left for him in the rental car. He had told them to expect him at 9:00 Friday morning, so he figured he'd need to leave Ottumwa by 8:00, giving himself an hour to find the place. He set his travel alarm clock for 6:30 and went to bed.

At ten minutes till nine the next morning, he pulled off the narrow country highway onto a dirt track that served as the Peters's driveway. As he drove toward the house, he looked around him. The barns all seemed to be in good shape: good roofs, fresh paint, yards clear of debris. The few pieces of farm equipment that were out and about showed signs of use but also signs of care and attention. He could see a mixture of crops, cow pastures, and woods from the road, but he had no idea how much belonged to the Peters. The farmhouse was a two-story frame house with wide porches, several chimneys poking out of the roof, and huge trees in the yard. It looked like it had been standing there for at least fifty years, probably longer.

Several dogs came out from under the porch when he pulled up in front of the house and parked the car. As he stepped out of the car, one of them approached, sniffed, and gave his hand a quick lick. Then, seeing the lead dog's sign of approval, the rest of the pack came towards him, wagging their tails.

While he was petting the dogs, the front door opened and a woman stepped outside. She was wearing a plain dress, an apron, ankle socks, and cheap tennis shoes. Her hair had been pulled back in a ponytail, but a few strands had escaped the rubber band and were hanging down around her face. As she wiped her hands on her apron, she cocked her head to one side and asked, "Mr. Stewart?"

Pallor nodded, still petting the dogs.

"We've been expecting you. Mr. Peters is out at the barn seeing to the one of the cows. He'll be in directly. Come on in."

15

Pallor nodded and followed her into the house. She led him through the living room into the kitchen where a big pot of something was steaming on the stove.

"I'm canning vegetables today, so we'll have to sit in here and talk so I can keep an eye on things. Can't afford to waste a pot full of beans." She picked up a big wooden spoon and stirred the pot a couple of times. Then she turned away from the stove and waved Pallor towards a chair at the kitchen table. After he set down, she asked, "Care for some coffee? I perked it about 4:30 this morning for breakfast, but there's still a little left in the pot. I've been keeping it hot just in case."

Pallor pictured the thick black sludge that would be left in the bottom of the pot after hours of sitting on a hot stove and said, "No, thank you. I'm fine."

Mrs. Peters nodded and turned back to the stove.

A few minutes later, a man walked through the back door. He was wearing a pair of dirty coveralls, a short-sleeve tee shirt, and work boots. He wiped his feet on the little rug in front of the door and nodded towards Pallor. "Mr. Stewart, right?" Again Pallor nodded. Mr. Peters pulled out the chair opposite Pallor and said, "Well, let's get this over with. I've got work to do. Don't have time to be sitting in here jawing all day."

"I'll try to be as brief as possible," Pallor said. "First of all, why are you using a private adoption lawyer? Why not go through the state agency?"

"They take up too much of your time," Mr. Peters said. "Want you to come in for interviews with all kinds of people and take classes in how to raise a kid. People been doing it for thousands of years without no classes. Our parents sure didn't take any. No, we don't have the time to waste on all their mess."

"I see," Pallor said slowly. "Why do you want a child if you're so busy already?"

"To help out," Mr. Peters said as if that was the most stupid question he'd ever heard. "Everyone knows that farm families depend on their children to keep the farm going. We can't have none ourselves. My fault. Some kind of sickness when I was a kid. Anyway, we figure that we can count on maybe another twelve, fourteen years before I start needing some real help around here, help that we don't have to pay for that is. And if we get a boy now, he'll be ready to pull his share of the load about then."

Pallor nodded as if the man's explanations were the most logical in the world. "How do you feel about school?"

"Law says they have to go, they go. We finished school. Expect he will too, but most of what he needs to know, he'll learn right here."

"What if he wants to go to college?"

"No need of that," Mr. Peters said.

"Well, if he really wants to, we might let him, if we can find someone else to help out around here while he's gone," Mrs. Peters said, laying her hand on her husband's shoulder. "Wouldn't hurt to learn some of the things that they teach over at the college. We'll have to see how things are going."

Pallor nodded politely.

"Look, this kid'll have it made," Mr. Peters said. "If he plays his cards right, stays out of trouble, does what we tell him, and takes care of us when we get old, this place'll be his one day. Can't ask for much more than that."

"No, sir, you sure can't," Pallor agreed. Then he stood up and held his hand out to Mr. Peters. "I've taken up enough of your time. I know you're a busy man. Thanks for taking the time to talk to me."

Mr. Peters stood up too, held his hand out, and grasped Pallor's in a bone-crushing grip. "Glad to talk to you. Now when can we expect that kid?"

"I'm only conducting the initial interviews. I'll go back to the mother and tell her what you said and what you have to offer, but the final decision's hers."

"As it should be," Mrs. Peters said quietly. "A mother always knows what's best for her child."

Pallor nodded, hoping that she was right. "Thanks again for your time. I'll see myself out."

~ ~ ~ ~

After he left Ottumwa, Pallor drove back to Des Moines. His flight to New York wasn't until early Saturday morning, so after checking into his next motel, he wandered around town for a while, had an early dinner, and went back to his room to go through the folders on the Johanssons, his next interview.

Harold Johansson had just turned forty. He was an advertising executive with a small but growing firm. According to the investigator, he was quite good, good enough that his present firm had actively recruited him for over a year before convincing him to leave the firm he was with and come in with them. Christina Johansson was thirty-seven. She was a professional photographer, and considered one of the best in the field. She worked for the fashion industry and advertising agencies, free-lanced for newspapers, had done the photos for several travel books, and had a studio where she did private portraits. Their financial statement was impressive. They made good money, invested wisely, and spent less that they made. Their only outstanding debt was for their condo in New York. Their house outside Richmond was paid for. All in all, their future prospects looked solid.

On a personal level, the investigator noted that their housekeeper, Gladys Stokes, had been with them for the past ten years, moving with them each time they relocated and finally settling with them in New York. Before coming to work for the Johanssons, she had worked for Christina's parents for over twenty years. In addition to running the condo in New York, she also saw to the upkeep of their house in Virginia. She seemed to be more like a part of their family than their employee.

Pallor's flight landed in New York around lunchtime Saturday. After he checked into his hotel, he called the Johanssons to confirm his meeting with them for 7:00 that evening. They were both out, but Ms. Stokes assured him that they were all looking forward to meeting him.

At 6:45, Pallor was standing on the street outside their address, in the heart of Manhattan. Not many people could afford to live in Manhattan; the cost of a condo there was prohibitive. Even though he'd seen their financial statement, it didn't really hit him just how rich they were until he entered the lobby of their building. The place reeked of understated wealth.

There was a reception desk, just like at a motel, and since he was a little early for his appointment, Pallor sat down in one of the easy chairs that were scattered around the lobby and watched for a few minutes. He saw the clerk hand one lady her dry cleaning, another her mail, take a package and mailing instructions from another, accept another resident's dog from the groomer, call for one of the doormen to take the animal up to his home, accept the keys from a couple headed out, and make dinner reservations for another couple. All in under ten minutes.

About five minutes before seven, he walked over to the desk and announced himself. The clerk consulted a small calendar, smiled at him, and motioned him towards the elevator. When he got on the elevator, the attendant asked whom he was visiting. Pallor told him the Johanssons and the man set the little dial for the seventh floor. The gated door slid shut silently and the elevator rose smoothly to the seventh floor and gently stopped. The attendant opened the door and told him to have a good evening.

The carpet on the hall floor was lush and showed signs of having been vacuumed recently. The small pictures along the walls weren't chosen to impress, only to enhance the décor. When he reached the door to the Johansson's condo, he pressed the little buzzer and waited for the door to open.

A middle-aged woman in a light green pantsuit opened the door and held her hand out to Pallor. "Mr. Stewart. I'm Gladys Stokes. Please come in. We've been expecting you."

She led him down a short hall and into a living room that actually looked like it had been lived in. There were magazines and books on the coffee table and end tables, not set out for show, but set aside by someone who had been reading them. The mantel over the fireplace held what looked like family pictures, and there was a basket of newspapers beside one of the recliners.

"If you'll have a seat, I'll get the Johanssons. They're in Christina's darkroom looking at some of the proofs she shot for Harold's company today. Can I get you something to drink while you're waiting?"

"No, thank you. I'm fine," Pallor said as he sat down in one of the chairs.

A few minutes later he heard talking and laughing, and then Mr. and Mrs. Johansson walked into the room. Both were dressed in jeans, sport shirts, and good quality tennis shoes.

Mr. Johansson stepped over to Pallor and held out his hand. "Pleased to meet you, Mr. Stewart. I'm Harold Johansson." Then he turned towards his wife and said, "And this is Christina, the talented one of the family."

She punched his arm playfully and said, "He's just saying that so that I'll give him a discount on the work I did for his agency today. Don't pay any attention to him."

Gladys walked in with a tray with four glasses and a big pitcher of what looked like lemonade. She held the tray while Mrs. Johansson cleared a spot on the coffee table. After she set the tray down, she said, "I know you said you didn't want anything, but I brought you a glass just in case you changed your mind." Gladys poured three glasses, handed one to each of the Johansson's, and took a sip of hers.

Mr. Johansson took a deep swallow of his and nodded. "You really should try this. Gladys is one of the few people left in the world who squeezes her own lemons. She makes wonderful lemonade."

Pallor smiled and nodded at Gladys. She poured the fourth glass and handed it to him.

"Now, what can we do for you?" Mrs. Johansson asked.

"First of all, I'm curious as to why you're going with a private adoption when I'm sure you'd qualify with a state agency."

"Well, from what we've read, most adopted children eventually want to know who their natural parents are, and with a state adoption, that doesn't happen very easily," Mrs. Johansson said.

Pallor frowned. "You do realize that in this case, the natural mother doesn't want her son to even know he's adopted."

"Yes, and that's fine for now, but by the time he's grown, he'll probably figure it out. I don't know what his mother looks like, but unless she's blond with blue eyes, he's going to figure out that something's not quite right here, and when he asks, we want to be able to give him someone to turn to."

"But you're not going to know her name or where she is," Pallor insisted.

"That's okay. We'll have you. It'll be up to you to tell him what he wants to know," Mr. Johansson said.

His words were truer than he could possibly imagine. Pallor was at a loss as to how to respond. Finally he nodded and said, "Yes, I imagine the time will come when he'll have questions, but you must agree not to bring it up yourselves."

Both of the Johanssons nodded.

Then Gladys spoke up. "What does the mother look like anyway?"

"She has brown hair and brown eyes, and I wouldn't really say her skin is dark, but she's not as pale as most Scandinavians."

Gladys nodded. "And the father?"

18

Pallor paused. "I haven't asked, so I don't really know."

"I take it that it's not you then," Gladys said quietly.

"No," Pallor said as he shook his head. "I'm not related to the child in any way."

"Then why are you willing to commit yourself to being involved in this boy's life for the next twenty-some years?" Gladys persisted.

Pallor hesitated and then said, "Because she asked me to, and she's a very dear friend of mine."

"But not a lover?" Gladys asked.

Pallor shook his head again. Gladys nodded and sat back.

"I understand that you travel quite a bit. What arrangements are you planning to make for the child while you're away?" Pallor asked, directing the question to Mr. Johansson.

"Gladys will oversee things, but he'll have a nanny, too. We're really too involved in our careers at this point to be able to spare the time that an infant will take," Mrs. Johansson answered. "Later, when he's old enough, he'll accompany us when he's not in school." She smiled and got a dreamy look in her eyes. "I'm really looking forward to taking him to some of the places we've been. It'll be so refreshing to see things through his eyes as he sees the wonders of the world for the first time."

Mr. Johansson nodded and took her hand. "As you can see, we have a lot to offer a child: financial security, the excitement of life in New York, unlimited travel, the best education that money can buy, anything he needs, and he'll be free to explore any area that interests him."

Pallor nodded. "I take it you're thinking in terms of private schools."

"Of course," Mr. Johansson said. "He can attend any of the schools in the city that he wants to and live here with Gladys, or he can go to a boarding school if he'd prefer. It'll be completely up to him. Of course, we'll play a big role in his life on weekends and vacations, but when school's in session, Gladys will be the main caregiver."

"And this is all right with you?" Pallor asked, looking directly at Gladys.

She nodded and said, "I've been looking forward to raising Christina's child for a long time. I have to admit I was sort of hoping for a girl, but a boy will be fine." Then she grinned and said, "I love kids. They bring such a life to the kitchen, and they're so much fun to cook for. Baking cookies, cupcakes, brownies, cakes, decorating for all the different holidays. Much more fun than tossing a salad."

Mrs. Johansson laughed and said, "You're not going to spoil him, Gladys."

"Humph! Cookies and milk after school didn't do you any harm."

"No, I'll have to agree with you on that one." Mrs. Johansson looked at her housekeeper with genuine affection.

"Well, I think I've about covered everything," Pallor said as he stood up. "Thank you for allowing me to take up so much of your time, and thanks for the delicious lemonade. Now, unless you have something you want to ask me, I'll be on my way."

"I would like to know what you think," Mrs. Johansson said. "Are we going to get the boy?"

"I don't know," Pallor said honestly. "All I'm doing is interviewing prospective parents. His mother will make the final decision."

Mrs. Johansson nodded. "Well, we'd like to know as soon as possible. If he's not coming to live with us, we'll need to set something up with someone else. When do you think you'll be able to let us know something?"

"Probably in about a month."

~ ~ ~ ~

Pallor spent Sunday in New York, meeting with his editor and publisher about the book he had coming out in the new year. By the time he boarded his flight Monday morning, he was glad to be headed away from the city. His next appointment was on Key Biscayne that evening at 8:00. The motel Cynthia had booked him into was on the outskirts of Miami, near the airport. Again, while on the flight, he reviewed the folder for his next interview.

Albert Troxler was seventy-four years old. He had been married to his first wife for over forty years when she died of cancer ten years ago. He had three grown sons, and a host of grandchildren and great-grandchildren ranging in age from newborn to thirty-two. Eight years ago, he married Tracy Shoffner, an exotic dancer that he met in Atlantic City. She was only eighteen when they got married, six years younger than his oldest grandchild.

According to the financial statement, the old man had more money than he could spend in two lifetimes. His sons had grown up while he was making his fortune and understood the value of hard work. Each of them had managed to do quite well on their own without tapping into their father's money.

The investigator wasn't positive, but the impression he got from the few people who would talk to him was that Tracy had signed a prenuptial agreement stating that her inheritance would be limited to a yearly stipend of fifty thousand dollars, payable in monthly installments for the remainder of her natural life. The bulk of Troxler's fortune was being left to his sons.

The only reason that Pallor could come up with to explain why Albert was interested in adopting a child was for Tracy, but Pallor felt sure that she'd be married again before the grass grew over the old man's grave, so why were they even bothering? He shook his head and put the folder away. He was probably wasting his time on this one, but he'd already made the appointment, so he'd go out there.

He had time to check into his motel, shower, and have a quick dinner before he had to leave for Key Biscayne, so he was in a good mood and relaxed when he knocked on the front door of the mansion at the address he'd been given. He was fully expecting a maid to answer the door, but when it opened, he found himself face-to-face with a woman who looked like a streetwalker. Her face was heavily made up, her jumpsuit looked like it had been painted on, her heels were at least four inches high, and her bleached blond hair was almost white and worn in an old-fashioned bouffant style. She was making loud popping noises with the gum she was chewing and kept glancing behind her nervously.

"It's just the newspaper boy, dear," she called back into the house. "No need to bother yourself. I'll handle it." Then she pushed Pallor backwards away from the door and pulled it shut behind her. "I can't talk to you here. Meet me at The Barnacle on the other side of the bridge in thirty minutes." Then she turned and went back into the house, shutting the door behind her.

Pallor stood at the edge of the front porch for a minute and considered knocking again. Surely she must have mistaken him for someone else. But then again, maybe she knew exactly what she was doing. He decided to err on the side of caution, so he got back in his rental car, drove back towards Miami, found The Barnacle, went inside, sat down at a table in the back, and ordered a drink.

A few minutes later, she came prancing through the door to a myriad of whistles and howls. She waved them off and sat down across from Pallor, tossing her huge pocketbook in the middle of the small table.

"You're Mr. Stewart, right?" Pallor nodded, so she continued. "Look, I've only got a few minutes. He thinks I've run out to the store for some ice cream."

"I take it he doesn't know about the adoption application?"

"Heavens, no! He'd have a fit. What's he need another son for? No. I'm the one who needs a kid."

"I'm afraid you've lost me."

"Okay, I'll spell it out. Look, the old man isn't going to live forever, and when he goes, so does that house, my car, everything but some little pittance. I've got to protect myself."

"How is adopting a child going to do that?" Pallor asked slowly.

"I'm not going to let him know the kid's adopted. Sheese, do you think I'm crazy? No way. That's why I've got to get this thing arranged as soon as the mother finds out she's pregnant. He may be old, but he's not stupid. I can't just suddenly hand him a kid and tell him he's the father. He's got to see me getting bigger and bigger, and then poof! We got a kid."

"How do you plan to get bigger and bigger?"

"Padding. I've checked into it. They have all kinds at costume stores. You know, the ones who sell stuff to theaters and all. I can get padding for all stages of pregnancy, and he'll never know."

"He never actually touches you?"

She glared at Pallor and said, "Of course he does, fool. Why do you think he married me?" She stood up, struck a pose, slowly and sensually ran her hands down her sides, and grinned as the bar erupted in applause. "He loves to get his hands on my stuff, but I won't let him while I'm pretending to be pregnant. I'll even make him sleep in his own room. After all, we wouldn't want to take any chances on hurting the baby, would we?"

Pallor shook his head.

"So, when can I get the kid?"

"Ahh, I'm interviewing a lot of prospective parents. It's up to the mother to decide who'll raise her child, but in any event, he isn't due to be born until the middle of March."

Tracy nodded. "That's okay. He should last until then. Look, is she showing yet?"

Pallor shook his head no.

"Good. Now, when can I get this thing settled? I need to get it nailed down. If she decides to go with someone else, I'll have to start all over again, and I don't have all that much time."

"I'll let you know something within a month, either in person or through your lawyer."

Tracy nodded and stood up. "Okay."

Pallor stood up, too. "Thank you for your time. Hope it didn't cause you any inconvenience."

Tracy shook her head. "It'll be all right when I get back with the ice cream. I'll just tell him there was a line at the store. It's hot enough out there that he'll believe it. Keep in touch," and with that, she turned and left the bar.

~ ~ ~ ~

When Pallor got back to his motel that night, he was too uptight to sleep, so he went out to walk on the beach. He didn't understand humans. Of all the people he'd interviewed, only the Johanssons were actually interested in having a child around, and he got the feeling that it was more for their housekeeper than for themselves, and although she seemed more than capable of raising a child, there was a very real danger that the boy could get attached to her. Obviously Mrs. Johansson had. And that would cause major problems later, when it was time for Badec's son to return to Terah.

The memory of Badec and Yvonne sitting on that bench in the garden flashed through his mind. If he put their child in any of those homes, he was going to have to relocate. He had thought that he could do this from Seattle, just flying out a couple of times a year to check on the boy, but that wasn't going to work. He was going to have to keep a close eye on things, a really close eye.

~ ~ ~ ~

Pallor's flight into Memphis Tuesday morning was delayed because of thunderstorms, so by the time he landed and picked up his rental car, he didn't even have time to run by his motel, much less eat dinner, before his meeting with the O'Reillys. As it was, he was five minutes late when he pulled into their driveway.

Their house was in one of the older residential sections, the ones that cost a small fortune and can't be upgraded without approval from the local historical society. It was a southern colonial, complete with wide porch and columns, tall windows covered with lace sheers, and a third-floor balcony. Trees that were probably planted while the Chickasaw Indians still lived in the area graced their front yard.

According to the information that he'd been given, the O'Reillys were relatively new to Memphis. Both of them had been born and raised in the Northeast, but when Mr. O'Reilly had graduated from law school, a Memphis firm had made him a very attractive offer, part of which included this house for a very reasonable price. Matthew O'Reilly had been with the firm for about ten years now, and was hoping to make partner soon. Nora O'Reilly didn't work outside the house, or inside either. She spent her days at the local club, playing tennis, golf, bridge, or drinking tea with the wives of the other lawyers in her husband's firm.

As Pallor approached the front door he tried to picture a child playing in the yard and a dog sleeping on the porch, but somehow it just didn't seem to fit. He knocked on the door and waited for someone to answer. A few minutes later, a middle-aged woman in a light blue uniform opened the door and moved aside. As soon as Pallor stepped inside, she quietly shut the door and asked him to follow her. She led him down a long hall, through a set of French doors and out onto a back patio. Mr. and Mrs. O'Reilly were seated around a wrought iron table covered with a white lace tablecloth. On the table was a platter of cheese, meat, and crackers, as well as a carafe of wine. Mrs. O'Reilly poured Pallor a glass of wine while her husband stood to greet him.

"I'm sorry to be late," Pallor said as he sat down. "My plane was delayed leaving Miami this morning."

Mr. O'Reilly nodded and said, "That's all right. We have just managed to sit down ourselves. It's been one of those days. Now, I understand that you would like to talk to us about possibly adopting a child that you're representing?"

Pallor hesitated. In one sentence, the man had turned the tables. He made it sound as if they would adopt only if Pallor could convince them that the child was worthy of them. "Before we get to that, I'd like to ask you why you're choosing to go with a private adoption rather than a state-sponsored agency. You're an attorney, so you know the ins and outs of the procedure."

"While that's true, we prefer the confidentiality that surrounds a private adoption. We do not wish to advertise the intimate details of our family life. We don't see it as anyone else's business," Mr. O'Reilly said stiffly.

"I see. So you're planning to pretend that your wife's pregnant?"

"I don't see that that concerns you," Mr. O'Reilly started, but then his wife interrupted.

"Oh, for heaven's sake, Matthew. You're making it sound so … I don't know. Anyway, yes, we're going to let the world think that he's our son. I think it would be best all the way around. That way no one would taunt him about his natural mother giving him up."

Pallor nodded. Good answer. Why didn't he believe it? "Do you think you'll be staying in Memphis? Or do you have plans to go back up north?"

"Again, I don't see that our plans should concern you, but to answer your question, we plan to stay. I'm up for partner in about a year, and I intend to make it."

Again Pallor nodded. He was sure there was something else going on here, but how to get to it? "You are aware that if my friend agrees to let you raise her son that I'll have to be involved in his life, right?"

"From what I understand, your 'involvement' would be limited to two visits a year and access to school and medical records. I hardly call that involved in his life."

"Well, I would expect to have input on important decisions concerning his future, such as schools."

Mr. O'Reilly sat quietly for a moment, and then nodded his head exactly once. "I guess that can be arranged, provided you're willing to pick up the tab if you want to send him someplace more expensive than the school we're considering."

22

"Fair enough," Pallor agreed. "Now, Mrs. O'Reilly, I have a couple of questions for you. You said that you're going to pretend that the child is yours. I understand that you don't work outside the home. Does that mean that you'll be the principal caregiver?"

"Good heavens, no!" Mrs. O'Reilly said vehemently. "I may not get paid, but the socializing I do is an important part of my husband's success. I'll have dinners to plan, parties to attend, teas to pour … I really don't have the time to see to a child. No, we'll hire a nurse or a nanny."

Pallor hesitated and then decided to take a chance. "From what I can see, you're both perfectly happy with your lives the way they are. Why bother with a child?" He looked at Mrs. O'Reilly. "As you've just stated, you don't have the time to raise a child, and neither do you," he said, cutting his eyes over to Mr. O'Reilly. "I understand that you put in approximately eighty hours a week at work. That doesn't leave much time for playing baseball with a kid."

For a few minutes, no one said anything. Pallor could see the struggle Mr. O'Reilly was having keeping his temper in check. Mrs. O'Reilly just looked frightened. What was going on here?

Finally Mrs. O'Reilly said, "I think we'd better level with him, Matthew." Then she turned to Pallor and said, "We wouldn't have this problem up north, or at least I don't think we would, but down here, children are considered a stabilizing factor in a marriage. No one in Matthew's firm has ever become a partner who didn't have at least one child. Men without families aren't considered suitable. The partners think they're more likely to pack up, leave the firm, and take their clients with them." She reached out and tentatively placed her hand over her husband's. "Mathew'll only be considered for partner one time, and if he's turned down, that's the end of it, and the end of our lives here. Everything has gone so well up until now. He deserves to become partner. He's pulled in more clients and billed more hours than any of the other associates who came in with him. We've tried and tried to get pregnant, but it just hasn't happened. We can't allow a little thing like a child to stand in our way!"

"So why not adopt openly? Surely the partners would consider that an act of charity."

Mrs. O'Reilly shook her head fiercely. "Donate money to an orphanage? Absolutely. Take an orphan into one's home? Never." Mrs. O'Reilly sighed and folded her hands on the table in front of her. "Taking a child from unknown parentage into one's home is risky at best, and could open the family to horrible scandals if the child turns out to be a bad seed, and any scandal that affects any of the partners would bleed over onto the firm. The other partners would never be willing to take that chance."

Pallor frowned, but before he could say anything, Mr. O'Reilly snapped out, "You don't have to understand. That's just the way it is." Then he turned and glared at his wife. "Nora, you really shouldn't have said anything. Now he's in the perfect position to blackmail us."

Pallor's frown deepened. "Blackmail? What are you talking about?"

"Whether we take the child you're representing or not, we're going to have to find a child to adopt. And when we do, you'll know it's not ours," Mr. O'Reilly hissed. "And you know that adopting a child would make me ineligible for a partnership, which would give you a perfect opportunity to pick up a little extra cash by threatening to expose us."

Pallor stared at the man for a few moments before answering. Then, in a calm, quiet voice he said, "I find your suggestion insulting, to say the least. I have no reason to blackmail anyone. I don't know whether you recognized my name or not, but I'm a well-known author and I make more money than I need already. I certainly don't want any of yours."

Mrs. O'Reilly stood up and said, "I'm sure my husband didn't mean to insult anyone. This has been worrying both of us for several years now, and we have found the only solution we feel is open to us, even though neither of us is very happy with it. We need a child, and if not yours, then we need to find someone else's. But either way, we'll just have to trust you not to divulge our secret. Now, if you two will excuse me, I've had about all of this conversation that I can stand. Have a good evening, Mr. Stewart, and please, help yourself to the refreshments."

After Mrs. O'Reilly went back inside the house, the two men sat silently for a few minutes, and then Pallor said, "I was serious when I said you had nothing to worry about as far as I'm concerned."

Mr. O'Reilly nodded stiffly. "Thank you." Then he stood, too, and said, "Mr. Stewart, we're running out of time. If we adopt your friend's child, we'll abide by the terms of the contract, even to the point of allowing you limited access to the boy, but I will insist on a confidentiality clause. We can't take any chances on anyone, not even the child himself, finding out that he is not our child biologically. But whether we adopt the child you represent or another, we really do have to find a baby. How soon do you expect to know something?"

"I hope that the mother will make her decision in about a month. I'll let you know when she does."

~ ~ ~ ~

Wednesday afternoon, Pallor was on a flight from Memphis to Los Angeles. He had a window seat and gazed out as the plane began its descent. It looked like there was a gray dome sitting over the city. He hated the idea of sinking into that mess. He shook his head. Poor Earth. The humans were slowly ruining the whole planet. At least they wouldn't be able to do that to Terah. The other races would never stand still for it.

After he checked into his motel and ordered room service, he pulled out the final folder from his stack. The Livingstons. Phillip Livingston was forty-seven years old and worked as an engineer for the city. Amanda Livingston was twenty years younger than her husband and worked as a bank teller. Although he made pretty good money, and their combined income would be considered comfortable, they lived up to their income and had very little set aside for emergencies. They liked to socialize, especially on the weekends, and mainly in out-of-town places. No household employees were listed on the financial statement, so either they were paying someone under the table, or Mrs. Livingston took care of the house herself.

Pallor pulled up in their driveway a few minutes before seven the next night. Their house was a white ranch with large doors and wide windows. A young woman in a white uniform opened the front door and led him through the house to the deck out back. Mr. and Mrs. Livingston were relaxing on lounge chairs sipping tall drinks with bits of fruit floating in them. The maid indicated the third lounge chair and asked Pallor if he'd like a drink. He said he was fine and sat down on the side of the chair, facing the Livingstons.

"Nice night, isn't it?" Mr. Livingston asked. "We like to relax for a bit before dinner. Helps the digestion."

Pallor nodded. "I won't keep you long, but I would like to ask you a few questions, if you don't mind."

"Fire away," Mr. Livingston answered.

"First of all, why are you going through a private adoption? Wouldn't it be easier for you to go through the state?"

Mr. Livingston shook his head. "Not really. They insist on interviews, physicals, psychological tests, parenting classes, and the list just goes on and on. We really don't have the patience for all that hoopla."

"Plus the fact that I absolutely refuse to get involved in any of this," Mrs. Livingston mumbled.

"I'm sorry," Pallor said, facing her. "I didn't quite catch that."

She shook her head. "Never mind."

"So, you're trying to expedite the process?" Pallor asked.

Mr. Livingston nodded. "If you've got enough money to grease the bureaucratic wheels, why not use it?"

24

"I see. Okay. Let me ask Mrs. Livingston a couple of questions," Pallor said, again turning to face her. "I understand that you work at a bank. Are you planning to quit your job? Or are you just going to take a temporary leave of absence?"

"Neither one," she answered. "I have absolutely no intention of getting involved in any of this in any way. This is something he wants. Not me. I have never had any interest in having or raising a child, and I don't intend to be saddled with one now. If he wants a son, he can have one, but he's going to have to take all the responsibility for it. I don't plan to alter my life one bit."

Mr. Livingston's face turned slightly pink, but he managed a little chuckle and said, "She's just kidding. She's as up for this as I am."

"You keep saying that, and I keep telling you you're wrong. Guess you're going to find out just how wrong once that kid gets here and you find yourself knee deep in dirty diapers"

Mr. Livingston looked at Pallor. "She'll come around. You'll see. She'll fall in love with him and it'll all work out great. She just hates change. You should have seen her when I bought this house and we were going to have to move. You'd have thought the end of the world was coming the way she carried on, but now that we're here, she loves it."

"Adopting a child is a bit more of a commitment than buying a house," Pallor said.

"Not really," Mr. Livingston said. "Both involve change, but once the change is made, everything will work out. You'll see."

Pallor nodded. "Have you given any thought to schools?"

Mrs. Livingston laughed. "With all the taxes we pay, he can go to public school, just like we did."

Mr. Livingston pursed his lips for a moment, like he was trying to keep the words from coming out, but he lost the battle. "I've been thinking about that, honey. Public schools aren't quite the same today as when you were there, and I'm not sure I want any son of mine in one. We'll just have to wait until it's time for him to go and see, but I'm thinking private school."

"And what are you planning to use to pay for that?" she asked.

"We can cut down on some of our spending. It's not like we really need three cars."

Mrs. Livingston rolled her eyes. "I'm not giving up anything. If you want to spend good money on a private school, you can take it out of your check."

"Well, we have time to work that out," Mr. Livingston said. "But in answer to your question, Mr. Stewart, I'm hoping that we'll be able to find an acceptable private school in the area so that he can live at home. I really do hate the idea of boarding school."

Pallor nodded. "I'm sure your lawyer told you that the adoption contract would contain a clause giving me access to the child at least twice a year, to his school records, and to his medical records. Right?"

Mr. Livingston nodded. Mrs. Livingston had picked up a magazine and was thumbing through it.

"Well, I'll need to be involved in any decisions regarding the school he attends."

Mrs. Livingston slapped the magazine down on her legs. "I don't think so, not unless you're planning to pick up the tab. Phillip, if you go along with that, he can say that that kid has to go to the most expensive school around, even if it bankrupts you. No. Do not go along with that. You can find some other kid to adopt."

"She does have a point," Mr. Livingston said.

Pallor nodded. He was tempted to say that he'd pay for the school himself, but he remembered Mr. Blalock's advice and kept his mouth shut. "Well, we can work on some kind of agreement along those lines at a later date." Then he stood up and thanked them for taking the time to talk to him.

Mr. Livingston escorted him to the front door, and as Pallor was leaving, he asked, "Do you have any idea when you can let us know something? It'll take me a while to get Mandy acclimated to the idea of giving up her exercise room for a nursery, but I don't want to get into that argument unless it's a sure thing."

"Sometime next month someone will let you know one way or the other," Pallor said, although he was tempted to tell the man that he wasn't going to have to get into any arguments with his wife, at least not over Badec's son.

~ ~ ~ ~

On Friday morning, September 12, Pallor caught a flight from Los Angeles to Seattle, and by late afternoon, was back in his office. He had planned to spend the rest of the day going through his notes and writing up a coherent report on each of the six couples, but he was just too tired and depressed.

He decided to take a nap and tackle the reports later. After all, he didn't have to be at Kalen's until dinnertime on Saturday, and that was twenty-four hours away.

Chapter 4

Plans and Preparation

Kalen spent Saturday morning cleaning and freshening three of the guest rooms at the Gate House. While he worked, he reminisced about his three hundred years as Keeper of the Gate and the changes he'd seen, as well as the changes his father had seen before him.

The Gate House was probably the oldest building on Terah, and as far as Kalen knew, it had always been run by a dwarf. It had been built by the same group of sorcerers, elves, dwarves, and dragons who had designed and built the two Gates Between the Worlds.

Both gates consisted of an inner circle of bluestones and an outer ring of sarsen stones. After all of the stones were set in place, the dragons fired the rings, creating an intense field of magical energy. Any sorcerer or magical being who entered the circle of stones could tap into that power to gain access to the stream of energy that flows between Earth and Terah, and use that stream to travel from one world to the other. On Earth the gate was known as Stonehenge.

For centuries, magical beings traveled freely between the two worlds and the Gate House on Terah was like a busy passport control office, and the Gate Keeper was primarily responsible for registering arrivals and departures and playing host to any overnight guests. The Gate House itself was a grand mansion surrounded by beautiful gardens with a full staff of housekeepers, cooks, grooms, and groundskeepers to see to the comfort of the guests.

But eventually magic became synonymous with evil on Earth and magical creatures as well as sorcerers were hunted and killed. The gate became an avenue of escape, and the Gate House became a temporary refuge for those seeking asylum on Terah. More and more magic was erased from Earth and the existence of the magical creatures became the substance of legends and fairy tales.

Although the gate on Terah was maintained in good working order, the gate on Earth quickly deteriorated after the exodus of magical creatures, so the Council of Sorcerers, in conjunction with the dragons, elves, and dwarves, made four keys that would open the energy flow from anywhere on either world. All the key holder had to do was concentrate on his destination and turn the key. One of the keys was given to the Master Sorcerer, a second to the dragons, a third to the dwarves, and the elves had the fourth key. Years later, as a safety measure, the keys were altered so that intense feelings of fear would automatically activate them, transferring the holder and, unfortunately, anyone near him to the gate on Terah.

Over the years, the responsibility of the Gate Keeper gradually shifted from welcoming visitors from Earth to protecting the secret of Terah's existence, and with the changing function of the Gate Keeper, the outward appearance of the Gate House had been altered.

When approached from the gate, it appeared to be an old cabin, made of logs and thatch, with a stone chimney held together by mud. There were no windows, only a couple of small holes in the wall covered by scraps of cloth, and there were no lawns or gardens, only forest.

That cabin was all that people from Earth ever saw. As soon as they arrived, they were escorted back to the gate and sent back to Earth. Returning them was never a problem; they were more than willing to go, and they were very willing to attribute any memories they had to dreams or hallucinations once they woke up back on Earth.

However, once someone actually entered the house, the illusion vanished. The front room was larger than most houses on Terah, with wide bay windows overlooking well-kept lawns and gardens. The huge kitchen could be used to prepare meals for one or banquets for hundreds. There was a small table for four in the kitchen, an elegant table for twenty in the dining room, and a separate banquet hall that could seat several hundred. There were a dozen guest rooms in the main house and several guest cottages nearby. The stable had thirty horse stalls and eight large open stalls for visiting pegassi and unicorns. A large wagon, several small wagons, and a few carriages were stored in a nearby shed for the convenience of the guests.

Looking after all of this was too much for one dwarf, and since there was no longer a housekeeping staff, the local brownies helped out, especially when Kalen was expecting guests, but this time Kalen had quietly prepared everything himself. He didn't want anyone else to know about this meeting.

Kalen was in the kitchen fixing dinner when Pallor suddenly materialized at his elbow.

"Why can't you use the door like everyone else?" Kalen fussed as he wiped up the stew he had sloshed out of the pot at Pallor's abrupt appearance.

"Sorry," Pallor answered as he swallowed a chuckle. "The stew looks good."

"Well, have you found someone to take the child?"

Pallor laid a stack of folders on the counter and tapped them. "I'm not sure. I've interviewed six couples, but after you read these reports, you may want me to keep looking."

"I hope not. I want this thing settled. And I'm sure Badec does too," Kalen said as he turned back to the pot. "I've been thinking about this a lot, and I don't think it would be a good idea for any of us to know the names of any of these people or where they live. You have to, but we don't, and anything we don't know, we can't tell."

"I understand what you mean, but it's too risky for only one person to know where the child is. Something could happen to me. I could get killed."

"I still think it's best if none of us knows anything. I'm sure our meeting with Badec didn't go unnoticed, and when Yvonne dies and the child disappears, it won't take very long for someone to put it all together. I don't want the information in my head."

Pallor thought about it for a few minutes and then shook his head. "This is Badec's son we're talking about, the future Master Sorcerer. Someone on Terah has got to know where he is. Who, if not one of you? Badec?"

"I doubt he'll want it in his head either, but I may have a solution. We'll talk about that later. What I'd like for you to do right now is go through your folders and mark out anything that could be used to identify these people." Kalen poured a big mug of scog and handed it to Pallor. "You've got a couple of hours. Use my desk."

~ ~ ~ ~

After dinner, Kalen cleared the dining room table and set out a fresh pitcher of scog and four clean mugs. Once everyone was settled, Pallor took over. "I hired a lawyer who has some experience dealing with the type of adoption that we're interested in. We need couples who for one reason or another don't want to go through the regular procedure."

"Why?" Duane asked.

"Because I need to keep a close eye on the child, and with regular adoptions, that would never be allowed. Everything would be kept secret. I wouldn't even be able to find out who had him."

"Oh," Duane said quietly.

Pallor waited to see if there was anything else, and then continued. "Our lawyer contacted some of the lawyers who specialize in private adoptions and found six couples who were willing to agree to let me visit the child a couple times a year. I just spent the past two weeks interviewing them."

"Have you decided which one you want to go with?" Laryn asked.

Pallor shook his head. "I'm not willing to make that decision by myself. I want all of us to be in agreement about which couple takes this child. If I need to, I can go back and try to find some others, but frankly, we need to get this settled as soon as possible." The others nodded, so Pallor continued, "Kalen has suggested that it would be best if none of you actually know the name or location of any of the foster parents. I understand his concerns, so I've gone through the folders and marked out all identifying information. I have a financial statement and a background search as well as my own report on each of the couples, and each of you will have a chance to go through those before we make a final decision, but I thought I'd give you a brief summary first." Pallor paused, looked around the table, and began.

"First, couple A," and Pallor described his reaction to the Haverstons, their reasons for wanting to adopt a child, and their dependence on his mother's good graces for their income.

"What about the place where they live? Is it suitable for a child?" Kalen asked.

"I can't speak for all the houses, but the one I visited was lavish, with white furniture, white rugs, expensive glass vases everywhere, and high-priced paintings on the wall. Not at all the kind of a place where you picture a young boy running around. They seemed to be the type who likes to flaunt their wealth, even though they had nothing to do with earning it."

"I don't know about anyone else," Duane said, looking around, "but I don't like the sound of this couple. I hope they aren't all like that."

"They aren't, but none of these situations is really ideal. We can't tell them anything about him, about his parents, about his powers, or about the role he'll have to play on Terah. For all they know, he's just some child whose mother can't be bothered to raise him. Under those conditions, the type of parents we'd normally pick would never consider having an outsider oversee the way they raise their son."

"I guess you're right, but I still don't like them, even if they are willing to let you keep an eye on things," Duane said as the others nodded.

"Our second couple, couple B, live on a farm," Pallor said, and then he described the Peters, their farm, and their views on school. He also pointed out that although on paper they looked well off, their money was so tied up in the farm that they were living one season to the next, and one bad year could wipe them out. "They want a son so that he can help out while he's growing up and take over the operation of the farm once he's grown. They fully expect him to support them in their old age."

"A farm's not a bad place to grow up. In fact, considering that life on a farm is the closest thing Earth has to life on Terah, it might have some definite advantages," Laryn said. "But it sounds to me like this couple is more interested in cheap labor than a child."

"That may be true, but even so, they'd feed him and clothe him, and they'd teach him what he needs to know to run the farm. Would it be fair to them to let Badec's son grow up there?" Kalen asked. "He won't be there to take over when they get old."

"True enough," Duane agreed.

"Couple C lives in one of the largest cities on Earth. They are quite wealthy, but they don't flash it around. Their living room is comfortable, a place where a child could play without causing a lot of damage, and both of them are down to earth. No pretentiousness, no arrogance, just plain simple people who happen to be incredibly well off," Pallor said as he began to describe the Johanssons, their work, their travels, and their housekeeper, who would probably end up raising the child.

"Their lives sound so full already," Laryn said thoughtfully. "Wonder why they decided to get a child?"

Pallor hesitated and then said, "I'm not sure, but I think they're doing it for the housekeeper."

"Why?" Kalen asked, frowning.

"I think she pretty much raised the wife, and it was obvious that she's more a member of the family than anything else. The man and his wife were looking forward to specifics, like places they could take him, things they could show him, experiences they could give him, almost like a favorite aunt and uncle, but the housekeeper talked about everyday things, like milk and cookies, like a mother."

Duane frowned. "That could be a problem when the time comes for him to return to Terah."

Pallor nodded and then continued, "Couple D was a bit strange." He described his first reaction to Tracy Troxler and the way she was dressed. "When I got there, the wife all but pushed me off the porch in her hurry to get rid of me and told me to meet her at a small tavern a few miles away. She didn't want her husband to see me."

"So her husband doesn't know she's thinking about adopting a child?" Laryn asked with a frown.

Pallor shook his head. "She's in her twenties, he's in his seventies. He already has three grown sons, a bunch of grandchildren and even some great-grandchildren."

"So why bother?" Kalen asked.

"Money," Pallor answered and proceeded to describe Tracy's motives and her plans to deceive her husband.

"And she thinks he won't know she's lying?" Duane's eyebrows were arched almost to his hairline.

"That's what she thinks," Pallor answered, "She said that she plans to use padding and insist that he sleep in another room while she's pregnant, but I have my doubts that a man smart enough to have made the fortune he's made is going to be foolish enough to fall for this one."

"I think we can rule her out right now," Laryn said, shaking her head.

"The next couple, couple E, has tried and tried to have a baby of their own, but it just hasn't happened, and they're running out of time," Pallor said.

"Out of time?" Laryn asked. "Is she that old?"

Pallor shook his head. "They're in their mid-thirties. The time issue has to do with his job," Pallor began as he described the O'Reillys, their home, his job, her social life, and the fact that his becoming a partner in his law firm hinged on their having a child.

"I'm not sure I like the idea of my nephew being used to secure a promotion, but at least they'd have a good reason for not letting him or anyone else know he's adopted," Laryn said. "Do you think she'll take care of him herself?"

Pallor shook his head. "I asked. They're planning to hire someone to do that."

Laryn nodded and waited for Pallor to move on to the last couple.

"Our last couple makes quite a bit of money, but they live up to their incomes, so if anything were to happen to either of their jobs, or if they ran into an unexpected expense, they'd be in trouble," Pallor began as he described the Livingstons, his desire for a son, and her complete disregard for the whole process and refusal to take part in any of it, including caring for the child. "He's sure that she'll change her mind, but I don't think so. I think she'll end up leaving him if he adopts a child."

Kalen shook his head and said, "Can't help but feel sorry for the guy. He married the wrong woman. Happens like that sometimes."

"Sounds like it pretty much comes down to couple C or E," Duane said quietly. "What do you think Laryn?"

"Couple C sounds good, but I'm almost afraid he'd like them too much to be willing to give them up. I bet he'd have a good time growing up in their home though," she answered with a sigh. "Couple E sounds better than any of the others, but I don't like the fact that they want him for a job promotion. What happens if the man still doesn't get the promotion? Are they going to want to give him back? Or worse, give him to someone else?"

Pallor shrugged. "I have no idea."

"Another thing about them bothers me," Duane said." They're going to be determined to keep anyone from finding out he's adopted. How are we going to convince him he's not their son when the time comes for him to return to Terah?"

Pallor grinned. "Well, both of them have light red hair. Badec and Yvonne both have brown hair, as did their parents, so I imagine their son will too. By the time he's grown, he's going to wonder where his brown hair came from. It's not much, but it's a start."

"What about the other couple? C?" Laryn asked.

"Both of them have blond hair and blue eyes," Pallor said. "He wouldn't look like them either."

Laryn nodded. "I think we can rule out couple D and the last one, the one where the wife doesn't want a child, but before we make a final decision, I'd like to think about each of the other couples and look through their folders. This is Badec's son we're talking about and our decision will have an enormous impact on his life."

"I would too," Kalen agreed. "Let's take the rest of the folders into the living room and get comfortable. We can make a decision tomorrow morning. Agreed?" As everyone nodded, stood up, and stretched, Kalen added, "I'll bring in some coffee and cake. Duane, light the fire in there, would you?"

Kalen walked into the kitchen to put on a pot of coffee and cut the cake. When he carried the tray into the living room, the others were sitting in silence, each concentrating on one of the folders. Kalen picked up the last one, opened it and began to read.

~ ~ ~ ~

The next morning, while everyone was sitting around the table after breakfast, Kalen placed four sheets of paper, four pens, and a clean mug on the table. "Before we get into any discussion, let's see where we stand. Write down the letter of the couple you think we should allow to raise Badec's son, fold the paper, and drop it in the mug."

After all four slips of paper had been dropped in the mug, Kalen poured them out on the table. All four of them had "E" written on them.

"I guess that it's then," Pallor said.

"I hope we've made the right decision," Laryn said quietly.

"What's next?" Kalen asked.

"I understand why you said you didn't want to know any of the details, but someone on Terah needs to know the identity of the foster parents and where they live," Pallor said. "However, I still have a lot of work to do and some things I need to sort through with the lawyers, and we may hit a snag with this couple and have to find someone else, so why don't I prepare a folder about the foster parents along with the adoption agreement and give it to someone on Terah for safekeeping when I pick up the child?"

"That's fine, but who are you going to give it to?" Duane asked.

"Well, I don't want to be responsible for the details, and I'm sure Badec doesn't either," Laryn said.

"I have a suggestion," Kalen said. "I haven't asked him, but I bet Glendymere would be willing to keep the folder."

Laryn tilted her head to the side. "That's not a bad idea."

"Glendymere? Who's going to take it to him?" Duane shook his head and continued, "I've had to wake him up before, and he wakes up with a big nasty yawn, spewing smoke and fire. You could end up toast before he recognizes you."

Laryn grinned. "He has a gong at the entrance to his cave now, Duane. You don't have to worry about that anymore."

"The dragons don't like to get involved in human affairs. Don't you think he might consider this as becoming too involved?" Pallor asked.

Laryn shook her head. "I doubt it, but let me see what Badec thinks. The request should come from him anyway. I'll let you know."

"What's next?" Duane asked.

"Has anyone given any thought as to how we're going to get the child to Earth?" Kalen asked. "If Pallor shows up at Badec's castle at about the same time that the child vanishes, anyone who's paying any attention at all will know he's on Earth."

"Not that it would do them much good," Pallor mumbled.

"It would be best if no one even knew you were connected to any of this, Pallor," Kalen answered.

"I've got an idea," Laryn said. "Duane, why don't you and Xantha pick him up at the castle, bring him up here, and Pallor can meet you here?"

"That might work," Kalen said with a slow nod. "But it would be even better if no one knew about it. If everyone at the castle was used to seeing Duane come and go they probably wouldn't even notice. But what reason could he possibly have for hanging around the castle?"

"Shelandra," Laryn said with a mischievous twinkle in her eye.

A slow blush crept up Duane's face. "I don't know what you're talking about."

"Oh, yes, you do," Laryn insisted. "You've had a crush on her ever since the first time you saw her. You're just too shy to do anything about it."

"Cousin!" Pallor said as he slapped Duane on the back. "Congratulations! I wondered when you were going to find a nice woman and settle down." Then he turned to Laryn and asked, "Are you talking about that gorgeous elf I saw there last Christmas? Long slender legs, hair down past her waist?"

"That's the one," Laryn said with a grin. "Duane, if you play your cards right, you could end up with a wife out of this. I know for a fact that she likes you."

Duane's blush deepened. "How do you know?"

"She told me."

Duane's eyes took on a dreamy look.

Kalen rolled his eyes, shook his head, and sighed. "We have about six months before the birth of the child. What else do we need to do?"

No one spoke immediately, so Pallor said, "Well, I have plenty to arrange, but I have to go back to Earth to do it. So, if there's nothing else, I'm off."

"I think that's all for now, but I feel sure we're going to think of other things as time goes on. Check in with me once in a while," Kalen said.

Pallor nodded, took out his key, and vanished.

~ ~ ~ ~

Six months later, on the sixteenth of March, a falcon landed on Kalen's windowsill with a letter from Laryn. She said that Badec's son, Myron, had been born the day before, and that although Yvonne was weak, she was in relatively good shape.

Kalen sent a message to Pallor, and then settled down in his living room to wait. As he sat there staring into the fire, he let his mind wander ahead twenty-five years, to the time when Myron would return to Terah. How would the boy feel, coming home to a culture so completely different from Earth's? Myron would be safe from Badec's enemies while he was on Earth, but how safe would he be when he returned to Terah? How could they prepare him for life here, much less for his role as Master Sorcerer?

After a while, Kalen stood up, walked around the room, and decided that the present was going to be difficult enough to deal with. He told himself to wait until the child was safely on Earth before he started worrying about bringing him back.

As if on cue, Pallor popped in. "Where is he?"

"He's not here yet. He's only a couple of days old," Kalen said as he sat back down. "Yvonne's weak, but she's doing all right at this point. You might as well sit down and relax. I think we may have a bit of a wait ahead of us."

Pallor slumped down in a chair near the fireplace. After a few minutes, he said, "When I got your message I called the adoptive parents and told them that they could go ahead with the birth announcement, but that it would be a few days before he arrived. I told them that my friend wanted to spend a little time with her son before she signed him over."

"Are you sure that was a good idea? What if they start worrying that she might change her mind?"

"Let them worry. I don't care. I don't completely trust Yvonne's vision. She may live, and if she does, there's no way that Badec's going to send his son to Earth."

"You really don't like these people, do you?" Kalen asked quietly.

Pallor slowly shook his head. "The only thing they're interested in is his job. They act like the child is some kind of possession, something they can take off a shelf when they want to show it off and then put it away again when the company's gone. They had a decorator fix up a little room for him, but there isn't an adult-sized chair anywhere in it. They've hired a nurse, and she's all right, but once he starts school, she'll move on to another job, and from what I'm seeing, he's pretty much going to be on his own after that."

"I'm going to go get a mug of scog. Do you want some? Or would you rather have something else?" Kalen asked as he stood up to go to the kitchen.

"Scog's fine. Then I think I'll go get some sleep. I'm tired." Pallor sat quietly while Kalen was in the kitchen. When Kalen returned with the two mugs of scog, Pallor asked, "Do you think we're doing the right thing, Kalen?"

Kalen handed Pallor one of the mugs, sat down, and took a sip of his before he answered. "I don't know, but this is what Badec and Yvonne want. We'll just have to trust that they know what they're doing."

"Yeah, I guess so." Pallor drank his scog in silence and then said, "Well, I'm off to bed. See you tomorrow."

Kalen sat in the living room watching the fire for a couple more hours. He couldn't make up his mind whether it made him feel better or worse that Pallor had some of the same doubts that he did.

~ ~ ~ ~

The next three days were nerve-wracking for Kalen and Pallor as they had no way of knowing what was happening in Milhaven. Around dawn on the twentieth, Xantha landed in the backyard of the Gate House. Kalen and Pallor were sitting in the kitchen when Duane entered with the baby in his arms.

"Is it over?" Kalen asked quietly.

"No, not yet, but Yvonne's getting weaker every day. She can't care for the child any longer, so Badec thought that it was time to send him to his foster home." Duane looked at the child in his arms. "No one at the castle has figured out that Yvonne's dying. They're still celebrating Myron's birth. There was a feast going on in the dining room while Badec was telling his son good-bye. There were tears in his eyes when he handed Myron to me. How he's handling all of this is beyond me." Duane took a deep breath and slowly exhaled. "I really hate this." He tickled Myron under his chin. "We live so much longer than humans that we end up burying a lot of our friends. Yvonne's such a good woman, and she's been so good for Badec."

Pallor got up and poured a mug of scog for Duane. As he set the mug on the table, he said, "Here, let me have him. You must be tired after holding him during the flight."

"I hate to give him up, but I've got to head back tonight and I need some sleep. Do you mind if I go lie down for a couple of hours?" Duane asked Kalen as he handed the child to Pallor.

"Go ahead. Your room's ready." Kalen nodded towards the hall. "But I want to talk to you for a few minutes before you leave. It's important."

Duane nodded as he picked up his mug of scog and headed towards the hall.

"By the way Duane, how's Shelandra?" Pallor asked with a grin.

"Oh, she's fine – in every sense of the word," Duane answered with a smile. "In fact, I think she might agree to marry me before the month's out. I haven't asked her yet, but I've been sort of hinting around about it, and she hasn't put me off."

"Let me know when the wedding is," Pallor said. "I want to be there."

"Will do," Duane answered as he headed off to bed.

"At least one good thing will come out of all of this then," Pallor said softly while he looked at the baby in his arms. Myron was blowing little bubbles up at him. "I guess I should head back to Earth now. Do you need me for anything before I go, Kalen?"

"No. Just be careful. And Pallor, I expect to hear from you on a regular basis. Do you have the folder with the specifics about the parents?"

"I put it in the top drawer of your desk. It's sealed in a big yellow envelope."

"That's fine. I'll handle it. Take care of yourself, and of him," Kalen said as Pallor turned his key and vanished.

"Well, Myron, I guess I'll see you in twenty-five years, give or take a few days. Have a good life," Kalen whispered to the empty room.

~ ~ ~ ~

Later that day, while Duane and Xantha were getting ready to leave, Kalen said, "We're going to have to figure out some way to prepare Myron for Terah."

"I don't know how much anyone can do until he gets here," Duane answered.

"I know, but when he returns to Terah, it'll probably be through the Gate. Who's going to meet him? Who's going to tell him who he is? Who's going to explain things to him? We've got to figure out how we're going to present this world to him."

Duane nodded as he mounted Xantha. "I guess we do need to talk about it, but we'll need Laryn. I'll mention it to her later, after it's all over."

"Good," Kalen said. "We have a little time, but twenty-five years will go by very quickly, and I don't want him coming here until we know what we're going to do. We need a plan."

Shortly after Duane and Xantha left, a falcon arrived from Laryn. Yvonne had passed away. Kalen nodded to himself. The team had done a good job. The child was safely off of Terah before anyone had any reason to start looking for him.

Chapter 5

March 15, Three Years Ago

On Myron's twentieth birthday, Badec paced back and forth in his office as he waited for Pallor to pop in to make his yearly report. Laryn watched her brother pace and smiled to herself. It was only in the past couple of years that he had shown any interest at all in the future, and his eyes, which had looked so empty after Yvonne had died, had begun to sparkle with life again, especially whenever his son was concerned.

"Where is he?" Badec grumbled as he paced.

"Why don't you sit down," Laryn said. "He'll be here in a few minutes. You know Pallor. He's always late."

"You'd think he could be on time for this." Just as Badec jerked his chair out from under his desk and plopped down, the air shimmered and Pallor appeared.

"Well, it's about time," Badec growled.

"And hello to you, too. And yes, I'm doing fine. Hope you are, too," Pallor said as he tossed an envelope on Badec's desk. "Sorry I'm late, but I've had a busy day."

"What's this?"

"Just something I thought you might enjoy seeing."

As Badec opened the envelope, some pictures slid out. He picked up the one on top and stared at it. "My son?"

Pallor nodded as he sat down. "That's Kevin. I know you said you didn't want to know what he looked like when he was younger, but I thought it was about time for you to see him."

Laryn stood up and walked around the desk to look over Badec's shoulder. "Every time you call him Kevin, I have to stop and think who you're talking about. I wish they'd kept his name the same." She gazed at the picture for couple of moments and then said, "He looks a lot like Yvonne, doesn't he?"

Badec nodded. "Especially his eyes. And that hair."

"But he has your mouth and chin," Pallor said from his chair.

"How did you do this? Did you paint it?" Laryn asked as she reached out to touch the picture.

Pallor shook his head. "No, it's something called a photograph. You aim a camera at someone, push a button, load it up on your computer, and print it out. I just took these today when I went by to see him. That's why I was late. I had to go by my house to print them out."

Badec shook his head and said, "I don't understand a word you just said." He kept thumbing through the pictures. They showed Myron in his dorm room at college, outside on the steps, standing under a tree, and sitting at a wooden table with a drink in his hand.

"I've taken pictures of him on his birthday every year," Pallor said while Badec studied the photos. "I've got the rest at home. Anytime you're ready, I'll bring them over."

"So how's he doing?" Laryn asked.

"All right, I guess," Pallor said. "He's doing great in his classes, but he still doesn't make friends that easily. About the only people he sees outside of class are the ones he's working on projects with."

"How about physically?" Badec asked, looking up from the pictures. "He doesn't look very strong to me."

Pallor shook his head. "I've tried, Badec, but he just isn't interested, and he's not very good at anything physical either. Remember when I enrolled him in self-defense classes while he was in high school? He hated them, and after a few sessions even the instructor was in favor of letting him give them up. He was afraid Kevin would end up hurting himself."

Laryn nodded. "I'm not surprised. Sounds like our father. Mother was the athletic and outgoing one. Most of us took after her."

"Except where magic was concerned," Badec interjected. "You're the only one who took after her there."

"Speaking of which, what about Myron? Has he shown any signs of having magic in his blood? Has he moved anything yet? Sent up any sparks?" Laryn asked.

"Not that I know of," Pallor said, "but like I told you last year, it's there."

Laryn frowned. "Are you sure you aren't just sensing the elven magic that flows through his blood?"

"I'm sure, Laryn. I know what strong human magic feels like. It's different from ours. I can feel it now, from Badec."

Laryn shook her head. "Yeah, well, Badec has elven magic in his blood too. I'm still not convinced you can tell the difference."

"Trust me, Laryn. It's there."

"I hope you're right. A lot is going to be riding on his shoulders one day."

"How do you think he's going to like Terah?" Badec asked.

Pallor shrugged. "I have no idea. Every time I tried to introduce the idea of magic, dragons, elves, anything like that, his parents got in the way. Whenever I gave him books of fairy tales, they took them away from him, saying that they didn't want him wasting his time on foolishness. They even told him that stories about Merlin were silly, and they're almost classics on Earth. I don't know what's going to happen when he comes face to face with Kalen or Xantha, much less Glendymere."

"Is there anything we can do to help him adjust?" Laryn asked. "I'm afraid he's going to feel really out of place here."

Pallor nodded enthusiastically. "You have no idea how true that is. He won't have any of the stuff that he's used to, no television, no computer, no cars, no microwaves…"

Before Pallor could say anything else, Badec held up his hand, palm out. "We get the idea. So what do we do about it? How do we make this world more, I don't know, maybe more acceptable? Less bizarre?"

"Well, there's not much we can do to keep it from feeling alien to him," Pallor said slowly. "For one thing, he's going to feel like he's gone through a time warp, like he's gone back at least a couple of hundred years. I tried taking him on a few camping trips when he was younger, just to see how he handled it. I told you about that, remember?"

Badec chuckled, "Quite a disaster as I recall."

"It was funny then," Pallor continued, "but now that it's getting closer to time for him to come home, I've been getting a little concerned."

"Do you have any suggestions?" Badec leaned forward and folded his arms on his desk.

"I think he's going to need some kind of anchor, something to hold on to, or he's not going to make it," Pallor began. "Look, I know your first reaction to what I'm going to suggest will be to veto the idea, but before you do, think about it. What if we were to bring a few people over with him, people he knows and likes? People who would have the same memories he does, who have shared the same experiences, who would know just how strange this world is to him because it's strange to them too, people he could really talk to."

Neither Badec nor Laryn spoke for few minutes. Then Laryn said, "Actually, I've wondered about doing that too, but we'd have to be really careful. The people we bring over would have to be able to fit in here, to adapt to our way of life, and they would have to be willing to leave Earth for good."

"We have a duty to protect Terah, too," Badec said slowly. "We can't bring over anyone who would use anything he knows to take advantage of anyone here. The people we choose would have to have a strong sense of right and wrong, and they'd have to be incredibly tolerant. But above all, they must be completely and totally loyal to my son."

"How are you going to find people like that?" Laryn asked Pallor. "It's not like you can interview candidates or take applications."

"I know. I've been thinking about it a little. Kevin doesn't have many friends right now, but he still has another couple of years of college. And hopefully he'll make some friends when he gets out on his own. I'll check them out and see which ones would be suitable companions. He's got another five years on Earth. That should be plenty of time."

Badec shook his head slowly from side to side. "I don't know. This may be harder than you think. For one thing, the people we bring over can't have any close family or ties, and they'd have to be pretty dissatisfied with the way their lives are going on Earth to be willing to try something so totally different."

Pallor nodded. "I still think I can find a few. Five or six maybe. So, do I start looking or not?"

Laryn and Badec looked at each other for a moment, and then Badec nodded.

"Good, but I do have one question," Pallor said. "They'll be coming through the Gate, and I'll have to be on Earth to cover their supposed deaths, so who'll meet them and explain what's going on? And who's going to tell Kevin who he really is?"

Laryn started laughing and said, "Not Kalen."

"No, not Kalen," Badec agreed with a smile. "Can you picture him trying to deal with a houseful of humans, much less humans from Earth? No, either Laryn or I will have to be there, maybe both of us if things are reasonably quiet around here."

"Someone needs to tell Kalen about this though," Laryn said. "It's not the type of thing we can spring on him at the last minute."

"He won't mind, as long as someone else is handling everything," Pallor said. "But I can stop by the Gate House before I head back to Earth and tell him if you want me to."

Badec nodded. "I'd appreciate it. Tell him that I'll be up to talk to him before we bring them over. We'll sort out all the details then."

Pallor nodded and stood up. "Anything else before I leave?"

"Not that I can think of," Badec said as he handed Pallor the pictures back. "I appreciate you bringing these, but you'd better take them back. I don't want them around here for someone else to find. It's rather obvious who he is, and it's also pretty obvious that's not Terah in the background. Take care and we'll see you next year."

Chapter 6

Saturday, March 3, Present Day

The winter before Myron's twenty-third birthday had been a particularly dreary one, but the first Saturday of March dawned clear and bright in Trendon, and although the breeze couldn't really be called warm, there was a touch of spring in the air. To make the day just that bit better to all the people who worked at the castle, it was also the day of the monthly meeting of the Council of Sorcerers, which meant that, for a few hours at least, Rolan, the Seated Sorcerer of Brendolanth, would be gone. Guards relaxed, the maids chatted as they worked, the young pages joked, and laughter could be heard in the halls.

Shortly before lunch, the guard at Rolan's bedroom door heard him banging around in his room as he changed out of his formal tunic and robes back into his regular clothes. The sorcerer was back.

Hushed whispers quickly spread the word throughout the castle that Rolan had returned. Tension filled the air as conversations stopped mid-sentence and guards snapped to attention.

As Rolan walked down the hall towards his office, the page standing next to his door opened it for him and then stepped aside.

"I don't want to be disturbed," Rolan said gruffly as he passed through the open door. "See to it."

The page nodded and quietly pulled the door to.

Rolan sat down behind his desk and allowed himself a few minutes to gloat. All of his work, all the planning and finagling, was finally going to pay off. Sometime this evening a package would be delivered to the kitchen at Badec's castle in Milhaven, a gift for the Master Sorcerer, a special tea that no one would ever suspect contained a deadly poison. With any kind of luck, Badec would be dead before the week was out, and best of all, there was absolutely no way it could ever lead back to him.

As soon as Badec was gone, the Master's Chair would be declared vacant. The Council wouldn't have any choice. There was only one heir, Badec's son, Myron, but he hadn't been seen or heard from since he was born. No one on the council had any idea whether or not he was still alive, but even if he was, he wasn't old enough to have started training yet, so there was no way he could hold the Master's Chair. No, Myron wasn't going to figure into this at all. Badec was all there was.

When Badec died, someone was going to have to act quickly or there was going to be another magic war, and Rolan planned to be that someone. On the day that the seat was declared vacant, which, if everything went according to plan, would be at the next council meeting, Rolan was going to address the Council of Sorcerers and suggest that Damien take the seat.

Damien had several things going for him. For one thing, he was one of the strongest sorcerers on the council, so not too many of the others would be willing to challenge him for the seat. For another, he minded his own business and he let the other sorcerers mind theirs. He'd bend over backwards to avoid any type of conflict, and they all knew it. Third, he got along with the dragons, at least the ones who lived in Calandra, including Glendymere. And that in itself was a major selling point.

Rolan frowned as he thought about his speech to the council that day. It would have to be good, really good. Several of the other sorcerers were going to have their eyes on that chair the second that they heard that Badec was sick, and if he couldn't convince them to go along with Damien, things could get dicey. A magic war would probably end up killing them all, if not in the actual fighting, in the fallout that would follow, himself included. But it was too late to worry about that now. Things had already been set in motion. He'd just have to be good enough to get everyone to fall in line, including Damien.

At first, Rolan had considered trying to find a way to get himself named Master Sorcerer, but he'd quickly abandoned that plan. There were too many other sorcerers out there as strong or stronger than he was. He wouldn't survive a week. But putting Damien on that chair would be the next best thing. Once he was seated as Master Sorcerer, the key to the Gate Between the Worlds would be turned over to him, and then it would be within Rolan's grasp. Damien was a trusting soul. If Rolan approached him just right, he was sure Damien would hand it over without giving it a second thought. And that was the prize. Rolan could almost feel it in his hand.

He smiled as he fantasized about that other world, the one Badec had described to his father all those years ago, in what they had thought was a private conversation. From what he had overheard, it was similar to Terah, but without magic. There wouldn't be any dragons to stop him or any sorcerers to challenge him. He could do whatever he wanted while he was there and no one would be able to do anything about it. It would be perfect.

He rubbed his hands together in anticipation. His plan was coming together. Another month, maybe two. He could hardly wait.

Chapter 7

Laryn was getting a little uneasy. Badec hadn't shown up at breakfast, and now, an hour later, he still hadn't put in an appearance. He hadn't said anything to her about an early morning appointment, and he always let her know if he was going to be out of the castle. Finally, she got up from her desk and went upstairs to make sure he wasn't still in his room.

When she knocked on his door, there was no answer, so she opened the door and stepped inside. A chill ran up her spine when she saw her brother still in bed. She'd never known him to sleep in, not even as a child.

As she approached his bed she noticed that his chest was rising and falling with steady breaths, so the first jolt of panic subsided a bit. Maybe he just had a touch of a cold or something. She felt his forehead, and although it felt fine, no sign of fever, he didn't open his eyes or do anything at all to imply that he knew someone else was in the room, and with his powers, that was beyond unusual.

Laryn softly called his name as she placed her hand on his wrist, searching for a pulse. It was there, not quite as strong as usual, but definitely there, and steady. Finally she took hold of her brother's shoulder and gently shook him, hoping to wake him up, but once again, no luck.

Laryn glanced around the room, looking for anything that might give her a clue as to what was going on. His evening tray with one tea cup was on the table beside his chair, just like always, and he had on the same old nightshirt he'd worn to bed for the past ten years. From all appearances, everything had been normal when Badec went to bed last night, but things were definitely not normal now.

After trying once more to rouse her brother, Laryn left his room and went back downstairs to the office. She asked Ariel, one of Badec's pages, to go to the Chapel of Light in Milhaven and ask Sister Agnes to come up to the castle as soon as possible.

~ ~ ~ ~

That evening, Kalen was in the kitchen of the Gate House when a falcon landed on the kitchen windowsill and pecked on the glass. When Kalen opened the window, the falcon held up his leg for Kalen to untie the note, and then immediately flew away, without even waiting for an answer. As soon as Kalen saw Badec's seal, a cold knot formed in his stomach. He sat down at the table, took a couple of slow, deep breaths, and opened the letter.

Kalen,

I regret to inform you that Badec seems to be in a coma. He was fine yesterday, but when I tried to awaken him this morning, I could not rouse him. I sent for Sister Agnes, but she was unable to rouse him either. He is breathing regularly and his heart seems to be fine, but he is unresponsive.

If he is not up and about by the beginning of April, I will have to report his condition to the Council of Sorcerers. They will not declare him dead as long as he is breathing, but they will vacate his chair in one year if he does not awaken, or if he is too weak to carry out the duties of Master Sorcerer.

I see no alternative other than to send for Myron immediately. We must get him to Glendymere as soon as possible, yet secretly and safely. I fear for Myron's life once news of Badec's condition becomes known.

I realize that we have not discussed plans for Myron's introduction to Terah, but there is no way that I can leave Milhaven right now. You have my complete support for any plan that you devise. I wish you luck.

I have sent a falcon to Duane with a copy of this message and have dispatched a phoenix with a message for Glendymere. I leave it to you to inform Pallor.

Yours sincerely,

Laryn

Kalen sat staring at the note until midnight. He had to agree with Laryn. Their only option was to send for Myron. Unfortunately, they weren't ready. It was too soon.

He put in an emergency call to Pallor, went into the living room, lit the fire, and sat down to wait for the elf to pop in. Kalen felt like he had only been staring into the flames for a few minutes when Pallor popped into his living room a couple of hours later.

One look at Kalen's face and the elf knew something was horribly wrong. Kalen didn't even seem to know that he was there. Pallor walked to a spot directly in front of the dwarf and asked, "What's going on?"

Kalen didn't answer. Instead he handed Pallor Laryn's note.

Pallor sat down on the edge of a chair and read through the note a couple of times. Finally he said, "I'll try to have Kevin and some companions on Terah in about two weeks."

"Who's going to explain all of this to them? Who's going to tell Myron what's going on? Who's going to tell him that he's Myron?!"

Pallor stood up, shrugged, and said, "I guess you are."

"Me?! I can't do this, Pallor. Someone else is going to have to."

"Who, Kalen? I can't. I'll have my hands full back on Earth explaining what happened to them."

"But I'll make such a mess of it." Kalen's face was the picture of misery.

Pallor put his hand on Kalen's shoulder and said, "I'm sorry about all of this. Badec wanted to be here and take care of this himself, but now … Look, just do the best you can, and don't blame yourself for any of this. No one could have foreseen this." Pallor handed the note back to Kalen. "Why don't you send for Duane? Maybe he and Xantha can help. I hate to leave you like this, but I've got to go. I've got a lot to do." Then he took out his key, gave it a quick turn, and disappeared.

Chapter 8

Another Search Begins

As soon as Pallor was back on Earth, he was hit with the closest thing to a panic attack that he had ever experienced. There was no way he could have Kevin and six or seven of his friends on Terah within two weeks. He had no idea which of Kevin's friends would even be suitable. He hadn't started working on that yet. He was supposed to have at least two more years to figure it out, not two weeks!

Pallor paced around his small office and tried to work his way past the panic. He stopped in front of the window, but nothing out there either relaxed him or gave him any ideas. All he could see were houses, cars, and tall buildings.

Omaha wasn't all that big when you compared it to places like New York, Los Angeles, or Chicago, but for an elf who loved the outdoors, it was suffocating at times. At least when he was living in Seattle he could see mountains in the distance. Here, nothing but city.

He had moved to Omaha a year ago when Kevin had accepted a job with Beasley, Dixon, Matherson and Co. PA. He had expected to be stuck here for at least a couple more years, but now it looked like his days in Omaha were coming to a close. As soon as he could figure out how to get Kevin and his friends on Terah, he could leave. He could go back to the Seattle area.

That thought alone helped ease the panic. So he took a deep breath, grabbed a pencil and notepad, and sat down at his desk to make a list of Kevin's friends. As Pallor stared at the notepad, he realized that there was no one to list. Kevin had not made any close friends while he was in college, and, as far as Pallor knew, Kevin had never even made it to first name basis with anyone in Omaha. He would have to send complete strangers to Terah with Kevin. As the panic started to build again, he forced it down and tried to tackle the problem logically.

First, he had to find some suitable candidates. He needed people without strong ties, basically loners, so he began by listing some quiet restaurants in the area that would appeal to loners. Then he added a few coffee shops near the college where the more independent types hung out.

Next, he listed several of his contacts who would have information on new arrivals in town. Maybe he'd luck up on someone who was a drifter, working at odd jobs, seeing the country one piece at a time, a modern day explorer.

After that, he picked up a stack of old newspapers that had piled up on the floor beside his desk and started going through them. He wasn't sure what he was looking for, but he made notes on anything that caught his eye. A couple of hours later he had found a few articles that he wanted to check out, but only one that really tweaked his interest.

On the sports page of a week-old paper, there was a follow-up article about a college football player who had been injured in a game a few months ago. The thing that caught Pallor's attention was a quote from the young man: "Football is my life. There's nothing else. I can't even imagine my life without it."

According to the article, the doctors would soon know how successful they had been at trying to save his career. Pallor made a note of the athlete's name, his coach's name, and the orthopedic surgeon in charge of his case.

Wednesday morning, he began calling his contacts. One was a woman in a real estate office that managed several apartment complexes. After they joked around about his only calling when he wanted something, Pallor said, "I've got a character who's going to have to pick up, move across the country, and take a new job in a strange city. I want to talk to someone who's doing that to get a better feel for my character. Do you have anyone moving in soon who would fit the bill?"

"Give me a couple of hours to look through the new rentals," she answered. "Male or female? Or does it matter?"

Pallor paused for a moment. "My character's male, so maybe I'd better stick to males."

"Okay. Do you want someone who's already moved in? We had a few who took possession over the weekend."

"I'd rather get his thoughts when he arrives, as he's moving in, but I guess I could work with someone who hasn't been here long." Pallor said. "But I don't want him to know he's being interviewed. I need his real reactions, so don't tell anyone."

"Don't worry," she said with a little laugh. "I don't want to lose my job. But you owe me! Again. Call me back this afternoon," she said, and then she disconnected.

Pallor's next phone call was to the young football player's coach. When he finally got through, he introduced himself and said that he had been asked to write a series of feature articles for one of the local papers. "Right now, I'm working on an in-depth feature on college football. I've been reading about your quarterback, the one who was injured, and I'd like to interview him and get his perspective on the sport. Do you know when he's meeting with his doctors to get their final evaluation?"

The coach hesitated. Pallor waited a few moments and then added, "I want to wait until he knows one way or the other."

"Next Tuesday morning," the coach finally said. "But don't crowd him if it's bad news. Give him a chance to … I don't know … come to terms with it, I guess."

"You're expecting bad news then?" Pallor asked. Then he added, "Off the record."

"I've seen a lot of knee injuries. I knew it was bad when he got hit."

"Have you told him what you think?"

"I've tried to prepare him, but he's not hearing me, or at least that's the way he's acting." The coach was quiet for a moment. Pallor felt like he had more to say, so he just waited. Finally the coach sighed and said, "He's a smart kid. I'd be willing to bet he's figured it out for himself, but he's not going to acknowledge the possibility that it's over until the doctors say so. After all, until they say no, there's always hope."

"Yeah," Pallor said softly.

"Just give him a little breathing room. He's a good kid. He didn't deserve this," the coach said. Then he disconnected.

Pallor left his house and went to a few of the restaurants on his list, looking for likely candidates, but the only thing he got was indigestion. When he got back home, he called his contacts back to see if any of them had come up with anyone.

He struck out on his first two calls. The newspaper hadn't had any requests for new subscriptions within the last few days and no one had applied for a new library card either. But when he called the real estate company, his contact there told him that they'd had four rentals move in over the past weekend, but all four of those were married couples, two with children. The only one that sounded the least bit promising was Chris McAllister, a twenty-six-year-old marketing director scheduled to arrive on Friday. According to the information on his rental application, he was single and had lived in New York City all of his life. He had stated that the reason for the move was that he had been offered a new job in Omaha.

Pallor almost didn't bother with him. Anyone who had spent his whole life in New York City would find Terah even more alien than Kevin would. But he made notes of all the specifics and got directions to the apartment complex all the same. It wasn't like he had an over abundance of prospects.

Pallor didn't have any luck at all on Thursday, but Friday morning he stopped at a small diner just inside the city limits. One of the waitresses caught his eye. Her accent didn't sound native to the area and from the bits of conversation he overheard, she had to have lived some place rural. She even looked the part with sandy hair, blue eyes and a down-to-earth way of carrying herself. She came across as being perfectly comfortable with who she was.

He had taken a seat at the counter and ordered a cup of coffee when he walked in, but once he had his coffee, he picked up the newspaper he was carrying as a prop, and moved to one of the empty booths in her area. When she stopped by to refill his cup, he noticed her nametag: Joan. It fit. A no-nonsense name for a sensible lady.

"You aren't from around here, are you?" Pallor asked.

She grinned, shook her head, and said, "My husband and I had a farm in Missouri until last fall. After the drought last summer, we decided to call it quits."

"Do you like living in the city?" he asked.

"Truthfully, I think we both miss the open spaces and peace of the country, but we'll adjust," she said with a smile. "Now, what would you like to go with that coffee?"

Pallor ordered a small pastry and settled in to observe her while he pretended to read the paper. She was friendly and attentive without being intrusive. He hadn't really considered using a married couple, but he could see some advantages to it, and there was a definite advantage to sending someone with an agrarian background. The more he thought about them as prospective companions for Kevin, the more he liked the idea.

While she was writing up his check, he asked, "Do you have any children? There are a couple of pretty good museums uptown that cater to children."

She shook her head and said, "No, it's just me and Karl," as she handed him his bill. "Thank you, and come again."

"I certainly will," Pallor said, and added to himself, *every morning*.

After Pallor left the diner, he drove out to the apartment complex to wait for Chris. He had the make, model, and tag number of the car that Chris would be driving. He cruised through the lot to see if Chris had already arrived, but the car wasn't there, so he parked his car at the end of the lot and settled in to wait.

A couple of hours later, a large truck pulled up in front of the apartment building and two burly men climbed out. They opened the back of the truck and started unloading a bed. Pallor got out of his car and walked over towards them.

"Is that for Chris McAllister by any chance?" he asked the larger of the two men.

"Yeah. Are you McAllister?" the man answered.

"No, but I'm a friend of his. He isn't here right now," Pallor said.

The man grunted, looked at his paperwork, and said, "Load it back up, Mac. He's not here. We'll have to come back this afternoon." Then he turned to Pallor and asked, "Do you happen to know which floor his apartment's on?"

"Third."

"And I'll bet there's no freight elevator," the big man grumbled as he climbed back up in the cab of the truck and drove off.

Pallor headed back over to his car to wait. About the middle of the afternoon he saw a car pull into the parking lot that matched the description he'd been given, right down to the New York license tag. The car backed into an empty space near the entrance to the apartment building and the driver climbed out. From a distance, all that Pallor could tell was that he had a fairly good physique and dark blond hair.

44

While the driver was stretching and looking around, Pallor got out of his car and walked over. When he reached the driver he held out his hand and asked, "Chris McAllister by any chance?"

"Guilty as charged," the driver said with a lopsided smile. "Are you the manager?"

"No, I was out here waiting for my girlfriend when a couple of guys in a big truck came by looking for you. I think they had a delivery to make," Pallor said. "My name's Paul Stewart."

"My bed! Do you have any idea what they did with it?"

"They said that they'd come back later." Pallor motioned towards Chris's car. "Are you moving in today?"

"Yeah, I just arrived from New York," Chris said as he unlocked the trunk of his car. The car and trunk were both jam-packed.

"New York? As in the City?"

Chris nodded.

"That's a long drive," Pallor said. Then he pointed towards the car. "My girlfriend is running late. Do you need some help?"

"I'd love it, but you might want to reconsider your offer," Chris said and tipped his head towards the building. "I have a third floor apartment, and I don't remember seeing anything about an elevator in any of the material the agency sent me."

Pallor shrugged. "Hand me a load and point me in the right direction. I may not be able to help you get it all upstairs, but I can take a couple of loads."

While they unloaded Chris's car, Pallor found out that not only was Chris single, he wasn't even seeing anyone. All the girls he'd dated in New York had been more interested in building their careers than in working on a long-term relationship, which had suited him just fine. He was from a large family, and although he got along okay with his parents, brothers, and sisters, he wasn't particularly close to any of them. Each of them had moved out of the house when they'd gone to college, and after college, they'd pretty much gone their own way.

When Pallor asked Chris about his job, Chris said, "I've been working for the same firm ever since I graduated from college. I was getting bored with my job, and a couple of weeks ago I realized that I was as high in that company as I was going to go. It was family owned, and only family members could be project manager, which was the next rung on the ladder, so I started looking for something else."

"Any particular reason you chose Omaha?" Pallor asked.

Chris shook his head. "I had already decided that it was time to get out of New York. I know it's supposed to be the most exciting place to live in the country, and there is a lot to do there, but to be honest, it can be depressing at times. I wanted some place new, some place different. And then I saw an ad in the newspaper for a marketing director out here. I sent my résumé to a post office box, and the next week I got a phone call. It was a conference call and I'm not sure how many people were on the line, but I was interviewed right there and then. I got another phone call the next day, offering me the job, so I took it."

"Just like that? You didn't want to come out here and check things out first?"

"No, not really. They told me that I would be heading up a marketing campaign for a new line, which was what I wanted to do, and they offered me more money than I was making in New York, so I figured it was worth a shot. If I don't like it, I'll start looking again."

The more Pallor heard, the better he felt about Chris as candidate for Terah. After a couple more trips, they were pretty much done. When they went back downstairs, Pallor made a few admiring remarks about Chris's car.

Chris smiled. "I don't know anything about cars. Fortunately one of my brothers does. He found this one for me last week. The price was right and he said that it would get me out here, so I bought it."

"You didn't have a car in New York?"

"No. I've never owned a car before. It costs too much to park it in the city, and since I almost never left the city, I couldn't see any reason to bother with one. I'd driven before, I even got a license when I turned eighteen, but I never bothered to renew it. I had to go get another one last week so that I could drive out here."

Pallor laughed and said, "You're going to need a mechanic then. Mine's good and his rates are pretty reasonable. I'll get you one of his cards next time I see him."

"Thanks," Chris said. "And thanks for helping me unload."

"I enjoyed it." Pallor took out his wallet and fished around in the back for a moment. He kept a well-stocked pack of business cards, listing a wide variety of occupations. He pulled one out that identified him as the proprietor of a modeling agency. "Here's my card. If you need anything, give me a call. I know how it is to move to a strange city and not know where anything is."

Chris smiled and put the card in his pocket. "Thanks. I may take you up on that."

~ ~ ~ ~

Over the weekend, Pallor searched through the newspaper to see if he could spot anything that might give him a lead on someone else, but he couldn't find a thing. He felt good about Joan, her husband, and Chris. Darrell Simmons, the football player, was another possibility, depending on what the doctors had to say on Tuesday. But that was only four. He'd like to have six or seven companions to send with Kevin and time was running out.

Monday morning, he ate breakfast at the little diner, but he got there during what must have been the diner's busiest time, so he didn't get to say much more than hello to Joan. He thought about hanging around until most of the customers were gone, but he was afraid he'd make her suspicious, so he left with the crowd.

After he scanned the morning paper, he started going around to the small restaurants on his list. About 1:00, while he was on his fifth light lunch, he spotted a man sitting off by himself near the back of the restaurant. Most of the waitresses stopped by his table to speak to him and a couple even sat down with him for a few minutes while he was lingering over his coffee.

Pallor guessed that he was probably in his fifties. His brown hair was speckled with gray and longer than most men his age wore their hair, almost as if he had forgotten to get it cut. Pallor watched as the man stood up and made his way to the front of the restaurant. He was not quite six feet tall and a little stocky, but overall he appeared to be in relatively good shape.

A couple of minutes later, while Pallor's waitress was making out his ticket, he asked, "Do you know that man's name? The one who was sitting near the back? I feel like I know him, but I can't quite place him."

"That's Steve Patterson," she said.

Pallor shook his head as if he was trying to remember, but just couldn't quite get hold of it. "I can't place the name, but I'm sure I know him from somewhere. Do you know where he works?"

"He's a retired teacher. He taught at the high school around the corner for thirty years. Maybe you know him from there. Almost everyone in this section of town was either in his class or had kids in his class," the waitress said. Then, after a moment, she added, "It's really sad about his wife, Cathy. Did you know her? She was so sweet. They used to come in here for dinner every Friday. She held his retirement party here." The waitress shook her head and gathered up his dishes.

"What happened?" Pallor prompted.

"What? Oh, you mean to Cathy? Well, about six months after he retired, she died. Poor thing had cancer. They found out about the cancer right before he left teaching. Such a shame. They had such wonderful plans for his retirement," she shook her head again and wiped off the table. "Now he just sort of drifts. He comes in here everyday for lunch. You never see him with anyone, always by himself. Really sad."

"How long has it been?" Pallor asked.

"Let's see. He's been retired for about three years now, so I guess she's been gone for a little over two years."

"Maybe he just needs a new interest, a distraction of some kind," Pallor said, thinking that he might be a good candidate for Terah.

The waitress giggled and said, "We think so too, and every one of us has tried to be that distraction, but mister, I just don't think he's interested in being distracted right now."

Pallor laughed and handed her a nice tip.

After Pallor left the restaurant, he walked uptown to the library to see if he could find a newspaper article about the retirement or about the wife's death. It took a couple of hours, but he discovered that Steve Patterson had taught history and political science to high school juniors and seniors, and that he was well-thought-of in his field. He had won several teaching awards and his students had won quite a few local competitions. As far as he could tell from the newspaper articles, Steve had never had any children. In fact, he didn't seem to have any family left at all.

The more Pallor thought about it, the more he liked the idea of Steve as an advisor, especially if Badec didn't recover and Kevin had to take on the role of Master Sorcerer. Now all he had to do was figure out some way to get to Steve.

~ ~ ~ ~

Tuesday morning, Pallor got up before daybreak and drove over to Chris's apartment complex. He had decided that it would be easier to explain their "deaths" if he could get Kevin and all of his companions in one placed and have them all "killed" by the same event. He hadn't worked out any of the details yet, but if he was going to maneuver Chris into position, he figured it was probably going to involve disabling Chris's car and then offering him a ride. And in order to do that, he needed to know what time Chris left for work, so he parked in a dark and crowded corner of the parking lot and kept an eye on Chris's car.

Finally, at 7:30, Chris emerged from the building with a steaming cup in his hand, got in his car, and left. Pallor nodded to himself. That was about the time he had figured Chris would leave. Chris would want to give himself plenty of time to get downtown, find a parking space, and get to his office. Just to be on the safe side though, Pallor planned to be in the parking lot by 7:00 every morning for the rest of the week, just in case Chris's schedule changed once he settled into his new job.

When Pallor left Chris's, he killed a little time riding around so that he wouldn't hit rush hour at the diner again. It worked. The diner was nearly empty by the time he walked in.

While he was eating, he asked Joan where her husband worked.

"Karl works at Home Depot, in the gardening section," she answered.

"That should be right up his alley."

Joan nodded. "It is, but sometimes I think it depresses him. He would much rather be the one buying seed than the one selling it."

"He'd rather be farming?"

"We both would. We hated to give it up, but it was one of those rock and a hard place choices. We finally came to the conclusion that we just couldn't afford it anymore, so here we are."

"Well, at least in a city the size of Omaha, if he doesn't like his job, it should be easy enough to find another one."

"That's sort of what we were thinking when we moved here. Lots of options." She topped off his coffee and then asked, "Now, do you need anything else?"

"No, that'll do it for today," Pallor said.

~ ~ ~ ~

When Pallor left the diner, he headed out to the hospital to see if he could find out what the verdict was for the young football player. While he was driving, he thought back over his conversations with Joan. The more he learned about Joan and Karl, the more certain he became that they would be a good fit. But once he arrived at the hospital, he put all thoughts of everyone else out of his mind and concentrated on Darrell.

It took him a while to find the orthopedic surgeon's office and he was half afraid he might have missed Darrell, but shortly after he got there, the office door opened and the doctor escorted a young man out of the office.

The picture in the newspaper must have been taken when Darrell was quite a bit younger, before his muscles had fully developed, because the young man in front of Pallor had a lot more definition. The accompanying article had described Darrell as African-American, but this young man's skin looked more golden than brown and his features looked Mediterranean. Even so, there was no doubt in Pallor's mind that he was looking at Darrell.

The doctor had his hand on the young man's shoulder and Pallor could see by the somber look in Darrell's eyes that the news had not been good. After they spoke for a couple more minutes, the doctor shook Darrell's hand and turned to head back to his office.

Darrell wandered aimlessly up and down the hospital corridors after he left the orthopedic wing. Pallor followed at a discrete distance. When Darrell passed the cafeteria, he went in, got a Pepsi, and headed for a table near the back of the dining area.

Pallor went through the line, ordered a cup of coffee, and sat down where he could keep Darrell in sight. An hour later, Darrell was still sitting there, so Pallor got up, got another cup of coffee, and drifted over in Darrell's direction until he was standing next to the chair across the table from Darrell.

"Hi, my name's Paul Stewart. I'm waiting for a friend to have a few tests done. Mind if I join you?" Pallor asked as he pulled the chair out from the table.

"Actually, I'd be lousy company," Darrell said without looking up. "You'd be better off sitting somewhere else."

Pallor sat down. "Bad news about the knee?"

Darrell looked up, surprised.

"I've followed your career. All-state in high school, then first string at the university your freshman year. Almost unheard of. I was looking forward to great things from you in a few years," Pallor said sympathetically.

"Yeah, me too," Darrell sighed. "Guess that's all over now."

"What did the doctors say?"

"I can lead a perfectly normal life, even play most sports, but no more football."

"Tough break. Do you have any idea where you're going to go from here?"

Darrell shook his head. "I haven't really thought about it. I figured the doctors would come up with a way to fix it. I knew it was a possibility, but until today …"

"I know what you mean." Pallor sipped his coffee and waited a couple of minutes before continuing. "But you might not have to give up football completely. There are ways to stay involved with the game, even if you can't play."

Darrell shook his head. "I don't think so. I don't really want to coach."

"Actually, I wasn't thinking about coaching. I was thinking about broadcasting, about sports commentary." Pallor took out a business card that he had made up especially to give to Darrell. It said that he was the manager of one of the local radio stations. "It's not much, I know, but we broadcast a high school game every Friday night during the season, and the college games on Saturday. Think you'd like to handle the play-by-play from the booth?"

Darrell fingered the card Pallor had handed him and thought about it. "I don't know if I'd be any good at it, but it sounds interesting."

"Good. I'll set up a sound test. We'll show you a game on tape and let you do the commentary for a demo tape," Pallor said. "It won't hurt to give it a try."

Darrell didn't say anything for a minute, and then he nodded. "Okay. Let's do it. When do you want me? And where?"

"I'm not sure yet. Let me get your phone number and I'll call you as soon as I can get the arrangements made."

Darrell gave Pallor his phone number, shook his hand, and left the cafeteria, walking a little taller than he had when he came in.

~ ~ ~ ~

By 10:00 Wednesday morning, Pallor was in his third coffee house. The first two had more business people than students, but the atmosphere in the third was just right. He ordered a cup of coffee and looked around for a place to sit.

A young lady sitting by herself at a small table off to the side caught his eye. The first thing he noticed was the long, dark hair cascading down her back. When he walked around to where he could see her face, he saw that her eyes were full of tears.

Pallor sat down across the table from her and said, "Hi, my name's Paul Stewart. I couldn't help but notice that something's upsetting you. I've got some time if you'd like to talk." He smiled and looked at her eyes.

"No, no. Everything's fine," she said, as she wiped her eyes with her napkin. "I'm all right, really."

Pallor waited to see if she'd say anything else. When she didn't, he said, "Look, this isn't a line. I'm old enough to be your father. I'm not trying to pick you up."

"Oh, I'm sure you're nothing like my father," she said with a touch of bitterness in her voice.

"So, he's the problem. Let me guess … he doesn't like your boyfriend, right?" Pallor said with a grin.

The girl laughed, but it was strained. "If only. No, I'm afraid I've got the opposite problem. I don't like the fiancé my father found for me."

Pallor's mouth dropped open. He slowly shut it, and then said, "You are kidding, aren't you?"

The girl shook her head. "Well, to be honest, I don't know him well enough to know whether I like him or not, but the rest is true." She took a deep breath, wiped her eyes again, and held out her hand. "Hello, I'm Theresa Maderina. It's nice to meet you."

After they shook hands, Pallor said, "Your father chose your fiancé? That's archaic!"

"Finally! Someone who agrees with me!" Theresa said with mock enthusiasm.

Pallor raised his eyebrows. "What about your mother?"

Theresa shook her head. "She thinks Mr. Lopez is perfect. He's about forty, a bank officer, completely respectable, reasonably well-off, just terrific."

"Have you told her how you feel?"

"Several times. She always defers to my father."

"Well, have you explained how you feel to him?"

"Only half a dozen times. At first I tried to talk to my parents in a mature manner, as one adult to another. When that didn't work, I tried everything I could think of. I've argued, I've screamed and cried, I've begged and pleaded, I've stormed and raged … nothing has done any good. I even tried to get our parish priest to intervene, but he's on their side. He thinks it's a perfect match."

"What about your brothers and sisters? Surely they're on your side."

"I'm an only child," Theresa said with a sigh. "Actually, I think that's part of the problem. My parents have always been completely focused on me, and I haven't helped matters by never fighting them. I've always done what they wanted. Now all they can think of is getting me married off. I feel so trapped. I wish I could just disappear, vanish, and wake up in a brand new life." There was as much frustration in her voice as in her words, and when she finished speaking, Pallor saw the tears well up in her eyes again.

"You know what they say, be careful what you wish for," Pallor said with a laugh to break the tension.

Theresa managed a small, tight grin. "I should be so lucky."

"What about school? Are you going to graduate this year?"

"No, I'm only a sophomore. My parents don't consider school very important for a woman, and neither does Mr. Lopez. It's like my plans, things I want, just don't matter."

"Do you have any idea how all of this came about?"

Theresa nodded. "Mr. Lopez mentioned to my father that he was ready to have children, so he guessed he'd have to find a wife. My father told him to look no farther, that he could marry me. And that was it. A done deal!" Theresa's eyes sparked with anger. "That was on a Sunday evening, right after church. Then, on Monday morning, at breakfast, my father told me to order a wedding gown, that I was getting married near the end of May."

"You know, maybe you're going about this the wrong way," Pallor said a little more quietly.

"Huh?" Theresa asked.

"Maybe you should find a way to make Mr. Lopez call the whole thing off."

Theresa tilted her head to the side, looked at Pallor, and asked, "And how would I do that?"

"I don't know yet. Let me think about it." Pallor leaned back in his chair and drank a few swallows of his coffee. Then he leaned forward and said, "I've got an idea. I'm an author, and I'm here to conduct a creative writing seminar for graduate students. Let me throw this out as a plot line and see if one of my students comes up with something."

Theresa looked panicked and shook her head no.

Pallor held up his hand for her to stop. "I won't use your name, and I'll disguise the whole thing. Maybe a first generation family from somewhere in Asia. This is what we do in the seminar. I give them a situation and they build a plot around it."

Theresa thought about it for a minute. "Okay. I don't guess it could hurt. Who knows? One day I may read about this in a book," she said with a nervous laugh.

"You never know. I may even write it myself," Pallor said with a grin. "My class meets tonight. Why don't I meet you here tomorrow morning about 10:00?"

Theresa shook her head. "I can't tomorrow. Friday?"

Pallor nodded. "Friday it is." Then he stood up and picked up his coffee cup. "See you then."

~ ~ ~ ~

That afternoon, Pallor called his mechanic. "Can I buy you a cup of coffee after work today in exchange for some information?"

"No, but you can buy me a beer," the mechanic answered with a chuckle. "You looking for a new car?"

"No, it's research for one of my books. What time should I meet you?"

"I should be done around six," the mechanic answered.

"Okay. See you then," Pallor said.

Pallor walked into the garage bay about ten minutes before six. His mechanic slid out from under a car, said, "I'll be done in fifteen minutes," and slid back under the car. Pallor wandered around the garage, looking at the different tools, trying to figure out each one's function. He turned around when he heard a car door open.

"Let me move this one around back and I'll be ready to lock up," the mechanic said as he climbed into the car and started the engine.

A few minutes later, they walked into a small bar near the garage. Pallor ordered a beer for his mechanic and coffee for himself.

When they were settled in a booth, he said, "I'm working on a story and I need a little help. One of my characters needs to disable someone's car, nothing serious, just something to keep it from starting. Any ideas?"

"Sure, that's easy to do, but it's also easy to undo. I take it that the person who owns the car wouldn't know a whole lot about engines," the mechanic said.

"About as much as I do," Pallor said with a grin.

The mechanic nodded. "He can't pop the hood without help."

"I'm not quite that bad. Close, but not quite."

"Well, it's not too hard then. A loose wire would probably be the easiest way."

"Just any wire?"

The mechanic rolled his eyes. "No, not just any wire." He took a long draft of his beer. "What do you want? Put the key in, turn the ignition, and nothing? Or do you want it to grind away, just never catch? Or maybe a clinking sound?"

"I think I'd like nothing. The car will be in a crowded area and I don't want it to be the type of thing that would attract attention. It needs to be quiet."

The mechanic nodded. "When we get back to the shop, we'll pop the hood on your car and I'll show you exactly what your character would need to do. Will that help?"

"That would be perfect," Pallor agreed. "Here, let me buy you a refill."

Pallor signaled the waitress but his mechanic put his hand over his glass and shook his head. "I've got to drive home. One's the limit until I get my car parked, but I'll be happy to let you buy me a six-pack for later tonight."

Pallor smiled and said, "Done. Ready to go?"

When Pallor got back to his house that night, he pulled his car into the garage and shut the door. He practiced disabling his car and then fixing it back until he felt sure he could do it in the dark. Then he turned out the lights and proved to himself that he could.

~ ~ ~ ~

Thursday evening, Pallor showed up at Chris's door at 6:30 with a pizza and a bottle of wine. "My girlfriend just got called back to work. I was wondering if you'd like to help me dispose of this pizza. I thought we might as well drink the wine I bought to go with it, too," Pallor said when Chris opened the door. "That is, if you don't have plans."

"No, no plans. Come on in," Chris said. "Sorry, but I haven't gotten any furniture yet. I've been eating on the card table." Chris nodded towards a rather battered card table and a couple of folding chairs that were set up in the middle of the living room. The only other furniture was an entertainment center with a television, a DVD player, and a big boom box. Boxes of books, CDs, and DVDs lined the wall. A small lamp was perched on top of one of the boxes.

"Fine with me," Pallor said as he set the wine and pizza box on the card table while Chris disappeared into the kitchen.

"Paper plates and mugs okay? I haven't unpacked anything else yet," Chris called from the kitchen.

"Perfect," Pallor called back.

Chris brought two mugs, paper plates, and a roll of paper towels into the living room and laid them out on the table. "Let's eat before it gets cold," he said, pulling out a chair and clicking on the TV at the same time. "Mind watching the basketball game?"

"Not at all," Pallor said as he picked up a piece of pizza.

After they finished eating, Chris folded up the card table and they stretched out on the floor to watch the rest of the game. At halftime, Pallor asked Chris about his new job.

Chris told him all about the company, the people he'd met, and the general atmosphere in the office. Then he frowned. "It's a good company, I guess, but it's not exactly what I was expecting. They hired me to head up the marketing department for their new line of children's clothes. Monday

I found out that I'm the whole department. I have no staff, not even a secretary. I've got a desk in what I swear looks like an old storage closet."

"Not a good sign," Pallor agreed.

"They think school uniforms are going to become really popular over the next few years, so they've come up with a few designs, but everything's still in the talking stage. They want me to outline a campaign strategy and present it to the board in a month. To be honest, I know next to nothing about the market, the competition, or what's already out there, and without a staff, I'm not only going to have to do all of the research, I'm going to have to do all of the grunt work as well." Chris sighed. "It's not exactly what I was expecting. I'm beginning to think coming here might have been a big mistake."

"Well, if you decide you want out, you can always have a job with my firm as a model. I bet the pay's better, and I know it would be a lot more fun."

"Me? A model? You've got to be kidding."

"No, you have that classic All-American look that we watch for in models. I could put you in casual or dress clothes and you'd look the part. You'd make a great model," Pallor insisted, but Chris still looked doubtful. "Seriously, you'd do fine."

"I don't know about that, but if things don't improve at work, I may end up giving it a try. We'll see."

They watched the second half of the game and then Pallor got ready to leave. "You've got my card, right? It's got both my home and office numbers on it. Give me a call sometime and we'll go out for a few beers."

"Thanks, I will," Chris said as he shut the door.

~ ~ ~ ~

Friday morning, Pallor dropped by the diner for breakfast after the 7:00 rush was over. Joan looked tired, but she also looked depressed. When she came over with his coffee, he said, "You look a little upset this morning. Is everything all right?"

"It will be," Joan said with a half-smile. "I bet I've looked at twenty apartments in the last two weeks, but I can't find what I want. It gets a little discouraging after a while."

"What's wrong with where you're staying now?"

"Oh, it's horrible," Joan said, frowning.

"Why did you rent it then?"

'Because we didn't see it before we rented it," Joan answered. "I know, not the smartest thing, but when Karl decided to take this job, we had less than a week to move. So we called a real estate agent up here and told him we needed an apartment and that we didn't have time to look around. We told him that we would have to trust his judgment." Joan looked at the ceiling and shook her head. "He described it as a spacious four room garden apartment with a modern kitchen and bath."

"I take it you don't agree?" Pallor asked with a grin.

Joan laughed. "Not hardly!"

"Tell me about it. Seriously. I'm an author. I'm always looking for good settings."

"Okay, but let me get their order first, "Joan said with a nod towards a family that had just come in.

A few minutes later, she returned with a pot of coffee, a cup for herself, and a pastry for Pallor. She refilled his cup, poured hers, and sat down in the chair opposite him. "Are you sure you want to hear about that place?"

Pallor nodded.

"Okay. There are four rooms, but that's where any similarity to the agent's description ends. The rooms are all in a row, one behind the other, like train cars. You walk in the front door and you're in a living room so small that two chairs and a TV make it feel crowded. There's no hall. To

52

get to the kitchen from the living room, you have to walk straight through both of the bedrooms. The first bedroom is the master bedroom because it's the only room in the apartment large enough for a double bed. After the master bedroom, there's a child's bedroom, but you better have only one child or else you're going to need bunk beds. There aren't any closets, so for right now I'm using the second bedroom as storage."

Pallor chuckled. "Where's the bathroom?"

"It takes up half of the second bedroom, which is why there's only enough room for a single bed. It has two doors, one from each bedroom, but you can't have them both open at the same time. The sink is opposite the toilet, but it's so close that if you sit on the toilet, your knees are under the sink. And the shower stall is so small that Karl's elbows stay bruised. You really do need to be a contortionist to live there. And I don't know where all of the hot water goes, but neither of us has had a hot shower since we came to Omaha."

"Didn't your agent say it was modern? I thought modern baths were roomy."

Joan grinned. "Yeah, so did I. The kitchen's just as modern as the bath. It has one of those little half refrigerators, like the ones college kids have in their dorm rooms. The stove is a hot plate that's been bolted to the counter top. The sink is maybe half a foot deep and at full force, the water dribbles out of the faucet. There's one small cabinet above the counter with just enough room for a few dishes and utensils. I have to keep any groceries I buy stored in boxes stacked against the wall, and we're eating on TV trays because neither of my tables will fit in there."

"I lived in an apartment once, but it was no where near as bad as that one. One of the things that bothered me was that every time my neighbors argued, I could hear every word. I felt like an eavesdropper."

Joan nodded and said, "I know what you mean. Our walls are so thin that we don't even bother to turn on our television. We just listen to the neighbor's. And I'll just let you imagine what else we hear."

Pallor laughed. "I hope you didn't sign a year's lease."

"No. The only good thing about this place is that we rent it by the week. As soon as I can find another place, we're out of there, but in the meantime …" Joan shook her head. "Oh well, things will be better soon." Then she stood up and took out her order pad. "Now, what else can I get you for breakfast?"

Joan waited on a few other customers while Pallor ate his breakfast. As he was finishing, she stopped by his table to fill up his coffee cup again.

"I've got an idea," he said. "I own a rental house about five miles on the other side of Council Bluffs. It's the last house on a dead-end road and it's becoming vacant this weekend. It would probably add twenty or thirty minutes to your commute, but would you and your husband like to see it? I was going to run an ad in the newspaper this weekend, but if you want to see it, I'll hold off on the ad."

"When can we look at it?" Joan's eyes lit up.

"Let me see what it looks like when they move out. I'll drop by Monday and let you know when I can show it. Would that be okay?"

"Perfect!" Joan said as she pocketed his ticket. "You just made my day. Breakfast is on me!"

~ ~ ~ ~

When Pallor left the diner, he rushed over to the coffee house for his appointment with Theresa. She was sitting at a small table in the back. Pallor got a cup of coffee and joined her.

"I was beginning to think you'd stood me up," Theresa said with a grin.

"No, just running a little late this morning. Still engaged?" Pallor asked.

Theresa frowned. "Unfortunately, yes. Mr. Lopez wants us to select an engagement ring this weekend. Did your seminar group come up with anything?"

"Well, there was one interesting idea. A couple of the guys said that they'd run for the hills if the girl started asking them to spend a lot of money on her, especially along the lines of jewelry or clothes, things that would be exclusively for her, things she would be able to keep if they broke up."

Theresa frowned. "You mean ask him to buy me things before we're married? I'm not sure I could do that. It seems so … I don't know."

Pallor laughed. "Theresa! Do you want to marry this man or not?"

"No!"

"Then you're going to have to make him break it off, and you can't do that by being nice. You need to come across as a conniving, money grabbing bitch."

Theresa took a deep breath. "Okay. How do I do this?"

Pallor offered a few suggestions and then he said, "Treat this like a class assignment. Write a scene between a greedy, manipulating hussy and the older man who wants her. Use a jewelry store for your setting and buying an engagement ring as the focus. Have her pick out an extravagant ring, and then demand all kinds of accessories. You know, necklaces, bracelets, earrings, maybe a brooch. Get outrageous with it. Ask some of your friends for ideas. Then when the time comes, just step into the role and play the scene."

"That's a good idea," Theresa said, her eyes sparkling. "I bet I could do that."

"I've got a friend who owns a jewelry store. Let me talk to him and see what I can arrange. I'll even play the role of the eager sales clerk who wants to sell you everything in the store. If we set this up for when the store is closed, like a private showing just for the two of you, there won't be any chance that someone who knows you will walk in and ruin everything."

"That would be great, but I hate to get you involved in this. You don't even know me."

"I hate to admit it, but I'm looking forward to it. I used to do a bit of community theater when I was younger, but I haven't been on a stage in years. This is going to be loads of fun. Well, for everyone except Mr. Lopez," Pallor said with a smile. "Do you think you can put him off about the ring until the first of next week?"

"I'm sure I can. I can always have a headache."

"Okay. Let me talk to my friend over the weekend and see what I can set up. Meanwhile, get that scene written." Pallor stood up to go. "Can you meet me here Monday?"

Theresa nodded. "10:00?"

Pallor nodded and said, "See you then."

~ ~ ~ ~

Immediately after leaving the coffee house, Pallor dashed to the little restaurant where Steve Patterson ate lunch. Steve was already seated when Pallor arrived. He walked over towards Steve's table and asked, "Mind if I join you, Mr. Patterson?"

Steve didn't recognize the man, but he figured that he was either a former student or the parent of one of his students, so he smiled and nodded towards the empty chair.

"How are you enjoying your retirement?" Pallor asked.

"To be honest, it's not as much fun as I'd hoped it would be. In fact, sometimes, it's downright boring," Steve admitted.

Pallor nodded. "I was sorry to hear about your wife. That was a rough blow, I'm sure."

Steve nodded and felt the familiar lump form in his throat. "Yes, well …"

"My name's Paul Stewart, Mr. Patterson. You don't know me. I'm a writer. I did a piece on your retirement party for one of the local papers."

"That was quite a while ago. I'm surprised you recognized me."

"To be honest, I came here today looking for you," Pallor said. Steve frowned, but he didn't say anything, so Pallor continued. "I spotted you in here earlier this week, and an idea hit me. I thought I'd mention it to you and get your reaction."

"Okay, shoot."

"Like I said, I'm a writer. My area is primarily fantasy, but lately I've been thinking about trying a historical novel. Unfortunately, I'm under contract with my publisher, so I have to keep going with the fantasy series. If I'm ever going to get anywhere with the other book, I need someone to help me."

Steve shook his head and said, "Mr. Stewart, I'm not a writer. I don't think I could be much help to you."

"I don't need help with the writing. I need help with the research. I don't have time to dig through libraries or search the Internet. That's what I'd like to hire you to do."

Steve looked thoughtful. After a few minutes, he nodded. "I might be interested, but I'd need to know more about the book before I could promise anything."

"Understandable," Pallor said with a smile and a slight nod. "All of my notes are in my office at the house. Maybe we could get together for dinner sometime next week and go over the outline I've written and talk about the specifics a little. Would you be willing to meet with me?"

"Definitely," Steve said with a little more enthusiasm.

"Great! I'll call you and we'll set it up," Pallor said as he stood up to leave.

~ ~ ~ ~

After lunch, Pallor called Mr. Beasley, the senior partner of Beasley, Dixon, Matherson and Co. PA. Shortly after Kevin had accepted a job with them, Pallor had moved his considerable assets to their care.

When Mr. Beasley came on the line, Pallor said, "This is Paul Stewart. I'm going to need Kevin O'Reilly to handle a couple of things for me next week. I'm not sure when yet, but it may entail time outside of the standard office hours. Will that be a problem?"

"No, of course not. I assure you that he'll be available whenever you need him, regardless of the hour. You have my word."

"Thank you, Mr. Beasley. I'll hold you to that. I'll be back in touch next week with the details."

"Very good, Mr. Stewart. We're at your disposal."

~ ~ ~ ~

Friday evening, Pallor collapsed in his recliner, shut his eyes, and mentally took stock. He felt pretty sure that he could maneuver Joan, her husband, Theresa, Steve, and Darrell into position. He hoped that by disabling Chris's car, he could get him into position, too. Another phone call to Mr. Beasley would pretty much guarantee Kevin.

The best way to fake someone's death without having to produce a body was a storm at sea, but considering Omaha's location, that was not an option. However, between the Missouri River and the various local lakes and forests, a body sometimes turned up years after a person was reported missing, long after the authorities had given up looking.

The only way Pallor could come up with to explain the disappearance and presumed deaths of Kevin and his companions was to get them all in one place and hit them with a really big tornado, one that would carry the debris for miles. The tricky part was going to be keeping the storm from harming anyone else, and with those thoughts floating around in his head, Pallor fell asleep.

Chapter 9

Pallor's Plan Comes Together

Saturday morning, Pallor went to a remote wasteland on Terah and spent the day creating tornadoes, controlling their direction, speed, and strength, and then calming them down. When he got back home that evening, he mapped out the city bus routes and selected one that ran out to Mall of the Bluffs in Council Bluffs.

Sunday afternoon he tracked down the man who drove that route during the week and conned the driver into letting him make the last run every night for a few days by pretending to be a private investigator in the middle of a sensitive case. Of course a valid commercial driving license and a fistful of dollars helped his case.

Sunday evening Pallor pored over weather maps to see when the atmospheric conditions would be the most favorable for what he had in mind. After several hours, he came to the conclusion that Tuesday evening was going to be his best shot.

Pallor's first stop Monday morning was the diner. As soon as he sat down, Joan brought him a cup of coffee and a cheese danish, but she was too busy to stop and talk. He took his time eating and then lingered over several cups of coffee waiting for the crowd to thin out. When she brought his check, he said, "I went by the rental house last night. The people are gone, but their furniture and packing crates are still there. They left a note saying that the movers won't be able to get to it until tomorrow morning. Unfortunately, I have to go out of town Wednesday morning and I won't be back until after the weekend."

Joan's face fell, but she said, "That's fine. No rush."

"Well, I was wondering if you and your husband would like to see it tomorrow night. I know you won't be able to see much of the yard, but at least you'd get a good look at the inside."

"Tomorrow evening would be great!" A grin spread from ear to ear on Joan's face. "What time do you want us to meet you? Where is it? How do we get there?"

"It's sort of hard to find at night if you're not familiar with the area. Why don't you take the last bus out to Mall of the Bluffs tomorrow night and meet me at the main entrance? I'll take you out to the house and then I'll drop you off at your apartment on my way home."

"Are you sure?" Joan asked. "I hate for you to go to all that trouble."

"No trouble at all," Pallor said as he stood up to go. "Besides, I'd like to get a look at that apartment you're in. You never know, it might show up in one of my books one day."

~ ~ ~ ~

His next stop was the coffee shop. Theresa was seated so that she could see the door. She was watching for him and her eyes lit up when he walked in.

Pallor got a cup of coffee and joined her. "So, did you get it written?"

Theresa nodded. "I called some of my friends Friday night and laid out the scene for them over the phone. By the time we got together Saturday morning, they had all kinds of ideas and lines, and we came up with even more once we started talking. It was actually a lot of fun. Then, when I got home, I told my mother that I had a bad headache and didn't want to be disturbed. I spent the whole day in my room, writing and rewriting."

"Have you got it with you?"

Theresa pulled a folder out of her bag. Pallor held his hand out, and after a moment's hesitation, she handed it over. While he read, she played with her hair, bit her lips, and squirmed. Finally he laid the folder down on the table and grinned at her.

"That's good work, Theresa. If you're half as demanding as your female lead, he'll run for the hills. Can you play the part?"

"I'll be nervous, but I can do it." Theresa had spent all day Sunday in her room, practicing her lines in front of her mirror, trying out different facial expressions and hand movements, working on it until it felt almost natural.

"As soon as you come into the store, concentrate on me. Play the scene for me. Don't worry about Mr. Lopez. He has a minor role. We're the actors."

Theresa laughed and nodded.

"Now, here's what I want you to do," Pallor said. He told her to take the last bus out to Mall of the Bluffs Tuesday evening and have Mr. Lopez meet her at the jewelry store. "My friend and I went through everything he had in stock this weekend and picked out the most exquisite pieces for me to show you. Be sure you pick them up and try them on while you're telling him that he has to buy them for you, and when he resists, really pour it on. If you play it like you wrote it, it'll scare him off for sure."

"I hope this works," Theresa said. "Well, I've got to get to class." She gathered up her papers and put them back in her book bag. "Thanks, Mr. Stewart. Keep your fingers crossed!"

Pallor nodded and gave her a thumbs-up.

~ ~ ~ ~

After lunch, Pallor called Darrell and told him that he had reserved a recording studio for late Tuesday evening, and asked him to take the last bus out to Mall of the Bluffs and meet him at the entrance. Then he said, "We'll take my car out to the recording studio and when we finish up there, I thought we'd drop by a new sports bar that I want to check out."

Darrell hesitated a second and then said, "Okay."

"Don't worry. The only thing I drink at a sports bar is coffee. It's all business for me. Have you tried doing a play-by-play with one of your old games yet?"

Darrell chuckled.

Pallor said, "I'll take that as a yes. Good. How did it go?"

"I got so tongue-tied the first time I tried to do it that I nearly gave up. I don't know whether I'm any good or not, but at least I'm not choking on my own words anymore."

Pallor laughed. "The first time's always the worst, but that one's behind you now. I'm sure you'll do fine. See you tomorrow."

After Darrell hung up, all the confidence he had built up by practicing over the weekend flew out the window. His hands began to sweat and his stomach began to churn. He felt just like he always did right before a big game.

~ ~ ~ ~

Steve had spent his weekend visiting computer stores, trying out different models, talking to salesmen, and collecting information sheets and prices. Monday morning, he had gone online at the library to check out different Internet service providers and software packets. By the time he got home Monday afternoon, he had decided that unless the subject matter of the book was objectionable, he was going to take the job.

He had just walked in the door when the phone rang.

"Mr. Patterson? This is Paul Stewart. Are you still willing to meet with me and discuss my outline?" Pallor asked.

"Yes I am," Steve answered. "As a matter of fact, I'm looking forward to it."

"Good! I'm glad to hear it. Would late tomorrow evening be all right with you?"

"Fine. Where should I meet you?"

"Why don't you take the last bus out to Mall of the Bluffs? I've got a late appointment out there, but I'll be done by 9:00. If you'll meet me at the entrance, I'll take you to a small restaurant I know that's right outside of town for a late dinner. They stay open until 1:00, so we'll have plenty of time to talk about the research topics. I can drop you off at your house on my way home."

"Sounds good to me. See you tomorrow night," Steve said as he disconnected.

~ ~ ~ ~

When Pallor showed up to drive the last bus route Monday evening, he was wearing glasses, a fake mustache, and a beard. His cap was pulled down over his hair and his jacket was zipped up to hide the padding he had used to add weight to his slim figure.

The regular bus driver stared at him for a few minutes and then grinned. "Almost didn't recognize you. Look, I don't mind helping you with your investigation, Mr. Carter, but I can't let you take this bus without checking you out. I'll ride along with you tonight and if all goes well, you're on your own tomorrow. Okay?"

Pallor hesitated just long enough to keep the man from getting suspicious and then he nodded. When he parked the bus at the garage two hours later, the regular driver shook his hand and said, "She's all yours for as long as you need her. Good luck with your case."

~ ~ ~ ~

Around 3:30 in the morning, Pallor dressed in black, drove out to Chris's apartment complex, and parked in the shadows. After thirty minutes, he got out of his car and walked over to Chris's. He opened the door, popped the hood, loosened the wire exactly like his mechanic had told him to, quietly closed the hood, and walked back to his own car. He waited twenty minutes before starting his car and driving home.

When he got home, he changed clothes again and settled in his office to wait until 7:00, when he would drive back over to Chris's apartment to rescue him.

Pallor pulled into the parking lot just as Chris climbed out of his car. He stood beside it shaking his head and looking totally helpless. Pallor parked beside him and got out. "Car problems?"

"Yeah. It won't start and I have no idea what to do," Chris said with a shrug. "Are you headed over to your girlfriend's at this time of the morning? I hope she's expecting you."

"She's on nights this week. She'll be getting home in about fifteen minutes. I was going to surprise her and take her out for breakfast, but I can do that another day. Come on. I'll take you to work," Pallor said as he got back in his car.

"Are you sure?" Chris asked. "I hate to mess up your plans."

"No big deal, really. She isn't expecting me. Do you want me to call my mechanic and have him take a look?"

"Would he be willing to come out here? I mean, I can't get it started, so I can't exactly take it to him," Chris said as he settled into the passenger seat of Pallor's car.

"No problem. He has a tow truck. If he can't fix it here, he'll tow it to the shop. I'll call him as soon as I drop you off. He'll probably have it fixed by the time you get home tonight," Pallor assured him.

"That'd be great. I really appreciate it."

"I have to see a client out at Mall of the Bluffs this evening, but after that, I don't have any plans. Like I said, my girlfriend is on nights. Do you want to meet me, go get some dinner, maybe have a few drinks?"

"Okay. Where do you want me to meet you?"

"Why don't you take the last bus out to the mall and meet me at the main entrance? The bus stop is only about half a block from your office building. I'll show it to you when we pass it."

A few minutes later, Pallor pointed out the bus stop and told him what time to be there. "Is that going to be too late for you?"

Chris shook his head no. "I've got so much work to do I could stay here until midnight every night and still not get it all done."

When he stopped in front of Chris's building, Chris said, "Thanks," and then as he got out of the car, he added, "See you tonight."

~ ~ ~ ~

When Pallor got home, he called his accounting firm. Once he had Mr. Beasley on the phone, he said, "I have some instructions for Kevin. Would you please see that they are followed to the letter? It's important."

"Certainly, sir. Would you like for me to tape your instructions?"

"No, that's not necessary. Just be sure to pass them along. A briefcase will be delivered to your firm this evening, probably around 8:00. I want Kevin to sign for it, take the last bus to Mall of the Bluffs, and bring the briefcase to me at the main entrance. Afterwards, I'll drive him back home. I need to talk to him anyway."

"Certainly, sir. I'll see to it."

After Mr. Beasley hung up, he buzzed Kevin and asked him to come to his office. When Kevin arrived, Mr. Beasley told him about the phone call and that he was to follow the instructions precisely, no variations, or it would be his job.

~ ~ ~ ~

When Pallor sat down behind the wheel of the bus Tuesday evening, he was in the same disguise he had worn the night before. The only passengers he allowed to board the bus were the seven people he wanted to send to Terah. As they traveled through town headed for the expressway that would carry them to the mall, his passengers were too absorbed in their own thoughts to notice how seldom he stopped. The bus company was going to get a few phone calls from some irate customers that evening, but by morning those same people were going to be very glad that the bus had passed them by.

All day long, as Chris had struggled with stacks of surveys and catalogues without any help, thoughts about Paul's offer of a job with the modeling agency had floated through his head. By the time he left his office, he had made up his mind to talk to Paul about it that night. He was trying to think of a tactful way to bring it up when remnants of a quiet conversation near the front of the bus distracted him.

"Just don't get your hopes up, honey," a rugged, outdoors-type man said to the woman beside him. "Wait and see. We don't have to move tomorrow." He put his arm around her and gave her a quick hug.

Joan playfully poked him in the ribs with her finger and whispered, "You want out of there every bit as bad as I do, Karl. I've got a good feeling about this one. You'll see. We'll be out of that place by the end of the week."

That afternoon, she had put a bottle of wine in the refrigerator to chill. If this house worked out, she was planning to invite Paul in for some wine and cheese to celebrate. She gave Karl's hand a little squeeze and glanced around the bus. One of the other passengers caught her eye, a young woman who kept wiping her hands on her skirt and fidgeting. The way her head and lips were moving, she was obviously engaged in some kind of conversation, but Joan couldn't tell if she was mumbling to herself or rehearsing lines for a play.

Theresa had butterflies in her stomach and her hands were damp. She didn't think she could have been any more nervous if she'd been going on stage and no matter how many times she played through the scene in her head, she couldn't relax. Finally, in an effort to distract herself, she looked around at the other passengers on the bus, trying to guess where they might be going by the way they were dressed.

One of the passengers was about her age and looked very familiar, but she couldn't quite place him. At first she thought he might have been in one of her classes, but that didn't feel right. She had a feeling that she'd seen his picture recently, maybe in the newspaper.

Darrell was almost as nervous as Theresa. He had planned to drive his own car so that he could leave when he wanted to, but around lunchtime, he'd started getting uneasy, and as the afternoon had worn on, he'd become more and more jittery. Finally he'd decided that he was too tense to drive, so he'd taken the bus.

While he was looking around the bus, he noticed someone else who seemed edgy: a slim, relatively short man who was probably older than he looked. He wore glasses that he kept taking off and putting back on, and he was squirming in his seat. He looked more like a high school nerd than anything else. The old beat-up briefcase resting on his lap didn't really fit with his expensive, tailor-made suit. It made the whole picture seem off, like something was out of place.

The briefcase was heavy and Kevin wanted nothing more than to be rid of it. He didn't know what was in it, and he didn't want to know. The whole situation was weird, almost like part of a game. He liked his job, even if it was pretty boring most of the time, and he didn't want to lose it, but many more errands like this one and he'd have to quit. That afternoon, Mr. Beasley had acted like this was a normal function of an accounting firm, but Kevin knew better.

His anxiety over the briefcase made him feel like everyone on the bus was watching him. In fact, the man seated in front of him looked like what Kevin thought an undercover cop would look like. He was an older man dressed in jeans and a sweater, and he had a baseball cap in his hands. He looked alert and thoughtful, and that made Kevin uncomfortable.

Steve felt like fate had intervened and sent him a project just when he was ready for one. That morning, he had gone back to one of the computer stores and bought a new computer, scanner, and printer. After he had his system up and running, he'd made a couple of phone calls, and by late afternoon he had Internet service. He could hardly wait to find out what the book was about and get started doing the research. He felt like he was finally beginning to come out of mourning.

The bus was less than a mile from the mall when sharp lightening lit up the sky and the wind began to howl. The bus rocked against the wind, and when Chris looked out the window, the sky looked eerie and he saw a strange looking cloud.

A few seconds later, Steve glanced out the window and yelled, "On the floor! Everyone! On the floor!"

Kevin looked at Steve, momentarily stunned by the sheer horror on Steve's face.

Karl grabbed Joan, pulled her to the floor, and tried to cover her with his body.

Darrell grabbed Theresa and half threw, half dragged her to the floor. Chris fell on top of them.

Steve grabbed Kevin and pulled him down just as the tornado hit.

The bus was lifted off the road and started to spin. Glass blew out of the windows with a crashing sound, and the metal in the bus screeched as it was being pulled apart.

The last thing that Chris saw was a brilliant bluish-white light; then everything went black.

Chapter 10

Wednesday, March 21

Kalen was pacing back and forth across his living room, mumbling. He had no idea what was going on, how many people to expect, when they would arrive, nothing. All he knew was that time was quickly running out.

When Pallor popped in, Kalen blurted out, "It's about time you got here. How many did you bring? Did you tell them anything about Terah? Or about Myron?"

When Kalen paused for a breath, Pallor shook his head. "None of them know anything, Kalen. They don't even know each other."

"What?! I thought the companions were all going to be friends of his!"

"I know. That was the plan." Pallor shrugged. "But he didn't have any friends."

"No friends?!" Kalen gasped. "What's wrong with him?"

"Nothing's wrong with him. He's just never had any friends. It's the way he grew up."

For a moment, Kalen stood there with his mouth hanging open. Then he asked, "What am I going to do? How am I going to get them to go with him? And protect him?" Kalen shook his head, completely bewildered. "Complete strangers?!"

Pallor nodded. "Look, I'm sorry, but that's the best I could do under the circumstances. I hate to dump all of this on you, but I've to get back. Good luck." Pallor handed Kalen the briefcase, turned the key, and vanished.

~ ~ ~ ~

When the passengers from the bus came to, they found themselves in a large, circular meadow. Around the outside of the meadow was a ring of huge stones standing about five feet apart, with slightly smaller stones balanced on top, giving the appearance of a stone wall with a lot of doors. Several feet inside that circle was a second circle, made up of smaller stones. A dense forest surrounded the whole area and there was no sign of any other people anywhere.

After they introduced themselves to each other, they talked about the tornado, wondered what had happened to the driver, and marveled at how lucky they were to be alive and relatively unharmed. At a lull in the conversation, Karl asked if anyone had any idea where they were.

"We've got to be in some kind of museum or park," Chris said as he motioned towards the stones. "Doesn't this look a lot like Stonehenge, or rather what it must have looked like when it was first built?"

Steve nodded and said, "But I've never heard of a replica being built anywhere near Omaha." Then he walked over to one of the closest stones and examined it for a moment. "These stones are real, not concrete, and they look like they've been here a while."

"Could it be an old Indian mound of some kind?" Theresa asked. "Maybe a sacred burial area or something?"

"I don't think any of the Indians from this area built anything that looked like this," Karl answered. "I agree with Chris. It must be some kind of exhibit, but I don't see any signs that people have been here, not even any litter. Why build something like this unless you want people to come look at it?"

Darrell slowly turned all the way around, looking for a gap in the trees. "There has to be a road around here somewhere. Those stones are huge. You'd need heavy equipment to set them up."

"Maybe we should walk around the perimeter and see if we can find an entrance of some kind," Chris suggested.

"Wait a minute," Steve said, frowning at Kevin. "You were wearing glasses on the bus. Do you need them to see?"

Kevin shook his head. "The glasses were just plain glass. I bought them to fit the image. No one trusts an accountant with good eyesight. I'm fine."

As they began to spread out, Kevin cleared his throat and said, "But while we're looking around, could you keep an eye out for an old battered briefcase? I was supposed to deliver it to a client, and I really need to find it. My job depends on it." The others nodded and headed out towards the woods.

The undergrowth was so thick that the forest was virtually impenetrable. After a while, Kevin spotted a narrow and overgrown path leading away from the meadow, right through the thickets. "Hey! I found something over here," he yelled and motioned for the others to join him. By the time everyone else got there, the path looked wider and clearer than it had at first. Kevin blinked his eyes a couple of times and then forgot about it.

"I guess this must be the way then," Karl said. He reached for Joan's hand and stepped towards the trail.

Kevin stepped back as the others started to follow. Steve looked at him with raised eyebrows. "I haven't found that briefcase and I really can't leave without it," Kevin explained. "The rest of you go on. I'll catch up later."

Steve shook his head. "If whatever was in that briefcase was all that important, your client should have picked it up himself. There's no telling where it is now."

"And if there was anything really valuable in it, I'm sure he had it insured. No one can hold you responsible for a tornado," Karl added.

"Come on, Kevin. We need to stick together," Joan said. "There's no telling how far it is to a main road or even if this path leads to a main road."

"Okay," Kevin answered slowly. "I guess you're right. I can always come back later and search for it."

~ ~ ~ ~

Three hours later, they were still walking through the woods. They were all getting tired, but Theresa was about ready to call it a day. She didn't want to hold the others up, but she honestly didn't know if she could make herself go much farther in her heels. Of all times to get dressed up.

Chris was having similar problems. His feet felt like they were so swollen that if he dared take his shoes off, he'd never get them back on. If he'd had any idea how his day was going to turn out, he never would have worn these shoes. They were only about a month old and definitely not broken in enough for a hike. He was on the verge of suggesting a nice long rest break when he saw something off to the side of the trail.

After a few moments, he realized that he was looking at a small cabin sitting in a thick grove of trees. It was dark and gloomy, but there was a thin trail of smoke coming out of the chimney so someone had to be there.

"Hey!" Chris said to get everyone's attention. Then he pointed towards the cabin. "Look. See that smoke? Someone's got to be there, or else close by. Maybe he has a phone."

As Chris started to head for the cabin, Steve grabbed his arm. "Hold on. Wait a minute." Steve looked around the woods in that area and shook his head. "I don't see any sign of a road, electrical lines, or telephone lines. I think we've either stumbled across a hunting cabin or some kind of hermit. Either way, whoever's in there is probably well-armed."

Karl nodded. "And without knowing anything about whoever's in there, I don't think it would be a good idea for all of us to go storming up to his front door."

"Okay," Chris said slowly. "But someone has to. If nothing else, whoever's in that cabin can point us in the right direction."

"I agree," Karl said. "The only question is who's going to go up to that door. I sure don't want Joan to, and I don't think Theresa should be the one to go either."

"Why not?" Joan asked. "Wouldn't it be a lot less threatening to see a woman out here in the middle of nowhere than to see a strange man?"

"Maybe less threatening to whoever's in there, but not less dangerous for you," Karl answered.

"She does have a point," Chris said slowly.

"I agree with Karl," Darrell spoke up. "Why don't I go up there by myself? One man, by himself, wouldn't be much more threatening than a woman, and maybe whoever's in there would be less likely to get physical with someone who can get physical right back."

Steve nodded. "I think you're right as far as the one man part goes, but I'm the better candidate. You're young and obviously strong. No one would have any doubt whatsoever that you could take care of yourself, which some people might read as a threat. I'm older, and there's no way anyone would think I was dangerous. And besides, I'm the only one dressed for the part of a lost hiker. I'm going."

As Steve took a step in the direction of the cabin, Chris stopped him. "What if he shoots first and asks questions later?"

Steve shrugged. "If you see a gun, duck. I know I will."

As Steve made his way to the cabin, the others backtracked a little ways down the trail so that they would be out of sight from the door of the cabin. Then they settled in to wait.

When Steve knocked on the door, it slowly swung open revealing a bright and cheerful room with soft white walls and beautiful rugs scattered over the floor. Large windows looked out over exquisite gardens and spacious lawns.

The entrance room was larger than the whole cabin had looked from the outside, and appeared to be a combination living room and office. There was a big fireplace on one side of the room with shelves full of strange knickknacks on each side of it. On the other side of the room was a modern executive-style desk. In between, were couches and big overstuffed chairs, each with its own lamp table, but the tables had small black boxes on them instead of lamps. From the front door, Steve could see a hall leading to other rooms, and a very enticing aroma of freshly cooked food drifted from that direction.

A gruff voice emanating from somewhere deep in the house called out, "Well, don't just stand there, come on in, and tell the others to come on in, too! You must be starving. Dinner's been ready for hours. What took you so long?"

Steve wasn't sure whether he should enter the cabin or wait at the door until the owner of that voice made an appearance. It was clear that the man was expecting someone, but Steve wasn't sure he should take advantage of the man's hospitality. He decided to err on the side of caution, so he waited at the door.

After a couple of seconds, a man stepped out into the hall carrying a large mug. At first glance, Steve placed his age at anywhere from forty to eighty. He was maybe four feet tall and at least two feet wide, but there didn't appear to be an ounce of fat on him. His face and hands looked like seasoned leather and seemed a bit too large for his body. He wore black leggings, black boots, and a brown tunic, gathered at the waist by a wide leather belt. His thick grizzled hair hung several inches below his shoulders, and a full gray beard reached halfway down his chest. At the center of his chest, right at the point of his beard, was a large pendant, and in the center of that pendant was a light blue stone shimmering with deep violet bands. All in all, he did not look that friendly.

"Don't just stand there with your mouth hanging open. Call the others," Kalen demanded.

Steve turned to the woods and signaled to the others to come in. Then as he stepped through the door into the large front room, Kalen offered him the mug. Steve took it and raised it to his lips. As he smelled the cold dark liquid to see if he could identify it, a strange sense of well-being came over him. When he sipped it, he found the taste unusual, but quite pleasant.

Kalen pointed to one of the chairs, and Steve gratefully accepted the invitation to sit down with his drink. Then Kalen disappeared into the kitchen for a minute and returned carrying a tray with enough mugs of scog for everyone. As the others entered the cabin, he handed each of them a mug. Almost immediately, Kalen knew which one was Myron. He looked just like Yvonne.

Once they were all settled on the couches and chairs, Kalen introduced himself and told them that he was pleased that they had finally arrived.

His visitors looked at each other in confusion. Finally Chris spoke up. "You act like you were expecting us, but that doesn't make sense. We don't even know where we are. The last thing any of us remember before we woke up in the meadow was our bus being hit by a tornado."

"Maybe someone has been through here looking for us," Joan said to Chris. Then she looked at Kalen and asked, "Are they searching this area? Do they know we're here?"

"Don't worry about the details right now. We'll talk after you've eaten," Kalen said. "Dinner will be on the table in about fifteen minutes. In the meantime, enjoy your scog." Then he turned and walked back down the hall toward the kitchen.

"Scog? What's scog?" Theresa whispered. She had yet to raise the mug to her lips.

"I think it's our drink." Joan sipped the dark liquid again. "I don't think I've ever tasted anything quite like it, but it's nice."

"If I were you, I'd drink it slowly," Steve said. "I was pretty tense when I came in here, but now that I've had a few sips I feel much more relaxed."

"I'm glad it's not just me," Darrell said quietly. "I feel almost tranquilized." He sat back and closed his eyes for a moment. "Did anyone else notice that he had the right number of mugs on that tray? Was he really waiting for us?"

"I don't see how he could have been," Karl answered. "Perhaps it's just one big mix-up."

"As long as he feeds us before he figures it out," Chris said with a sigh. "I'm starved."

While they waited for their host to reappear, an easy silence filled the room.

A few minutes later, Kalen returned and asked them to follow him to the dining room. The first thing they noticed about the dining room was its size, and the second thing they noticed was the long table loaded with platters of meat, bowls of vegetables, freshly baked bread, fruits, and pastries.

Kalen motioned to the chairs, and as his visitors seated themselves he told them to enjoy their meal, and that he would wait for them in the living room.

The food, delicious by any standards, was particularly good since it had been so long since any of them had had anything to eat. Finally, when everyone was finished, they went back to the living room, and had a seat.

Joan was the first to break the uneasy silence. "Thank you for dinner. We really enjoyed it."

Kalen nodded and mumbled, "You're welcome."

After another minute of tense silence had passed, Chris asked, "Could you tell us where we are? And do you have a phone? We need to call our families and let them know we're alive and where we are."

"We need to call in to our jobs, too," Karl added.

Theresa stared at her hands, clasped in her lap, and whispered, "I don't care whether anyone finds out where I am or not."

Joan was the only one who heard her. She gave Theresa a questioning look, but Theresa didn't say anything else.

"I'm sorry, but I'm afraid you won't be able to contact anyone from the other side," Kalen said.

"The other side?" Chris asked. "The other side of what?"

"The other side of the gate," Kalen answered quietly. He didn't know how to go about telling these people that they would never see Earth again, and he had no idea how they might react. It was going to be awkward at best, and he felt sure that he'd probably bungle it.

"What gate?" Darrell asked quietly. "Just where are we anyway?"

"You're on Terah, Earth's double," Kalen replied. "You left Earth when the tornado hit the bus. The meadow where you woke up is on Terah. The tall stones around the meadow make up the gateway."

"Okay," Karl said slowly. He figured it would be best to humor the man. "How do we get back to Earth?"

"I'm afraid that you can never return to Earth," Kalen said with a deep sigh. "By now, everyone on Earth thinks that all of you are dead."

"Look, is there a phone anywhere around here?" Joan asked impatiently. She wanted to call her parents and let them know that she and Karl were all right.

"We don't have telephones on Terah. We communicate with letters delivered mostly by falcons." Kalen looked a little embarrassed.

"All right then," Steve said in a conciliatory tone. "Where's the nearest town?"

"About fifteen miles away, but I can't let you go into town at this point," Kalen answered.

"What do you mean you can't let us?" Chris asked. "What's going on here?" He leaned forward as if he was going to stand up.

"Look. I'm putting all of this very badly. I really don't know how to explain it to you." Kalen looked around the group, hoping for some kind of clue as to how to approach this. "Maybe I should start at the beginning. Twenty-three years ago, a son was born to Badec, of the House of Nordin. He's the Seated Sorcerer of Camden and the Master Sorcerer of Terah. His wife, Yvonne, died shortly after the boy was born. To protect the heir to the Master's Chair from his enemies, Badec arranged for an elf named Pallor to take the child to Earth and place him with foster parents." Kalen took a deep breath, looked into Kevin's eyes and said, "You are that child."

Kevin's mouth dropped open. After a moment, he stammered, "What? What are you talking about?"

"An elf?" Joan asked.

"Master Sorcerer?" Steve asked.

Kalen nodded. "I know this sounds like a fantasy story to you, but believe me, it's all quite real." Kalen paused, stood up, and slowly turned around so everyone could get a good look at him. "I'm a dwarf. Surely you've noticed that I don't really look like the humans you're used to, right?"

No one said anything. They just looked back and forth at each other, so Kalen sighed and continued. "All of you must have met Pallor at one time or another, but you probably knew him as Paul Stewart. That's the name he's using on Earth right now. Do you know who I'm talking about?"

"Paul? An elf? No way!" Darrell said. "I was supposed to meet him out at the shopping center. He's the reason I was on that bus!"

Chris sank back into the cushions of the couch and frowned. "My car wouldn't start. I thought it was a stroke of luck that Paul happened along right when I needed a ride."

Steve shook his head. "I checked him out. He's a writer who has lived in Omaha for the past year. Before that he lived in Memphis."

Kevin sighed. "I used to live in Memphis, too. He moved to Omaha when I did. He's my godfather."

Karl shook his head and said, "I'm having a really hard time believing any of this."

"Let me continue with the story." Kalen turned to Kevin and said, "Your mother was a seer. She knew that she was going to die shortly after you were born, so she wanted all the arrangements for your childhood made before your birth. She and Badec decided that Earth would be the safest place for you, so Pallor found a young couple who wanted a son. When you were about a week old, he carried you to Earth, and he's kept a close eye on you ever since. Your father planned to send for you when you reached your twenty-fifth birthday so that you could return to Terah and begin your study of magic."

No one spoke, but their disbelief was almost tangible. Kalen sighed and concentrated on convincing Kevin. "Think about it. Do you remember the stories that Pallor told you when you were a child? Do you remember the books he gave you? He was trying to let you know that there was something beyond what you could see and touch. Magic flows through you; it's in your blood. It's who you are."

For several seconds Kevin stared at Kalen in shock. Then he shook his head vigorously, as if he were trying to clear it. "What are you talking about? This is crazy!"

Kalen was not upset by Kevin's outburst. He just continued talking. "Haven't you ever wondered how you ended up with brown hair and brown eyes when both of your parents had red hair and green eyes?"

Kevin's mouth dropped open. "How do you know what my parents look like?"

Kalen smiled. "I know a lot more than that. I know your father works for a law firm, and that he made partner shortly after your birth. I know that your mother went to her mother's in Montana while she was supposed to be pregnant with you. I know that you had a nurse when you were young, and that your parents didn't spend much time with you while you were growing up."

Kevin frowned and shook his head. "How could you possibly know all of this?"

Kalen gave Kevin a moment to think before he continued. "Haven't you always felt like you were somehow different? Like you didn't really belong? Haven't you ever wondered if maybe you were adopted? Have you ever had dreams about people and places that you couldn't identify? You probably inherited some of your mother's gift of sight as well as your father's magic." Kalen continued to look deep into Kevin's eyes. Kevin's face had slowly drained of color as the truth of Kalen's words sank in, but his eyes were full of disbelief. "You know I'm telling the truth, don't you? Somewhere deep inside, you know it, Myron. Yes, that's your real name. Myron, of the House of Nordin."

Kalen looked around at the others to see how they were taking all of this. The disbelief was beginning to give way to confusion, so he continued. "You had an old briefcase with you on the bus. It held the key to the Gate Between the Worlds. The key had to be in your possession to ensure your safety. It activated automatically when you saw the tornado, and everyone around you was transported with you. Your fear activated the key because you're from Terah."

Kevin was slowly shaking his head, but the other passengers were looking back and forth between Kalen and Kevin. Kalen could tell they didn't really believe him yet, but at least they were thinking about what he'd said.

The whole thing sounded absurd to the other passengers, but so did the fact that all of them had survived a direct hit by that tornado with basically no injuries. And Kalen's house looked so small and primitive from the outside, but it was so large and comfortable on the inside. They all had to admit, at least to themselves, that something weird was definitely going on.

Then Kevin suddenly remembered something that Kalen had said that was definitely wrong. Maybe if that was wrong, so was the rest of it. "Wait a minute. According to the story you just told us, if I really am the son of this Badec guy, I was supposed to be brought back to Terah when I turned twenty-five. Well, I'm not twenty-five. I've just turned twenty-three. So something's wrong here."

A look of deep sadness flashed over Kalen's face. It was gone almost as quickly as it appeared. "Unfortunately, your father has become gravely ill. He's in a coma and no one knows whether he will wake up or not, but if and when he does, he will probably be too weak to assume his place as the Master Sorcerer. His sister, Laryn, is his second. She'll have to notify the council of his condition at the meeting in April."

Then Kalen looked away from Kevin and spoke to the group as a whole. "I need to explain a little about Terah so that you'll understand the significance of Badec's illness. The humans of our world are governed by the Council of Sorcerers. The council is made up of thirteen sorcerers, each representing a province. The only two ways that a sorcerer can get on the council are to inherit the chair or to challenge a seated sorcerer for his chair. The Master Sorcerer is the chairman of the council, and the only people who can challenge him are the other seated sorcerers."

Kalen once more turned towards Kevin and said, "Your father has been the Master Sorcerer for the past thirty years, ever since his father's death. Few have dared to challenge him because his magic is so strong."

Kalen turned back to the others. "If a sorcerer resigns, dies, or for some reason can't continue, the chair passes to the oldest child with magical ability. The sorcerer's second is allowed to hold the chair as a non-voting member of the council for exactly one year if the heir has not reached his thirtieth birthday in order to give him time to hone his skills." Kalen looked back at Kevin, and said, "So, we had to bring you back early. I'm sorry, but you have one year from the beginning of April to be ready to take over as Master Sorcerer." Kalen looked around the room. He couldn't help but wonder if any of what he was saying was sinking in.

"I don't understand," Joan said quietly. "You said that the heir has one year to hone his skills before he has to take the chair. Why? What kind of skills?"

Kalen took a deep breath and let it out in a long sigh. "His magic skills, especially the ones he needs for self-defense. A challenge between seated sorcerers is basically a magical duel, and it's fought to the death. So …"

Joan's eyes opened wide as the implications registered. "If I understand this right, you're saying that Kevin has one year to learn how to defend himself magically against sorcerers who have been at this for years? And that if he loses, he dies?"

After a couple of minutes of strained silence, Kalen nodded. Then he looked at Kevin and added, "I guess I should also warn you that there will be people searching for you as soon as Badec's condition becomes known.

"A few of the stronger council members would like to see you take your seat so that they can challenge you for the Master's Chair. But there are other sorcerers who are afraid that given the opportunity to develop your skills, you'll become as powerful as your father, so they'll probably send out assassins to try to kill you before you can learn to protect yourself. That would leave the Master's Chair vacant.

"If that were to happen, the stronger sorcerers would fight it out amongst themselves for the right to sit in that chair. With no one setting any rules or limits, everything in their paths would be destroyed. That happened once before, hundreds of years ago. We cannot allow that to happen again."

Kalen paused and took a deep breath. "It is our hope that no one, including the council members, will know where you are until you're able to defend yourself."

Chris was the first to recover enough to speak, but his voice was strained. "Okay. That explains why Kevin's here. But what about the rest of us? Why are we here? And what happened to the bus driver? Did you guys just let him die?"

"We didn't let anyone die. Pallor was the bus driver. When the tornado hit the bus, he was transported along with the rest of you. He retrieved the key and returned to Earth before you regained consciousness. Right now, he's handling all the odds and ends about the accident and your supposed deaths." Kalen paused to let that idea sink in.

"Look," Darrell said, "I can understand that you don't want anyone on Earth to know about Terah. We wouldn't tell anyone. After all, who'd believe us? They'd lock us up. Just give us another key and we'll be on our way. Your secret's safe with us."

"I'm afraid it isn't quite that easy," Kalen said. "You really can't go back. If you ever went through the gate again, you would return at the precise moment when you left, and there is no way that you could survive a direct hit by that storm."

"But you just said that Paul, or Pallor, or whatever his name is, went back! Did he end up back in the tornado?" Darrell asked angrily.

"Pallor's an elf! And he's from Terah. He doesn't have to use the gate. You do." Kalen stood up and slowly gazed around the group. "As to why the rest of you are here, Pallor was supposed to find a small group of people from Earth to go with Myron and help him fulfill his destiny. You're that group."

"So you just kidnapped us? And now you think you can force us to work for you?" Darrell asked, even angrier.

"We did not kidnap any of you, and no one's forcing you to do anything. Pallor had a reason for choosing each of you. I don't know what it was, but I'd be willing to bet that each of you were at a turning point in your life, looking for something, wanting a change. He was giving you a chance to be part of something really important." Kalen's patience was running out. "But whether you choose to help us out or not, you cannot go back to Earth!"

"I'll admit that I wasn't exactly happy with the way things were going, but who knows what tomorrow might have brought? You really had no right to do this, you know. Not without asking." Chris was angry, too.

"Be careful what you wish for," Theresa softly mumbled, "That's what he said to me the first time I met him." Then she glanced around at the others and said, "Well, I don't know about the rest of you, but I'm tired. Is there anywhere around here where we could lie down for a bit. I feel like I've had about all that I can take for one day."

"I have a lot of questions, but I agree with Theresa, not tonight," Karl said. "I'm too tired to listen to any more right now."

"Of course. I have the guest rooms ready for you. Oh, I need to tell you about our lights. We use glowstones," Kalen said as he pointed to a small black box on one of the end tables. When he opened the box, light streamed out and lit up the room. When he closed it, the light vanished. His guests looked puzzled, so Kalen shrugged and said, "We don't have electricity on Terah. When you want light, open the box. Close it when you don't. It's easy." Kalen moved towards the long hall, "Now, Myron, your room is the first door on the left. Chris, yours is next, and Darrell yours is the last. On the right, we have Theresa, then Karl and Joan, and the last room is Steve's. Is there anything that I can get for any of you?"

"I wouldn't mind a brandy. Do you have that here?" Steve asked quietly.

"No. I'm sorry. How about another mug of scog? Or maybe a glass of wine?" Kalen offered.

"I think I would like another mug of scog. Maybe it will help me sleep."

"Anyone else? No? Well, Steve, I'll bring your scog to your room in a minute. Good night." Kalen escaped into the kitchen.

After Kalen left, no one could think of anything to say. They were all too bewildered. After a bit, Theresa said, "Maybe we'll all wake up tomorrow and find that this has been a dream. I'm going to bed. Which room did he say was mine?"

"I'll come with you. Your room is next to ours," Joan said. Then she looked at Karl. "Are you ready to go get some sleep?"

Karl nodded. Then he looked at Steve and asked, "Do you think there's any truth to what he's saying?"

"I don't know," Steve replied. "But I do know that something's strange here. Did you notice how small the cabin appeared from the outside? And how big this place is on the inside?"

"Yeah," Darrell said as everyone else nodded. "That's one of the things that scares me about all of this. I'm afraid he might be telling the truth. I might not have had much of a future at home, but what am I supposed to do here? I'm not a soldier, and I don't know anything at all about being a bodyguard."

"None of us do," Chris said. "And I doubt if Kevin knows anything about being a sorcerer either. Let's wait and see what Kalen has to say tomorrow."

No one had started down the hall yet. It was almost as if they were afraid to. Finally Steve took the lead, and the others followed. When they reached their rooms, they stood with their hands on the doorknobs and looked at each other. This time Karl took the initiative and opened the door to his and Joan's room. When nothing strange happened, the others opened theirs.

After the hall cleared, Kalen sighed. He shook his head and poured Steve's scog. He could send them back to Earth if he wanted to. He could send them back to their own bedrooms if he chose, but he wouldn't, not now. They knew too much about Terah, about Myron, and about Paul Stewart. His duty to Terah came first, above all else.

Maybe they should have found a way to interview the people who would have to help Myron, but even if they had been able to come up with a way, there wouldn't have been enough time. So much was riding on this. He had to make them understand. He had to make them help.

Kalen felt like the weight of the world had descended on his shoulders.

Chapter 11

The Next Day

Steve was the first of Kalen's guests to wake up the next morning. When he left his room, the smell of fresh coffee led him to the kitchen. He helped himself to a cup, took it to the living room, and drank it slowly as he walked around, gazing out of the windows.

Kalen entered the room from the hall and stood quietly, watching. When Steve turned around, Kalen motioned to two overstuffed chairs near the fireplace.

After they sat down, Steve sighed. "I'm having a hard time accepting all of this."

"I'm not surprised," Kalen said quietly. "But I assure you, it's all true."

"Could you tell me a bit more about Terah?"

Kalen nodded. "Let's get another cup of coffee first."

When they stood up, Steve glanced at his watch. "My watch seems to have stopped. Do you have any idea what time it is?"

"Oh, that's right," Kalen said as he walked over to the large desk. "I have new timepieces for all of you. According to Pallor, everyone in your area wears one, so I thought you might want one here." He opened one of the drawers and rummaged around inside for a moment. "Yes, here they are. Which one would you like?"

Kalen showed Steve a collection of watches that looked like wind-up pocket watches, but each was on a wristband of brightly color cloth rather than a chain.

While Steve looked through the watches, Kalen explained, "For years, every time Pallor came back from Earth, his timepiece would stop working. He said it was because of the energy field. Then, about ten years ago, he found one that could survive the trip, so he brought over an extra one for me to keep here."

"Don't the people of Terah wear watches?" Steve asked as he picked one up and fastened the band around his arm.

Kalen grinned and said, "They didn't used to, but it's starting to catch on. I showed the one that Pallor brought over to a friend of mine and the next thing I knew, he'd taken it apart. He said that he liked the small timepiece and was going to make one for himself. He did, and it spread from there." Kalen took the rest of the watches out and laid them on top of the desk. "Good thing, too. When I found out that we were going to have to bring Myron back earlier than we had planned, I contacted him and had him send me some. I didn't much think Pallor would remember to bring any over."

As Steve and Kalen walked into the kitchen to get another cup of coffee, Joan and Karl walked in. While Kalen was pouring coffee for them, Chris walked in, followed closely by Darrell. Before Kalen could get them served, he heard Theresa and Kevin talking in the hall, on their way to the kitchen too, so Kalen told everyone to have a seat in the dining room and started fixing breakfast.

After they had finished eating and joined him in the living room, Kalen explained about their watches and showed them the ones he had on his desk. After everyone had chosen a watch, he asked them to have a seat.

"Before the rest of you got up, Steve asked me to tell him a little more about Terah. I'm sure all of you have questions you'd like to ask, but before we get into those, let me give you a little background," Kalen said. "Long ago, the two worlds were very similar. Both worlds had sorcerers, dragons, elves, dwarves, and so on. Almost all of your myths and legends about magical creatures or other races were based on actual events, just like the legends about Merlin."

Kalen's guests looked at each other, but no one spoke. Kalen could still see doubt in their eyes, but nowhere near the level of disbelief that he had seen the day before. "Well, science and magic don't get along too well, and eventually the humans on Earth started leaning towards science and away from magic, and the more they learned about science, the more they hated magic, mainly because science couldn't explain it. Before long, anything even remotely connected with magic was hunted down and destroyed, so most of the magical creatures left Earth and came to Terah. From what Pallor has told me, most humans on Earth now believe that there's no such thing as magic, and on the rare occasion when they are confronted with evidence of it, they label it evil. But magic does exist and just like anything else, it's good when it's used for good and evil when it's used for evil."

Kalen paused for a moment, and then continued. "Of course, magical creatures and sorcerers weren't the only ones who had to leave Earth. Dwarves, elves, goblins, giants, and so on had to leave too, but not because they were magical. They had to leave because they were hated, hunted down, and killed just for being different. Humans aren't exactly known for being tolerant of others on either world, but at least on Terah, they aren't quite so open about it."

"Okay, for the sake of argument, say all of this is true," Chris said. "Why are we here?"

"I explained that last night. We needed someone to help Myron, and Pallor chose you."

"Help him how?" Chris asked.

"Myron has the power to become a great sorcerer, but he will need a lot of specialized tutoring. Badec has arranged for him to study with Glendymere, the most powerful sorcerer on Terah. He lives in a mountainous region southwest of here. We hope that the rest of you will escort Myron to Glendymere, and then help him get to Camden in time to take his seat on the council."

Chris and Darrell looked at each other. Darrell mouthed "bodyguard" and Chris nodded.

"Okay," Steve said slowly, "but I don't see how I fit into any of this."

"Pallor was responsible for assembling a team that would give Myron the best possible chance to succeed. I'm not sure exactly how any of you fit in, but I am sure that each of you is essential to the team." Then Kalen frowned and looked directly at Steve. "I have to admit, you were a bit of a surprise to me. I expected all of the companions to be about Myron's age. What did you do on Earth?"

"I taught history and political science."

"Maybe that's why you're here," Kalen said quietly.

"What do you mean?"

"I think Pallor chose you to be an advisor after Myron's seated on the council."

"Okay, that makes sense," Chris said, determined to pin Kalen down. "But what about the rest of us? You just mentioned that you want us to escort Kevin to some sorcerer named Glendymere, and yesterday you said that there are going to be people out there who want to kill him. Are you expecting us to be bodyguards?"

"We're hoping that you'll be able to protect Myron until he's able to protect himself, but that's not …"

"How are we supposed to do that?" Darrell interrupted. "I know absolutely nothing about being a bodyguard!"

"Me either," Karl agreed, "and neither does Joan."

Theresa had been sitting off to the side during all of this, listening. When she realized that the others were waiting for her to say something, she quickly shook her head and said, "Don't look at me! I don't even know how to protect myself!"

Kalen cleared his throat and tried again. "We want you to accompany him, to be his companions, and to do whatever you can to help him. Protecting him is only one small part of it. We hope it won't come to that, but we wouldn't let you leave here without giving you some weapons and teaching you how to use them."

Steve looked around at the others for a minute, and then said, "Kalen, we need to talk about all of this, privately. Could you just tell us exactly what our options are?"

Kalen took a deep breath and exhaled it in a long-suffering sigh. "First of all, you can go back to Earth, but only if you're ready to die. Secondly, you have the right to refuse to help, but, in that case, we won't help you either. You might last a little while if you pull together, but I guarantee you that you would not survive the magic war that will break out if Myron does not take his place on the council. Your third option would be to do your best to help Myron make it to Camden in time. If you succeed, all we can do is offer you our thanks," Kalen paused, and then added as an afterthought, "Although I'm sure you'd be welcomed by the people of Camden after Myron assumes his chair."

"Thank you," Steve said as he put his arm around Kalen's shoulders and walked him towards the kitchen. "Now, if you would just leave us alone for a few minutes and let us talk about all of this, we'll let you know when we have more questions or when we've made a decision."

As Steve turned to go back to the living room, he pulled the kitchen door shut.

After Kalen got over his shock at being so coolly shut out, he smiled. At least they were making the decision as a group.

"Well, I guess that's it. What do you want to do?" Steve asked when he got back to the living room.

"I'm not at all sure that I'm willing to risk my life for these people, and it does sound dangerous. Who would we be fighting anyway? Other people? Sorcerers? Or something else? He mentioned dragons at one point," Darrell said. Then after a moment, he added, "But, on the other hand, I'm not so sure that I'm willing to try to make it here without a little help from the natives. From the looks of things, I'd be at a loss as to where to begin." Then he shook his head. "I'm still having a lot of trouble believing this."

Chris sighed. "It sounds like a rather risky proposition at best and it really gets me that they didn't even bother to ask if we were willing to do this before they brought us over. The least they could have done was ask."

"I don't know how they think I can help," Theresa said, "but at least while I'm here, I don't have to get married, so, I guess I'm in, for whatever good it will do."

"Personally, I don't really want to go back to Omaha," Joan said slowly.

"From everything he's said, I don't think you need to worry about that," Karl answered as he put his arm around his wife. "You know, I'd love to go back to farming. Maybe if we help Kevin get to his throne, or whatever the Master Sorcerer sits on, we'll be able to find a bit of land and start over. What do you think, Joan?"

"Sounds good to me," she answered with a nod.

"Well, Kevin? You haven't said a word all morning. What's your reaction to this whole thing?" Steve asked.

"I don't know why they think I'm a sorcerer, or could ever become one, but even if I could, why would I want to? I don't believe half of what he's said, but if even a small portion of it's true … Assassins? Duels to the death? Magic wars? Why would any of us want to be in the middle of all of that? Look, let's just leave, go somewhere, anywhere, as long as it's a long way from here."

"Where would we go?" Chris asked.

"I don't know where at the moment, but I don't think this place is some strange 'other world'. I think Kalen's just trying to scare us to get us to do what he wants, and I have no idea what that really is."

"I'm not sure we should be too quick to discount what he's told us," Steve said slowly. "Remember what this house looked like from the outside, and what it looks like now. There's definitely something strange going on here."

"Okay," Karl said. "Say this is another world. Other than the fact that magic is fairly common here, what do we really know about it? He hasn't given us much practical information. Maybe it's not as bad as it sounds."

"Or maybe it's worse," Darrell added quietly.

"Which is a very good reason to hang around here for a while and see what we can find out," Chris said.

"Let's take a vote," Steve said. "All in favor of going along with Kalen, at least for a while, raise your hand."

At first, no one moved, and then hands starting going up slowly and hesitantly until the only one whose hand was not raised was Kevin. Steve looked at Kevin and raised his eyebrows.

Kevin shook his head. "No way."

"Okay, how can we help him if he doesn't agree to go?" Joan asked.

"Good question." Steve looked at Kevin and asked, "Are you sure?"

"I'm sure. There's no way I'm going along with any of this."

Steve nodded and said, "Then I guess that's that."

Then he walked over to the kitchen door, opened it, and looked for Kalen. He wasn't in the kitchen, but the back door was open, so Steve stepped outside. What he saw made his legs go weak. Standing in the backyard was a snow white pegasus. And standing beside him was a very tall, very thin man with long pointed ears talking to Kalen.

When Kalen saw Steve, he motioned him over. "Steve, this is Duane. He's a warrior elf. I asked him to help you train in hand-to-hand combat and with the weapons that we have here on Terah." Then he turned to Duane and said, "You need to meet the rest of our guests. Why don't you join us in the house? Xantha, there are some oats in the barn if you'd like a snack."

"Hope you have some of the nutty oats this time, Kalen. Last time they were all plain." Xantha began walking towards the barn. *"I'll be around if you need me."*

"I could have sworn I just heard him answer you, but in my head," Steve said without taking his eyes off of Xantha. "Is that telepathy? Are all animals capable of telepathic communication here?"

"No, only the magical ones. Pegassi, unicorns, and dragons mainly. But they are really picky about who they talk to," Duane answered. "I'm surprised that Xantha allowed you to hear him. He must like you."

When Duane spoke, Steve really looked at him for the first time. Other than his diamond-shaped eyes that glowed like tiny red coals and his pointed ears, he looked human. He was dressed in leggings, boots, a tunic, and a cloak. A sword hung from his belt and he had a long bow in his hand. All in all, he looked like a very handsome Robin Hood.

Kalen led Steve and Duane back to the living room. After he introduced Duane, he said, "Well, then, did you reach a decision?"

"Yes and no," Steve answered with a slight frown.

"What do you mean, yes and no?" Kalen asked.

"We took a vote about going along with your plans," Chris said. "Only one person voted no."

"Who has chosen not to? And may I ask why? Perhaps there is some way that we can convince you to change your mind," Kalen said in a placating tone.

"The one lone hold out is rather critical from what you've told us," Darrell picked up the lead. "It's Kevin."

Kalen sat down. "Whaaaaaat? Myron? Don't you understand what's at stake here?!"

"I know what you've told me is at stake here. I also know that what you have planned for all of us sounds dangerous to say the very least. And from what you've said, even if I make it to my father's house, it won't end there. I'll be in danger for the rest of my life, and eventually, they'll get me. So why should I go along with any of this? Why not just go hide somewhere, not tell anyone who I am, and live a nice quiet life?"

"You can't do that. You really have no choice," Kalen spoke slowly and quietly, but with an edge to his voice, like an angry parent dealing with an unruly toddler.

"You have no idea how sick I am of hearing that," Kevin interrupted. "Of course I have a choice. We all do. You act like you can pull the strings and we'll all jump just like puppets. Well, I'm not jumping."

"Myron, talent breeds talent. You're not going to be able to hide yours much longer, and you look just like Yvonne. It won't take anyone very long to figure out that you're Badec's son. There's going to be a price on your head as soon as news of your father's coma gets out. You're scared. Who wouldn't be? But go to Glendymere. Learn how to use your power. Then decide what to do," Kalen said, trying to buy some time.

"If he doesn't agree to take his place as head of the House of Nordin, I'll kill him myself, today," Duane said. "It would be kinder than letting the sorcerers get hold of him. I owe Badec that much." He turned around and left the living room.

Kevin glared at Duane's departing back and said, "Go ahead. At least that would put an end to all of this."

"Kevin, look out the window," Xantha said privately to Kevin.

Kevin had heard that voice many times over the years, but always in his sleep. He walked over to the window that looked out over the front yard. Xantha was standing in the middle of the clearing. As their eyes met, Xantha pawed the ground three times and bowed his regal head. At that moment, Kevin knew beyond any doubt that everything Kalen had been saying was true.

The others walked over to see what Kevin was looking at. Xantha lifted his head, pawed the ground again, and spread his wings. No one said a word. They could hardly breathe. Xantha was magnificent.

Finally Kalen said, "I'd like for all of you to meet Xantha. He came with Duane."

"Okay," Kevin said softly. Then he spoke louder. "If I do decide to go along with this, if we all do what you want, what do we get out of it?"

"You get to live, at least for today," Kalen hissed at Kevin. Then he turned around and left the room. Shortly afterwards, they heard the back door slam shut. For a few uncomfortable minutes, no one said a word or even looked at anyone else.

"I don't know about the rest of you, but I sure could use a cup of coffee. Think I'll go put another pot on," Theresa said softly.

After Theresa left for the kitchen, Chris said, "Come on, Kevin. What have we got to lose?"

Kevin stared at Chris. "You could lose your life! Don't you get it? If what he's saying is even half true, what chance do any of us have of surviving?"

Darrell shrugged. "I don't know, but I'd sort of like to give it a try."

Karl nodded and quietly said, "Anything beats Omaha as far as I'm concerned."

Kevin studied the faces around him, shook his head, and said, "I give up." He took a deep breath and exhaled slowly.

Karl nodded and said, "All right. If we're going to do this, we need to find out as much as we can about this place. Where are we? Where are we going? And how are we going to get there?"

Chris nodded. "We need maps."

"Kalen said something about Duane teaching us combat and weapons," Steve said. "We need to know what skills we already have. I was in the Marines for three years but that was over thirty years ago. At that time I was pretty good with a rifle, but I haven't shot one in over 25 years."

"I was never in service, but I'm pretty good with a gun, and not too bad with a bow and arrow," Karl said. "I've worked in rodeos. I can handle horses and I know how to use a rope, but I've never been a fighter and I've never learned much about it."

"Well, you're both better off than I am," Chris said. "I've never been in service, and I've never even fired a gun. The only arrows I ever shot were the little plastic ones with rubber tips. I ran cross-country in high school, but I didn't really work at it. I swam with a local swim club, but I wasn't fast enough for college competitions. I belonged to a boxing gym in New York for a couple of years while I was a teenager, but that was a long time ago. I really don't see that I'm going to be much help at all."

"The only thing I know how to do is play football, but I can throw a football, and aim is aim. Maybe that's something we can build on," Darrell paused and a far-away look settled over his face. "Actually, I used to be pretty good with a shuriken, too."

"I may sound dumb, but what's a shuriken?" Joan asked.

"It's a small Asian weapon, sometimes called a throwing star. Supposedly, the Ninjas used them at one time. I'm sure you've seen them in movies. I'd almost forgotten about all of that," Darrell said a little hesitantly.

"Do you mean that you know Karate?" Chris asked quickly. "Maybe you could teach us a little of it. It might come in handy."

"It was some form of martial arts, but I'm not sure which one. My next-door neighbor, Martin, was retired from the military. I saw him working out in his backyard one day when I was maybe eight or nine. I asked him to teach me, and he did. He taught me to throw the stars and fans too, but I haven't touched any of those things since I was fifteen. Martin moved to Florida then."

"Well, I've never had to fight, but I suppose I could learn," Joan said. "I'm pretty good at target archery. I don't think I could shoot a deer, but a man? I don't know, maybe, under the right circumstances, if it were him or us."

Since Kevin was the only one who had not spoken up, the others looked at him sort of expectantly. He shrugged and said, "No one ever told me that sorcerers and assassins were going to be out to kill me. I never even went to PE in high school. They let me write a paper about something instead. And when I was in college, I convinced my PE Instructor that I would be more valuable to him as an aide than as a student. Paul did try to get me to take some self-defense classes when I was a teenager, but he didn't tell me why, so I never gave it much effort."

"Joan, could I see you for a minute?" Theresa called from the doorway to the kitchen.

When Joan reached the kitchen Theresa was putting seven cups, the sugar jar, spoons, and a cream pitcher on a tray. She asked Joan if she was familiar with herbs and healing plants.

"A little. Actually I know more about the herbs used in cooking and preserving than I do about healing herbs. I recognize the aloe plant over there and I know it's for burns, but that's about as far as it goes."

"My grandmother has an old wood stove, similar to this one, but her door handle's covered with something so that it stays cool. When I opened this door to put in another piece of wood, I didn't think about the handle and I burned my whole hand."

"Let me see it!" Joan said as she reached for the aloe plant.

"No, no, it's okay. And I mean it's really okay. Look at it." Theresa held her palm out for Joan to see. There was no sign of any injury, definitely not of a bad burn. "It was fiery red and starting to swell by the time I cut a piece of the aloe plant. As soon as I touched the burns with the juice –

gone! Totally healed. I've never seen anything like it. I've used aloe for burns all my life, but this was unreal. That burn was bad, and there's no way our aloe could have done anything like that."

Theresa looked at her hand again. "My grandmother's a healer, and she believes in magic, witches, the whole bit. She says that long ago, when the witches were powerful, the herbs were more powerful. I was thinking, since Terah is more magic oriented, do you suppose the herbs here are stronger than the ones on Earth? If so, I know some good ones for wounds, pain, upset stomachs, colds, sore throats, and so on. I could make up a sort of first aid kit out of herbs."

"Let's talk to Kalen about this. I don't know much about herbs, but if you show me what to look for, I'll be happy to help you gather and prepare them. We can probably find some cloth for bandages, too." Joan turned back to the stove. "The coffee smells like it's ready, don't you think? Let's take it in to the guys."

Theresa carried the tray and Joan carried the pot. When they reached the living room, the men were standing around talking about the Final Four in college basketball. All the guys had an opinion about which teams would make it and they were arguing fiercely for their favorites. Joan smiled. It sounded just like the conversations she had heard between Karl and his friends every spring back at home. It sounded right.

Just as Joan poured the first cup of coffee, Kalen walked in. "Duane wants to see each of you individually to get an idea how you move and to find out what you can already do so that we can make out a training plan. Darrell, why don't you go first?"

Darrell nodded and walked towards the door, mumbling, "I was really looking forward to that coffee."

After Darrell left, Chris asked, "Do you have any maps of the area? We'd like to know where we are and where we need to go."

"That's an excellent idea. Here we go," Kalen walked over to the desk and pulled out a drawer. It was full of folded bits of paper.

"Are these your maps?" Steve asked, a little disappointed.

"Yes. The brownies make them. They're really quite good." Kalen opened one that had been folded over several times and took it into the dining room. As he straightened it out on the table, the map almost tripled in size. At first it looked blank, and then, as they watched, the markings became clear and dark.

"Hey, that looks like North America," Karl said.

"Your North America, our Calandra."

"Where are we now?" Karl asked.

"Here." Kalen pointed to a spot that would have been just south of Lake Winnipeg, Canada, on Earth. "We're in Brendolanth, but we're not too far from the northern border of Camden. Here, this river is the boundary between Brendolanth and Camden." Kalen pointed to the river that the others recognized as the Mississippi.

Steve asked, "Do you have mountains where we do, deserts and rivers where we do? Are the two worlds really alike physically?"

"Pretty much, at least on this continent." Then Kalen opened a second map, one that showed all of Terah. "The last magic war took place overseas." Kalen pointed to a blank area that was where Europe was on Earth. "Only within the last hundred years have grasses and small shrubs started growing there again. Where you have mountain ranges, we might have flat lands or even craters." Kalen shook his head sadly. "Things got rather wild. Rivers evaporated, and then some of them filled up with dirt during the winds that the war unleashed. As far as I know, none of the animals have returned yet. One day life will once again flourish there, but none of us will live to see it. We don't even have any maps of that area, but other than that, the two worlds are pretty much alike."

His guests were quiet for a moment, picturing the destruction that Kalen had described. Then Steve pointed to the map of Calandra again. "Where do we have to go to find Kevin's tutor, this Glendymere?"

Kalen pointed to a spot that would have been in the middle of Colorado on Earth. "Glendymere lives in a cave in the mountains of Nandelia. We'll provide much more detailed maps for you before you leave, but this is the general area that you want to head for. Then after you leave Glendymere, you'll want to head here." He pointed to a spot in what was eastern Tennessee to them. "Badec's castle is located here, in the town of Milhaven. Again, you'll have detailed maps of that area, too, before you leave, but this should give you a good idea of where you need to go."

"I have a question. I don't see anything that looks like a major highway on this map, just small local roads. Are there other maps for the highways?" Joan asked.

"Well … uh … that's one of the differences I was talking about. I know all of you are used to traveling by car. Pallor has told me all about them. We don't have anything like that here."

"Then how do you travel?" Joan asked.

"By wagons, carriages, on horseback, or on foot."

"You are kidding, right?" Theresa asked apprehensively.

"Uh … no … actually, I'm very serious." Kalen fiddled with the maps while he tried to come up with something to help ease them over this hurdle. Pallor had warned him that this might be a stumbling block. "Xantha can help any of you who don't know how to ride. We haven't selected horses for you yet because we thought you might want to do that for yourselves. There's a fairly large herd grazing near here. Most of them are saddle broken, but a few haven't been trained yet. We thought some of you might prefer to train your own."

They were all still staring at him. Kalen didn't know what else to say, but he kept talking anyway, waiting for the shock to subside. "You'll need a couple of horses for each wagon, too. We weren't sure how many wagons you'd want, but you'll need at least one for supplies. We figured that a couple of you would probably rather handle the wagon than ride. Of course, handling wagon horses can be a bit tricky. You know, like when you're climbing over mountains, crossing streams and rivers, during storms, things like that. You really do need to know what you're doing to control the horses properly. It's more complicated than it looks."

"I have never been on a horse in my life! And you want me to ride to Colorado on one?!" Chris blurted out.

"Well, you could walk if you prefer, but it's a long way to Glendymere's, and we do need to get you there as soon as possible," Kalen said, trying to sound reasonable.

Karl nodded. "It's not that bad, Chris. I've been riding all my life. I've also taught a lot of other people to ride, and most people catch on quickly. The worst part is that it does make you sore the first couple of times you ride." Then he turned to Kalen, grinned, and asked, "When can we see the herd?"

Before Kalen could answer, Duane called through the back door. "Kalen! Come out here! You've got to see this to believe it!"

What now? Kalen thought as he headed outside with everyone following him.

"We've been sparring for at least fifteen minutes, Kalen, and I haven't been able to touch him. I mean it. Watch!" Duane began circling Darrell, preparing to strike. But whenever Duane threw a punch or a kick, Darrell dodged it. He swung low, jumped, moved to the side, twisted, and in general seemed to flow from one stance to another. Then Duane picked up a wooden practice sword and tried to score on Darrell, but he didn't have any luck with that either. Darrell out-maneuvered him every time. It was beautiful to watch.

When Duane finally stopped, Darrell said he was going to go get some water.

Chris walked into the kitchen with him. "I thought you said you only had a little training. I'm no expert, but that looked like black belt stuff to me."

"I don't know what's going on, but I was never that good." Darrell filled a glass with water, turned it up, and drained it. "It's almost like … I don't know … like I'm as good as I always wanted to be, like what little skill I had was magnified when we went through that gate. And another thing, those moves should have killed my knee, but they didn't. I'm not sure any of us knows what we're capable of over here, but I don't think we should mention any of this to Kalen or Duane just yet."

"We'd better try to warn the others before someone gets hurt though," Chris replied.

"Warn us about what?" Kevin asked as he and the others came through the kitchen door.

Darrell glanced towards the door to make sure that Kalen had stayed in the yard with Duane, and then he quietly said, "I don't understand it, but I'm a lot better at blocking and dodging over here than I ever was on Earth, so be careful. You might be stronger and quicker than you expect. Take it easy until you see what you can do, but at the same time, don't let on if anything you do surprises you. Just act like it's perfectly normal until we get a handle on what's going on here."

"If we ever do," Kevin mumbled.

Chapter 12

The Tellurians

Duane spent the rest of the morning outside, sparring with the guests. Steve's military experience, Darrell's martial arts, and Chris's boxing experience gave them an edge over the others in hand-to-hand combat, but everyone except Kevin and Theresa showed good potential for fighting. Right before they broke for lunch, Duane handed out some wooden swords and let them spar with each other. Chris had a real knack for the give and take of swordplay, but the only ones who seemed more likely to hurt themselves than their opponents were Kevin and Theresa.

After a quick lunch, Kalen brought a pretty little quarter horse out of the barn and introduced her as Buttercup. He led her over to Karl and handed him the reins. Karl swung up in the saddle in one fluid motion and rode as if he and the horse were one. Joan rode next, and although she took it a little slower than Karl, she was just as comfortable in the saddle as he was. When she dismounted, she held up the reins to see who wanted to ride next, but no one was willing to take the reins.

None of the others had ever been on a horse before, and even mounting Buttercup turned into a comedy of errors for most of them, so Karl, Joan, and Kalen took turns leading her around the yard so that the others could get the feel of sitting on a moving horse. When everyone had had a turn, Kalen told them to go join Duane while he took care of his horse.

While the guests had been busy with Kalen and Buttercup, Duane had set out targets for the longbow, crossbow, spear, and throwing knives. Karl, Joan, Darrell, and Steve all did well with the bows and arrows, and although Chris wasn't very accurate, he at least hit the outside of the target. The only ones who were pretty much hopeless with the bows were Kevin and Theresa.

When they got to the spears, only Darrell and Karl showed any real aptitude. Darrell was a natural with the throwing knives, but the only ones who showed absolutely no potential were, once again, Kevin and Theresa.

Towards the end of the afternoon, Duane gave them wooden daggers and let each of them have a try at attacking him. Joan came into her own with a dagger, but Theresa couldn't manage to keep a grip on hers, and Kevin's flipped out of his hand with his first thrust.

Both Kevin and Theresa were embarrassed by their lack of aptitude for violence and their inept performance with all of the weapons, and although the others tried to assure them that they would be fine with a little time and training, neither of them believed it. They both felt totally useless.

During dinner that evening, Karl asked if they could get some good ropes. When Kalen looked a little surprised by the request, Karl explained that ropes came in handy for a multitude of tasks, including self-defense. Kalen asked for a few specifics about the type of ropes Karl wanted and said that he would do what he could. Duane just nodded.

Then Steve asked about rifles and handguns.

"Guns?" Duane asked the question as if he had no idea what Steve was talking about.

"We don't have guns here," Kalen said quietly.

"Do you mean that you don't have any guns here, or that you don't have any guns on Terah?" Karl asked.

"We don't have guns on Terah."

Karl and Steve looked at each other for a moment and then Steve nodded, "I should have known. That's why you use swords and bows and arrows. It's like medieval Earth. We'll just have to think Middle Ages."

After dinner, everyone retired to the living room. Kalen and Duane had made some notes during the afternoon and had mapped out a training plan while they were preparing dinner.

"We've come up with a training schedule and we want to see what you think about it," Kalen began. Then he nodded towards Duane.

"We've scheduled about three weeks for training," Duane said. "The weather will still be a little uncertain for a while, and there's no sense in your starting off for Glendymere's before then. Even then, you might run into a stray snowstorm, but the worst of it should be over." Duane looked at Darrell and said, "Darrell, we would like for you to begin training everyone in what you call martial arts. Would you be willing to do that?" Darrell nodded, so Duane continued. "We would also like for you to draw fairly detailed pictures of the throwing stars and fans that you mentioned this afternoon. We'll send the drawings to Palladin and have him make some for you." Then Duane looked around at the others. "We realize that three weeks is nothing in the study of any combat skill, but it's a beginning, and I'm sure all of you will continue training after you leave here, while you are on your way to Glendymere's, and then while you're waiting to escort Myron to Camden."

They all nodded.

Then Steve asked, "Who's Palladin?"

Kalen smiled. "He's an old friend of mine. He's the one who made those watches you're wearing. He does exceptional metal work. I've asked him to make swords for you and he can make the stars, too."

When no one else said anything, Duane continued. "We'd like to do most of the training in small groups of maybe one or two. Xantha will work with you on horsemanship. You've all met Buttercup, and we have another horse, Star. He's not quite as gentle as she is, but he's not really spirited either. I'll work with each of you on hand-to-hand combat, daggers, and archery, and Kalen will work with you on swords, spears, and throwing knives. However, Darrell will probably want to work with you as a group to go over basic moves. Right, Darrell?" Again, Darrell nodded. "Do any of you have any objections or suggestions concerning the overall plan?" Duane looked around, but no one had any comments.

After a couple of minutes, Theresa said, "I have a question, but it has nothing to do with any of this."

"Certainly, my dear," Kalen said gently. He was afraid that she might try to back out now that she had been exposed to the violent aspects of this adventure.

"I noticed the aloe plant that you have in your kitchen. Or, at least, aloe's the name that I know it by. Do you have medicinal herbs on Terah?"

"Herbs are the only medicine we have here. Why?" Kalen asked.

"Well, I know a little about the herbs found on Earth," Theresa said. She took a deep breath and plunged ahead. "My grandmother uses herbs for treating wounds and illnesses. She taught me as much as she could whenever my father let me visit her. I'd like to gather some herbs and prepare a first aid kit for the journey."

"Is your grandmother a healer by any chance? Can she use her hands to slow bleeding, warm muscles, and soothe pain?" Kalen asked quietly.

Theresa blushed. "I know a lot of people don't believe in that type of thing, but I know it works. She's used it on me, and I've even done a little of it myself."

Kalen turned to Duane and said, "We need to get Drusilla."

Duane nodded.

"Excuse me, but who's Drusilla?" Theresa asked.

"She's the Sister of the Chapel of Light in Drisden. It's about 15 miles southwest of here. I think you should talk to her, Theresa. She'll be able to answer your questions about herbs a lot better than we can. She's a healer herself," Kalen answered. Now he understood why Pallor had chosen Theresa. A healer would be a wonderful addition to the group. Things were beginning to look up.

"It's been a long day and it's getting sort of late. If there's nothing else, I'd like to go for a short walk around the yard before going to bed," Steve said as he stood up and stretched.

"Oh, before you go, there are a few more things that I'd like to mention." Kalen looked at Steve, who nodded and sat back down. "I'd like for you to put some thought into the types of supplies you might need for the trip to Nandelia. We'll need some time to get everything together. I've already bought some staple goods, and a few months ago I bought another wagon that you can use. Palladin has it right now, making a few minor adjustments. He'll bring it when he comes in two weeks. Actually, the timing on that's pretty good. He usually visits when winter breaks, so no one will think anything about it when he closes up his smithy and comes up here for a vacation. Anything he can bring with him will help. We don't want to arouse any more suspicion around here than we have to."

Kalen leaned back in his chair and continued. "I have a collection of human clothing and boots that I've accumulated over the years. As I'm sure you've already figured out, we've been planning this for quite some time. I know you don't want to go through them tonight, but you need to do it soon so that we can get the clothes you want to wear cleaned up and altered. You need to get used to wearing them and moving around in them so that you'll blend in with the rest of the humans when you leave here."

Darrell laughed. "We're going to attract attention when we leave here no matter what we're wearing. Look at us. I'm black, Theresa's Hispanic, Karl looks Indian, and the rest of you may be white, but no one would believe you're related."

"You've got a point. You can do a lot with clothing, but you can't disguise race," Chris said.

"What do you mean, race? You're all human, aren't you?" Kalen asked, confused by their comments.

"We may all be human, but we're not considered the same race, and there are some places on Earth where that matters, where being a different race is grounds for getting beat up or worse," Darrell said.

"I knew things used to be bad on Earth, but I thought that they were getting better. I guess humans always have to have someone to hate. Here, a lot of them hate dwarves, or elves, or brownies, or so on, but not other humans simply because of skin color." Kalen paused before saying any more. He wasn't sure that now was the right time, but he went ahead anyway. "But there is one prejudice that you do need to be aware of. There are a lot of people out there who hate Myron because his great-grandmother was an elf. He has elven blood in him. Some humans consider him a half-breed." Kalen shrugged. "Of course, that same elven blood is what makes Myron's power so strong, and in order to keep it strong in his family line, his son will probably need to marry an elf, but that's something we'll worry about later."

"Yeah, like after he's born," Kevin muttered. "And that's assuming I live long enough to have children."

"You know, there's an old saying: 'If you want to hide something, hide it in plain sight,'" Steve said.

"Well, you'll be in plain sight when you leave here, but I don't see how that's going to help," Kalen said.

"No, what I mean is we need to invite people to look at us," Steve said. "All through history, there are stories of people, from murderers to kings, who traveled incognito by traveling with a circus, with minstrels, or with a carnival. People look at what you do, but not really at you."

Joan nodded. "That's true. Half the time our friends didn't recognize us when we were working at the Pioneer Village. They watched us, and they watched what we were doing, but they didn't see us."

"We also don't want people wondering where we're from, or where we're going. We need to be like gypsies, like traveling is our way of life. I don't suppose you have a traveling circus hiding in the wings, do you, Kalen?" Steve asked with a twinkle in his eye.

"In the wings? What do you mean?" Kalen frowned, very confused.

"It means that you have one waiting for us somewhere. You don't, do you?" Steve asked.

"Sorry, no. I didn't think of that, but I would have been afraid to do it even if I'd thought about it. The more people who know about you, the more danger you're in. Before Yvonne died, she told Badec that Myron would be seated as the Master Sorcerer one day. We aren't sure whether she was saying that as a seer, or as a mother, but she definitely didn't say anything about the rest of you. We'd like to see all of you come through this in one piece."

"Believe me, so would we," Joan mumbled.

"It was just a thought. We may be able to come up with something later. Right now though, I'm going for a walk. Good night all." Steve stood up and left the room.

Conversations broke off into small talk, and after a bit, Kevin slipped out the front door and walked to the edge of the woods. The sky was full of bright stars. As he stood there staring up at the sky, he felt someone approaching.

"You okay?" Chris asked as he walked up behind Kevin.

"Yeah, just thinking."

"Mind some company?"

"Not at all," Kevin answered.

"You haven't said much since this morning. How do you feel about being Superman for this place? Or maybe Merlin?"

"It would be funny if it weren't so real. The scariest part is that everyone else seems to assume I can do this."

"Well, you have to admit, they've gone to a lot of trouble to pull this off. They must have some reason to believe you're the one to do it."

"Chris, I don't even believe in magic." After a couple of minutes, he asked, "Do you remember what Kalen said about that war in Europe? I can't get that out of my head. It sounded like a nuclear blast, and I'm supposed to go up against something like that?!"

"No, from what I understand, you're supposed to prevent it."

"I have a feeling those 'challenges' that he mentioned are going to be the same thing, just on a smaller scale, with me, and probably all of you, right in the middle."

Chris shrugged and said, "I never did plan to die of old age, did you?"

"Never really thought about it to be honest." Kevin looked back up at the night sky. "I'd kill for a cigarette right now, and I haven't even wanted one since I left college."

"I never smoked. Too scared of cancer. Seems almost funny now. I really don't think cancer is going to be a worry for either of us, do you?"

Kevin laughed. "No. Heart attack, maybe. Like the first time some guy in a long dress and a pointed hat says 'Wanna fight?'"

Chris laughed and asked, "What makes you so sure it'll be a man? I imagine sorcery is an equal opportunity employer."

"Now there's a thought. What do I do if some woman wants to fight?"

Chris shrugged. "Whatever you have to do to survive. But don't worry about that now. You're not a sorcerer yet, and I thought you didn't even believe in sorcery."

"I don't. This is a case of brainwashing. If everyone else assumes that I'll become a sorcerer, and says so often enough, I'll end up repeating it, even if I don't believe it."

"Well, if it makes you feel any better, I'm not so sure about it either. I realize everything seems to depend on it, but I have a hard time picturing you working spells."

Kevin laughed again and seemed to lighten up a little. "I wonder if I'll have to have a big black cauldron, eyes of newt, bats' wings, spider webs and all that other mess – ugh! Just thinking about it makes my skin crawl."

They both laughed at the idea of a big pot boiling away with Kevin standing over it, stirring with a big black stick. Then the laughter died away as a meteor streaked across the sky and drew their eyes back to the night sky.

After a while Kevin broke the silence. "There's something that Kalen said tonight that's sort of bothering me. I may be reading something into it that isn't there, but I wonder if you noticed it, too."

"You mean that comment about the fact that they've been working on this little party for quite some time now? Yeah, it hit me. It probably hit all of us."

"Maybe this team was not a last minute random thing. After all, there's the fact that Theresa's grandmother's a healer, and I get the feeling that that's hereditary, too."

"But that came as a surprise to both Kalen and Duane. They had no idea that she was a healer," Chris said.

"True, but didn't Kalen say that the team was Paul's responsibility? What if he spent the last couple of years finding everyone and maneuvering all of you into position?"

Chris thought for a minute and then shook his head. "I don't see how. No one told me to interview for that job, or to move to Omaha. I just happened to see the ad in the newspaper. Anyway, how we came to be here really doesn't matter at this point."

"If everything they're saying is true, I would have had to come, but the rest of you didn't. You should have been given a choice," Kevin said quietly. "If they had asked, what would you have said?"

"I'm not sure. There's a part of me that has always wanted this type of adventure, but basically I'm a coward. I don't know what I would have said is someone had asked," Chris answered. Then he shrugged and said, "Oh well. I guess we should go back in before they send out a search party."

As they approached the house, they heard someone singing. When they entered the living room, they found that Joan was singing lead, with Theresa harmonizing and singing backup. Karl waved to them and motioned them to a seat. Everyone else, including Steve, was already seated.

When the song was finished, Karl said, "We were thinking about what Steve said, about hiding in a group. What if we were the group? Joan and I have both sung on stage at the Pioneer Village. Theresa's sung solos at church, so she's used to singing in public, too. Do either of you sing?"

"Well, when I was in college, I was the drummer with a group. We played in some clubs and for some local dances. I even did a little backup singing, but I'm not what I'd call a singer," Chris answered.

"Once again, count me out. I can't carry a tune in a teapot. And musical instruments were not on the list of approved activities in my household when I was growing up, too noisy. Sorry." Kevin was beginning to wish that he really were a sorcerer. At least then he would have something to contribute.

Karl looked over at Steve and raised his eyebrows. Steve said that he had sung with a faculty glee club, but he had never sung by himself except in the shower. Darrell said that his singing experience was pretty similar to Steve's.

"I still bet we could come up with a pretty good traveling minstrel show," Karl said. "I wish we could get hold of some of our old instruments. I used to play the fiddle and the bass. Joan is great on a harp and she also plays the recorder and flute. She used to play an old fashioned fife at the Pioneer Village."

"Well, I used to play the guitar," Theresa said. "I've even played a little banjo. When I was in high school, I played the flute and recorder too. I tried the piccolo once, but I didn't have too much luck with it. Probably because I didn't practice."

"Is there any way we could get some of these instruments, Kalen?" Joan asked. "This idea might work if we have the right props."

"I can probably figure out a way to get a harp and some type of fiddle. We have those things on Terah." Kalen turned to Duane and said, "Duane, can you get the flutes?"

Duane nodded. "I'll have to send Xantha though. It's too far for any of the birds to try to carry one back. Let me go see if he could fly out tonight. At least then no one would see him." Duane stood up and headed out the door.

"I do wish we could get some type of guitar. There's so much you can do with one," Theresa said.

"Could we make one?" Kevin asked. "We could use some of the same materials that they use for the fiddles. If we change the size and shape of the sound box and alter the length of the strings, we might be able to get the right sound. What do you think?"

"It won't hurt to try," Karl said, nodding. "Kalen, could you get us several fiddles, and some extra string, lots of it, and some glue for making the sound boxes? We'll need some fine wood too. It'll probably take several tries to get something we can use."

"I'll see what I can do, and I'll see if Palladin can bring a harp, but he won't be here for a couple of weeks. I'll try to have the rest of the stuff here within five days, but I can't promise anything. You know, you'll need a lot of practice if you're going to try to put on a professional performance," Kalen said hesitantly. He wasn't at all sure that he liked this idea. "Are you sure you want to do this? They may not like your group. They don't always like traveling minstrels, you know."

"What's the worst that they could do to us, boo us off the stage? Tell us to get out of town? They don't kill people for a bad performance, do they?" Karl asked.

"No, the worst thing that could happen is that you might find the town inhospitable. Usually, minstrels are housed and fed in exchange for a performance. But if they don't like the performance, housing might be in the stable, and the food might be kitchen scraps," Kalen answered.

"Well, in that case, what have we got to lose? It'll give us a good reason to be traveling through with our wagons, and it'll stop a lot of the questions people always ask strangers. I say let's do it!" Joan's eagerness crept into her voice.

"What are we going to use for songs? We don't know any from Terah, and that will become obvious real fast," Theresa said.

Kalen shook his head. "One of the reasons people enjoy a minstrel show is that they get new songs. You need to be able to sing a few of the old favorites, but I'm sure Drusilla knows a couple and can teach them to you. But the new songs will be your strength."

"I know a lot of songs, but I don't know how well any or them will fit in here," Joan said.

"I think we should stick mostly to love songs until we get a feel for Terah. You can't sing songs that are supposed to be funny until you find out what other people find humorous," Steve said.

Chris snapped his fingers and said, "I've got an idea. What if we use the minstrel show as an advertising campaign for Kevin here?"

"I don't know about that. Maybe you should just play that one real secretive, not mention Myron," Kalen cautioned. "After word of Badec's illness gets out, everyone will be wondering where he is. Bounties will be set, and assassins will be hired. The last thing you need is for someone to start thinking of him in connection with your little group. It could be dangerous, even fatal, if they think any of you know anything at all about him or where he is. And if you make it sound like he is some kind of favored son, you just might enrage some of the other sorcerers. That could be fatal, too."

"Okay. I understand what you mean about making it seem like he's destined to be Master Sorcerer, but we don't really need to talk about that. We could write songs that deal with his birth and about him growing up in some exotic place, maybe on an island. We could concentrate on the child. We could write something like the stories about Merlin taking Arthur soon after his birth and hiding him until the time was right. We could even use the same legends. No one here would recognize them, would they?"

Kalen shook his head and said, "No, I don't think so."

Chris continued, "If we keep the songs simple, with easy lyrics and catchy tunes, everyone will soon be singing the songs, and before long, they'll think that whatever the song says is true. Anyway, I'm not talking about having the entire program centering on Myron, just a couple of upbeat songs."

"He's right about music influencing the way people think," Steve said. "That's why there's always such an abundance of patriotic music during wartimes. But we would need to keep the songs vague, and far away, both in time and distance."

"All right. We can do that. We'll have to write the lyrics and fit them to tunes that we already know," Joan said. "I'm too tired to start on any songs tonight, but we need to schedule some time each day to work on this. If we're going to disguise ourselves as minstrels, we better be good. And we need a name for the group, too."

"I've been thinking about that," Chris said. "How about the Tellurians?"

"I've never heard of that. Did you make that up?" Joan asked.

"No. It just means someone who's from Earth," Chris said. Then he shrugged and added, "I used to do the crossword puzzle in the newspaper every Sunday. 'Tellurian' was used once, and for some reason, it stuck in my mind."

"I like it," Karl said. "It fits, sounds different, and we're the only ones who'll know what it means."

When Joan glanced around, everyone nodded. "Good. Then that's settled. Well, I don't know about anyone else, but I'm off to bed."

"Can I ask one thing first?" Darrell said quietly. "If we aren't any good at this, will we admit that we aren't, scrap this plan, and go to something else? I'm afraid that we'll develop tunnel vision and that could be the death of us – literally."

With solemn nods, the others agreed, and then they all went off to bed.

Kalen sat by the fire for a while, thinking about everything that had happened that day. When Duane returned from talking to Xantha, they talked about the pros and cons of using a minstrel show as cover.

Then, as Duane was leaving for his camp in the woods, he said, "You know, this could be a good sign. I don't know that the minstrel idea will work. Maybe, maybe not. We'll see how good they are in a week or two. But the important thing is that they're thinking and working together. We need a good, solid, cohesive unit, and it looks like they may become one. Considering that they were complete strangers two days ago, they certainly have come a long way."

Chapter 13

Thursday Night, March 22

Later that night, long after everyone at the Gate House had gone to sleep, Rolan lay in his bed in Trendon wide awake. That morning, he'd received a message from his spy in Milhaven. Badec was ill, in a coma, but still alive. How could that be? He had been told that no one survived Sleeping Angel for more than two weeks, and most were dead within a week. It had already been two and a half weeks. Why wasn't he dead?

Rolan got out of bed and ordered his personal slave to go get him some scog. While he waited, he paced. He finally came to the conclusion that the elven blood in Badec's veins was probably just slowing the poison down. The half-breed should never have been allowed to be on the Council of Sorcerers in the first place; it was supposed to be for human sorcerers, but that wasn't important at this point. Nor was it really important that he wasn't dead yet. All that mattered was that he die before the next council meeting.

What was important, and what was keeping him awake, was something he'd overlooked when he was planning all of this to start with: Gwendolyn.

Rolan's slave returned with the scog, poured a little into a separate cup, drank that, and then handed Rolan's drink to him. Then the slave went back to his pallet on the floor of what was once a large closet.

Rolan drank some of the scog and then shook his head sharply, trying to force himself to focus on the problem at hand. Gwendolyn. She was one ambitious old woman. And strong too. How was he ever going to get her to fall in line with his plan? He'd been fooling himself thinking that a speech in front of the council would ever sway her. It was a good thing he'd come to his senses about that before it was too late. The council meeting was a little over two weeks away. That left plenty of time to go see her and work something out.

He'd have to come up with some reason to see her though. It wasn't like they were friends or anything. Maybe he could begin by telling her that Badec was sick and not expected to recover. He seriously doubted she'd know anything about that unless she had her own spies in the castle, and if she did, she wouldn't want to let on, so she'd act like it was news to her. All right. He had his opening. Where could he go from there?

Rolan paced some more. Finally he decided that his best approach would be the truth, or at least a very limited version of it. He'd ask her what she thought about supporting Damien as the new Master Sorcerer. At that point, she'd probably act insulted. After all, she was one of the strongest sorcerers on the council and a very likely candidate herself. How could he soothe over the fact that he wasn't thinking of her for the job?

A few minutes later the perfect approach hit him. He'd pretend that he'd never considered her because he figured she wouldn't want it, not with all the hassle and aggravation it brings with it. No, that wasn't quite right. She might take it that he thought she wasn't up to it. That would never do. He paced some more. Maybe he should act like he thought of it as a job, sort of menial, like the Master Sorcerer was some kind of lackey doing the biding of the council, definitely beneath a sorcerer of her standing.

Rolan nodded to himself. That would work, but he needed to back it up. So why would it be beneath her? The reason had to be personal, things about her that made the position unacceptable. Rolan picked up the pace as he walked around his room. What did he know about her? They hadn't had a lot of contact. He wasn't even sure how many children she had, but he did know that she absolutely hated anyone or anything that she couldn't control, which was probably one of the reasons that she hated Badec so much. Every time she looked at him, her eyes filled with loathing.

Maybe that was something he could use, Rolan thought. The Master Sorcerer had to deal with the other races all the time, especially with Glendymere since he was the chairman of the Federation of Terah. And that old dragon didn't kowtow to anyone.

Rolan knew he'd have to be clever in the way he pointed that out though. If she took it that he was implying in any way that Glendymere was her equal, much less her superior, it would make her all the more determined to claim the Master's Chair just to prove him wrong. He needed to present dealing with the dragon as an unpleasant chore that was only one of the irksome duties of the Master Sorcerer.

He would also have to slip it in somewhere that if she were Master Sorcerer, she would be expected to help out with emergencies all over Terah, that she'd be on call all the time, no matter what she had going on herself. She was selfish enough to really resent that one. But if he was going to slip it in sideways, he'd need examples. Rolan continued pacing as he thought. He knew there had been quite a few disasters in the past few years, if only he could remember what they were. He shook his head as if he could shake loose the memories. They hadn't involved him, so he hadn't paid much attention. Now what were they? He paced quicker, trying to remember.

Ah, yes. There had been that tidal wave off the coast of Havernia last year. And there was also something about a volcano somewhere, and wasn't there a big forest fire a couple of years ago, and hadn't there been some bad floods in Landoryn a while back? That was Gwendolyn's province. She'd remember those if she didn't remember the others. Rolan frowned. He wasn't positive, but it seemed like he remembered that she'd really pitched a fit that Badec hadn't brought more sorcerers to help rebuild that area. And hadn't she ranted on and on about his leaving early, before all the work had been done, leaving her and her sorcerers to finish up? He could use that, telling her that if she decided to take the position herself, she could make sure things were done properly because she'd be in charge of doing them.

Now, what other arguments could he use? Maybe something about being a target? No. Rolan shook his head. He didn't need to mention anything that might imply that she wasn't capable of taking care of herself. She was too arrogant. What else? Rolan paced, and thought, and paced, and thought. What other drawbacks were there to being Master Sorcerer?

At the moment the only other one he could think of was that whoever was Master Sorcerer had to listen to complaints from sorcerers, from non-magical humans, and from members of the other races, especially if the complaint had to do with the abuse of magical power by a human. That had to get old, really old. Of course if Gwendolyn were seated on the chair, it wouldn't be long before no one would dare complain about anything. Word would get around as to how she handled complaints, provided she did the same thing as Master Sorcerer that she did in her own province. Whenever anyone complained about anything in Landoryn, Gwendolyn took care of the complaint by killing the person who complained. So having to handle complaints probably wouldn't seem like a very big deal to her. Rolan shook his head. He wouldn't be able to use that one, and he couldn't think of any more right now. It was time to move on to the next part of his plan anyway. The carrot.

There was no way Gwendolyn would throw her support behind Damien without expecting something in return. What could he offer her? Rolan paced some more. She was probably the wealthiest sorcerer on the council. Anything she wanted that she didn't already have, she simply took. What would appeal to her?

Rolan thought through everything he knew about her. The only thing that came to mind that he might be able to work with was the fact that she seemed to crave slaves the same way a hungry man craves food. She was always sending out slavers. What did she do with all of them anyway? He knew she sold a lot of them, but not nearly all that her slavers captured, if the stories he'd heard about their hauls was true. In most provinces, the families were kept together and leased to villages as a group. But from what he had been told about Landoryn, families were usually split up unless someone wanted to buy the whole group. He'd heard that she gave children and teens as gifts to some of her captains, ministers, and sorcerers to do with as they pleased. He didn't know whether or not that was true, but he did know she went through a lot of slaves.

Maybe that was what he should offer her: slaves. He could easily promise to supply her with five slaves a month, and even promise to deliver what she wanted: male, female, young, old, even down to skin and hair color. Granted, with all the slaves she went through, five was only a drop in the bucket, but she'd think he was raiding his own villages to get them, and that in itself would please her.

But he wouldn't need to do that. He'd get them from that other world, the one the key would take him to. He could pick up enough for Gwendolyn, and even a few extra for himself, without anyone ever being the wiser. And there wasn't anyone who could stop him. Yes, that would work out nicely. And it was just the carrot to dangle in front of her face.

Rolan laughed to himself. Once again, he'd figured out how to overcome the obstacles in his path. Sometimes he amazed himself. Manipulating others was pretty easy once you figured out what they wanted, but it was the figuring out how to hook them that took skill. Too bad no one else knew what he was doing and could appreciate how clever he was, but then, if anyone else knew, the plan would be ruined. No, better that no one suspect how shrewd he really was.

Rolan took a deep breath and sat down on his couch. He'd been pacing for nearly an hour while he was coming up with his plan, and it was well past midnight. He needed to get some sleep. He called for his slave once again and told him to go fix him a sleeping draught.

Rolan knew that his father had planned to free the man and let him go his own way as a chapel aide, but Rolan had no such intentions. Why should he? The man was a slave and had been all of his life. Rolan was glad his father had sent the slave to study at the chapel though. He loved having someone at his beck and call who knew all the secrets of the herbs. There were so many times when that came in handy.

Of course, Rolan always made the slave take the first swallow of anything he prepared for him. No need to take any chances. After all, he didn't want to end up like Badec.

Chapter 14

Specialties Emerge

The next morning, Kalen dragged the chests down from the attic and his guests spent several carefree hours trying on clothes before selecting the outfits they would wear. The men's clothes were similar to the ones that Kalen and Duane wore: tight leggings, tunics that fell to mid-thigh, cloaks, and hats. Some of the tunics were made of wool, but most were made of a material that felt like cotton. The cloaks were knee length, warm, and had some type of slick finish that Kalen said would keep them dry during rainstorms.

The dresses for the women had full, floor length skirts, and although most were lightweight, a few were quite heavy. Some of the skirts were made like culottes, and Kalen pointed out how much more convenient those would be when riding horseback. The women's cloaks were similar to the men's except that they were ankle length and had hoods.

Kalen suggested that they choose clothes for all seasons since they would be on the road for a year before they reached Camden, but since space was limited, the Tellurians decided to concentrate on what they would need to reach Nandelia, and worry about the trip next winter later. As they selected clothes, Kalen marked any repairs or tailoring that was needed and set them aside.

After those few light-hearted hours, things turned serious.

Drusilla arrived that afternoon and immediately took charge of Theresa. The rest of the Tellurians spent their days with Duane and Kalen, training for combat. The evenings were devoted to writing and practicing songs.

By the end of the first ten days, Kalen was getting concerned about Theresa spending all of her time with Drusilla because she wasn't getting any self-defense training. On the morning of the eleventh day, he cornered Drusilla in the kitchen.

"We need to talk, Dru."

"Can't it wait, Kalen? Theresa and I need to gather herbs this morning. They take a while to dry and we don't have a lot of time left if they're leaving in ten days."

"That's my point. I feel like Theresa needs to spend some time learning to protect herself. She hasn't been in any of the training sessions since you got here, and she can't use any of the weapons. How is she going to defend herself?"

"Kalen, I've traveled all over Calandra and I've never needed to defend myself against any type of attack. I really don't think she needs to worry about that."

"Dru, you're a Sister! Your pendant protects you! No one would dare attack a Sister."

"I know. So why are you pushing self-defense for Theresa?"

"She's not a Sister!"

Drusilla just raised her eyebrows and looked at Kalen.

After a couple of moments, Kalen said softly, "You mean she is?"

"I would never share all my knowledge and skills with anyone who had not pledged to the Sisterhood. You should know me better than that."

"How? When? I mean …"

"I initiated her when I first got here. I didn't have to spend more than a couple of hours with her to know that she's a healer."

"Why didn't you tell me?"

"I didn't think it was necessary to inform you. You asked me to come, didn't you? 'To work with her', I think your message said. What did you expect?" Drusilla was on the verge of anger.

"No, no, that's quite all right. A Sister of Healing. Does she understand her obligations as a Sister – no, never mind. That was a stupid question. If you initiated her, you made sure she knew what she was doing," Kalen said. Then he leaned back against the counter to watch Drusilla prepare lunch for herself and Theresa. She was beautiful. He'd never been attracted to any other human female, and in the 500 plus years of his life, he'd been around plenty of them. But Dru was different. The sun made her hair look like spun gold, and her eyes were the blue of an October sky. She was slim, delicate, almost fragile in appearance, but fierce as a tiger when riled. She was kind and tender to those who needed her help, but stubborn and shrewd when opposed. Kalen had felt that Dru should have been born a dwarf ever since he'd first met her.

Drusilla finished packing their lunch. Then she turned to Kalen and said, "A healer rounds out the group pretty well, don't you think? If she's ever in any danger, the Sisterhood will come to her aid, and to the aid of those she protects."

"While that's usually good, it could be bad in this case."

"Not really. We don't tell our secrets. You know that," she said as she walked out the door.

When Kalen stepped out into the yard, Duane looked at him and raised his eyebrows.

"Don't worry about Theresa. She'll be fine," Kalen said in answer to his unasked question.

Duane nodded and went back to grooming the horses.

~ ~ ~ ~

The work on the minstrel act was going better than anyone had expected. Steve was their source for legends and stories. Theresa and Chris made a pretty good lyrics team, and Joan found tunes to fit the lyrics. Drusilla taught them four popular folk songs and served as a music critic for the ones they wrote. After ten days, they had a collection of about twenty songs on paper.

While the others were busy writing songs, Karl, Darrell, and Kevin worked on instruments. So far, they had a fiddle and bow, several flutes, a couple of drums, a set of bongos, and a cymbal, but the guitar was proving to be a challenge. All of them, except Kevin, were beginning to identify with the new roles they were playing. They weren't just preparing a minstrel act; they were becoming minstrels.

All of them except Theresa and Kevin were performing better physically than ever before, and they were improving more in one day on Terah than they would have in a month on Earth. They were becoming adept at hand-to-hand combat and competent with all of the weapons, but each of them had discovered that they had special talents in one or two areas.

Darrell adapted his talent for throwing a football to throwing spears and knives, and his martial arts skills made him a formidable opponent in hand-to-hand combat. Chris's boxing background gave him an edge with the sword and with all types of close combat. Thanks to his experience as a sharpshooter for the military, Steve excelled with all of the bows, but he was especially proficient with a long bow. Joan's skill with the long bow was second only to Steve's, but she really came into her own when she was fighting with a dagger. Karl had used a crossbow on Earth, so he preferred that over the other bows, but like Steve, his aim was true with all of them, and his skill with throwing knives was second only to Darrell's. Along with their new skills came a conviction that they could handle whatever Terah had to offer.

Theresa was learning how to use the power in her hands to heal, and knowing that her skills were recognized and valued gave her a level of self-confidence that she had never experienced before. She had not simply adjusted to Terah; she felt that she belonged more to Terah than to Earth.

90

One morning near the end of the second week, Kevin walked out into the yard a little earlier than the others.

Xantha said, *"You don't really want to work out this morning, do you?"*

"No, I don't. I know I'm not any good at any of this, but I have to try."

"None of this has anything to do with you." Xantha pawed the ground and tossed his head. *"Come on. We need to talk. I'll tell Kalen we're going off for a while. You need to learn more about your family."*

"You know my real family? Why haven't you said anything before?"

"Didn't think you were ready to listen." Xantha walked over to the edge of the clearing. *"Get on my back and hold on. You can't fly yet."*

Kevin wasn't sure that this was such a good idea after all. He had enough trouble trying to ride a horse that stayed on the ground.

"What do you mean, can't fly yet?" Kevin asked as he tried to get up the nerve to mount Xantha. "Am I going to have to learn how to fly?"

"Sure, if you're good enough."

That didn't sound too good to Kevin either, but since he could never tell whether Xantha was serious or not, he decided to assume that the pegasus was joking. He took a handful of Xantha's mane and asked, "Where are we going?"

"There's a lovely meadow with some sweet grass not too far from here. We won't be disturbed there. Come on, let's go." Xantha knelt down to make it easier for Kevin to mount.

As soon as Kevin was settled, Xantha spread his wings and Kevin shut his eyes.

"Don't worry, Kevin. I won't let anything happen to you," Xantha said with a snort. *"We need a live sorcerer, not a dead accountant."*

A few minutes later, Kevin slowly opened his eyes and looked around. They were soaring above the clouds. Calm settled over Kevin as memories flooded back. He'd done this before, but only in his dreams. As a child he'd always felt safe and free on Xantha's back, and some of that feeling of contentment settled over him now. It was the first time he'd relaxed since landing on Terah.

All too soon, Xantha swooped down and landed in the meadow. He started grazing while Kevin stretched out on the ground in the sun.

"I'm expecting to wake up and find out that this has all been a dream. Maybe I'm unconscious. Maybe I'm the one in a coma," Kevin said. "I might be lying in a hospital bed right now, hooked up to monitors, waiting to come back to life, my life, my reality."

"I'd worry if I thought you really believed any of that," Xantha said.

"The day that you arrived with Duane, our first full day on Terah …"

"Yes?"

"Were you reading my thoughts then? Is that why you showed up outside the window?"

"I was in your mind. I knew what you were trying to do."

"Yeah, well, it didn't work," Kevin said quietly. Then he added, "I recognized you as soon as I saw you. Were you really there, in my dreams all of those years, or were you just a memory from long ago, from the time before I went to Earth?"

"You were on Earth before you were a week old. I seriously doubt that even a sorcerer's memory goes back to the first week of life," Xantha said with a snort. *"But to answer your question, yes, I was actually there, at least mentally. The first time I appeared in one of your dreams, you were only a couple of years old. Something was chasing you and you couldn't get away, so I helped you out. Since then, I've dropped in on a fairly regular basis. I'm not sure how much humans remember about their dreams, but I knew you'd recognize me when you saw me."*

"Why were you reading my mind when I was two years old?"

"I set up a mind link with you before you left the castle."

"Do you have to have a mind link to read someone's thoughts?"

"No. I can read anyone's thoughts if I want to. A mind link means that the channel is always open. I'm always in your mind. All of your thoughts flow through to me."

"You've always known every thought I've ever had? How I've felt about everything in my entire life?" Kevin sat up and stared at Xantha.

"Of course. I had to be sure that you were all right and that you were coming along as you should. You had to be worthy of your destiny."

"What about my rights to privacy?!"

"I respected your privacy. I never once told anyone what you were thinking or feeling. All I did was reassure your father that things were going along just fine."

"As if he cared."

"He does, very much. You've never been far from his thoughts."

"If he cares, why did he give me away when I was born? Just because my mother died?"

"No. That had nothing to do with it. If she had lived, you would have stayed with them until you were about a year old, but he would have had to foster you out by then."

"Why?"

"Because you are a sorcerer's son. Sorcerers have to foster their children out to keep them away from magic while they're growing up." Xantha wandered over to a fresh patch of grass and began grazing again. "Children tend to mimic adults, and a sorcerer uses magic on a daily basis. If a child were around magic all the time, and had the ability, he would just have to experiment. And uncontrolled magic is not a pretty sight. Control, absolute control, is necessary to make magic safe, and children just do not have that much control. Most sorcerers don't even begin to study magic until they're about twenty-five years old."

"Do all of the sorcerers put their children on Earth?" Kevin asked.

"No. As far as I know, you're the only one that's ever been sent to Earth. Most of the time children are fostered with non-magical friends. Seated sorcerers have to be a little more careful about protecting their children while they're growing up, but since there are usually quite a few of them, they're relatively safe. Of course, not all of the children inherit the magic strain, like Laryn, your father's sister. When it became obvious that she was non-magical, her parents brought her back home to live with them, but Badec had to live with his foster parents until he turned twenty-five. If you had not been an only child, Badec would have done the same with you."

"Wasn't he an only child as far as magic was concerned?"

"No, he has three brothers and two sisters who are sorcerers, too."

"Why didn't my father remarry after my mother died? Doesn't this world allow it?"

"Yes, but no other woman has ever interested him for more than a few days, and since you were safe on Earth he didn't feel like he had to remarry."

"But anything could have happened to me, a car accident, a fire, anything."

"I know. I tried to tell him, so did Laryn, and probably quite a few other people, but apparently Yvonne had told him that you would be the heir, so he didn't worry about it. The rest of us did though."

"Laryn is his second, right? I don't really understand the idea of a 'second'."

"A second is 'second in command'. A second's more than a secretary, more than an advisor, more than a best friend. A second is the highest position a non-magical human can achieve. Even the governor of a province answers to the seated sorcerer and to the second."

"Will Laryn become my second?"

"No. Whenever a sorcerer dies or retires and the heir takes over, the second must retire. The heir has to find his or her own second."

"Then I'm going to have to find someone else?"

"Eventually, but not yet. You don't have to formally declare a second until you have an heir. Then you have to register your second with the council. That way, if anything happens to you, there's someone to hold the chair for a year to give your heir time to get ready to take over, unless your heir is thirty years old or older."

"What if the heir is a child? What happens then?"

"The child has one year to learn how to use magic, or he or she will die at the end of that year."

"What?! What do they do? Execute them?"

"No, of course not! They're not barbarians," Xantha snorted. "The child will almost certainly be challenged at the end of that year, and if he isn't good enough, he'll lose, and to lose a challenge is to die. Just another incentive to make sure you're good enough, and careful enough, to hang around until your children grow up. Your second is supposed to help out on that score, too. One of a second's duties is to watch the sorcerer's back."

"I don't think I'll ever get married. I don't want to subject any child of mine to all of this."

"Don't even start to think that way. As Master Sorcerer, you're responsible to all of Terah, not just one child. You have to make sure that the line of succession is clear and that your powerful strain of magic survives." Xantha paused as he glanced around the meadow, searching for another tasty spot. "Actually, you'll need several children, just to be on the safe side. Badec took quite a chance, never marrying again and having more children. You should not do the same. You cannot leave the highest chair on the council up for grabs. But foster them well, or they'll fight amongst themselves to inherit the Master's Chair."

"Why? You mean someone might actually want all of this?"

"You are so naïve. You have no idea how much power you'll have, and most humans will do anything to get power."

"From what I've seen, with power comes responsibility, and the more the power, the more the responsibility. Who wants it?"

"I'm afraid you may find out all too soon just how many others do want it." Xantha turned his head towards Kevin and took a good long look at him. "At least you see the drawbacks. Most humans are hypnotized by the power."

"Is my father one of those?"

"No, he's more like you. He never really wanted it, but he knew it was his destiny, so he accepted it, same as you will."

Xantha found a new spot and grazed some more while Kevin thought about the future. He felt like he couldn't get a clear grasp of what his life would be like in a month, in a year, or in ten years, should he live that long. For the first time in his life, things were not neatly mapped out.

Finally he said, "I have no idea what I'm heading into. Even with everything you and Kalen have said, I don't know."

"And you won't, not for a while. Sometimes being a sorcerer is really fun, and sometimes your magic will help people, and sometimes it will protect them, but sometimes it won't be enough. Sometimes bad things will happen, no matter how good or how careful you are. It's just the way it is. You're going to have to accept that, and you need to start now."

"What do you mean?"

"You've got to stop feeling responsible for everybody else. Pallor was the one who assembled the team. You didn't force them to come here. You didn't put them in danger. You even tried to give them a way out by refusing to go along with all of this."

"A lot of good it did," Kevin mumbled. Then he said, "Xantha, I don't think they realize what Kalen is saying. They could all die. I figure I'm dead regardless, but they don't have to be involved. Or at least they didn't at that point."

"Well, first of all, I don't figure you're dead regardless, and I wish you would try to have a little faith in us, and a lot of faith in Glendymere. And as far as the others are concerned, they feel like they're doing something important. That's why they're all working so hard. They have a reason to get up every morning, and that reason is a lot more important to them than anything they had back on Earth. They're happy right now, and I'm not picking up any regrets. You have nothing to feel guilty about. Some of them may die, but they think it's worth the risk. When you take that chair, they will have done their part in averting a disaster, and no one can ever take that away from them. That's the way they see it."

Xantha walked over to the far side of the field and continued to graze. Kevin felt a little better at first; then a new responsibility started to sink in. If they were willing to risk their lives to get him to his tutor and then to Camden to take the Master's Chair, he owed it to them to be good enough to hold it.

"Now you're getting it," Xantha chimed into his thoughts. *"You were feeling guilty because you couldn't use those weapons or sing. That's nothing. Your responsibility lies in a totally different direction. You have to become the most powerful human sorcerer on Terah. That needs to be your focus."*

After Xantha had left Kevin to his thoughts for a while, he added, *"And you do have to do one other thing."*

"What's that?" Kevin asked.

"Produce heirs! Lots of them! And soon!"

"Not until all of this is settled."

"Never too soon to start looking for a mate. Want me to help?"

"No, I do not! I'll find my own 'mate', thank you. Just not yet. There will be time enough for that later."

"Maybe, maybe not. Well, I'll just keep reminding you in case you forget."

"Are you ready to go back?"

"Yes, I guess so. It's about time for Duane to feed the horses. Maybe he has some fresh oats." Xantha knelt for Kevin to mount. They he stood up and said, *"Hang on,"* as he stretched his wings and took off.

Xantha and Kevin landed at Kalen's in time for lunch. That afternoon Kevin participated in the training exercises, but it was obvious to everyone that his mind was elsewhere. During dinner that night, he asked Kalen how long he thought the journey to Glendymere's home would take.

Kalen told them that it was close to eleven hundred miles, so his best guess was about seven weeks for the trip. Then he told them that they would need to allow about eight weeks for the trip to Camden, and that they would need to arrive there at least two weeks before the April council meeting next spring to give Myron time to prepare for it.

"Then that means that we have to leave Glendymere's by the middle of January," Steve said, "and since we probably won't get there until the beginning of June, that leaves less than eight months for Kevin to work with Glendymere. Right?"

"That's about right," Kalen agreed.

"Okay. So I'll have about eight months to become strong enough to defend myself against sorcerers who have had years of experience. Is this normal?" Kevin asked. "How long is someone usually a student or an apprentice? How long do sorcerers usually practice their skills before they fight? And if I get challenged, do I have to fight?"

"Yes. That's one of the hazards of being on the council. Other sorcerers can refuse a challenge, but not one who has a seat on the council. And you will be challenged, make no mistake about that. Maybe not immediately, but it will happen," Kalen answered as he stood up to begin clearing the table.

"You sort of skipped over a couple of his questions, didn't you?" Darrell asked. "I'd like to hear the answers. How long do sorcerers normally train before they consider fighting to the death?"

"Well, it varies. Some apprentices have more talent and intelligence than others. There's no one easy answer," Kalen hedged.

"Quit stalling! We owe them the truth," Xantha interjected.

Kalen frowned and then cleared his throat. "Most sorcerers apprentice with an experienced sorcerer for ten to twenty years before they go out on their own. Then they usually practice for another five years or so before they consider challenging another sorcerer." Kalen did not look at anyone as he answered. He directed his attention to stacking dishes.

"Wait a minute! That's a minimum of fifteen years before they face off. And Kevin has eight months? That's suicide! Or more accurately, murder!" Chris yelled. His face had gone beet red.

Kalen glanced around the table as anger rumbled through the group. "No! Wait! Chris, listen to me! Myron is not a typical sorcerer! What normally happens does not apply to him." Kalen paused a second, hoping things would calm down a little, but instead of calming down, everyone seemed to be getting angrier. Even Joan was looking at him with daggers in her eyes.

"Most sorcerers only have a small store of magical energy inside," Kalen explained. "They have to supplement their natural magic by gathering it from the flow of magical energy around Terah and storing it inside their bodies, and every time they use any of the magic that they've stored, they have to replace it. That's a tough thing to do, and takes a long time to master. Myron won't have to gather magic, it's already there, waiting to be used, an unending supply, right at his fingertips! I know you don't understand what I'm talking about, but it's almost like he has an unfair advantage to start with because he's part elf. And he won't really be an apprentice either. Most sorcerers have to act as a servant to their teacher and learn little bits and pieces as they go along. Myron will be a student with a tutor dedicated to teaching him. That's another big plus!"

For once, Kevin was the calm one, although his face had gone a couple of shades whiter than normal. He nodded to Kalen and quietly said, "If eight months is all the time I have, then eight months will have to be enough. Now, there's something else that I want to bring up." Kevin paused for just a moment. "I'm no good with any of the weapons or with hand-to-hand fighting. I know it and all of you know it. This afternoon I started thinking about just how much we do not know about this place, the customs of the people, how they live, their laws, their beliefs, and in less than two weeks we're going to be trying to pass ourselves off as natives. I think my days would be better spent finding out all I can about Terah before one of us does something to cause people to start wondering where we're from, or one of us breaks a law, or even worse, a taboo. Xantha knows all of this and he can explain some of it to me over the next two weeks."

"That's a good idea," Steve said.

Kalen nodded eagerly. "I think that can be arranged. If Xantha agrees, I see no reason why you can't begin tomorrow." Relief was written all over his face.

"Xantha agrees," Xantha said to Kevin privately.

"I sort of thought you would," Kevin answered mentally.

"Oh, and one more thing," Kevin said as they were all standing up, "I want all of you to call me Kevin. I don't have anything against the name Myron, and I'll be perfectly willing to answer to Myron in a year, but if there are assassins and sorcerers out there searching all over this world for 'Myron', I want to be 'Kevin'."

After everyone else had left the dining room to work on the minstrel act, Kalen finished stacking the dishes and carried them out to the kitchen. Duane came through the back door as Kalen was putting them in the sink.

"Xantha told me about the dinner conversation tonight," Duane said. "I asked him if he put those thoughts in Kevin's head. He said he didn't."

"I wondered. I was afraid he'd back out when he found out how long most sorcerers train, and even though I could tell it scared him, he took the news pretty well." Kalen added hot water from the kettle on the stove to the dishes in the sink. "The suggestions he made were pretty good, too."

"At least now we can stop worrying about accidentally killing him while we try to teach him to defend himself!" Duane chuckled as he picked up a dishtowel and began drying the dishes as Kalen washed them.

~ ~ ~ ~

Later that evening, Duane and Kalen sat down at the kitchen table to outline a new training schedule. The target date for the group to leave for Glendymere's was the twelfth of April, and they figured that the eleventh would be spent packing. That left only seven more days for practice. They wanted the team to spend that time concentrating on building its strengths.

While they were working, Drusilla came in and sat down at the table. She told Kalen that she felt that she had left the chapel in the hands of her aide for about as long as she could and that she really needed to get back to Drisden. "I've told Theresa that I'd like for her to go with me. There are a lot of herbs that do not grow around here, especially this time of year. I have everything she'll need in my workroom, but we'll need some time to go over their uses and preparation."

"I understand, but I really don't want to break up the group, Dru. What about the minstrel act? Theresa will miss a lot of practices if she leaves now," Kalen argued.

"Kalen, you know that she can pick that up easily enough, and she already spends her days with me," Drusilla persisted.

"Well," Kalen said hesitantly, "I guess it'll be all right."

"Can we take the wagon that she's going to drive with us so we can get the herbs loaded?"

Kalen nodded.

"Fine. Then we'll plan to leave right after breakfast tomorrow morning. I told Theresa to pack her things tonight," Drusilla said as she stood up to go.

After Drusilla left the dining room, Duane asked, "What would she have done if you had really been against Theresa going to Drisden?"

"They would have gone anyway," Kalen said with a shrug. "I've never won an argument with that woman." Then he stood up. "The extra food I bought for them to take with them is in the pantry, and we need to pack their sleeping tarps and bedrolls, too. Come on. Let's go get the wagon loaded."

Chapter 15

Palladin Arrives

First thing the next morning, Duane checked the load in Theresa's wagon, hitched the horses, and parked it next to the barn. The wagon was a covered wagon just like the ones that the American pioneers used when they traveled west in wagon trains. Canvas flaps served as doors at the front and back, and storage compartments were located inside the wagon along both sides and under the driver's seat. All of the cooking utensils, food, sleeping tarps, bedrolls, and herbs were going to be stored in Theresa's wagon. Several days earlier, the women had gone through Kalen's kitchen cabinets and appropriated everything that they thought the group might need.

After breakfast, they all gathered around the wagon to wish Theresa and Drusilla a safe journey. As soon as the two women drove out of sight, Kevin turned towards Kalen and asked, "Do you need me for anything else?"

"No, not really. We're going to go over the new training schedule now, but that doesn't involve you."

"Then I'm going to find Xantha. See you tonight," Kevin said as he turned towards the stable.

~ ~ ~ ~

At dinner that evening, Chris asked Kevin what Xantha had told him about Terah that day.

"He just talked about the towns and stuff, nothing really critical," Kevin said.

"Well? You need to fill us in," Karl said.

Everyone nodded, so Kevin said, "Okay, but when you get bored, just remember, you asked. Most of the towns have around a couple of hundred people, if you count the outlying farms. There's usually a tavern with a few rooms for rent upstairs, a dry goods store, a farmers market, and a stable. The stable master often doubles as the town blacksmith. If the town is large enough, there might be a Chapel of Light, the closest thing they have to a hospital."

"What do the people in the towns that don't have a Chapel of Light do for medical care?" Darrell asked. "Or does every town have a local sister?"

Kevin shook his head. "No, there aren't that many sisters. Some of the sisters travel around with herbs and hold healing clinics whenever they're asked to, but most of the sisters live at chapels. A lot of the smaller towns don't have regular access to a sister."

"I imagine it's the same as it is in a lot of rural places on Earth. People have the basic medicines and treat themselves, only here, they'd have herbs," Joan said and glanced towards Kalen to see if she was right. He nodded.

"Xantha also said that there are a lot of villages that are too small to be called towns. They usually have a tavern and maybe a small dry goods store, but that's about it. Most of the time, one of the local men has a barn large enough to board a couple of extra horses or store a wagon if someone traveling through really needs to stay overnight," Kevin continued. "And, on the other end of the scale, there are some fairly large towns, but they're rare. There might be a couple of inns, several taverns, a couple of dry goods stores, a cobbler's shop, a saw mill, a grist mill, a large stable with a separate smithy, a wagon yard, and probably a good size Chapel of Light, often with more than one sister in residence. A few large towns along rivers or on natural harbors might even have boatyards, but there again, those are pretty rare."

"Who's in charge?" Steve asked. "Is there a sheriff or something?"

"Not exactly," Kevin answered. "I got the feeling that the army doubles as a police force. But each town has a director, sort of like our mayors. Then each district, which is sort of like our state, has a minister, and the province, like our country, has a governor for civil affairs."

"What do they use for money here?" Chris asked.

"There are several different types of coins, but the value of the coins varies from town to town, and often from merchant to merchant. Most people prefer to barter for what they want."

Kalen chuckled and said, "That's putting it mildly. Haggling over barters is serious business here. A good haggler is one of the most respected men in town, but no one wants to do business with him. You know you're going to get taken before you even start. One thing you need to remember when you leave here though is never accept the first price offered for anything. Nothing would make people suspicious any faster than that."

"Aren't most people pretty much self-sufficient?" Steve asked.

Kevin nodded. "People make their own furniture, do their own repairs, make their own clothes, can their own vegetables, churn their own butter, things like that."

"What about the houses? Does each family make its own house, too?" Darrell asked.

"No, from what Xantha said, all the men in the community help each other when it comes to the big stuff, like raising a house or a barn," Kevin said.

"Do they have running water?" Chris asked.

"Yes and no. Most of the kitchens have a water pump, but that's it. No other running water," Kevin said. "They get hot water by heating it on a wood stove, which is used for heating as well as cooking."

"They don't have electricity, so I'm assuming they use glowstones for light, right?" Darrell asked.

Kevin nodded.

"No electricity means no refrigerators, no freezers, and no microwaves, doesn't it?" Chris asked. "That's depressing."

"Sorry, Chris," Kevin said with a grin. "Well, that's about all we talked about today."

"Then let's get the table cleared and get to work," Joan said. "I'd like to run through all of our songs tonight. We haven't done that yet."

"What about Theresa's part?" Chris asked.

"I'll take it for now," Joan said. "Come on, let's get moving."

Since Kevin couldn't sing, he became the stage manager, handing them instruments when they were needed and setting them aside when they weren't. In addition to the fiddle, flutes, drums, bongos and cymbal, they had added a triangle, sticks, a couple of bells, and even maracas. The guitar still wasn't quite right, but they were getting close.

The next couple of days passed without any interruption to the new routine, but on the third day, Palladin arrived. They heard him long before he reached the house. His voice bellowed out of the woods as he commiserated with his horses over the heavy load and the poor road, and berated Kalen for not taking better care of it. When he reached the house, the Tellurians were surprised to see that he was even shorter than Kalen. In fact, he looked like a shrunken version of Kalen, except that his beard and hair were a bit longer and much grayer. He wore a dark green tunic with black leggings, boots, and heavy leather gloves, and there was a large ax anchored to his chest by thick leather straps that crisscrossed his chest. Attached to his belt on his left side was a long sheath that held a sword. The sword was angled so that its tip swung behind him, and even though it looked almost as long as Palladin was tall, he had no trouble moving with it fastened to his side. All in all, he looked ferocious, but his twinkling eyes and lop-sided grin gave away his good nature as he approached Kalen and grasped him in a bear hug.

"Well there, Kalen. How are you getting along with all these guests? Are they driving you mad yet?" Palladin asked in a whisper that could have been heard on the other side of the yard.

"No, not yet. Things have been going just fine. Here, let me introduce you to the Tellurians, our minstrels," Kalen said as he gestured for them to come over. "One of our ladies turned out to be a healer, so she's in Drisden with Drusilla right now. They'll pick her up on the way down to Glendymere's. And Myron, Badec's son, is off with Xantha. He'll be back this evening. Oh, he's asked us all to use his other name, Kevin." Then Kalen introduced the rest of the Tellurians to Palladin.

Palladin shook hands with everyone and then he pulled an eight-pointed shuriken out of a large pocket on the front of his tunic. "And who did I make these for?"

"I asked for those," Darrell said. "May I see it?" When Palladin handed it to him, he held it in his hand and juggled it a bit to test the balance as he walked towards the target he had been using with the knives. He stopped about fifty feet from the target, set his stance, swung his arm like a backhand in tennis, and flicked his wrist as he released the shuriken. One of the eight blades hit the middle of the bull's eye, and the shuriken sliced into the target. Darrell retrieved it and handed it back to Palladin with a smile. "Thanks. These will work just fine."

Palladin hadn't realized that he had been holding his breath until he started to speak. He frowned, shook his head, and said, "I had a feeling that I was making some new kind of weapon. I don't know if I should be pleased or worried."

"Be pleased," Kalen answered. "Darrell's on our side." Then he put his arm around Palladin's shoulder and turned him towards the house. "It's just about time for lunch. Let's eat now and unload your wagon later."

Palladin made lunch a boisterous and jovial affair and it lasted twice as long as normal. Afterwards, they all went outside to his wagon. It looked like the ones the traveling snake oil salesmen used in the days of the Wild West, an enclosed wooden box with the driver's seat mounted on the front.

He opened the back door and began removing a large crate from the interior. Darrell stepped up to give him a hand, but Palladin smiled and said, "Thanks for the offer, but you'd better let me get this. We don't want any of you to get hurt." Palladin picked up the crate and carried it over to the exercise yard. He motioned for the others to join him.

Kalen stepped over to walk beside Darrell. "Remember, things are not always as they seem," he said quietly. "The weakest dwarf is stronger than the strongest human and mountain dwarves are the strongest of the dwarves. Never let a dwarf hand you anything unless you know what it is. Have him set it on the ground and check it out yourself before you try to lift it." Then Kalen added with a chuckle, "But if a wagon wheel comes off and there's a dwarf around, ask him to hold up the wagon while you replace the wheel. It would be child's play to him, and you won't even have to unload."

Darrell nodded. "I'll remember that. You aren't planning to find a dwarf to go with us just in case we get stuck in the mud, or drop a wheel in a ditch, are you?"

"No, sorry," Kalen answered. "In general, dwarves and humans do not travel together well. Humans tire too quickly and dwarves are always in a hurry."

By the time they reached the exercise yard, Palladin had removed the top of the crate. There were at least twenty-five swords in there. Palladin, Kalen, and Duane began unloading the crate, drawing the swords out of their scabbards and laying each sword on top of its scabbard on the ground.

A few of the swords were fairly short, only about two feet long, while others were nearly four feet long with two-handed grips. There were swords as narrow as rapiers, and there were swords with blades three or four inches wide. Some were curved and some were straight as an arrow, but all of the cutting edges had been honed to razor sharpness.

Some of the handles were made of hardwood and some were metal. Some of them had finger grooves, some were covered with spun cord, and a few were covered in leather. Most of the handles had round or oval pommels on top, some engraved and some plain.

The cross guards separating the blade from the handle varied as much as the handles. Some were short, extending about half an inch on each side of the blade, but most extended three or four inches. Some curved towards the blade, some curved towards the handle, and a few were relatively straight.

As the humans wandered around looking at the swords and admiring the craftsmanship, Palladin urged them to pick them up and try them out. At first they hesitated, thinking that he was like a traveling peddler, trying to sell his goods, but then Kalen told them that Palladin had brought the swords specifically so that each of them could choose one.

"Well, it won't be completely up to you, you know," Palladin said. "The sword will choose you as much as you will choose the sword. It has to be mutual, or it won't work well for you."

"What do you mean, the sword will choose us?" Joan asked.

"You'll see. Walk around, pick them up one at a time, and hold them in your hands. If it's for you, you'll know it," Palladin assured them.

Chris and Darrell exchanged skeptical looks, but each reached for a sword to test out and soon the others followed suit. Palladin walked among them, encouraging them. He told them to feel the perfect balance between the blade and the handle, to try a fighting stance, and to take a couple of jabs with the swords. As soon as one of them put a sword down, Palladin was right there to point out another.

After a few minutes, Joan gasped, "It's vibrating! Palladin, what's going on?!" Joan had one of the shortest swords in her hand. The blade was only about eighteen inches long.

Palladin nodded and said, "Like I said, you'll know when a sword chooses you. And that's a fine choice for a woman. It's lightweight, less than two pounds, and it's a defensive weapon. No one will think that you're looking for a fight with that sword by your side, but it also serves notice that you won't back down either. Excellent choice!"

As she held the sword in her hands, she felt strangely attracted to it. She looked it over carefully, tracing the ivy design that had been etched in the cross guard with her finger and then polishing the pommel with its delicate etching of an eagle in flight. Then she turned back towards Palladin and smiled.

"Try the scabbard. It should fit nicely on your belt. See how it feels."

Once the scabbard was on her belt and her belt was fastened back around her waist, Joan placed the sword carefully in the scabbard.

"Now, draw your sword."

When Joan reached for her sword, it seemed to leap clear of the scabbard and into her hand of its own volition.

"Yes, that sword will suit you nicely," Palladin said with a smile. Then he looked around at the others. "Has anyone else found a sword yet?"

After watching how the sword had reacted to Joan's touch, everyone else began picking up the swords with a new enthusiasm. Steve was the next to find his. It was a thin sword with a blade about two feet long and a medium sized handle that would feel comfortable with either a one-handed or a two-handed grip. The cross guard was straight and narrow, and the tip of his handle was not a pommel as much as a small cap.

Karl's choice was heavier than anyone else's and had a wider blade. The three-foot blade curved slightly towards the left at the tip, and the two-handed grip curved slightly towards the right. The head of a lion was engraved on the pommel.

Darrell's sword was straight and narrow like Steve's, but it was nearly as long as Karl's. The handle was designed for a two-handed grip, but it was light enough that it could be used one-handed. A roaring cougar was engraved on its pommel.

Chris was beginning to get discouraged. He thought he had tried all of the swords when his eyes fell on one that had been left in the crate. The sword was still in its scabbard, but he could see the hilt. The handle had two hardwood grips separated by a metal spacer. Chris asked Palladin if he could try it, and when Palladin took the sword out of its scabbard and handed it to Chris, sparks jumped from the sword to Chris's hand and the sword began to hum softly.

"Yes, I'd say that one's yours," Palladin said with a nod as he walked back towards Kalen.

Once they had all selected a sword, Palladin, Duane, and Kalen started collecting the extras.

"Wait a minute," Chris said. "What about Kevin and Theresa? Don't they need swords, too?"

"He may be right," Duane said hesitantly. "Although neither of them has shown any interest in having one."

"Theresa doesn't need one," Kalen said. "She's a sister now, and they never carry a sword, but she'll need a dagger. As for Kevin, sorcerers never bother to carry a sword, so if for no other reason than that, he'll need one. What do you think, Palladin?"

"Well, since he probably has no intention of using it, I'm not sure any sword will really select him, but I've got one here that I'd love to see him carry. It's one of my favorites." Palladin turned to the crate, and dug down to the very bottom. The sword he pulled out of the crate had a twenty-inch blade but only the bottom fifteen inches had cutting edges. Although the sword was light enough to be used one-handed, the five-inch section of the blade closest to the cross guard had small rounded knobs on the edges, which could be grasped in the second hand to deliver a powerful two-handed thrust.

"Yes, I think that will do just fine for Kevin," Kalen said as Duane nodded his approval.

Duane and Kalen continued collecting the extra swords, sheathing them, and stacking them beside the crate. Palladin pulled a large leather bag out of the bottom of the crate and then began packing the extra swords away.

After the humans had all fastened their scabbards to their belts, practiced drawing and sheathing the swords, and fought imaginary opponents for a while, Palladin said, "Now, for my next toys." He picked up the leather bag and opened it. The bag was full of what appeared to be walking sticks and canes. "From what Kalen told me, you're going to travel as a group of minstrels. You can't really wear your swords on stage, but there's no reason not to have a couple of these around while you're performing."

Palladin emptied the contents of the bag on the ground. There were three carved walking sticks and three walking canes with large curved handles.

Steve picked up one of the canes and took a few steps with it. "Does everyone on Terah use some kind of stick or cane?"

"No, of course not. Watch." Palladin took hold of a cane, flipped it over, grabbed the end, and used the curved handle to grab Kalen by the neck. "If I had jerked on it, he would have ended up on the ground at the very least. They're great for pulling someone off a buddy during a fight, and so easy to use." Palladin grinned as Kalen struggled to regain his balance. "And if that's not enough," Palladin flipped the cane again, grasped the handle, gave it a twist, and pulled a thin, sharp blade out of the shaft of the cane, "you can always run him through!" Palladin made a playful lunge towards Kalen. "Now do you think you might like to carry my little toys along?"

Darrell picked one of the canes up and twisted the handle to pull the blade out. He frowned and said, "Are all of the canes on Terah this lethal? Or is this something new?"

"It's new at the moment, just like those things you had me make for you to throw, but all you have to do is use them once and other people will start making them, too. If I were you, I'd stick to swords, daggers, and throwing knives if at all possible, and save the new weapons for emergencies," Palladin answered.

"What about these? Is there anything special that we need to know about them?" Karl asked as he picked up one of the walking sticks.

"Not much really. All I did to those was run a cast iron bar down the center of the shaft. Here, look at the bottom end and you can see where I filled the borehole. But after it's used as a walking stick for a while, no one will be able to spot it. It's a little heavier than other sticks, but it'll pack a good wallop and it won't break. It'll even stop a sword if you can hang on to it. Now let's put those back in this storage bag. Could someone take the bag into the house along with Kevin's sword? We've still got another crate to go through."

As soon as the yard was cleared up again, Palladin carried the crate with the extra swords up to the barn and stored it in one of Kalen's spare wagons. Then he unloaded the second crate from the new wagon and carried it to the exercise yard.

When everyone had gathered around, Palladin pried the lid off. The crate was separated into three sections. One section contained daggers, one contained throwing knives, and the third contained several dozen throwing stars.

Palladin explained that a dagger was not like a sword; when it was used, it was left in the victim. He told everyone to choose two daggers, one to be worn on the belt in plain sight, and a smaller one to be worn somewhere else on the body, hidden by clothing.

The daggers were as unique as the swords. Some had wavy blades, some had triangular blades, and some had thin narrow blades. Most of the handles were slightly curved to fit the palm of the hand, although a few were almost "L" shaped and a few were straight. While the others chose daggers for themselves, Kalen chose daggers for Kevin and Theresa.

As soon as he had selected his daggers, Darrell started going through the throwing stars. Palladin had used Darrell's sketches as a basis for constructing them, but after he had made a few, he had created some patterns of his own. Some of the stars had triangular blades, some had arrowhead-shaped blades, some had blades that swirled off in a circular motion, and a few had spikes.

Palladin watched as Darrell carefully examined the stars. Then he handed Darrell a small leather bag with sections inside, almost like an accordion file. It would hold eight stars and would fit in a tunic pocket. There were leather straps on both sides so that the bag could be secured to the tunic through small holes in the pocket or tied to a belt. Darrell placed eight of the stars in the bag and immediately dropped it in his pocket. He turned to Palladin to thank him, but Palladin had already moved on.

He was giving everyone two small leather sheaths with leather straps attached to all four corners. "Now, you need to choose some throwing knives. They are all pretty much alike, so this shouldn't take but a few minutes. One of the sheaths that I just gave you should fit nicely on your forearm. Here, let me show you," Palladin said as he took Joan's from her hand and tied it around her forearm. "Notice that the wide part has slots for four knives. Now if you'll remove your boot, I'll show you how to attach the ankle sheath," Palladin said to Joan.

After Joan had taken her boot off, Palladin tied the sheath so that the pouch would be on the inside of her leg. "This sheath will hold six if you really want to carry that many in your boot. But if you do, be sure you allow for that when you buy your next pair of boots. More than likely you'll find that three or four knives are all that you can wear comfortably with the boots you have on now. By the way, notice people's boots if you think you might have to fight them. Boots that are loose around the calf are a dead give-away that the person's carrying knives."

Soon everyone had the sheaths tied on and knives stored in the pouches. Palladin picked up the rest of the knives and put them in a wooden box. "I have just the spot for these. You know, once you throw a knife you probably won't get it back, so you'll need spares. If this supply starts running low, you'll need to buy some more. Just be sure that they're made by a dwarf. You want good quality. After all, if the balance isn't right there's no telling where the knife might end up when you throw it."

Then Palladin put the box of knives back in the crate with the stars and extra daggers, picked up the crate and started back towards the wagon. When he reached the wagon he set the crate on the ground.

"Before I can show you the hidden compartments I built, I really need to get this harp out of the way." Palladin lifted the harp out of the wagon and set it on the ground next to the crate. "And who did I lug this thing all the way up here for?" he asked with a smile as he looked directly at Joan.

"Yes, it's for me," Joan answered as she walked around the harp, fingering the exquisite design carved into the wooden frame. "Did you make this? It's beautiful!"

"No, I can't take credit for this one, but it is good work. I don't know who made it, but I'd bet it was an elf. I traded a man a horse for that harp a while back. I was going to put a 'for sale or trade' sign on it and stick it out in front of the shop, but I never got around to it. Then I got the message from Kalen requesting a harp."

Joan strummed the harp a few times and said, "Karl, why don't you and Darrell see if you can get the harp into the house. I want to set it up in the living room so I can practice with it. I'll get the door."

"That's all right. I'll get it," Palladin offered.

"No, Palladin, please let them. If we're going to carry this harp with us and use it in our performances, we need to be sure that we can move it ourselves, unless you plan to travel with us, of course," Joan said.

"No thank you. I wouldn't mind seeing how all of this works out, but I have a shop to run. I think I'll have to pass on that one."

Darrell and Karl picked up the harp and carried it carefully into the house. It wasn't really heavy, but it would be awkward for one person to carry. They set it up in a corner of the living room.

After they came back outside, Palladin showed everyone the regular storage compartments and then the hidden compartments that he had built inside the wagon. They stored the extra daggers and knives in one of the hidden compartments near the back door. Then he showed them the compartment he had built under the driver's seat. No one would guess that part of the seat was hollow and contained a small metal lock box that could be opened by twisting a key that looked like a nail that hadn't been hammered quite flush with the wood. The driver could open the box and reach in without dropping the reins, getting off the bench, or even bending over more than he would to rest his elbows on his knees.

By the time they finished exploring the wagon, it was time for dinner. Xantha and Kevin returned just as everyone was heading into the house. Kalen waited for him so that he could introduce Palladin, and then he took Kevin inside to show him the sword and daggers that they had selected for him.

Kevin was surprised to find that he actually liked the little sword and that it felt right in his hand. He tied the scabbard onto his belt and went outside to practice drawing it while everyone else was getting ready for dinner.

Duane stood by the backdoor for a few minutes watching him. Then he turned towards Palladin and said, "I think you made a good choice. That's the first time he's shown any interest at all in weapons. He seems to like that little sword, so maybe he'll make a real effort to learn how to use it."

Palladin just smiled in return.

Chapter 16

Reality Sinks In

Kevin was relieved that Palladin kept the dinner conversation lively that evening because no one thought to ask him what he and Xantha had talked about during the day. Xantha had told him that slavery existed virtually everywhere on Terah, and that capturing, transporting, and selling slaves was considered a business venture. He knew that the idea would be as repulsive to the rest of the Tellurians as it was to him, and he was wondering how to go about telling them when he noticed a lapse in the conversation. The others had finished eating and were sitting back enjoying their scog.

After a few minutes, Joan said quietly, "You know, so far this has been like preparing an act for the Pioneer Village. I hadn't really thought of it as real, but today I had weapons strapped to my waist, my arm, and my ankle. In five days we'll be leaving here, and I'm wondering just what we're heading into. Are we going to have to fight our way to Glendymere's? If we are, I don't know that I can handle it." She kept her gaze on the table because she could feel the tears burning in her eyes.

"I know what you mean," Chris said slowly. "I've been thinking about that, too."

"Well, don't dwell on it," Kalen said. "More than likely nothing will happen. You'll probably travel from town to town quite peacefully, and get to Glendymere's without having to draw a weapon once, but we couldn't gamble on it. We had to do everything we could to make sure that if you suddenly found yourselves surrounded by a group of bandits you would have a good chance of surviving the encounter."

"Or assassins," Darrell said.

"I don't think anyone is going to figure out who Kevin really is. You won't be in any one place long enough. So, I'm not too worried about that threat," Kalen answered.

"Well, I think I'll just keep on worrying about it until this is over," Darrell said.

"Not a bad idea," Palladin agreed.

"We'll also have to be on the lookout for the slave traders," Kevin said before he realized it.

"The *what*?" Karl gasped. His frown was so deep that he appeared to have one long eyebrow stretched across his forehead. He looked first at Kevin and then at Kalen, who was suddenly busy clearing dishes, a sure sign that what Kevin said was true.

"Oh, no," groaned Joan.

"Just out of curiosity, when were you planning to tell us about this? Or were you going to just let us discover it on our own?" Karl's voice had a knife-edge to it.

"I was afraid of this," Steve said quietly.

Darrell's eyes became cold and hard, and Chris's face turned red with anger.

"I didn't know how to bring it up, but no, I wasn't going to let you leave without warning you. I really don't think you'll run into any slave traders though. They tend to raid near large bodies of water. Look, let Kevin tell you about it. I'm sure he can explain it better than I can." Kalen continued stacking the dishes. "Besides, I need to start washing up." He picked up a stack of dishes and disappeared into the kitchen.

"Coward," mumbled Kevin. Then he turned to the rest of the group. "From what I gathered, humans only enslave other humans. They don't bother the dwarves or the elves for some reason." Kevin paused and looked at Palladin and Duane as if waiting for them to explain.

"I can tell you why they don't bother the dwarves," Palladin said. "In general, dwarves are pretty easy going as long as you let them go about their business in their own way, but we go berserk when we're threatened."

"Berserk?" Joan asked. "What does that mean?"

Palladin fingered the edge of his ax. "I'd rip my battle-ax off, right through the straps and start swinging. Before I came out of the frenzy, I'd have destroyed everything around me and killed everyone in the area. Most humans are pretty careful around dwarves."

"I bet," Darrell mumbled. Then he turned towards Duane and asked, "Do elves go berserk, too? Is that why slavers don't go after them?"

"No. We're just too hard to catch," Duane said as he stood up. "Here, Palladin, grab my arm."

As Palladin reached out to grab Duane's arm, Duane vanished.

"See what I mean? No one can capture an elf," Duane said from the other side of the room. "We can translocate. Most of us can't go much farther than half a mile, but that's usually enough. We train for battle, especially when we're young, and we're armed when we travel, but that's more due to custom than necessity." Duane walked back towards his seat and sat down. "Although some elves who do enjoy a good fight. They usually hire themselves out, mostly to human armies, but there are a few who have joined gangs of bandits or signed on with slave traders."

"So who do the slavers go after? What criteria do they use? Skin color, hair color, eyes, what?" Darrell asked.

"I don't think any of that matters to the slave traders. They prefer families, but from what I could tell, that's about it," Kevin said. "Xantha said that slavery began as a way to meet the quota in local army units. All of the male peasants and townspeople who are eighteen to twenty-five years old are required to serve in the local unit, but it's on a part-time basis. They meet one day a week for drill and training, and other than that, they are only called out in case of attack or natural disaster. Apparently the provincial army is a lot like our National Guard. Anyway, if there aren't enough able-bodied men to fill out the unit, the town director petitions the district minister for enough slaves to fill the empty slots."

"You mentioned attack. Who attacks the towns? Invading armies from other provinces?" Karl asked.

"No, at least I don't think so," Kevin said. "From what I gathered, the only people who attack are slavers."

Chris frowned. "It's a vicious circle. They need slaves to build up the armies to protect the citizens from slavers."

"What's to keep the slaves from just walking away?" Darrell asked.

"I asked Xantha the same question," Kevin said. "A man by himself probably would. That's why the slavers go after families. If a man is sent to a village to serve in that village's army unit, his family is also sent to the director, sort of like hostages. Children might be sent to work at one of the local farms, or to help out at the stables. Women might be used to help out on a farm, in one of the local shops, or even in someone's home. When the man's not training with the army unit, he might be sent out to one of the farms or village shops to work. You really can't blame the locals for using slave labor; after all, they're paying the tab."

"Do you mean the slaves are owned by the town?" Joan asked.

"Not exactly. The village doesn't usually buy them. They lease them from the minister. The ministers either buy slaves from the slave traders, from each other, or they can lease them from the governor. The governor buys slaves to work in the sorcerer's castle and in the governor's house, and he usually has some extras that he can lease out or sell to his ministers."

"Then individual people don't actually own slaves? Only the government does?" Karl asked.

"For the most part," Kevin said. "Sometimes a wealthy family doesn't want their son to have to serve in the army, so they buy a slave to take his place, or they might buy a couple of young girls to work at the house, but it doesn't happen often."

"Who are the slavers?" Chris asked. "Are they just a bunch of renegades?"

"Slave traders are businessmen. They don't have much contact with the people they sell," Kalen answered. "The actual raiding parties are usually made up of free-lance soldiers. Most professional soldiers work as officers in the armies, but some become bandits, and some sign on with the slave traders. The raiding parties consider any travelers that they happen to come across as fair game, but mainly they raid outlying villages and farms. Makes it easier to get away. Once they capture the people, they split them up by family units and ship them off to be sold in distant provinces."

"No wonder Palladin brought us so many weapons," Darrell said.

"I didn't really bring the weapons because of the slavers," Palladin said, trying to reassure them. "Slavers are something you need to be aware of, but you aren't going to be near any large rivers or oceans, at least not on the way to Glendymere's, and those are the danger zones. It's not like there are raiding parties stalking all the roads. There just aren't that many slavers out there."

"The way I see it, I think the slavers pose a bigger threat than the assassins," Steve said. "As long as we manage to keep Kevin's identity under wraps we can probably avoid the assassins, but the slavers are random. We could run into them anywhere."

"I wonder how many more nasty little surprises this world has in store for us," Joan said quietly. "Well, you guys can sit here and talk about this as long as you want to. I'm going to the living room and practice with the harp."

~ ~ ~ ~

The next three days were spent in a flurry of activity. Everyone, even Kevin, spent a couple of hours each morning sparring with the new swords. Kevin spent his afternoons with Xantha while the others practiced combat skills. After dinner each evening, the group continued practicing for the minstrel shows.

The night before they were to leave, they held a dress rehearsal and asked Kalen, Duane, and Palladin to act as their audience. Even though all three of them had heard the Tellurians practice from a distance every night, seeing the show from beginning to end was different. When the show was over, the audience cheered, and even Kalen admitted that he was impressed.

After the rehearsal, they loaded the instruments in the wagon that Palladin had brought. When they were done, Kalen handed each of them a bag of coins, some copper, some silver, some a funny grayish color, and some gold. He went over the relative values of each and told them about how much they should expect to pay for food, lodging for themselves, stable fees for the horses, new shoes for the horses, and so on. He also reminded them that they should be able to exchange a performance for most of their needs, but that if they had to use the coins, not to accept the first or even the second price.

Then Kalen and the Tellurians gathered around the dining room table to review the maps and go over the routes that they needed to take. When Kalen was satisfied that they knew where they were going, he folded the maps and handed them to Karl, who took them out to the wagon and packed them into one of Palladin's little hidden compartments.

Later that night, after the Tellurians were asleep, Kalen, Duane, and Palladin sat in the living room, drinking scog. "I think they're about as ready to go as we can make them," Kalen said with relief.

"I don't know what else we could have done to prepare them in the short amount of time we've had," Duane said. "It scared me a bit the other night when Kevin broke the news about slavery. For a minute, I thought that they were going to bolt."

"I don't understand why they reacted like they did. Don't they have slavery on Earth?" Palladin asked.

"Yes, but from what Pallor says, most Americans either don't know that it exists, or don't want to know. They prefer to think that it was abolished a hundred years ago. I was afraid we'd lost them there, too. I wasn't planning to say much about it, but I guess Xantha felt like they needed to be aware of it before they left here," Kalen answered with a shrug.

"You know, there's something else that we haven't found a way to mention, and I wonder if maybe we should tell them tomorrow morning before they leave," Duane said.

"What?" Palladin asked.

"We haven't told them about Glendymere," Duane answered.

"I know," Kalen said. "I don't know how to bring it up. I'm sort of surprised that Xantha hasn't told Kevin."

Palladin frowned. "I'm sure I've heard his name mentioned while I've been here. Don't they know that Glendymere is going to train Kevin?"

"Oh, they know that. And they know that Glendymere lives in a cave in the canyons of Nandelia. What they do not know is that Glendymere is a dragon," Kalen replied.

"Whoops," Palladin said softly. "With the way a lot of humans react to dragons, that's a rather significant detail. What are you going to do?"

"I'm going to keep my mouth shut," Kalen said. "I'm afraid that finding out that they're going to travel over a thousand miles to meet a dragon and live with him for eight months might be more than they can handle right now."

"So what happens when they meet him?" Duane asked.

"I really don't know. I'll send Glendymere a note after they leave and let him worry about it," Kalen said with a sigh.

Chapter 17

The Journey Begins

Thursday morning dawned bright and clear, and within an hour of daybreak, the Tellurians were loaded and ready to go. Two horses were hitched to the front of the wagon, two spare horses were tied behind it, and Kevin was seated on the driver's seat. Everyone else was mounted.

Kalen, Duane, Palladin, and Xantha had gathered in the yard to see them off.

"Will you be joining us at any point?" Kevin asked Xantha mentally.

"Probably, but I'm not sure when. Duane and I are going to go home for a while when we leave here. He hasn't seen his wife in over a month."

Kevin nodded, turned to Kalen and said, "Thanks for your hospitality and all of your help, Kalen. And you too, Duane. And Palladin, thanks again for the weapons and this wagon."

"All of you have really been wonderful," Joan added. "Duane, Palladin, have a safe trip home. And you too, Xantha."

"Thank you," Duane replied as Palladin nodded. Xantha tossed his head and pawed the ground.

"It was the very least we could do," Kalen said graciously, quickly pushing aside a twinge of guilt as the truth of his statement hit him. "You need to get on the road if you're going to get to Drusilla's in time to load the other wagon tonight. Take care and Godspeed!"

"See you in Camden," Karl said with a mock salute as he turned his horse and headed west down the little dirt road that led away from the Gate House and into the woods. Joan and Chris fell in behind him, followed by Kevin and the wagon, with Steve and Darrell bringing up the rear.

After about five miles, they came out of the woods into a large meadow, and the road disappeared. While the others waited, Karl rode on through the thick shrubs and grasses to see if he could spot where the road continued. Finally, on the other side of the meadow, he came across a well-traveled road running north and south, but there was no sign of the little road they had been following. He turned around in his saddle and motioned for the others to join him. As they crossed the meadow, Kevin brought up the rear, carefully and slowly maneuvering the wagon through the dense underbrush.

While they were waiting for Kevin, Darrell stood up in his stirrups and looked back across the meadow. "I can't see any sign of the road to Kalen's house. Hope we don't have to try to go back there."

"We shouldn't," Steve said. "You know, I bet that road is actually a driveway. The only people who used it while we were there were Palladin and Drusilla, and they're both friends of Kalen's. I doubt he has many other guests."

"You're probably right," Chris said, looking around. "If that road was used much we'd be able to see the tracks through the meadow. Must get pretty lonely out there."

"Or pretty private," Karl said. "I didn't get the impression that Kalen was one for a lot of entertaining. I imagine he enjoys the solitude."

About that time, Kevin reached the road and stopped. "Before I pull out onto the road, which way are we going? I don't want to have to turn this wagon around."

"The maps and directions Kalen gave us more or less start at Drisden," Chris said with a frown. "I thought the road we were on would take us straight into town. It'd be sort of funny if we got lost on the first day out, wouldn't it?"

Kevin grinned. "I can almost see Kalen now, shaking his head and mumbling, 'They'll get it together. They have to.' "

They all chuckled. Then Karl turned to Steve and raised his eyebrows.

Steve shrugged his shoulders and said, "Well, Drisden is supposed to be on our way, and we know we're heading south, so I vote that we head south."

Karl looked at the others but no one else had any other suggestions, so he turned his horse toward the left and said, "South it is."

At the end of the meadow the road entered a hardwood forest that was just beginning to come back to life after the long cold winter. Around lunchtime, the forest gave way to farmland. Long, narrow driveways led from the road to the barns and silos that were tucked away behind the small farmhouses. Smoke drifted out of most of the chimneys and the smell of wood smoke and cooking mixed with the smell of farm animals, hay, and manure. Sounds of children laughing and dogs barking mingled with the sounds of men working. Chickens roamed around the front yards while horses, cows, goats, and sheep grazed in nearby pastures.

It was mid-afternoon by the time the Tellurians rode into Drisden. The village houses had small front yards, with fruit trees and little flower gardens where tiny green stalks were beginning to poke through the dirt. The large backyards held stables, sheds, and vegetable gardens as well as large shade trees. The houses were closer together than the farmhouses were, but they weren't as close as houses in most of the housing developments on Earth.

After the houses, the road widened to form the village square. Wide wooden boardwalks separated the buildings from the hitching posts and water troughs that lined both sides of the road. A tavern with rooms for rent upstairs, a cobbler's shop, a blacksmith's shop, and a stable were on the left-hand side of the square. A dry good's store, a farmer's market, and a relatively large building with a sign in front that had a starburst on it were on the right. Then the road narrowed again and passed between a few more houses before the village gave way to more farms.

As they rode through the town square, people stopped and stared, pointing at the wagon and talking excitedly. The Tellurians were all beginning to get a little nervous, especially Kevin.

Joan rode up beside Karl and whispered, "I don't like this. Do you know where we're supposed to meet Drusilla?"

"I have no idea," Karl mumbled.

About that time, the front door of the building with the starburst sign opened and Drusilla walked out onto the large front porch. She waved to them as she stepped off the porch and headed towards the road. When she reached Karl, she said, "I'm glad you made it all right. Take your horses around back. Harald's waiting back there to help you."

As Karl nodded, Drusilla turned around to head back to the chapel, but before she had taken a step, she turned back to Karl and said, "By the way, park the wagon next to the back porch rather than in the barn."

Karl raised his eyebrows and opened his mouth to ask why, but before he could get the words out, Drusilla grinned and said, "Just do it. I'll explain later."

Karl and Joan led the others down the small drive that curved around the chapel to the backyard. A tall, skinny young man in his mid-teens was filling feed buckets with oats, but when he saw Karl, he set the oats aside, opened the corral gate, and waved them through. While the others tended to their horses, Kevin parked the wagon and he and Harald unhitched the team and the spare horses. As soon as all of the horses were in the corral, Harald closed the gate and everyone pitched in to get them watered and fed.

Karl carried the tack into Drusilla's barn, and while he was there, he checked the supplies in Theresa's wagon. The first couple of cabinets on the left-hand side of the wagon held kitchen equipment, and the next two held flour, sugar, coffee, and other staples. Dried fruits and vegetables were stored in the cabinets under the driver's seat.

Theresa's herbs were on the right-hand side of the wagon. The dried and powdered herbs were in neatly labeled containers and were packed in the cabinets closest to the driver's seat. The cabinet closest to the back of the wagon had netting over the front instead of a door, and some of her potted herbs were stored in there, but most of the pots were in a wooden trough which had been anchored to the top of the cabinets on the right-hand side of the wagon. Bags of cloth bandages were tied to special metal rings that had been attached to the metal hoops that supported the canvas top. Their bedrolls were stacked on top of the left-hand cabinets and the tarps were piled on the driver's seat. About half a dozen coils of rope were lying on the ground beside the front wheel. Karl nodded to himself, satisfied with their provisions.

While the others were still outside, busy with the horses, Drusilla and Theresa had set out some platters of bread, cheese, and fruit along the kitchen counter. Joan was the first one to come into the kitchen, and as soon as she washed up, she started setting the table. When Theresa brought over some silverware for Joan to set out, Joan noticed that she was wearing a pendant just like Drusilla's. While the others were washing up, she quietly asked Theresa if she was wearing the pendant because she was a sister.

Theresa nodded and whispered, "I'll tell you all about it, but not here, later, once we're on our way."

After the Tellurians had finished eating and were relaxing around the table, Drusilla ginned and said that she had a big surprise for them. "Most of the townspeople have met Theresa and know that she's going to travel with a group of minstrels to Nandelia. I thought it might be a good idea for you to put on your first show in front of a friendly audience, so I've invited everyone in town to come here for a performance this evening."

"Today?" Joan gasped.

Drusilla nodded.

"But we haven't rehearsed with Theresa in over a week," Darrell said.

"That's not a problem," Drusilla assured him. "Theresa shouldn't sing with you tonight anyway. You're supposed to be meeting her here for the first time, remember? She wouldn't know your routine."

"What time are we supposed to begin?" Karl asked.

"They'll start drifting in after they've eaten dinner, so you should plan to start in about three hours."

Steve nodded and asked, "How many songs should we do?"

"Well, the show should last anywhere between one and two hours, but if the audience starts getting restless after an hour, bring it to an end. If they're caught up in it, sing as long as you like, but two hours is long enough. You'll be worn out by that time."

"But I don't know if we can be ready in three hours!" Joan's face had gone slightly pale. "We need to practice!"

"You'll just have to be ready. I assure you that your audience will be," Drusilla said matter-of-factly. "When you're on the road, you'll usually perform within an hour or two of your arrival, and that includes time for tending to your horses and eating dinner yourselves. It won't take but a few minutes for you to unload your instruments, and you can sing in whatever you happen to have on, but there won't be a lot of extra time for you to practice."

Karl nodded again and asked, "Where are we going to perform?"

"I thought we'd use the front porch. Most of the time your stage will be a spot near the back of a tavern, but it might be the sidewalk in the town square. You won't know what to expect until you get there, so you'll just have to be flexible."

"What about the people? Where do they sit?" Chris asked.

"Tonight they'll sit on the front lawn. If you're in a tavern, they'll sit on chairs, sit on the floor, or stand. They'll be fine. They know what to expect."

Joan let out a deep sigh. "I never expected to feel this scared."

"You aren't the only one," Darrell said. "I feel positively sick. I wish I hadn't eaten."

"Look, these people are friends of mine, and they plan to have a good time tonight. They're not coming here to judge, only to enjoy," Drusilla said with a smile. "I figured you'd probably be a bit nervous before your first performance. That's why we had something light for you to snack on. You've got three hours to get over it before you have to go on stage. We'll eat dinner later tonight, after it's over."

"Well," Kevin said with a grin, "I have to admit I feel relieved. I was getting really spooked today when we rode through town. Now I know why they were looking at us like they were."

"Easy for you to say," Chris mumbled. "You don't have to go on stage."

"Okay," Karl said as he stood up from the table. "The best cure for opening night jitters is to get busy. Let's unload the instruments and run through a couple of numbers in the front room before we set up outside. That should settle us down. Now, Drusilla, where would you like for us to stack the dishes?"

"Leave them here. I'll take care of those while you get set up," Theresa said as she started gathering the empty plates. She took a stack of them over to the sink as the men went out back to begin unloading the wagon. Joan followed her with several of the mugs, and by the time the instruments had been unloaded and set up in the front room, the dishes were done.

After they'd practiced for about an hour, Joan called it quits and told everyone to take an hour off and then meet back in the front room so that they could get set up on the porch.

Before the hour was up, people began arriving for the show. They came in wagons, in carriages, on horseback, and a few arrived on foot. Horses were tied to whatever happened to be handy, including other wagons. There were teenage couples, young married couples, parents with children, elderly couples, and a few adults who appeared to be single. Some brought blankets or tarps to sit on, some brought wooden crates, and a few brought chairs. One elderly couple drove up in a small wagon that had two rocking chairs loaded on the back. After they parked their wagon, they climbed in the back, sat in the chairs, and waited for the show to start. Most of the women had packed picnic baskets with snacks, and the innkeeper had moved a couple of kegs of scog out onto the sidewalk to sell to the gathering crowd. By the time the Tellurians began to set up on the front porch, the yard was filled and the road was blocked.

Steve began the show with a quick welcome. He introduced the group as the Traveling Tellurians, the same name that Chris had painted on the side of the wagon. Then he stepped to the side as Joan began to play the opening number on the harp. After a few minutes, the others joined in and the performance was underway.

The enthusiasm of the crowd was contagious, and soon the performers forgot about being nervous and started having a good time, which made the show even better. After they had been on stage for about an hour and a half, and had gone through all of the songs they had planned to do, Steve stepped forward to thank the audience and to bring the show to a close. The crowd gave them a standing ovation and asked them to perform just one more song. Steve looked around at Joan, who nodded and mouthed, "Country Roads" to everyone.

During their last week at Kalen's they had altered John Denver's lyrics a bit to make the song fit Terah. It was one of their favorite songs, but they weren't sure how the people from Terah would respond to it since Drusilla hadn't been around to give them her opinion. Joan doubted that they

111

would ever have a more receptive crowd to try it out on, so she decided to give it a shot. When they finished the song, the crowd was absolutely silent for a couple of heartbeats, and then they broke into a rousing cheer.

The Tellurians walked to the edge of the porch, joined hands and bowed deeply while the crowd roared. After the applause died down a bit, they began to gather their instruments and take them back inside, and the people in the audience started packing up their picnic baskets, blankets, and chairs. By the time all of the instruments had been stored back in the wagon, the front yard was completely empty.

Drusilla had prepared dinner for them during the show and had set the table while they were packing up. After everyone was seated around the table, she said, "You were really good. This town will be talking about that show for months. If you put on performances like that while you're traveling, no one will ever doubt that you really are minstrels."

"I can't believe how well it went," Joan said with a smile. She hadn't been able to stop grinning since the last ovation.

"After the first couple of songs I forgot about being scared and started enjoying it," Darrell said. "No wonder people wanted to get into the concert scene at home. It's fun."

They talked about the show and about small changes that they wanted to make while they were eating. As they finished dinner and the talk started dying down, fatigue settled over them like a mantle.

With a deep sigh, Karl said, "I'm really tired. I guess we were all on an adrenaline high for a while there, but I feel like the tide just washed out. I have nothing left. Let's get ready for bed."

Joan and Theresa helped Drusilla clear up from dinner while the men went outside to check on the horses and be sure that everything was secure for the night. By the time they returned, the dishes were done and everyone headed for bed.

The chapel was not set up for healthy guests. There was one small bedroom for Drusilla, another small one that Theresa was using, and a large room with a long row of cots for those who were too sick to go home. Fortunately, all of the cots were empty.

Shortly after dawn the next morning, everyone was up. After breakfast, the men went outside to hitch the teams to the wagons and saddle the other horses. Joan stayed inside long enough to help clear up from breakfast, but then she went outside to help with the horses and to give Theresa a chance to say good-bye to Drusilla in private. By the time Theresa and Drusilla walked out on the back porch, Theresa's wagon was parked beside the steps. Kevin had turned his wagon around and had pulled it behind Theresa's. Everyone else was mounted and ready to go.

Theresa hugged Drusilla, wiped the tears from her eyes, smiled, and climbed up on the wagon seat. Drusilla had taught her how to drive a team over the past week, so she felt at ease as she gathered the reins in her hands, released the side brake, and looked at Karl.

"Well, Drusilla, I guess we need to head out. Thanks for everything," Karl said as he moved to the front of Theresa's wagon. As he waved and started down the drive to the road, Joan moved up to ride beside Theresa, Chris moved back to ride beside Kevin, and Steve and Darrell brought up the rear.

Drusilla stood on her porch until they were out of sight. She never expected to see any of them again. Even if, by some miracle, they did manage to survive the next year and make it to Camden, her work was in Drisden. It would be many years before she returned to Camden to live, and she seriously doubted that any of them would still be around there by then. She sighed, wiped a tear out of her eye, and went back inside.

~ ~ ~ ~

For the first couple of hours the road passed through farmland. Then it passed through a lightly wooded area until mid-afternoon when the woods gave way to more farms. They pulled in to the next town a little before dinnertime.

It was about the same size as Drisden, but there was no sign of a Chapel of Light. When they reached the town square, Karl rode over to the hitching post in front of the inn, dismounted, tied his horse, and went inside to see what arrangements he could make for their room and board.

The door opened into a lobby area that ran the full length of the building but was only about six feet deep. A narrow stairway on the left-hand side of the desk led upstairs and a hall on the right-hand side led to the tavern located behind the lobby.

Karl could hear laughter and bits of conversation coming from the tavern area and the smell of fresh cooked food made his stomach growl. He approached the desk and asked the man behind the counter if he was the innkeeper. When the man nodded, Karl asked if he would like to have the Traveling Tellurians perform for his customers that evening.

"And how much would it cost me?" the innkeeper asked brusquely.

"Room and board for us and our horses."

"How many are we talking about?"

"We have seven people, eleven horses, and two wagons."

"What?! No!" the man said, shaking his head. "The price's too high. I'll let you have one room and dinner. You pay for the other rooms, breakfast, and stable fees for the horses."

"Two rooms, dinner, breakfast, and all stable fees for the horses."

"I'd lose money on that deal! Two rooms, dinner, and half the stable fees. And that's my final offer."

About that time, Theresa opened the door and walked over to stand beside Karl. "Do you have a Chapel of Light here? I didn't see one when we rode in," she said to the innkeeper. Then she turned towards Karl and said, "I thought I might stop in for a few minutes to see the local sister."

The innkeeper's mouth dropped open as he saw the medallion around Theresa's neck. "Sister, are you traveling with the minstrels?"

As Theresa turned to face him, she smiled one of her sweetest smiles and nodded. The innkeeper turned to Karl and growled, "You should have told me that a sister was traveling with you." Then he turned back to Theresa and said in a very gentlemanly tone, "Of course we'll offer you room and board, and we'll stable your horses for you, too."

Theresa smiled again and said, "Why thank you, sir. That's very generous."

"Sister, could I prevail upon you for something for my stomach?" the innkeeper said in a hushed voice. "It seems that I'm troubled more and more by my wife's cooking. When I was younger I could eat anything, but now …"

"I'll be happy to fix something for you as soon as we take care of our horses," Theresa said in a demure tone. "Now, if you'll just tell us where to fine the stables, and what we should tell the stable master concerning his fees, we'll be on our way."

"Tell him that Janon said to put up your horses for the night and to let you pull your wagons inside, too. Here, give him this." The innkeeper picked up a quill pen and scribbled a note on a piece of rough paper. Then he handed the paper to Theresa.

"Thank you, sir. And I'll return shortly with something for your stomach," Theresa said as she turned to leave.

Karl nodded to the innkeeper and followed Theresa out of the lobby. When he caught up with her, he grinned and said, "Your timing was perfect. We couldn't have done that any better if we'd planned it. What made you decide to come in anyway?"

"I thought it might help. Drusilla said that people would become a lot more helpful if they knew that a sister was involved. Just thought I'd give it a try."

"Well, it definitely worked. You had him eating out of your hand." Karl gave her a hand up to the seat of the wagon and walked back over to his horse. After he untied it, he mounted and led the group over to the stable.

As they approached the stable yard, Karl moved to one side to let Theresa pull her wagon up beside him. When the stable master came out of the barn, Theresa handed him the note from the innkeeper. The man took it, read it, nodded, and opened the barn doors. Theresa and Kevin pulled the wagons to one side, climbed down and began unhitching their horses while the others dismounted and started unsaddling theirs.

As soon as the stable master saw Theresa start to unhitch her team, he walked over and took the reins out of her hands. "No, Sister, let me. You should rest. I'm sure you've had a tiring day."

Theresa smiled at him and said, "Why thank you. I'd really appreciate that. We're going to be performing at the tavern in a little while and there are a few things I need to do in the back of my wagon before I go over there. Thanks again." Then she walked around her wagon, lifted the canvas flap, and climbed inside to prepare a packet of tea for the innkeeper's stomach.

Before they left the stable, Karl made arrangements for two of the Tellurians to sleep in the loft to keep an eye on the wagons. When they returned to the inn, the innkeeper hurried them into the tavern, where all but one of the tables had been removed. As soon as they sat down, the waitress brought out plates of steaming food. While the Tellurians ate dinner, the innkeeper and a couple of other men set up chairs and crates for the audience.

Almost the very instant that the Tellurians finished eating, their plates were whisked away and the table was carried out of the tavern to make room for their stage. When they left to go get their instruments, the innkeeper opened the door to the tavern and the audience poured in. By the time the Tellurians returned, they had to go through the kitchen to get to the stage area. Although there was standing room only, the crowd fell silent as soon as Steve stepped to the front to introduce the group.

Theresa may not have practiced with them for over a week, but her performance was flawless. The ninety-minute program ran without a hitch. When the cheering began to die down at the end of the show, the innkeeper came out of the kitchen carrying a large tray loaded with seven mugs of scog. He wandered around the stage area offering each of the Tellurians a mug as he congratulated them on a terrific performance. When he came to Theresa and Joan, he also handed them the key to their room and suggested that maybe they would like to go on upstairs while the men took care of storing the instruments.

As Joan opened the door to their room and stepped inside, she let out a small sigh. The room was so small that three pieces of furniture made it feel crowded. The door was in one corner of the room and a bed that looked to be a bit smaller than a regular double bed was set flush against the next corner. Between the bed and the door was a small table, just large enough for a pitcher of water, washbasin, and a small glowstone box. On the other side of the narrow room, at the foot of the bed, was a small straight-back chair. Above the chair, there was a tiny window covered by a piece of canvas.

"Oh well, I wasn't really expecting Holiday Inn," Joan said.

"No, but this room is hardly big enough for the two of us. How are the guys going to manage three in a room this size?" Theresa asked.

"I have no idea, but better them than us. Now I know why Karl was so quick to volunteer to sleep in the stable loft."

Joan left the door open a bit so that they could see the guys when they passed by to go to their room.

A few minutes later, Chris knocked on the door and eased it open. "Just thought we'd check on you on the way to our room. Do you need anything?" Chris asked from the hall.

"No, but thanks," Joan said. "I do have a question though. How are the three of you going to manage to sleep in a room this size?"

"I don't know. It is kind of small, isn't it," Chris answered as he looked around the room. Then he turned his head towards the hall and said, "Either one of us is going to have to go back to the stable and sleep in the loft with Darrell and Karl, or someone's going to have to sleep on the floor. There's no way all three of us are going to fit on one of those beds."

"I don't mind either way," Kevin said. "I like a hard mattress, so the floor won't bother me. As long as I have a blanket, I'll be fine."

"Okay. Well, I guess that takes care of that. Good night, see you in the morning," Chris said as he started to shut the door to Joan and Theresa's room. Just before the door shut, he added, "We'll just wait out here to make sure your lock works."

Chris finished shutting the door, but didn't walk away until he heard the tumblers in the lock click.

"I'd be willing to bet you money that Karl asked him to do that," Joan said with a little laugh after she locked the door. "Well, shall we flip a coin to see who gets stuck against the wall?"

Chapter 18

A Night Off

By the middle of Saturday afternoon, Joan felt really tired. She had not had a good night's sleep since Palladin had given them their weapons, and she just didn't think she could face another strange town and another performance that night. She rode up beside Karl and asked him to wait for the others.

Since the road in that area was fairly wide, Kevin pulled his wagon up beside Theresa's. Once they were all together, Joan said, "Look, I don't know how the rest of you feel, but I need a break. We haven't been by ourselves since we landed on Terah and I want a night off. How would you feel about finding a secluded spot in the woods and camping out tonight?"

"I'm all for it," Chris answered quickly.

"We'll have to stand guard through the night if we set up camp," Darrell said.

"That's not a problem," Steve replied as the others nodded.

"Shall we try to find a spot now or do you want to go on for a while?" Karl asked, looking at Joan.

"I'm ready to find a spot now," Joan said. "I'm afraid that if we go much farther we'll come out into farmland and be stuck staying in town again. The forest isn't very dense along here. I think the wagons will go through okay, don't you?"

"Yeah, but why don't I ride in a little ways and see if I can find a good campsite? That way we won't get the wagons in there just to have to turn them around and get them back out. I won't be gone long," Karl said as he turned to ride into the woods.

About thirty minutes later, Karl returned and told them that he had found a nice quiet clearing large enough for both wagons with plenty of room left over for their sleeping tarps and a campfire, and that there was a second clearing not too far away with a small stream running through it that would be perfect for the horses.

By late afternoon, the horses had been cared for and were securely tethered in the second clearing. The tarps had been set up like tents and a fire was burning in a shallow pit. A stew was cooking over the fire, and coffee was perking. Everyone was seated around the fire, relaxing for the first time in days.

"This was a good idea, Joan," Chris said. "I think I was more tired than I knew. I love the idea that we don't have to do anything else tonight."

"Well, we do have to come up with a watch schedule," Darrell said. "I was thinking about it while we were setting up camp. Since there are seven of us, I thought we could use three shifts. I feel like Karl and Joan should have the same watch."

"I guess I could put up with her for a little while," Karl said as he slid his arm around Joan's waist.

"As far as the rest of us are concerned, it really doesn't make that much difference," Darrell said. "I was thinking that maybe Kevin and Chris could share a watch, and then Steve, Theresa, and I would make up the third. What do the rest of you think?"

"Fine with me," Chris answered. The others nodded their agreement.

"How are we going to split up the night?" Joan asked.

"I was thinking of three-hour shifts," Darrell answered. "How about nine to midnight, midnight to three, and three to six?"

"Okay," Joan said. "But who gets which shift tonight?"

"Well, the worst one is the midnight to three shift," Darrell said. "We won't be camping every night, so it's not like we'll be doing this all the time. We could draw straws for the shifts for tonight, and then whoever gets the early shift tonight takes the middle shift next time we camp, and so on."

"That'll work," Steve said with a nod.

"Here, I'll break these three twigs off at different lengths," Karl said. "One person from each group draws one of the twigs. The shortest twig is the first shift, middle twig is the middle shift, and the longest twig will be the last shift."

"I'll draw for us," Chris said and pulled out the shortest twig.

"Theresa, you draw for your group. Joan and I will take the one that's left." Karl turned towards Theresa to let her draw.

"I think we've got the longest one," Theresa said. "Karl, let me see which one you have left." Karl opened his hand and held up the twig that was left. He had the middle twig. "We have the early morning shift," Theresa said to Darrell and Steve. Then she turned towards Joan and said, "I guess that means we make breakfast, right?"

"Sounds good to me," Joan answered.

After guard duty was settled, conversation around the campfire lapsed into a comfortable silence as each of the Tellurians entertained private thoughts while gazing into the fire.

Theresa fingered her pendant, thinking about its power. She could feel the heat that came from the fire that danced deep inside the black opal in its center, and the faint coolness that came from the turquoise stones surrounding it. After a bit she said, "While we have a few minutes, I want to tell you about this pendant. All of the sisters wear them. The turquoise stones around the outside are healing stones. They help us focus our powers. They're harmless, but the opal is a very dangerous stone."

"Dangerous?" Chris asked.

Theresa nodded. "Do you remember hearing any legends on Earth about the fire in the opal being connected with the soul of its rightful owner?"

Several of the Tellurians nodded.

"Well, the fire in this opal is not only connected with my soul, it's also linked with my mind and my emotions."

"What do you mean?" Joan asked.

"If I'm threatened, if anyone tries to hurt me, the flame in the opal will reach out and burn them. I'm not sure how, but from what I understand, it can burn from quite a distance."

"Does it kill the person it hits?" Darrell asked.

Theresa shook her head no. "I saw a man who had a long narrow burn on his forehead while I was in Drisden. Drusilla said that it was the mark of an opal. She said that no sister will ever treat him or give him any herbs, and I noticed that the people in town wouldn't have anything to do with him either. Anyway, I'm not sure that the opal would know the difference between friend and foe once the fire begins to strike, so just be careful about getting in the middle." Theresa took a deep breath and looked around.

"No wonder Drusilla told Kalen that you didn't need any self-defense lessons," Steve said. Then he frowned, "He did know about the pendants, didn't he?"

"According to Drusilla, everyone on Terah knows," Theresa answered. "But she didn't tell him that I'd been initiated into the Sisterhood until a few days before we left for Drisden, and after she told him, he relaxed about the self-defense, but I notice he sent me a dagger anyway."

"Yeah, like you might actually need it with that thing around," Darrell said.

"Well, you never know," Kevin said. "Getting burned might not stop some people. They might try even harder to hurt you since the opal had marked them for life."

"I don't know," Karl said. "If that thing is meant to protect her, it might keep on burning him until he either gave up or died."

"You could be right," Theresa said. "I don't know very much about it, and I don't know how to stop the stone from striking. I'm not even sure that I can."

"Are there any other little surprises we need to know about?" Joan asked with a touch of wariness in her voice.

"Well, there is one more thing," Theresa said quietly. "Don't ever try to take my pendant off my neck, even if I'm dead. Only another sister can safely remove it. Drusilla said that the fire in the opal would explode and consume anyone else who tries to take it."

"What if someone tries to take it while you're alive?" Chris asked. "What happens to you? Do you get burned, too?"

Theresa took a deep breath. "I don't know. Maybe it would just burn them. I hope so, but Drusilla didn't really make that distinction and I was afraid to ask. I didn't want to seem ungrateful."

"I imagine the opal's need to protect you would override everything else," Joan said reassuringly.

"I hope so," Theresa sighed. "But you know how things work on Terah. They tend to go to extremes."

For a few minutes, no one said anything. Then Darrell said, "I want to change the subject."

Theresa smiled and said, "Please," as the others nodded.

"We need to schedule some time on a regular basis for sparring. It's easy to backslide if you don't practice."

"That's a good idea, but how?" Steve asked. "When we stay in town we spend the whole day on the road and then we're busy with the performance until time for bed."

"Setting up camp and having some time to ourselves is sort of nice," Chris said. "What if we plan to camp out every third or fourth night? We could work out for an hour or two before dinner."

"We're not the only ones who need a break," Karl said. "I've been thinking that we need to try to take a day off every week to rest the horses. We'd have the whole day, so we could really get a good workout then."

"Not the whole day," Joan said. "At some point, clothes are going to have to be washed, things mended, and so forth, and that's going to have to be taken care of on our day off, too."

"What do you think about trying to work out for an hour or so at lunch everyday?" Darrell said. "At least it would get us out of the saddle and let us move around a bit."

"I'm not too sure about stopping for an hour," Chris said. "We won't know how far away the next town is, and we might not make it before dark if we stop for too long."

"What if we try thirty minutes and see how it goes?" Steve asked.

"Okay. Just as long as we get in some regular practice," Darrell said.

By then, dinner was ready so Joan dished up a plate of stew and warm bread for everyone while Theresa poured their coffee. After they finished eating and the dishes were all stored away, Joan made a fresh pot of coffee and everyone settled back down around the campfire. It wasn't dark yet, but the sun was going down, and it would be dark within the hour.

"You know, I haven't been able to stop thinking about what you told us about slavery here, Kevin," Darrell began.

"I know. I haven't been able to shake it either," Kevin answered.

"I feel like maybe that has something to do with why we're here," Karl added.

"How?" Joan asked. "I mean, what can we do about it anyway?"

"I don't know," Karl answered quietly. "I just feel like we were sent here to do something about it. You know we can't just go along with it."

"Don't you even think about going off on some suicide mission to kill raiders and free the slaves! I won't have it! You are not going to leave me alone in a strange new world Karl Stanton! And I mean it!" Joan was on the verge of tears, picturing her husband riding off like an avenging angel.

"Whoa, I'm not even thinking about doing anything like that," Karl said as he put his arm around his wife. "Settle down, honey. You know better than think I'd ever leave you."

"Well, I have to admit that the thought of trying to track down a few slavers and take them out did cross my mind," Darrell said, "but I just can't see how it would be worth the risk. As soon as we took out one group, another would pop up to take its place. It's sort of like the drug dealers back home. Attacking them isn't going to really help the situation in the long run."

"Maybe we should try attacking the demand since we can't do much about the supply," Chris said. "You know, like the 'say no to drugs' campaign to stem the demand for drugs?"

"I'm afraid it probably wouldn't work any better here than it has against drugs," Kevin said. "I imagine most of the peasants would love to say no. After all, they're the ones who get captured and taken away as slaves. It's the ones who use slaves that we need to target and they aren't likely to say no to something that makes their lives easier."

"I haven't really had a chance to think it through," Steve said slowly, "but what if we could find out exactly why they think they need slaves, and then find a better way to meet that need? We might be able to get the people of Terah to put an end to slavery themselves."

Darrell shrugged and said, "From what Kevin said, they mainly need slaves to protect them from the slavers."

"No, there has to be more to it than that," Steve said. "I know that they need slaves to fill out the army now, but I bet it all began because someone wanted servants and there weren't any people willing to do it, so someone else went out, captured some relatively helpless people, and sold them to the highest bidder. Maybe that's where we need to start."

"I sort of understand what you're saying," Joan said. "If we could find some way to make being a servant an honorable way to earn a living, then there would be people who wanted to work as servants, shutting down the market for slaves."

Steve nodded.

"How do we do that?" Karl asked.

"I don't have the faintest idea," Steve said. "Of course we can't do anything yet. We're just a band of traveling minstrels at the moment. But when Myron becomes the Master Sorcerer, he might be able to do something about the tradition of owning slaves."

Kevin frowned. "If he becomes the Master Sorcerer, and that is still one really big if, he can definitely ban the use of slaves at the castle where he'll be living."

"Yeah, and since free people work better than slaves, we could show that our way is better," Darrell added.

"Maybe better by our standards, but we have to be able to show that it's cheaper in the long run, more efficient, and more satisfactory," Steve said. "And we'd have to be subtle about it. If the upper class thinks that their privileged way of life is being threatened in any way, they'll fight it tooth and nail and we won't get anywhere." He paused and thought for a moment. "If we're going to have any impact at all, we're going to have to show them a better way and make them want to copy it, or better yet, give them a reason to want to stop using slaves and let them come up with an alternative themselves. That would be best." Steve paused again, thinking. "You know, we need a battle plan. We'll be in Nandelia for nearly eight months. Maybe we can come up with some ideas then."

"That's a good idea," Karl said. "We'll have plenty of time to work on something while we're there."

"But keep in mind that even if we come up with a workable plan, we'll be lucky to see any results within the next twenty years," Steve said. "A custom that has lasted for centuries won't just die overnight. I seriously doubt if any of us will live to see the end of slavery, but maybe we can trigger the beginning of the end. That's about the best we can hope for."

The crackling of the fire was the only sound for the next few minutes. Then Theresa spoke up. "I didn't want to say anything earlier, but I wasn't there when Kevin apparently told the rest of you about this slavery bit. Steve, you and Darrell can fill me in during our watch tonight, but now, if no one has any objections, I'm going to turn in. Does it matter which of the tarps I take?"

"No, you can have whichever one you want," Steve said as he stood up and stretched. "We set out four. One is for you and one is for Karl and Joan. The rest of us could bunk with the person we have watch with."

Theresa nodded and said, "Then I'll take the one next to my wagon."

"Okay," Steve said. Then he turned towards Darrell. "Which tent do you want to use? It makes no difference to me."

"The one closest to Theresa's would be best since she's on watch with us," Darrell answered as he too stood up.

"Shall we take the one next to Kevin's wagon, Karl?" Joan asked. "I'm ready to get some sleep, too."

"Fine with me," Karl answered. "I'll join you as soon as I check on the horses one more time."

After a couple of minutes, only Kevin and Chris were left at the fire. Chris poured himself another cup of coffee and offered some to Kevin. Then he built the fire up a bit and sat back down to watch it burn. After a while he said, "I could get used to this. No briefcase to lug around, no high pressure sales meetings, no memos."

"No hot showers, no stereos, no computers …" Kevin added, a touch of longing in his voice.

"Except for the hot showers, none of the rest particularly bothers me. I never did care much for TV, and telephones could be a real nuisance," Chris said. "Although a microwave would be nice."

"I have to admit I miss my computer."

"Not me. A computer was just a tool that I used at work. I never owned one myself."

"I've had my own computer for as long as I can remember. In fact, Paul gave me my first one," Kevin said. "It was a Mac. I loved that machine."

"Did you know Paul well?"

"Not really. He was my godfather, according to my parents, or according to the people who I thought were my parents. It's strange, but finding out that they're not really my parents doesn't surprise me. In fact, it's almost a relief. I knew that I didn't fit in with them and now at least I know it wasn't my fault," Kevin paused and gazed into the fire for a bit. "Anyway, Paul would show up about twice a year and take me out for the day. Come to think of it, I don't think he ever told me anything about himself. I knew he was a writer, and that he lived fairly close by, but that's about it. He always wanted to hear about what I was doing, what I thought. He was the only adult who ever showed any interest in my life."

Kevin picked up a stick and stirred the coals of the fire for a while. Then he laughed and said, "My mother's chief complaint about Paul was the way he dressed. He always showed up in a tee shirt or sweatshirt, jeans, tennis shoes, and a baseball cap. He even kept the cap on when he was in the house, and that really set her off."

"I guess he had to wear the cap to hide his ears. Didn't Kalen say that Paul was an elf? I bet his ears were just as large and pointed as Duane's."

"You're probably right. You know, my parents never seemed to like him. Actually, they seemed a little bit afraid of him. I always wondered about that. Mother would stay right behind the maid for a couple of days before he came to make sure the house was perfect, and if he was planning to eat dinner at the house, she would change the menu ten times."

"I wonder if he had some kind of contract with your parents where he could remove you from their home if he wasn't satisfied with it."

"Maybe, I don't know. I'm not sure they'd have cared if he had taken me away, just as long as no one blamed them." Kevin poured himself another cup of coffee. "Until I was about seven or eight years old, I had a nanny, but after that, I was on my own. They had their lives and I stayed out of the way. To be honest, I don't remember seeing them all that much while I was growing up. I will give them credit for making sure that I had the best clothes, the best school supplies, and a room full of things to entertain myself with though."

"Didn't Paul ever try to let you know what was in store for you?"

"He used to bring me books with stories about dragons and leprechauns and things like that, but my mother would take them away from me as soon as he was gone and I'd never see them again. Paul did ask me if I liked one of the stories once, and when I told him that she had taken all the books away, he got pretty angry. I can see why now, but apparently he didn't do anything about it at the time, because she didn't give me any of the books back." Kevin paused and stared at the flames. "I can't help but wonder what my real parents were like. I know Yvonne died when I was born, but it would have been nice to at least meet my father. I thought about insisting that Xantha take me to see him before we left Kalen's house, but if he's in a coma …" Kevin shrugged.

"They wouldn't have let you go anyway," Chris said. "It really would have been too risky. There's no way you could have gotten in to see him without being recognized. Everyone at Kalen's said you favored Yvonne, and I'm sure the castle's full of people who knew her."

"I know." After a few minutes Kevin asked, "What was your childhood like? Were you close to your parents?"

"Yes and no. We ate breakfast and dinner together almost every day and they kept pretty close tabs on what was going on in our lives, but there were seven kids. My parents both worked two jobs trying to keep us in shoes and food. I was closer to my swimming coach while I was in high school than I was to my father because I spent more time with him. My parents tried to make it to as many of my swim meets as they could, just like they tried to make it to the different football, soccer, basketball, and baseball games that one of my brothers or sisters was playing in. And then there were the musical recitals, dance recitals, plays, and so on. They tried, but there was no way that they could make it to everything. Sometimes I think about what it must have been like for them. You know, they're the real heroes, them and all the other parents just like them. And through it all, the whole time I was living there, I never heard them complain or argue," Chris said proudly. Then, after a bit, he added, "I didn't keep in touch like I should have after I moved out and I know the news of my death must have come as a horrible blow to them. I might have agreed to come to this world if I'd been asked, I don't know, but I never, not in a million years, would have let my parents think that I'd been killed like that. I would have found a better way." Chris sat quietly and stared at the fire for a few minutes. Then he stood up and said, "Think I'll go check on the horses. Back in a bit."

When Chris came back, the conversation stayed light and focused more on the things they had seen since leaving Kalen's house. They laughed about the room at the inn and decided that from now on two men could sleep in the inn to be near Joan and Theresa, but the other two could join Karl in the stable. And they thought that a rotation there might be in order, too. After all, the stable had to be more comfortable than that room had been. Almost before they knew it, it was time to wake Joan and Karl, and as soon as they got up, Kevin and Chris headed off to their tent.

Chapter 19

Sunday, April 15

Sunday morning Rolan woke up with a headache, both figuratively and literally. He couldn't shake the feeling that something in Laryn's statement before the council a week ago was going to cause him problems, but he couldn't put his finger on what was bothering him. She had told everyone about Badec and that although he was still in a coma, the local sister felt sure that given a bit of time, he'd come out of it and be able to resume his duties. That comment in itself had shaken him for a moment until he realized that without knowing exactly what was wrong with him, that was about all that they could say. But there was something Laryn had said after that, something he'd missed. What was it?

While he was eating his breakfast, he thought back through the beginning of the meeting, trying to remember every thing he'd heard, the comments of the other sorcerers when it became evident that Badec wasn't going to be there, and the murmurs that had run through the council when Laryn had explained why. Damien had been sitting next to Rolan and had said something about what a tragedy it would be if Badec didn't recover. It was while he was agreeing with Damien that Laryn had said something else, something about next year. What could she have been talking about? What did next year matter?

Rolan got up and started pacing. Face it; he wasn't going to remember because he hadn't heard the whole thing, so he'd just have to figure out what she had been talking about from the little bit he did hear. He distinctly remembered her saying something about next April. What was the significance of next April?

As he paced around the room his headache got worse and worse. If he didn't get something figured out soon, he was going to have to make his slave give him something for the pain, but anything that would get rid of the pain would also make him sleepy, and he didn't want to sleep until he got this figured out.

Rolan grinned and thought if only he could get rid of the pain caused by the House of Nordin as easily as he could get rid of the pain in his head.

Then Rolan's head jerked up and he snapped his fingers. That had to be it. The House of Nordin, the heir, Badec's son. That's what the year meant. She must have said that he was going to start his training so that he'd be ready to assume the seat in a year if his father didn't recover. That was the significance of next April. That was when Myron would have to take over or the seat would be declared vacant. The son. The one Rolan had thought must be dead. Apparently he wasn't dead after all. Laryn would never have mentioned him unless she planned to produce him in a year. But there was no way he'd be ready.

Rolan frowned. This could really mess things up. He was sure the boy wouldn't be able to keep the chair; he'd be an easy target. Every sorcerer on the council could defeat him. A year was nothing in the study of magic.

What was Laryn thinking? Rolan paced some more. She must believe that he'd actually be good enough in one year to be able to hold the chair. He shook his head. That's what happens when you let non-magicals make decisions about sorcerers. They just had no idea what they were talking about. But you'd think growing up surrounded by sorcerers like she had would have given her at least some idea of the kind of time it takes to become strong enough to duel. Or maybe it was just a last ditch attempt to keep the chair in the family. Maybe she knew it was hopeless, but had decided to go through with it anyway.

Rolan swirled around and his frown deepened. She was going to ruin everything. There was no way he'd ever convince Damien to challenge the boy. It wouldn't surprise him if Damien declared himself the boy's protector for the first few years, and that would never do.

No, the only way to take care of this was to get to the boy before he was ever named Master Sorcerer. That would be the only way to keep his plans on track. Myron had to die.

Chapter 20

Theresa's Role as a Sister

Over the next few days, the Tellurians settled into a routine. They got up as soon as it was light, were on the road shortly afterwards, worked out for about half an hour at lunch, and pulled into the next town during the late afternoon or early evening. After they bargained with the innkeeper for room and board in exchange for a performance, they took care of the horses, put on a show, and fell into bed around midnight, exhausted.

After three nights spent in towns, they were all looking forward to another night off, but during the morning, dark clouds started rolling in. Karl stopped to ask the others if they wanted to take a chance and set up camp anyway, or if they wanted to go on to the next town. While they were talking about it, Theresa dug out the cloaks. They had barely put them on when the rain started, so they decided to go on. It wasn't a heavy rain, but it was steady, and by the time they reached the next town they were cold, damp, and tired. After making arrangements for room and board with the innkeeper and tending to the horses, they went into the tavern to eat dinner.

Almost as soon as they sat down, an older woman approached their table and said, "Sister, I hate to bother you, but my husband's sick and there isn't a Chapel of Light for over thirty miles. Could you please come see him after you finish your dinner?" She looked to be near exhaustion herself.

"Of course," Theresa said. "Why don't you sit down while I eat, and then I'll go with you?" She motioned to one of the empty chairs nearby.

"Oh no, I couldn't do that. I'll wait for you outside. Enjoy your dinner," the woman said and then quickly turned and left.

"I'd better go see about her husband," Theresa said as she stood up to follow the older woman. "I'll eat later."

"I don't think you should go by yourself," Darrell said as he pushed his chair back to get up. "Karl, save our dinners for us, okay?"

Darrell and Theresa got their cloaks and followed the older woman to her house on the edge of town. He waited on the porch while she went in to see her patient. After a few minutes, she came back out and Darrell walked with her to the stable.

"Are you going to be able to help him?" he asked.

Theresa nodded. "He has a touch of pneumonia. Unfortunately, there's no penicillin, but I do have some other things that should work. It won't take but a minute for me to mix up what I need," Theresa answered. Then she climbed into the back of her wagon and started pulling out different herbs. "While I'm treating him, would you mind getting some firewood into the house for her? I doubt if she can do too much more tonight before she just gives out."

"No problem. I'll take care of it," Darrell said as he reached up to help Theresa down from the wagon.

When they reached the house, Theresa went in the front door and Darrell went around back. He found the woodpile off to the side of the small barn and started carrying wood to the back porch.

After he had enough for several days piled right outside the back door, he opened the door to start stacking wood inside.

Seated at the kitchen table were two young girls, and when they looked up to see a strange man coming through the back door, they started screaming. The older woman ran out of the bedroom to see what the problem was. Theresa followed her into the kitchen.

"What are you screaming about, child?" the older woman asked as the younger girl jumped up and buried her face in the woman's skirt.

"That … that man. Who is he?" the older of the two whispered.

"He's a friend of mine," Theresa said as she walked over towards Darrell. "He's going to put some wood in here for you." Then she turned to the older woman and asked, "Are these your children?"

The woman shook her head. "They used to live in the house next door, but their parents died a few months ago from a fever. That's one reason I've been so worried about Derek. Anyway, they have an aunt who's going to come for them, but they needed a place to stay until she can get here, so they're staying with us."

"No wonder you're worn out," Theresa said, more to herself than to anyone else. Then she turned towards the older woman and said, "I brought some herbs for you too, to keep you from getting the fever, but I just brought enough for today. I'll mix up some more and bring them by tomorrow morning before I leave. I want you to have enough for at least two weeks. You are to make yourself a cup of tea using these herbs twice a day, every day, once in the middle of the morning, and again in the middle of the afternoon. You are to sit down and inhale the steam as the tea steeps, and then slowly drink the tea. In all, you'll need to sit still for about thirty minutes each time. Do you understand?"

"Thirty minutes?" the woman said hesitantly. "That's a long time, but I'll try."

"No, don't just try, do it. Stay seated for the full thirty minutes. You can't afford to come down with the fever, and this will help you stay healthy. Derek and the children can manage without you for that long." Theresa turned to the older girl and said, "I want you to see to it that she follows my directions exactly. Will you do that?"

"Yes, ma'am," the girl said shyly.

"Okay," Theresa said as she nodded at both of them. Then she turned towards Darrell and said, "Would you please bring in a bit more wood? I'd like for her to have enough in here to keep the house nice and warm tonight." Theresa pointed to a bare section of flooring on the other side of the kitchen and asked, "Can he pile the extra wood over here?"

"That would be fine," the older woman said with a slow nod. Then she turned to Darrell and said, "Thank you. It's really nice of you to go to all this trouble."

"You're welcome, ma'am," Darrell said as he set the wood that he had in his arms down on the floor. "I'll have some wood stacked up for you in no time."

When they left the older woman's house, Darrell asked Theresa what type of tea she had given the old woman.

"Just some apple and cinnamon tea, with a touch of sugar," Theresa answered him with a grin.

"What was all that about sitting down for thirty minutes, smelling the steam, and slowly sipping it then?" Darrell asked.

Theresa laughed. "It was the only thing I could think of to make her sit down for a few minutes a couple of times during the day. If I had simply told her that she needed to take a break, she would have ignored me, but now, since she thinks that she has to inhale the steam and then sip the tea, she'll probably sit still for at least fifteen minutes and that's better than nothing. Her husband should be all right in a week or so, but looking after him and those kids has just about done her in. I'm going to see if I can find a little help for her when we get back to the inn."

When they returned to the inn, the innkeeper had cleared the tavern and was setting up for the performance. He motioned to Darrell and Theresa to come over. "My wife has your plates in the kitchen. Go right through there," he said, pointing to a door on the other side of the tavern. "My wife is the older lady in the red apron."

Theresa and Darrell thanked him and set off for the kitchen. The innkeeper's wife motioned towards a small table near the stove where two places had been set. Their plates were sitting on the edge of the stove next to the table.

"Thank you," Theresa said. "Do you happen to know the older couple who live in the next to the last house on the southern end of town?"

"Sure," the innkeeper's wife answered. "I've known them most of my life. Why?"

"That's where we've been," Theresa explained. "Her husband's quite sick and she's also taking care of two orphan children until their aunt can get here. Is there anyone in town who might be able to help them out a bit?"

"I didn't know Derek was sick! Sure, I'll send them some food, and we'll help with the kids, too," she said as she turned to one of the waitresses. "Here, take this extra food down to Derek's house. And take that bread. Let's see, I think I had a couple of pies left, too." The innkeeper's wife and the waitress packed a basket of food and then the waitress put on a cloak and set off for the house.

Darrell and Theresa were just finishing their dinner when Steve came in to see if they were ready to go on stage. The performance was supposed to begin in ten minutes.

The innkeeper had followed Steve into the kitchen and when Darrell and Theresa stood up to head out to the stage area, he asked Theresa if he could have a quick word with her. When she nodded, he said, "Sister, do you think you could hold a healing clinic tomorrow morning? It's been months since a sister has passed through our town and the people around here would really appreciate it."

"Well, I suppose I could, but I'd need to talk to my friends before I said yes," Theresa said. "Where would we hold it?"

"We could set it up in here if that would be all right with you. We'll pay you, of course. Would provisions for all of you for a week be enough?"

Theresa had no idea how much a sister was usually paid for holding a clinic, but it sounded like a generous offer to her, so she nodded. "Give me a minute to talk to my friends and see what they have to say."

The innkeeper nodded and then quickly added, "By the way, the next town is only about twenty miles away. If you leave here by lunch you should have plenty of time to get there before dark."

Again Theresa nodded, and then she turned towards Darrell and said, "I need to talk to everyone about this. Would you ask the others to step in here for a minute?"

As soon as Darrell came back with the rest of the Tellurians, she explained that she had been asked to hold a healing clinic the next morning. "I know it'll give us a late start, but I really should do it. Would you mind?"

No one said anything at first, but most of them shook their heads no.

"I don't see any problems with it," Karl said. "What can we do to help?"

"I'm not sure. I've never done anything like this before," Theresa answered quietly. "I know I'll need help getting set up, and Joan, I'll need you to help me with the herbs."

Joan nodded.

"If we have much of a crowd, I may need some of you to sort of direct traffic." Then Theresa added as an afterthought, "Oh, and the town is going to pay us in groceries. He said they'd give us about a week's supply."

"That's fine," Karl said. "We'll load the groceries into your wagon after you finish with the clinic."

While the others returned to the stage area, Theresa found the innkeeper and told him that she would be happy to hold the clinic after breakfast the next morning.

During the performance, the innkeeper circulated among the crowd, quietly telling them about the clinic and asking them to spread the word. After the show, he asked Theresa how she wanted him to arrange the tavern.

Theresa glanced around and said, "I need a couple of different work areas. Is there any way we could string up a curtain so that the patients would have a little privacy?"

The innkeeper nodded. "We can mange that. Would those two corners be all right?" He pointed to the ones closest to the kitchen.

"That would be fine. I'll also need a couple of tables set up in the kitchen for my herbs."

The innkeeper nodded again and told her that he would have things set up before he went to bed.

~ ~ ~ ~

The next morning, Theresa woke up a little earlier than usual. She was a bit nervous as well as excited about holding her first clinic. She made her way downstairs quietly, expecting to find that everyone else was still asleep, but people were already standing in line outside the tavern door, waiting to see her. It was drizzling rain and they were huddling under the eaves of the buildings trying to stay dry.

Theresa made her way to the kitchen, grabbed a cloak hanging by the back door, and ran over to the stable. Although she was trying to be quiet, Karl woke up as soon as she opened the door. He climbed down out of the hayloft and said, "Do you realize that it's not even 6:00 yet? You should still be in bed."

Theresa led him over to the stable door and pointed to the line forming outside the front door of the inn. "There's no telling how long they've been lined up out there. I need to get started."

Karl nodded and said, "Okay. You go on back to the tavern. I'll drive your wagon over as soon as I get the horses hitched up."

When she returned to the kitchen, the innkeeper's wife was stoking the fire under a big pot of coffee. Joan walked into the kitchen about the same time that Karl pulled the wagon up to the door, so she helped Theresa unload the herbs and get them sorted. By the time they finished with the herbs, the innkeeper's wife had finished cooking breakfast and the rest of the Tellurians had gathered in the tavern.

As soon as everyone had eaten, the innkeeper opened the doors to let the crowd in. Kevin and Chris kept the line moving, sorting the problems as the people came in. Theresa had set Karl and Steve up with a good supply of woundwort, hops, and bandages, so anyone who needed to have wounds cleaned and dressed was siphoned off to them. Theresa saw the patients who were complaining of illnesses, chronic problems, or who had open wounds. Joan stayed in the kitchen, mixing the various poultices, teas and powders that Theresa prescribed. Darrell entertained the children as they either waited for their turn to see Theresa or waited for their parents to be finished.

By mid-morning, the last of the patients had been seen and the only sound in the tavern was the sound of rain on the roof. Joan carried a large tray with cups and a fresh pot of coffee in from the kitchen and set it down on one of the tables. Then she started pouring coffee, handing a cup to each of the Tellurians.

"When you two get done, pack up the herbs and get the wagon ready to go," Karl said, looking at Joan and Theresa. "Steve, you and I are going to find out about the provisions that they offered us in exchange for the clinic. Darrell, Chris, could you two take care of getting our horses ready? And Kevin, when you get your team hitched, how about pulling your wagon in front of the inn?"

They all nodded and continued drinking their coffee. When the pot was empty, Joan loaded the tray with the cups and returned to the kitchen.

Theresa followed her into the kitchen where she bagged up some apple cinnamon tea. When she was done, she said, "I'm going to take a couple of minutes to go check on the man I treated last night. I'll feel better about leaving if I look in on him first."

"Sure, go ahead. I'll start packing up," Joan answered.

Theresa walked down the road to Derek's house. She knocked on the door, and opened it slowly. The house was warm and smelled of food and the mustard poultices that she had told the woman to put on her husband's chest every couple of hours.

The woman walked into the front room wiping her hands on her apron. She was smiling and looked a bit younger that morning than she had the night before. "I was hoping to see you before you left. I wanted to thank you. Derek is resting so much better today. I think he'll recover now. And thank you for the food. I know that Caryn sent it over from the tavern, but you must have said something to her. I didn't realize just how tired I was until she came over later and took the kids home with her. I just collapsed. I wish I knew of some way to repay your kindness."

"I'm just glad I could help out, and I wanted to remind you not to forget about the tea I fixed for you. Be sure you drink it just like I told you," Theresa said as she handed her the bag. "Now, could I just check on my patient before we leave?"

"Of course. Derek, you have some company," the woman called to her husband.

When Theresa entered the room, Derek was sitting up in bed. He was still quite sick, but his face was no longer deathly pale. "You do look quite a bit better, but you're still very sick. I know you're feeling better, but you absolutely must keep the poultices on for at least three more days, and stay in bed for at least a week." Theresa turned to his wife and said, "If the fever starts up again, start the poultices again. He's not to get out of that bed for more than a couple of hours a day until he's been clear of fever for three full days. Understood?"

The woman nodded and looked over at her husband. "See, I told you that you weren't ready to go back to work yet!"

"No, you aren't," Theresa said to Derek. "Unless you want your wife to become a widow, you don't need to even think about going back to work for at least three weeks. Is that clear?"

"But how are we going to survive if I don't get the shop opened back up?" Derek asked, looking at his wife.

"Don't you worry about that. We'll be fine. You'll see," the woman said as she patted her husband on the shoulder. Then she turned to Theresa, "Thank you for stopping by this morning. I know you've been busy with the clinic. Are you planning to leave town today or are you staying over?"

"No, we're leaving in about an hour. In fact, I need to get back and load my wagon. Take care," Theresa said. The woman walked her to the front door and waved as Theresa headed back towards town.

By the time she got back to the inn, Joan had the herbs packed and ready to load. Theresa climbed into the back of the wagon and stored the herbs as Joan handed them to her. Karl walked into the kitchen just as they were finishing, and asked them to pull Theresa's wagon over to the dry goods store to load the provisions, but before Theresa could climb up on the wagon seat, the innkeeper's wife called her back into the kitchen.

"I wanted to thank you for all you've done here. You didn't have to take the time to see Derek or to hold the clinic, and I know it put you behind schedule. I thought it might save you a little time on the road today if I packed a lunch for you. Here," she said as she handed Theresa a large sack.

Theresa thanked her and carefully set the sack of food inside the back of the wagon.

Joan had already climbed up on the wagon seat and had the reins in her hands. As soon as Theresa joined her, they drove over to the dry goods store.

The food that was stacked in front of the dry goods store was quite a bit more than Theresa had expected. She looked at Steve questioningly.

"I know," he said quietly as he helped them both down. "We would never have taken this much. They already had it stacked up out here."

"Where are we going to put it all? We don't have that much room," Joan said in a whisper.

"We'll just have to try. I think it's a point of honor with them. They seemed a bit insulted when I tried to get them to take some of it back. Apparently they feel that this is a fair exchange for Theresa's services," Karl answered softly.

"We may be able to exchange some of it for other things we need in the next town," Steve said quietly, "but I think we need to find a way to take it with us."

"We're going to need Kevin's wagon, too. I'll go get him," Joan said as she headed over to the inn.

The spare team was tethered behind Kevin's wagon and his wagon was facing away from the dry goods store, ready to head out of town. When Joan told Kevin that his wagon was needed at the store, he had to drive it back into the stable yard to get it turned around. After they loaded the food into the two wagons, Karl shook the dry goods store owner's hand and wished him well. Then they mounted up, got the two wagons turned back around, and finally headed out of town.

They had traveled about five miles when Theresa remembered the lunch that the innkeeper's wife had packed for them. It had stopped raining for the moment, so she called to Karl to stop, jumped down, walked to the rear of the wagon, and took out the lunch bag. There was cheese, bread, meat sandwiches, and about a dozen small tarts.

While they were eating lunch, Karl asked them what they wanted to do that night, whether they wanted to go on to the next town or find a campsite. Joan said that she really wanted a night off, but she didn't know if trying to set up camp in the rain would qualify as a night off.

"Maybe we should stay in town tonight and plan to find a spot for a couple of nights tomorrow," Steve said. "You wanted to give the horses a day off about every week, right? Well, we left Kalen's house a week ago today."

"Can everyone take one more night in town before we have a night off?" Karl looked around at everyone, but especially at Joan, as he asked that question.

"Yes, one more performance," Joan sighed. "But I want to have camp set up by lunch tomorrow, hopefully near a stream. We need to wash some clothes."

"And I've got to gather some herbs. We used a lot today, especially woundwort," Theresa said.

"Okay. Mount up then. From what the innkeeper said, we've got about fifteen miles to go before we get to the next town, and it's already a little past noon," Karl said as he headed for his horse.

~ ~ ~ ~

The town must have been a little farther than twenty miles because it was dinnertime by the time they got there. The innkeeper grunted that he guessed he could let them have two rooms and dinner for a performance, but said that they were on their own for breakfast and stable fees. Karl was too tired to argue, so he agreed.

After they settled the horses for the evening, they went back to the tavern for dinner, but the innkeeper already had the tavern set up for the show. When Karl asked him about their dinner, the innkeeper snorted that they took too long with the horses. Dinner was over. He added with a sneer that if their performance warranted it, he would have his wife prepare some sandwiches after the show.

Since they had eaten a late lunch, none of them were very hungry, but the man's attitude was insufferable, so Karl said that they would not perform until they had had something to eat, and all of

129

the Tellurians sat down. After a bit, the innkeeper went off in a huff and slammed his way into the kitchen.

A few minutes later, an older woman came out with a platter of bread and cheese and a jug of water. She whispered to the Tellurians, "Please perform. You don't know what he's like when he gets crossed. I promise I'll have some food ready for you after the show."

Joan looked at Karl and nodded. When Karl looked around at the rest of the Tellurians, they all either nodded or shrugged.

Finally Darrell said, "I figure we either have to perform, or we'll end up having to kill him, and I'd rather not have to do that."

"All right. Let's eat a bite and then we'll go get the instruments. I don't think we'll have much fun with this show though," Karl conceded.

They didn't do several of the usual numbers and ended the show after about an hour, but the crowd seemed pleased anyway. After the audience cleared out and they had packed up their instruments, the innkeeper's wife brought them a large platter of food and a couple of pitchers of scog. When they thanked her, she shook her head and said that it was she who should be thanking them, that her husband had enjoyed the show so much that he was in a much better mood.

"Well, maybe we did a public service by putting the town jerk in a better mood," Chris said quietly after the innkeeper's wife had gone back into the kitchen.

"I'd hate to have to live in the same house as that man," Theresa said, shaking her head. "That poor woman!"

"We don't know what's going on," Steve said. "You can't judge someone based on only one evening. He may have just had a really bad day."

"And he took it out on us," Kevin said. "At least we're leaving here tomorrow, never to see him again."

After they finished eating, everyone headed off to bed. About 3:00 in the morning there was a knock on Joan and Theresa's door. Joan grabbed her cloak and quickly opened the door. The innkeeper's wife was standing in the hall ringing her hands. She asked quietly if the other woman was really a Sister of Healing. When Joan said yes, the woman asked if she could please speak to her.

Theresa had awakened at the knock, but she didn't get out of bed until she heard the woman ask for her.

"Yes?" Theresa asked as she shrugged into her cloak.

"I hate to bother your sleep, Sister, but could you please come? It's my husband. He's in terrible pain and I don't know what to do for him."

"Of course I'll come," Theresa said as she put on her boots.

"I'm coming with you," Joan whispered to Theresa. "Wait until I get my boots on." *And grab my dagger,* Joan added to herself.

The innkeeper's wife led them to a small house out behind the inn. Her husband was white as a sheet, soaked with sweat, and his face was contorted with pain. When Theresa approached, he waved her away.

His wife said, "He didn't want me to disturb you. He thinks it'll just go away, but he's been like this for the past week, especially at night."

"Can you describe when it starts, where the pain is, how it feels? I need something to go on," Theresa said to her.

As the woman explained about her husband's illness, Theresa figured out what the problem probably was – kidney stones. She had some herbs that would alleviate the pain and help him to pass the stones, but they were in her wagon. She explained that she would have to leave for a few minutes to go get some medicine, but that she would be back shortly. In the meantime, she asked his wife to put on some water for tea.

"Tea?! I'm dying here and you want a cup of tea?!" the innkeeper yelled.

"Yes, tea. But not for me, for you. Now stop acting like a spoiled child or I won't bother to give you anything at all. And you're not dying, but I don't doubt that you feel like you are. Leave your wife alone and let her get the water ready," Theresa said in a stern tone. "Joan, why don't you come with me?"

When they returned, Theresa made a cup of tea and handed it to the man. "Drink this, and yes, I know it tastes terrible. That's life. If you want the pain to go away, you have to drink every drop of that tea."

The man turned the mug up. He nearly gagged on the taste, but he drank it all. About ten minutes later his face started relaxing, and he slowly sank back into his chair. After a few more minutes, he was asleep.

"He'll sleep like that until morning, but this isn't over," Theresa said. "He might be in pain for four or five more days, but it will pass. Just be sure that he drinks four mugs of tea everyday until the pain's completely gone. And the fourth mug needs to be right before he goes to bed unless he wants to hurt all night."

"Thanks, Sister. You don't know how much I appreciate this. And he does, too. He just forgot to say so before he fell asleep." His wife gently stroked the man's forehead. "Please don't tell anyone about this. He would hate for anyone to know."

"You're welcome, and we won't say anything. Now why don't you just throw a blanket over him right where he is? If you wake him up, the pain may start up again. You need to get some sleep yourself," Theresa said, as she got ready to leave the house. "I'll check with you tomorrow morning before we leave."

After they reached their room, while they were getting ready for bed again, Joan asked Theresa if there wasn't something she could have added to the tea to make it taste better.

"Sure. There are several things I could have added to give it a nice, soothing flavor," Theresa answered with a smile, "and I would have, if he hadn't been such a jackass."

With a laugh, Joan wished her a good night's sleep.

~ ~ ~ ~

The next morning dawned clear and bright, and the Tellurians were all in really good moods as they started packing up to leave town. The weather had finally cleared and all of them were looking forward to two days off, two whole days by themselves.

But before they could hitch the horses to the wagon, the innkeeper's wife walked into the stable and said, "Don't forget to come over to the tavern for your breakfast before you leave. I've made some fresh biscuits to go with your eggs, and we have butter and a nice blackberry jam to go with them. The coffee should be ready by the time you get there."

"Breakfast wasn't part of our agreement with your husband," Karl answered with a frown.

"That was then. This is now, and your breakfast is waiting. Please come before it gets cold," she said as she turned and left the stable to head back over to the inn.

"Well, will wonders never cease? I wonder why he had a change of heart," Karl said to no one in particular. Then he looked at the rest of the Tellurians, shrugged, and followed the innkeeper's wife out of the stable.

Theresa and Joan shared a private smile as they followed the others over to the inn for breakfast.

Chapter 21

Taelor Joins the Group

The Tellurians spent the next two nights in a large clearing beside a lake. Theresa gathered herbs while the others sparred and practiced with their weapons. They washed clothes, tended the horses, and reorganized the wagons, but most of all they relaxed. When they hit the road again, they felt completely refreshed.

Over the next couple of weeks they fell into a pattern of two nights in town, one camping, two nights in town, and then two nights at the same campsite. They crossed streams on wooden bridges, and rivers on ferries. They rode through forests, prairies, farmlands, and small towns.

The people they encountered along the way seemed relatively content and friendly. News about the people in and around a town traveled by way of the backyard grapevine, but the people in one town knew almost nothing of what happened in other towns, and didn't really care to know.

On the first Saturday in May, they reached the eastern fringes of the Badlands. The vast empty basins looked untouched, except for a cloud of dust that seemed to hang above the ground on the western edge of one of the basins, moving slowly off to the south. While they were trying to figure out what was causing the dust, they saw a figure that looked like a man stumble out from behind one of the spires and fall to the ground about a quarter of a mile away.

Karl remembered stories about bands of outlaws who hid in the Badlands on Earth during the days of the Wild West, and he wasn't at all sure that the man wasn't bait, but if he really needed help, they couldn't just leave him there to die. Karl glanced over at Darrell and raised his eyebrows. Darrell nodded, so Karl turned his horse and rode towards the fallen figure with Darrell following about twenty yards back.

While Karl and Darrell slowly approached the man, Joan rode around to the front of Theresa's wagon, unfastened her bow, and drew an arrow out of her quiver. Steve took up a position behind Kevin's wagon and unfastened his bow too. Chris stationed himself between the two wagons and loosened his sword in its scabbard.

Darrell stayed back, sword in hand, while Karl dismounted with his canteen and walked towards the man. From a distance, the man looked dead. His lips were parched and cracked, and there were dark circles around his eyes that made the sockets look empty. His clothes hung on his emaciated frame like a shroud. As Karl got a little closer, he could see the blood-drenched tunic slowly rise and fall. The man wasn't dead yet, but he wasn't far from it. When Karl pulled back the tunic, he found a gaping wound just under the collarbone. Infection had already set in.

Karl put his hand behind the man's head and raised it just enough to try to give him a sip of water. The man opened his eyes and looked at Karl in terror.

"No! Won't go back!" the man hissed through clenched teeth. "Kill me now!"

"I'm not going to hurt you," Karl said gently. "Here, drink some water." He tilted the canteen and let a little water dribbled over the man's mouth. "Who did this to you?"

"You … you're not … with the bounty hunters?" the man said, struggling to get the words out.

"No," Karl said, shaking his head. "Why are bounty hunters after you?"

"Escaped."

"Escaped? From jail?"

For a minute, the man said nothing. Karl wasn't sure he was still conscious. And then the man frowned and tried to shake his head no, but the movement was so faint that Karl nearly missed it.

"No … not jail," the man said in a whisper. Then he took a couple more breaths and said, "From Rolan."

"You were a slave?"

The man slowly nodded his head and moaned. Karl gave him a couple more sips of water. After a few minutes, the man continued, "Been hiding in a cave … yesterday…maybe the day before, went… looking …for food … one of them spotted me … got me with an arrow … hid." He took a deep breath, seemed to find a spark of strength from somewhere deep inside, and said, "They were closing in … tried to make a break this morning … not far behind me." He struggled, trying to sit up. "You go … get out of here."

"I'm not going to leave you here," Karl said as he slid his arm behind the man's shoulders. "Can you sit on my horse?"

"No!" The man shook his head and tried to push Karl away. "They'll kill you. Go!" he gasped.

Karl turned and signaled for Darrell. When Darrell reached him, Karl quickly explained the situation. There was no way that they could cover the runaway slave's trail or the tracks left by two men on horseback, so they didn't waste time trying. They hoisted the runaway slave across the saddle on Karl's horse and then Karl swung up behind the saddle and spurred his horse back to the road and the wagons.

As Theresa watched them more or less throw the man onto Karl's horse, she knew that he was either gravely wounded or desperately ill, so she climbed into the back of her wagon and began spreading out a couple of the bedrolls in the narrow alley between the cabinets for cushioning. Then she covered them with a couple of layers of canvas. She took out a good portion of woundwort in case he had been wounded, and a mixture of herbs for pain and infection.

By the time Karl and Darrell returned with the wounded man, Theresa was ready for him. Darrell lifted him off of Karl's horse and carried him over to the wagon. Theresa held the back flap to the side, and between the two of them, Darrell and Karl got the man settled on the pallet Theresa had made on the floor of her wagon. As soon as she could get to him, Theresa pulled back his tunic and started cleaning the wound.

"Karl, can we stay put until I get this bandaged?"

"I don't think so, Theresa," Karl answered, "He told me that he's a runaway slave and that bounty hunters are after him. I think that dust we saw a little while ago was from their horses. We need to get as far away from here as we can, and fast."

"Okay," Theresa said, "but I'm going to busy back here for a while."

"That's okay," Joan said as she tied her horse to the back of Theresa's wagon. "I'll drive."

After Theresa cleaned the wound, dressed it with woundwort, and bandaged the area, she mixed some herbs in water and had him sip it. As soon as he drank the potion, he fell asleep. Theresa leaned back and took a long look at him. He was older than a teenager and younger than middle age, but other than that, she couldn't say how old he was; he was in too rough a shape. His hair was jet black, and really thick, and from the looks of it, long enough to reach his shoulders. His skin was almost an almond color, though whether from his natural coloring or from exposure to the sun out in the badlands, she had no idea. He was relatively short for a man, maybe five feet nine or so, had a small frame, and was thin as a rail. Theresa covered him with a blanket and climbed onto the driver's seat beside Joan.

Karl rode over to the wagon as soon as he saw Theresa. "How is he?" he asked quietly.

"I don't know," she said, shaking her head. "Mainly he's going to need a lot of rest. I stopped the bleeding and cleaned the wound, and the woundwort will soon heal it, but he's half-starved and he's so weak that I'm not sure he can survive the loss of blood. A stronger man would probably be fine in a couple of days, but I just don't know."

"All right," Karl nodded with a slight frown and thought for a few minutes. Finally he said, "I don't think we should try to stay in town with a wounded man. It would cause too many questions."

Joan frowned and turned towards Theresa. "Is it illegal to help an escaped slave?"

"I don't know," Theresa said with a shrug. "The subject of slavery never came up with Drusilla, but at the same time we can't just let him die."

"And we can't just hand him over to those bounty hunters either," Joan added.

"We won't," Karl said.

"Let's just ride through the next town and camp tonight," Joan suggested.

"That won't leave us a lot of time to find a secure campsite before nightfall. Let me see what the others think," Karl said as he pulled his horse back to discuss things with the rest of the group.

While he was waiting for Darrell to ride up, he saw three men on horseback emerging from the Badlands about half a mile down the road. They stopped and spread out across the road, obviously waiting for the approaching wagons. One of the men urged his horse out in front of the others.

Karl rode back to the front of Theresa's wagon with Darrell close behind him. As they passed her wagon, Theresa said, "Don't be surprised if I act like I'm in charge. I've got an idea."

Karl nodded and kept riding.

When they were within twenty feet of the bounty hunters, Karl held up his hand to signal a halt. The wagons slowly rolled to a stop. Steve and Chris stopped their horses between the two wagons.

"Good day, and what can we do for you?" Karl asked in his most pleasant and non-threatening voice.

"We're looking for an escaped slave," the man in front said. "Have you seen a stranger in these parts?"

"We're strangers in these parts ourselves, but we haven't met anyone since we left that little town about ten miles north of here this morning," Karl said in a smooth voice.

"Well, then, I'm sure you won't mind if we search your wagons, will you?" one of the men in the back asked.

"I most certainly would mind," Theresa said in a soft yet firm voice

"We won't disturb your herbs, Sister. We just want to make sure that there's no one in your wagon," the man in the back row snorted.

"You'll just have to take my word for it," Theresa said as she rubbed her pendant. The fire in the opal was starting to glow.

The man cocked his head and sneered.

Theresa raised her eyebrows, looked down her nose at him, and said, "Or isn't my word good enough for you?" Her words were chiseled out of ice.

"No offense intended, Sister," the man in front said in a placating voice as he urged his horse towards her wagon. "We're just looking out for your safety. That crazy slave could be holding a knife on you to make you hide him." He noticed the fire in the opal begin to sparkle and dance, so he stopped in his tracks.

Theresa allowed her mouth to fall open as if in shock. She shut it, raised her eyebrows, and snapped, "Do you really think that would work?" The fire in the opal was steadily growing in strength.

"No, ma'am. I guess not. We meant no disrespect," the man in front said. Then he turned to his men and said, "Let them pass. The man we're looking for isn't with them." Then he moved off the road and signaled for his men to do the same.

The men rode off to the side, but the one who had spoken up from the back row didn't quite leave the road, and as Theresa's wagon rolled past, he reached out, grabbed the canvas flap, threw it up over the back of the wagon, and darted his horse around behind the wagon to peer inside. All he saw between the built-in cabinets were canvas tarps.

He shook his head at the man who appeared to be in charge just as Darrell reached the back of the wagon. Darrell dove from his horse, grabbing the man on his way down, and wrestled him to the ground. He had his dagger drawn and was ready to plunge it into the man's chest when Theresa yelled at him to stop. She had jumped off of the wagon seat and had nearly reached the back of her wagon by the time Darrell had the man pinned to the ground.

Meanwhile, another bounty hunter had ridden up behind Kevin's wagon and jerked its back door open. The only things between the cabinets in there were their clothes and Joan's harp. He signaled the lead man that the wagon was empty just as Chris rounded the far side of the wagon and stuck the tip of his sword at the man's throat.

"Don't move," Chris hissed. The man sat as still as he could and slowly raised his hands away from the weapons at his side.

Theresa turned to the man in charge of the bounty hunters and glared. "I want to know the name of the person responsible for this! Who are you working for?" Tiny sparks were starting to shoot out of Theresa's opal towards the men.

"We're just doing our jobs, ma'am. There's no need to get all riled up," the head man said as he urged his horse backwards. "No harm's been done."

"You haven't answered me," Theresa said as both her glare and the opal's sparks intensified.

"Rolan, of the House of Gergin, Seated Sorcerer of Brendolanth."

Theresa stood her ground and continued to glare at the man. "Take these men and leave us while you still can. Go!"

The leader of the bounty hunters turned to ride back out into the Badlands. Darrell allowed the man that he had tackled to get up and mount his horse at the same time that Chris eased his sword away from the other man's throat.

As the three bounty hunters rode away, Darrell kept his eyes on their departing backs and quietly said, "I think we need to get away from here, far away – now. And keep your weapons ready. They may come back."

As soon as Darrell was mounted again, Karl led the Tellurians down the road at a much quicker pace than they normally traveled. Darrell didn't stay behind Kevin's wagon like he usually did. He circled the whole group, watching for any sign that the bounty hunters were returning.

After about fifteen minutes Joan whispered, "Do you need to check on him?"

"Probably, but I don't want to crawl into the back of my wagon until I'm sure we're out of sight. They may still be watching," Theresa answered quietly.

"Quite a show you put on back there."

"I just hope I don't have to do that too often. I'm shaking all over," Theresa said with a little shiver.

"Why did you stop Darrell from stabbing that bounty hunter?"

"I didn't want to have to get to the woundwort to treat him," Theresa said with a sigh. "That was way too close."

In another thirty minutes, Theresa said, "I left my canteen in the wagon earlier so that I'd have an excuse for climbing into the back in case we were being watched. Think I'll go get it now."

"Okay. I'll try to hold the horses steady while you're back there," Joan said.

When Theresa climbed in the back, she was surprised to see that the rest of the tarps had been pulled down into the walkway between the cabinets. There was absolutely no sign that a person was under the canvas. As she lifted a corner of one of the tarps, the man opened his eyes and quietly asked, "Are...are they gone?"

Theresa nodded and whispered, "At least for now." Then she picked up her canteen and gave him a little water. "Try to sleep if you can."

Then she climbed back out on the wagon seat with her canteen and offered it to Joan. "I think he's okay, or at least he's no worse than he was," she whispered. "But I'll feel better when we're a few days away from here."

Joan nodded as she tipped the canteen up for a drink.

~ ~ ~ ~

About mid-afternoon, they rode through the next town without stopping. A couple of miles later, Theresa spotted a woman carrying a basket from a chicken coop to her house.

"How are we doing on eggs? Aren't we almost out?" she asked Joan.

"Yes, I used the last ones for breakfast Thursday morning."

"Karl, Karl, wait up a minute," Theresa called out. "I've got an idea."

When she and Joan caught up with him, Theresa pointed to the farmhouse and said that she wanted to stop and see if she could trade some herbs for a couple dozen eggs. Karl looked around, but he didn't see any sign that they were being followed, so he nodded.

"Just be quick," he said as she jumped off the wagon seat and ran up the drive.

As Theresa approached the back door of the house, the lady opened it and stepped out into the yard. After Theresa introduced herself, she explained that she would like to get a couple of dozen eggs, if the lady could spare them, and that she would be willing to trade some herbs for the eggs.

The lady nodded and said, "I use a lot of woundwort patching up my husband and sons, but what I really need is something for fatigue. I just don't seem to have the energy that I used to. Do you have anything that might help?"

Theresa smiled and told her that she had some tea that she had developed especially for those symptoms. "You need to drink a cup in the middle of the morning and then again in the middle of the afternoon." Theresa tried to look as serious as she could. "First you'll need to mix a heaping spoonful of the tea with either a spoonful of sugar or a spoonful of honey in a cup. Next, you pour boiling water in the cup, sit down, and slowly inhale the steam for ten minutes. Then after that, you need to sip the tea over a period of twenty minutes. The timing is critical here. If you drink it too fast, it won't help." The lady nodded as she listened carefully to the instructions.

"Shall I fix some up for you? Maybe a couple of week's worth?" Theresa asked.

"I'd really appreciate it if you would."

While Theresa walked back to the wagon to get the woundwort and some apple cinnamon tea, the lady went out to the hen house to get two dozen eggs for Theresa.

A few minutes later, the Tellurians were on their way again.

~ ~ ~ ~

That night they camped in a small clearing that was well hidden from the road. Karl was concerned that a campfire might attract the bounty hunters, so they ate cheese and bread for dinner, but by daybreak, everyone wanted coffee bad enough to risk it, especially since they would be back on the road within the hour.

Over the next couple of days, Theresa's patient slowly gained strength. She hadn't wanted to bother him with a lot of conversation, but she did manage to find out that his name was Taelor and to tell him a little bit about each of the Tellurians. By the morning of the third day, he was strong enough to get out of the wagon on his own. He walked over to the fire while Theresa and Joan were preparing breakfast.

"I guess I owe all of you my life," Taelor said with a touch of embarrassment. "I don't know how I can ever repay you."

"No thanks necessary," Joan said as she handed him a cup of coffee.

"You're looking a lot better," Karl said as he walked up with a load of firewood. "I didn't know if you would live through the day when we found you." After he put the firewood down, he looked at Taelor again and said, "But we really do have to do something about those clothes." He looked around for a minute and spotted Kevin over near the back of his wagon. "Kevin, can you come over here for a minute?"

"Don't worry about the clothes," Taelor said quietly. "They'll be fine."

"No, they won't. If anyone spots you in those clothes, they'll know something's going on," Karl said. "We'll probably stay in town tonight, and we don't want you to stick out."

"Oh, I hadn't thought about that," Taelor said, looking down at the ground. "Look, if I could just ride in the back of the wagon for one more day, I think I can make it. I can hide in there tonight. No one will even see me. I should be strong enough by tomorrow morning to strike off on my own. I can leave as soon as we get out of town. I don't want to be a burden to any of you."

"You're not a burden, and anyway, I doubt that Theresa is going to be willing to let you go off on your own by tomorrow," Karl said as Kevin walked up. "Kevin, do you think you could find some clothes for Taelor that would fit him better than the ones he has on?"

Kevin nodded, turned around, and walked over towards his wagon.

Taelor looked like he wanted to argue, but finally he gave in and turned towards Theresa. "Is there some way I could wash up a little?"

"Sure. You go with Kevin and get some clothes while I get a wash basin set up on the tailgate of my wagon."

All in all, Kevin's clothes were a pretty good fit, but Taelor did have to use some rope as a belt to keep the leggings up around his waist. After he finished washing up and changing clothes, he joined the group for breakfast.

While they were eating, Karl asked him what his plans were. Taelor said that the only plan he had at the moment was to get out of Brendolanth. Karl glanced around at the others and they all nodded in answer to his unspoken question. Then he said, "Taelor, we'd like for you to consider traveling with us for a while. We're headed for Nandelia ourselves, and we could use another man."

Taelor shook his head and started to speak, but Karl interrupted him. "When we camp, we all stand guard, but I'd like for Joan and Theresa to be able to sleep through the night." Karl looked at Joan who had started to protest. "No, I'm serious, Joan. When we're in town, you and Theresa are sometimes up half the night tending to sick people, and when we're camping, both of you get up before dawn every morning to get breakfast ready. I think that you two do enough without having to stand guard."

"I agree with Karl," Steve added.

"Same here," Darrell said as he looked directly at Theresa.

"And if Taelor would consent to joining our little group, at least until we get to Nandelia, then he could stand guard with Karl. That would give us two men for each of the three shifts and the women could get some sleep," Chris said.

"I don't know," Taelor said cautiously. "What if I'm spotted? Do you know how much trouble all of you would be in?"

"I know that you would have a much better chance of making it to Nandelia with us than you would on your own, and I know that I'd like for my wife to get some sleep," Karl answered. "As I see it, this way everybody wins."

"Well, I'd like to point out one potential problem," Kevin said slowly. "When we stay in town, the Tellurians will have to perform. I'm already working as the stage manager. If there are two of us who don't perform, won't that look a bit strange? Is there something else that he could do? Something that would give him a reason to be traveling with us."

Taelor looked around the group for a moment and then he looked directly at Theresa. "I worked in a chapel for about five years. I could pretend to be your assistant."

"Do you know enough about the herbs to be able to pull this off?" she asked. "We've had to hold a couple of healing clinics already."

Taelor nodded. "I know how to dress wounds, how to set bones, which herbs work best for which illnesses, how to gather and prepare herbs, and how to make potions and poultices." Taelor looked at Karl and added, "I've also worked in stables. I could take care of the horses and wagons whenever you stay in town. I would be more comfortable there than in an inn anyway."

"That'll work out fine then," Steve said, "and as Theresa's assistant, naturally you would ride with her and drive her team. That gives you an excellent reason to be on the wagon seat instead of on a horse."

"Okay. That's settled. Let's pack up. It's time to hit the road," Karl said as he stood up and drained the last of his coffee out of his cup before handing it to Joan. "Darrell, let's go get the teams hitched up while they load the wagons."

As Karl and Darrell walked off towards the horses, Steve, Chris and Kevin loaded the canvas sleeping tarps and the bedrolls while Theresa and Joan washed out the breakfast dishes and stored them in the wagon.

Taelor looked around uneasily and finally asked Theresa what he could do to help.

Theresa shook her head and told him to stay put. "I know how you feel, wanting to do your share and all, but right now, I'm more interested in seeing to it that you don't end up flat on your back again. Let's just take it easy for a couple of days. There'll be plenty of time for you to pitch in later."

Less than an hour later, they were back on the road. Taelor picked up the reins when he climbed up on the wagon seat, so Theresa sat back and enjoyed the ride. After a while, Taelor asked her where she was from.

"I trained in Drisden, but other than that, I'm not really from anywhere. I've spent most of my life traveling."

"Have you always traveled with the Tellurians?"

"No. We met up in Drisden. We were all going to Nandelia, so Drusilla suggested we travel together. I used to sing before I became a sister, so I join in whenever they perform." Theresa paused and then asked Taelor where he was from.

"I'm not sure," he answered. Then he explained that his mother had been captured by slavers while he was still an infant. Eventually, the slavers had offered them on the market in Trendon, the capital city of Brendolanth, and the seated sorcerer, Tsareth, had purchased them both. "Tsareth adored my mother, and he treated me just like he did his two non-magical children. We were all taught to read, write, and keep accurate records. We ate together, played together, and did chores together, especially in the stables. Then, when I turned sixteen, Tsareth asked me if I'd like to train as a sister's assistant. For the next five years, I lived at the chapel when I was on duty and at the castle on my days off."

"Sounds good. What happened?"

"When I was twenty-one, Tsareth died," Taelor said. For a few minutes, he didn't say anything else, and Theresa was beginning to think he had said all that he was going to, but then he shook his head and continued. "Rolan might be Tsareth's son, but he is nothing like him. Tsareth was kind and fair; Rolan is just plain mean. He hates everyone, even his brothers and sisters."

"Why do you say that?"

"He sent them away from the castle and told them that they could never return."

"Oh," Theresa said. Then, after a few minutes, she asked, "What happened to your mother?"

"Rolan made her work in the kitchens and he told me that unless I did exactly as I was told, he would kill her."

"What did he want you to do?"

"Be his personal servant," Taelor said. "I even had to sleep in his room, on a pallet in a closet, so that I would be available during the night should he want something. The only time I was able to slip away was when he had one of the village or slave girls with him. Then I could count on about an hour, but that was my only free time."

"What about your mother? Now that you've escaped, what will he do to her?"

"My mother died about six months ago," Taelor said. He paused before he continued. "Once she was gone, he told me that he was going to arrange for me to marry one of the local village girls. I think he figured that we'd have a baby before long, and then he could hold the child and its mother over my head for the rest of my life, so I left."

"Wasn't that dangerous? I mean, didn't everyone know that you were his servant? How did you manage to even get out of the castle, much less make it to the Badlands?"

"I was part of the furnishings. When he had guests, I poured their drinks and waited on them. When he entertained women, I showed them to his quarters. They all knew my name, but they never looked at me. I doubt if any of them would recognize me. Do you know what I mean?"

Theresa nodded. "I know I wouldn't recognize the waitress we had in the last inn we stayed in, or the innkeeper for that matter. I bet the people who watched us perform wouldn't recognize me without my flute. And the people who come to me for medicines only see the pendant. But even so, you took quite a chance."

"Not really. One day, about three weeks ago now, Rolan met with some of his guard officers. I was serving scog while they were talking, so I heard him give them their orders. He sent his two top squads out to search for a sorcerer named Myron. I knew he'd need the other two squads to guard the castle, so that left run-of-the-mill bounty hunters to come after me."

"Why is Rolan interested in finding this sorcerer?" Theresa's heart had jumped and begun to race at the mention of Myron, but she kept her voice even.

"It seems that Master Sorcerer Badec is in a coma, and they really aren't expecting him to make it. Rolan wants his men to find Badec's son, Myron, and kill him before anything happens to Badec so that the Master's Chair will become vacant. While they were talking, Rolan did mention something about Damien, the Sorcerer of Nandelia. I'm not sure what he was saying, I was in and out, but I got the impression that Damien's trying to prevent a magic war. Like I said, I don't know what Rolan was saying about that, but I do know that the only thing he's interested in is power, and for some reason, he really wants to see Myron dead. That was one thing that he did make crystal clear."

"He sounds like a dangerous man," Theresa said softy.

"He is," Taelor agreed.

"How did you manage to get away?"

"I waited about four days to give his guards time to get far away. Then I put a heavy dose of Valerian in his scog to put him in a deep sleep and I left during the middle of the night. I made it out of the village before daybreak, and I've been on the run ever since. I don't know when he sent the bounty hunters after me, but it was common sense that I would head for the closest border, so I took a roundabout route. It was just bad luck that they managed to get on my trail before I made it. I spotted them about a week ago, so I tried to hide out in the Badlands until they gave up and left. They were just more patient than I thought they'd be."

"What would he do if he caught you?" Theresa asked.

"He'd kill me," Taelor answered calmly. "But he would also have anyone who had helped me killed, and that's why I'm not sure that this is such a good idea."

"Well, let's not worry about that right now. After all, I doubt that even Rolan would be willing to kill a sister or those under her protection," Theresa said.

"Don't be too sure," Taelor said. "He doesn't play by the rules."

~ ~ ~ ~

By late afternoon, they reached the next town. Karl and Theresa made arrangements with the innkeeper for two rooms, meals for eight and accommodations for eleven horses. The innkeeper wanted to have an outdoor concert in the town square, and he wanted to have it before dark, so he told them that he would have a meal prepared for them afterwards.

Taelor took care of the horses while the others put on a show, and then after the concert, he joined them in the tavern for dinner. As soon as everyone had finished eating, he left with Karl, Darrell, and Steve to spend the night in the stable. No one in town gave him a second glance.

Theresa waited until she and Joan were alone in their room to tell Joan what Taelor had said about Rolan sending a couple of hit squads out after Myron.

"Should we tell Kevin?" Theresa asked.

Joan shook her head and said, "I'm not sure. Let me talk to Karl and see what he thinks." She wasn't sure that it would be a good idea for Kevin to know at this point, but then again, she wasn't sure it was fair to keep it a secret either. This could be one of those Catch 22 decisions, and she didn't feel that she was the one to make it.

Chapter 22

Kevin's Dream

Kevin was more exhausted than usual that night and fell into a deep sleep almost as soon as his head hit the pillow. Sometime after midnight, he became aware of the dreams that were floating through his sleep. Then Xantha appeared and the scenery evolved into the grassy meadow near Kalen's Gate House.

"Just thought I'd pop in and let you know that things are starting to heat up and get interesting."

"What do you mean?"

"Several of the seated sorcerers have commissioned assassination squads, and a couple have sent out protection squads."

Kevin felt a throbbing pain start behind his eyes. "What do we do now?"

"Nothing. No one has any idea where you are or what you look like. They're all out there chasing shadows. It's sort of funny really."

"I'm afraid I don't find assassins very funny."

"I was afraid of that," Xantha sighed. *"That's why I wanted to tell you about it myself before you heard about it somewhere else. You take things too seriously."*

"Someone trying to kill me is about as serious as it gets," Kevin insisted. "At least tell me which ones are my enemies and which ones are my allies."

"Allies?"

"Yes, the ones who sent out the protection squads. Aren't they trying to help me?"

"Help you get seated on the Master's Chair, but that's about it. They're not going to help you get to Glendymere or help you learn to protect yourself. They've got enough confidence in their own skills to challenge you. They figure they're strong enough to take the chair away from you and to stand up to anyone who wants to take it away from them. The only difference between them and the ones who sent out assassination squads is that they're far more dangerous."

"So basically I don't have any allies in this mess?"

"You've got a lot of allies. They just aren't on the council," Xantha said slowly. *"Kalen, Duane, Palladin, Laryn, Glendymere, Pallor, the people from Earth, me ... we're your allies, Kevin."*

"This is scary."

"You'll get used to it. Oh, by the way, Rolan, the Seated Sorcerer of Brendolanth, the province you're traveling through right now, has sent two death squads to Camden to look for you. Sort of ironic, isn't it?"

"Yeah, right!" Kevin said with a groan. "Sorry, Xantha. I just don't find anything amusing about any of this."

"All right. Let's change the subject then. How are things going for you? Found anyone you might be interested in mating with yet?"

"NO! And I don't plan to start looking for a long, long time, so just drop it."

In Kevin's dream, Xantha walked over to the other side of the small meadow and began grazing.

"Xantha, I've got a question," Kevin began hesitantly.

"All right," Xantha acknowledged. Then after a couple of minutes passed and Kevin hadn't said anything, Xantha prompted, "I'm listening."

"The person who sits in the Master's Chair is supposed to be the most powerful human sorcerer on Terah, right?"

"Yes, he would have to be, or he would soon lose it to someone else." Xantha picked up his head. Something in Kevin's tone intrigued him.

"What about Glendymere? Assuming that my father wants to protect our line, he would have asked one of the most powerful sorcerers to teach me, right? If Glendymere's so good, and if being the Master Sorcerer is such a big deal, and everyone wants it, what's to keep this Glendymere from taking me out himself? Even if he waits until after I've been seated, there's no way that I could become good enough in less than a year to protect myself from my mentor."

"The key word there is 'human'. You're in absolutely no danger from Glendymere."

"Glendymere's not human?"

"No," Xantha said slowly. "Kevin, Glendymere's a dragon."

"A dragon?!" Kevin gasped. "You are kidding, aren't you?"

"No, Glendymere is very much a dragon. Why are you so shocked? Naturally the most powerful sorcerers on Terah would be those who were magic to start with, right?"

"I can't believe this is happening. You're telling me that I'm going to apprentice with some dragon, and you can't understand why I look shocked?!"

"First of all, Glendymere is not just some dragon. He's more like the head dragon. He's the oldest and the wisest. You're incredibly lucky that he liked your father enough to agree to teach you. Do you have any idea how many young sorcerers would sell their souls for the chance to just visit him? And you're going to study with him!"

"Yeah, I feel really lucky," Kevin said with sarcasm dripping from his words. "Come to a strange new world, be held captive by a dwarf, spend a year with a dragon and learn to be a sorcerer, just so that someone who has been practicing sorcery for longer than I've been alive can blow me to bits in a showdown of magic, provided I manage to evade the assassins."

"Put like that, it doesn't sound so good to me either," Xantha said with a laugh.

"I think I'll just go back to Earth and take my chances with the tornado. Let one of those other sorcerers go work with Glendymere. I'm sure you can find someone who could hold the Master's Chair. Pretend he's me! No one would know the difference, and I sure won't tell!"

"Kevin, you really can't afford to get all bent out of shape over every little thing. You won't make it through the first year at this rate!"

"That's what I've been trying to tell all of you! You need a hero, and I'm a coward. I don't like violence. I don't like pain. I don't like the idea of blowing up someone else much more than I like the idea of being blown up myself. And I don't like the idea of dragons! Don't I get any say in any of this?"

"Not really. You don't know enough about any of this to make intelligent decisions, so we have to make them for you."

"I can always refuse to go along with this charade."

"You're overreacting again. You don't know whether you like dragons or not. After all, how many have you ever known?"

"That may be, but …"

"Look, Glendymere is the best there is, and while you're with him, no one can harm you. That's the one place on Terah where you will be completely safe."

Kevin paused, took a deep breath, and slowly exhaled it. Meanwhile Xantha went back to grazing. Finally he said, "Okay. Tell me about Glendymere."

"What do you want to know?"

"Well, what does a dragon look like? Is he as dangerous as I think he is? How do I communicate with him? By talking? Telepathy? I don't know what I need to know. Just tell me about him."

"See? It's like I told you. You don't know enough to make informed decisions. That's why we decide for you," Xantha said smugly. Then he answered Kevin's question. *"First of all, Glendymere is old, really old, but age makes a dragon stronger, not weaker. He'll communicate with you like I do, by telepathy. As to how dangerous he is, that depends. If he sees you as his enemy, he would be the most dangerous force you would ever encounter, and he would see to it that you cease to exist. But if he sees you as his friend, you would be safer when you're with him than you would be in your mother's womb, just as long as you don't wake him up. That can get a bit dicey. His yawns can pack a wallop!"*

"What does he look like? All I know about dragons is what I've seen on television on Earth."

"Well, I could give you a mental picture of him if that would make you feel better. Here." Xantha projected a memory of Glendymere standing beside Duane into Kevin's mind.

Glendymere's shoulders were twice as tall as Duane and his long neck snaked around from his shoulders to his huge, triangular head. His eyes were like glittering emeralds and showed no sign of age although he did have bushy white eyebrows. He had a lot of very big teeth, and a long white goatee that curved halfway to the ground. His huge torso was supported by legs that looked like tree trunks, and, even folded, his wings were massive. His clawed feet looked as deadly as his teeth, and his long tail curled around them just like a cat's. His golden scales sparkled in the sun, and around his neck, he wore a pendant with a huge blue sapphire in the center. Glendymere was magnificent, regal, and in a way, beautiful. Kevin was completely mesmerized by the image until Xantha allowed it to fade.

"Do you feel better now that you've seen him?" Xantha asked.

"I don't know." Kevin's voice was a bit shaky. "When were you and Kalen planning to tell me about this? And when are you planning to tell the others?"

"Kalen was planning to tell you before you left the Gate House but I guess he didn't get around to it. Not that it really matters. You know now."

"Who's going to tell the others?" Kevin asked.

"I guess you are, but be careful. You don't need to be overheard talking about Glendymere. If anyone knew that you were headed for his territory, tongues would start wagging, and eventually the wrong people would hear about it."

"I don't suppose you could show the others the same picture of Glendymere that you just showed me, could you?"

"Sorry, but I need a mind link to share one of my memories. I already have two mind links, you and Duane, and there are times when I think that that's two too many."

"But they need to know what to expect, too," Kevin argued.

"Why? Most of them probably won't even see Glendymere, at least not at first."

"What? I thought we were going to stay at Glendymere's."

"I'm sure he's made arrangements for everyone to stay nearby, but only another dragon would actually stay in his canyon with him. There are plenty of caves in the area where all of you can live quite comfortably, or you can build a house if you prefer."

"So I'm the only one who'll have any contact with him?"

"Well, someone will probably have to go with you as an assistant. Most sorcerers have a non-magical assistant, you know."

"No, I didn't know. Who's supposed to go with me?"

"That has to be your choice. After all, it's your assistant."

"How do I choose?"

"Carefully. You're going to be spending a lot of time with this person, and at times, your life may depend on him, or her."

"My life already depends on these people. They put themselves at risk everyday just by being around me. Now I have to ask one of them to live with a dragon?"

"Not exactly. You'll probably live with the others and just spend your days with Glendymere. But yes, you'll have to ask one of them to be with you when you're with Glendymere."

"Who?"

"That has to be your decision. Look, choose the one that you're the most comfortable with, the one you can talk to the easiest. Now, it's time for me to go. You need to wake up before long." Xantha leapt into the air and was lost in the clouds almost immediately.

Kevin tried to hold onto the meadow in his sleep, but it faded away almost as soon as Xantha did. As the meadow vanished, Kevin woke up enough to notice the faint sound of a rooster in the distance. He glanced towards the small window and saw a narrow crimson streak across the horizon. He sighed, closed his eyes, and tried to grab a few more minutes of sleep.

About half an hour later, Chris touched Kevin's shoulder to wake him up. Kevin jerked up and spun around with clenched fists. Chris took a step back and said, "Whoa, take it easy. You must have been dreaming. It's just me."

Kevin stared at him for a few seconds, and then, with a sigh, said, "Sorry about that. Nightmare."

While he was getting dressed, he considered telling Chris what Xantha had said, but he wasn't really positive that it hadn't been just a dream. If it had been only a dream, all that he would accomplish was embarrassing himself when Glendymere turned out to be some old man, and if it wasn't a dream, if Glendymere really was a dragon, well, they'd all find out soon enough. No need for anyone else to be worrying about that now.

Chapter 23

Taelor Pitches In

Joan didn't get a chance to talk to Karl about the assassination squads that Rolan had sent out until after lunch the next day.

"We knew that it was going to happen, but I'm a little surprised that it's already started." Karl said quietly. "Rolan didn't waste much time, did he?"

"Theresa asked what I thought about telling Kevin. Do you think we should?"

Karl thought about it for a moment. "Yes, but I don't want to make too big a deal out of it. I'll find a way to mention it to Darrell and let him pass the word to the others. In the meantime, tell Theresa to listen carefully to anything Taelor says about Rolan, but not to ask too many questions. We don't want him getting suspicious."

When they reached the town of Billows later that afternoon, Karl and Theresa went into the inn to offer to perform in the tavern that evening in exchange for room and board, but the innkeeper asked Theresa if she would consider holding a healing clinic that evening instead. "There's something going around that's making people awfully sick, and folks around here need a clinic a lot more than they need a show. No one's died yet, but I'm afraid it's just a matter of time until someone does."

Theresa asked him to describe the general symptoms. From what he said, she felt sure that they were dealing with a virulent strain of flu.

"Have you let anyone know that you need some help?" she asked.

The innkeeper nodded. "I sent a letter to the district minister and asked him if he knew of a sister who would be willing to come and stay here for a while, at least until the worst of this is over. When I saw your pendant, I thought maybe he'd sent you, but then when the two of you started talking about a minstrel show …"

Theresa shook her head. "No, I'm sorry. I can't stay, but we can hold a clinic."

"We'd be mighty grateful, Sister," the innkeeper said with a faint smile.

"Where would you like for Theresa to hold it?" Karl asked.

"We have a Chapel of Light, but I imagine it's a little dusty. We haven't had a sister in residence for quite a while." The innkeeper took a big door key out of a drawer in his desk and handed it to Theresa. "It's the big building next to the stable."

Theresa pocketed the key. "We'll go get set up." She looked at her watch. "It's 4:00 now. Let's say 7:00 for the clinic. That will give most people time to eat dinner first."

The innkeeper nodded. "I'll get the word out."

When Theresa returned to her wagon, she said, "We're holding a clinic in the old Chapel of Light this evening. We need to go get set up."

Taelor nodded and looked around. "Where is it?"

Theresa pointed to the old abandoned building next to the stable. There was a post in front of it, but there was no trace of a starburst sign. The grounds were overgrown with weeds and the porch was littered with old leaves.

Taelor nodded and drove the wagon around to the back of the building. Theresa and Joan went with him while the others took Kevin's wagon and the rest of the horses over to the stable.

When Theresa unlocked the door and the three of them stepped inside, Taelor took one look at the dust and cobwebs, told Theresa that he'd be right back, and disappeared out the door.

As Joan and Theresa made their way through the maze of rooms, they found acorn shells, dried remnants of apples, corn kernels, leaves, and animal droppings, but even the animals must have moved on because the cobwebs didn't look like they'd been disturbed in years, and there were no little footprints in the layer of dust that coated everything.

By the time they finished touring the building, Taelor had returned with brooms, feather dusters, buckets, pots, and an old wheelbarrow loaded with wood. He primed the old pump, started a fire in the wood stove in the kitchen, filled a couple of pots with water, and set them on the stove to warm. Meanwhile, Theresa and Joan took a couple of brooms and dusters and cleared out a few of the rooms.

When the others arrived from the stables, Theresa sent them over to the tavern to get some tables. After the tables were set up, she and Taelor started making up packets of herbs for the general malaise that accompanied the flu while the others helped Joan clean. A couple of hours later, four rooms were clean enough to use and Theresa was ready to begin the clinic.

Before she could open the front door, Taelor stopped her. "Theresa, I told the innkeeper you'd want to eat before the clinic started. They're expecting you for dinner."

"When did you go over there?" Theresa asked.

"When I went to get the brooms. I also told him that if they're really interested in having a sister come here to take care of this town, they needed to get the clinic cleaned up, repaired, and furnished," Taelor said as he ushered her towards the back door. "Go on over there and eat. I'll stay here and keep an eye on things."

"But what about you? When will you eat?"

"Just bring me something when you come back, maybe some cheese and bread. While you start the clinic, I'll take a couple of minutes to eat. It won't take me long."

"Okay, and thanks, Taelor," Theresa said as she stepped out onto the porch to join the others.

"All part of my job," Taelor said as he shut the back door.

~ ~ ~ ~

The clinic lasted until after midnight even though it ran more smoothly than any that they had held so far. Karl and Steve ran a small wound clinic, but most people needed flu medicine. Joan made hot Echinacea tea and the tavern waitresses served it to the people waiting outside. When the waitresses brought back the empty mugs, the innkeeper's wife washed them, dipped them in boiling water, and lined them up for Joan to use again. Chris and Kevin handled the crowd, and Darrell entertained the children who were there with their parents.

Taelor worked in the small examining room with Theresa, and anyone watching them would have thought that he'd been her assistant for years. He seemed to know what she needed before she asked for it.

By the time the clinic was over, they were all exhausted. The innkeeper brought over a barrel of scog and poured drinks for everyone who had worked at the clinic. Taelor gulped his scog down and went straight back to work. He had Theresa's herbs packed up and stored in the wagon before the others finished their drinks. As soon as the wagon was loaded, he told Theresa good night and drove it over to the stables.

When everyone else was ready to head off to bed, the innkeeper handed Karl two gold coins and said, "This clinic was worth a lot more than a couple of rooms and a few meals. We hope you'll accept these coins as a token of our appreciation."

Karl thanked him and handed the coins to Joan.

~ ~ ~ ~

The next morning, several people from outlying farms came into town in hopes of seeing Theresa before she left, so she and Taelor went back over to the deserted chapel and held another clinic after breakfast.

While they were busy with the clinic, Joan asked the others what they thought about using the money they had received for the previous night's work to buy some clothes and a blanket for Taelor.

Karl frowned. "Won't that draw a lot of attention to him?"

"Not if we divide up the purchases," Darrell said. "I'll get a hat."

"My tunics fit him fairly well," Kevin said. "I'll pick out a couple for him."

"And his waist is about as small as Theresa's. She could get a belt," Karl added, nodding. "I'll pick up a blanket."

"I'll get a cloak," Chris offered. "Steve, you get some socks."

Steve nodded.

"All that's left are some leggings, and Taelor can get those himself," Joan said. "And while we're shopping, I'll pick up the groceries we need."

After Theresa and Taelor finished the impromptu clinic, they all went over to the dry goods store. While they were shopping, Joan asked Karl if he was planning to make it to the next town that night.

"I don't think so. It's nearly noon now, and I don't want to push the horses that hard. They haven't had a day off in over a week."

"Well, do you want to find a good spot and set up camp for two nights then?"

"Sounds good to me," Karl said with a nod.

"Then we're going to need some more coffee. We go through a lot of it when we're camping."

Neither of them noticed the man who trailed along behind them, staying just within earshot.

By the time Joan finished stocking up on staples, the others had finished shopping and everything was stacked on the counter. The two gold coins covered all their purchases with enough left over for a couple of bags of rock candy.

As soon as they were out of town, Theresa insisted that Taelor climb in the back of the wagon and get some sleep. For once, he didn't argue. The healing clinics had drained him, and he fell asleep almost as soon as he lay down.

While Taelor slept, Karl pulled his horse to the side of the road to wait for Darrell. After Kevin's wagon rolled past, Karl signaled for Darrell to drop back a bit. Karl fell into place beside him and quietly told him about Rolan and the assassination squads.

"Well, I can't say it comes as a surprise," Darrell said. "I feel sure that Rolan's not the only one who's sent them out. Do you think we need to have three people stand guard and split the night into two shifts?"

"No, I don't think one extra person would make much difference whereas more sleep might. Also, if we change things now, Taelor's going to wonder why. He's paranoid enough as it is. I don't want to give him any reason to start wondering about us."

"You're right," Darrell agreed. "Okay. I'll tell Chris about the assassins this afternoon. Then I'll tell Steve while we're on guard duty tonight, and Chris can tell Kevin."

"Just do it quietly. We don't want Taelor to overhear us talking about it."

Darrell nodded, and then, a couple of minutes later, he said, "I think we need to start working out again – tonight."

Karl nodded and said, "Now's definitely not the time to get rusty. Maybe we'll have some time before dinner, and we definitely should have plenty of time tomorrow. Well, I'm going back up front with Joan before Taelor wakes up. You know, he sure was a big help with the clinics. We really lucked out there. He has a perfect cover. There's no way anyone in that town doubted that he was Theresa's assistant."

"He certainly did know what he was doing," Darrell said slowly. After a couple of minutes he added, "You do think he's legit, don't you? I mean … you don't think he's really one of the assassins, do you?"

Karl sighed and said, "That thought crossed my mind too, but I don't think so. If they know enough to target us, why not just kill us? Why go to all the trouble to plant someone on us?"

"I don't know, but those bounty hunters gave up a little too easily to suit me."

"Did you see Theresa's pendant? I think that had a lot to do with the way they backed off."

"Maybe, but Taelor did manage to get himself covered up with the rest of those blankets and tarps pretty well. For someone so close to death …"

"Yeah, but you can do a lot of stuff when you're life depends on it. Besides, if he was an assassin out to kill Kevin, he's had plenty of opportunities to do it."

"That's true, but he may not have any idea who Kevin is."

"I'm not following you. If he doesn't know who Kevin is, why would he be here?"

"What if it was just a ploy to get someone in with us so he'd have a good excuse to travel around and scope out the towns? The townspeople are pretty free and easy around us. It would be a good cover if you were looking for someone and didn't want to alarm the locals."

"But why here? It would make more sense if we were in Camden," Karl said.

Darrell shrugged and said, "I don't know. Of course, it's always possible that he's exactly who and what he says."

"Where's Xantha when you need him?" Karl frowned. Then he laughed and said, "Now I sound paranoid."

"Yeah, but just because you're paranoid doesn't mean that they aren't out to get you!" Darrell said with a grin. Then he got serious again. "We'll just keep our eyes open and our hands near our swords."

~ ~ ~ ~

They made camp that night beside a wide but shallow stream about a quarter mile from the road. On one side of the stream there was a small grassy clearing for the horses, and on the other side the forest was open enough for the wagons, their sleeping tarps, and a small cooking area. Between their campsite and the road was a huge tangle of bushes and shrubs. Someone on the road might be able to smell the smoke from their campfire, but they wouldn't be able to see it, and the only way to get from the road to their campsite was to come down the stream, just like they had.

By late afternoon, the horses were settled, camp was set up, wood had been gathered, and dinner was ready to go on the fire. Theresa offered to tend to dinner, and Taelor said he was going to look for herbs. That left the others with a bit of free time, so they worked out for a couple of hours while the stew simmered. Then, after dinner, everyone except Karl and Taelor headed off to bed. The last few days had been hectic and everyone was ready to take advantage of every minute of sleep they could get.

Karl and Taelor had not said more than a dozen words to each other since Karl had suggested that Taelor join the group, and Karl was hoping that guard duty would give him a chance to get to know Taelor a little better, if he could only figure out how to get him talking. At first, they talked about the weather and the horses, but those topics ran out pretty quickly, so they ended up sitting in silence.

Finally Taelor said, "You know, I envy you your type of life. Free to come and go as you please, no responsibilities, no ties, no worries, just taking life one day at a time."

"Well, it's not quite as worry free as you make it sound. I worry about where we're going to stay at night, how safe the girls are, where our next meal is coming from, and things like that. It just looks carefree," Karl answered.

"Maybe, but I like it. I hate feeling boxed in, trapped. That's the way I've felt for the past six years, ever since Rolan took over. I hate him almost as much as I loved his father."

"What happened to Rolan's father anyway? I never did know."

"Rolan told everyone that Tsareth passed away in his sleep, but the truth of the matter is Rolan killed him. Rolan demanded that Tsareth resign and pass the seat on to him. When Tsareth wouldn't do it, Rolan challenged him." Taelor took a deep breath and exhaled it in a long sigh. "That was a dark day for Brendolanth. I just wish one of Tsareth's other sons or daughters was strong enough to defeat Rolan."

Taelor put some more wood on the fire and watched the flames dance. After a while he said, "There might be one person who could defeat him. Tsareth had a daughter born after most of his other children were grown. She inherited his magic as well as his red hair. She looks more like Tsareth than Rolan does. I'm not sure that she and Rolan have ever even met. I know that they were never at the castle at the same time. She should be twenty-three, twenty-four by now. She probably hasn't even begun to train yet. I wonder where she is."

Taelor stared into the fire for a while as if it could answer his questions. "Rolan might have already had her killed, but if she's still alive, she might be able to defeat him one day." Taelor was talking to himself more than he was talking to Karl at this point. "Wish I knew where she was fostered. We were friends a long time ago, even though I was a slave." Taelor stood up, stretched, and said, "Think I'll go check on the horses."

Karl had a lot of questions, beginning with the name of the younger daughter, but he was afraid to show too much curiosity. He was trying to decide just how much he could ask when Taelor returned. "I didn't know that Tsareth had a daughter who had the gift for magic," Karl said. "From what I'd heard, Rolan was the only one of Tsareth's children to have inherited his magic."

"Several of Tsareth's children have the gift, but Rolan is the strongest so far. Tsareth was pretty sure that Landis was going to be more powerful than Rolan, but I don't imagine we'll ever know now. Tsareth isn't around to arrange an apprenticeship for her, and I can't see Rolan doing anything to help her. If she's even still alive," Taelor said quietly. He was afraid he might have already said too much.

They both became quiet, lost in their own thoughts for the remainder of their watch. At midnight, Taelor wished Karl a good night and headed for his bed in the back of the wagon. Karl woke Darrell and Steve and waited for them at the fire. As soon as they had a cup of hot coffee in their hands, Karl told them good night and headed off to his tent to join Joan.

Darrell waited about an hour to be sure that Taelor was asleep before he quietly told Steve about Rolan and the assassination squads. Then he chuckled and said, "Assassins, bounty hunters, slavers, bandits … I feel like we need a scorecard just to keep track of who's trying to kill us. It's almost funny."

"I know what you mean," Steve agreed, "but I'm not going to ask for credentials before I defend myself."

"I'll just be glad when we get to Glendymere's. At least we're going to stay put for a while. I feel so exposed traveling like this."

"Maybe so, but remember, we're hiding in our roles. Keep thinking of yourself as a minstrel. Don't even think of the other stuff. You never know who might be tuned in to your thoughts."

"I guess that's something we should sort of keep in mind, isn't it?" Darrell said quietly. "You, know, that's like the ultimate invasion of privacy."

"Yes, and one that we never had to worry about before we came here."

They spent the rest of their watch talking about plans for their time in Nandelia and before they knew it, their watch was over and it was time to wake Chris and Kevin.

After Chris checked on the horses and Kevin got a fresh pot of coffee going, they sat down next to the fire to wait for the coffee to perk. After Chris told Kevin about Rolan and the assassination squads, Kevin didn't say anything for a while, and Chris was afraid that the idea had spooked him.

"Look, don't worry about it," Chris said. "We knew this was going to happen. It's why all of us are so well armed and why we've spent so much time practicing. We'll handle whatever comes our way."

"No, it's not that. I was just trying to decide how much to tell you about something else," Kevin said slowly. "Do you remember the other morning when you woke me up and I jumped up like a madman? I told you that I'd had a nightmare? Well, Xantha had come into my dreams that night and told me several things, including the fact that Rolan had sent out two death squads. But from what Xantha said, we don't really need to be too concerned about them. They headed straight for Camden."

"That's good news. What else did he tell you?"

"Rolan isn't the only one who's sent out assassination squads. Quite a few death squads are out there, roaming around looking for Myron, and there are also a few protection squads looking for him, too."

"Great! Then all we need to do is find one of the protection squads, link up with them, and let them worry about the assassins. At least it proves Myron has some friends on the council. Right?"

"No, not really. According to Xantha, the sorcerers who sent out the protection squads are so sure that they can defeat Myron in a sanctioned challenge that they want to make sure he assumes his chair as soon as possible, and the squads that they sent out are charged with delivering Myron to Badec's castle in Camden immediately, with no side trips to Glendymere's. The ones who sent out assassination squads are a bit leery of challenging him, afraid of being defeated, so they want to kill him before he can get to the castle. So, no, I wouldn't say that any of this implies that Myron can look to anyone on the council for help."

"Oh. And Xantha told you all of this the other night? Why didn't you tell me?"

"For one thing, I wasn't positive that it wasn't just a dream. I mean, after all, I was asleep the whole time. But what Taelor said about Rolan backs up what Xantha told me, so I have to assume that the conversation really did take place, and that I didn't just dream it all up. And that's really scary."

"I have the strangest feeling that there's something you haven't told me. What is it?"

Kevin paused, trying to decide how much to tell Chris. Finally he shrugged and said, "I don't know if I should say anything about this or not, but according to Xantha, Glendymere isn't a human sorcerer."

"Well, in a way that makes sense. If he's as good as Kalen and Duane say he is, he would be on the council if he were human. So what is he? An elf?"

"Not exactly."

"Well??"

"Glendymere's a dragon."

"Whaaaaat?!?" Chris's eyes popped wide open, like white saucers with little black holes in the center. His jaw dropped and his face slowly drained of blood, turning a ghastly shade of white.

Kevin nearly laughed at the look on his face. "Shh! Don't wake the others."

Chris slowly closed his mouth, frowned, and stared straight through Kevin.

"I hadn't planned to tell anyone yet," Kevin said in a hushed tone, "and I probably shouldn't have mentioned it to you, but I sort of wanted someone else to know. Now be quiet!"

"Okay," Chris gasped. "I'll try. Did you say a dragon?"

Kevin nodded.

"Do you know if a dragon on Terah is the same type of thing we're thinking of?"

"Oh, yeah. It's what you're thinking of all right. Big, with lots of big sharp teeth. Looks a lot like a huge lizard with wings," Kevin sighed.

"How do you know?" Chris argued.

"Xantha showed me a mental image of Glendymere. His scales are golden by the way, and he has green eyes."

"Oh," Chris said slowly. Then he asked, "What do we do now?"

"We keep going," Kevin answered. "What other choice do we have? Besides, he's the one who's supposed to teach me how to defend myself, remember?"

"Are you going to warn the others?"

"I don't think I want to mention it yet. Let's wait a while. I'll tell everyone before we get there, but there's no need to worry anyone else with the news right now."

"Why not?"

"From what Xantha said, we won't be living in his cave, just nearby. I'll have to go to him everyday, but they probably won't see much of him."

"Oh. So you're the only one who'll have to deal with the fact that he's a dragon." Chris nodded his head, relieved.

"Not exactly," Kevin said hesitantly. "One other person will have to be around Glendymere everyday. I have to have an assistant. Xantha told me that, too."

"And you're telling me about all of this now." Chris paused and looked deep into the fire. "Why do I get the feeling that I'm going to be that assistant?"

"I'd like for you to be, but you don't have to," Kevin said quietly. "I could ask one of the others."

Chris groaned, shook his head, and said, "I didn't say that I wouldn't do it, but how about letting me think about it a bit and sort of get used to the idea? We'll talk about it some more later."

"Okay, but for now, let's just keep this between us."

"Sure. Fine. Who would I tell anyway? A dragon you say? I wonder if he can fly." Chris said as he drifted off into his own thoughts about dragons and magic.

Kevin smiled to himself. He felt good about his decision to ask Chris to be his assistant. He had the feeling that Chris would end up viewing life with a dragon as just one more adventure.

Then he put thoughts of Glendymere and magic out of his head. They were too distracting, and at least one of them needed to concentrate on keeping an eye on things around the campsite.

They spent the last hour of their watch gathering firewood. Around daybreak, Joan and Theresa got up and sent Kevin and Chris back to bed for a few hours. The evening before, the two women had decided to give the guys a chance to sleep in for a while so that they could get some things done without interruptions. Joan hung several pots of water over the fire, and by the time the men woke up, both Theresa and Joan had had their baths and had started on the laundry. By lunch, everyone had had a bath and the laundry was hanging on tree limbs and bushes to dry.

Theresa and Taelor headed out to gather herbs, and the others spent the afternoon practicing with their weapons and sparring with each other. While Joan prepared dinner, the guys brushed down the horses and checked their legs and feet. Shortly after dinner, everyone except Kevin and Chris went to their tents and quickly fell into an exhausted sleep.

Chapter 24

Trouble in the Night

Kevin and Chris were so tired that evening that they were afraid they'd fall asleep if they didn't stay on their feet, so they walked the perimeter of the camp, loop after loop. Shortly before midnight, Kevin realized that Chris had jumped at every sound all evening, so he asked Chris if anything was wrong.

"I've had a bad feeling all day, like there's someone out there, watching us. And it's getting stronger," Chris said, glancing back over his shoulder.

"Do you think it's tied in to the stuff we talked about last night?"

"No, I don't think so," Chris said. "I don't know how to describe it, but I've had this feeling before, several times."

"And did something happen when you had this feeling?"

Chris nodded, and glanced around nervously. "Oh, yes. The first time I had it, I was about sixteen, and I got beat up by some punk who wanted my jacket. The next time I was around eighteen and on my way to my date's apartment. I got mugged. The third time I felt like this, I didn't hang around to see what was going to happen. I walked into the nearest store to wait for it to pass. So what happens? A couple of guys burst into the store behind me, waving guns around and yelling for all of us to empty our pockets. That was about four years ago."

"Okay," Kevin said slowly. "Have you ever been jumped, mugged, or robbed when you didn't have that feeling?"

"No. I always thought of it as New York radar, 'picking up vibes from the street' type of thing. But out here … no New York … no streets … just that feeling closing in on me. Man, it's getting strong."

"That's good enough for me. Let's get the others. Now. But quietly," Kevin said.

Chris ran down to Karl's tent to wake him and Joan up while Kevin headed over to Darrell's tent to wake Darrell and Steve. Within a couple of minutes they were all on their feet and armed. Then Joan woke Theresa and told her that they thought there was someone in the woods. Theresa said that she'd wake Taelor and get some woundwort ready, just in case.

When Theresa got to her wagon and drew back the canvas flap, she saw that the floor of the wagon was empty. Taelor was nowhere to be seen and his bedroll was gone. But before she could react to his absence, she heard swords clanging. She whirled around just in time to see the startled faces of the five intruders as they realized that instead of sleeping victims, the people at the campsite were awake and ready for a fight. A couple of them actually looked panicked, like they hadn't expected to meet armed resistance and weren't quite sure what to do about it. Even though the light from the campfire was fairly dim, Theresa had the distinct feeling that she'd seen some of those faces before, she just wasn't sure where. A sudden yelp as someone got cut shook Theresa out of her trance and sent her scrambling into the wagon for her herbs and bandages. By the time she got everything she needed and climbed back out of the wagon, the battle was over. The invaders had turned tail and were running back towards the stream.

Then she heard Karl yell, "Catch one of 'em! We need to find out what's going on!"

Darrell dropped his sword and sprinted after the intruders, tackling the last straggler before he made it to the water. Darrell pinned him to the ground and waited for Karl and Chris to get there. Karl grabbed the man's sword while Chris placed the point of his sword at the man's throat. Darrell slowly got up off of the man and dragged him to his feet while Chris kept his sword ready at the man's chest. As soon as Darrell took a couple of steps back from the man, Karl handed Darrell the man's sword. They could hear the other invaders sloshing through the water as they made their way upstream towards the road.

"Well, looks like they've gone and left you behind, doesn't it?" Darrell said.

"Turn around. Head over there. Towards the fire. Now!" Chris said as he poked the man with his sword. Then Chris took up a position behind him and held the point of his sword at the man's back.

Once they were all back around the fire, Joan whispered to Karl that she had seen the man before, in the dry goods store in Billows.

Karl took a long look at him and asked, "Why did you attack us?"

"For your money," the man growled.

"Money? What money?" Kevin asked

"I saw the gold coins you gave the shopkeeper. We figured there had to be more where that came from," the man said with a snarl. "Why should the likes of you gypsies have gold coins when us hard-working farmers never have any? It isn't right! You probably stole it off somebody yourselves!"

"I don't believe this," Theresa said in exasperation. "We had those coins because that's what your town director gave us for holding the healing clinic, you idiot!"

"What were you planning to do?" Steve asked. "Kill us and go through our pockets?"

"Well, we hadn't really talked about it, but yeah, I guess so," the man said defiantly.

"Just how did you plan to get past my pendant?" Theresa asked.

"We figured those things aren't half as dangerous as people say, especially once you're dead," the man said with a sneer. "I figured I'd give it to my wife."

"You're crazy! Stark raving mad!" Joan said in disgust. "That thing would have killed you in a heartbeat. When you get back to your wife, tell her she has a fool for a husband."

"I hope you guys are better farmers than you are thieves," Karl said with a laugh as he put his arm around Joan.

"Who would have thought a band of singing gypsies could fight?" the man said in a loud voice, almost yelling. "You should have been easy to take!"

"Go, get out of here, before we come to our senses and kill you," Darrell said as he pointed towards the river with the man's sword.

The man looked at Darrell like he had just grown horns or something. He couldn't figure out what Darrell was planning. He didn't know whether to make a break for it, or just stand there and wait for them to kill him. Finally he took a few hesitant steps towards the stream. When no one came after him, he broke into a run and was going so fast by the time he reached the stream that he slipped and hit the water with a loud splash and a curse. He jumped up and half ran, half stumbled up the stream until finally the sounds of his footsteps splashing through the water faded away.

Theresa suddenly noticed that Steve's tunic sleeve was soaked in blood.

"Steve, you're hurt. Can you get your tunic off? Here, let me help you," she said as she led him to the back of her wagon. As Steve sat on the tailgate, Theresa lifted his tunic over his head and eased it off the injured arm.

"It looks a lot worse than it is," Steve said as Theresa started to wash his arm. "I think most of the blood belongs to someone else. I did get cut, but only a scratch."

"You're right. There's no way all that blood came from this cut," Theresa said as she turned to look closely at the others to see if any of them had been injured.

"I think it's from one of the bandits," Steve said. "I got in a few solid hits before they started running. I might not have been so aggressive if I'd known they were just a bunch of petty thieves, but I thought we were up against bounty hunters or assassins."

"They may have been just a bunch of thieves, but they'd have killed us just the same if they'd had the chance," Chris said. "Dead is dead, whether we're killed by part-time bandits or full-time assassins."

"Oh, I'm not feeling guilty, Chris. They opened the door to violence when they attacked us. They can't complain if more violence came back through that door than they were expecting," Steve replied. He felt a warmth seeping into his arm, and after a moment he felt a tingling sensation. "What's going on, Theresa?" Steve asked as he looked down at his arm. Theresa's hand was about an inch from his arm, directly over the wound.

"I'm closing the wound," she answered. "I've finished cleaning it and I want it to close before I put the bandage on."

"I had no idea," Steve said slowly. "Have you always been able to do that?"

"No. My grandmother could put her hand over a cut and the bleeding would slow down, but I'd never see a wound close like this until we came to Terah," Theresa explained. "Drusilla said that my healing powers became stronger when I passed through the Gate."

"Just like our athletic ability," Darrell said with a nod.

"I hate to change the subject here, but Taelor's missing," Theresa said as she finished bandaging Steve's arm. "He left before the attack. The wagon was empty when I ran over here to get some woundwort and bandages."

"Think I'll go check on the horses," Karl said as he started off towards the grassy clearing on the other side of the stream.

"Hold up a moment. Let me get my sword and I'll go with you. We don't know for sure that all the bandits are gone," Darrell said. He still had the bandit's sword in his hand. He tossed it down and grabbed his sword up off the ground where he had dropped it when he started running after the thieves. Then he ran towards the stream to catch up with Karl.

"Why would Taelor leave?" Chris asked.

"Maybe he heard us talking about waking up the others and figured that the bounty hunters had tracked him here," Kevin said.

"And if those guys had been bounty hunters, that would have been his best move, for us as well as for him" Steve said. "Of course, we won't really know why he left until we talk to him."

A few minutes later, they heard Darrell and Karl come back across the stream.

"One of the spare horses is gone," Karl said. He turned to Chris and asked, "When was the last time you checked the horses?"

"Actually, I was the last one to check on the horses," Kevin said. "And I checked them about forty-five minutes before we woke you up. I counted just to be sure none of them had managed to get outside the ropes and wander off. They were all there. And I walked around the perimeter too, to make sure the ropes were okay."

Karl nodded, "He probably left as soon as you started waking us up. At least he was careful. He tied the rope back so none of the other horses could take off." Then Karl thought about it for a moment. "If he had headed towards the road, someone would have heard him in the stream."

"Not if he waited until the fighting started," Chris said. "An army could have ridden through the water then and none of us would have heard it."

"True, but if he thought they were bounty hunters, he wouldn't have wanted to ride past them and take a chance that one of them had hung back, waiting for him to make a run for it," Darrell said. "I bet he went away from the road, farther back into the woods."

"Tomorrow morning I'll take a look around and see if I can find any horse tracks leading out," Karl said with a sigh. He wasn't at all sure that Taelor had left because of the bandits. Karl was wondering if he had taken off to try to find Landis. "It's just a few minutes past 1:00. Why don't we try to get a little sleep? We've got a long day ahead of us tomorrow. Steve, why don't you lie down for a while? I'll stand watch with Darrell."

"No, I'm fine, really. Anyway, it wasn't my sword arm that got cut. You go ahead and get some sleep. We'll wake you around 3:30. Joan, are you going to stand watch with Karl?" Steve asked.

Joan nodded. "Well, if you're sure you're okay, we're going to bed. Come on Karl." She took Karl's hand and led him off towards their tent.

"Guess we'll turn in, too, but wake us up if you feel like something's going on. I'd rather lose sleep than wake up dead," Chris said as he and Kevin headed off towards their tent

"I'm going to stay up with you two for a while. I'll put on a fresh pot of coffee," Theresa said. Then she walked off towards the fire circle, mumbling, "The least he could have done was say good-bye."

Chapter 25

Sunday, May 13

As the door to Rolan's office swung open, the messenger could see the sorcerer pacing furiously while two officers stood in the background. Rolan's face was contorted with anger, and fury flashed in his cold, dark eyes.

"Well? What is it?" Rolan roared. "What news do you bring me today?"

"I'm sorry, sir, but Captain Garen has had no luck finding anyone who knows anything about where Myron was fostered, or who he's apprenticed with," the messenger said nervously. "The Captain's sent his men out to eavesdrop in taverns and he's offered coins for information, but no one seems to know anything."

"So he sent a messenger to tell me that he's failed, huh?" Rolan began pacing again. Then he stopped, spun around towards the messenger, clasped his hands behind his back, and snarled. "Well, I have a message for you to take back to Captain Garen. Tell him that he is not to return until he brings me Myron, dead or alive. If Myron takes his chair next April, I will assume that Captain Garen and all of his men are dead, including you. That would be the one and only acceptable reason for failure," Rolan paced a few more steps, then turned back to the messenger and sneered. "But tell Captain Garen that my guards will make sure his wife and children remain here, safely awaiting his return, as will the families of the rest of his squad. And tell him to rest assured that I'll find someone to take in his wife and children in the event that he doesn't return, and if that someone isn't interested in bedding the wife, I'm sure that the daughter will be suitable. Do you understand?"

The messenger had gone pale with the cold cruelty of Rolan's words. "Yes, sir, and I will hasten to deliver your message to Captain Garen. If there is nothing else, I will be on my way now."

"Good, see that you leave for Captain Garen's camp immediately. Captain Yardner will escort you out of town and see you on your way," Rolan said.

"Yes, sir," Captain Yardner said as he ushered the young messenger out of the room.

Rolan turned to Sergeant Jermain, who was charged with overseeing the castle slaves. "Sergeant, any word on the escaped slave yet?"

"N … no … no, sir," Sergeant Jermain stammered. Then he took a deep breath and plunged ahead. "The bounty hunters have reported that they've lost his trail. They followed him into the Badlands, and they're sure that he was wounded by one of their arrows, but they haven't found his body so they don't know whether he's dead or alive."

"So? What are they doing about it?" Rolan prompted.

"There was a band of traveling minstrels in the area at the time, but the bounty hunters checked out both of their wagons and found no sign of Taelor. Now they think that he might have run into the minstrels later and persuaded the sister who was traveling with them to help him. They're still looking, but so far, nothing."

"Am I to be surrounded by incompetence forever?!" Rolan bellowed. "I want that slave found, and I want him found now! Do you understand?"

"Y … y … yes, sir," Sergeant Jermain said in a timid voice.

"Then get out there and find him! If you had been doing your job, he never would have escaped in the first place!" Rolan walked over behind his desk and sat down. "And bring him to me alive. I want the pleasure of watching the insolent bastard die. Now go!" Rolan slammed his fist down on his desk. "And do not return until you have him in hand!"

Sergeant Jermain bowed and backed out of the room. Once he shut the office door, he wiped the sweat off his face and set off to pack his belongings. He had no intention of ever returning to Trendon, with or without Taelor. He was going to set his path for the quickest route out of Brendolanth.

Rolan drummed his fingers on his desk. He hated loose ends, and he saw both Myron and Taelor as loose ends, things that needed to be taken care of immediately, before his plans began to unravel. He had mapped out the path to his goal years ago, and now that he was nearing the end, nothing was going to get in his way. Myron had to die before he had a chance to take the Master's Chair. That was all there was to it.

As for Taelor, Rolan wasn't positive just how much of a threat he really was. Rolan was certain that he'd never mentioned the Key to the Gate Between the Worlds around the slave, after all, he'd never even said the words out loud. And there was no way Taelor would be able to figure out that Rolan was behind Badec's coma. He had never mentioned anything about that anywhere near the castle. But he wasn't sure how much other stuff Taelor might have overheard, and Taelor definitely knew that Rolan was responsible for Tsareth's death. The slave was there. He saw it happen.

Rolan's hold over Taelor had ended with the old slave woman's death. Taelor might talk now, if he could find someone who would listen, someone who might believe him. That's why Rolan wanted the slave brought back alive. He had to find out if Taelor had talked, and if so, to whom. But as soon as he had the answer to those questions, Taelor was a dead man.

While Rolan was sitting there, thinking, another loose end came to mind: his half-sister, Landis. He was eighteen years old when she was born, and as far as he could remember, he'd never even seen her, but according to castle gossip, Tsareth had thought that her magic was strong enough that one day she'd be more powerful than Rolan. He had even heard that Tsareth had planned to hand over his seat to her. He wondered if his father had ever told her that. If so, that was just one more reason to find her now and destroy her while he still could, before she developed her powers. Landis would be almost twenty-four years old now. Time was running out.

Rolan didn't have any idea who the girl's mother had been, or where she had been fostered. It was a shame that his father's second had been killed along with his father. That had been an accident. He hadn't meant to kill the old man until he'd had a chance to question him, but sometimes he didn't know his own strength.

Rolan got up and opened his office door. The young page who was standing beside it stepped forward. "Tell Captain Yardner I want to see him when he gets back."

The page bowed and set off for the stables. Another page stepped up beside the door to take care of the next errand.

When Captain Yardner entered the office, Rolan said, "You were here as a castle guard when my father was alive. Who would my father have talked to other than his second? Was there anyone else around who might have known the family secrets?"

Captain Yardner thought for a moment, and then said, "The old kitchen slave who died about six months ago was a frequent guest in your father's quarters. He probably discussed a lot of things with her."

"My father and a slave? Are you sure?" Rolan found the idea repulsive. "I knew that he must have found companionship after my mother's death, but a slave?"

"She was a bit more than a slave, sir. She was the mother of his youngest daughter," Captain Yardner said.

Rolan laughed. "I figured the girl was a bastard, but the daughter of a slave? How delightful! She's nothing then."

"She isn't exactly a bastard, sir. While it's true that Tsareth never married the child's mother, the only reason was that they didn't know for sure that her first husband was dead. Tsareth publicly recognized the child and proclaimed her as his own, and he treated her mother as his wife. That's why Taelor was never treated as a slave. He only worked as a slave after Tsareth's untimely death," Captain Yardner said.

Rolan glared at Captain Yardner for his last remark. "Is there anyone else who might know the identity of her foster parents? A nurse maybe? Or the sister of the chapel? What about the man who was governor?"

"I really don't think so. There was no nurse. Landis's mother took care of her while she was an infant. As for Sister Candice, she's too young. She came when Sister Yano passed on, maybe two years before you came. I can think of no reason why Tsareth would have told Sister Candice anything. And as for the governor, you arranged for the man to have a rather fatal accident a couple of months after your father's death, remember? So if he knew anything, the knowledge died with him."

"Then there is no one left who knows the whereabouts of the child?"

"As far as I know, no one. The only other possibility that I can think of is Taelor, but I doubt if either his mother or Tsareth entrusted the young man with that knowledge. I'm not sure he even knows that Landis is his half-sister. He was only about three years old when she was born."

"I want that slave found. I want to see him dead, but I want to question him first. And I want that girl found, and found within the year." Rolan's voice was quiet and chilling. After a minute, he looked at Captain Yardner and hissed, "Send word to the bounty hunters that I'm doubling the reward, but he must be delivered to me alive, and tell them that I expect news of their progress within a month."

"As you wish, sir," Captain Yardner said. Then he bowed and left the room. As soon as the door closed behind him, he wiped his face with his hand. He always felt that he needed a bath whenever he left Rolan's office.

Chapter 26

Evelyne of Abernon

The Tellurians pushed hard for the next few days, and on a Tuesday near the middle of May, they crossed the Teran equivalent of the North Platte River, which Kalen had told them formed the boundary between Brendolanth and Nandelia, but there was nothing to indicate that they had gone from one province to another.

Thursday they crossed another large river, and their road curved to follow it, heading more west than south. Around mid-afternoon they found a secluded cove and set up camp for a two-night stay. That was the first time they had camped since they had been attacked and everyone was a little apprehensive, but after the first night passed peacefully, they relaxed a bit and enjoyed their second night.

According to the route that had been marked on their map, they were to continue west, following the river, for a couple of days until they came to a southbound road at a "T" junction in the middle of a town called Abernon.

Late Monday afternoon they rolled into Abernon. It was by far the largest town they had come across. Shops, stores, and taverns lined both sides of their road for several blocks. The blocks were formed by narrow crossroads. On the southern side of town, the crossroads were lined with houses, but on the northern side, they led to what looked like a large open meadow, which served as a buffer between the town and the river.

There were three inns in Abernon, the largest of which was located at one corner of the "T" junction. A combination restaurant and tavern was located at the other corner, and directly opposite the main southbound road was the largest Chapel of Light that they had come across. It was as large as a small hospital on Earth.

Karl stopped in front of the clinic as he considered which innkeeper he should approach for a night's lodging. As the others pulled up behind him, a sister came out of the chapel and walked towards them. Her auburn hair was streaked with silver and she was a little plump around the middle. Her tan face looked like she had spent a lot of time in the sun and her hands looked like they had seen a lot of years of hard work, but there was a youthful twinkle in her eyes.

"Is there a Sister Theresa traveling with you?" she asked Karl.

He nodded and looked over at Theresa, who had pulled her wagon up beside him.

"I'm Theresa, Sister."

"Good! Your assistant came through several days ago and told me to expect you. Here, let me show you to the barn," she said as she turned to walk down the drive beside the chapel.

"Uh, Sister, you do realize that I'm part of a fairly large group, don't you? We like to stay together," Theresa said hesitantly.

The sister nodded. "We have rooms set up for all of you and there's plenty of space in the barn. Come along now," the sister said as she resumed walking down the drive.

Karl looked at Theresa questioningly. Theresa shrugged, then nodded, and drove her wagon down the drive. As soon as Theresa pulled into the barn, a young man stepped out of the shadows to help her down. Once Theresa was safely on the ground, he climbed up and drove the wagon to the end of the barn so that the others could enter.

"I'm Sister Evelyne, the resident," Evelyne said as she took Theresa's hand. "If you'll come with me, I'll introduce you to my aides and staff." She leaned towards Theresa and whispered, "Taelor left a note for you."

Then she turned to the others and said, "There's a pasture out behind the barn. Why don't you put your horses out there? I hate to see them cooped up in tiny stalls in nice weather. You can set out some feed buckets for them if you like. Patrik will help you. Just let him know if you need anything. As soon as you've seen to your wagons and horses, come on in. We'll have some refreshments ready." After everyone had dismounted, Evelyne stepped over towards Karl and very quietly told him, "The horse that Taelor borrowed is in the pasture."

While the rest of the Tellurians were busy with the horses, Evelyne led Theresa on a quick tour of the chapel and introduced her to the staff. Then she and Theresa went to the kitchen to prepare the refreshments.

While they worked, Evelyne told Theresa that she had received a message from Drusilla asking her to be on the lookout for Theresa. "She asked me to help you replenish your stock of herbs and to answer any questions that may have come up along the way. I got the impression that you haven't been a sister for very long and that you're not from anywhere around here."

"You're right on both counts. I've only been a sister for about two months now," Theresa answered. "You said that you had a note for me from Taelor?"

"It's in my office. I'll get it for you later," Evelyne said as she continued slicing bread. "It's funny that Drusilla didn't mention him. She did say you'd be traveling with a band of minstrels, but not one word about an assistant."

Theresa took a deep breath. Drusilla had told her that sisters would never betray each other, and she sincerely hoped that Dru had been right. "Drusilla didn't know about Taelor. We found him passed out along the side of the road about two weeks ago. He had an arrow wound in his shoulder and was weak from loss of blood. I treated him and he traveled with us for a while."

"Why did he say he was your assistant?"

Theresa sighed. "He's an escaped slave. He needed to fit in with the rest of us, to have a reason to be traveling with us, so there wouldn't be any questions when we were in town. He had been trained in a chapel, so we pretended that he was my assistant. It worked out quite well. We held a healing clinic about a week after he joined us in a small town that had been hit with a flu outbreak, and he was really good. I hated to see him go."

Evelyne nodded. "I figured it might be something like that. He arrived late one night, and was gone before daybreak the next morning. None of my staff met him, and I didn't mention his being here to any of them, so you don't need to worry about that." Evelyne continued preparing the platter of cheeses, meats, and breads for the Tellurians. "You know, Theresa, you can tell me or ask me anything you want to. What is said between sisters stays between sisters."

Before Theresa could answer, Joan walked through the back door into the small kitchen. She felt sure she'd walked into the middle of a conversation. She glanced at Theresa and said, "Hope I'm not interrupting anything."

"No, not at all," Evelyne said as she wiped her hands. "I was just asking Theresa if she was running low on any of her herbs, but we can get to that later. Will the others be coming in soon?"

Theresa carried the platter that they had been fixing over to the table. Then she began to set out some plates and forks.

"The guys will be along in just a minute. They're carrying feed buckets out to the pasture," Joan answered as she stepped over to the table to help Theresa. "I love that pasture! The grass is so full and green, and the scenery's beautiful! It's almost a shame to waste it on the horses."

"It is nice, but I wouldn't want to live any closer to the river," Evelyne said. "It floods every spring. I've seen it up as far as halfway through the pasture, but that's rare. We had a nice surge go through here about two weeks ago, but the water didn't make it over the top of the banks. So far this spring's been fairly calm."

Joan heard the clomping sounds of boots on the back porch, so she walked over to the back door to open it for the guys. Evelyne poured some hot water into a big basin, tossed in a bar of soap, and grabbed a couple of large towels. She set the basin and towels on the counter on the other side of the room from where she and Theresa were setting out some cookies and tarts.

"Wash up, and then have a seat at the table. Theresa, would you get some mugs out of the cupboard over there?" Evelyne said, pointing to a cabinet over the washbasin.

Theresa found the mugs, set them out, and then filled a pitcher with milk while the others sat down around the table. As soon as everyone was seated, Evelyne placed the tray of sweets and the coffee pot on the table and told them to serve themselves. Then she poured herself a cup of coffee and sat down in an empty chair at the end of the table.

"Have you had any problems since you left Drisden?" Evelyne asked.

Darrell grinned at Theresa and said, "Not really. We had a small problem with some bounty hunters who wanted to search our wagons, but Theresa set them straight."

"And then we had a small band of thieves attack us around midnight one night, but we had them on the run within five minutes," Chris said with a touch of bravado.

Evelyne looked at Theresa. "Taelor failed to mention any of this. What happened?"

"It was nothing really. The bounty hunters stopped us and wanted to search through our things. Taelor was asleep in the back of my wagon and I didn't want him disturbed, so I refused to allow the search. They didn't really argue about it. And Taelor didn't know about the bandit attack because he left before it happened," Theresa explained.

"Yeah, the bounty hunters didn't argue, but one of them tossed the flap up on the back of her wagon as she started to drive past them. You should have seen her come off that wagon seat!" Darrell said with a chuckle.

"You did mark them, didn't you?" Evelyne asked.

Theresa could feel a blush creep over her face. She glared at Darrell and said, "No, it wasn't necessary. They apologized and rode off."

"You should have burned them anyway. I would have," Evelyne said. "What did they do when they saw Taelor in the back of your wagon?"

"They didn't see him. I had covered him with a blanket and put a sleeping tarp over the blanket."

"Good," Evelyne said. "Now what was that about bandits?"

"Chris saved the day there," Kevin answered. "He had a feeling that we were being watched, so we woke up the others. The bandits took off as soon as they realized that we were armed and ready for them."

"But why did they attack you?" Evelyne asked.

"One of them had seen us use two gold coins to buy a few things in town and figured we had more," Joan said with a shrug. "Theresa had held a healing clinic the night before and the town director had paid her with the coins. It was just one of those things."

"They'd have killed all of you if they'd had the chance," Evelyne said. "I hope you burned them."

Theresa shook her head no. "When Joan woke me up, my first thought was to get some woundwort and bandages ready in case any of us got hurt. By the time I got out of the wagon, it was over. The whole thing didn't last more than a couple of minutes. I only saw the one that Darrell captured."

"You captured one?" Evelyne asked.

"We wanted to know who had attacked us, so Darrell tackled one and we questioned him," Steve explained. "When we found out that they were just a group of bungling thieves, we told him to go home and stay there."

"You let him go?!" Evelyne asked, surprised. "Why?"

"We couldn't just kill him in cold blood, and we didn't want to have to watch him until we could turn him over to the authorities," Karl explained. "If we had tried to hold him, his friends would probably have felt compelled to try to rescue him, and if they had attacked us again, we wouldn't have had quite so easy a time of it. They would have been ready for us. At the time it just seemed like the best option."

"I see," Evelyne said with a sigh. Then she shook her head. "You certainly showed more charity than anyone else would have. Oh, well, I guess all's well that ends well."

After everyone had finished with the refreshments, Evelyne said, "If you like, I could get one of my aides to show you around town, or if you'd like to rest up a bit, I'll be glad to show you to your rooms."

"Would it be all right for us to work out a little behind the barn? Maybe do a little sparring?" Darrell asked.

Evelyne laughed and said, "Considering your knack for running into trouble, that might not be a bad idea."

Joan groaned. "I don't suppose there's any way I could get a hot bath afterwards, is there?"

Evelyne smiled and said, "I think that can be arranged."

~ ~ ~ ~

While the others were practicing hand-to-hand combat, Theresa and Evelyne went out to the shed that housed Evelyne's indoor herb garden and workroom. The room was dark and cool, and smelled of rich moist dirt. A large workbench sat directly under a skylight and there were storage cabinets along all four walls. Between the workbench and the cabinets, there were rows and rows of herb beds.

Evelyne motioned Theresa to one of the lab-type stools while she took a seat on another one. "I know you're probably running low on several herbs, but that can be taken care of later. I'll bring one of my aides in here tonight and she and I can get everything you need together in no time at all. I thought we'd just talk for a while," Evelyne said. "Tell me about your clinics. How did they go?"

Theresa told Evelyne about the healing clinics, about the herbs that she had used to treat various illnesses, and about the exhaustion she frequently saw on the faces of the women. Evelyne nodded and said that she saw a lot of that, too. She laughed over Theresa's tea breaks and said that she might try it with a few of her patients. Before either of them realized it, they had been chatting for over an hour and it was getting close to dinnertime.

"I'm going to have to go to the kitchen soon and check on dinner," Evelyne said. "Is there anything you want to ask me before we join the others?"

Theresa said that she did have one question that she needed to ask. "How does this pendant work? What do I have to do to get it to protect me?"

"All you have to do is focus on the person's forehead, picture the flame burning them, and the fire in the opal takes care of the rest."

"What if one of my friends steps in between us to protect me? Will the opal burn them too?"

"No, it will only burn the one you're focused on," Evelyne said. "Of course, if someone grabs you or attacks you, your fear will activate the opal, and it will strike out on its own, so you might want to warn your friends not to grab you."

Theresa nodded. "I did. And Drusilla also told me to tell them not to try to remove the opal if anything happens to me because it would burst into flame."

Evelyne nodded.

"Well, what if I'm unconscious and someone tries to take it. Won't I get burned, too?" Theresa asked.

"No. The opal would burst into flame, but you wouldn't be hurt," Evelyne said, shaking her head. "Dragon's fire can not burn anyone it protects."

"Dragon's fire?"

Evelyne frowned. "Yes, Glendymere's flame is in each of our opals. Haven't you ever heard the story of the opals?"

Theresa shook her head.

"You must be from a really isolated area," Evelyne said with a frown. Then she settled back on her stool and said, "A long time ago, about five hundred years, the sisters who traveled around Terah were often attacked for their herbs, potions, and healing gems. Some were even sold as slaves. Sister Drixanne thought someone should do something to protect them, so she went to see Glendymere, the grandfather of the dragons. He took her into his deepest cavern, the room where he keeps his jewels. They searched through the gems he had collected on Terah and the ones he had brought with him from the land of his birth, looking for just the right stones. Finally they came across his opal collection. All of the opals had a glimmer of fire in them, but the flame in the black opals danced as Glendymere approached, so he carried them up to the surface."

"Our opals?" Theresa asked.

Evelyne nodded. "Glendymere had some oil lamps stored in another one of his caverns and he told Drixanne to choose one. She selected a brass-based lamp with three oil bowls, one on top of the other. Then Glendymere carried Drixanne, the opals, and the lamp back to her home in Camden. When they landed behind the chapel, he laid the opals out in a circle, took a deep breath, and blew dragon's flame into the stones. Then he breathed on the old oil lamp to light its wick. Glendymere said that although the dragon's flame in the opals would lie dormant until awakened, the opals would protect the sisters as long as his flame burned in the lamp."

"How did she wake up the flame in the opals?"

"By holding the opal in the flame of the lamp until the spark inside the opal began to grow."

"Ouch!" Theresa rubbed her fingertips in sympathy.

Evelyne laughed. "Glendymere picked out an opal for Drixanne, suspended it in the flame, and then handed it to her. She mounted it in the center of her healer's pendant and slipped it around her neck. As she stroked the opal, Glendymere covered her in dragon's flame. According to the legend, Drixanne said that his fire breath felt cleansing and refreshing, that there was no sensation of burning at all, and all of the sisters who have been entrusted with the care of the lamp since then have said that the flame in the lamp feels cool on their hands when they place an opal in it."

"Because they have an opal on?"

"Yes, their opals protect them from the flame."

"Would your opal protect me? Or just you?"

"My opal won't burn you as long as you have your pendant on, but it won't protect you either. An opal identifies with the first person who wears it after the flame is awakened, and the dragon's flame continues to burn in that opal until it's removed, either by the person who's wearing it or by another sister after the person dies."

"What happens then?"

"The flame becomes dormant again and the opal is returned to the head of the Sisterhood."

"Who decides who the head of the Sisterhood is?"

"Drixanne was the first, and she chose her successor before she died. Since then, each head chooses her successor as soon as she assumes the responsibility for the lamp. The lamp is kept at the Chapel of Light in Timera Valley, just as it was five hundred years ago."

"Has anyone ever tried to steal the lamp?" Theresa asked.

"No, why would they? The only ones who are safe around it are the sisters. The flame inside the lamp would destroy anyone else."

"Who's the head now?"

"Brena. And Drusilla has agreed to take over after Brena."

"Will Drusilla have to leave Drisden and move to Camden then?"

"Yes, but she's from that area, so it'll be like going home."

"How many opals did Glendymere give Drixanne?" Theresa asked. It stuck her as quite a coincidence that the dragon of the legend should have the same name as the tutor that had been arranged for Kevin.

"Six hundred."

"So there can only be six hundred sisters at any given time?"

"Most of the time there are around five hundred practicing sisters. A sister can retire if she chooses, but she must return her pendant so that the opal can go to someone who can take her place," Evelyne explained.

"So not everyone who wants to be a sister can train to be one, there has to be an opening. Right?" Theresa asked.

"There are usually enough openings for those who have healing hands, but not everyone who wants to be a sister has the power to heal. Sometimes a woman can train for years and never develop healing hands, but she can learn which herbs to use for which illnesses, how to gather and prepare them, how to care for wounds, and with the help of the moonstone, how to assist with childbirth. Neither of the two aides I have now has shown any real potential for becoming a sister. As my aides, they can live in the chapel and work here as long as they like, but they won't be inducted into the Sisterhood and they won't ever wear one of the pendants."

"I had no idea that it was such an exclusive group. I almost feel guilty for taking one of the pendants," Theresa said.

"No, don't feel guilty. You have the gift. If you hadn't gone to Drusilla, one of us would have found you. We always search out the true healers. There aren't so many who are born with the gift that we can afford to overlook any."

A knock on the door startled both of them. They had been so engrossed in their conversation that they had completely forgotten about the time. When Evelyne answered the door, one of her aides asked if it would be all right to serve dinner in half an hour.

"That's fine. We're about done for now. I'll be in the kitchen in just a couple of minutes to help," Evelyne answered.

Then she shut the door once again and turned to Theresa. "Anything else?"

Theresa shook her head. Then she said, "I need to run out to my wagon before it gets dark and make out a list of the herbs that I need. If I go right now, I should have enough time to do it before dinner."

Evelyne nodded and said, "Right after dinner, I'll make my rounds of the patients in the chapel. Would you like to join me?"

"I'd love to, "Theresa answered.

~ ~ ~ ~

During dinner, the chapel staff questioned the Tellurians about life on the road. Since most of the staff was young, Darrell and Chris took turns telling stories about some of the towns they'd visited, the people they'd met, and their adventures on the road. By the time dinner was over, the young men on Evelyne's staff were envious, and most of the young women had crushes on one or both of them.

After the dishes had been collected, one of the aides turned to Joan and asked, "Would you like your bath drawn now, or would you like to wait a little while?"

Joan smiled and said, "I'd like to take a bath as soon as possible."

The aide nodded and said, "I'll draw it for you as soon as I leave here. Would lavender be all right in the bath water, with bayberry candles for aroma?"

Joan sighed with pleasure and nodded. Then she turned to Evelyne and said, "You do realize that you live in the lap of luxury here, don't you?"

Evelyne laughed. "I try to pamper myself at least twice a week with a long, hot, aromatic bath. Theresa, would you like a hot bath prepared for you after we check on the patients?"

Theresa's smile was answer enough.

The older aide laughed and said that she'd prepare the bath in Theresa's room in a couple of hours. Joan headed for her bedroom to get ready for her bath while the men adjourned to the back porch with mugs of scog. Evelyne and Theresa went to Evelyne's office.

When they reached the office, Evelyne suddenly remembered the note from Taelor. She took it out of a locked drawer in her desk and handed it to Theresa.

Theresa,

Please express my gratitude to those who travel with you, and know that I will always be in your debt. Not only did you save my life, but you also treated me as your equal. For that I am even more grateful.

I hated to leave in the dead of night without saying thank you and good-bye, but I knew that if I explained my intentions you would try to talk me out of it. There is something I must do, someone I must find. I owe it to Tsareth.

I hope I caused no inconvenience by borrowing one of the spare horses, but once I made my decision, I was eager to begin.

Please do not try to find me, for I fear that would endanger you as well as me.

Forever yours,
Taelor

Theresa folded the note back up and stuck it in one of her skirt pockets with a sigh. "I hope to run into him again one day. He really was a good assistant. Oh well. At least he's free to make his own choices now, and that's the important thing."

They left the office and began checking on the various patients in the chapel. Two hours later, when they were done, Evelyne took Theresa's list and headed out to the herb shed, while Theresa made her way to her room and the hot bath that was waiting for her.

~ ~ ~ ~

After breakfast the next morning, Evelyne sent one of the young men on her staff to help bring the horses in from the pasture. Then she told another to collect the herbs they had prepared for Theresa the previous night and take them out to her wagon so that she could get them stored. After everyone left the kitchen, Evelyne packed some sandwiches, fruit, and sweet snacks in a basket and carried it out to the barn.

An hour later the Tellurians rode out of Abernon on the southbound road. When they stopped for lunch, Theresa showed them Taelor's note.

"I was afraid of that," Karl said after he read the note. "He's probably going to get himself killed, but I have to admit, I admire him for trying."

"For trying what?" Joan asked. "What's going on?"

"From what Taelor told me, Tsareth had a younger daughter named Landis. She's only twenty-four years old, but her father said that she was going to be more powerful than Rolan. I think Taelor's planning to try to find her and see if he can find a way to help her defeat Rolan, provided Rolan hasn't already killed her."

"I wish him luck," Darrell said in a wistful tone. "If he helps her defeat Rolan, he'll probably have a lot of influence with her once she's on the council. We might have a real chance to make an impact on slavery then."

"There were a lot of 'if's and 'when's in there that haven't happened yet. It's a nice thought, but it's no more than that right now, and I think the best thing we can do for the present is to forget about it," Steve said.

"You're right," Karl said. "We have our own mission and we don't need to get sidetracked at this point. He'll either succeed or he won't, but right now there's nothing we can do to help him. Come on, let's mount up and get back on the road."

~ ~ ~ ~

They arrived at the next town late that afternoon, in plenty of time to get settled before their performance. Fortunately, there didn't seem to be any medical emergencies around, so Theresa was able to join Joan in their room right after the show. Once the door was shut and locked, Theresa told Joan the legend about the black opal in her pendant.

Joan listened to the entire story before she said anything. Then she said quietly, "You don't think there's any way ... surely not after five hundred years."

"No, but the same thought hit me. It's probably just a coincidence. I imagine Myron's tutor's parents just named him after the hero of the legend. I'm sure our Glendymere couldn't be the same one. That was five hundred years ago. Dragons don't live that long, do they?"

"I have no idea. I don't know anything at all about dragons. In all the stories I've heard, they were always out to kill people, not to protect them," Joan said thoughtfully.

"Surely Myron's tutor isn't a dragon. If he were, Kalen would have warned us, don't you think?"

"If he thought there was anything to warn us about. He wasn't the one who told us about dwarves going berserk or elves translocating. Duane and Palladin did."

"Okay, but dragons are different. Surely he would have mentioned that," Theresa insisted, but her voice didn't sound quite as convinced as her words implied.

"It's just a coincidence. It's got to be. We're being silly. No one would have sent us out to live with a dragon without warning us! Forget it!" Joan said emphatically.

"Okay, but do we tell the guys the legend, or should we just leave it for now?" Theresa asked.

"Leave it. If we jumped to the conclusion that the Glendymere in the legend is our Glendymere, imagine what Kevin will do! No, I think the best thing we can do is just keep this to ourselves until after we've met Glendymere and seen that he's as human as we are," Joan said with an air of finality. Then she quietly added, "I hope."

Chapter 27

Blalick Arrives

Friday morning the Tellurians were heading west across an empty prairie when the clouds that had lain on top of the mountains for days suddenly lifted. In less than an hour, there wasn't a cloud in the sky and they had their first clear view of the snow covered peaks.

Kalen had marked a pass between two of the mountains and told them to wait there for a guide, and up until that morning, the task of reaching that pass had been foremost in everyone's thoughts. Now the pass was literally in sight, and although everyone was relieved to be nearing the end of the first part of their journey, no one had any idea what to expect when they got there, much less what the next eight months might bring. The idea of being introduced to the world of magic was exciting on one hand and scary on the other. And like always, now that there was no one around to ask, everyone had loads of questions.

For the next couple of days the Tellurians traveled in relative silence, each lost in his or her own thoughts about the future. Joan mentally made lists of everything they needed to do to prepare for the trip to Camden in the dead of winter while Karl's thoughts centered on food and shelter for the next eight months. Theresa planned the workroom she was going to ask Karl to build and speculated about which herbs might grow wild in the area. Steve reflected on everything they had seen, learned, and experienced as he organized the journal he wanted to write. Darrell designed an athletic field in his mind and tailored a workout a program for everyone except Theresa and Kevin. Chris alternated between excitement and dismay over the prospect of being Kevin's assistant, and Kevin, who had no idea what he was headed into, just wanted to get there and get on with it.

The closer they got to the mountains, the more tension they felt. They finally rode into Sheridan around lunchtime on the last Sunday in May. It was a small town located at the base of the mountain range, and according to their map, it was the last town travelers would see for days, if not for weeks. Only one road went through Sheridan and when it left town it headed straight up the mountain. Common sense demanded that they stay in town Sunday night and start up the mountain early Monday morning, even though the last thing any of them wanted to do was to put on a performance.

Sheridan wasn't the smallest town that they'd performed in, but it was close. However, since so few people passed through Sheridan, a minstrel show was a really big deal and everyone for miles around came to hear them sing. Almost as soon as the Tellurians started performing they were caught up in the crowd's enthusiasm, and before they knew it, they had performed for a little over two hours and had enjoyed every minute of it.

Monday morning was gray and drizzly when they rode out of Sheridan, and although the drizzle ended around lunchtime, the clouds stayed with them until mid-afternoon.

When they reached the pass, they found an established campsite. There were a couple of three-sided sheds for storing wagons or carriages, and four larger sheds with fireplaces and wooden floors for people to stay in. A short ways from the campsite were several large corrals for horses, mules, and oxen. The area between the corrals and the sheds had been cleared, but a thick forest of pines surrounded the campsite on the other three sides.

The shelters were a welcome sight, especially with six inches of snow on the ground. They decided to use one of the sheds for sleeping and a second for cooking and storage, leaving the other two vacant in case anyone else happened to arrive at the pass that night. Since they had no idea how long they might be at the campsite or where they were headed when they left, they unloaded most of the food, cooking gear, and their clothes. By the time they unpacked, stored the wagons, and tended to the horses, it was evening.

Dinner was unusually quiet. After they had finished eating and were sitting around the fire, Joan asked, "How long do we stay here? I mean, how long do we wait for our guide?"

"I don't know," Karl answered with a shrug. "I guess we stay as long as it takes."

"I understand what you're saying, but what if no one shows up? How long do we wait?" Joan persisted.

"For right now we should probably plan to wait until either our food supply gives out or our supply of hay for the horses runs out. Then we'll have to decide what to do next. But don't forget, Glendymere's expecting us. If we don't show up soon, I'm sure he'll send someone out to check on things," Karl said. Then he turned towards Steve and asked, "Don't you think so?"

Steve nodded. "Let's give it a few days before we get concerned. We made pretty good time. They may not be expecting us to be here yet."

"I just wish we had some idea whom we're supposed to meet," Darrell said. "They should have told us something about our guide, something to identify him."

"Yeah, like a password," Chris agreed, "or a physical description. Something."

"They might not have known who would be meeting us," Steve said.

"Well, I don't like the idea of coming this far and then just going off with a complete stranger," Darrell said with a frown. "After all, there are a lot of people out there looking for us."

"You know, Kalen left out a lot when he was telling us about this journey," Karl said as he was staring into the fire. "Sort of makes you wonder what else he didn't tell us."

Karl didn't see the look that passed between Theresa and Joan, or the slight blush that crept up Chris's cheeks, but Kevin did.

"I don't know how to say this, but there is another bit of information that Kalen neglected to mention. Xantha told me in a dream soon after Taelor joined us." Kevin paused and took a deep breath. "Glendymere's not human." Once more Kevin paused, this time to look around. Chris was busy staring into the fire. Theresa looked at Kevin expectantly, and Joan's mouth had quietly formed an "o". Everyone else simply looked puzzled.

"Well, what is he then, an elf? That wouldn't surprise me at all," Darrell said off-handedly. "What's the big deal?"

"He's not an elf. In fact, he isn't any type of humanoid," Kevin said. "He's a dragon."

"A what?!" Darrell exclaimed. "A dragon?"

"Yes, but before you get too concerned, Xantha said that we wouldn't actually be staying with Glendymere, just in the same general area. Most of you won't have to be around him," Kevin said slowly, letting his words sink in.

"Most of us?" Steve asked. "What do you mean?"

"Well, Xantha also told me that I'd need an assistant. I've asked Chris if he would be willing to help me while I'm training with Glendymere and he's agreed to do it. But the rest of you will have very little contact with Glendymere, if any, according to Xantha."

"Chris, you've known that Glendymere is a dragon?" Karl asked. Chris just nodded. "Why didn't either one of you tell us?"

"That was my decision Karl, not Chris's," Kevin said quickly. "To be honest, I didn't see any reason to tell you. It was definitely a distracting thought and I didn't think any of us needed any more distractions than we already had. And there was nothing to be done about it anyway. Dragon or not, Glendymere's the sorcerer who has been selected to tutor me, so we had to come."

"I found out that Glendymere is a dragon while we were in Abernon," Theresa said slowly. "Or at least I found out that about five hundred years ago there was a dragon named Glendymere who came to the aid of the Sisterhood." Theresa's fingers absent-mindedly caressed her medallion. "It's his dragon's breath that burns in this opal."

"And Theresa told me about Glendymere the next night," Joan said. "We discussed bringing it up, but we really didn't think that the Glendymere of the legend could possibly by the same Glendymere as Myron's tutor, that was over five hundred years ago, but even if it was, what difference would it make? We still had to go."

"So Steve, Darrell, and I were the only ones who didn't know? Is there anything else that needs to be mentioned at this point?" Karl snapped. He was irritated with Kevin for not telling him, but he was angrier with his wife.

"Look, don't blame them. They probably figured that I'd freak out and call the whole thing off if I found out about Glendymere. I nearly did when Xantha told me," Kevin said quickly. "At first I thought it was just a nightmare, but then Chris told me what Taelor had said about the assassination squads. Xantha had warned me about them in the same dream, so I figured the part about Glendymere had to be true, too."

Darrell's face was a couple of shades lighter than normal. His mouth was slack and although his eyes were wide open, they had gone glassy and weren't focused. He looked like he was in a trance.

"It makes sense," Steve said with a slow nod. "If Glendymere is the best sorcerer on Terah, he would be the Master Sorcerer if he were human. Of course, that doesn't rule out an elf, but Kalen knew that the idea of an elf wouldn't bother us after being around Duane for so long, so he would have told us that. Therefore, Glendymere would have to be something that might spook us for Kalen to fail to mention it. It's like the slavery issue. If Xantha hadn't told Kevin about it, I don't much think Kalen would have brought it up. He didn't want to take any chances that we might refuse to go."

"You're probably right," Karl said, slowly nodding his head. Then he looked at Kevin and said, "But I still don't understand why you didn't tell us."

"Like I said, I found it unsettling and it hasn't really been out of my mind since Xantha told me. I had planned to tell you once we reached the pass, but I really didn't see any reason to mention it earlier."

"A ... a ... dr ... dr ... dragon?" Darrell stammered. Then he whispered towards Kevin, "Like in the stories? Breathing fire? Lots of big, sharp teeth? With wings?"

"Yeah, a dragon. In fact, his scales are golden, and he has a white goatee and green eyes. He's not really bad looking, if you can get past the teeth, and the smoke coming out of his nostrils."

"How do you know what he looks like?" Karl asked.

"I asked Xantha what he looked like, so he showed me one of his memories. I asked him if he could show it to all of you, but he said he couldn't."

"Why not?" Karl asked.

"He said he can communicate telepathically with all of you, but he'd have to establish a mind link to share his memories, and I doubt if any of you really want him to do that."

"Why not?" Joan asked.

"Because once a mind link is established, it's there for life. He would know every thought you ever have. Absolutely nothing would be private," Kevin explained. "He established a mind link with me before I left Terah and he has been in my mind ever since, but until that day at Kalen's, I thought he was just a figment of my imagination. The mind link must be pretty powerful to span the gap between the worlds."

"You're right," Karl said. "I don't want anyone to take up residence in my head."

"A dragon?" Darrell whispered.

"Come on, Darrell. Shake if off. Kalen and the others would not have gone to all the trouble of sending us here to meet him if we weren't going to survive the introduction. You'll get used to the idea. I did," Chris said, grinning. He took Darrell's arm and helped him to his feet. Then he put an arm around Darrell's shoulder and led him outside. "Let's go check on the horses before we head for bed. Come on."

~ ~ ~ ~

Kevin and Chris were on watch the next morning as day began to break. While Kevin put on a fresh pot of coffee, Chris went down to the corral to check on the horses. He stood at the gate and counted to be sure that none of them had wandered off, and when he turned around to head back, he stumbled over what looked like a slab of rock about two feet long. The rock seemed to be connected to a small tree trunk, but the trunk got larger instead of smaller as it went up. As Chris's gaze wandered up the strange tree trunk, he was astounded to realize that it was a leg and that the rock was a foot. Chris quickly backed up against the gate, and when he found that he could go no farther, he stopped and stared open-mouthed at the largest man he'd ever seen. Chris's head only came up to the middle of the man's thigh. He wasn't sure how tall the giant was, but he was more than twice as tall as Chris.

The man appeared human, just magnified. He wore black boots, black leggings, and a dark gray, long-sleeve tunic. Around his waist he wore a maroon sash with green geometric designs embroidered on it, and attached to the sash was a scabbard and sword. The sword hung from the man's waist to the middle of his calf, a good five feet at least. His bronze face was surrounded by a thick mane of black hair that tumbled down to his shoulders and was held out of his face by a headband that matched his sash. Directly under the headband were black eyebrows so bushy that they seemed to extend from one side of his head to the other, and peering out from under the canopy of hair were two eyes the color of jade. His long handlebar mustache blended into the full beard, which hung halfway down his massive, muscular chest. Peeking out from behind the thick beard was a large white opal that glittered with every color of the rainbow.

When the man opened his mouth to speak, Chris cringed, expecting a thunderous roar, but the man's voice was quite soft and melodic. "I have come in search of one named Ke-vin-O-Reil-ly. Do you know of such a man?"

"I think I do. Hold on and I'll get him for you," Chris answered as he started to edge his way around the giant.

"Hold on to what, sir?" the giant asked in a quizzical voice.

"Uh, nothing. Sorry. What I meant was for you to wait right here while I go get him," Chris said as he skirted the giant and started backing away toward the shed.

"Very good, sir. I will wait here," the giant said with a nod.

Chris turned and sprinted to the shed where Kevin was. "Kevin, you're not going to believe this. There's a giant out there. He asked for Kevin O'Reilly, only he said it like it was one word. It's got to be you. He must be our guide. Man, you are not going to believe this guy. He is huge!" Chris was talking so fast that his words ran together.

"Slow down. What are you talking about?" Kevin asked as he started towards Chris.

"Come here!" Chris grabbed Kevin's arm and hurried him over to the door. "Look, down towards the corral. Do you see him?"

Kevin looked towards the corral and then unconsciously took a step back when he saw the giant standing beside the pathway. "You say he asked for me? Are you sure?"

"I think so. Is your last name O'Reilly? I can't remember. It sounded like he said Kevin O'Reilly, but like I said, he said it like it was all one word, so I'm not really sure," Chris said without taking a breath.

"Okay," Kevin said hesitantly. "Here goes nothing. Let's go see what he wants. At least he asked for Kevin, not Myron." Kevin took a deep breath and walked slowly and deliberately out of the shed and down the path towards the giant, with Chris a half step behind him.

"Hello. My name is Kevin O'Reilly. I understand you were asking for me?" Kevin said, with only a small tremor in his voice.

"My name is Blalick, sir. Glendymere requested that I meet you here and escort you to the accommodations that have been prepared for you," Blalick said in a very precise but pleasant tone. "I understand that there are six humans accompanying you. Is this correct, sir?"

"Yes, it is. The others are still sleeping. When will you want to leave?"

"At your convenience, sir."

"We'll need to eat and pack up. Would a couple of hours be all right?"

"Very good, sir. I will return in a couple of hours," Blalick said. Then he bowed his head slightly towards Kevin, turned, and disappeared into the woods.

"How could anything that big disappear so quickly?" Chris whispered as he scanned the forest searching for a trace of the giant. "Did you get the feeling that you have a very large, very formal, butler?"

"Almost the gentleman's gentleman. Seemed a little weird," Kevin whispered.

"Which part? The very large, or the very formal? Come on. Let's wake the others. We've got a lot to do. If we'd known he was going to get here this morning we never would have unloaded everything," Chris groaned as he set off for the shed where the others were sleeping while Kevin headed back to the fire to start breakfast.

When Blalick returned after breakfast, he stood in the road beside the campsite, patiently waiting for the Tellurians to get loaded up. When Kevin introduced the rest of the group, Blalick was quite polite to everyone, but once everyone was mounted and ready to go, he looked to Kevin for permission to head out. It was obvious that he considered Kevin to be in charge.

The road down the other side of the mountain ran along a rocky ledge that was barely wide enough for the wagons. They had to ease their way around snowfields near the top, and then around watersheds as they worked their way down the side of the mountain. There were no trees to provide an illusion of safety, only some small scrub bushes and a few hardy wildflowers. The only consolation to the barren path was the panoramic view of the surrounding mountains and the slender evergreen valley that snaked its way to the north.

It took them most of the day to reach the foot of the mountain and the rocky terrain didn't give way to forest until they were almost on the valley floor. The main road appeared to continue west, heading up the side of the next mountain, but Blalick led them down a smaller road that turned off to the right. By the time they had traveled a few miles up the valley road, they decided to call it a day and set up camp for the night.

While Joan and Theresa prepared dinner, Karl and Darrell tethered the horses, and Steve, Kevin, and Chris unloaded the sleeping blankets and tarps. By the time their campsite was set up, dinner was cooking, and everyone gathered around the fire for coffee. Kevin was the first to notice that Blalick had disappeared again.

"I wonder where he's gone," Kevin said quietly.

"More to the point, I wonder when he'll return," Theresa whispered. "He makes me nervous."

"Probably because of his size. I really don't think we're in any danger from him," Steve assured her.

"I'm not scared, just a bit uneasy," Theresa explained. "I feel like he's watching us, judging us. It just makes me uncomfortable."

"I know what you mean. I get that feeling too," Joan agreed.

"I imagine he's supposed to report his observations and opinions to Glendymere," Darrell said. "If I had a group of people I didn't know coming to stay with me for eight months, I'd try to find out all I could about them, too. Don't worry about it. After all, we passed muster with Kalen and Duane, didn't we?"

"I don't know if we did or not," Steve said with a chuckle. "I got the feeling that they just took what Paul sent them and hoped for the best."

"Well, I'd like to ask Blalick a few questions," Karl said. "Kevin, maybe you should ask him to join us for dinner, or maybe he could join us for coffee afterwards. It wouldn't hurt if we had some idea of what we're heading into."

"I'll ask, but that doesn't mean he'll accept," Kevin replied.

"I imagine he will if you ask," Joan said. "He seems to look to you for instructions and orders, which is only right, all things considered."

Kevin spotted Blalick walking up the road toward their campsite. "Shh, here he comes. I'll go ask him to join us," Kevin said to no one in particular as he stood up and walked down the road to meet Blalick.

"Why don't you join us for dinner, Blalick?" Kevin asked.

"Thank you, but I have already eaten, sir. I came to ask what time you wanted to get underway tomorrow morning."

"I suppose we'll plan to leave about an hour after daybreak if that's all right with you."

"Very good, sir. Should I come by before daybreak tomorrow morning to see if there is anything in particular that you need before we begin?"

"No, that won't be necessary. Most of us won't be up until around daybreak. I know I won't. I was on third watch last night. Tonight I'll be on first."

"What is this 'watch'?"

"We divide the night into three segments, from nine to midnight, then from midnight to three, and then from three until daybreak. Joan and Karl take one watch, Chris and I take another, and Steve, Darrell, and Theresa take the third. That way someone is awake and alert in camp all night long," Kevin explained.

"Are you doing this as a safety precaution?"

Kevin nodded.

"Well, that is not really necessary here, sir," Blalick said with a smile. "If Glendymere did not want you to travel through this valley, this road would not appear to you. You would see only a tangle of undergrowth and impassable marshes. Also, the nocturnal animals have been informed of your presence and will watch over your sleep. No harm will come to you here. All of you may sleep through the night if you wish."

"Thank you," Kevin said. "You said something about coming for us in the morning. Where will you be?"

"I have my own campsite. I require a larger clearing to lie down."

"Well, why don't you at least join us for coffee after dinner? We'd like to get to know you a little better."

"As you wish, sir. I will return in an hour," Blalick said. Then he bowed his head towards Kevin, turned, and walked back down the road.

When Kevin returned to the fire, Joan handed him a bowl of stew. "I don't guess you had any luck getting him to join us, did you?"

"Actually, I did. He said that he would return in an hour," Kevin answered as he took his bowl. "He's already eaten so I guess he was giving us time to eat and get cleaned up. He's sleeping down the road a ways, in a larger clearing." While he was eating, Kevin told them what Blalick had said about the valley.

"That's nice to know, and I probably trust it about ninety-five percent, but I think we'll stand watch for the other five percent," Darrell said as he looked around at the others for signs of agreement. No one disagreed.

~ ~ ~ ~

Blalick joined them just as they finished washing up the dishes. Karl asked him how much farther they had to travel to reach Glendymere's canyon.

Blalick hesitated for a moment before he spoke. "I think the answer to your question is two more days. Our destination is not Willow Canyon, but a small valley nearby."

"Is that valley going to be our home for the next eight months?" Joan asked.

"I was not told how long you would live there, but yes, we have prepared ample rooms to accommodate all of you," Blalick answered.

"What do you mean, 'ample rooms'?" Karl asked. "Did you build a house large enough for all of us, or individual shelters?"

"We did not build any houses. We did build a fence around a pasture for your horses for when the weather is nice, but the rooms we set up for you are underground."

"You mean we're going to be living in caves?" Theresa asked apprehensively.

"Yes, the rooms are caverns, but they are well-ventilated, dry, and have a pleasant temperature year round," Blalick answered. "I think you will find them quite comfortable."

"Blalick, you said 'we' a minute ago. Who helped you?" Chris asked.

"My wife and children, of course," Blalick answered with a frown.

"Oh, do you live in the area then?" Steve asked.

"I am sorry. I thought you knew who I am. My family attends Glendymere."

"What do you mean, 'attends'?" Chris asked.

Blalick's eyebrows knitted together like he was working out a puzzle. "When someone needs to speak with Glendymere, he contacts me and, if Glendymere agrees, I make the arrangements," he explained. "Of course, a few of Glendymere's friends can contact him directly, but one would need a phoenix to do that. And the only way to get into Willow Canyon without my assistance is to fly, but I would not recommend that unless Glendymere had issued an invitation."

"Oh, then you work for Glendymere?" Theresa asked.

"What do you mean, 'work for'?" Blalick asked.

"You know, like he pays you to take care of all of this for him," Theresa explained.

"No, I most certainly do not work for pay. It is my honor to serve someone as venerable and august as Glendymere, the foremost dragon on Terah." Blalick's chest seemed to get a little bit bigger as he talked. "My father served Glendymere as did his father before him, and on back for hundreds of years. When my son, Macin, is ready to assume the responsibility, I will pass it on to him, as he will to his son, and so on until the end of time."

"Do you only have the one son?" Joan asked.

"Only one son, but I also have a daughter, Sari," Blalick answered slowly.

"What will she do? Stay with your son and help him?" Joan asked.

"No." Blalick's frown deepened. "She will marry into a different family of giants and join her husband's family in caring for one of the other dragons. My wife's family attends the silver dragon, Saradelia. I met her when I accompanied Glendymere to Saradelia's home, and when we left, Ashni came home with me." Blalick slowly looked around at the Tellurians and then he asked in a rather skeptical voice, "How is it that you do not know that giants attend the dragons? I can understand that if you are from far away you might not recognize my name, but this is the custom throughout Terah. Where exactly are you from?"

"There were no dragons near the place where we lived. It's a place called Omaha. Perhaps you've heard of it?" Joan asked in an effort to waylay Blalick's suspicions.

"No, I have never heard of this Omaha, but there is at least one dragon in every province on Terah. How is that you do not know?" Blalick was becoming increasingly uneasy.

"Blalick," Darrell said calmly, "didn't you say that you and your family had prepared for us to stay as Glendymere's guests? And that he asked you to meet us?"

Blalick stared at Darrell for a couple of seconds and then let his gaze wander over the others as if he were trying to find the answer to a riddle. Then, all of a sudden, Blalick's eyes popped wide open and he stared at Kevin open-mouthed, as if he were really looking at him for the first time. "Myron," Blalick whispered and his cheeks went from a deep bronze to a bright red almost in the time it took him to say the word. "I am sorry, sir. I did not know. Of course, that explains everything. Welcome." Blalick continued to stare at Kevin.

No one knew what to say, so no one spoke. Finally after a few minutes, Kevin said, "Thank you, Blalick. But I'm sure you'll understand if I ask you to continue to call me Kevin."

"As you wish, sir. I must say, sir, you do resemble your mother. Had I looked at you more carefully, I would have known immediately." Blalick finally broke his eyes away from Kevin and turned to address the rest of the Tellurians. "And now I understand why you use a rotating watch schedule, and why you might hesitate to trust the forest to protect you, but all of you may sleep tonight. I will stand watch myself. I do not really need to sleep more than a few hours a week, and I am well-rested at the moment. If you do not mind, I will just go get my things," Blalick said as he stood up.

"Really, that's not necessary. We're used to standing watch. I sort of enjoy it. It gives me some time to just sit and talk with my wife," Karl said. "Don't worry about it, we'll be fine."

"Sir," Blalick said directly to Kevin again, "if anything were to happen to you while you were in my charge, I would never be able to face Glendymere again." Then Blalick turned towards the others and said, "You may stand watch if you wish, but whether you do or not, I assure you, I will." Blalick bowed, turned back towards the road, and disappeared into the night.

"Well, what do you think? Do we trust him? I don't like the idea that he's figured out what's going on," Darrell said quietly.

"I don't like it either, but I don't think we have any choice but to trust him. After all, he must be from Glendymere. He knew my last name, and I haven't told anyone on Terah my last name. Supposedly, at least from what Xantha told me, only Glendymere, Xantha, and Paul knew all of the details. If the bad guys have gotten hold of that much information, we're all dead anyway," Kevin said with a shrug. "So what do you want to do about standing watch? Yes or no?"

After a few minutes discussion, they decided that they were not quite ready to hand over the responsibility for their safety to anyone else, so they chose to continue to stand watch at least until they got to the valley that Blalick had told them about.

Blalick returned less than an hour later, sat down near the sleeping tarps, and settled there for the night.

~ ~ ~ ~

Wednesday Blalick led the Tellurians north through the narrow valley to a small box canyon where the road seemed to come to a dead end. When Karl questioned Blalick about it, he just smiled and told Karl that the way would become clear in the morning. After dinner, Blalick once again settled down near the sleeping tarps to guard the campsite during the night.

Shortly after daybreak Thursday morning, Karl was wandering around checking on the horses when he saw what looked like a crevice in the rock wall on the western side of the canyon. He hadn't noticed it the night before. When he returned to the campsite he mentioned it to Blalick and asked if they were going to go through it.

Blalick smiled and said, "Yes, our road does indeed go through the crevice."

"I'm surprised that I didn't notice it last night. I'm usually more observant than that."

"You could not have seen it last night. The entrance was hidden by large boulders."

"What happened to them?"

"I moved them after dark. I did not want to take the chance that anyone could observe the order in which I removed them. If one were to remove them in the wrong order, one would be crushed," Blalick said quietly. "That crevice leads to a mountain pass, and from the pass, a trail leads directly into the valley where you will be staying. I really do not think that there is anyone following us, but I decided that it might be best to play it safe. Sorry if it seems that I have deceived you, but I felt it necessary."

"Blalick, never, ever apologize for protecting our backs," Karl said.

~ ~ ~ ~

As soon as all of the Tellurians had passed through the entrance to the crevice, Blalick replaced the boulders to once again hide the path. The climb through the rocky crevice to the rim of the gorge was difficult at best. There were several stretches where the wagons had only a couple of inches to spare, and the rocky terrain was so rough on the horses that they had to stop frequently to let them rest. They didn't get to the rim until well after lunchtime. Once they reached the top, they could see back into the box canyon, which was now to their east, but a dense forest obstructed their view to the west.

Blalick headed into the forest and motioned for them to follow. Karl could not see any sign of a road or a pathway and he was a little concerned that the wagons might not make it through the woods, but Blalick seemed to know exactly how much clearance was needed. Around mid-afternoon, they emerged onto a ledge overlooking a lovely valley that led to the west.

The valley was a couple of miles long and about a half-mile wide, and was framed by steep mountainsides covered in thick forests. A winding stream tumbled over boulders as it ran through a meadow of grasses and wildflowers on the north side of the valley and then seemed to disappear into the mountain near the western end. In the forest on the southern side of the valley, apple trees bloomed among the hardy evergreens and aspens.

Before he led them down the path into the valley, Blalick turned to the Tellurians and said, "Welcome to Rainbow Valley. This will be your home for the next few months."

Joan frowned. "I didn't notice a valley by that name on our maps."

"I do not know if anyone else calls it Rainbow Valley, but that is the name my mother used."

"Is there any particular reason why she gave it that name?"

Blalick nodded. "There is a waterfall almost directly beneath us. When the late afternoon sun hits the spray just right, it casts a rainbow over the falls. I am sure that you will see it often while you are here."

Then he turned back towards the forest and led them down the side of the mountain into the valley.

Chapter 28

Rainbow Valley

By the time the Tellurians reached the valley floor, the sun was beginning to sink behind the mountains. They rode slowly through the middle of the valley, between the fenced-in pasture and the woods. When they reached the other end of the valley, Blalick led them through a narrow strip of woods and into a large dark hole in the mountain.

The entrance was at least ten feet wide and probably twice as high. As soon as they entered the mouth of the cave, they lost the faint rays of sunlight that were lingering over the valley, and just as Karl reached the point where he could no longer see anything at all, he heard Blalick call out for all of them to stop where they were.

A couple of minutes later, Blalick appeared in front of the Tellurians in a ball of light, carrying some sticks that looked a lot like Lacrosse sticks. They had long handles and mesh pockets at the top, but instead of balls, the pockets held glowstones stored in black pouches. Blalick handed one to each of the Tellurians, and as they removed the glowstones from their pouches, the limestone inside the cave caught the light and reflected it, adding bits of color and dispelling the gloom.

The floor of the cave was hard dry clay, and the footsteps of the horses echoed as they continued down the tunnel. After about a hundred feet, a smaller passage veered off to the right.

Blalick turned to Kevin, and said, "I thought you might want to get the horses settled before we go on to the living quarters. We have fixed a temporary stable in a room at the end of this hall."

"That passage looks sort of small. Will the wagons make it through?" Kevin asked.

Blalick pointed to a large opening in the wall opposite the small passage "We have cleared that room out for storing the wagons." Then he turned towards Karl and said, "I will take you down to the stable area, and while you are taking care of your horses, I will return to help Theresa and Kevin get the wagons parked and their horses unhitched." Blalick looked back at Kevin to see if the plan met with his approval. When Kevin nodded, Blalick led the others down the passage on the right.

The narrow corridor led to a large chamber with a ceiling at least fifty feet high. Black boxes were attached to the side walls at five foot intervals, and as Blalick opened a clasp on each of the boxes, the sides swung down exposing the glowstone housed inside. After all the boxes had been opened, the room appeared as light as a bright sunny day.

On the left-hand side of the chamber were two alcoves. Bales of hay and barrels of oats had been stacked in the larger one, and the smaller one had been made into a tack room. Along the back wall there were twelve large box stalls, each with its own gate, feed basket, and water trough. All of the water troughs were connected and were fed by a natural stream of fresh water that had been diverted so that it flowed through the troughs and then emptied back into the stream. There was a long hitching post in the middle of the chamber, with plenty of room on each side for horses.

As the Tellurians dismounted, Blalick opened the gates on the stalls and then he left to go help Theresa and Kevin store their wagons. While the others began unsaddling their horses, Karl tethered his and followed Blalick back to the main hall so that he could get the spare team that was tied behind Kevin's wagon.

The wagon room was about twenty feet deep and extended several feet on each side of the opening. There were two black boxes mounted inside the room, one on each side of the wide doorway, and when Blalick unclasped the lids, the effect was the same as turning on two spotlights. Blalick guided Theresa as she backed her wagon into the room. Then he helped Kevin maneuver his wagon so that he could back it into the room beside Theresa's. Once the two wagons were parked and the brakes were set, Blalick and Kevin unhitched the teams and the three of them led the wagon horses to the stable.

When all of the horses were settled for the night, Blalick fastened the black boxes back around the glowstones, but after he finished, the room was not quite dark. Glowstone boxes had been fastened near the top of the walls and on some of the stalactites, creating a soft glow that was about the same as a clear moonlit night.

After they left the stable area, Blalick led them down the main passageway, once again by torchlight. They snaked around limestone columns for about the length of a football field, and then the passageway opened into a huge chamber. Blalick hung his torch in one of the holders attached to the wall near the doorway, stored the glowstone back in its pouch, and motioned for the Tellurians to do the same. Directly in front of them, an entrance hall separated a large sitting room on the left from the dining room and kitchen on the right. Smells of homemade bread mingled with the smells of stew and fresh strawberries.

To their right was a large table with four chairs on each side and one at each end. Seven places had been set with plates, bowls, mugs, and flatware. There were two candlesticks on the table, but instead of candles, they held tiny glowstone cases. Above the center of the table, there was a stalactite which had glowstones attached to it, giving it the appearance of a chandelier. The rug covering the dining room floor looked like it had been woven with variegated yarn using deep, rich, earth tones.

Beyond the dining room, there was a "U" shaped kitchen. Along the left-hand wall, there was a stack of wood, a small opening that led into a pantry, a table, and a wood stove. Continuing around the "U", along the back wall, there was a large sink. Water ran into the sink from a pipe anchored to the wall above it, and then drained into a pipe that went through the floor below it. Next to the sink, there was a second table, and two large metal buckets with lids. Beside the two buckets, coming up the right-hand wall, there was a third table, and a large cupboard with two sets of double doors.

A woman who was a couple of feet shorter than Blalick was bending over the stove, stirring the stew. Although everything in the kitchen was full-size for humans, the picture she made standing there was comparable to an adult in a child's play kitchen. She had on a light brown dress similar to those worn by Indian maidens in western movies, and her thick black hair fell in one long braid down the middle of her back. The sash at her waist highlighted her slim figure and was just like the one Blalick wore, but instead of a sword, she wore a long dagger at her side. She was as dark as her husband, but she was willowy where he was sturdy. Her features were soft and friendly, and her light green eyes sparkled when she smiled.

Blalick moved to his wife's side and put his arm around her possessively. "I would like for all of you to meet my wife, Ashni," he said with a deep smile.

Ashni welcomed them to Rainbow Valley and asked them if they would like to have a mug of scog in the sitting room while she put the finishing touches on dinner. Joan and Theresa opted to stay in the kitchen to help with dinner, but the men headed for the sitting room with mugs and a large pitcher of scog.

The sitting room was set up in three main areas. In the center of the room, two couches faced each other with a coffee table in between. A dark green rug covered the floor between the couches, and there was a vase of fresh flowers on the table. Small tables with glowstone lamps had been placed at each end of both couches.

A second area consisted of three large armchairs that sat in a semi-circle on one side of the couches. A brown rug covered the floor between them, and there was a small lamp table beside each of the chairs.

On the other side of the couches, there was a table about the size and shape of a card table with four chairs pulled up to it, one on each side. The table top was clear but there were a couple of glowstones attached to the stalactite hanging over the center of the table.

After the men sat down, Blalick said, "I am going to leave you in Ashni's hands now, but I will return after dinner to lead you to the rooms which have been prepared for you. Is there anything you need before I go?"

The men looked at each other, but no one said anything, so Kevin answered, "No, we don't need anything else, but you are going to join us for dinner, aren't you?"

"Thank you, sir, but no. Ashni and I will eat later with our children. Now, if you do not mind, I do need to check on a few things outside."

"Of course, and thanks for everything, Blalick," Kevin said.

The men settled back in the comfortable furniture drinking scog and talking quietly amongst themselves while soft conversation and laughter drifted from the kitchen. About half an hour later, Joan called from the dining room. "Okay guys. Dinner's on the table. Come on before it all gets cold."

As soon as the Tellurians were settled around the table, Ashni quietly left.

During dinner, they could hear a melody that sounded like a flute, accompanied by occasional "baraaack" sounds in the distance. The sounds didn't grow any louder, but they didn't fade away either. When Blalick and Ashni returned, Theresa asked them if they had any idea where the music was coming from.

"That was Sari playing her flute," Ashni said with a smile. "She was up in Luci's room."

"I know that Sari's your daughter," Joan said. "Blalick told us about her and Macin, but he didn't mention Luci. Is she a permanent resident, or a guest like us?"

Ashni laughed and shook her head. "Luci is a giant condor. She has a perch in one of the caves near the top of the mountain, but she has been here so long that she seems like a member of the family. She often sings along when Sari plays her flute."

"A giant condor?" Steve said wistfully. "I'd love to see her. Maybe Sari will let me go with her sometime and watch from a distance."

"I feel sure that that could be arranged after you have been here for a while," Blalick answered. "Luci flies over the valley several times a day. She will get used to seeing all of you around before long."

Since everyone had finished eating, Joan started gathering the dishes. "I want to thank you for our dinner, Ashni. It was delicious."

"I am pleased that you enjoyed it," Ashni said with a shy smile as she picked up the dishes that Joan had stacked. "I am sure you are anxious to see your rooms, so I will clear the table while Blalick shows you around. I felt sure that you would be too tired to bother with unpacking this evening, so I took the liberty of placing a nightshirt on everyone's bed for tonight. They are old ones that Sari and Macin have outgrown and I know they will probably be quite big on you, but if you like them, feel free to keep them."

"Now, if you do not mind, I would like to show you to your rooms," Blalick said.

"Blalick, I hate to hold you up, but I'm afraid that I'm going to insist on helping Ashni with the dishes," Joan said as she gathered more dishes to take to the kitchen.

"It really won't take a moment with all of us helping," Karl said as he began collecting mugs. "Just give us a few minutes, Blalick, and we'll be right with you."

"Certainly, if that is your wish," Blalick said with a slight nod of his head. Then he turned to Kevin and said, "May I speak with you for just a moment?"

Kevin nodded. "I'll be right with you. Just let me take these into the kitchen," he said as he picked up several mugs and a handful of flatware.

Blalick nodded and headed towards the sitting room.

Kevin carried the mugs and flatware out to the kitchen where Ashni was pouring hot water into a bucket for washing the dishes. As he set them down on the table, he said, "I want to thank you for all that you and your family have done for us. You didn't have to go to so much trouble, and we really do appreciate it."

A slight tinge of color crept up her cheeks as Ashni turned towards him. "We are honored to help you in any way we can, Myron. Your parents were wonderful people."

Kevin nodded and then walked towards the sitting area with a lot of questions floating around in his head. When he reached the sitting room, Blalick was standing near the far end, next to an arched opening that led to a second passageway.

"Sir, have you chosen your assistant yet?" Blalick asked quietly.

"Well, yes. Chris has agreed to be my assistant. Why?"

"We have bedrooms set up for all of you, but the rooms are in pairs. I wanted to know whom we should put in the room next to yours."

"You mean we will all have our own bedroom? Great," Kevin said with a sigh. "I figured we would be in some type of barracks."

"Barracks? What is a barracks?" Blalick asked.

"It's one big room with a long row of beds, and no, I do not want to stay in a barracks. It's just what I was expecting. Thank you for preparing individual rooms," Kevin said quickly before Blalick decided to rearrange things.

"Of course, sir," Blalick said. Then he got the torches from the holders beside the main passageway and began removing the glowstones from their pouches. Kevin helped him, and by the time they finished, the dishes were done, and everyone was ready to continue exploring their new living quarters.

Blalick led the Tellurians through the arch and out of the sitting room. After they had walked about forty feet down a twisting walkway, a smaller hall led off to the left. Blalick turned into that hall and continued walking until they came to a fork. Blalick led them down the left fork to a heavy wooden door that completely blocked the passageway. "Joan, Karl, this is your room," Blalick said as he swung the door open.

Joan led everyone through the door and then stopped dead in her tracks. Her jaw dropped as her gaze wandered over her new living quarters. The room consisted of two distinct areas. The main area was the bedroom and was larger than her whole apartment back in Omaha. The other area was an alcove to the immediate right of the door that had been made into a sitting area. There were two large easy chairs angled towards each other with a table between them and an ottoman in front of them. The table had a couple of shelves under it, and a glowstone lamp and serving tray on top. A deep yellow circular rug covered most of the floor in the alcove.

Along the wall to the left of the doorway was a large double bed covered with a quilted bedspread with a design of interlocking circles. A pale yellow blanket was folded across the foot of the bed, and two nightshirts were folded on the pillows. On each side of the bed, there was a night table with a glowstone lamp, and an oval rug made of the same deep yellow material as the one in the alcove. The end wall had pegs for cloaks and there was a shelf about a foot off the floor for boots. In the corner was a small table with a wash basin on top and a pot with a lid underneath. Two large chests of drawers stood against the wall directly opposite the bed, and next to the chests there was a large wooden desk with a straight back chair. On top of the desk, an inkbottle and quill stood ready for use beside a small stack of notepaper. A glowstone lamp was attached to the wall directly above the center of the desk.

Joan walked slowly around the room, touching the furniture as if to make sure that it was really there. When she turned back towards Blalick, she quickly swiped her eyes to catch the tears that threatened to spill over. "It's absolutely beautiful! It's the loveliest room I've ever had. I can't tell you how much I appreciate this. It's really wonderful."

At Joan's gushing praise, a hint of pink crept up Blalick's cheeks under his dark skin. "Ashni prepared this room for you. We hope you will enjoy it." Then he backed out of the door and suggested that they move on to Theresa's room.

They went back down the short hall that had led to Joan and Karl's room and took the right-hand fork. A couple of minutes later, they came to a second door. When Blalick opened that door, Theresa led the way. Her room was not quite as large as the one that Karl and Joan were in, but it was still spacious. It was furnished very much like Joan's except that the bed was a little smaller, there was only one chest of drawers, and there was only one chair in her sitting area. Her bedspread was also quilted, but the designs were floral and the blanket folded at the foot of the bed was light blue, to complement the dark blue rugs on the floor.

Theresa's room had a second door. After she walked around her bedroom for a moment, she stepped over to the door, put her hand on the door knob, looked back at Blalick, and raised her eyebrows.

Blalick nodded and said, "That door leads to another room. We thought you might need a workroom for you herbs."

Theresa opened the door and everyone followed her down the short hall into the second room. Blalick, Karl, and Steve opened the glowstone boxes that lined the walls and soon the workroom was flooded with light.

The room was almost square and had a small stream running along the far wall where six troughs had been set up for cultivating herbs. In the center of the room, there was a long worktable. Along the left-hand wall was a large storage cabinet and a big sink. Extra shelving had been attached to the right-hand wall, and sitting to the right of the door was a wheeled cart.

As Theresa looked around, Blalick said, "I hope this workroom is satisfactory. Sari knew that a sister was coming to stay for a while and insisted on preparing this room herself."

"It's perfect. And I love the herb beds. We can set them outside for the growing season and then store the seeds and bulbs in here when the frost begins," Theresa said as she wandered around the room, inspecting everything. "I can't wait to meet Sari and thank her for all of this."

"You will meet Sari and Macin tomorrow morning. They plan to help you unload your wagons. But Theresa, I do need to warn you. Sari has always been interested in healing and the medicinal herbs, so she will probably ask if she can assist you while you are here."

"I'd love to have her help, Blalick, for as long as it lasts, but most of the work is just plain backbreaking and no fun at all, so don't be surprised if she starts losing interest before long," Theresa said with a smile.

After they left Theresa's rooms, Blalick led them back down the hall past the fork and on to the walkway they had taken from the sitting room. When they reached the main walkway, he turned left, and led them farther away from the sitting room. After another fifty feet or so, a second corridor led off to the left. As they turned down that hall, Blalick announced that the next bedrooms belonged to Chris and Kevin.

The doors to both of the bedrooms were at what appeared to be the end of the hallway. Chris's room was off to the left and Kevin's room was straight ahead. Both of the rooms were large and almost square. The furniture was the same as Theresa's, but their bedspreads and rugs were done in earth colors. The only difference between the two rooms was that Kevin's room had a second door on the opposite wall, just like Theresa's.

When Kevin asked about it, Blalick replied, "The tunnel continues through that door, and eventually leads to our house at Wildcat Pass, and then on to the peak of the mountain. Later I will show you which tunnels to take to reach our house, but for now, it would be best if you do not venture out on your own. There are a lot of side tunnels that wind around inside the mountain going nowhere, but there are also deep shafts that drop hundreds of feet into rock pits or underground pools of water."

Blalick then changed the subject by using Kevin's door to illustrate how to latch their doors once they were inside their rooms. "This latch will not really stop anyone who is determined to get in, but it will slow them down a bit, and they will make enough noise trying to break through that you will definitely be awake by the time they get in."

"Do you really think we might be attacked here?" Darrell asked.

"No, I do not. However, I believe in preparation. I feel certain that all of you plan to keep your swords handy, even though you are tucked away inside a mountain. That is the same reason we put latches on your doors. Now, shall we move on to Darrell's and Steve's rooms?" Blalick asked as he motioned them back out of Kevin's room.

Once they had returned to the main walkway, they once again turned left, away from the sitting room. This time they only had to go a short ways before they came to a corridor that went off to the right. Before they headed down that hall, Blalick pointed to a small alcove at the end of the main walkway. "You might want to use that area for some extra storage. We can put a door across it if you wish. It is not very big, but it might be useful."

Then Blalick led them down the hall to a fork. He pointed to the right and said, "Darrell, your room is that way. The door is only a few feet down the hall, but the hall curves so you cannot really see it from here. And Steve, this is your room." Blalick pointed to a door that was down the left fork.

Steve opened his door and walked into his room at about the same time that Darrell opened his. The rest of the Tellurians split up, half following Darrell and half following Steve. Their rooms were not quite as square as Chris's and Kevin's, but they were just as large.

After everyone had looked around the rooms for a few minutes, Blalick said, "Shall we go back to the sitting room? I imagine you would like another mug of scog before turning in for the night, and I feel sure that Ashni has prepared a snack."

The walk back to the sitting room seemed quite short now that they knew where they were going.

Ashni had already set a tray with a large pitcher of scog and seven mugs on the coffee table, and was taking oatmeal cookies out of the oven just as the Tellurians walked in.

When Ashni brought in the tray of cookies, Joan said, "Ashni, those rooms are lovely. Did you make those quilts? They're gorgeous!"

"Thank you. I am pleased that you like them," Ashni said. "Sari and I made them."

"I love those patterns, and the stitching is so delicate. Do you think you could teach me how to make quilts like that while we're here?" Joan asked. "And where did you get those rugs?"

"I would be happy to show you. It will not take you long to pick it up. As for the rugs, I have a loom on which I made them. If you like, I will have Blalick make one for you," Ashni said. "I set the coffee pot and coffee on the table beside the stove ready for the morning. I will come down around 8:00 and help you fix breakfast, if that is all right. The children will come down a little later to help you unload the wagons and store your things." Ashni put her hand on Blalick's arm. "We will say good night now, if there is nothing else that we can do for you tonight."

"Thanks again for everything," Steve said as Blalick and Ashni started towards the passage. "We really do appreciate all the trouble you went to."

After the giants left, Joan poured scog into the mugs and handed them out while Theresa passed the tray of cookies around.

Once everyone was settled, Joan asked, "Do you believe those rooms? Who would have thought that life in a cave could be so luxurious?"

Chris nodded and said, "Once you get past the chamber pot and the wash basin, our rooms rival any four star hotel I've ever stayed in."

Joan frowned and asked, "Why not a five star hotel?"

"Can't say," Chris said with a shrug. "I never stayed in one."

After the chuckles died down, everyone drank their scog and ate cookies in relaxed silence. Finally Steve stood up and said that unless someone knew of something that absolutely had to be done that night, he was going to head for his room and stretch out on a real bed for a change. When no one said anything, he picked up his mug and started to take it out to the kitchen.

"Leave your mug on the tray, Steve," Kevin said. "Chris and I'll clear up tonight."

"Hold on a minute, Steve," Darrell said as he finished his last swallow of scog. "I'll walk down with you."

~ ~ ~ ~

After everyone else had left the sitting room, Kevin and Chris straightened up the area. As they carried the mugs out to the kitchen, Kevin asked, "What do you think about the fact that I have a room with a second door in it? Is it just a coincidence?"

"No. I don't think anything connected with Blalick is coincidence. He's far too organized and careful for that. He had a reason for putting you in that room," Chris said thoughtfully. "Why give you a room with an extra door to defend?" Then after a minute he added, "Unless it's an escape route."

"But if it's an escape route, wouldn't he have shown me which way to go to get out of the caves, or at least told us that that's what it was?"

"It doesn't make a lot of sense, does it?"

"I got suspicious when he tried to scare us out of exploring it. Do you think it might lead to Glendymere?"

"I hadn't thought of that."

"Guess we'll find out soon enough," Kevin said as they finished washing up the mugs. "Let's get some sleep. I have a feeling you and I are going to need all the rest we can get."

Chapter 29

Settling In

By the time everyone woke up the next morning, got dressed, and showed up in the kitchen for coffee, it was nearly 8:00. Darrell was the last one to saunter in.

"Good morning," Steve said as he handed Darrell a mug filled with hot coffee. "Did you sleep as well as the rest of us?"

"I slept like the proverbial log," Darrell said with a sheepish grin. "I can't believe I slept nearly ten hours without waking up once. I've never done that before. I must have been more tired than I realized."

"We're all worn out," Theresa said. "We've been on the road for seven weeks." Then she sighed and added, "I'm so glad we're finally here, and do you believe we actually made it on time? Today's the first of June."

Karl nodded. "When we left Drisden, I wasn't sure that we'd make it at all, much less on time. I wish there were some way we could let Kalen know."

"I have a feeling that he'll know soon, if he doesn't already. I bet Blalick sent him a message last night," Kevin said. The conversation paused as Joan used the last of the coffee in the pot to top off everyone's cup.

"What did you think of your nightshirts?" Theresa asked. "Mine was so soft and warm I hated to pull it off to get dressed this morning."

Darrell nodded. "I hope Ashni meant it when she said we could have them. I'd love to have a couple more of those."

"They were probably so soft because they're been worn a lot," Joan said as she put a fresh pot of coffee on the stove to perk. "Those nightshirts were tunics that her children had outgrown. There's no telling how old they are."

"I never got anything that comfortable when I was wearing my brothers and sisters old clothes at home," Chris said. "She can feel free to offer me hand-me-downs like that any time."

Ashni walked into the kitchen with a basket on her arm in time to hear Chris's comment. As she began to unload the groceries, she said, "I may be able to find a few more old tunics if you really are interested, Chris."

"You bet I am."

"They were made out of llama's wool. I was afraid that they might be too warm."

"Llama's wool?" Karl asked in surprised. "You have llamas around here?"

Ashni nodded. "In the valley on the other side of Wildcat Mountain. We have llamas, big horn sheep, and a few goats. I spin the wool into thread or yarn, and then either weave it into cloth, use it for knitting, or use it to make rugs. We also have about ten dairy cows and a couple of dozen hens."

"I don't suppose you'd be willing to teach me how to do all of that, would you?" Joan asked, a little embarrassed. "I hate to seem so ignorant, but we bought our cloth pre-made where we came from."

"Of course. I will be happy to show you how to do it. It really is not hard; it just takes time. Blalick can make you a spinning wheel after he makes you a loom. Now, shall we get breakfast ready so you can start unpacking? Blalick and the children will be here in about an hour."

Blalick walked in with his son and daughter right as the Tellurians were clearing the table. Macin was about ten feet tall, and looked and moved like a teenager in the midst of a growth spurt: his feet seemed to be too big for the rest of his body and his movements were a little awkward. His squarish face looked young, about thirteen or fourteen, but they knew that he was twenty-four years old. His eyebrows were thick and bushy, like Blalick's, and his eyes were the same deep jade. The belt that he wore around his tunic was a replica of his father's, and although the sword he wore at his side was a full four feet long, it looked small when compared to Blalick's. When Macin said hello, his voice cracked, which increased his general discomfort and embarrassment.

Sari wasn't quite as tall as Macin, only about eight and a half feet tall, and she favored her mother. Her thick black hair hung loose to her waist and was held out of her face by a headband like Blalick's. Her face was oval with delicate features, and her eyes were the same shade of green as her mother's, not as dark as her father's and Macin's. She had the same regal stature as her mother, although she was not yet as willowy and graceful. Her dress was similar to Ashni's and, like Ashni, she wore a dagger at her side. Sari looked and acted like a shy young girl eleven or twelve years old, even though she was twenty. She kept her eyes either on her parents or on the floor, not risking even a glance at any of the Tellurians.

After Blalick introduced everyone to his children, he asked, "Shall we get started?"

"I'd like to take the horses out to the pasture first," Karl said.

Blalick nodded. "Come along, Macin. You can help with the horses."

After the men left, Joan said, "Theresa, why don't you and Sari get started on your wagon?"

"Okay. Sari, let's go get the cart from the workroom. It'll make unloading all my stuff a lot easier," Theresa said. Then as she started walking towards the hallway to her room she added, "I understand you're the one I have to thank for my workroom. You really did a great job in there."

"Thank you, miss," Sari said in a quiet voice, but her eyes sparkled with pleasure as she turned to follow Theresa.

By the time Joan and Ashni finished washing the dishes and putting everything away, Theresa and Sari had returned with the cart, so all four of the women headed for the wagons to start unpacking.

While they were walking down the passageway towards the wagon room, Sari edged over next to her mother and whispered excitedly, "Theresa asked me to help her collect herbs for the beds."

"That is nice, Sari, but remember, she will have other things to do too, so be careful not to overstay your welcome," Ashni whispered back.

"I will be careful." Then Sari walked a little faster to catch up with Theresa again.

The men were just coming in from turning the horses loose in the pasture when the women got to the wagon room. Karl looked at the two wagons and said, "Let's tackle Theresa's first."

Darrell climbed up in the back of Theresa's wagon and started handing things down to the others.

"Darrell, just pile the blankets and tarps on the seat for now," Joan said. "I want to air them out before we store them."

After everything except the herbs had been unloaded, Theresa climbed up in the wagon and started handing jars of powdered herbs out to Sari to load on the cart. Everyone else grabbed an armful of kitchen supplies and headed for the kitchen.

Joan and Ashni stayed in the kitchen to sort the food and cooking utensils while the others went back to help Theresa and Sari. When only the potted herbs were left, Theresa said, "I need to find a place to set up an herb garden. I don't want to move all of these twice. Why don't all of you take a break for a few minutes while Sari and I go outside and look for a good spot?"

"Let's all go outside for a bit," Darrell suggested. "I could use some fresh air."

The men stretched out on the ground right outside the cave entrance while Theresa and Sari wandered around looking for the perfect spot for the herbs. About half an hour later, they found a small clearing that would work just fine.

While they were looking it over and planning how they would organize the plants, Sari said, "Would it help if we had some tables to set the pots on?"

"That would be nice, but we didn't bring anything like that with us," Theresa said.

"Would you like for me to ask Father to make us some tables?" Sari asked.

Theresa considered it for a moment. "I hate to ask, but it really would help."

Sari grinned and headed back to the cave entrance. By the time Theresa caught up with her, she had already asked Blalick to build a couple of tables for the potted herbs.

"How long would you like for the tables to be?" Blalick asked Theresa.

"Six or seven feet would be great," Theresa answered.

Blalick nodded and said, "Would you like them waist high? Your waist, that is? About three feet?"

"If it's not too much trouble," Theresa said. "I really hate to ask you to do this, Blalick. You've already done so much."

"It is no problem. Come along, Macin. Let us go get some wood and a few tools," Blalick said as he stood up.

"Do you need some help?" Karl asked as he stood up and stretched.

"No, we will be fine. You still have some unpacking to do," Blalick said. "We will be back in a little while."

By the time all of Theresa's potted herbs had been carried out to the clearing, it was time to break for lunch. While they were eating, Blalick and Macin returned.

"We left the wood and tools outside in front of the cave," Blalick said. "When you are done, you can show me exactly where you want the tables and we will get them put up for you."

As soon as Theresa finished her lunch, she, Sari, Blalick, and Macin left to go set up the tables in the herb garden.

"I'll take care of clearing up from lunch. Why don't you go ahead and unload Kevin's wagon?" Joan said to the guys when they had all finished eating.

"Let's just leave the instruments in the wagon for now," Karl said. "Next week I'll borrow some wood and tools from Blalick and make a case for the harp and a cabinet for everything else."

Joan nodded.

"What about the weapons? Where are we going to put those?" Darrell asked.

"We'll only have to store the extras," Steve said. "I'm sure we'll all want to keep our own weapons in our rooms."

"We could use that alcove that Blalick showed us, but we need to get some cabinets built down there first," Karl said. "Maybe we should just leave them in the wagon, too."

"I want one of the long bows in our room where I can get to it," Joan said. "I plan to practice with it quite a bit while we're here."

"And I want to keep the stars in my room," Darrell said.

"Karl, would you get Theresa's bag and put it in her room for her?" Joan asked.

"Sure, and I suppose you'll want me to get yours, too," Karl said with a grin.

"Unless you'd rather wash dishes," Joan said, ginning back.

After they finished with the dishes, Ashni said, "Let us go through the pantry so that you can get a good idea of what you have and what you are going to need. Macin will leave for his monthly trip to Abernon on Sunday, so you will need to give me your shopping list by tomorrow night. Include everything that you think you will need for the next month, not just food. If Theresa needs anything from the Chapel of Light in Abernon, tell her to add that to the list. Macin can stop by and pick it up for her."

"How long does it take him to get there?" Joan asked.

"It takes him three days to get there, one day to pick up the supplies and to deliver the goods that we send in, and three days to get back."

"Three days? You're kidding! We traveled for ten days to get here from Abernon."

"They must have sent you the long way around."

"Must have," Joan said, shaking her head. "You mentioned sending things to Abernon. What do you send?"

"Different things. I make wine from berries and grapes, so sometimes I send a few casks of wine. Sometimes I send some cloth, and occasionally a few quilts or rugs. In the fall, I send preserves and jams if I have any extra. Now, shall we get started on the pantry?"

As they were going into the pantry, Chris and Kevin walked through the sitting room on the way to their rooms, each holding one bag and carrying a cloak.

Ashni frowned. "They do have more clothes than what is in those bags, do they not?"

"No, that's it. We each have four outfits, including the one we're wearing," Joan said. "I know we're going to need warm clothing for the winter, but there was no way we could bring it with us. There wasn't a lot of spare room in those wagons. I figured that we'd be close enough to a town that I could get some bolts of cloth and some thread. We've still got most of the coins that Kalen gave us, so we have the money, and once I get some material, it won't take me long to make tunics and leggings."

"Let us go through my attic first. I have a lot of winter clothes that Sari and Macin have outgrown. Maybe we can alter some of them. And we will need to have a new pair of boots made for everyone, a little larger than the ones you are wearing now, so that we can line them with fur. Did you say that you are leaving here in eight months? That is the end of January, the worst possible time of the year to cross the prairie." Ashni shook her head. "We will make thick, bulky sweaters. We will use a double strand of wool, and…"

Joan interrupted her. "Ashni, we can't take very much with us. Remember, we only have two wagons, and those wagons have to hold all of our instruments, weapons, food, camping supplies, and Theresa's herbs. There isn't going to be a lot of room for clothes."

"Do not worry about that. I will have Blalick make another wagon. You will need it," Ashni said firmly. Then she stepped into the pantry. "But, for right now, we need to see what you need for the next month. I hope you do not mind, but I started ordering extra supplies a couple of months ago to get you started. Shall we see what we have here?"

~ ~ ~ ~

A couple of hours later, Joan and Ashni had finished making the grocery order, Blalick and Macin had finished making Theresa's tables, and the wagons were as unloaded as they were going to be for a while. As the work was finished, people began congregating in the sitting room.

At one point, Macin walked over to Kevin and quietly asked if he could speak with him for a moment. They walked into the kitchen for a little privacy.

"Glendymere is expecting you tomorrow morning, and my father has requested that I escort you to his cave," Macin said. "Would it be all right if I met you at your room about 7:30?"

"That will be fine, Macin, but would you rather I meet you somewhere else?"

Macin looked a little confused. "No, your room will be fine, sir."

"By any chance are we going to Glendymere's by way of the tunnel that leads from my room?"

"Yes, sir. I am sorry. I thought you knew. Willow Canyon is on the other side of Wildcat Mountain. It is quicker to go through the mountain than to go over it."

"7:30 tomorrow morning will be fine. Will Chris go with us, or does Glendymere want me to come by myself tomorrow?"

"Father told me to escort you and your assistant. Is Chris your assistant?"

Kevin nodded.

"Then Chris is supposed to go, too. "

"Thank you, Macin."

Macin nodded, bowed his head towards Kevin, and walked back to the sitting room to join his parents.

Chris glanced over towards Kevin when he saw Macin leave the kitchen and raised his eyebrows. Kevin nodded, so Chris quietly slipped out of the sitting room and walked over to the kitchen.

"What's up?" Chris asked.

"Tomorrow morning the show gets under way."

"Already?" Chris moaned. "I was hoping we'd have a couple of days before we had to meet him."

"I know. But look at it this way, by this time tomorrow, we will have already spent a whole day with him," Kevin said with a grin that was not at all convincing.

"What time are we leaving? And is anyone else going, or is it just the two of us?"

"Macin's going to escort us, but it's just the two of us out of our group. He's meeting us at 7:30. And guess where he's meeting us?"

"Here? Outside? I don't know."

"My room," Kevin said quietly.

"Your room? You mean … the tunnel? So that really is where it goes?" Chris asked, almost in a whisper.

Kevin nodded. "Our own private passageway to Glendymere's cave."

"Are you going to tell the others where we're going to be tomorrow?"

"Yes, sometime after dinner. Any second thoughts?"

"Tons! But don't worry. I'm not going to back out on you," Chris said as he grabbed a cookie that had been left over from the night before. "We'd better get back in there before everyone wonders what's going on." Then Chris headed back to the sitting room with his cookie.

Kevin poured himself a cup of coffee and stood in the kitchen slowly drinking it. While he was standing there, he overheard Blalick tell Sari and Macin that it was time to head back home, so he walked back towards the entrance hall to say thank you and good-bye.

A few moments later, Blalick herded his family towards the door to a chorus of 'thank-you's from the Tellurians. Macin was ready to go and quickly vanished down the passageway, but Sari hung back, not wanting to leave Theresa.

"Sari, would you be free to help me for a little while tomorrow morning?" Theresa asked. "I'd like to start cataloging the herbs that we have in the storeroom and getting them organized on the shelves and I really would appreciate the help if you have the time."

Sari's face lit up and her smile seemed to spread from one ear to the other. "Yes, miss. I will be happy to help. What time would you like for me to be here? I could be here as early as 6:00 if you wish."

Theresa laughed and said, "I'm not that energetic. Why don't we wait until around nine to begin?"

"9:00 it is. Thank you, Sister."

Ashni put her arm around her daughter's shoulder and. mouthed "thank you" to Theresa over Sari's head as she steered her daughter out of the room. Blalick wished them all a good evening and disappeared through the door behind his wife.

~ ~ ~ ~

During dinner, Joan told the others that Macin would be leaving for Abernon on Sunday, so they needed to make a list of any and all supplies that they wanted him to pick up. "Ashni and I have pretty much finished the grocery list, but if there is anything special that any of you want, now's the time to speak up. It'll be a month before he goes again. I have to give him the list tomorrow night."

Theresa smiled a wistful little smile and said, "I don't suppose you included anything like chocolate on your list did you?"

Joan laughed. "Actually I did put baking chocolate on the list. I don't know if they have it, but we'll give it a shot. Anything else?"

Steve said, "It isn't in the grocery category, but I would like some writing paper, quite a bit of it actually, and maybe a couple more bottles of ink. I'd like to start a journal."

"I'd like some more paper and ink too," Theresa said. "I want to make some notes about the different herbs and their preparations."

"Okay. I'll add paper and ink to the list. Anything else?" Joan asked.

No one could think of anything, so Joan reminded them again that once she gave the list to Macin, that was it for a month. She said she'd hold onto the list until dinner the next night, but after that it would be too late.

Then Kevin said, "Macin's going to take Chris and me to Glendymere's cave tomorrow morning. We're leaving at 7:30."

"So soon?" Joan asked.

Kevin shrugged. "From what Kalen said, we have a lot of work to do and not much time, so I guess the sooner the better."

"How about you, Chris? Are you up for meeting a dragon tomorrow?" Theresa asked with a mischievous grin.

"No, but then I don't think I'd ever be up for it, so I might as well go ahead and get it over with. I'm sure the idea is worse than the reality," Chris said with a sick-looking smile.

"I don't know about that," Darrell said shaking his head. "All I can say is that I'm glad it's you and not me. I'd probably faint dead away at the sight of him."

"I hope not. You'll have to meet him eventually," Kevin said.

"But not tomorrow," Darrell said. Then after a moment, he added, "Kevin, do us all a favor. If you know that I'm going to have to meet Glendymere, don't give me too much warning. I don't think it would help, and it would give me that much more time to panic. Okay?"

"Okay," Kevin said as they all laughed.

~ ~ ~ ~

Although Kevin had gone to bed early, he was still awake around midnight. He decided to go get a glass of cold milk, hoping that it would help him drop off to sleep.

When he got to the kitchen, he found that Chris was already there, heating some water on the stove. "Thought I'd fix a cup of tea. Want one?" Chris asked.

"No, what I really want is a big bowl of ice cream, but I'll settle for some milk."

"Did you have trouble falling asleep, too?"

"Yeah. I keep looking at that door and wondering what's waiting for us at the other end of that tunnel," Kevin said as he poured a mug of milk.

Chris sighed and said, "I have no idea what we're walking into or what we're going to have to do, and I find that idea scarier than the idea of meeting a dragon."

Kevin nodded and drank his milk. "I don't know how long we may be gone tomorrow. Maybe we should take some food with us, at least for lunch."

Chris held up a small sack. "I just finished cutting some cheese and bread for us to take. I also threw in a couple of mugs. I was trying to figure out what we could use to carry some water with us when you came in. Do you have any ideas?"

"Not off hand. I'll look around while you drink your tea," Kevin said as he started for the pantry. A few minutes later he found a jug that had a wooden stopper in the top. The jug looked like it would hold about a half gallon, so they set it beside their sack, ready for the morning.

After Chris finished his tea and Kevin drank another mug of milk, Chris asked, "Feeling any better?'

Kevin grinned and shook his head. "Not really. How about you?"

"No, can't say that I do," Chris answered as he rinsed out the mugs. "Oh well, guess we should at least lie down for a while. Who knows? Maybe we'll get lucky and fall asleep. Let's go."

Chapter 30

Glendymere

Kevin got up around 6:00 Saturday morning and headed towards the kitchen. The aroma of fresh coffee greeted him before he reached the sitting area. Chris was up, dressed, and pacing back and forth across the kitchen with a steaming cup of coffee in his hand.

As Kevin poured himself a cup, he asked, "Did you get any sleep at all last night?"

Chris shook his head. "I tossed and turned for about four hours, and then I gave up. How about you?"

"I dozed a little, but that was about it."

The two of them drank a whole pot of coffee during the next hour and had just put on a fresh pot when Joan walked in. She offered to fix them some breakfast, but Chris said that he was much too nervous to eat, and Kevin said that he had already eaten some cheese and a piece of bread.

A little after seven, Macin walked into the kitchen, spoke to Joan, and asked Kevin if he and Chris were ready to go. When Kevin nodded, Macin led them down the hall to Kevin's room, opened the door to the tunnel, and led them through a corridor wide enough for all three of them to walk abreast.

About a quarter of a mile later, they entered a large round chamber. Four tunnels led out of the chamber at right angles.

Macin stopped at the door and said, "You need to think of this room as a big compass. The hall we entered from is west." Then Macin pointed to the hall to the left. "That hall is north. It winds around through the mountain for several miles before coming to a dead end. The east tunnel leads up to our house and then on to the peak of Wildcat Mountain, and the south tunnel leads to an underground lake."

"Which tunnel do we take?" Chris asked.

"None of those," Macin said. "We go northeast."

"Northeast?" Chris frowned as he looked at what appeared to be a solid wall.

"Northeast," Macin said with a grin as he started across the room.

As they got closer to the wall, Kevin and Chris saw a small dark alcove, about the size of a closet, set back in the shadows. Macin walked into the alcove and seemed to disappear. When Kevin stepped into it, he could see the light from Macin's torch off to his left. There was a narrow opening in the wall of the alcove, just behind the chamber wall. Kevin stepped through the opening and found that he was in an "L" shaped passageway. After he and Chris turned the corner, the passageway widened and they were at the beginning of another large corridor that extended beyond their torchlight.

"That doorway is the main reason Father asked me to show you the way. It is a rather tight fit for him," Macin said. "This entrance to Glendymere's cave is private, so do not tell anyone else about it unless Glendymere says it is all right."

The corridor was relatively level and straight, and after they had walked about half a mile, Kevin noticed a faint smell in the air. At first it came in whiffs and was too faint to identify, but after a while it became stronger and Kevin recognized it as the smell that lingers after a fire has been extinguished.

Eventually they came to a large wooden door with a heavy iron knocker shaped like a flying dragon and mounted on an iron shield. Macin lifted the knocker, slammed it against the iron shield four or five times, stepped back, and waited.

"What are we waiting for?" Chris asked nervously.

"Several years ago, Glendymere was sleeping when a friend of his, an elf, came to visit. Glendymere is always aware when someone is nearby, but he does not necessarily wake up. When the elf entered his chamber, Glendymere yawned in his sleep and caught the elf's clothes on fire. It gave the elf quite a scare and shortly after that Glendymere had my grandfather install this door and knocker. We wait for him to answer so that we know he is awake." Macin reached for the handle and started to open the door. "It is safer that way."

"I thought you said you waited for Glendymere to answer," Kevin said with a slight frown.

"He did. He told me to come in and to bring both of you to his inner chamber," Macin replied.

"I didn't hear anything," Chris whispered.

"He was not talking to you," Macin said quietly.

"Telepathy," Kevin said. "Like Xantha."

Macin nodded and led them through the door and down the hall to a fork. He pointed to the right and said, "That leads to Glendymere's entrance hall, where he receives most of his guests." Then he started down the left fork. "This leads to Glendymere's sleeping chamber. Very few are allowed to enter this area."

The hall led to a large circular room. A football stadium, complete with bleachers, could have been set up in there with room left over. The ceiling was about a hundred feet high and a shaft about ten feet wide opened to the sky directly above the center of the room. Along the right-hand wall was a large rock basin filled with water. Fresh water fed into the basin from a spout in the wall and the overflow drained into an underground stream through a lip in the rim.

Glendymere was curled up like a cat along the opposite wall. His enormous head was resting on his front paws and his tail was wrapped around his body. As the trio entered the room, Glendymere raised his head, cocked it to one side, eyed the two humans and said, *"Welcome to my home."*

Kevin stared at Glendymere in awe. He was exactly as Xantha had remembered him, only more so. His movements had a fluid grace and elegance that was animalistic, but his eyes radiated an intelligence that far surpassed anything a human could even hope for.

Chris froze in mid-step. He was mesmerized by the sheer power and imminent threat that Glendymere embodied.

"Macin, would you please give Chris a drink of water before he faints," Glendymere said with a chuckle. *"Myron, I'm happy to meet you at long last. I've looked forward to this day, but I always thought Badec would introduce us. I am very sorry about your father's illness."*

Kevin was a little surprised that he felt relatively at ease in Glendymere's presence. "Thank you. I wish I had had the opportunity to know him," he answered. Then after a moment, he continued, "I want to thank you for agreeing to tutor me, but I have to admit that I have absolutely no idea what a sorcerer does, or what kind of powers he has. I'm afraid that you have an impossible task ahead of you."

"Nonsense. You have the power. All we have to do is direct it," Glendymere said. *"I see that you think of yourself by your Earthly name, Kevin. Would you be more comfortable if I were to address you as Kevin?"*

"Yes, I would. I know that when I get to Camden, I'll need to answer to Myron, but for now, I would prefer Kevin if you don't mind."

"Fine by me, and if you choose, you can continue to call yourself Kevin after you're seated, but we'll talk about that later. Right now, I'd like for you to try to get your assistant moving again so that the two of you can fix up that room over there." Glendymere nodded towards a small room that was located next to the water basin. "You'll need a place to work, and there will also be times when it will be necessary for you to stay here over night. You'll find some human furniture in the adjoining storeroom. Pick out a couple of beds, tables and chairs. When you have the room squared away, we'll begin." Then Glendymere turned his head towards Macin, "Thank you for escorting them, Macin. You may leave now if you like. I know you have things that you need to do to prepare for your trip to Abernon."

Macin nodded to Glendymere, turned back towards the tunnel, and left.

Chris was barely able to move, but he managed to stumble across to the small room that Glendymere had indicated. As he and Kevin started going through the furniture trying to find two suitable beds and a couple of tables with chairs, he began to loosen up a bit.

"I have a feeling that Glendymere had us set up this room to give you something to focus on, something to get your mind off your fear. Are you going to be okay here?" Kevin asked.

"Yeah. Just give me a couple of years to get used to being around something that could destroy me with a snort," Chris said in a half-hearted attempt at humor. Then he added seriously, "I hadn't really thought about just how dangerous he is, but as soon as I saw him …"

"I know what you mean, but I keep remembering something that Xantha told me: 'If he sees you as his enemy, he would be the most deadly force you would ever meet. If he sees you as a friend, you are safer with him than you were in your mother's womb.' Those aren't his exact words, but that's the general idea. He is dangerous, but not to us," Kevin said quietly. "Think you can get past this fear thing?"

Chris slowly nodded. "Just give me a little time."

About two hours later, when they were almost done, Glendymere said, "I forgot to mention that you'll need a candle. You should be able to find one in the storeroom."

"A candle? Won't we use glowstones?" Kevin asked.

"No. A glowstone won't work for our first exercise. You'll need a candle."

Chris walked out of the storeroom with a couple of candles and candlesticks to see which one Kevin wanted. Kevin chose a slender candle and a brass candlestick. He set it in the center of one of the tables and then said to Glendymere, "Well, unless there's something else that we need to get out of the storeroom, I guess we're done."

"Good. Come on out here and have a seat," Glendymere said. "Kalen sent me a message saying that he had not found a way to tell you that I'm a dragon before you left the Gate House. I wasn't sure how I was going to let you know before you walked in here. I didn't want to ask Blalick to tell you because he would have been deeply offended if any of your group had balked at the idea of working with me. Fortunately, Xantha took care of the problem. If he hadn't, Chris might have had a heart attack. Are the rest of the humans in your group afflicted by dragon-fear?"

"I think Darrell is, but the others didn't seem to be too upset with the idea," Kevin said as he and Chris walked back into the large chamber.

Glendymere nodded his massive head. "I guess we need to get down to business now. First of all, we need to talk about magic. I've searched through your minds, and neither of you has the faintest idea what it's all about. No, Chris, we don't use bat's wings, spider's webs, or eyes of newt. I don't think any of the real sorcerers on Earth ever did either. That's just something that someone made up to sound good in stories."

"That's good. I was dreading having to go out and collect them," Chris said in a valiant effort to seem at ease, but his shaky voice betrayed him. Now that they were back in Glendymere's presence, his knees threatened to buckle, so he slowly and carefully sat down on the cave floor across from the dragon.

Kevin sat down beside Chris. "So what do I need?"

"Only yourself. The power of magic is all around you, but the best source is within your own body. You're very fortunate. You have the best of two worlds, the elven world and the human world. From the elves, you have a unique relationship with nature, one that humans without elven blood cannot hope to achieve. And you also have the magical power that resides in the mind of certain humans: the seeing eye, the outstretched hand, and the energy bolt," Glendymere said as he studied Kevin. *"How much do you know about elves?"*

"Not much at all. We've only met two, Duane and Paul, but we didn't know that Paul was an elf until we got to Kalen's house," Kevin said. "Actually, Kalen called him Pallor, but Paul is the name we knew him by."

Glendymere nodded. *"Elves are elementals, as in the four elements of nature: fire, water, air, and soil. An elf can project a part of his essence into the forces of nature. For example, an elf can become one with the wind and clouds. As long as the clouds are already there an elf can join with them, pull them together, influence the wind to stir things up, and create a storm, but the basic elements must already be in place. Going the other way, an elf can join with a violent storm system and settle it down, but an elf could not make it simply vanish."* Glendymere stopped because Chris's mouth suddenly dropped open. He waited for Chris to speak.

"I've got a question. That tornado, the one that triggered the key that transported us to Terah, seemed to come out of nowhere. There was no way that Paul could have counted on a tornado forming at that precise time and place. That's been bothering me ever since we got here. Did he cause it?" Chris asked.

"I'm sorry, but I have no idea what you are talking about," Glendymere said. Then, as Chris opened his mouth to describe the sudden storm, he added, *"No, no need to explain, just let the memory surface. I'll look at the memory and see what happened."* After a couple of seconds, Glendymere nodded and said, *"Ah, yes, I'd say that tornado was definitely Pallor's work. And a good job of it, too. He didn't have a whole lot to work with, just a few clouds and a little wind. He did a fine job of controlling it. I doubt if I could have done much better myself,"* Glendymere said in such a way that Kevin and Chris both knew that he had just paid Pallor his highest compliment. *"Do you see what I'm talking about when I say that an elf can join with nature?"*

"For the sake of argument, let's say that I can sort of imagine something along that line, especially since I was in the middle of that storm, but that does not mean that I think for even one minute that I could do it," Kevin answered.

"Fair enough. I'll accept that for the moment. Now, about the human magical powers ... let's see, maybe a little demonstration would help. Come with me."

Kevin and Chris stood up and waited for Glendymere to get up. As Chris watched Glendymere slowly unwind and stretch, his eyes got bigger and bigger, and by the time Glendymere was standing, Chris's face had gone chalky white and he was swaying on his feet. Kevin took hold of his shoulders and gently eased him back to the ground.

"Take a deep breath, Chris," Glendymere said gently. *"You'll be all right in a moment."*

Chris nodded his head in jerky movements and said, "It's just … that … you're … you're so big."

Glendymere chuckled and said, *"Guess I am compared to you. Would it help any to know that I'm not the largest dragon around? In fact, I'm almost a runt."*

Chris shook his head. "No, that doesn't help at all."

"Didn't think it would. Now, do you think you can stand up again?"

Chris nodded and slowly climbed back on his feet. He wasn't swaying, but he didn't feel all that steady either. "I think I'll be okay now."

"Good. Let's go then," Glendymere said as he led the way down the huge passageway that led out of his chamber.

They passed through several large rooms before they came to a massive cave that opened into the canyon. The cave was almost square and large enough that several dragons could lie down comfortably without crowding each other. There was a small alcove near the cave opening that contained chairs ranging in size from one that would fit in a child's dollhouse to one that would suit a giant. Three bronze gongs, one small, one medium, and one large, stood near the alcove, and a dozen mallets, from tiny to huge, leaned against the wall. A flying dragon was engraved in the center of each gong.

Glendymere continued through the cave and walked out into the sunlight that filled the small canyon. The floor of the canyon extended about fifty yards on each side of a gentle stream that ran down the middle of the canyon. Small bushes and wild flowers dotted the rocky ground, but the only trees in sight were the willows that grew along the stream banks. The little valley was surrounded by steep mountain walls, giving it the appearance of a box canyon.

By the time Glendymere stopped and turned towards them, Chris was feeling almost normal again. Glendymere glanced over at him, gave a quick nod, and then turned towards Kevin.

"See that dead tree trunk over there? The one next to that big boulder. Watch it closely now," Glendymere said as he indicated a tree trunk about three feet in diameter and four feet long lying on its side.

Kevin and Chris both turned to look at it. A couple of seconds later they saw a bright flash and the tree trunk disintegrated into dust and ash.

"What happened? What did you do?" Kevin asked.

"You might say I threw a lightning bolt at the tree trunk, although it really isn't lightning. It's more like a bolt of pure energy. Now watch the boulder next to it."

The boulder rose slowly through the air, floated to the other side of the stream, and settled gently on the ground beside one of the willow trees. Neither Kevin nor Chris spoke. They just stood there, staring. If either of them had held onto any lingering doubts about magic, they were gone now.

"That was what we will call the outstretched hand for lack of any better description. I picked it up by reaching out with my mental energy, moved it, and set it back down. Now, let's see if I can come up with a demonstration of the seeing eye." Glendymere looked around for a bit. Then he said, *"Chris, I want you to pick three different color flowers about the same size."*

Glendymere nodded as Chris started to pick three flowers. *"That's right. Just make sure they're different colors. Now I want you to walk around to the other side of that boulder and face me."*

After Chris was in position, Glendymere continued, *"I want you to hold the three flowers behind your back. Now throw down two of the flowers."* Glendymere paused for a moment while Chris did as he asked. *"You're still holding the pansy with the purple head. Kevin, check it out."* Glendymere waited while Kevin walked to the other side of the large boulder.

"You're right," Kevin said. "He has the purple pansy in his hand. The other two are on the ground." Chris picked up the two flowers that he had dropped and then he and Kevin walked back out in the open to join Glendymere.

"I guess the best way I can explain that one is that I projected an extension of my own sight through an imaginary eye that I held over Chris's head. I can guide the eye anywhere I want it to go. I can see what's on the other side of that boulder, what's going on in the sitting room in your caverns, or who has entered the next valley and what they're doing."

"This is all really great, but I can't do any of this stuff," Kevin said.

"No, not right now, but given time, you will." Glendymere paused and gazed into Kevin's eyes. *"Kevin, you have the ability, you were born with it. Forces of magic are everywhere, all around you, and I can feel it flowing through your body. But it's in raw form. To learn to channel it, to control it, to make it work for you will take a great deal of effort on your part. At the level that you'll be competing, victory will go to the one who has devoted the most effort to refining that control. And if that's you, you'll survive. Otherwise, you won't."*

"I don't have long, Glendymere. I have to be in Camden by the middle of March. From what Kalen said, most sorcerers spend at least ten years learning how to do all of this. I have eight months. It seems like a losing proposition to me," Kevin said honestly.

Glendymere nodded. *"I understand your concern, but I think maybe you're confusing time with effort. They are not the same thing. It's going to be hard, and the hardest tasks will be the first ones. It will get much easier with use and practice. We'll begin with four small tasks, and then, after you master those, we'll move on to bigger and better things. But first and foremost, you must believe in yourself. Magic comes straight from your mind, Kevin, and the secrets to powerful magic are confidence and focus. Doubt and distraction are your worst enemies.*

"One of the tasks that I want you to work on is to create a mental spark that will light the candle that you put on your table. To do that, you must see it happening. See the candlewick burst into flame. Feel it happening. Concentrate the energy in your mind into a flicker of flame that extends from your mind to the top of the candle.

"Another task is to use your mind to move a pebble across the table. To do that, envision a hand extending on a long arm from your mind to the pebble. Use that hand to push the pebble along on the table.

"Third, I want you to see which flower Chris has in his hand. He'll need to have three again, of different colors. Now, lucky guesses don't count. You have to actually 'see' which one he's holding as you look down on him from an eye that you've created and positioned over his head.

"The fourth task that I want you to work on involves the wind. I want you to feel the wind, feel it rise and fall, join with it and try to change its direction or speed. Try to make the wind move the branches in the willow trees, or if it's already blowing, try to calm it to the point that the branches of the willows lie still.

"These will be the hardest tasks that I'll ever ask you to perform, but only because they're the first. So, I guess it's time for you to get to work. Do you have any questions?"

"I don't know," Kevin said slowly. Then he asked, "How long do you think it will take me to be able to do them?"

"It will take as long as it takes. Now go eat your lunch and get started. I'm going to take a nap." Glendymere turned and walked back into his cave and through the tunnels to his inner chamber.

By the time Kevin and Chris reached the inner chamber, Glendymere was curled up and snoring softly.

"I don't think we should stand out here in the open while he's sleeping, Kevin," Chris said, thinking about what Macin had told them about Glendymere's yawns. "Let's get in our room."

Kevin nodded and they quickly left the large open chamber for the relative safety of their small room. After they ate their cheese and bread, Kevin set the candle in the middle of one of the tables and sat down in one of the straight back chairs with his back to the door. While Chris watched, Kevin tried to envision a flame on the end of the candlewick. He concentrated on the candle for over an hour before he finally shook his head, stood up and walked around for a few minutes. Then he said, "Okay, let's try the thing with the flowers. Do you still have the three flowers that you picked earlier?"

"Yeah, right here. Where do you want me to stand?" Chris asked, glad to finally be of use.

"Why don't you stand next to that table over there, just keep your back to me," Kevin answered. When Chris was in place, Kevin said, "Now, put two of the flowers down on the table. Just be sure that you put them down where I can't see them."

Kevin sat back down and tried to imagine a giant eye positioned over Chris's head and focused down on Chris and the table, but try as he might, he could not see anything except the back of Chris's shirt. After an hour of frustration, Kevin gave up and told Chris to take a break. Chris set the three flowers in the center of the table next to the candle and stretched

"Don't get discouraged, Kevin. This is only the first day," Chris said.

"I know. I'm just tired."

"Why don't we get out of here for a few minutes, go get some fresh air?"

"You go ahead. I'm going to sit down for a bit and try to move that pebble. Really, go explore the valley. There's no reason for you to have to stand here and watch me do this." Kevin picked up the stone and tossed it from hand to hand for a few moments and then placed it in the middle of the table.

"If you're sure," Chris said hesitantly as he looked at Kevin before heading out.

Kevin nodded and waved towards the door.

When Chris returned two hours later, Kevin was still sitting at the table in exactly the same position, staring at the pebble. He was concentrating so hard that he hadn't heard Chris come in, and he jumped when Chris touched his shoulder. When Kevin looked up, Chris was appalled at how completely drained he looked.

"Come on, Kevin. Let's call it a day," Chris said quietly. "If we're going to be back in Rainbow Valley in time to eat with the others, we need to get going."

Kevin stood up and stretched. "All right. I hate to give up, but I'm too beat to keep trying to do this right now," he said with a flick of his hand towards the table. "In fact, walking back to our side of the mountain almost sounds like more than I can manage." He bent down to stretch the muscles in his back. "That bed over there's looking pretty good about now."

"You'll feel better once you move around a bit, and the others are going to want to hear about our day," Chris said as he gathered up their torches and their lunch sack. "Should we wake Glendymere to let him know that we're leaving?"

Kevin remembered Macin's story about the elf and said, "No, I don't think so. Glendymere didn't mention anything about it, and Macin said that he's always aware of anyone coming in or leaving whether he's awake or asleep. He'll know we've gone."

"Good! I definitely was not looking forward to waking him up," Chris's voice perked up with relief.

~ ~ ~ ~

The hike back to the round chamber went quickly, and by the time they reached Kevin's room, he was feeling a little better, although he was still quite tired. "I bet we both sleep a lot better tonight than we did last night," he said as he looked longingly at his bed.

"If I sleep at all, I'll sleep better than I did last night," Chris said with a laugh. "Come on, let's go find the others and tell them all about Glendymere."

Joan was just getting ready to set the table for dinner when Chris and Kevin walked into the sitting room. "Well, I see you survived your first day with Glendymere," Joan said from the kitchen. "How did it go? What's he like? Wait, don't tell me. Everyone's dying to know and if you tell me, you'll just have to go through it all over again when the others get here."

Joan had poured two mugs of scog while she was talking. She carried them to the sitting room and handed one to each of them. "Karl, Steve, and Darrell are bringing the horses in for the night. They should be about done by now. Theresa's in her workroom. She just sent Sari home. They've been sorting and cataloging herbs all day. She should be coming along any minute." Then Joan walked over to the big cabinet near the dining room table and started to take out the plates and mugs for dinner. "Chris, here are the plates and mugs, and the flatware's in that drawer. How about getting the table set?"

"I'll take care of it, Joan," Chris said from the sitting room. "Just give me a minute to finish my scog."

With a quick nod Joan went back to the kitchen to put the finishing touches on dinner.

By the time the table was set, Joan had the food ready. Theresa arrived in time to help her carry the serving dishes to the table, and almost as if on cue, Karl, Steve, and Darrell walked in. As soon as everyone was settled around the table, the questions began.

Chris was a natural born storyteller, so Kevin sat back and let him enjoy it. Chris described his first reactions to meeting Glendymere in such a way that even Darrell was laughing. While he was explaining how elves work their magic, the others started looking at each other, some of them frowning.

Finally Karl said, "Wait a minute. Didn't Kalen say that that Paul guy was an elf?"

"I was thinking about that, too," Darrell said. "You don't suppose …"

Chris grinned. "I asked the same question." And then he told them how Glendymere looked into Chris's mind to look at his memory of the storm and then confirmed that Paul had created and controlled the tornado.

"I don't know how I feel about that," Karl said with a frown, and for the next few minutes, Paul and the tornado were the topics of a lively discussion. When things settled down a bit, Chris went on to describe the demonstrations that Glendymere gave of the three types of mental powers that human sorcerers use.

At that point, Kevin yawned and said, "I'm sorry, but I'm pretty tired, and unless there's something that you need me to do tonight, I'm going to turn in."

Joan asked him if there was anything that he needed to add to the shopping list, but Kevin said that he couldn't think of anything. Then he thanked her for dinner, took his plate to the kitchen, told everyone good night, and left for his room.

Everyone fell quiet for a few moments after Kevin left. Then Steve asked, "Did something happen over there that you haven't told us?"

"Well, sort of," Chris answered. "You see, after Glendymere demonstrated the various magical powers, he gave Kevin four tasks to work on. They're supposed to be the four fundamental skills. From what Glendymere said, after he masters these, he can begin to learn how to be a sorcerer, but he has to be able to do these first. One task is that Kevin's supposed to join his spirit with the wind somehow and influence it to blow harder and then calm it back down. The second is to light a candle basically by willing it to burst into flame. For the third task, he's supposed to mentally push a pebble across a table. And the fourth is to look through an eye that he creates mentally and positions over my head to see what I'm holding while I've got my back to him."

Chris stopped for a moment and took a long drink of coffee. Then he continued. "Kevin concentrated on the last three of those tasks for over four hours this afternoon without a break. At one point, I tried to get him to go outside for a breath of fresh air, but he wouldn't do it, so while he was trying to move the pebble, I went outside for a while. I was hoping he'd come out and join me, but he didn't. When I decided it was time to call it quits for the day, I went back inside, but he was concentrating so hard that I had to touch him to get his attention. When he looked up, his face was pale and he looked like someone had given him two black eyes. There were deep circles under them, black shadows over them, and both of his eyes were blood red." Chris shook his head and sighed. "He looked like he had aged twenty years. His face had pretty much gone back to normal by the time we got back over here, but I'll never forget what he looked like today. It was scary to see what this is taking out of him."

"Do you really think he can do that stuff?" Darrell asked.

"Yesterday, I'd probably have said no. But I saw Glendymere do it, and since everyone says that Kevin has the genes, I guess he can, too, but even if he can, I think it may take him a while to get the hang of it." Chris paused for a moment and then added, "Unfortunately, I'm not at all sure that Kevin believes that he can do this, and according to Glendymere, a sorcerer's belief in his own ability is crucial."

"Is there anything we can do to help?" Theresa asked.

"I don't know." Chris thought for a moment and then said, "Don't ask him too many questions right now. Give him a little time and space. Oh, and could I get you to put chocolate on that list, Joan? Lots of it?"

"It's on there already. Everybody's craving it," Joan answered. "Is there anything in particular that you want it for?"

"It's like Kevin has no concept of time or anything else while he's concentrating. For a while, I think my main function's going to be making him take breaks, and for some reason, chocolate breaks came to mind. I used to live on Hershey bars and coffee during exam time in college, and that's exactly what today felt like, crunch time before exams."

"The chocolate won't be here until Macin returns from Abernon next week, but I'll bake some oatmeal cookies with nuts tonight so you can take them with you tomorrow. We have several coffee pots. Do you have a stove over there?" Joan asked.

"No, but I wish we did," Chris said. "I didn't see anyplace that looked like any type of kitchen. From what I've gathered, people sometimes visit Glendymere, but it's like having an audience with a king or the Pope. They come, state their business, and leave."

"Why don't I ask Blalick about it? If there's a stove around, he'll know where it is. If not, maybe we can get one for you," Karl suggested.

"I hate to put anyone to any extra trouble," Chris said, "but we both could have used a cup of coffee half way through the afternoon today."

"It's no problem," Karl said. "I'll check with him tomorrow."

Steve nodded and added, "We have no idea how to help you two, so we're counting on you to let us know when there's something we can do to help."

"Thanks," Chris said. "Well, to tell the truth, I was so nervous I didn't sleep at all last night and I'm pretty bushed myself. So, if you don't mind, I think I'll head for bed."

As Chris stood up, he picked up his plate to carry it out to the kitchen. Joan laid her hand on his arm and said, "Just leave it for now. I'll get it with the others. Go ahead, and sleep well."

Chris thanked her, told everyone good night, and left for his room.

After Chris was gone, Steve said, "He's got his work cut out for him."

"Which one?" Karl asked.

"Actually I was thinking of Kevin when I said it, but you're right. Chris does, too," Steve answered.

"We can't do anything to help with the magic part, but we can handle everything else," Joan said as she began clearing the table. "Now, while I'm doing the dishes, all of you go on into the sitting room and start thinking about what we're going to need for the next month, for the next eight months, and then for our trip to Camden. We have a winter to prepare for."

Chapter 31

Things Start Looking Up

Sunday morning Chris got up around six, dressed, and opened his door. He saw a light under Kevin's door, so he knocked on it softly to see if Kevin was awake and ready to join him for coffee. When Kevin didn't answer, Chris gently pushed on the door. It was unlatched, so it slowly swung open. Kevin was seated at his desk, staring at a pebble lying in the center of the desktop. Chris quietly shut the door.

When he got to the kitchen, he found a sack of food on the counter. Joan had wrapped bread, cheese, and a dozen oatmeal cookies in cheesecloths, and she had set a small basket of fresh strawberries on top. The coffee pot was on the table ready to go on the stove, and there was a note leaning against it that said, "Hope today goes well."

After the coffee perked, Chris poured two large mugs and carried them down to Kevin's room. This time he banged on the door with the toe of his boot, making enough noise to rouse Kevin out of his intense concentration. When Kevin opened the door, Chris handed him a mug of coffee and said, "Come on. Let's drink our coffee in the sitting room. Then we'll fix some breakfast and get ready to go."

They left for Willow Canyon an hour later, carrying their torches and Joan's bag of food. The closer they got to Glendymere's cave, the more tense Kevin became. When he reached up to knock on the wooden door with the iron knocker, they both heard Glendymere say, *"It's all right. You can come in. I'm out in the valley."*

Kevin asked, "Do you want us to join you or should I start working on those four tasks?"

"Work on the tasks. We can't go any farther until you master at least one of them," Glendymere answered.

Kevin spent all day Sunday concentrating on those four skills, but to no avail. Chris was determined not to let Kevin work himself into a state of exhaustion, so he insisted that Kevin get up, stretch, walk around, drink water, and eat a little something at least once every hour. Since working with the wind could only be done outside, Chris used that as an excuse to get Kevin to go outside for some fresh air every few hours.

Around 5:30, Chris decided that it was time to call it a day, so he started getting their things together. When Kevin looked up and frowned at him, Chris said, "We've got to get moving. If we don't leave here within the next few minutes, we'll be late for dinner."

"So we'll eat later," Kevin said with a shrug.

"If it were just the two of us, that would be fine," Chris agreed. "But the others will wait for us, and then everybody'll end up having a cold dinner. Joan can't keep it warm forever." Actually, Chris had no idea whether the others would wait for them or not, but it sounded like a good argument.

"Okay, okay," Kevin grumbled as he got up from the table and headed into the adjoining storage room.

"Where are you going now?" Chris asked.

"I'm going to find another candle and candlestick to take back to my room."

"Why?"

"So I can keep working over there."

Chris rolled his eyes, but he kept his mouth shut.

~ ~ ~ ~

As soon as Kevin finished eating dinner Sunday night, he excused himself, saying that he wanted to return to his room to rest. Chris waited a little while and then slipped away to check on him. He gently opened Kevin's door and saw him once again sitting at his desk, focusing his attention on the pebble. As he quietly shut the door, Chris couldn't help but wonder how long Kevin could keep up that level of strain.

Monday, Tuesday, and Wednesday were carbon copies of Sunday. Wednesday afternoon as they were getting their things together to leave, Glendymere said, *"Kevin, I feel doubt growing in your heart with each passing day. You must believe in yourself before your talent can rise to the surface. It will come, but only if you conquer your doubts."*

Then he told Chris privately, *"If this is going to work, not only does he have to believe that he can become a sorcerer, he must also want to become one. The desire as well as the confidence must come from within him. Neither one is something that either of us can give him."*

Chris nodded to indicate that he understood as he followed Kevin down the hall.

~ ~ ~ ~

That evening after dinner, Kevin returned to his room as usual, but instead of trying to move the stone or light the candle, he put all of his glowstones in their cases, stretched out on his bed in the dark, closed his eyes, and began to think about what Glendymere had said. He knew that Glendymere was right; something was wrong. He just didn't know what.

While he was thinking about everything that had happened since he stepped onto that bus, he became aware of a faint light near his desk. It grew in intensity, until it proved enough of a distraction that his thoughts were interrupted. When he opened his eyes and sat up to investigate, he saw a woman standing in the center of a shimmering oval of light. As he watched, she nodded her head once, very slowly, and then sat down on the edge of the desk chair. Her hair was light brown, and although Kevin couldn't see the color of her eyes, he somehow knew they were light brown also. She was wearing a pale blue robe that was gathered around her waist by a small silver belt, and her feet were encased in dainty black slippers.

After a couple of minutes the apparition spoke. "Myron, you've grown into a handsome man. I had hoped that you would have your father's build, but never mind. You have his magic, and that's much more important."

Kevin scooted back in the bed until his back rested against the wall of the cave. He stared at the woman seated across the room, trying to capture a faint memory that he never knew he had. "Are you Yvonne?" he asked softly. He was amazed to realize that he was neither afraid of the apparition, nor surprised by its presence in his room.

"Yes, I'm your mother. I do hope sending you to Earth wasn't a mistake. You don't know how Badec and I agonized over that decision. It was definitely the safest place for you, but there were so many disadvantages to cutting you off from Terah and our way of life. I just hope we didn't end up doing you a disservice while trying to preserve your life."

"What do you mean?"

"Well, Glendymere's right. I've been watching you for the past few days, and the only thing stopping you is your own doubt, and I'm afraid that you got that from Earth. We knew that was a possibility, but we really thought Pallor would be able to counteract the prejudice that the people of Earth have against magic."

"He tried. He brought me books that had stories about magic and dragons and things like that, but my parents took them away from me. They said that there was no such thing as magic and that the stories were silly. Oh, sorry, I mean my foster parents," Kevin said in Paul's defense.

"No, that's all right. They were the only parents you knew. You do realize that the only reason you didn't grow up knowing who your real parents were and spending time with us was because I died, don't you?"

"Yes, Kalen explained all about that, and so did Xantha. I was sort of relieved to find out that the O'Reilly's weren't my natural parents. We had almost nothing in common. I used to wonder what went wrong, if babies had been switched in the hospital or something. At least now it all makes sense." Kevin shrugged as if to say that it was no big deal.

"Well, if knowing about Terah, Badec, and me answers some of the questions that have been troubling you, and helps things in your life make sense, why do you have so much trouble believing that you can do the things that Glendymere describes?"

"I've been thinking about that for the past hour. I don't think the problem is that I don't believe in magic, or in Terah, or in all the things that I've seen since I've been here. What I don't believe in is me as a sorcerer. I don't want to be a sorcerer, much less the Master Sorcerer. That's an important position and the person who holds that post has a lot of responsibility. Decisions he makes affect the lives of a lot of people."

"Yes, so?"

"So, I'm just an ordinary guy. Well, maybe a little smarter than average, but certainly no genius. I don't know how to be an important person whose decisions affect other people's lives and I don't want to be one. I never even wanted to be a supervisor. Just being a desk jockey was fine with me. I can't stand the idea of having to fire someone from their job, and here they're talking about challenges where sorcerers fight to the death. I definitely don't want to die, but I don't want to cause someone else to die either. If I do become a sorcerer, then I've got to accept the baggage that goes with it, and I just don't know if I can do that."

"Myron, I understand, and believe it or not, so would your father. You're right that there's a lot of responsibility involved, and there are risks. Badec would never have challenged another sorcerer, and he really tried to talk anyone who challenged him out of fighting, but when he had to fight, he did, and so will you."

"Why? Why fight? In the end, someone better, someone stronger, will come along and kill me. Why not just go ahead and get it over with? Why have to live with other sorcerers' deaths on my conscience when it won't do anything but put off the inevitable?" Kevin asked in an explosive voice.

Yvonne waited a moment before answering. "For one thing, some of the sorcerers out there are just plain evil; they are power hungry monsters. They'll kill anyone who gets in their way. Your father was dedicated to seeing that none of them got a chance to sit in the Master's Chair, and the only way he could do that was to keep it himself. And the only way to keep it is to be so good that the bad guys know that you have the power to destroy them if they try to take it away from you, the good guys know that you can hold onto it, and the ones on the fence don't have to choose sides. Badec practiced constantly and used every opportunity he could find to publicly demonstrate just how powerful he was. In the thirty years that your father served as Master Sorcerer, he only had to accept two challenges, and his victory was celebrated all over Terah in each case. Son, sometimes you just have to stand up for what's right and fight. I wish it weren't so, but it is."

"I understand what you're saying, and I could probably justify it to myself if an evil sorcerer challenged me and I happened to win, and I'll grant you that preventing evil from gaining control is a valid reason to risk my conscience or even my life. But how can I be sure that I'd be any better in the Master's Chair? I don't know anything about Terah, about how this culture really operates. I could do some serious damage here by accident!"

"You know the difference between right and wrong, and as long as you put the welfare of others above your own, you can't go wrong. Trust your instincts."

Kevin leaned forward and said, "Okay, let me give you an example of what I'm talking about. Slavery is accepted on Terah. To me it's wrong, pure and simple. The idea of raiding a village, taking families away from their homes just to sell them into slavery somewhere else is abhorrent. There is no way I can go along with that."

"I agree, and so does your father. Every province on Terah has laws concerning the capture and sale of its citizens. The armies try to protect the citizens from capture, and anytime slavers raid a village, the soldiers really do try to catch the slavers before they can get out of that province. When they catch them, they either imprison the slavers or execute them, so you'd think that would slow things down, but it doesn't." Yvonne paused and then went on. "I guess it's because there's so much money tied up in the slave trade. Government officials, wealthy landowners, and sorcerers stand in line to buy people who were captured in other provinces at the same time that they're issuing orders for soldiers to hunt down the very same slavers if they pull a raid in their province. It just doesn't make sense and Badec has been trying unsuccessfully for years to get people to recognize the hypocrisy inherent in the slave trade. Actually, he was beginning to make a little headway. A couple of the other sorcerers on the council were starting to look at slavery the same way Badec does, and then he …" Yvonne didn't finish her sentence. She looked off into space as if listening to her own thoughts.

"What happened to him anyway? All I've heard is that he's in a coma. Was it a stroke? Or a heart attack?"

"I don't think so. Badec was one of the healthiest men on Terah only a couple of days before he fell into that coma. I don't know what happened," Yvonne said slowly.

"You think someone tried to kill him, don't you?" Kevin asked after a couple of minutes of silence.

"I don't know, but let's just say it wouldn't come as a complete surprise. In fact, I think it's probable."

"Any idea who?"

"I'm not going to speculate as to who might have done it until we know what happened, but if you can find proof that the coma wasn't due to natural causes, I might have a few ideas."

"So, all of this is probably because someone either doesn't want to give up their slaves or is making a lot of money off of the slave trade?"

"Not necessarily. If someone tried to kill Badec, it could just as easily be a sorcerer who knows he or she has no hope of defeating him and figures you're an easier target. Or it could be someone who wants to see the stronger sorcerers kill each other off in the war that will take place if you don't make it to Camden by April. Or it could be because of something that neither of us knows anything about at this point," Yvonne said with a shrug. "But I won't be surprised if it turns out that the coma's not natural."

Kevin settled back against the wall for a few minutes. Then he said, "I'm going to change the subject if you don't mind." Yvonne nodded. "What are you? A ghost?"

Yvonne laughed and said, "I guess that's about as good a description as any. My body died, but not my spirit."

"Are you real? I mean, can I touch you?" Kevin asked as he stood up from the bed.

"You can touch the space where I am. It's not like touching another person, but you can tell there's something here. Why?"

"Oh, no reason really. I just wondered what it would be like to kiss my mother's cheek."

Yvonne smiled. "Why don't you find out?"

Kevin walked over to the apparition and kissed her cheek. His lips touched something cool and soft, not quite solid, but definitely there. "Will I see you again?"

"If you wish. I can't do this often though. It takes a lot of concentration to hold a visual image. In the meantime, I'll always be close by," Yvonne said as she stood up and reached for her son's hand.

Kevin cupped his hands around hers. "I'd like to spend some time with you, talking to you. I'd like to get to know you. Have you always been nearby? Why haven't you ever come to me before?"

"A spirit is confined to the world where the body died. I thought about having Badec transport me to Earth right before I died so I could watch over your childhood, but to be honest, I thought you might need me more once you returned to Terah, so I stayed here. I hope I made the right choice." Yvonne's aura was beginning to fade.

"You did. I need you here. I made it through childhood just fine," Kevin said. "You're starting to fade. Does that mean that you have to go now?"

"Yes, son. I've held this image for about as long as I can. Take care," Yvonne said as the shimmering light closed around her, dimmed, and then vanished from the room.

~ ~ ~ ~

Thursday morning Chris was waiting for the coffee to perk when Kevin walked into the kitchen. He looked ten years younger than he had at dinner the night before. There was a sparkle in his eyes and a spring in his step. Chris nodded and said, "You're in a good mood this morning. Anything happen with the stone or candle?"

"No, not yet," Kevin answered as he cut a large slice of bread and began spreading strawberry preserves on it. "I just slept better last night than I have in quite some time."

"Your good mood wouldn't have anything to do with your visitor last night would it?" Chris said with a grin.

Kevin didn't answer immediately. He leaned against the table, eating his bread and thinking. He decided that he might as well tell Chris. "How much do you know?"

"Not much. I just know that when I went to my room last night there was a faint glow under your door and a very feminine voice coming from inside."

"Chris, I'm going to tell you what happened, but I'm not sure that I'm going to tell the others just yet, so keep this between us for now, okay?"

"Sure."

"Yvonne came to see me last night."

"Yvonne?" Chris asked. "As in your mother?"

Kevin nodded. "We had a good talk. Unfortunately, she couldn't stay very long. There are a lot of questions I would like to ask her."

"I thought your mother was dead," Chris said slowly.

"She is. When I said that she came, I meant her spirit."

Chris stopped slicing the bread he was fixing for his breakfast, turned, and stared at Kevin. Finally he asked, "What did she look like? Was it like a ghost?"

"Kind of. There was a sort of glow around her, but she didn't float or anything, and I couldn't see through her like they show in the movies. She was standing when she first appeared, and then again right before she vanished, but most of the time she sat on the chair at my desk. We talked, just as if she had been … I don't know … human I guess. It was just like talking to you."

"Did she say anything that I need to know about?" Chris asked. He was curious, but he didn't want to pry. He poured a large mug of coffee for each of them and handed Kevin's to him.

"Actually there are a couple of things you'd be interested in. One, Badec had been trying to get the council to take a stand against slavery before he got sick," Kevin said, and then he took a long, slow swallow of coffee.

"Darrell would love to hear that. So would the others."

"I know. We'll tell them later, but I'm not ready to share this with everyone yet. The other thing she told me is that she's pretty sure Badec's coma did not come from natural causes. She feels fairly certain that someone was trying to get him out of the way." Kevin stopped for a moment, sighed, and added, "She didn't come right out and say so, but I got the feeling that she's not expecting him to recover."

"Then I guess it's going to be up to you to find the people responsible, isn't it?"

"Eventually, I guess. But I can't get sidetracked with that right now. Are you about ready to go? I'm anxious to get over there and get started."

"Give me about ten minutes and I'll be ready to leave. Have another cup of coffee." Chris picked up the pot to top off both of their mugs. "What's your rush this morning anyway?"

"I don't know. I'm just ready to get going."

~ ~ ~ ~

When Chris and Kevin knocked on Glendymere's door, they got an immediate response. *"I'm out in the valley. Come on out and join me."*

They stopped by their room just long enough to drop off the torches and their lunch bag and then headed down the hall to the mouth of the cave. When they stepped out into the sunlight, they saw Glendymere gliding on air currents as he circled the canyon a couple of hundred feet above the ground. He looked like he was thoroughly enjoying himself.

"He seems to be in a good mood this morning, too," Chris said with a grin. "You know, that does look like fun."

"It is. Want to go for a ride?" Glendymere asked.

"Uh, no. I think I'll keep my feet on the ground for now, but I might take you up on it later," Chris said, laughing at his own cowardice.

"All right, but it's your loss." Glendymere circled down and settled gently on the ground in front of them. *"Kevin, I thought we'd take a trip today."*

"Where are we going?" Kevin asked.

"In search of a storm to play in. Come on, climb on up. Sit between two of the spines on my neck and hold onto the chain I wear around my neck. It'll feel a bit awkward at first, but it's not any harder than riding Xantha." Glendymere knelt and extended his foreleg so that Kevin could scramble up his arm to his massive shoulders and then on up to his neck.

While Kevin was getting settled, Glendymere said to Chris, *"Blalick will be along in a few minutes. He said something about the two of you installing a stove somewhere in the caverns this morning. We'll be back around lunchtime."*

Then Glendymere asked Kevin if he was settled, and when Kevin said yes, he rose, stretched his wings, and slowly and gracefully ascended into the sky, disappearing beyond the canyon walls. Chris walked back inside the huge entrance hall to wait for Blalick.

Kevin could tell that Glendymere was flying in a southerly direction but he had no way of estimating how fast they were traveling. All he knew was that they were flying a lot faster than he had ever flown with Xantha. After a while, Kevin saw storm clouds in the distance over what looked like desert canyon lands.

Glendymere slowed down as they approached the clouds, circled for a few minutes looking for a good place to land, and finally settled on a barren butte a couple of miles from the clouds and directly in their path. When Kevin climbed down, Glendymere told him to stand near the edge of the cliff and watch the storm.

Kevin took a couple of steps towards the cliff and watched the wind swirl the clouds around. When the rain began, it looked like someone had dropped a dark gray translucent cloth from the bottom of the clouds to the ground. A few minutes later he saw the lightning begin as the storm intensified.

"Now, I want you to join with the storm. Feel its power, its strength, become one with the wind," Glendymere said.

204

"How? How do I do that?" Kevin turned to face Glendymere.

"Don't worry about how. Don't even think about what you're trying to do. Just give yourself over to your instincts and let it happen," Glendymere answered gently.

Kevin turned back to the storm, took one step closer to the side of the cliff, closed his eyes and tried to erase all thoughts from his mind and just feel. After a few minutes, he became aware of a sensation of rising, of floating above the ground, of racing with the wind. He felt pockets of cool air clashing with hot gusts of wind. The rain slashed at his body as the fury of the storm washed over him. Lightning darted all around him, leaving him with a tingling sensation.

As the storm intensified, he felt cut off from everything and everyone, isolated in the core of the swirling winds. He surrendered his senses to the power of the storm and felt the energy surge through him, building inside him. He had no idea how long he remained in the center of the storm. It could have been a minute or a day. There was no sensation of past or future, only the moment at hand.

Then the storm began to wane, and after a few minutes, Kevin became aware of his surroundings again. He was surprised to find that he was still standing on the butte not more than ten feet from Glendymere. His hair, his clothing, and the ground where he was standing were all perfectly dry. He turned to Glendymere with a look of awe in his eyes.

"Magnificent storm. Did you enjoy it?" Glendymere asked.

"I don't know what to say. It was the most incredible experience I've ever had," Kevin said, almost in a whisper.

"And there are a lot more experiences out there waiting for you that are just as incredible as that one." Glendymere stood quietly for a few minutes to let Kevin savor the feeling. Then he said, *"I felt a change in you this morning. I thought you were ready for this. I hope you don't mind, but I scanned your memories to see what caused the change. Yvonne is a delightful woman. I'm glad you finally met her."*

Glendymere knelt for Kevin to climb back up. As soon as Kevin was seated, he rose into the sky and soared off to the north. After a while, he continued, *"And I'm glad that you've come to terms with your doubts. We'll talk more about that later, but you're right, the only way you're going to get through this without either killing another sorcerer or getting killed yourself is to be so good that no one would be willing to risk challenging you."*

"Do you think I can do it?"

"I don't know. Possibly. Your elven blood gives you an advantage in the raw talent area, but the real key is hard work. You'll have to practice and practice, and then when it's perfect, you'll have to practice some more, and it won't end until you pass the Master's Chair on to your heir. But for now, take it one day at a time and don't try to look too far ahead. Let me worry about the future."

~ ~ ~ ~

By the time Kevin and Glendymere returned to Willow Canyon, Blalick and Chris were almost finished installing the stove. It was a small potbellied stove with room on top for either a coffee pot or a saucepan, but not both. They had put it in a corner so that a natural crevice could be used for the chimney.

Glendymere raised his eyebrows and said, *"You know, if you wanted hot water, all you had to do was say so. I'm sort of the original furnace."*

Kevin laughed and Chris said, "I never even thought of that. Oh well, at least this way we won't have to bother you when we want a cup of coffee."

Then Glendymere yawned carefully and settled down for his afternoon nap while Kevin and Chris went to their room for lunch. While they were eating, Kevin told Chris about the storm and how its power seemed to surge through him. "It was almost like I was part of the storm, not just in it. I've never felt anything quite like it. I felt the rain all around me, but when I came out of it, I was completely dry. It was almost like my mind was there but my body wasn't. Really weird, but amazing."

After lunch, he sat down at the table and focused his attention on the candle for over an hour with no luck. Then they tried the seeing eye, but that was futile, too. After a short stretch break, Kevin sat back down at the table with the pebble in front of him and concentrated on it for another hour. By then it was getting close to 5:00.

Chris pulled his chair out across the table from Kevin, sat down, leaned back, and stretched his legs out under the table. "Give it a rest. You've been at this all afternoon. You accomplished one task today; you joined with the wind. Be happy with that and let's knock it off for today."

"I just feel so frustrated," Kevin said in exasperation. "This morning was the most exhilarating experience of my life. I felt like I could do anything, but now … I just don't know what else I'm supposed to do. How do you make a pebble move anyway?"

"You're probably trying too hard. It can't be that tough or no one would ever get the hang of it. Maybe if you relax a bit," Chris suggested.

"Relax?! I suppose you think that stone will just move by itself, huh?" Kevin flicked his hand towards the pebble, and the pebble flew off the table, straight into the middle of Chris's forehead. "Chris! Are you okay?" Kevin sputtered as he jumped up from his chair.

Chris just sat there, stunned. He gingerly felt his forehead with his fingertips, and then looked at them to see if there was any blood on them. When he realized that he wasn't bleeding, he started rubbing the spot where the pebble hit and grinned, "Well, you just accomplished the second of the tasks. You definitely moved that pebble!"

"I did, didn't I?" Kevin said in a dazed voice as he sank back down in his chair. "But how? What did I do that worked?"

"Well, for one thing, you weren't concentrating so hard. You were talking to me. What did you see in your mind right before it flew off the table?" Chris asked.

Kevin thought for a minute, and when he spoke, he was talking to himself more than to Chris. "When I said 'move by itself,' I got a mental image of the stone taking off – almost just like it did."

"Okay, there's your answer. Just imagine that same thing again, only wait until I move out of the way this time. I think I'll stand behind you. It should be safe enough there," Chris said as he got up and walked over behind Kevin. "Go on, try it again."

"I'm afraid to. I'm afraid that that was just a fluke and it'll never happen again," Kevin admitted.

"So what have you got to lose? It never happened before, did it? Go ahead. Just picture your hand reaching out for it and pushing it along. Don't try to force it. Be gentle," Chris said quietly.

Kevin turned back to the table and took a deep breath. This time he didn't try to block out all other thoughts. He didn't lose sight of everything else around him like he had done every time before. He just pictured the stone moving along the table. After a few seconds, the small stone scooted along the table for about six inches.

"You did it! Kevin, you really did it! And this time it wasn't a fluke! You've got it. You've really got it! I can't wait to tell everyone! I can't believe how exciting this is!" Chris was jumping around the room in his excitement. "We've got to wake Glendymere up and tell him!"

"You've already done that," Glendymere said with a laugh. *"I think things should start moving along nicely now. See you tomorrow."*

"See you in the morning," Kevin said in as steady a voice as he could manage as he began to slowly gather their things together. What he really wanted to do was to dance around the room and whoop and holler, just like Chris.

Chapter 32

The First Month

The next morning, a big goose egg had come up on Chris's forehead. Joan came into the kitchen while Chris was making the coffee and asked him what had happened.

"Do you remember the four tasks that I told you that Kevin was working on?" Chris asked. When Joan nodded, he continued, "And one of them was to move a pebble across a table?" Again, Joan nodded. "Well, let's just say he did it."

"Are you saying that Kevin hit you in the head with the pebble?" Joan asked, laughing. When Chris nodded, Joan said, a little more sympathetically, "Do you want Theresa to look at it? Maybe she has something that would take the swelling out."

"No, it'll be okay. It doesn't hurt unless I touch it."

"Maybe it would be a good idea to stand behind Kevin while he's working on his magic."

"Actually, I do try to stay out of the way while he's working, but this happened while we were sitting at the table in our room over at Glendymere's, just talking."

"Talking? And the pebble just jumped up and hit you in the head?"

"Not exactly. He was frustrated about not being able to move the pebble and I told him to stop concentrating so hard, to relax about the whole thing. He sort of blew up. He asked if I thought the stone would move by itself, and he flicked his hand as he said it. The next thing we knew – Whap! The pebble flew through the air and nailed me between the eyes!" Chris poured a mug of coffee for himself and one for Joan. "Actually, I think it surprised him more than it did me. Then, a couple of minutes later, he moved it again, slowly, gently, and only a few inches, but he moved it. And yesterday morning, he and Glendymere went off to find a storm, and Kevin managed to join with it. He said it was the most exhilarating experience of his life."

"Why didn't the two of you tell us about this last night?"

"He asked me not to say anything yet. I think he's a bit self-conscious about the whole thing." Chris drank a few sips of coffee.

"Chris, try to get him to talk to us about what he's doing and to demonstrate it for us." Joan took a long swallow of her coffee. "None of us have any experience with this kind of stuff. It's totally new to us."

"I know, but there really hasn't been anything to tell until yesterday." Chris poured a mug of coffee to take to Kevin. "Give him a little time. He's not exactly comfortable with any of this yet. I'm sure he'll loosen up once he masters the basics."

~ ~ ~ ~

Over the next couple of weeks, things settled down into daily routines for the Tellurians. Karl, Steve, and Darrell spent their early mornings on horseback, riding over the valley, mountainsides, and crests, searching for any signs that they had been discovered. Joan usually joined them for about an hour before lunch to work out and spar.

Karl spent his afternoons with Blalick, working on various building projects, tending the animals, or gathering fruits and vegetables from Blalick's orchard and garden. Joan spent her afternoons with Ashni, spinning fleece into thread and yarn, weaving cloth, canning, preserving, and baking. Darrell and Steve spent their afternoons constructing a target range, an exercise field, and an obstacle course.

Theresa and Sari spent most of the day combing the woods for herbs, transplanting some and gathering others. In the late afternoon, they worked in Theresa's workroom, processing the herbs they had gathered while Theresa taught Sari how to prepare and use them.

Kevin and Chris were completely occupied with magic. Kevin began to make slow and steady progress, but each small success brought new and more difficult challenges.

The only one of the four original tasks that was still giving Kevin problems was lighting the candle, and he was almost becoming obsessed with it, working on it for hours everyday while they were at Willow Canyon and then every night in his room.

"Do you realize that it was exactly two weeks ago today that I first moved the pebble?" Kevin asked while he and Chris were eating lunch in their room in Willow Canyon.

"Yeah," Chris said as he gently touched his forehead. "You've come a long way in two weeks." Chris reached for his mug, just as it started moving slowly across the table towards his hand. As the mug reached his fingertips, it gently stopped, this time without splashing any hot coffee on Chris's hand. "You're definitely getting better with that. The first time you moved a mug of water across the table, you sloshed most of it out. I'm waiting for you to get good enough to carry the mug to the pot, pick up the pot, pour the coffee, and then put it in my hand."

"Why don't we give it a try?" Kevin asked as he mentally picked up his own mug, carried it over to the coffee pot and held it in the air a few inches away from the pot. "I've never tried to control two objects at one time before. Maybe I should start with something else first. I'd hate to loose all the coffee. Let's try a pitcher of water." Kevin set the mug down on the small table that they had set up beside the wood stove.

Chris got up, picked up a pitcher, and took it out to the spout above the water basin. When he brought it back in, he set it down on the floor. "I know that's not what you were thinking, but if it falls, the water won't splash quite as far." Chris walked back over to the table and sat back down. "I didn't fill it up. There's just enough for you to be able to pour some. Go ahead. Give it a try."

Kevin mentally moved his mug down to the floor beside the pitcher, but he didn't set it on the floor. "The main idea here is to control two objects at one time. Let's see. Maybe I should think in terms of having two hands," Kevin mumbled to himself as he began to concentrate on the pitcher. After a couple of minutes, the pitcher moved, but instead of tipping over to gently pour the water, it flipped over and dumped the water on the floor. "All right. Let's try that one again."

"Do you want some more water? Or do you want to try a dry run?" Chris asked with a laugh.

"Let's try it without water." Kevin lifted the pitcher in the air and tried to ease it over on its side. The pitcher moved a little slower, but just as it reached the point where it would begin to pour, it slipped and fell to the floor again.

"One more try. I'll get it this time," Kevin said to himself as he mentally reached out, righted the pitcher, and picked it up again. This time he managed to hold the pitcher and the mug steady, tip the pitcher just a bit as if to pour, then right the pitcher again, but he lost it before he could set it back on the ground.

"Oh well. That one will take a little practice. Right now, I want another cup of coffee." Kevin stood up, mentally picked up his mug and floated it to his hand, carried it over to the stove, and poured the coffee. "You know, I could get really lazy with this. It's as bad as remote controls for television. With enough practice, I could just sit in that chair and get anything I want without ever having to get up."

"I don't think that's the objective here," Chris said with a grin. "When we get back tonight, why don't you try setting the table? They haven't seen you do any of this stuff yet. I bet Joan would freak out."

"I don't want to break all the dishes." Then Kevin thought about it for a moment. "But if we set them on the table first, and then I moved them around one at a time … yeah, I think I could do that okay. Might be fun at that."

"Well, it's time to get back to work. What do you want to work on now?" Chris asked.

"The candle I guess," Kevin said with a sigh. "I don't know why I can't get the hang of this one. Nothing I've tried has worked. I think the only way that candle is going to get lit is for me to find some matches, strike one, and light it!" Kevin flicked his hand like he was striking a kitchen match.

As he flicked his hand, flames flew out from his fingertips in a cone-like pattern. Most of the flames landed on the floor or table and went out almost instantly, but some landed on the blanket and pillow on his bed and ignited the cloth.

Chris yelped as he grabbed the pitcher and ran out to the water basin.

Kevin was so surprised that he couldn't do anything but stand there and gape at the dancing flames for a couple of seconds. Then he darted over to his bed and jerked the blanket and pillow off before the mattress could catch on fire. By the time he had his bedding on the floor, Chris had run back in with a pitcher of water to douse the flames. In a matter of seconds, all of the flames had been snuffed out.

"Well, I guess you found the secret to that one," Chris said as he tried to choke back a chuckle.

The smell of smoke woke Glendymere up from his afternoon nap. *"What happened? I thought we had my chambers clear of anything that would burn,"* he said as he looked around, trying to figure out what was smoldering.

"It wasn't you," Chris laughed. "Kevin finally made some fire. Unfortunately, his aim was a little off."

"Oh, good. Now that you've found your internal spark we can start working on other things. We'll get started first thing in the morning," Glendymere replied with a yawn.

"Great, I can hardly wait," Chris mumbled as he and Kevin cleaned up the remnants of Kevin's blanket and pillow.

~ ~ ~ ~

They returned to Rainbow Valley a little early that night so that Kevin could offer to set the table. He took the dishes and mugs out of the cabinet and set them down on the table. Then he leaned against the dining room wall and began mentally moving them around to each place. While Kevin was moving the plates and mugs, Chris took the flatware out of the drawer, laid it down on the table, and walked away to watch. Kevin moved the knives, forks, and spoons into their proper positions around the plates.

Joan didn't see Kevin move the plates because she had her back to the table, but she turned around in time to see pieces of flatware moving around on the table and sliding to a stop next to the plates. At first she frowned, and then her face lit up. "Kevin! Are you doing that? You're going to have to do this again when the others get here. I'm not kidding! Karl will think I've lost my mind if I tell him about this. He has to see this for himself! What else can you do?" Joan said without taking her eyes off the table.

"Oh, there are a few other things. This afternoon I set our room over at Glendymere's on fire, but so far, this is the most useful thing I've been able to accomplish."

Joan raised her eyebrows and turned to look at Kevin as she asked, "What do you mean, you set your room on fire?"

"Well, it wasn't on purpose. We were talking about the fact that I couldn't seem to get the hang of lighting the candle, and when I said that I needed a match to light it …"

Chris grabbed Kevin's hand just as he started to flick it. "And that's how he set the room on fire, by flicking his hand like he was striking a match. Man, you have got to learn to talk without moving your hands until you get this magic stuff down."

"Sorry," Kevin grinned sheepishly. "And that's exactly how it happened."

"Well, just don't try to light candles on my table yet," Joan replied. She reached out to gently touch her tablecloth, almost protectively. "Now, take the plates and silverware up so that you can set the table again when everyone else gets here."

Kevin and Chris stacked the plates back up, set the mugs in a circle around the plates and gathered the flatware into a pile. Then they sat down to wait for the others to come in.

That evening, after he'd gone back to his room, Kevin smiled as he thought back to the demonstration he'd put on for the rest of the Tellurians before dinner. He had enjoyed showing them what he could do and answering their questions. Maybe he was becoming a bit more comfortable with the idea of Kevin the Sorcerer. When it worked, magic was fun. But even so, he still had some serious problems with the idea of Myron, the Master Sorcerer.

~ ~ ~ ~

On Saturday evening when Kevin and Chris returned from Willow Canyon, they found a large cake sitting in the middle of the dining room table with one lone candle stuck in the top. Chris asked Joan what the cake was for.

"We decided that it was time to celebrate. Do you realize that today is June 30? We've been in Rainbow Valley for a month. That's what the candle is for. We've asked Blalick, Ashni and the kids to come down for cake and coffee after dinner. We thought we'd pull out the instruments and put on a show for them," Joan replied.

"Sounds like fun," Chris said.

"Why don't we hold the performance outside?" Kevin suggested. "The weather's nice and the giants can stretch out on the ground. It really is a little cramped for them in here. We could take the cake outside and make coffee over a campfire."

"Good idea, but we'll need something large enough to hold the cake, plates, and mugs," Joan said as she looked around to see if she could spot something suitable.

"How about the square table in the sitting room?" Chris suggested.

Joan nodded. "That'll work." Then she turned her attention back to dinner.

Everyone had a good time that evening. After the Tellurians ran through their usual show, they put the instruments away and joined the giants around the campfire for cake and coffee. Over the past month, the giants had become almost family and conversation was easy and relaxed, and even the occasional silence was comfortable. For the first time in a long time, the Tellurians felt at home, like they actually belonged right where they were. Even Kevin, with all his misgivings about his future, was content.

Later that evening, after the giants had returned to the mountain peak and all of the Tellurians had retired to their rooms, Chris decided that he wanted a cup of hot chocolate. He stopped by Kevin's room to see if he wanted one, but Kevin wasn't there. Chris walked down to the kitchen to see if Kevin had had the same idea, but he wasn't in the kitchen either, so Chris decided to look around outside. He found Kevin at the edge of the forest, gazing at the stars.

"Want some company, or did you just want some time to yourself?" Chris asked.

"No, that's okay. I just wanted to look at the stars for a while. I hadn't thought about it until tonight, but we've already been here a month."

"I know. In a way it's flown by, and in another way, it seems like we've been here a lot longer than just one month."

"It's like when we were in school, the days drag by, but the weeks fly."

Chris nodded and said, "That's it exactly. But then, I guess that's as it should be."

Kevin grinned. "Yeah, I'm enrolled in Willow Canyon University taking Magic 101."

"And your professor is not only the head of the department, he's the university founder and president."

"Well, I wish someone would give us a course outline. Right now, I'm only up to Elementary Parlor Tricks, and I have a feeling that I have a long way to go before we get to the chapter on Dueling Strategies and Defenses."

"Yeah, but we'll get there. You know how professors are. They're always rearranging and adjusting the curriculum to make sure they cover the important stuff before the term runs out," Chris said with a shrug. "Glendymere knows that we have to leave here in less than seven months."

"If not sooner."

"What do you mean?"

"What if Badec dies? Granted we don't know the customs here, but surely a son is expected to show up at his father's funeral. And then what? Do I just turn around and leave Laryn holding the bag while I head back to school? Or do I try to take over as the Master Sorcerer?" Kevin asked quietly.

"Don't borrow trouble, Kevin. Besides, I'd be willing to bet that there's a contingency plan already in place for just that possibility."

Kevin gave Chris a startled look and then chuckled, "I bet you're right. I hadn't thought of that. Kalen probably had that worked out before we left the Gate House."

"I wouldn't be surprised if he had it worked out before we ever arrived on Terah. Kalen probably took care of that while Paul was busy rounding all of us up."

After a few minutes, Kevin said, "I guess it's about time we went back inside. I'd like something warm to drink before we turn in. How about you?"

"As a matter of fact, I was on my way to fix some hot chocolate when I discovered that you weren't in your room," Chris answered. "You know, with the number of people who are searching for you, it might be a good idea if you let me know when you go outside to look at the stars. That way, I'd know you're missing on purpose."

"Oh, sorry. I hadn't thought about that. This valley is so peaceful that it's easy to forget we have people after us. Too bad we can't just stay here forever," Kevin said as he started walking back towards the cave entrance.

Chapter 33

Saturday, June 30

The messenger from the bounty hunters rode into Trendon around sundown that evening. Rolan had said that he wanted word by the end of the month and the messenger had ridden hard to get there before the deadline. When he finally made it to the castle, he was taken to a bench outside Rolan's office and told to wait there for Rolan to finish his dinner. No one bothered to offer him anything to eat or drink. He could only hope that his horse was faring better than he was.

An hour later he heard harsh orders and directives accompanied by heavy footsteps and a few seconds later Rolan burst out of the dining room and turned towards his office. Captain Yardner followed at a respectful distance.

As soon as the messenger saw Rolan, he jumped up and stood at attention.

"Who are you, and what is your business here?" Rolan demanded as he drew abreast of the messenger.

The messenger stood even straighter and looked straight ahead, not at Rolan, as he answered, "Sir, I'm here to report on the progress of the bounty hunters. I would not have bothered you so late in the day, but it was my understanding that you wanted the report before the end of the month."

"Well, if I'm to receive the report before the end of the month, you had better get in here and tell me the news. The month will end in a couple of hours," Rolan growled as his page opened the office door. Captain Yardner followed Rolan in, and the messenger followed Captain Yardner. The page shut the door behind them.

The messenger waited for Rolan to speak, but Rolan only glared at him. Finally, he cleared his throat and said, "Sir, we have questioned the locals and searched all of the villages near the badlands area, and we have reached the conclusion that Taelor was with the minstrels when they arrived in Billows. A man answering his description assisted the sister with a healing clinic, and from what you've told us about Taelor, he would have been able to do that. We think it was probably him."

"So, where is he? When will the others arrive with him?" Rolan asked.

"We don't exactly have him, sir. We know that the minstrels and the sister continued traveling south and west. We tracked them all the way to Sheridan, but we haven't been able to find anyone who remembers seeing Taelor with them after Billows. It's like he just vanished," the messenger said quietly.

"Vanished? Vanished? No one just vanishes! Have you questioned the minstrels?"

"Sir, we haven't been able to catch up with them yet. We followed their trail into the mountains, and we know that they camped at the pass above Sheridan, but we don't know where they went from there. We're still looking, but it's going to take a while to track them over the mountains."

"Don't waste your time trying to track them through the mountains. Think about it! Obviously they're not headed for North Amden. They're headed for the human settlements farther to the south, along the coast. There's nowhere else for them to go. Send a couple of men to the coast to wait for them. News of minstrels travels quickly. They should be easy enough to find. And when you find them, bring them to me. I want to question them." Rolan walked over to the chair behind his desk and sat down as if the interview were over.

"Sir, what about the sister? You don't really expect us to bring her, too, do you?"

"Do you have a problem with that?" Rolan glared at the messenger as he answered.

"Uh, no, sir, I don't guess I do," the messenger stammered. "Do you want me to tell them to concentrate on the minstrels and the sister then?"

"No, I want them to find Taelor." Rolan spoke slowly, as if he were addressing a child. "But since their only lead seems to be the minstrels, find them! Question them! And then have someone bring them here to me! But not all of the men are needed to go after a bunch of minstrels, are they?" Rolan paused long enough for the messenger to shake his head. "No, I didn't think so. The rest of the bounty hunters should stay on Taelor's trail. He went somewhere. Check the villages to the east and west of the minstrels' route. He didn't just disappear. He's out there. Find him! Do you understand?"

"Yes, sir. I understand perfectly. If there's nothing else, I'll be on my way tonight with your instructions." The messenger waited a moment to see if Rolan had anything else to say, but when it was clear that he didn't, the messenger turned, opened the door, and fled the office.

As the office door shut behind the messenger, Captain Yardner asked, "Do you think it's wise to turn the bounty hunters loose on a sister? If you alienate the Sisterhood, they could pull all of the sisters out of Brendolanth."

"They wouldn't dare."

"Actually, they would, sir. It happened once before in Jardin, back before the House of Tassori. The sorcerer ordered the arrest of a sister who had treated the wounds of one of the sorcerer's enemies. In the end, all of the sisters left the province and refused to return until the sister was released and the sorcerer was gone. Since then, no sorcerer has tried to interfere with any of the sisters."

"That doesn't mean that they can break the law," Rolan countered, "and aiding an escaped slave in any way is against the law."

"True, but if he was wounded, the Sisterhood will maintain that her vows to treat the wounds of any and all who need her help come first, above any other laws. Even if the bounty hunters can somehow convince her to come with them, the Sisterhood is going to be upset about it and you're going to have quite a battle on your hands, and it's one that you won't win," Captain Yardner said in a calm voice.

"Fine. We'll release her as soon as she gets here. I'll just say that I ordered the capture of the minstrels and that the bounty hunters took it upon themselves to grab the sister, too. No one can blame me for their actions," Rolan said with a shrug. "Now, draft a letter to Damien telling him that I have some bounty hunters on the trail of a thief, and that the minstrels helped him escape. Tell Damien that the bounty hunters have orders to bring the minstrels here to answer some questions about his whereabouts. Don't mention that there's a sister with the group. No need worrying him with the details."

"Thief, sir?"

"Yes, thief. Badec's got Damien questioning the practice of slavery and I don't want to make him choose sides. I need to keep him happy right now. Even Badec himself couldn't object to my sending bounty hunters after a thief."

"Yes, sir."

"Have the letter ready for me to sign in the morning. Now, if there's nothing else, I'm going to get out of here," Rolan said with a wicked grin. "I have someone waiting for me in my chambers."

"Have a good evening, sir" Captain Yardner said with a bow. Then he left Rolan's office and walked down the hall to his office to draft the letter to Damien.

Chapter 34

Long Days of Summer

Glendymere was waiting outside when Kevin and Chris reached Willow Canyon the next morning. He was standing beside a big sand pit similar to the type used in track and field competitions on Earth.

"I thought we'd begin your flying lessons today."

"My what?" Kevin asked, certain that he had misunderstood.

"Flying lessons. You know, up in the air, moving around. You get the general idea, right?"

"Are you sure this is a good idea?" Kevin asked. "I don't much like heights."

"Nonsense. You'll be fine. Step over here and stand in the middle of that sand pit." Once Kevin was in position, Glendymere said, *"Now use your outstretched hand to push against the ground. The farther you push it away, the higher you'll rise."*

Kevin frowned, trying to figure out how to do it.

"Sort of like push-ups", Chris suggested. When Kevin still frowned, he added, "You know, like in gym class."

Kevin cut his eyes over at Chris and said, "Never went to gym class, remember? But I get the idea." Then he closed his eyes and focused on the image of a large hand pushing against the ground.

For the first couple of hours all he managed to do was throw himself off balance, but then, right as he as about ready to call it quits for a while, he felt himself start to rise. As soon as his feet left the ground, he began to wobble around and as he tried to steady himself, his arms fluttered through the air, just like a circus clown standing on a large ball. When Kevin was about a foot off the ground, he completely lost his balance, tipped over, and fell.

"Let's try that one again," Glendymere said while Kevin was dusting the sand off. *"Try to keep the hand that's lifting you directly under you. I think you slipped off to the side a little that time."*

Kevin regrouped, concentrated on pushing against the ground, began to rise, and once more began to falter and pitch from one side to the other as he tried to maintain his balance. After about a minute of floundering around, his feet flew out from under him and he crashed back to the ground.

"At least you were quicker that time. We need to work on those landings though. It would be better if you could land in an upright position."

"Right. Upright. Believe me, I would if I could. Okay, let's give it another shot," Kevin said once he was back on his feet.

"Wait a minute. I've got an idea," Chris said. "Forget the push-ups. Think about a hydraulic lift instead. Let your hand be the base of the lift. Then picture a metal platform on top and yourself standing on that platform. Then use the hydraulic lift to push against the ground."

Kevin nodded slowly. "Okay. Let me try it." He closed his eyes to get the picture firmly in his mind, opened his eyes and began to concentrate on lifting the imaginary platform. After a couple of minutes, he began to rise in the air.

When he had reached a height of about eight feet without wobbling, Glendymere said, *"That's it. I think you've got the idea. Now stop and see if you can just hold that height for a minute."*

Kevin pictured the lift coming to a stop and holding steady. His eyes were open, but he was concentrating so hard that he wasn't focusing on anything. He knew he was up in the air, but he had no idea how high.

"Good. Now I want you to picture yourself being lowered to the ground. Take it slow and easy," Glendymere coached.

Kevin began to lower himself slowly towards the ground. When he was about half way down, he stopped, focused his eyes, realized that he wasn't on the ground yet, lost his balance, and fell the remaining four feet. But this time when he dusted himself off, he was grinning. "I think the hydraulic lift idea's going to work. I think I can do it if I just make sure I'm on the ground before I lose the image. Let's try it one more time."

"Only one more time today though. I don't want you to get so banged up that you can't get out of bed tomorrow. This time keep your eyes focused so you know how high you're going. I don't want you to get too high until you learn how to get back down."

"Okay, but I don't know if I can hold the image if I look around." Kevin closed his eyes for just a couple of seconds to bring the image of the lift back into his mind, opened his eyes, and began to rise almost immediately. When his feet were about ten feet off the ground he stopped, held the height for a couple of seconds, and then began to lower himself slowly back towards the ground. He didn't fall, but he didn't land gently either. He stayed on his feet, but it was a bone-jarring landing, like he'd suddenly stepped off of a curb without realizing it was there.

"Good, much better. I want you to work on that over the next few days, but don't go any higher than you did today. Let me know when you can land on the sand and walk away without leaving any footprints."

~ ~ ~ ~

Over the next couple of weeks, Kevin spent every waking minute either practicing tasks that Glendymere had assigned or thinking about how to use what he was learning. He had progressed from lighting a candle to lighting a small campfire, and then to throwing a burst of energy roughly in the direction he intended. He was lifting larger and heavier objects, and moving them with more precision. He was getting much better at influencing the speed and direction of air currents, vertically as well as horizontally. His skill with his seeing eye had improved to the point that he could use it to map out the location of the trees, boulders, stream and pools in small canyons or valleys. Using the eye to find Chris in the canyon or in the caves had become so easy that Kevin had spiced it up a bit by floating small pebbles out over Chris's head and dropping them on him as he hid.

Around the middle of July, Chris decided that it was time to come up with a new challenge for the seeing eye. He was in the kitchen waiting for the coffee to perk one morning when an idea hit him. As soon as Joan came in, he asked her if she thought the rest of the Tellurians would mind helping out with one of Kevin's exercises that evening.

"No, of course not. What do you want us to do?" she asked.

"Play a game of hide and seek with him."

Joan frowned.

"I'm serious. A couple of times a day I hide, either somewhere in Glendymere's caves or out in the canyon. Kevin gives me a few minutes to get set, and then he uses his seeing eye to find me. He's gotten really good at it, but we need to see if it's just me, or if he can find other people, too."

"Oh, okay."

"Do you think you could get everyone to hide somewhere out in the valley late this afternoon? If everyone's already hidden by the time we get here, he'll have to scan the valley to locate them. I think that would be a good test." Chris poured three cups of coffee, handing one to Joan.

"I'm sure that won't be any problem at all, but how do you know when he finds you?" Joan asked.

"Well, he lets me know by hitting me on the head with pebbles."

Joan thought for a moment. "I have a suggestion. Instead of pebbles, why don't I make some chocolate drops this morning? I could tie up three or four in a small bag and he could drop those down to each person when he finds them. Or do you think the bags might be too heavy for him to work with?"

"They won't be too heavy. The shape might give him a little trouble, but the whole idea is for him to learn to handle new situations. And candy would be a lot more fun than pebbles. We'll plan to return a little earlier than usual this evening, say around 4:30?"

"That's fine. I'll fix a pot of stew this morning and we can heat it up after we're done," Joan said as she sipped her coffee.

"You'll ask the others to hide?"

Joan nodded. "I'd ask the giants to hide too, but they're so big that they might have trouble finding a good hiding place."

"I doubt it," Chris said as he picked up the other two cups of coffee to take back to Kevin's room. "Remember when we first met Blalick? Up at the pass? I was staring right at him when he stepped into the woods and seemed to vanish. I bet they can hide better than any of us can. Ask them if they'd like to join in the fun. They might enjoy it."

~ ~ ~ ~

Joan was so busy that morning, that it didn't even cross her mind to tell the others what Chris had said. By the time she thought about it, they were all scattered for the afternoon.

She found Karl and Blalick outside the cave entrance. Karl was helping Blalick make the loom that she was going to use to weave cloth, as soon as Ashni taught her how to do it. Joan smiled to herself. She knew her husband. He might be in the position of helper right now, but by the time they were done, he'd be able to build all the looms she'd ever want all by himself. They kept working while she explained what Chris wanted, and when they agree to do it, she had the distinct impression that neither of them had the faintest idea what she'd said. As she turned to go find Theresa, she shrugged to herself. She'd just have to come back when it was time to hide, take their tools out of their hands, and tell them again.

Theresa had fully expected the young giant's enthusiasm for gardening to wane after the newness wore off and the work became tedious, but Sari was like a sponge, soaking up all she could learn and always ready for more. When Joan found them in the herb garden, Theresa was showing Sari how to grow a new plant by layering. Joan waited until she finished with the plant she was working on before she explained what Chris wanted them to do. Sari started to object, saying that they had a lot of work to do, but Theresa overrode her and said they'd be happy to help.

On her way out to the practice range, Joan saw Steve sitting on a large rock, concentrating on something in his lap. As she drew closer, she could see that he had a pen in his hand and a board with several sheets of paper on top of it on his lap.

As she approached, she saw a bird sitting on a limb a few feet from Steve, almost as if it were posing. The bird suddenly became aware of her and flew away.

"I'm sorry, Steve," Joan said as she sat down on the rock beside him. "I didn't mean to frighten him away."

"No problem, I was done with him anyway. I was working on the background," Steve said as he looked up from his work.

"This is really good," Joan said as she took a closer look at his sketch. "I had no idea you could draw."

"This is the first time I've done any sketching since Cathy got sick," Steve said. "She and I used to spend our Saturday's out in the woods. I'd sketch and she'd write poetry. Just us, the birds, and the breeze." Steve smiled as the pleasant memories flooded his mind. Then he came back to the present and said, "I'm sure you didn't just happen on me by accident. What can I do for you?"

"Nothing at the moment, but Kevin needs us to help him a little later this afternoon. We're all supposed to hide somewhere in the valley and he's going to try to find us using his seeing eye. When he locates you, he's going to drop a small bag of chocolate drops on you to let you know you've been spotted. Are you game?"

"Sure. I'm guessing that the chocolate drops were your idea. I bet Kevin and Chris were thinking more along the lines of a rock or something, right?"

Joan laughed as she agreed.

Steve gathered up his supplies and stood up.

"Don't you want to stay and finish your sketch?" Joan asked.

"I'll finish it tonight. I was about ready to stop for now anyway. I'm supposed to meet Darrell in a few minutes and I need to walk around and stretch out first."

"Well, I'm going to get out of here and leave you to it. Just remember to hide by 4:30, okay? See you later," Joan said as she stood up to leave.

Darrell was working out when Joan reached the exercise field. He spotted her as she crossed the field, so he stopped, wiped the sweat off of his face, and smiled in greeting. "Hi. What brings you out here? Did I forget that I was supposed to do something this afternoon?"

"No, but I do want to ask you to do something a little later today," Joan said. Then she explained about Chris's request. After Darrell agreed, she brought up another subject. "Darrell, how would you feel about letting Macin hang around, work out with you, and help you with the exercise field when he's not going to and from Abernon? Ashni asked me to talk to you about it. He's been hiding in the woods watching you work out."

"Yeah, I know. I spotted him in the woods a couple of days ago."

"He's really impressed with the way you move."

"I have to admit, I did show off a little," Darrell grinned. "Why didn't he come join me?"

"He wanted to, but remember, even though the two of you are about the same age in years, he's only thirteen or fourteen emotionally. He wants so badly to learn from you, but he's embarrassed to ask you to teach him."

Darrell nodded. "I know how hard it was for me to approach Martin. I'll ask him to help me with the field, and we'll take it from there. Tell Ashni to have him join in the hunt and I'll ask him when it's over."

"Thanks, Darrell," Joan said as she squeezed Darrell's hand. "Now, I'd better get back and bag up the chocolate drops. Remember to be hidden by 4:30."

On the way back to the cave, Joan stopped by Theresa's herb garden and asked Sari to run up to her house and invite Ashni and Macin to join in the hunt. "And tell your mother to insist that Macin join in."

"Why?" Sari asked.

"Because Darrell wants to talk to him afterwards."

"Should she tell him that Darrell wants to talk to him?"

"No, she just needs to be sure he's here. Darrell will take it from there. Now get going. It's going to be time to hide in about an hour, so you don't have any time to waste. Sorry about stealing your help, Theresa," Joan said as she started off towards the cave entrance.

"No problem. We were about ready to call it a day anyway," Theresa said to Joan. Then she turned towards Sari and said, "Run on now. We'll finish working with the rest of these herbs tomorrow."

~ ~ ~ ~

By the time Kevin and Chris got back from Willow Canyon that afternoon, the caves were empty and eleven small bags of chocolate drops were sitting on the table in the dining room.

Chris counted the bags, grinned, and picked one up. "Joan made one for each of us, too."

Kevin's mouth watered as Chris popped a chocolate drop in his mouth. He could almost taste it himself. "I guess I should wait until after I've found everyone."

"Why?" Chris asked as he tossed one of his chocolate drops to Kevin. "Now, while you and your seeing eye are out there looking for everyone, I'm going down to the waterfall. Let me know when the hunt's over and it's time for dinner."

"How?" Kevin asked.

"You owe me a chocolate drop," Chris said as he walked out of the kitchen.

Less than an hour later, while Chris was stretched out on the grass near the splash pool, a chocolate drop fell on his stomach, telling him it was time to head back for dinner.

~ ~ ~ ~

The next morning, Glendymere watched Kevin practice rising up to a height of about ten feet and then lowering himself back to the ground. His landings had improved to the point that they were no longer dangerous, but he still hadn't managed to land without leaving his footprints in the sand.

"You're getting better, but this time when you get up there, stop and hold your position. I want you to try doing a little more."

Kevin rose up about ten feet and stopped

"Now I want you to move yourself over to the left. Don't try to walk over, that won't work. You have to imagine that your support is moving. Picture it moving to the left, with you on top."

When Kevin tried to move to the left, he leaned in the direction that he wanted to go and lost his balance. He struggled for a few seconds before he started to fall. Just as he was about to hit the ground, he felt himself land on a soft cushion, almost like a giant air bag. He was able to stand back up without injury. Kevin and Chris both looked at Glendymere with questions in their eyes.

"Yes, that was me. I was planning to go over how to do that later today, but maybe you need to learn how to catch something before we go much farther with the flying." Then Glendymere turned towards Chris and said, *"I need an egg."*

"An egg?" Chris asked.

"Yes, an egg. Let's go inside. I asked Blalick to bring some down yesterday. They should be in the storeroom. Would you go get one for me, Chris? On second thought, get several."

Once they were back in the inner chamber, Glendymere said, *"When you're trying to catch something small, like an egg, you could just reach out with your mind's hand and grab it out of the air, but if you aren't really careful, you might break it. An air cushion is the safest way to catch something. And the nice thing about an air cushion is that it'll work for anything from an egg to a man, or even a horse and wagon."*

"How do you make one?" Kevin asked.

"You make the air near the ground really dense and then you build up the pressure until there's enough force to support the weight of what's falling. You don't have to worry about building up too much pressure though. It's not going to explode or anything. Once whatever you're trying to catch is riding on top of the air cushion, you release the air nice and slow and let it sink to the ground. Ah, here comes Chris. Watch as I catch the egg." Glendymere waited for Chris to join them. *"Chris, I want you to hold one of the eggs out in front of you at shoulder height. Yes, that's right. Now drop it."*

Chris dropped the egg, but before it hit the ground it came to rest on an invisible cushion about six inches above the ground. It bobbed up and down for a moment and then slowly sank to the floor. When Kevin picked the egg up to examine it, the shell wasn't even cracked.

"Now, you try it," Glendymere said to Kevin.

Once again Chris held the egg out at shoulder's height and released it. A couple of seconds later the egg splattered all over the floor. "Well, at least we know he wasn't using a hard boiled egg for the demonstration," Chris said with a chuckle.

"Let me know when you can catch the egg without breaking the shell. Then we'll move on to something more interesting, like catching Chris when he jumps off a cliff," Glendymere said with a twinkle in his eye.

"You are kidding, right?" Chris asked as he pictured the cliff on the east side of the canyon. It was a vertical wall at least a thousand feet high.

"Not really, but we'll get to that later. Right now, the egg. Wake me up when you can catch the egg three times without breaking the shell," Glendymere opened his mouth in a big yawn. *"I'm ready for a nap,"* he said as he curled up, closed his eyes, and began to snore.

"He was kidding, wasn't he?" Chris asked.

"I have no idea, but don't worry about it. If I miss, you probably won't feel a thing when you hit. They say that a person dies of a heart attack before he hits the ground," Kevin teased.

Chris ignored him and stooped down to clean up the broken egg. "Why don't we try a rock or something first? Then when you figure how to make the air cushion we could go back to eggs. Otherwise we're going to spend all our time cleaning the floor."

"Good idea. And if we use a rock, we can work on it in my room after dinner tonight," Kevin replied, and grinned as Chris groaned.

~ ~ ~ ~

A couple of weeks later, Theresa and Joan were making a grocery list for Macin to take with him to Abernon when Ashni walked in.

"I know Macin picks herbs up at the Chapel, but I don't know who fills the orders," Theresa said. "By any chance does he know Sister Evelyne?"

"Yes, he knows Evelyne," Ashni answered. "She and I often exchange notes. She helped with the birth of both of my children."

"Would Macin be willing to deliver a note for me? I thought I'd ask her if she'd like to come for a visit while I'm here, or maybe I could go into Abernon with Macin sometime to see her. But I don't want anyone else knowing where we are, so he would need to put the note directly into her hands."

"I am sure that would be no problem. I will send her a jar of strawberry preserves."

Theresa raised her eyebrows, but she didn't ask any questions.

Ashni grinned. "A few years ago, Blalick took a couple of jars of my preserves to the Chapel for Evelyne and left them with her staff. By the time Evelyne found out about the preserves, all that was left was empty jars. When Macin started making the trips to Abernon, she gave him strict orders not to leave the preserves with anyone but her."

"Good. Then no one will notice the note. I'll write it tonight and give it to him tomorrow. Thanks."

~ ~ ~ ~

Glendymere had asked Kevin and Chris to meet him outside in the canyon first thing the next morning, but when they got there, Glendymere was nowhere to be found. While they waited, Kevin practiced rising, moving horizontally, descending a little, moving horizontally again, then rising again, and so on. Chris was leaning back against a large boulder watching him when he spotted Glendymere off in the distance. A few minutes later, Glendymere swooped down.

"Sorry I'm late," he said as he settled on the canyon floor. *"Got to talking with some of my friends and lost track of time."*

"Do you go visiting often?" Chris asked.

"No, not really, which is one reason time got away from me. After I asked them if they'd be willing to spar with Kevin, we started talking and since we don't see each other very often, there was a lot to say."

"Wait a minute," Kevin said. "Back up. Did you say you asked someone to spar with me?"

"Yes, that was the purpose of the trip. I was lining up some magical sparring matches for you for later this fall. Anyway, don't worry about that now. We have something else to work on."

"Hold on. Magical sparring matches," Kevin repeated. "Exactly what are you talking about?"

"Just what it sounds like. I've asked a few friends of mine to spar with you. It'll be good practice for when you have to fight for real. Don't worry, like I said, they're friends of mine. They won't be trying to kill you."

"But that could happen, right?" Chris asked. "When we spar, there's always the chance that someone could get hurt. And as powerful as magic is … are you sure this is a good idea?"

"Kevin has to learn to protect himself sometime, doesn't he? What better way than to duel with a dragon?"

"You set these sparring matches up against dragons?" Kevin gasped.

"Of course. Who else would I ask?"

Chris shook his head and held his hands up, palm out. "No! Not against a dragon! There's no way he could win. He won't stand a chance!"

Glendymere tilted his head and bunched his eyebrows. *This isn't about wining. It's about learning to fight. What's the point of training if you don't train against the best? This way he'll learn to defend himself against sorcerers more powerful than any that he'll ever face in combat. I don't know what you two are so upset about, but you can worry about it later. We have other things to think about today,* Glendymere said as he looked around the clearing, searching for something. *"Ahh, that's a good one."* Glendymere mentally picked up a rock about the size of a basketball and set it down about five feet in front of Kevin. *"Now, I want you to tap into the same energy that you use to light the candle and concentrate on heating that rock."*

Kevin shook his head, trying to cast all thoughts of sparring with dragons out of his mind. "All right, I'll give it a shot." About half an hour later, he walked over towards the rock and put his hand out over it to see if he could feel any heat coming from it. "I didn't think I was getting anywhere with this. What am I doing wrong?"

"You aren't doing anything wrong; you just aren't doing it right. Now try it again."

Kevin concentrated once again on the rock, but this time he focused so hard that it made his head ache. After a few minutes, the rock blew apart, throwing hot chunks of rock all around the clearing. Kevin and Chris would both have been hit if the chunks hadn't been stopped in mid-flight by some kind of invisible barrier.

After the dust settled, Chris looked at Glendymere and mouthed, "Thank you."

Glendymere nodded. Then he turned to Kevin and said, *"All right. You have the general idea. Now let's try for something somewhere between nothing and destruction. You need to release the energy in a controlled manner. Build it slowly until you find the right level for what you want to do."*

Kevin looked around for another rock while he thought about what Glendymere had said. "I've got a question. It seems to me that my major breakthroughs have always come when I have the least amount of control, when frustration has built up to the point of anger. Like the time with the pebble, or the time that I set my bed on fire, or just now. I was angry, and something seemed to explode in my head just before the rock exploded."

"So, what is your question?"

"It just seems to me that lack of control is the key, not control."

"For the explosion, yes. But how useful is the explosion? Did the pebble go where you wanted it to go? Did the candle get lit? Did the rock give off a useful warmth? After the explosion, comes the control, and you must control the magic. Otherwise it controls you. We want all the explosions to happen here, where I can sort of keep a lid on things, before you get strong enough to cause real damage."

Kevin thought about what Glendymere had said for a moment and then nodded.

"Now, back to the rock. See if you can get a nice warm glow out of it. Could come in handy on a cold winter's night out on the prairie."

~ ~ ~ ~

A week later, Kevin and Glendymere were on top of the cliff on the east wall of Willow Canyon. Kevin was trying to stir up enough turbulence in the air to produce a rain shower, but he wasn't having much luck. He had managed to push some clouds together and he had even created a few up and down drafts to mix warm and cool air, but it wasn't enough to cause the drops of moisture to become large enough to fall as rain.

While he was concentrating on the wind and clouds, Glendymere spotted Macin's wagon as it wound its way up the side of Wildcat Mountain towards the peak. *"You might want to wait until Macin unloads his wagon before you start the rain."*

"Like I'm really going to be able to make it rain," Kevin said, irritated that his efforts had yet to produce any results. "This place is in for one long draught if it only rains when I cause it!"

Well, why don't you take a break for a bit and let him get inside before you play in the clouds anymore. Who knows? You might do it right for a change."

"Yeah. Just my luck, to do it right at the wrong time," Kevin said as he sat down on the edge of the cliff. About that time he felt a few raindrops hit his head. As he looked up at the sky, the cloud opened up and rain pelted down all over the area. At first Kevin just sat there with his mouth hanging open and his hands out for the rain drops to hit. Then he looked at Glendymere and asked, "Did you do that?"

Glendymere shook his head no.

Then Kevin jumped up and started dancing around in the rain, yelling, "I did it! I finally did it! I made it rain! I did it!"

"Yes, you do have a knack for doing it right at the wrong time," Glendymere said with a quiet chuckle. *"Why don't you fly over there and help Macin unload? Unless, of course, you've figured out how to make it stop. I'm not going to do it for you."*

"No, I haven't gotten there yet," Kevin said as he rose a little above the treetops and worked his way sideways towards Macin.

After Macin and Kevin unloaded most of the goods at the giants' house, they drove the wagon down the side of the mountain to Rainbow Valley and pulled into the cave entrance where Karl and Blalick were waiting somewhat patiently for the sudden rain shower to end.

"That sky was pretty much clear a little while ago, Kevin," Karl commented. "I don't suppose you had anything to do with this sudden rain shower, did you?"

"Well, yes, sort of. Sorry about that. But I did it! And it feels great!" Kevin broke out in a big grin. "Well, since you two are here to help Macin, I'm going back over to Willow Canyon and see if I can do it again. See you at dinner."

After Kevin left, the other three unloaded the wagon and carried the groceries to the kitchen. When they got to the dining room there was a large tray of cookies sitting on the table next to a pitcher of milk. Theresa and Joan were heading for the table with mugs in their hands.

"After you put the groceries down, grab yourself a mug and join us," Joan said. "We'll put them away in a few minutes."

Once the men joined them, it didn't take any time at all for the cookies and milk to disappear. As the men were heading back outside, Macin handed Theresa a sealed envelope. It was from Evelyne. She quickly ripped it open and skimmed the two-page note.

Dear Theresa,

Macin delivered your note this morning. I am writing this while he collects the supplies that he's taking back to his family. I hope this letter finds you safe and in good health.

You mentioned coming here for a visit. I really do not think that is wise at this time. For the past month some rough looking men have wandered in and out of Abernon, asking a lot of questions about the minstrels, you, and most especially about Taelor. From what I've been able to gather, they are bounty hunters sent by Rolan with orders to arrest all of you for aiding an escaped slave.

Since you stayed at the Chapel while you were here and did not go out into the town, they have not been able to find out much. I know that they have questioned my staff, but there was very little that any of them could say.

I was the only one who talked to Taelor when he came by late that night. No one else even saw him. I imagine he planned it that way. So, as far as the bounty hunters know, he was never in Abernon. As for the rest of you, the only thing my staff knows is that a Sister Theresa stayed here one night, accompanied by some minstrels, and that all of you left the next morning.

For some reason the bounty hunters have been hesitant to question me. But do not fear. Even if they do try to get information out of me, I have none to give. You never mentioned your plans or your destination. I know that you headed south when you left Abernon, and that much I will gladly tell them if it will get them away from here.

I have warned Macin not to talk while he is in Abernon, but he is a quiet boy and is used to keeping his own counsel. The giants never discuss any of their guests with the townspeople of Abernon, so his reticence is not seen as unusual.

As long as all of you stay away from any of the roadways and towns around here, you should be safe. There are too many valleys and canyons for the bounty hunters to consider searching all of them. They seem to be waiting for one or all of you to surface. They have pretty good descriptions of all of you, but they don't have any names other than yours. The people of Billows remembered Sister Theresa, the sister who treated them during the recent illness that swept through their town, and they also remembered the young man who assisted her.

Take this seriously, Theresa. Be careful, and stay out of sight. Maybe when things settle down I will be able to take a short vacation. We'll see. I certainly could use one.

With regards,
Evelyne

After Theresa read Evelyne's letter, she passed it on to Joan, who stopped putting away groceries, sat down with a cup of coffee, and began to read. When she had finished, she said, "I think we need to tell the guys, don't you?"

Theresa nodded. Then she slowly shook her head in dismay. "It wouldn't hurt to bring the giants up to speed on this, too. You never know. We might have inadvertently involved them."

"What a mess. Oh well, let's finish putting away these groceries and get dinner started," Joan said as she got back up and continued sorting through the groceries.

~ ~ ~ ~

That evening, Theresa passed Evelyne's letter around so that everyone could read it. Chris was the first to comment. "It's almost funny. We made it all the way from Kalen's to Glendymere's without anyone catching on to who Kevin really is, only to get a gang of cutthroat bounty hunters on our trail."

Darrell nodded. "I'd rather not have anyone looking for us for any reason, but I'm surprised it took them so long to connect us to Taelor's disappearance. I expected them to be hot on our trail within a day at least."

"Maybe they'll give up before we have to leave for Camden," Theresa said hopefully.

"I don't think we'd better count on that, especially not if Rolan has put prices on our heads as well as on Taelor's," Darrell replied.

"Even if the bounty hunters do move on, everyone will know there's money involved in our capture. That's not a very comforting thought," Chris said.

"Everyone's going to be looking for a troupe of minstrels and a sister," Steve pointed out. "The only reason we traveled as performers was so that no one would pay any attention to Kevin. Now we simply need to come up with new roles to hide in."

"Yeah, you're probably right. I just hate to give up a routine that worked so well," Karl said. "And it was nice that we were able to travel pretty much for free using the minstrel show."

"We won't be able to do Healing Clinics on the way to Camden either, so we can't use that to trade for room and board," Joan added.

"I'm still bound by my vows. If we come across anyone who needs help, I have to help. It's not optional," Theresa said quietly.

"Okay, but not as Sister Theresa. Sister Theresa is wanted for assisting a runaway slave," Karl said. "Is there anything in your vows against using a different name?"

"No, at least not as far as I know. I guess I could use Marie, my middle name, if you really think it's necessary," Theresa replied. "Or maybe Teri."

"Well, we have plenty of time to work out the details, but we'll need a new cover story for traveling together, and maybe some kind of simple disguise," Karl said.

"You know, we could split up. If the bounty hunters are looking for seven people, maybe we should travel as five and two," Kevin suggested. "Then no one would look at us twice. Chris and I could go first. In fact, I could go as Myron. That would certainly distract any bounty hunters out there. They would be too busy trying to collect the bounty on my head to worry about the rest of you."

"I appreciate what you're trying to do, but I'd rather come up with a way for all of us to travel together. I still think it would be wiser to make it to Camden before you let anyone know who you are," Karl said. "After all, the only reason any of us are even on Terah is to get you to Camden and to Badec's castle safely. That has to be our primary focus."

"And if we do travel together, your magic would be like a secret weapon, held in reserve until needed," Darrell added. "I sort of like the idea of having a powerful sorcerer to act as backup should we have to defend ourselves."

"Well, I don't know how powerful I'll be by then. I could be more of a hindrance than a help. At any rate, we don't have to decide tonight, but keep splitting up in mind as an option," Kevin said.

"Whether we stay together or travel separately, we'll need to do something about the instrument wagon," Chris said. "It's a dead giveaway as it is now."

"I don't want to leave the instruments behind though," Joan said.

"We may have to," Karl said. "How could we explain having all of those instruments if our things were searched? I'm not sure we should chance it. We might be able to take your harp though. Let's see what we can come up with for a cover story."

"Steve, you've been awfully quiet over there. What do you think about all of this? Do you have any ideas?" Joan asked.

"As a matter of fact, I might. Take a look at these sketches," Steve said as he handed a sheet of paper to each of the Tellurians.

On the left-hand side of the papers, Steve had sketched each person as he or she had looked on the trip to Rainbow Valley. On the right-hand side, he had sketched the same person, but with significant differences.

"First of all, we'll be traveling in the dead of winter. If we could get hold of some thick sweaters to wear under our tunics, we would all look a bit heavier and rounder. Of course, that would also mean that we would need larger tunics, but we're going to need new clothes for the trip to Camden anyway." Steve looked around as everyone nodded in agreement. "I had already decided to stop shaving and let my beard and hair grow out, but I wasn't thinking in terms of a disguise. I was thinking it would help with the cold winds we're going to run into crossing the prairies. But if all the men grow beards and wear their hair long, and Joan and Theresa pull their hair back over their ears and braid it, we won't look anything like the minstrels that the bounty hunters are looking for. Top it off with clerical hats or maybe fur-lined caps that come down around our necks, add long dark cloaks, and I don't think even Evelyne would recognize us."

"I like it," Karl said as he studied the pictures. "I think that would definitely work for a disguise. Can we come up with the clothes we'll need to pull this off?"

"Let me talk to Ashni. We were already planning to make more clothes. This will just alter the things we need to make a little," Joan said. "I think we have enough time to get it all done, but I may need some of you to help with spinning and weaving. Karl, we're probably going to need another spinning wheel and loom."

Karl nodded. "All right, but to make this work, we'll have to come up with some kind of compelling reason for traveling across the country in the dead of winter." Karl stood up and stretched. "Let's think about it for a while, and talk about it some more later. As for now, I'm ready to get some sleep."

"Joan, you'll have to let us know when you need our help. I'm going to count on you to do that. Otherwise, I'm going to stay out of the way. You too, Karl. If there is anything that any of us can do to help, just let us know," Steve said as he gathered up his papers and pens.

As everyone got ready to head off to bed, Kevin offered to take care of straightening up the living room and washing the mugs. Chris stayed behind to help.

"Do you really think it would be best for us to strike out on our own?" Chris asked when they reached the door to his bedroom.

"I don't know," Kevin admitted. "It might be safer, for them at least, but then again, maybe not. As it is now, we have enough people to be able to stand guard through the night when we camp. If we split up, neither group would have enough people to be able to post a guard. I keep remembering that night when the bandits attacked. If we had not had someone on guard duty, I think we would all have been murdered in our sleep."

"I know. That thought crossed my mind, too. Oh well. We don't have to decide tonight. We have time to come up with a plan," Chris said as he entered his room.

Chapter 35

North Amden

Taelor knew that if he was going to have any hope at all of finding Landis, he was going to have to find her foster parents, but all he knew about them was that her foster father's name was Hayden and that he was an elf. Since most of the elves lived in North Amden, which was on the west coast, Taelor set his course by the sun and headed west when he left Abernon.

Whenever possible, he followed streams and rivers as he worked his way through the mountains, and although he came across a few wandering shepherds, for the most part, the wilderness was uninhabited. Along the way, he gathered and prepared herbs, which he used to barter for food when he came across a farm or a village.

The valleys to the west were a little more populated, but he kept a low profile and avoided established roads. The few towns that Taelor came across were usually no more than tiny villages, with maybe a tavern and a dry goods store. Travelers were rare in this area, and most either camped out in the woods or bartered with a local farmer for an empty stall for the night. Weather permitting, Taelor slept in the woods.

No one paid much attention to him. He was just a skinny young man who was passing through. The biggest problem he encountered was that other young men occasionally wanted to join him. Traveling with others could provide a certain amount of cover and safety, but at the same time it could cause a lot of problems. Companions expected conversation, and there were few topics Taelor could safely discuss, including his destination. His plans to go to North Amden would make even the most disinterested of companions curious. Humans just didn't go there.

Taelor's first sight of the ocean came as a bit of a surprise. He hadn't realized how close he was until he climbed a hill one morning in August and saw the deep blue waves shimmering in the distance. When he reached the coastline, he wasn't sure which way he should go, but north felt like the better choice, so he that's the way he headed.

A couple of days later, he came across a large sheltered bay. On the east side of the natural harbor, there was a town about the size of Abernon. A sign near the docks welcomed him to South Port. Taelor was hesitant to enter the town until he saw that the inhabitants were elves.

None of the elves in North Amden would be interested in capturing him and returning him to Rolan. They didn't recognize human laws, and as long as humans left them alone, they didn't bother humans. At the same time, they were just as likely to ignore him to the point of refusing to help him in his search.

When Taelor entered South Port, he attracted quite a few stares. He needed to talk to someone in authority, but he had no idea how to go about finding out whom that might be. Since he wasn't sure what to do, or where to go for help, he ended up just wandering around town.

After a couple of hours, he became aware that there were a couple of elves keeping an eye on him from a distance. Finally one of them approached and asked if he could be of any assistance.

"I hope so. I'm looking for someone who lives in North Amden, but I have no idea where. I have a name, and a little information, but not much. Is there anyone around who might be familiar with some of the outlying families?" Taelor asked.

"Why are you searching for a resident of North Amden, sir?" the elf asked warily.

"I have a message to deliver, concerning someone who has passed away. Unfortunately, he died before he could tell me exactly where to find the elf."

"Let me take you to Weldon, the head of the Council of Elders. I'm his assistant. He can advise you," the elf replied.

Taelor knew that the elf was turning him over to the authorities as much as he was helping him out, but the end result was the same. He would get a chance to present his case to the elders, and if anyone in South Port had any idea where Landis might be, it would probably be one of them.

Weldon conducted council business from a room in the back of one of the taverns. He welcomed Taelor to South Port and then said, "I understand that you're looking for someone who lives in North Amden."

"Yes, sir. I'm looking for an elf named Hayden."

"I imagine that there are quite a few elves named Hayden in North Amden. It's not an uncommon name. Can you be a little more specific?"

"I don't know very much about him. The last time I saw him was in Trendon about seven or eight years ago. He was visiting Tsareth, the Seated Sorcerer of Brendolanth. From what I gathered, he and Tsareth were good friends."

"Many elves have human friends, but since the humans seldom visit North Amden …" Weldon shrugged.

"Well, there is one other thing that might help. Hayden was fostering Tsareth's youngest daughter, Landis, so he would have a human girl living with his family."

"I don't suppose you could describe this girl, could you?" Weldon asked.

"She would be about twenty-four years old now. She has red hair and dark green eyes, and would probably be about medium height and build for a human woman."

"Hmm. You seem to be able to describe her better than you can describe the man you're looking for," Weldon said, a little suspiciously.

"I knew her better," Taelor said. "Whenever they visited the castle, Tsareth would ask me to keep an eye on her."

"I see. Anything else?"

"I do remember that they talked about someone named Rhee, or at least that's how it sounded," Taelor said. When Weldon gave Taelor a puzzled look, he added, "I had the impression that Rhee might have been Hayden's daughter."

"Did you meet this Rhee?"

"No. I just remember the name. I can't even say why I think she's Hayden's daughter. I could be wrong about that."

"You don't seem to know this Hayden very well at all. Why have you come such a long way looking for him?"

"I need to talk to him concerning Tsareth's death," Taelor said. Weldon raised his eyebrows and gave Taelor an appraising look. "I know. That was six years ago. I should have come sooner, but this is the first chance I've had."

Weldon did not look completely satisfied with Taelor's answer, but he let it go. "Would you like to give me the message so that I can relay it to Hayden, when and if I find him?"

"No, sir. No disrespect intended, but the information I have is for Hayden's ears only."

"Very well. I'll see what I can do. In the meantime, what are your plans? Where do you plan to stay while you're in South Port?" Weldon asked as he took out a pen and a sheet of paper.

"I haven't really thought about it. I hadn't planned to stay in South Port. Do you know if any of the merchants in town could use some help in exchange for room and board? Most of my experience has been in stables and in healing chapels."

Weldon wrote a note on the paper, folded it, and placed his stamp on the outside. "Take this note to Chandra, the elf who owns the stable up the road. He doesn't really need help right now, but I'm sure you can find a way to make yourself useful. He'll let you bed down in the loft. Won't be fancy, but at least it'll be dry, and his wife's a good cook. I'll look into this and let you know something in a few days. Oh, I don't recall that you ever said. What is your name?"

"Taelor, sir. I don't expect that Hayden will recognize the name, but Landis should."

"Very well," Weldon replied. Then he turned to the elf who had escorted Taelor in. "Please show Taelor the way to Chandra's stable. When you return, I have another errand that I would like for you to take care of."

The elf nodded and replied, "Certainly, sir. I'll only be a few minutes. Come along, Taelor."

~ ~ ~ ~

After the elf dropped Taelor off at Chandra's, and privately made sure that the stable owner understood that he was to keep an eye on Taelor and have his wife find out everything that she could about the man, he returned to Weldon's office.

When he walked in, Weldon had just finished drafting a note and was waving it around in the air to dry the ink.

Hayden,
    I had a visit today from a young man who calls himself Taelor. He was asking for you and he knew about Landis. I've had Chandra put him up for the next couple of days. Please let me know how you would like for me to handle this.
    Weldon

"Would you mind delivering this to Hayden? I want to be sure that it makes it to Hayden and no one else. I have a funny feeling about all of this." Weldon folded the note, stamped his seal on the outside, and handed it to his assistant.

His assistant nodded. "No problem, sir. I should be back by next Tuesday if all goes well."

~ ~ ~ ~

The next week passed quickly for Taelor. Although Chandra's stable was not busy, a lot of repair work needed to be done, so Taelor found plenty of things to do to pass the time. After breakfast the next Wednesday morning, Weldon walked into the barn while Taelor was brushing one of the horses.

"If you are who you say you are, you are one of Rolan's slaves," Weldon said.

"I see that you were able to locate Hayden," Taelor said without looking at Weldon or missing a stroke with the brush.

"You're a cool one, I'll give you that," Weldon said as he sat down on the edge of the tack table. "How did you manage to escape?"

"I waited until Rolan was occupied with other things. Then I just walked away one night, and kept on walking." Taelor stopped brushing the horse and turned towards Weldon, looking him straight in the eye. "Are you planning on collecting the reward for my return?"

"No, I'm just surprised that you managed it with everything I've heard about Rolan. I would have thought that he would have sent troops after you just for the principle of the thing."

"He did. They just haven't caught me yet," Taelor said as he returned to brushing the horse.

"It seems to me that the smart thing for you to do would be to put as many miles as possible between yourself and Rolan. We have overseas ships in our harbor right now. I could probably arrange a berth for you on one of them if you'd like."

"I need to talk to Hayden before I make any long-range plans. After that, I may take you up on your offer." Taelor walked the mare over to her stall and closed the door after she went in.

"I have a question to ask you before we talk any more," Weldon said. "The last time that Landis visited Trendon, she didn't want to leave. She was in the stable preparing to go when you gave her something. What was it?"

Taelor grinned. "A test to see if I really am Taelor? I gave her a kitten to take home with her. It was small, hardly old enough to leave its mother. I made a pouch that Landis could wear around her waist to keep the kitten safe and warm while they were traveling and a leash so that she could let the kitten walk around when they stopped."

Weldon nodded. "Hayden sent a horse and map for you. When would you like to leave?"

"I'd like to be on my way as soon as possible."

"Fine. I'll tell Chandra that you're leaving while you get your things together."

~ ~ ~ ~

Taelor rode out of South Port around lunchtime, and by dusk he had entered the redwood forest. Thick overhead branches formed a canopy a hundred feet high, allowing little light to penetrate the deep shadows of the forest. Mosses and ferns cushioned the damp forest floor, muffling even the footsteps of his horse. It was a place of peace.

The forest enveloped him, and although there was no tangible sign of animals, he could envision deer, elk, unicorns, and pegassi wandering through the quiet forest, stopping to drink at the small streams that he heard more often than saw. The haunting beauty of the dark woods struck a chord deep inside Taelor.

After his two-day journey through the redwood forest, Taelor felt the calmest that he had felt since the day of Tsareth's death. He no longer felt the need to hide in shadows or check over his shoulder to see if anyone was hunting him. For the first time in years, he felt safe.

Around lunchtime on Saturday, he heard the sounds of rushing water. A few minutes later, he broke out of the forest and into the sunshine that beamed along the banks of the Crinsor River. He followed the river upstream as it curved around one mountain and then snaked its way between two more. According to the map he'd been given, Hayden's home was in the valley between the two mountains, known locally as Crinsor Run.

When Taelor reached the little valley, he saw five houses fanned out in a horseshoe, with the largest at the heel. The houses resembled wagon wheels, each with a central hub and several long spokes leading away from it. The courtyard framed by the houses and bordered by the river was full of flowering bushes, plants, and trees, with a few small waterfalls and pools scattered about. Two gazebos, one on each side of the courtyard, were connected by winding pebbled walkways.

Taelor turned away from the river and started down the small drive that separated the gardens from the houses. He caught a glimpse of red hair in the closest gazebo only seconds before Landis spotted him. He dismounted as she ran down the steps to greet him.

"Taelor, I can't believe it's you! You're really here," Landis cried as she hugged him. "It's so good to see you." Then she asked, "Why did you come? Did Rolan send you?"

"You look all grown up now," Taelor said as he held her at arm's length to get a good look at her. "How are you?"

"I'm fine, great actually. Come on and say hello to Hayden and Gwynn," Landis said as she led Taelor towards the largest house. "We were hoping you'd get here today. Everyone's coming for dinner tonight to meet you. Gwynn's been in the kitchen cooking all day."

"I hope no one went to any trouble on my account," Taelor said quickly.

"Of course they did!" Landis laughed. "After all, it isn't every day that my closest and dearest human friend comes to visit! Tell me everything about Trendon! What's Rolan like? Do you think I'll like him?"

"Trendon is just the same old Trendon. As for Rolan, he's not at all like your father. In fact, if Tsareth had not vouched for the fact that Rolan is his son, I'd think he was an imposter. You look more like your father than Rolan does."

"Is he married? Does he have any children? How about my other brothers and sisters? Do I have any nieces and nephews yet?"

"No, he's not married. I'm not sure how many nieces and nephews you have. None of your other brothers and sisters remained in Trendon after your father's death."

Landis frowned. "I would have thought that they would have stayed to help Rolan. Oh, well," she said with a sigh. "We never were a close family, but then I imagine most sorcerer's families are like that, aren't they? We didn't get to know each other while we were growing up. A shame really."

"Where do we need to take the horse?" Taelor asked, changing the subject. "Is there a pasture or something around here?'

"There's a tack room out behind the house. We'll put the saddle and reins in there."

"Don't we need to take the horse out to the pasture where the other horses are grazing?"

Landis shook her head. "The horses are free to roam around wherever they want to here. Cassie knows the area. She'll find the others." Landis led Taelor behind the house to the tack room. While Taelor removed the saddle and blanket, Landis slipped the bridle off Cassie's head. As soon as Cassie was free, she walked towards the woods.

"You're sure she'll be all right?" Taelor asked.

"She'll be fine, seriously. She's home now. She can take care of herself," Landis answered. Then she opened the back door and led Taelor into the kitchen.

The rooms in the central hub were open, separated only by the arrangement of furniture. In addition to the kitchen, there was a spacious sitting room and a dining room which could easily seat twenty or more. Large windows overlooked the courtyard and river out front and the redwood forest in the back Skylights that opened the ceiling to the treetops gave the house a light and airy feel. In good weather, all of the windows could be removed, opening the house even more. Individual sitting rooms and bedrooms were in the long separate wings that resembled spokes on a wheel.

Since Hayden's wife, Gwynn, was in the kitchen, Landis introduced Taelor to her before she led him to the guest bedroom where he would be staying. She left him there so that he could unpack and freshen up while she prepared a snack to hold him over until dinner that night.

The sitting area and bedroom in Taelor's wing were separated by an arched doorway with the sitting area closest to the main hub. All of the furniture in the sitting area was arranged in the center of the room facing out. Two wingback chairs faced the front towards the garden, and a lounging chair faced the forest out back. The only other piece of furniture in the room was a small table between the two wingback chairs.

The bedroom was sparsely furnished, too. There was a narrow but long bed, made primarily for tall, skinny elves, two slender clothes chests, one of each side of the arched doorway, and a wash basin set in a wooden tripod.

Taelor unpacked his meager belongings and put them and his bag in one of the chests. Then he sat down on the foot of the bed just to see how it felt. It wasn't really soft, but it wasn't hard either. He leaned back, stretched his arms out over his head and just lay there for a few minutes. He had no idea what the mattress was made of, but it felt like he was floating on air. It was the most comfortable bed he'd ever stretched out on.

While Taelor was lying there, Hayden knocked on the door to the sitting room. Taelor jumped up and reached the sitting room just as Hayden walked in.

"Hello, Taelor," Hayden said from just inside the doorway. "It's good to see you again. Mind if I join you for a few minutes?"

"Not at all," Taelor said as he shook hands with the elf. "Thank you for allowing me to come."

"I have to admit to a certain amount of curiosity about your visit," Hayden said as he sat down on one of the wingback chairs. "You didn't tell my brother much about why you came."

"I thought Weldon must have known you to have been able to find you so quickly," Taelor said as he sat on the other wingback chair. "I'm sure you have a lot of questions, but let me assure you that I came out of concern for Landis, not to cause her harm."

"I have no doubt of that. Why don't you get a bite to eat and then you and I will go for a long walk and talk. I don't imagine Landis will be very happy at being left out, but I think it would be best if we talked first."

"I think that would be a good idea. Give me about fifteen minutes to join her for a snack, and then I'll meet you out back."

~ ~ ~ ~

When Taelor met Hayden outside, they walked off towards the woods. Once they were out of earshot of the house, Hayden asked, "How did you manage to get away from Trendon?"

"I just left one night."

"From what I've heard about Rolan, I doubt he's very happy that one of his slaves walked out on him. Is he looking for you?"

Taelor nodded. "He has bounty hunters out looking for me. They nearly got me at one point when one of them shot me with an arrow, but I haven't seen anyone on my trail in quite a while. I don't think I led anyone to you."

"Don't worry about that. We can handle any bounty hunters who come our way," Hayden said. "But why did you come to North Amden? Why didn't you just leave Calandra?"

"Because of Landis. I was afraid she might decide to go back to Trendon one day to meet her brother. I have no doubt that once he sees the magic in her, he'll find some way to either kill her himself or have her killed."

When Hayden remained quiet, Taelor continued. "I don't know how much you know about Rolan, but he's evil. The story about Tsareth dying in his sleep isn't true. Rolan killed him. And then he told all of his brothers and sisters to leave Trendon and never return. He told them that if he heard they were even thinking about coming back, he'd kill them, their children, and everyone else in their family."

Hayden nodded. "Tell me what happened with Tsareth."

Taelor took a deep breath and slowly exhaled. "As soon as Rolan arrived at the castle, he demanded that Tsareth retire and hand over his seat on the council. Tsareth told him not to be so impatient, that it wasn't time yet, that he would resign as soon as Rolan learned to control his temper, his ambitions, and his magic. Rolan was furious. He stormed around the castle creating all kinds of havoc with his magic. Then that evening he challenged Tsareth to a duel. Tsareth tried to reason with him, but it did no good. The duel took place the next morning."

"Are you sure they fought?"

"I was there," Taelor said slowly.

"Who else was there? Were there any other witnesses?"

"Tsareth's second and I were the only witnesses. Rolan didn't have anyone with him." Taelor paused to take a deep breath, trying to exhale all the emotions that had surfaced as he recalled the events of that day. "They were supposed to meet at daybreak in a field that Tsareth had set aside for sorcerers to use for practice, competitions, whatever. When we got there, Rolan was already there. He told Tsareth to remove the Key to Terah and set it on the ground at the side of the field. Tsareth did, and then he turned around to come back to his side of the field. As soon as Tsareth's back was to him, Rolan roared and the next thing I knew, I was on the ground and someone was kicking me in the stomach, telling me to get up and get moving. Tsareth and his second were both gone. Rolan was the only one left."

"So you're the only surviving witness to the fact that Rolan murdered his father."

Taelor nodded.

"I never met Rolan, but I knew that Tsareth was worried about him. Seems he had good reason," Hayden said sadly.

"I didn't know what to do after Tsareth died. I couldn't leave Trendon while my mother was still alive. Rolan would have killed her for spite, but after she passed away last winter, I decided that the time had come for me to do something. My plan was to go to Camden and talk to Badec. I knew that Tsareth trusted him, and I was hoping that after he heard what I had to say he might be able to do something. If nothing else, he could take care of making arrangements for Landis, provided I could find her. But before I could make my break, I heard that Badec was in a coma." Taelor shrugged.

"Badec would have been my first choice, too," Hayden said as he continued to walk.

After a few moments, Taelor said, "The only other thing I could think of was to try to find Landis and see if there was any way that I could help her myself. I know I can't do much. I'm not a trained soldier. In fact, I might be more of a liability than anything else, especially with bounty hunters on my trail, but I felt like I had to try to do something."

"I understand," Hayden said quietly. Then he turned and faced Taelor. "There's something I need to tell you. Are you aware that you and Landis are related?"

"Related? I don't see how. My mother and I weren't from Trendon. We were from a land across the ocean, and I think Tsareth's father was the Seated Sorcerer of Brendolanth before him, so his ancestors would not have had a chance to mingle with mine. You must be mistaken."

"What you said is true enough, as far as it goes. Taelor, do you know anything about what happened to your father?"

"No. All I know is what Mother told me. She said that he was a fisherman. He had already left our house and gone out to the docks when the slavers raided the village. Mother didn't see him during the raid so she chose to believe that he had already cast off and was out of sight when the raid took place. Otherwise, he must have been killed, and she didn't want to think that he was dead," Taelor sighed. "Not that it really mattered. There was no way he could have found us."

"Keep in mind that she had no way to find out, no way of knowing what happened to him, or where he was."

"Where are you going with this?" Taelor asked in confusion.

"Your mother was a very special woman. Not just to you, but to others, too. She and Tsareth were very close."

"I know. He loved to spend his evenings with her, listening to her sing and play the harp," Taelor said with a smile, remembering how Tsareth doted on his mother.

"Well, they were a little more than just friends. She was Landis's mother." Hayden paused for a moment to let his words sink in. When Taelor didn't react, he continued. "Tsareth wanted to marry her, but your mother wouldn't agree to it. She said that she had no way of knowing that she was a widow, so she wasn't free to marry anyone. It was her decision that neither you nor Landis were to be told that she was Landis's mother."

Taelor frowned. "I don't understand. Why not? What was she worried about?"

"The future. Look at the way things worked out," Hayden said. "Your mother was a very wise woman. Just think how Rolan could have used the information that he had Landis's mother and half-brother right there in the castle."

Taelor shuddered at that thought. "I can't believe he doesn't know. Everyone who lived at the castle when Landis was born must have known. Surely someone would have told him."

"That's a possibility. He may just consider Landis to be no threat to him. In fact, I hope he is underestimating her," Hayden replied. "But it could also be that everyone who was there at the time feels more loyalty to Tsareth than to Rolan. Who knows?"

"Should we tell Landis about all of this? How will she feel about the fact that her mother was a slave?"

"Oh, I don't think she'll mind that. I think she'll be thrilled that you're her brother. And she saw the way Tsareth treated your mother. He never treated her like a slave. He didn't treat you like one either."

"No, he didn't," Taelor said with a wistful sigh. "But things changed after his death. Rolan made me his personal slave and he assigned my mother to the kitchens. I think she died of exhaustion as much as anything else. If I could have figured out a way to kill Rolan when she died, I would have, but I couldn't, so I just left."

"It was probably for the best that you didn't try to kill him. Even if you had been successful, you'd probably have died in the attempt and you wouldn't have been able to help anyone then."

"No, but at least he'd be out of her way."

"True, but she's not ready yet. And you never know, that might have opened the door for someone even worse. Better the devil that you know …" Hayden shrugged.

"I guess. Anyway, how much of this do you think we should tell Landis?"

"All of it. Everything. Including how Rolan killed her father. I wish I could keep her here as an innocent child forever, but I can't. She's a grown woman now, and next year she'll begin to train as a sorcerer. She has to understand what she's up against." Hayden put his arm around Taelor's shoulder and said, "You did the right thing, coming here to try to help her. A very unselfish thing. Tsareth would have been proud of you."

"Thank you. That means more than you know."

"Let's get back to the house. I think we should tell Landis before dinner tonight. And we might as well tell Gwynn and Rhianna at the same time. Otherwise I'll have to go through it all over again later."

"Is Rhianna your daughter? I remember Landis mentioning a Rhee when she was younger."

Hayden nodded. "She's a little younger than Landis, but they're inseparable. I don't know what's going to happen when it comes time for Landis to leave here. Oh well, let's handle one crisis at a time," Hayden said with a laugh.

As they turned back towards the house, Taelor asked who else lived in Crinsor Run, so Hayden filled him in on the rest of his family. In addition to Rhianna, Hayden and Gwynn had another daughter, Serena, and two sons, Duane and Mickel. The other three were married and lived with their families in three of the houses along the arc. The fifth house belonged to his nephew, Pallor, who was away about eleven months out of the year, but who had dreams of one day finding the right elf and settling down, so he had built a house next to Duane's.

When they reached the house, Gwynn, Landis, and Rhianna were all in the kitchen putting the finishing touches on the food for the evening meal. Hayden asked them to join him and Taelor in the sitting room for a few minutes.

Hayden talked first, explaining that Taelor and Landis were blood relatives.

When he finished, Landis put her arm around Taelor and beamed. "I can't think of anyone that I would rather have as a brother. How long have you known that we have the same mother?"

"About an hour," Taelor answer. "I had no idea until Hayden told me, although I really should have figured it out a long time ago."

"I'd love to see Mother again," Landis said wistfully. Then she frowned and asked, "Why isn't she with you? Is she all right?"

Taelor looked a little pained. Then he took a deep breath and told Landis that their mother had passed away the previous winter.

Tears filled Landis's eyes. "Why didn't she come to see me after my father died? Or at least send for me? Didn't she want to see me?"

"Landis, that's not it at all. She couldn't. She wasn't free to do what she wanted to do. We were slaves. Tsareth bought us both when I was a baby," Taelor explained. "After he died, Rolan sent my mother to work in the kitchens and made me his personal slave."

"What?! Why didn't someone tell me? I could have explained the situation to Rolan. Both of you could have come here to live," Landis protested.

"No. You don't know Rolan. And that brings me around to some of the other things I have to tell you." Then Taelor told her how Rolan had murdered her father and banished all of Tsareth's other children from Trendon. "I don't know if Rolan even knows that you exist, but he would probably kill you if you were to show up in Trendon. As soon as he realized how strong your magic is, he would see you as a threat, and he deals with anyone he perceives as a threat quickly and decisively. He kills them."

"Then what am I going to do? How will I train?" Landis asked. "If I ask someone to let me train with them, won't I make them a target for Rolan?"

"Probably," Hayden answered her. "But there are still some sorcerers out there who are powerful enough that Rolan's anger wouldn't concern them. Let's not worry about that yet, Landis. You can't begin training for nearly a year anyway, and there's no law that states that you have to begin training as soon as you turn twenty-five. We'll figure something out. Don't worry." Then Hayden turned to Taelor and said, "Taelor, I'd like for you to stay with us, for as long as you like."

"I appreciate that, but I hate to impose," Taelor said.

"It's no imposition. You're the only family that Landis has left that she can rely on. I don't know what your plans are, and I can certainly understand if you want to put as many miles between yourself and Rolan as possible, but let me assure you that he cannot reach you here unless he's willing to declare war on the elves, and I doubt if even he is that foolish."

"I hadn't made any plans other than to find Landis and tell her about Rolan. I would love to stay here for a while, but I don't want to put any of you in danger," Taelor answered.

"Don't worry, you won't," Hayden said as he stood up. "It's settled then." Hayden turned to his wife, stretched and asked, "What's for dinner anyway, and when are the others going to get here? I'm hungry!"

Chapter 36

Fall Settles Over the Valley

During the month of August, Kevin's skills progressed faster than he had dared to hope. He could boil a cup of water for tea, or he could heat a large tub of water for a bath. He could pick up anything from a feather to a boulder and move it two feet or two hundred. Not only could he catch eggs on a cushion of air, but he could also catch boulders, and his energy bolts were strong enough to crumble small rocks.

He could soar through the sky beside Glendymere, dive for the ground, catch himself, and land so gently that he left no footprints in the sand. With his ability to catch himself came the confidence to try other tasks while flying. He could move objects, stir air currents, light a candle, ignite a bonfire, or use his seeing eye to peek in on the activities in another valley, all while flying a hundred feet above the ground. And he was getting better with each passing day.

One morning near the middle of September, Kevin and Chris were outside practicing some of Kevin's skills when Glendymere walked up. *"Mind taking a break for a little while? I'd like to talk to you."*

"Fine with me," Kevin said as he sat down on the nearest boulder. "What's up?"

"I've asked some elves and dwarves to join us in about six weeks for some mock battles. You need to learn how to defend yourself against all kinds of attack, so I thought we would start with the basics: arrows, knives and swords."

"I'm not sure I understand," Kevin said slowly. "Are you thinking that I'm going to defend myself with a sword?"

"No. Most sorcerers don't even carry a sword. You'll have to use non-lethal magic to defend yourself."

"Are they going to be using non-lethal weapons?" Chris asked.

"No, they'll be using the same ones they always use. They know that they're going to be fighting a sorcerer and his guards, so they'll come prepared."

"Guards?" Kevin asked. "What guards?"

"You know, the ones you travel with, your friends."

"Are they going to be involved in this, too?" Kevin asked.

"They'll have to be if you're going to learn to fight as a team."

"Are you going to be there?" Chris asked.

"Of course."

Chris and Kevin looked at each other.

"Maybe they should get to know you before the battle," Kevin said.

"That's one of the things I wanted to talk to you about."

"How do you want to do this? Are you going to come to Rainbow Valley, or do you want us to bring them here?" Kevin asked.

"I think it'll be best if they come over here. You can bring them through the tunnels."

"When do you want us to bring them over?" Kevin asked.

"How about tomorrow morning? They can stay until about lunchtime. That should be enough for the first day. And have them bring their swords, bows, and arrows."

"Okay," Kevin said. "We'll tell them after dinner tonight."

"Good. Now you can go back to what you were doing. I'm going to take a nap," Glendymere said as he turned and went back to his chamber.

~ ~ ~ ~

After dinner, when everyone had gathered in the sitting room, Kevin said that he had something he needed to tell them. "Glendymere has set up some mock battles so that we can get some experience fighting together. He's invited some elves and dwarves to make up the opposing team. They're supposed to be here in about six weeks."

Darrell nodded. "Good idea. We need to practice our combat skills. Sparring against each other isn't going to help us improve that much."

"I'm assuming that no one is actually going to be trying to kill anyone else, right?" Karl asked.

"It's a mock battle, but the weapons will be real," Chris answered.

"What weapons?" Joan asked.

"From what Glendymere said, we can expect to be attacked with arrows, swords, knives, anything and everything except magic," Kevin answered.

"How do we defend against arrows?" Joan asked. "What if one of us gets hit?"

Chris shook his head. "Glendymere won't let that happen."

Joan looked at Chris for a moment, frowned and said, "Huh? What do you mean?"

"Glendymere set this up so that I can learn how to use non-lethal magic to defend us during an attack. I'm not sure what he's talking about, but I do know that he'll be there in case I mess up, so everyone will be okay," Kevin answered.

"Wait a minute," Darrell said with a deep frown. "What do you mean, he'll be there?"

"He'll be watching, from the sidelines," Chris said.

"Glendymere will be there? Where we are? We're going to have to fight a battle while he's close by?" Darrell asked. "Kevin, I don't know if I can do that."

Chris said, "I know what you mean, Darrell, but you'll get past it."

"No, no, I don't think so," Darrell said shaking his head. "I could end up being perfectly useless during the battle." Then he looked at Kevin. "I don't think this is going to work. Maybe you better count me out."

"That's why Glendymere wants us to bring all of you over to Willow Canyon tomorrow morning," Kevin said slowly, trying to engage Darrell's eyes. "He wants you to get comfortable being around him so that he won't be a distraction during the battle."

"Tomorrow morning? I've got to meet a dragon tomorrow?" Darrell squeaked.

"Darrell, think of it this way, by this time tomorrow you'll be over your fear of dragons," Chris said.

Darrell stared at Chris like he was looking at a ghost.

Kevin looked around the group and said, "Glendymere said that he wants to start working on battle skills tomorrow, so take your swords, and your bows and arrows, too."

"Are we going to be sparring?" Karl asked. "Is he going to coach us?"

Chris shook his head no. "I think he was talking about Kevin's battle skills. I got the distinct impression that we're going to be the enemy."

"You mean we're going to attack Kevin?" Steve asked with a frown.

Kevin nodded. "I wasn't too thrilled about that part either."

Karl stood and stretched. "Well, it's been a long day. Think I'll head towards bed. I have a feeling we're all going to need to be well-rested tomorrow."

Darrell shook himself a little and then mumbled, "I won't sleep a wink all night."

"I can fix some tea that will help you sleep if you want me to," Theresa offered.

Darrell shook his head no. "I need to psych myself up for this."

"Do we need to take lunch with us?" Joan asked.

"I don't think so," Chris said. "Glendymere said something about working with us until lunchtime. I think he's planning to send you back around noon."

"Come on, Karl. Help me gather up the mugs." Joan held out her hand for Karl to help her up.

Darrell reached for the pitcher and poured himself another mug of scog. "Don't bother. Go on to bed. I'll clear up later."

~ ~ ~ ~

The next morning, everyone except Kevin was in the kitchen by the time Chris walked in. There was hot coffee but there was no sign of breakfast.

"Have you already eaten?" Chris asked.

"No, I think everyone's too nervous to be hungry," Joan said.

"I felt the same way the first time I met Glendymere," Chris said as he picked up a loaf of bread and began slicing it, "but today I need something to eat,"

"Cut enough for everyone," Joan said. "I'll slice some cheese. Theresa, get out some jam. Maybe once the food's on the table we'll be able to eat a little something."

When Kevin walked in, Chris handed him a cup of coffee and motioned towards the table. "Have a seat. Breakfast will be on the table in less than five minutes. Come on, everyone grab a plate and sit down."

Everyone sat down with a plate, and although everyone except Darrell managed to nibble on their food, only Kevin and Chris had any appetite.

After breakfast, Kevin told everyone to get their weapons and meet him in his room. When Kevin led the others through the second door in his room, Darrell hung back, taking only a couple of hesitant steps towards the door. Chris stepped back beside him and tried to distract him with conversation, but even though Darrell did start walking forward, he and Chris were soon well behind the others. When Kevin and the others reached the compass chamber, they had to wait several minutes for Chris and Darrell to catch up. Kevin slowed his pace after that, but even so, Darrell and Chris lagged behind.

Once they had all reached the door to Glendymere's caverns, Kevin picked up the old iron knocker and hit the shield a couple of times. While they were waiting, Chris told them the story of the elf who dropped in to visit Glendymere with near tragic results.

"As if things weren't bad enough," Darrell moaned. "Now I have to worry about him roasting me in his sleep."

"Not if you knock first, Darrell. Welcome to Willow Canyon. Would you join me outside, please?"

"What? What was that? Did I hear something?" Darrell whimpered.

"That was Glendymere," Kevin said. "You didn't talk to Xantha much while we were at Kalen's, did you?"

"Only a couple of times," Darrell said. "Didn't much like it."

"Well, you'll get used to it," Kevin said as he opened the big wooden door and led the others through the caverns.

When they walked out into the canyon, they saw Glendymere circling above. He swooped down, and settled gracefully on the ground about fifty feet from them.

"You need to do something about Darrell," Glendymere said to Kevin and Chris privately.

"What do you mean?" Kevin answered in his head.

"His mind has shut down."

"What?!" Kevin and Chris both exclaimed mentally.

236

"I'm holding him up right now. Chris, give Kevin a hand. See if you can set him down against that boulder."

"Is he ... is he dying?" Chris asked mentally as he and Kevin took Darrell by the arms and gently eased him to a seat on the ground in front of a large boulder. His limbs weren't exactly stiff, but they weren't cooperative either.

"No, he's just gone," Glendymere answered.

"From dragon-fear?" Kevin asked.

"Yes."

"Is this normal? Do many people react like this?" Chris asked.

"No, not really. Some have a touch of dragon fear, but I haven't seen a case this bad in several thousand years, not since the last time I was on Earth," Glendymere answered.

"How long will he be like this?" Kevin asked.

"I don't know. Most come around eventually, but a few never recover."

"Never? What are his chances?" Kevin asked.

"Chances? I don't know. He'll either recover or he won't. In the meantime, you need to pay a little attention to Karl and Joan. They're still standing, but not by much. Help them sit down or their knees are going to give out. Theresa's in pretty good shape, just a little nervous. Get her to look after Darrell. Once she has someone to take care of, she'll be fine. Steve's all right. No reaction at all other than curiosity."

As Kevin took Joan's arm and led her to a seat beside Darrell, he said, "Theresa, you might want to keep an eye on Darrell. I think he's pretty close to passing out."

Chris helped Karl to a seat beside Joan while Theresa stepped around and knelt beside Darrell. He had clammy skin, glassy and unfocused eyes, a rapid pulse, shallow breathing, and twitchy muscles. Within seconds Theresa had completely forgotten about Glendymere in her concern for Darrell. Meanwhile, Steve was completely focused on Glendymere, trying to memorize every detail.

"Chris, go get some water for Karl and Joan. Kevin, why don't you try to distract them? Give them something else to think about," Glendymere suggested.

When Chris turned to head back into the cave, Steve asked, "Is there anything I can do to help?"

"Come on," Chris said. "I'm going to get a pitcher of water. You can bring the mugs."

After Chris and Steve left, Kevin said, *"I don't have any idea what to do. What would distract them?"*

"Have they seen you fly yet?"

"I don't think so."

"All right. Move into their line of sight, rise a couple of feet off the ground, shift around a bit until their eyes are following you. Then, once you're sure their eyes are on you, rise slowly maybe a hundred feet, hover a little, and then dive for the ground, pulling out of it at the last minute and landing gently in front of them. If nothing else, that should startle them enough to break that empty stare. Once that's broken, they'll start coming out of it. In the meantime, I'll see what I can do with Darrell."

When Chris and Steve returned with a couple of mugs and a pitcher of water, Chris handed Theresa a damp cloth. "I thought a cool cloth might help"

She nodded her thanks and began sponging off Darrell's forehead.

"I'm going to try to distract Joan and Karl," Kevin said to Chris, Steve, and Theresa. Then he explained exactly what he was going to do. "Chris, if they do start to come around, try to hand them a mug of water. They'll have to focus on the mug to take hold of it and that should help."

Chris nodded.

Then Kevin slowly rose a couple of feet through the air.

"You're not in their line of sight yet," Chris said. "Move a little to your left." Kevin began to drift in that direction. Once he was lined up right, Chris signaled for him to stop. "Now move around a little, clown it up, do something to shift their focus to you."

"Such as?" Kevin asked.

"I don't know. Pick up something and juggle it. How about that boulder over there?" Chris pointed to a boulder about the size of a basketball.

Kevin reached out mentally, picked up the boulder, and then pretended to be dribbling it. Eventually Joan and Karl's eyes began to lose a little of their glassy gaze. When Chris felt fairly sure that they were at least somewhat aware that Kevin was floating around, he nodded. Kevin mentally held the boulder in front of him as he began to rise. When he was about a hundred feet in the air, he tossed the boulder and then dived after it. When he dived, Steve and Theresa both gasped even though they had been expecting it. Joan let out a little scream and clasped her hand over her mouth. Karl tried to jump up, but his legs wouldn't work, so he ended up bobbing up and down on the ground.

Chris put one hand on Karl's shoulder to steady him and the other on Joan's. Meanwhile, Kevin mentally slowed the boulder enough so that he could dive past it, come up under it, and turn in time to appear to catch it before it hit the ground. When he gently lowered himself to the ground with the boulder resting on his right hand, everyone was focused on him except Darrell, who remained in a catatonic state.

"Chris, now you can give Joan and Karl a sip of water. That should bring them around a little more."

Chris handed each of them a mug, but their hands were shaking so much, they couldn't drink any of the water.

"Kevin, they need to move around a little and loosen up. Why don't you and Chris show them your room? I know there's nothing in there for them to see, but the walk will do them good, and it won't hurt them to be away from me for a few minutes either."

Kevin squatted down in front of Joan and Karl. "Welcome back. Let's walk down to our room in the cave and you can splash some water on your face. It'll make you feel better." He stood up as Steve moved beside Joan to help her, and Chris took Karl's hand to help him. Once they were all standing, Kevin led them toward the caves.

"Theresa, you can join them if you like. I'll look after Darrell," Glendymere said privately to Theresa.

"Thanks, but I think I'll stay with him for now," she answered.

Once he was in the tunnel, Karl wiped his hand over his face and took a deep breath.

Chris laughed and said, "I know exactly how you feel. There are no words to describe it."

Karl grinned at him and nodded.

"I can't believe I reacted like that. I knew I was nervous, but …" Joan said. Then she just shook her head.

"Like I said, there are no words to describe that feeling," Chris said. "But it's over now. When we go back out there, you'll be fine."

"Think so?" Joan asked with a weak grin. "I'm not so sure."

After they washed their faces and walked around in Glendymere's chambers for a few minutes to loosen up, Karl said, "Well, I guess we should go back out there and get this show on the road. Where are Darrell and Theresa?"

Kevin and Chris just looked at each other. Steve spoke up. "Darrell reacted a little more strongly than you two. He's still a bit out of it. Theresa's with him."

"Is he all right?" Joan asked.

"Glendymere seems to think he'll come out of it in a little while," Kevin hedged. "Let's go back and see what he wants us to do next."

Once they were all back outside, Glendymere spoke to Kevin and Chris privately. *"Darrell's mind isn't quite as frozen as it was before. From what I've been able to gather, he seems to have a strong inclination towards protecting others. The image he has of himself is that of a sword carrying warrior. Is that about right?"*

Both Kevin and Chris nodded.

"Good. I want to try something with Darrell. I'm not sure that Joan and Karl are quite ready to see me stand him up, so for their sake, see if you can help him into a standing position. I'll support him after that."

Kevin and Chris walked over to Darrell and gently eased him up on his feet. Theresa backed off a little, but she stayed within arm's reach.

Then Glendymere said to everyone, *"I want all of you to pile your swords over by the cave entrance. Then I want you to back up about twenty or thirty feet. Kevin you need to stand on the other side of the pile. Karl, would you help Chris with Darrell?"*

Glendymere kept Darrell upright while Chris and Karl turned him around and walked towards the cave, supporting Darrell between them. They added their swords to the others and put Darrell's sword on top. Then they turned him back around and led him to a spot about twenty-five feet from the cave entrance.

"Chris told me that Palladin made your swords. He's a master swordsmith. You couldn't have found a better one. I'm sure he told you that you'd know it when you had the right sword, that you'd feel it, didn't he?" Glendymere asked. Chris, Steve, Joan, and Karl nodded. *"And since then, you've worn them pretty much everyday, practiced with them, and probably had them close by when you slept, haven't you?"* Again they nodded. *"By now your sword knows you. Kevin is going to lift the pile of swords and toss them about ten feet into the air. When he does, I want you to hold your sword arm out with your hand open. Your sword will come to you."*

"Are you serious?" Joan asked. The only sign that she was still a little uneasy was that her words were a touch slower than usual. "The swords will come to us?"

Glendymere nodded. He turned towards Theresa and said, *"You might want to step over here, dear. I doubt that you even have a sword, do you?"*

"No," Theresa said as she shook her head and took a couple of steps towards Glendymere. "Drusilla said that sisters don't carry swords."

"She's right. With your pendant, you don't need one."

Glendymere waited a few moments for Theresa to move farther away from the others. While Theresa was moving out of the way, Chris guided Darrell's arm until it was outstretched. Then Chris helped him open his hand.

As soon as everyone was ready, Glendymere said, *"All right, Kevin, toss the swords."*

Kevin mentally picked up the pile of swords and tossed them into the air. The swords curved off and flew towards their owners, and within a couple of seconds Karl, Joan, Steve, and Chris were armed.

Joan's eyes opened wide and a grin spread across her face. "Will it always do that?"

At the same time, Chris frowned and asked Glendymere, "Did you do that?"

With a chuckle, Glendymere said, *"No, that was your sword. Thank Palladin for that little trick, not me. And yes, Joan, it'll always do that."*

Darrell's sword had struck the palm of his outstretched hand, but his fingers had not closed around the handle. Glendymere mentally caught the sword and held it suspended in the air, not even an inch from Darrell's hand.

Karl struck a fighting pose, lunged a couple of times, then straightened back up and asked, "Why didn't they tell us that our swords could do that? That's a rather important detail."

"For one thing, only a sword which has chosen you will do that. And for another, the sword will fly to you, straight to you, and heaven help anyone in its way. It's something that really isn't used very often. It's just too dangerous. But you're right, it is an important detail. Watch out if you ever see anyone else start to toss a sword."

Then Glendymere concentrated on Darrell. "Reach out and take your sword, Darrell," he said in a coaxing tone. "A warrior needs his sword. You don't want it to hit the ground. Just close your fingers. That's it, that's right, just a little more and you'll have it." Slowly Darrell's fingers began to close around the handle of the sword. After a minute or so, he held it firmly enough that Glendymere could let go. "He's starting to come out of it. He should be over the worst of it soon. Let's go on and see how he does."

Chris reached up and gently took the sword from Darrell's hand. Then he helped Darrell lower his arm.

Glendymere asked them to line up in a straight line, with their bows and arrows, facing Kevin. Then Glendymere asked them to fire an arrow at Kevin, one at a time down the line and then start back over until he told them to stop. Kevin's task was to use his outstretched hand to bat the arrows out of the air before they reached him.

What if he misses? Joan thought. We could kill him!

"I'll be here. If he misses, I won't," Glendymere reassured her privately. Then he said to Chris, "You tell them when to fire. Keep the arrows coming."

Chris fired the first arrow and as soon as Kevin batted it away, Chris signaled for the next arrow to be fired, and worked his way down the line until he reached Darrell. Karl put Darrell's bow in his hand, strung the arrow and closed Darrell's fingers around the notch. Then he helped him pull it back, but when Chris told Darrell to fire, his release was so slow that the arrow fell harmlessly at his feet.

"He's coming around. He realized he was supposed to shoot, so he's hearing you. He's just operating in slow motion," Glendymere said as Karl helped Darrell get the next arrow ready.

The exercises continued for an hour. By the last round, Darrell was able to pull the string back on his own, but his hands were shaking so badly that he still couldn't notch the arrows, and his release was so ragged that the arrows didn't go anywhere near Kevin. He kept glancing nervously over towards Glendymere every few seconds, but although he had yet to speak, it was clear that he understood what was going on around him.

For the next hour, Glendymere had Kevin catch the arrows rather than bat them away and stack them in a pile next to one of the boulders. After that, Glendymere called for a break. By then, Darrell was moving better, but whenever he opened his mouth to speak, nothing came out.

While they were relaxing near the stream, Glendymere said that he'd like to work with them three mornings a week for the next few weeks. He asked if that would fit into their schedules, and looked straight at Darrell for an answer. Darrell cleared his throat and answered with a very hesitant and creaky yes, but at least it was intelligible.

Since it was nearly lunchtime, Glendymere said that they had done enough for the first day and suggested that Chris lead the others back to Rainbow Valley. Then, as they were gathering their weapons and getting ready to leave, Glendymere turned to Chris and said, "You don't need to come back this afternoon. Take the rest of the day off."

Chris didn't argue, and he didn't wait around for Glendymere to change his mind. It was his first free afternoon since coming to Rainbow Valley and he wanted to take advantage of it.

~ ~ ~ ~

After Kevin had eaten his lunch, Glendymere led him to an arched opening. "I'm going to show you how to weave a protection ward over this tunnel entrance."

"What's a protection ward?"

"It's like a magical net. You can use it to seal a door, keep someone else from opening a chest, anything like that."

"Sort of like a booby trap?"

"I don't know." Glendymere searched Kevin's memories for examples of booby traps. "Yes, I guess you could compare a protection ward to a booby trap."

"What do I need to make one? Some rope? String?"

"No. All you need is your own magical energy."

Kevin looked puzzled.

"Think of a long strand of flowing energy, somewhat like a ribbon. You manipulate that ribbon, move it around, and stretch it out. Then you use it to protect a door, or any opening, even a lid on a chest, by weaving the ribbon of magic back and forth as intricately as you wish, and then, to close the ward, you slide the ends together to make one continuous loop. When you want to remove it, you separate the ends and unwind the ribbon of energy. Just be sure that you remove it exactly backwards from the way you put it on."

"What would happen if I goofed?"

"That depends on how strong you made the ward. A weak one might give you a shock, a moderate ward might burn you, but a strong one could incinerate you on the spot. Of course there are any number of levels in between. Keep that in mind if you ever have to remove a ward that another sorcerer has formed. You won't know its strength unless you break the loop, and then it's too late, especially if it's one of the stronger ones."

"It sounds a little like an electrical current on Earth. As long as the circuit remains closed, no problem. Break it, and it flows into you. Depending on the current, it might tingle, it might grab you, it might throw you across the room, or it might fry you."

"Yeah, that's a pretty good comparison. Think of the ribbon of magic as your flow of electricity."

"Where does it come from? I mean the energy that I would use to create the strand to start with. How do I get it?"

"It's all around you, in the wind, the light, the heat, everywhere, even your own life force. All you need to do is concentrate on feeling the flow and channeling it into the form you need. One advantage that you have is that the elven part of you acts as a conduit for the forces of nature through no effort on your part. Human sorcerers have to consciously tap into the forces of nature and convert it to an energy that their minds can store, ready for use, and that's hard to learn how to do. A human sorcerer could actually run out of magical energy in the middle of using it and be left powerless until he restocks. You won't ever run out."

"If being part elf is such an advantage, why don't more sorcerers marry elves so that their children will have both sets of genes?" Kevin asked.

Glendymere shrugged his massive shoulders. "I don't know. It always made sense to me. Elves have longer life spans than humans do, too. With your elven blood, even as watered down as it is, you can expect to live at least a hundred and fifty years. You'd think that humans would want to improve the species for their offspring, but humans are funny creatures. It's like they think they're better than everyone else and marrying someone who isn't human is beneath them. They aren't any more intelligent than the other races, they have short life spans, they don't have the agility of the elves or the strength of the dwarves ..." Glendymere shook his head. "You do know that most humans will look down on you as a half-breed, don't you?"

Kevin nodded. "Kalen told me about it, but it doesn't bother me. On Earth, when I was a kid, the other kids looked down on me because I was a nerd, so you might say I'm used to it."

"Nerd? What's a nerd? No, I get the image: a skinny little kid with big round glasses and an armload of textbooks. Let me guess, a nerd is someone who's smart."

"Yeah. I didn't wear glasses, but otherwise, I fit the stereotype."

"And that was a bad thing to be? I won't even ask why, I'll take your word for it. Now, let's get back to this protection ward. I want you to envision a long, thin strand of energy. When you have it, join the ends together to make a loop." Glendymere watched as Kevin formed a long rod of shimmering energy. As he was trying to force the ends towards each other, the strand gave a shudder and vanished. *"I think you're trying too hard. Just guide the ends towards each other. They should join together easily."*

Kevin created another strand, but this time he backed off a little, and the energy strand that had the flexibility of a rope. He eased the two ends towards each other, and as they touched, the ends disappeared and the strand became a loop. Kevin got so excited that he lost his concentration and the loop vanished into thin air. "I did it! Did you see it? Did you see the way those ends slid together?"

"Yes, that was much better. Now, do that again, but this time hold the image long enough to do something with it."

Kevin created another loop almost effortlessly. It curved around and floated in the air like a string on top of a pool of water. "What do I do with it now?"

"Find the two ends that you joined together. When you want to remove a ward, you have to separate the two ends so that the energy no longer flows in a loop."

"I thought breaking the loop could cause a big bang that might be hazardous to my health."

"Not if it's separated at the precise point where it was joined."

"So how do I find the two ends?"

"Look at the loop. It won't stand out, but you should be able to see where it's joined if you really look at it."

"Oh, I think I see it. All right, now what do I do, just move the ends away from each other?"

"Yes, but slowly. If you separate them too quickly it becomes unstable and who knows what it'll do then."

"What do you mean, who knows? Don't you know?"

"No. No two of these things are the same. It could simply vanish, or it could cause one of those big bangs you're not too fond of, or anything in between."

"How slow is slow enough?"

"Slow."

Kevin very slowly manipulated the loop until the ends seemed to separate all by themselves. "Okay," Kevin said as he began to breathe again. "They're separated and we're still here, so I guess that was slow enough. Now what?"

"You could get fancy and try to absorb the energy, but the safest method is to let it seep into the ground. Just lower one end of the strand until it touches the ground."

Kevin maneuvered the strand so that one end pointed towards the cave floor, and then he lowered it until it touched the ground. The strand slowly sank into the floor, like a pole into quicksand. After it was gone, Kevin sat down on the cave floor, exhausted.

After a minute, Glendymere said, *"Now, make another strand of energy. Then use it to make a net over the doorway. When you're satisfied with the net, join the two ends together."*

Glendymere watched quietly as Kevin made another strand and concentrated on weaving it around the arch, crisscrossing the lines of energy over the opening, and finally joining the ends. After Kevin was done, he asked, "Did I do it right? How strong is it? What would happen if someone tried to go through that arch?"

"I have no idea how strong you made it. We'll have to test it. Here, stand behind this boulder and look over the top." Once Kevin was behind the boulder, Glendymere backed up and stood off to the side, keeping another boulder between his torso and the archway. *"All right, I'm going to toss this stone towards the opening. Let's see what happens."* Glendymere mentally picked up a small

stone and threw it at the center of the doorway. There was a flash of light, a loud sizzling pop, and the stone disintegrated into a pile of dust. *"Guess you made that one a little strong. Maybe next time you should try a lighter, thinner strand."*

"How are we going to get rid of it?" Kevin whispered, awed by the power of the ward.

"Oh, you're going to have to do that. After all, you put it there. Just be careful. If you break that strand, all that energy will rush into you, and you'll end up just like that stone."

Kevin stood beside the boulder, looked at the pile of dust, and gulped.

"Come on, you'll be fine as long as you undo it exactly opposite of the way you made it. You do remember how you made it, don't you?"

"I think so, but what if I make a mistake?"

"Don't worry. If you make a mistake, you'll never know it. But let me get out of range first," Glendymere said as he stepped back behind his boulder. *"Go ahead. I'm out of the way now."*

Kevin thought sarcastically, *I'm so glad you're safe. My biggest concern is that one of my particles might fly off and burn you as I disintegrate.*

"I heard that," Glendymere said. *"Quit stalling and concentrate. You can do it."*

"Yeah. If you really believed that, you wouldn't be hiding behind that rock."

"I do believe that you can do it. I just don't believe in taking any unnecessary chances. Now get on with it," Glendymere said with finality.

Kevin took a deep breath and separated the two ends. Once he began dismantling the ward, he was surprised at how easy it was. The net seemed to unravel by itself, almost as if it were alive. Once he had removed the strand from the archway, he touched one end to the cave floor and watched as it disappeared into the ground.

Glendymere said, *"That wasn't too bad for a first try. Now I want you to do it again, only this time, don't make the strand quite so thick. Then toss a stone at it to test it. After you dismantle that one, make another one, even thinner, and so on. Notice how strong the ward is in relation to how thick the strand is. You'll also need to come up with a design you like and then make all your wards using the same pattern so that you can remove them quickly, and in the dark if you have to. But don't make it too simple, or even an apprentice will be able to remove it. After you master creating and dismantling your own wards, we'll work on dismantling one that someone else has created."*

Kevin just stared at Glendymere, so Glendymere raised his eyebrows in an unspoken question. Kevin shook his head and said, "It seems like everything I learn leads to a dozen more. It's mushrooming so fast that sometimes I feel like it's hopeless. And one of the most frustrating things about it is that I really do think I could get all of this if I had enough time."

"What's enough time? You've got the time you've got. That's all any of us ever has." Glendymere sighed as he looked into Kevin's mind. *"If you're asking me if you'll be ready for your first fight, the answer is no. No one ever is, or ever will be. Even if you survive a hundred challenges, you still won't be ready. The best you can hope for is to be just that bit more prepared than your opponent. And the way you prepare is ..."*

"Practice, practice, practice. Go on. Take a nap. I know that's what you want to do," Kevin said with a grin.

"Umm. Think I will. Naps are wonderful. When you get to be my age, you'll treasure them, too."

"How old are you anyway?" Kevin asked.

"I don't really know. I quit counting a long time ago, when I was somewhere around five thousand years old. Wake me when you're done and let me see what you've learned," Glendymere said.

As he headed for his chamber, Kevin's comments replayed through Glendymere's mind, so he took a few minutes to really examine the progress Kevin had made in the short time he had been in Willow Canyon. Glendymere felt that it was entirely possible that Kevin's skills would surpass

Badec's, and if they did, there would be very few sorcerers out there who would be foolish enough to challenge him. Maybe it was to Kevin's advantage that he had grown up on a non-magical world. He had no basis for comparison, so he didn't realize just how good he really was. At least there wasn't much chance that he would get cocky and slack off. It would be interesting to see how he performed against the dragons that Glendymere had lined up for sparring matches.

Chapter 37

Duane's Invitation

Duane wasn't expecting to hear from anyone, so the falcon that landed on his windowsill around midnight startled him. He clipped a light cord around the falcon's leg, set out some food and water for him, untied the note, and began to read:

Duane,

Our young man is showing a great deal of progress and I have high hopes for his future.

I have arranged some war games for November. He and his friends will oppose a squad of about fifteen elves and dwarves. I feel confident that if they can learn to hold their own against my friends, they will fair well against any human squads they may meet on their journey.

I thought you and Xantha might be interested in observing the games.

Glendymere

"Xantha, would you like to go?" Duane asked mentally.

Xantha was grazing on the other side of the valley, but he was aware of the contents of the note through his mind link with Duane. *"Sounds like fun."*

"Do you want to go down a couple of days early? Just to visit and watch them practice?"

"Sure."

"Then I'll tell Glendymere that we'll arrive around the end of October. I might even participate in the games."

"I don't know about that. I have no desire to return you to Shelandra with any extra holes in your body," Xantha said with a laugh.

"Ha, ha!" Duane said as he sat down to write the note to Glendymere.

~ ~ ~ ~

The next morning, Duane wandered through the woods, thinking through an idea that had come to him overnight. Finally he decided that it was time to discuss it with his father. He found Hayden working in the gardens.

"I'd like to run an idea past you. Have you got a few minutes or would you rather I wait until later?" Duane asked.

"I'm always looking for a good reason to stop weeding," Hayden said as he stood up. "Why don't we go for a walk while we talk. I need to stretch my legs."

After Duane helped his father gather his tools and store them in the shed, they headed out into the forest.

"Now, what's this idea of yours?" Hayden asked.

"I've been thinking about Landis. She's going to need to apprentice with a sorcerer soon, and I may know just the sorcerer," Duane answered.

"Who?"

"What do you think about apprenticing her with Myron, of the House of Nordin?"

Hayden frowned. "Myron? But we don't know if he's even still alive." Then Hayden stopped and looked at Duane. "Or do you know something I don't?"

"He's alive, and right now he's with Glendymere in Willow Canyon," Duane answered. "Yvonne knew that she was going to die, so she and Badec asked us to make arrangements to foster Myron on Earth. Xantha and I took him from the castle as soon as Yvonne became too weak to take care of him and met Pallor at the Gate House. Myron was on Earth by the time she died. That's why no one on Terah had any idea where he was."

"I see. That explains why you were hanging around Badec's castle so much about that time, and here I thought you were just smitten with Shelandra," Hayden said with a grin.

"Oh, I was in love with her all right, from the first day I saw her. Having to come up with a reason to hang around Badec's just gave me the courage to pursue her. It worked out great for me."

Hayden nodded. "So Myron grew up on Earth? When did he return to Terah?"

"Remember last spring when Badec became ill and I left for about a month? I was at Kalen's, with Myron. Pallor brought him back last March."

"How old is he now, twenty-three? Isn't he a little young to be training to be a sorcerer?"

"He wasn't scheduled to return until his twenty-fifth birthday, but we really had no choice under the circumstances."

"No, I don't suppose you did," Hayden said. "And he's with Glendymere now? How in the world did you convince Glendymere to tutor him?"

"We didn't. Badec made all of the arrangements with Glendymere right after Yvonne died. When Pallor brought Myron back to Terah, Kalen, Xantha, and I tried to teach him as much as we could about life on Terah in the short period of time he was at the Gate House, and then we sent him on to Willow Canyon."

"Did Xantha fly him down?"

"No, we thought he needed to spend a little time traveling through Terah, to sort of get a feel for the place, so we sent him down on horseback."

"Wasn't that a bit risky? What if he'd been attacked? Or is he a warrior?"

Duane laughed. "No, far from it. He has none of Badec's physical prowess. Fortunately, Pallor brought over six companions to help him, and they were far more adept at defending themselves than he was, or at least five of them were. The sixth turned out to be a healer. One of the reasons we kept them at Kalen's for three weeks was to teach them how to use our weapons."

"So we have seven people from Earth wandering around on Terah. Are you sure this is a good idea?"

"So far it seems to have worked out pretty well. They weren't too thrilled at first, but as time went by, they really got into the spirit of things."

"And now they're living and working with Glendymere. That's got to be interesting. I wonder how Blalick is handling all of this," Hayden said with a chuckle. "Do you have any idea how things are going?"

"I got a note from Glendymere last night. He said that Myron's progressing well. He didn't say anything about the others, but he's arranged some war games for November. He wants to put Myron and his companions up against a squad of elves and dwarves, so the others must be working out all right. He asked me if Xantha and I wanted to come observe. We're going down around the end of October."

Hayden frowned. "Are you planning to talk to Myron about taking Landis on as an apprentice now?"

"No. I was thinking about telling Glendymere about Landis and asking him if he thinks Myron will be ready to accept an apprentice by the time Landis is ready to start training."

"Is there any particular reason you want to apprentice her with Myron?"

246

"For one thing, Myron's not really an apprentice, he's more like a student, and I think he would be more like a teacher with Landis than most sorcerers. A lot of sorcerers use their apprentices as glorified servants."

"That's true."

"Another thing is that any sorcerer who accepts Landis is going to incur Rolan's wrath. Glendymere would know if Myron's going to be strong enough to protect her, don't you think?"

"Yes, I suppose he would. If nothing else, Myron's elven blood should give him an edge over Rolan," Hayden said thoughtfully. "But doesn't he have to assume his seat at the council meeting next April?"

"Yes, that's the deadline."

"How long has he had with Glendymere? Four months? And he'll have to leave in another four or five months? That's not much time to learn to be a sorcerer. You do realize he may not survive his first month as Master Sorcerer, don't you?" Hayden asked quietly.

"That's another reason I wasn't going to say anything to Myron yet. I was just going to bring up the idea with Glendymere and get his reaction to it, but I wanted to talk to you and see what you thought about it before I mentioned it to him."

"If Myron's half the man his father is, I would have no problem at all entrusting her safety to him, and if he's anywhere near the sorcerer that Badec was, he could definitely train her to protect herself. I trust your judgment, Duane. So, talk to Glendymere, see what he has to say. If he thinks it's a viable plan, I'll find a reason to visit Myron after he's settled in Camden. We can discuss it then."

Chapter 38

Practical Applications

During lunch the next Saturday, Kevin and Chris were discussing the upcoming war games and defensive strategies.

"I especially liked the idea of sending the arrows back on the enemy, although it was a bit scary to be on the receiving end," Chris said.

"Yeah, I sort of liked that one, too. I've been thinking about trying to ignite the ends as I return them, sort of like flaming arrows. What do you think?"

"I like it." Chris nodded. "Maybe you should try it the next time we practice."

"Yeah," Kevin agreed. "But one thing is really bothering me about all of this."

"What?"

"Defending against the arrows takes all of my concentration. I have to block everything else out. Someone could walk up behind me and I'd never even know they were there. If this were real, I'd be completely vulnerable."

"Don't forget, if it's ever for real the rest of us will be there to watch your back. Besides, it'll get better with practice. It always does," Chris assured him. "Give it a little time."

"You're probably right."

"Maybe you should try holding your seeing eye over the battlefield so that you can see what's happening."

"I don't think I can manage that yet, but it would be a good defensive strategy. Maybe later," Kevin said as he ate the last bite of his sandwich. "Want some coffee?"

Chris nodded. "I've been thinking about something else. One of the things that you want to do is to appear invincible so that the other sorcerers will be afraid to challenge you, right?"

"I'd like to, but that's a tall order, and I have no idea how realistic it really is."

"The key word here is 'appear'. You don't have to be invincible, just appear to be. That's a totally different thing."

"I'm not following you," Kevin said with a frown. "What do you mean?"

"I'm talking about showmanship. Sometimes athletes intimidate their opponents by the way they dress, the way they walk, the way they stand, and so on. It's all advertising. I was thinking that you could add a little pizzazz to your performance, make it look easy, like you could do all of this in your sleep. That would give the impression that your powers are so strong that these things are hardly worth your bother," Chris answered. "Do you see what I mean?"

"I think so, but I don't know if I could pull something like that off."

"Sure you could. I sat in on several commercial rehearsals when I was in college. There are things you can do to create the illusion of supreme competence, even superiority. All it takes is a little practice."

"Sorry to be eavesdropping, but Chris has something here. It's worth a try," Glendymere said.

"But how do I do it?" Kevin asked both of them. "What should I change?"

"One thing that might help is if you'd stop thinking of yourself as an accountant."

"Huh?"

"Remember when we first landed on Terah? You had lost your glasses. When Steve asked you if you needed them, you said that they were just for looks, so you'd fit the accountant image."

"Okay," Kevin said with a slight frown.

"Back on Earth, I bet you got up every morning, put on a suit, picked up your glasses, slid a serious look on your face, and stepped into the persona of the young accountant, right?"

"Well, I hadn't really thought about it, but yeah, I guess so."

"And you're still doing it."

"What do you mean?"

"When you start working with magic, you dip your head a little, bunch your eyebrows, and set your mouth in a straight line, and you usually sort of clench your fists. You never smile. You never loosen up. You're the epitome of a young executive taking his work seriously."

"This stuff is serious, Chris. If I mess up, bad things can happen."

"But after you learn how to do something, after you're comfortable with it, you need to relax and have fun with it." He looked around for a moment and then pointed to a small boulder on the other side of the river. "Suppose you were going to lift that rock. Here's you." Chris held his arms down to his side, clenched his fists, tilted his head forward, frowned, glared at the rock, and strained. "You don't need to do all of that. You're not picking the thing up with your muscles. It isn't heavy to your mind. Try it like this."

Chris turned sideways and stood casually with his weight on one leg and the other slightly to the side. He turned his head so that he could see the rock out of the corner of his eye, smiled, bent the elbow of the arm closest to the rock, and raised his hand with his palm open and his fingers curled slightly upwards. "And lift the rock," he said as he flipped his fingers up. Then when you want to set it down," he said as he turned his hand over and patted the air, "Almost like you're doing it all with your fingertips." Then Chris stepped back and looked at Kevin. "Now which one makes the sorcerer look stronger?"

Kevin nodded. "Okay, I see what you mean."

"Every time you start to practice, put on the sorcerer persona, not the accountant one. Loosen up. Do it with flair. Strut your stuff. Show the world that this stuff is so easy a baby could do it. Play the role."

"I'm not sure I can carry it off without looking really stupid," Kevin said, "but I guess I can give it a try."

~ ~ ~ ~

That evening, while they were all relaxing in the sitting room, Steve said, "We've been so concerned about getting to Camden that we haven't given a lot of thought as to what's going to happen once we get there."

"What do you mean?" Karl asked.

"What's going to be expected of Kevin as the Seated Sorcerer of Camden? Does he have any regular duties? Or does he just sit around waiting to meet with the council once a month? And as his friends, do we have roles that we're supposed to fill? Or do we just fade away into the background? Should we even show up at castle? Or should Kevin arrive on his own? Anyone from Terah would have a pretty good idea of what to do and what to expect. None of us has a clue, and I'm afraid it's going to be pretty obvious."

"Good point," Karl said. "And who do we ask? Just asking the question ..."

Kevin nodded. "I'll mention it to Glendymere tomorrow morning. Maybe he'll know."

"And if not, maybe he'll have some suggestions as to how we can find out," Chris added.

~ ~ ~ ~

The next morning, Kevin brought up Steve's questions as soon as he and Chris arrived in Willow Canyon.

Glendymere was quiet for a couple of moments, and then said, *"I should have thought about that. He's right. As far as the everyday work that sorcerers do, it's pretty much a matter of using your skills to help people do what needs to be done. You might be asked to help build a dam, or clear a field, or find a child who has wandered away from home. Sorcerers who apprentice with other sorcerers get plenty of experience in the 'grunt work'. I don't think you'll have any trouble picking up on it, but I'll set up some practice with those kinds of things. Just give me a few days to get it together. But as to the other stuff, the non-magical duties, I don't really know. Let me see if I can find someone who can explain how the government works in Camden and what role you'll have to play. "*

When Kevin and Chris went outside to practice, Glendymere asked Blalick to send a note to Laryn explaining that their guests needed someone to explain the government of Camden to them and ask if she had any suggestions. He wanted to see if she came up with the same person that he had thought of: Tyree.

~ ~ ~ ~

Monday morning, while they were taking a break from preparing for November's war games, Theresa asked Glendymere how many sorcerers there were on Terah.

"I have no idea," Glendymere answered. *"Most of the humans who left Earth and came to Terah were sorcerers, so a lot of the people here have magic in their family history. Over the years some of the families have pretty much lost the trait, some families have a little talent, and some have a lot, but unless a sorcerer's ambitious and wants a seat on the council, he probably wouldn't be that well known outside of his village or district. "*

"What do they do?" Karl asked. "I mean the ones who aren't on the council."

"It depends. Some prefer not to depend on sorcery for their livelihoods. They lead pretty much normal lives. They might hire out for individual jobs such as helping a farmer clear a field in exchange for a portion of the crop. However, anyone who has completed an apprenticeship in sorcery is supposed to register with their town director. They would probably be asked to help out in an emergency, but it's up to them whether they do or not. Sorcerers are under no obligation to risk their lives unless they've been hired by the town or district. "

"How do they get hired? I mean is there some kind of list of sorcerers and the ministers choose from the list?" Chris asked.

"Not exactly. Usually a novice sorcerer writes to the seated sorcerer to let him know that he's interested in serving as a district or town sorcerer, and asks to be considered if any openings come up. Then, when an opening comes up, if the applicant can demonstrate that he has the needed skills, and if no one else has applied for the job, he gets hired. If there are several applicants, they hold a competition to determine who gets the job, " Glendymere explained.

"What kind of competition?" Kevin asked.

"Someone from the district, either the minister or some other local official, meets with the seated sorcerer to come up with several tasks to test the skills that are most needed in that area. Then each of the applicants is asked to perform those tasks. After everyone has finished, the local officials usually decide which applicant gets the job. The seated sorcerer has to be there, but it's more in an advisory capacity than in a decision-making role. " Then Glendymere turned his head towards Kevin and said, *"Since you'll have to help plan and supervise every district competition, you'll need to know the needs of each of your districts. The local representative may have a good grasp of what a local sorcerer needs to know, but a lot of times they don't. Not all districts are the same. "*

"What do you mean?" Kevin asked.

"Districts along the borders or near major rivers are often targets for slavers, so their sorcerers see more military action. They need someone who can hit targets with energy bolts,

deflect arrows, disarm the enemy, and do all of this while flying. Districts in mountainous regions need sorcerers who are good at search and rescue, so they need someone who is skillful with the seeing eye and who can support someone else while flying. Sorcerers who excel with the outstretched hand are usually matched with inland farming communities where there are fields to be cleared and a lot of construction work to be done. Although all sorcerers should be competent in each of the three major areas, their level of mastery will vary. If a district is really lucky, they'll find a sorcerer who has the skills they need, who is able to think on his feet, and who is willing to work for what they're willing to offer, but more often than not, they have to settle for the one they can afford."

"But how do you test a sorcerer's skills?" Kevin asked. "Say the district was a farming community. I have no idea what tasks they would need a sorcerer to perform. How could I come up with an appropriate competition?"

Karl laughed. "Farming is about the only thing I do know something about. First, have the sorcerers clear a small stretch of land, and choose the rockiest land you can find, and if there were a couple of massive old tree trunks in the way that would be even better. Then see if the sorcerer could water the field using water from a stream or pond. For a third test, you could have the sorcerer help build a silo."

"Not bad. I had a little trouble with the word 'silo', but that would be a good competition. In the first test, a good candidate would clear the land and the farmer wouldn't have to clean up before plowing. A poor one would leave the field riddled with debris. As for watering the field, an unskilled sorcerer probably wouldn't be able to do it at all. One of medium skill might get some water over the field, but it would probably just get dumped. A highly skilled sorcerer would handle a little at a time and let it drizzle down. It would take a lot longer, but it would be a lot more effective.

"Devising skill tests isn't hard once you understand what the sorcerer needs to be able to do. Talk to several of the local people, not just the officials, and see what they need. Then pick the most important tasks and set up the competition, but once the competition begins, don't take your eyes off the test. Anyone can claim to be a sorcerer, and there's nothing more dangerous than a little magical ability. You may have to intervene to keep bystanders from getting hurt."

"Assuming I'm good enough to protect them," Kevin said.

"When you devise the tests, give some thought to all the things that can go wrong, and set up the field so that the spectators are a safe distance away. Remember, you're in charge, so you can do it any way you want to. Suppose one of the tests involves energy bolts. Set up your targets on the other end of the field, away from everybody. It won't be all that hard to protect the observers if you just think it through."

"How would you test a sorcerer's skill in battle? Set up some war games? Maybe against the local military unit?" Darrell asked.

"Possibly, but that could get rather dangerous," Steve answered. "Someone would have to make sure that no one got hurt. Guess that would be your job, Kevin."

"There would be more to it than that. Most sorcerers can handle deflecting arrows, but the test would be how well a sorcerer handles multiple tasks. How would he fare if he had to defend against another sorcerer as well? You would probably have to get directly involved if you wanted to find out, and at the same time, you would have to provide protection for the army as well as the spectators."

"I can't do all of that by myself!" Kevin gasped.

"Not yet, but you will be able to. That reminds me, I've invited my friends to come back in early January for a second round of war games. I thought it might be a good idea for all of you to have some experience fighting a group that was backed up by magic, so I've asked Jonquin to come in January, too."

Chris frowned. "Isn't it a bit risky letting another sorcerer know that Kevin's here?"

Darrell nodded in agreement. "From what we've heard, there's probably quite a bit of money being offered for information about where he is, and that's assuming that Jonquin doesn't want to kill him himself."

Glendymere looked confused for a second and then he said, *"You're thinking Jonquin's human. He's not. He's a dragon."*

"You mean we're going to have to go up against a dragon?" Darrell sputtered.

"No, Kevin will be going up against a dragon. All you will have to worry about are the elves and dwarves. It should be quite a lot of fun."

"You do have the strangest idea of fun," Chris muttered.

Glendymere ignored him and continued, *"But before we can start preparing for the games in January, we need to get ready for the ones that are going to take place in November. Now, if there are no more questions, let's get back to work."* Glendymere stood up and stretch out his wings.

"I have one more quick question," Theresa said. "You keep saying 'he'. Women can be sorcerers too, can't they?"

Glendymere nodded. *"Yes, of course. Actually there are several on the council. Anything else? Good. Now, I want to try something a little more interesting today."* A large stick popped up from the ground and traced a circle about thirty feet wide in the dirt. *"I would like for Joan, Chris, and Karl to spread out around the circle and shoot arrows towards Kevin. Then I want Darrell, Theresa, and Steve to try to cross the circle and reach Kevin. I don't care whether you spread out, or if you try to rush the circle together, but try to get in. Kevin, I want you to collect the arrows and stack them next to that boulder, and at the same time, prevent anyone from crossing that circle."*

"Isn't that a little risky? I mean, what if we hit one of the three who are trying to cross the circle?" Joan asked as she picked up her bow.

"Don't worry. Kevin won't let that happen," Glendymere said.

"You'll make sure no one gets hit if I miss an arrow, right?" Kevin asked mentally.

"Of course, but it does no harm for them to think that you're doing it all yourself. After all, someone has to have confidence in you, and right now that someone doesn't seem to be you," Glendymere answered Kevin privately. *"See if you can put on a show while you're defending the circle. Go out there and, as Chris says, 'Strut your stuff!'"*

~ ~ ~ ~

While Kevin and Chris were eating lunch that afternoon, Kevin said, "You know when Glendymere was talking about the sorcery competitions this morning? He mentioned rescue missions, remember?"

"Yes?"

"Well, one of the skills he brought up was the ability to support someone else while flying."

"Yeah, I noticed that, too," Chris said hesitantly.

"I've never tried to do that."

"Let me guess," Chris said with deep sigh, "You want to try it now, right?"

"Well, I need to learn how to do it."

"And you're thinking I'm going to agree to let you experiment with me?"

"I know how to catch you if you fall."

"That may be true, but I don't much care for the idea of falling in the first place," Chris said. "Look, your first attempts at something aren't usually all that successful. Let's start with something else, like maybe a big rock. Then once you've got the hang of it, we'll give it a try. But when we do, I want Glendymere around."

"Why?"

"Backup, just in case you happen to have a moment of panic when you drop me."

"I don't freeze up as bad as I used to," Kevin argued. "But if it'll make you feel better, I'll try flying with a rock after we finish eating, and if that goes well, we'll get Glendymere back out here and see how it goes with a person."

"Let's just see how the rock goes for now," Chris mumbled.

"Chicken," Kevin teased.

"You got that right!"

After Kevin flew around for half an hour with the rock by his side, Chris pointed to a log about six feet long and asked Kevin to try flying with that next. After Kevin circled the canyon with the log a few times, Chris could come up with no more valid objections, so he reluctantly agreed to let Kevin fly him over the valley, provided Glendymere would come back outside to back Kevin up.

Glendymere quickly chimed in that he was on his way. Then he said, *"Chris, I haven't been able to get you to fly with me and now you're going up with Kevin. Should I be insulted?"*

"No, I still don't want to fly, but you said that sorcerers need to be able to support someone else in flight, and I don't see a whole lot of volunteers standing in line out here."

"Guess you have a point there," Glendymere said with a bit of a snort. *"But don't worry. Between the two of us, I feel sure we can take care of you."*

"Yeah, well …"

"What is it about flying anyway? Are you afraid of heights?"

"Yes and no. I'm not really afraid of heights, I'm afraid of falling from heights. And floating through the air seems like a mighty good way to fall," Chris answered.

"I won't drop you. Just relax and don't start fighting me when we lift off," Kevin said as he stepped over beside Chris. "Okay, we're going to lift off now. Let me do all the work."

They began to slowly rise. When they were about twenty feet off the ground, Kevin said, "Now we're going to start going sideways. Don't try to do anything, just let me do it," and they began to float over towards the stream.

Chris had closed his eyes as soon as he felt himself lifting off the ground. He slowly opened one eye and sort of peeked out to see where he was. There was no reassuring pressure on the bottom of his feet, but it wasn't as bad as he had expected. Finally he worked up enough courage to look around. "Hey, this is sort of neat. I guess this is what's known as a 'bird's eye view,' huh?"

"Not exactly. If you'd really like a bird's eye view of this canyon, I can take you up higher," Kevin said with a grin.

"No, no. This is high enough. But it is sort of nice. I could get used to this."

"Good. I need the practice and you need to get over your aversion to flying with me. You never know when you might need to do it for real. Let's plan to fly around the canyon after lunch everyday for a while, and when you're comfortable with it, we'll go up higher," Kevin said. "But for now, I guess we need to land and get back to work."

~ ~ ~ ~

A couple of weeks later, Glendymere and Kevin flew to a nearby valley where a local farmer had begun clearing the land in hopes of tilling the area before the snows set in. He was having trouble with some old tree trunks and large boulders, so he had offered Blalick a fourth of next year's harvest if he'd help him. When Blalick mentioned it in passing, Glendymere saw an opportunity for Kevin to get a little experience in the more mundane tasks that sorcerers are expected to handle, as well as a little practice throwing energy bolts. He told Blalick that he and Kevin would take care of it.

They reached the valley shortly after dawn. Glendymere pointed out the boulders and stumps that needed to be removed. *"Any sorcerer could clear this field, but a good sorcerer would leave it ready for the plow. When you blow up a boulder or a tree trunk, don't leave chunks of it scattered around for the farmer to have to clear. Hit them again and again, until they're dust. That's how you build a reputation, by taking care of the little things, the details."*

Then Glendymere flew back up to the top of one of the surrounding mountains to take a nap while Kevin cleared the field.

Around lunchtime Kevin flew up to join him. He sat down beside the dragon and opened the bag that contained his lunch and a jug of water.

"Glendymere, can I ask you a question?" Kevin said quietly.

"Sure."

"Why did you agree to tutor me? Do you do that a lot?"

"No. You're only the fifth human sorcerer that I've agreed to help, and the first three were on Earth. After I came to Terah, I decided not to do it anymore," Glendymere said. *"About forty years ago, a young man about your age sent me a letter requesting an audience. It was Badec. In the letter he said that he had something very important that he needed to discuss with me. I was intrigued, so I agreed to see him. When he came to my cave, he asked me to train him as a sorcerer. Usually the father makes apprenticeship arrangements, so I asked him why he was doing this himself. He said that when he had approached his father with the idea, Nolan had told him that if he wanted me, he'd have to arrange it himself."*

"Why didn't my grandfather want you to tutor him?"

"Nolan and I had been friends for years and he would have been embarrassed to ask me to tutor his son. With a human sorcerer, he could strike a bargain, pay him in some way for his time and trouble, but what can a human offer a dragon? He would have felt like he was taking advantage of our friendship and putting me in an awkward position if I didn't want to do it. Anyway, I told Badec that I'd have to think about it. He said he'd wait for my decision, no matter how long it took. I'm still not sure why I said yes, but about a year later I sent word that I would accept him as a student when he reached his twenty-fifth birthday." Glendymere stood up and stretched his huge wings. *"I could hardly refuse Badec's request that I also tutor his son when he came to see me right after Yvonne's death. I could see how devastated he was. I figured it was the least I could do, so I agreed. Now, are you ready to go back to Willow Canyon? Or are you just taking a break?"*

"No, I'm done. Let's go," Kevin said as he tied his lunch bag to his sash and rose in the air to fly home beside Glendymere.

~ ~ ~ ~ ~

Later that week, Glendymere told Kevin and Chris that he had a job for Kevin to do in another canyon. There had been a rockslide during a sudden downpour the day before, and one of the few roads in the area was blocked.

"This is another typical job for a sorcerer, and I thought you could use the experience. Come on, climb on board, Chris. It's time you flew with me." Glendymere knelt down and extended one of his forearms so that Chris could climb up on his back. When Chris was settled, Glendymere said, *"Don't worry. Just hold onto my chain. You'll be fine,"* and gently rose into the air.

When they reached the canyon, Glendymere and Chris landed on top of the cliff on the opposite side of the canyon from the rockslide. The rocks had formed a six-foot high barrier across the narrow road that ran between the small river and the canyon wall. A few of the boulders had rolled into the river, but not enough to obstruct the flow of water.

As soon as Kevin landed on the road, he heard the unmistakable sound of a rattlesnake. He quickly looked around to his left where the sound seemed to be coming from, and right there in the rocks, not more than five feet away from him, was the grandfather of all rattlers, a monstrous snake, coiled and ready to strike.

"Yikes!" Kevin screeched, and he was suddenly fifty feet down the road, heart pounding and feeling faint, but well out of reach of the snake.

"I see you've figured out how to translocate," Glendymere observed. *"Very good. That might come in handy later."*

"What are you talking about?" Kevin asked, gasping for breath.

"The way you just jumped away from that snake. That's translocation."

"Are you under the impression that I did that on purpose? All I know is that when I saw that snake, I thought I was dead."

"That's all right. Now that we know you can do it, you've just got to figure out how to control it."

"You make it sound so easy," Kevin said as he crept up the road towards the rock pile. "Where'd that snake go?"

"Oh, don't worry about him. You scared that poor rattler so bad he won't come out of his lair for days. Just try not to hurt him while you're cleaning up this mess," Glendymere said as he stretched out in the sun.

"Right, my biggest worry right now is going to be hurting that poor rattler!"

"As it should be."

Kevin shook his head and carefully began floating the boulders away to clear the road.

Chris quietly asked Glendymere, "You knew the snake was there, didn't you?"

"Yes."

"Why didn't you warn Kevin? He really could have gotten hurt."

Glendymere shook his head and said, *"That snake wasn't going to bite. He's a friend of mine. My only worry was that Kevin might hurt him."*

"Did you set it up?"

"Yes."

"Why?"

"I wanted to see if Kevin could translocate, and I found out that he can. Right now it only works when he's scared, but at least that's something."

Chris slowly nodded his head. Then he settled down beside Glendymere to wait for Kevin to finish clearing the rockslide. A little more than two hours later, Kevin joined them on top of the cliff wall.

Glendymere stood up to get a good view of the canyon so he could check Kevin's work. The road was cleared and smoothed out. The boulders had been broken up into gravel and scattered along the road. There was no sign that a rockslide had ever blocked it.

"Now that's the way to build a reputation, Kevin," Glendymere said. *"The gravel is a nice touch, good use of the boulders. Couldn't have done it any better myself."* Glendymere stretched out his foreleg and said, *"Come on then, Chris. Climb on up. Time to head for home."*

Chapter 39

Looking Ahead

They returned to Willow Canyon around lunchtime, so Kevin and Glendymere followed Chris as he headed inside for lunch. Chris stopped as soon as he stepped into Glendymere's chamber, and a few seconds later, Kevin plowed into him. Glendymere peeked around the corner to get a look at what had startled the guys.

A magnificent bird at least three feet tall was perched on Glendymere's water basin. His chest and topknot were the color of wheat, his beak and claws were blue-black, and his eyes sparkled like two huge rubies. When he fluttered his six-foot wings, there was an explosion of color. His feathers were a mixture of violet, crimson, and scarlet, all with flaming orange tips. His piercing shriek shattered the silence of the cavern.

"Good morning, Freddy. Do you have a message for me?" Glendymere said, including Kevin and Chris in the conversation.

"Aye, that I do," the phoenix answered. *"But my message is for your ears only."* The phoenix lowered his wings and glared at the two humans.

"Open you eyes Freddy and you'll know who this is," Glendymere said as he nodded towards Kevin.

The phoenix turned his cold stare on Kevin for a few moments. *"Sure, and it's his heir, isn't it? But that changes nothing. My message is still for your ears only."*

"Very well," Glendymere nodded.

In a private telepathic conversation, Freddy said that Laryn thought Tyree would be a good tutor for Glendymere's guests. She had already asked him if he would be willing to go to Nandelia for a couple of months as her emissary, and he had replied that he'd be honored.

Glendymere nodded and continued their private conversation. *"Please ask Laryn to let Tyree know that I'll pick him up on the last Monday in October, and tell him to plan to remain here until the middle of January, maybe longer."*

"Anything else?"

"No, I think that's all. You don't need to rush off though. Why don't you stay awhile and get to know Myron and Chris?"

"No need. I know all I need to know. I scanned them both when they came in."

"And?"

"Aye, they are both good men. I found no hint of evil lurking in their souls."

"I thought so, but it's always nice to be sure," Glendymere replied.

"If there's nothing else, I'll be on my way," Freddy said, this time including Kevin and Chris in the conversation. Then with a bone-chilling screech, he circled the chamber and rose towards the opening in the ceiling. As the sunlight caught his wings, the colors shimmered and Freddy seemed to vanish.

"What happened? Did he turn invisible?" Chris asked.

"No, you just can't see a phoenix in flight. They fade into the sky."

"I wish Steve could have been here," Kevin said.

"Why? Oh, I see. So that he could sketch Freddy. Steve will have plenty of chances once you get to Camden. Freddy's roost is in the castle tower."

"He lives at the castle?" Chris asked.

"Yes. He's lived in Camden ever since he came to Terah over a thousand years ago, but he didn't take up residence at the castle until Nolan became the Master Sorcerer. When Nolan died, Freddy stayed. It may just be that the tower suits him, I don't know, but I hope he'll stay at the castle while you're there."

"Any particular reason, other than sending messages?" Kevin asked.

"A phoenix has the ability to sense whether a soul is good or evil. A lot of people would love to have a phoenix in residence, but the phoenix chooses you, you can't choose him. However, if Freddy should happen to leave, you can always reach me by sending a falcon to Blalick. The message will get here. It just won't be as quick."

"Speaking of messages, if that message was from Camden …" Kevin said a little warily. He didn't want to pry into Glendymere's business, but if Freddy's message had come from Camden, it was probably as much his business as it was Glendymere's.

"Yes, yes. I nearly forgot. The message was from Badec's sister, Laryn. She and I both think Tyree would be a good choice as a government tutor for all of you. She's already asked him if he would be willing to travel to Nandelia for a few months on her behalf. He's agreed to come, but he has no idea where or why."

"Who's Tyree?" Chris asked. "How do you know him?"

Glendymere explained that he had first met Tyree years ago, back when Badec's father, Nolan, had been the Master Sorcerer. Tyree's father had been the Governor of Camden during the last twenty-five years of Nolan's tenure, and Tyree had been his father's assistant for the last eight of those years. He had an excellent understanding of how the government worked, and was completely loyal to the House of Nordin. *"I asked Freddy to tell Laryn to let Tyree know that I'll pick him up on the last Monday in October."*

"Does Tyree know you?" Kevin asked.

"Yes, but he's never flown with me before. Maybe I should ask Blalick to make some kind of safety harness so that Tyree will feel more secure and comfortable. Think I'll do that now, before I forget. I also need to ask him to prepare a room for Tyree," Glendymere said.

"I don't think there's another room near us. At least, I haven't come across one," Chris said.

"No there isn't, but he won't be staying with you. Blalick has a couple of spare rooms in his house for visiting dignitaries. Tyree will be fine up there."

~ ~ ~ ~

After dinner that evening, Chris told the others about Freddy and Tyree. "Glendymere's expecting Tyree to stay with Blalick, but if he's going to talk to all of us about life on Terah, it'll have to be in the evenings, so that means we only have two weeks to come up with our cover story for the trip to Camden."

"What do you mean?" Theresa asked.

"Well, we don't know this guy, and Glendymere hasn't seen him in thirty years. Laryn knows him, but he's not part of Badec's government, so she probably hasn't spent a lot of time around him lately either. Just how far are we willing to trust him?" Chris asked.

Darrell nodded. "I don't think we should discuss any of our plans while he's in the area."

"You and Chris are being paranoid again," Kevin told Darrell, with a chuckle.

"Maybe so," Chris answered, "but I'm of the opinion that a little paranoia once in a while might be the secret to a long life in this world."

Joan laughed and said, "He may be right, Kevin. After all, this guy is going to realize that you're Myron, and your plans would probably bring a pretty penny."

"Okay, okay, I agree. I just said it's paranoid." Kevin grinned and held his hands up, palms out, as if to fend off an attack.

"So, does anyone have any ideas about our cover story?" Karl asked.

When no one answered, Theresa said, "If any of you are interested, I have a lotion that should help your hair grow a little faster and thicker. I sent a message to Evelyne right after you first mentioned growing beards to see if she knew of anything that might help, and she sent me a recipe that her mother had used for her father. I've made up a little of it. Does anyone want to volunteer to try it?"

"I will," Kevin said. "And then, if it does anything weird, like turn my hair green or make it all fall out, I'll use that as my disguise." He grinned at Theresa. "I'll try it for a couple of weeks and see if there are any bad side-effects. Then, if it works, you can make up some for all of us."

Theresa nodded. "I'll bring it to your room tonight. You need to apply it morning and night, especially at first."

"Ashni and I have altered some of the old tunics she had in her attic and we've made some new ones. They're larger and heavier than our old ones," Joan said.

"How many new tunics are we going to be taking with us?" Chris asked.

"Right now we have enough for each of us to have three," Joan answered.

Darrell frowned and asked, "Will we have enough room to take our old ones, too?"

"We should," Karl answered.

"I'm also planning for each of us to have two sweaters," Joan said. "I've got enough yarn to start making them and I'm thinking about crocheting them with a double strand of yarn to make them bulkier and warmer. Ashni also suggested that we might want to try on some of the cloaks that Sari and Macin have outgrown. They're already made, lined, and are waterproof. Plus, they've been worn, so they won't look new. I'm going to bring them down this week so we can all go through them. Then I'll know if I need to make any more."

The others nodded.

"Next, why are we traveling?" Steve asked. "There has to be a compelling reason for us to cross the Great Plains during the dead of winter. No one would do that just for fun."

After a couple of minutes of silence, Karl said, "Why don't I go get our maps? If we spread them out on the table and look at where we're going, maybe an idea will hit one of us."

Theresa stood up when Karl did, stretched and said, "If I'm going to do any serious thinking tonight, I need a cup of coffee. Anyone else want one?"

The others nodded, so Theresa and Joan went to the kitchen to fix the coffee and find some snacks to go with it. By the time Karl returned with the maps, Theresa had the coffee on the stove, Joan had a platter of cookies and seven mugs ready, and everyone else was seated around the dining room table.

Karl spread their maps out over the table. "We're somewhere near here," he said, pointing to a spot a little west of Abernon. Then he pointed to the town that Kalen had marked in eastern Tennessee. "And Milhaven's right here."

Darrell focused on the section of the map that covered Abernon and the surrounding area. "I've got a question. When we leave here, where are we going? We really shouldn't go through Sheridan or Abernon again."

"Maybe we could head north, by-pass Abernon, and get back on the road that follows the river," Karl said. "I bet we could follow the river all the way to the Mississippi."

"Here it is." Joan put her finger on the road and traced it. "It runs beside the river all the way. How are we going to cross the Mississippi?"

"I'm sure they have ferries somewhere along there," Karl said. "I'll ask Blalick and see if he knows where."

"I've got another question," Darrell said. "Where are we going to be coming from? I mean, people are going to ask us where we're from and where we're headed now that we aren't traveling as minstrels."

"How about this? We had farms out here," Steve said, pointing to a spot about three hundred miles north of Abernon. "There aren't many roads or towns in this area, so we could say we had farms about a hundred miles south of Trendon."

"And we were our own little community," Karl agreed. "Joan and I would be a married couple. How do we explain the rest of you?"

"I can say that my wife died a couple of years ago, so I'm covered, but in that case, I'd have to have my own wagon and it would have to be loaded with household-type stuff," Steve said.

"Blalick and I have already discussed altering the minstrels' wagon. You could use that one. We're planning to build another wagon, too, so that one could be for Joan and me. Then, of course, Theresa would have hers," Karl said.

"But why are we traveling in the dead of winter?" Joan asked.

"And how are we going to explain the rest of us?" Chris added.

The coffee had perked, so Theresa stepped into the kitchen to get the coffee while Joan brought out the cookies and mugs. When they got back to the dining room, Theresa started pouring coffee in the mugs and handing them out.

Steve took a sip of his and said, "Let's try this. Karl and Joan had a farm that was next to mine. In late November, a bad storm was brewing and two soldiers knocked on your door and asked if they could stay the night. You agreed, and during the evening, the soldiers explained that they were sick of the cold and ice, had resigned their commissions, and were heading to southeast Camden, to a more agreeable climate. They figured they could hire out easily enough once they got there. You listened, and the more the soldiers talked about Camden, the more tempting it sounded. So, all of you struck a deal. The soldiers would provide protection on the journey in exchange for meals along the way." Steve looked around at the others. "When the storm cleared, Karl came over to my place and asked me if I wanted to join them and move to Camden, so I packed up my belongings, and we all left within the week."

"Let me guess, Darrell and Chris are the soldiers, right?" Kevin asked. "You know, that's not bad."

"And all of you were camped on the side of the road one evening when my assistant," Theresa said, nodding at Kevin as she set a cup of coffee in front of him, "and I pulled up and asked if we could join you for the night. Then, since we were all headed in the same general direction, we decided to travel together."

"Where are we all going?" Darrell asked.

"Well, Kevin and I would probably be headed for Timera Valley, the home of the Sisterhood. Here it is, not too far from Milhaven," Theresa said, pointing to a spot on the map. "And if I were really going there, I would probably go to Milhaven and then follow that road right there. It seems to lead through the mountains and up towards Timera Valley."

"Where are the rest of us headed?" Joan asked.

"We could be planning to take this road," Karl said, pointing to a road that wound through the mountains and then on to the coast. "See that town? Dayton? That looks like a good spot. Plenty of open country around, not too many towns. Looks like good farming country to me."

"But how would we know? I mean, what reason would we give for heading to that particular spot?" Joan asked.

"No reason, other than it's on the other side of the mountains, a road leads to it, and it's on the map," Karl answered. "We could always say that we figured if we got there and it's too crowded, the local people would have some suggestions for where we could settle, but we're traveling through the winter so that we can find a piece of land in time for spring planting. Steve and I will work together on the same piece of land, clearing it, plowing it, and planting our crops this spring. Then this summer, we plan to raise a house and a barn."

"I think that'll work if we have the right props. We'll need to carry farming equipment, a little household furniture, kitchen utensils, and some bedding. Are we going to be able to get everything we need?" Steve asked Karl.

"We should. The plows are the only things I'm concerned about. They're heavy, bulky, and big, but they're essential if we're going to masquerade as farmers. Maybe we could have one between us, one that we've shared over the years, working together to plow and plant both our fields. Would they do that on Terah?"

"I don't know, but what if we were family? What if my wife had been Joan's sister? Then we'd have a good reason for living near each other, working together, and staying together. No one questions family," Steve answered.

"Good. I think we've got it then," Darrell said. "Theresa will have all of her herbs and tools, so she and Kevin have their props. We have plenty of weapons for me and Chris, so we can masquerade as soldiers easily enough."

"Blalick and I will start working on some furniture and farming tools," Karl said. "But we're going for simple, the type of stuff peasants would have, nothing fancy. Just a table, a couple of chairs, bed headboard, mattress pad, a loom, a spinning wheel, maybe a small chest of some sort. But this gives us a good reason to carry your harp, Joan, and I'll take a fiddle. We'll put a couple of flutes in Steve's wagon. They could have been his wife's. I don't see how we could carry much else without inviting suspicion though."

"I can take one of the guitars," Theresa said.

"All right, but that's it. Let's not push our luck," Karl answered.

"We'll review the plan again before we leave, but I think it's simple enough to work," Steve said.

"Do we have a target date yet?" Darrell asked.

"I've been thinking that we'd leave around the twentieth of January," Kevin answered. "If it takes us eight weeks, that will put us in Milhaven around the middle of March, giving me a couple of weeks to get ready for the April council meeting. That's cutting it fairly close, but I don't want to leave here until we absolutely have to."

"We'll probably get there in under eight weeks. It will be cold, but if we really were farmers and soldiers, we wouldn't stay in inns very often. That way we won't have to stop in the middle of the afternoon simply because we've reached a town," Karl said.

Chris frowned and said, "You know, there must be a reason why Kalen had us travel by wagon to Glendymere's, and now we're traveling by wagon to Milhaven. Xantha could have flown Kevin down here, and he would have had that much more time with Glendymere. And Glendymere could fly us to Milhaven just as easily, giving Kevin until the middle of March to stay here and work on his magic. Why haven't they suggested that?"

"I've wondered about that too," Darrell said.

"I think they want us to be immersed in the day-to-day life on Terah before we get to Milhaven, and one of the best ways to absorb the concerns, problems, and dreams of local people is to sit around in the tavern and listen to them talk. We didn't listen all that much on the way down here because we were performing, but even so, we picked up quite a bit," Steve said. "If we camp out all the time, we may be shortchanging ourselves. At the same time, camping is nicer. We don't have to watch what we say, we can relax, and even with standing guard, I sleep better when we camp than I do when we stay in town."

"I don't sleep well when we stay in towns either," Darrell agreed.

"All right. Let's plan on about three or four nights a week in town and three or four nights out," Karl nodded. "When we do camp, we'll need something really warm to sleep under, Joan, and we're going to need some heavy horse blankets."

"I know," Joan said. "Ashni and I have already talked about that. Macin's already gotten several blankets for us and he's going to pick up three or four more each month. No one will notice that amount, especially since some of the local farmers ask him to get stuff for them, too. And as for us, I'm going to make sleeping bags. We've been gathering and preparing down from the chickens and we set aside some of the wool from the llamas. We won't have zippers, but I'll sew the bottoms together, and I'll sew ties along the side. The ties will be a couple of inches from the edges so that once you tie them, the sides will pretty much stay together. We're also going to make some mats filled with straw and a little wool for us to sleep on to keep the ground cold out."

"We'll probably sleep in just one or two tents. It might be a little crowded, but it'll be warmer," Karl suggested.

"If it gets too cold, I'll heat some rocks and we can use them for bed warmers," Kevin offered.

"Oh, I just thought of something. Theresa, have you decided what name you want to use?" Chris asked. "I know my paranoia is showing again, but I don't think we should call you Theresa around Tyree."

Kevin and Darrell laughed, but they nodded in agreement.

"I think I'd really prefer Teri. But do you think that's too close? Should we go with something completely different?" Theresa asked.

"I think it'll be okay, don't you?" Joan asked Karl.

Karl nodded. "If anyone comments on the similarity, just smile and agree that it's quite a coincidence. If we don't make much out of it, no one else will pay much attention to it."

"I agree," Steve said. "Our reaction is the key. We'll also have to watch how we react if anyone asks if we've come across the minstrels, Taelor, or Myron in our travels."

"Play the role," Joan said. "We can probably carry that off by now."

"I think this scenario will work," Darrell said with a nod. "Now, unless anyone can think of anything else we need to work on tonight, I'm for clearing up the table and going to bed." When no one could think of anything else, Darrell gathered up several of the mugs, took them to the kitchen sink, and started washing them.

~ ~ ~ ~

On the last Friday morning in October, Glendymere was waiting out in the canyon when Kevin and Chris arrived.

"Things are going to get hectic around here soon. I'm going to go get Tyree Monday, and the elves and dwarves will start arriving by the middle of next week. Oh, and have I mentioned that Duane and Xantha are coming to observe the games? They should be arriving near the beginning of next week, too."

"How long are they going to stay?" Kevin asked.

"I'm not sure, but they'll be here long enough to see all of you in action."

"Where are they coming from?" Chris asked. "Kalen's?"

"No, at least not as far as I know. Duane was at home when he answered my note."

"Where's home?" Kevin asked.

"A valley called Crinsor Run. His parents live there, as well as his brother and sisters, their families, and Pallor, when he's on Terah."

"Where's Crinsor Run? I mean, how far away, which direction?" Chris asked.

"It's near the western coast, a little north of where we are now, in the redwood forest," Glendymere said. Then he changed the subject. *"I've been thinking about battle strategies. Sometimes it helps to break your enemy's concentration, to direct his attention to something other than yourself."*

"How do we do that?" Kevin asked. "What could possibly distract a warrior in the heat of battle?"

"It would have to be something threatening, more threatening than the enemy," Chris answered with a frown. "But what could be more daunting than having a sorcerer throw your own arrows back at you? Add a few lightning bolts, and you'd have my undivided attention."

"How about a tornado headed your way?"

"Now, that would be a distraction," Chris said with a nod. "But where are we going to get a nice tame little tornado that will attack the enemy but leave us alone?"

"From Kevin, of course."

"You mean like the one Paul made?" Kevin asked shaking his head. "I've just gotten to the point that I can get a good thunderstorm going."

"Don't you think a tornado would be a better distraction than a thunderstorm?"

"Oh, definitely, but can you really control one of those things once it gets going?" Kevin asked.

"I can. And apparently Pallor can. It remains to be seen whether or not you can, but you'll never know until you try." Glendymere stretched his wings and extended his foreleg. *"Come on up, both of you. I don't want to stir things up too much around here. We'll go south to the canyon lands."*

After Chris and Kevin were seated, Glendymere soared into the sky. When they reached the deserted canyon lands, Glendymere settled on the same butte he had perched on when he had brought Kevin to the area back in June. After Kevin and Chris dismounted, Glendymere walked over towards the southern edge of the butte and concentrated on creating the warm and cool masses of air necessary for unstable weather. He generated some warm updrafts and cold down winds to get things started, and then he stirred it up with some energy bolts until he had a good thunderstorm brewing.

"Kevin, I want you to join with that storm just like before. You have to experience the formation of a tornado before you can spawn one. Just let yourself go," Glendymere said. Then, while Kevin was concentrating on the storm, he privately told Chris that he had wanted him to come for two reasons. *"First of all, I want you to pay attention to the way a tornado forms so that you'll be able to recognize the signs. Secondly, I want you to see what it's like when Kevin projects himself mentally. Watch him closely. You need to be familiar with the physical signs that Kevin has left his body. He won't see you or hear you, and if you touch him, he won't feel it, unless you touch his forehead. That's the only way you can call him back, but only do that in the event of a dire emergency, like if the two of you are about to be attacked."*

Kevin gave himself over to the storm, joining with the wind and rain, and reveling in the immense power of the storm swirling around him. Lightning streaked by him as it leapt from cloud to cloud, and a strong updraft swept up from the ground and punched through the clouds above. As the updraft grew, it began to spiral, and as the storm gathered in intensity, the spiraling motion became faster and tighter, until a funnel formed and snaked its way down towards the ground.

Kevin was centered inside the immense vortex. The deafening roar shut out all sounds and became a numbing silence. The swirling dust blocked all light out of the vortex except for the thin shaft of sunlight that beamed through the eye of the storm. Kevin felt completely isolated.

Chris watched Kevin closely as the funnel reached out to grab the ground. Kevin's eyes took on the vacant stare of the dead as the tornado made contact, and if he was breathing at all, his breaths were too shallow and too slow to move his chest. Chris barely resisted the urge to grab Kevin's wrist to feel for a pulse.

"Glendymere!" Chris shouted above the roar of the distant tornado. "Is Kevin all right?"

The dragon was thoroughly enjoying the storm and had completely forgotten about his human companions. *"What? Oh, sure, he's fine. Isn't the storm grand?"* Glendymere answered without taking his eyes off the approaching tornado. *"I wish you could see one of those things from the inside! They're awesome!"*

"No thanks. I saw one from the inside, and that was enough to last me a lifetime," Chris mumbled as he nervously inched closer to Kevin. "What about Kevin? Shall I touch his forehead and bring him back? Don't we need to get to safety?"

"No, no, we're fine. I'm going to start calming things down in a few minutes anyway. I don't want the storm to do any damage. We'll give it just another minute or two ..." Glendymere's voice faded as he lost himself in the storm again.

Chris was so concerned about Kevin that he didn't notice the funnel lose its grip on the ground and flounder around in the air. By the time Chris looked towards the storm again, the funnel was trailing after the cloud like the tail on the end of a kite. Glendymere stretched and turned towards them just as Chris noticed Kevin blink and try to focus his eyes.

"How did you like that, Kevin? Fabulous inside a tornado, isn't it?"

"It was incredible, and horrifying! I don't know of anything like it," Kevin gasped as he tried to steady himself. After a couple of deep breaths, he continued, "Last time, with the thunderstorm, it was exhilarating, and even with lightning crackling all around me, I wasn't afraid. And at first, this storm was just like that. But when that updraft started swirling and the funnel formed ... I couldn't hear anything and all I could see was this weak beam of light, like a giant flashlight shining into a long tube, but the light faded out before it reached the ground. I felt completely cut off from everything. It was terrifying. I don't know if I want to learn how to make one of those monsters or not."

"Don't you want to be able to stop one if it's headed towards you?"

"Of course!"

"Make one, unmake one, all the same," Glendymere said with a sigh. He was a little disappointed in Kevin's lack of enthusiasm. *"Why don't you walk around a little and clear your head. Then I'll make another one and you can stop it. You can learn to create one later, after you get used to them."*

After Kevin and Chris walked all the way around the butte a couple of times, Kevin joined Glendymere at the edge and Chris sat down and leaned back against a boulder to watch. After the first couple of hours of watching Glendymere stir up tornadoes so that Kevin could practice calming them down, Chris fell asleep.

Towards the middle of the afternoon, Glendymere decided that they had worked long enough for one day and asked Kevin if he and Chris were about ready to head back home.

"Can you give us a few minutes to walk around and loosen up first?" Kevin asked.

Glendymere nodded and settled down to wait.

After Kevin woke Chris up, the two of them started walking around the edge of the butte again.

"So, did you manage to stop Glendymere's tornadoes?" Chris asked while they were walking.

"Yes, so far anyway. It's not hard to calm one down if you catch it right as it's forming, but once one gets going good, it's nearly indestructible. You can't calm it until you break its connection with the ground, and that's like trying to unwind a tight spring. I can do it, but it takes time and a lot of effort. Unfortunately, while I'm working on that, the tornado is still destroying everything in its path," Kevin explained. "I won't feel comfortable around a tornado until I know I can stop it quickly, and I'm afraid that's a long way off."

"Well, can you influence its path? Turn it away from where it's headed? Send it off in a new direction?" Chris asked.

"Yes, I finally figured out how to do that. The bad part is that while I'm concentrating on turning it, I can't do anything about stopping it. I sort of have to make a choice, either control it or destroy it. I'm not strong enough to handle both at once."

"Do you think you'll get there? Or is this one of those things where that's as good as it gets?"

"I don't know. For now, I'm just happy that I managed to stop them. I want more practice though, a lot more practice. Before we head out this winter, I want to be absolutely sure that I can either turn one away from us or stop it before it gets to us," Kevin answered. "We're going to have to travel through the heart of tornado alley on the way to Milhaven."

"Are you going to try to learn how to start one? Or have you decided not to bother with that?"

"I think I'm going to give it a try. I still think they're monsters, and I don't want to make anything that I can't control, but Glendymere's right. If I can get to the point that I can control where it goes, it would be one awesome weapon, don't you think?"

"Oh, it would be awesome all right. Just as long as it doesn't end up destroying what you're trying to protect," Chris said hesitantly. "I just hope that we're never in a position where you have to resort to such drastic measures."

"Same here, but don't count on it."

"Can all sorcerers create and control storms like that? Or is this one of the things that you can do because of the elven genes?"

"I'm not sure. Let's ask Glendymere," Kevin said.

"I heard the question. Several human sorcerers have been successful at stirring up a storm by raising the temperature in the air mass close to the ground and then charging the air with bolts of energy. But as far as controlling it enough to get a tornado out of it, I don't think so. At least I haven't heard of any who have been able to do it."

"That could make it even better. No one would be expecting it," Kevin said. "Can we come back out here tomorrow afternoon and work on this some more?"

"Yes, if you want to," Glendymere said as he stretched his leg out for them to climb up. *"Let's head back. It's getting late and I'm ready for a nap."*

After Kevin and Chris climbed aboard, Glendymere soared off towards Willow Canyon.

~ ~ ~ ~

That evening during dinner Kevin told the others that Duane and Xantha were coming and should arrive sometime during the next week.

"I can't wait to see what Duane thinks of Kevin as a warrior now," Joan said with a grin.

"I've been thinking about something ever since Glendymere mentioned that Duane's coming," Chris said slowly. "He's probably going to ask about our trip down. How much are we going to tell him?"

"Are you being paranoid again?" Joan teased.

"Probably. I just don't know how he and Kalen would react to the thought that there are bounty hunters out there looking for us and that there's a price on our heads, all because we helped a slave escape from the Seated Sorcerer of Brendolanth," Chris explained.

"Umm, when you put it like that, it doesn't sound like a very smart move on our part, does it?" Karl agreed.

"We can tell him about the healing clinics, our performances, even the bandit attack, but maybe we should keep anything to do with Taelor our little secret," Steve said.

"Are we going to tell him that we're changing our cover for the trip to Camden?" Darrell asked.

"If we do, should we mention that we don't plan to tell Tyree?" Theresa asked. "If Duane knows Tyree, he might be insulted that we don't trust Tyree enough to tell him our plans."

"We might just have to risk it," Kevin said. "Darrell, you and Duane spent a lot of time together at Kalen's. How do you think we should handle this?"

"From a defensive point of view, the fewer people who know our plans the better. I'll tell Duane that that's why we're not going to tell Tyree anything about the minstrel cover we used on our way down here or about our new cover for the trip to Milhaven. He would agree with that, but what reason can I give him for changing our cover story?"

"You could tell him that no minstrel in his right mind would cross the Great Plains in the dead of winter, and we were concerned that there might be a lot of questions and speculations if we stayed with that cover, especially in the areas where we had already performed. So, we switched to a new cover that we hope will be a little more believable," Steve said.

"That sounds good," Darrell said. "We're going to have to be careful what we say, and where we say it."

"It won't be that bad. I've been listening lately, and none of us talk about Taelor or the trip down anymore," Steve said.

"I just thought of something," Joan said. "Theresa, you're going to be Teri while Tyree is here, right?"

Theresa nodded.

"How are we going to explain that to Duane?"

"We'll tell him it's just a nickname if he asks, but I bet he won't even notice. Duane might not call you Teri, but if the rest of us do, Tyree will think of you as Teri, and that's all that matters," Karl said as he stood up. "I'm ready for coffee. Anyone else want some?"

Chapter 40

Tyree Arrives

Duane and Xantha arrived Monday morning while Glendymere was gone to get Tyree. After lunch Xantha invited Kevin to go flying with him while Duane visited with the others.

"So, you're finally getting used to the idea of being a sorcerer," Xantha said.

"I still don't like the idea of being the Master Sorcerer, but being a regular sorcerer has its moments."

"I was hoping some girl would catch your eye while you were traveling down here. Want me to check around? See if any of the local girls would be a good candidate? I'll have plenty of time while I'm here."

"No, and don't get started on that topic. There are a lot of things I need to take care of before I can even think along those lines," Kevin said in exasperation.

"All right, but as soon as you're seated, you're going to have to get serious about finding a mate. You need heirs!"

"I may not even last a month, and in that case, the whole idea of heirs becomes moot. Besides, when the time is right, I'll find my own girl, and I won't need any help."

"That's what you think," Xantha mumbled.

As they were flying over Willow Canyon, Kevin spotted a shadow near the horizon. "Isn't that Glendymere?"

"Yes, it is. Let's land and wait for him." Xantha said as he swooped down to the canyon floor.

After a few minutes they heard the sound of Glendymere's wings as he circled the canyon before landing. Once Glendymere settled on the ground, he extended his foreleg for Tyree to climb down, but Tyree didn't move.

"Kevin, would you mind helping Tyree down?" Glendymere asked. *"I think the trip was a little more than he bargained for."*

"What happened?" Kevin asked.

"I'm not quite sure. It's not dragon fright," Glendymere said, *"but he doesn't seem to be able to move. I don't think he can let go of my chain."*

"I know just how he feels," Kevin said with a grin as he scampered up Glendymere's leg. When he reached the dragon's neck, he found Tyree clutching the chain in a death grip and staring straight ahead.

"It's all right. You can let go now," Kevin said as he tried to gently pry the chain out of Tyree's fingers.

After a few minutes, Tyree looked at Kevin, jerked his head in a nod, and tried to unclench his fist. Kevin unbuckled the safety harness and sat down beside the older man to give him some time to relax. "I felt the same way the first time I flew. You'll feel better soon."

Tyree looked like he was about seventy years old, but Kevin figured that was partly due to fear. His black hair was speckled with gray, and his beard had gray streaks running through it, but it was still predominantly black. As the color started coming back into his face and his facial muscles began to relax, he dropped about fifteen years.

"I ... I've flown before, just never on the back of a dragon," Tyree gasped. "I've known Glendymere for years. I don't know why I reacted like this." Tyree finally managed to release his grip on Glendymere's chain and shook his hands to get the blood circulating again. When he tried to stand, he staggered like a drunk.

"Here, let me help you down. Let's go slow and easy here," Kevin said as he tried to help Tyree stay on his feet. Tyree was a little shorter than Kevin, but they probably weighed about the same and every time Tyree wobbled, he pulled Kevin off balance. "Wait a minute. I've got an idea. Close your eyes and don't open them until I tell you to. Trust me. It will help."

"I don't see how, but I'll try anything," Tyree mumbled, clutching Kevin's tunic to try to keep his balance.

Kevin waited until he was sure that Tyree's eyes were shut. Then he gently eased Tyree off Glendymere's back and flew him to the ground. Once they were standing on the ground, Kevin said, "All right. You can open your eyes now. You're down."

"What? Did Glendymere do that?" Tyree asked. "Or are you a sorcerer?"

"I had nothing to do with it," Glendymere answered. *"Tyree, may I introduce Myron, son of Badec, of the House of Nordin."*

"Myron?" Tyree grasped Kevin's hand. "I'm so pleased to finally meet you. I can't tell you how relieved I am that you're all right! So you're the reason Laryn wanted me to come out here. How may I be of service?"

"How much do I tell him?" Kevin asked Glendymere mentally.

"That's up to you, but if you want him to tell you and your friends about Camden, you're going to have to give him some kind of explanation as to why you don't already know," Glendymere answered Kevin privately.

"Tyree, I need someone who has been on the inside of the government to give me and my companions a quick course in how things work. I always thought my father would explain things to me once I came of age, but unfortunately ..." Kevin said.

Tyree nodded. "It's been a long time since I served in my father's office, but I'll be more than happy to try to answer your questions. You mentioned your companions? Are they going to be your officers?"

"They're my advisors."

"Have you chosen your governor?"

"No, not yet," Kevin said. *"Does the sorcerer appoint the governor?"* Kevin shouted out mentally to Glendymere and Xantha.

"Don't ask me. I have no idea," Glendymere said.

"I don't either. But, isn't that why he's here, to answer questions like that? Ask him!" Xantha said.

"Tyree, I'm not sure who does what, or how any of the positions get filled. I'm not even sure what the positions are. I want you to go over everything with us from the beginning, even the stuff you feel sure everyone knows, just as if none of us had ever set foot on Terah before," Kevin said.

Tyree hesitated for a beat and then nodded. "I'll do my best. When would you like to get started?"

"Why don't you rest up this evening? Our days are pretty full right now, so we'll need to meet with you in the evenings. Could you join us for dinner tomorrow evening? I can introduce you to my companions then."

"That would be fine. That will give me some time to get my thoughts in order. Do you want me to go over the organization of the army, too?"

"Yes, and anything else that you think we might need to know," Kevin answered. "Now, we need to get you settled. Did you bring anything with you?"

"Yes, I brought a small bag. Now where did I put it? I know I had it when we took off," Tyree said as he looked up towards Glendymere's back.

"Hold on. I'll see if it's still up there," Kevin said as he flew to Glendymere's shoulder. He untied the bag and carried it down to Tyree. "Now, to find Blalick."

"I called him before we landed," Glendymere said. *"He should be coming out of the cave about now."*

A couple of minutes later, Blalick walked out of the cave towards them. Blalick nodded at Kevin and took Tyree's bag while Kevin made the introductions. Then he led Tyree to the path that snaked its way up Wildcat Mountain.

"Well, I think that went well," Kevin said.

"Until he realizes that you know absolutely nothing about government, taxes, the army, or any of the rest of it," Glendymere said with a chuckle.

"Xantha filled me in on a lot of the stuff while we were at Kalen's. It's not like we won't know enough to be able to ask intelligent questions," Kevin said in self-defense.

"We'll see. Just keep in mind that we would not have invited him here to tutor you if he were a stupid man," Glendymere said. *"He won't be easily fooled."*

"And if you end up having to tell him where you're from, what's the harm?" Xantha added. *"He's completely loyal to the House of Nordin."*

"From the way Kalen talked, I got the feeling that it was our duty to try to conceal that detail," Kevin argued. "I was under the impression that most of the people on Terah don't even know that Earth exists."

"Well, it wouldn't do to go around advertising that fact, but Xantha's right," Glendymere said. *"Tyree knows how to keep his mouth shut or Laryn never would have recommended him for this. After all, she knows where all of you are from, remember?"*

"I keep forgetting about her," Kevin said with a touch of a frown. "I guess you're right, but I still don't feel comfortable trusting strangers with details about my life."

"Probably a good idea to keep thinking like that," Glendymere agreed. *"Just consider Tyree the exception to the rule should the need arise to tell him."*

"Besides," Xantha added, *"if he's as smart as Glendymere seems to think he is, you probably won't have to tell him anyway. He'll figure it out for himself."*

~ ~ ~ ~

Kevin introduced Tyree to the others Tuesday evening. The dinner conversation was the polite non-conversation of strangers who end up sharing a table. They discussed the weather, the coming winter, and the scenery. After the dishes had been cleared from the table, Steve asked Tyree to tell them a little about Camden.

Tyree took a map of Camden out of his pocket and spread it out on the table. "As you can see, Camden is surrounded by water. The good thing is that there are no disputes over the boundary line. The bad thing is that we have to defend our entire border against slavers."

"Is that a major problem?" Kevin asked. "I mean, are there frequent raids?"

"I don't know if I would call them frequent, but I'd say that ten to fifteen families are captured each month."

"That's around a hundred and fifty a year!" Darrell exclaimed.

Tyree nodded. "True, but remember, we're talking about ten thousand miles of open border."

"Aren't there army units in all of the towns?" Karl asked.

"Yes, each town has at least a ten-man unit, and in the event of an attack, all of the men in the village would turn out, armed and ready to fight, but the towns are usually twenty miles or so from the water, and there are a lot of open miles between the towns. If the slavers raid the outlying families, they would be long gone before help could arrive, probably before anyone in town even found out that help was needed. The farmers and fishermen who live near the coast have to pretty much take care of themselves."

"Do they do anything to try to protect themselves?" Joan asked.

"Well, they live in clusters of four or five families so that they can try to protect each other, not that it does much good. The slavers are trained warriors, and farmers and fishermen are easy targets. Even though they're skilled hunters, shooting a person is different from shooting a deer. The slavers don't hesitate to kill, the local men do, and that as much as anything leads to their defeat."

"Does the army do anything to discourage slavers?" Chris asked.

"There isn't much that can be done as long as the slavers are so well paid. We capture a few every year, but for every one that we capture, dozens go free, so that's not much of a deterrent."

"How many districts does Camden have?" Steve asked.

"There are eighty districts, each around a hundred miles square. Some of the mountain regions have more territory, but smaller populations."

"So there are eighty district ministers. Do they ever get together to discuss things like slaver raids?" Steve asked.

"Yes, they meet once a year with the governor in Milhaven to discuss problems, concerns, and taxes," Tyree answered.

"When do they meet?" Karl asked.

"Usually during the summer. A lot of the district ministers are farmers, and spring and fall are busy times, and the weather in winter is so unpredictable that no one wants to schedule anything then."

"How long does the conference usually last?" Karl asked.

"About a week. They all communicate during the year, so most of their concerns are well known before the meeting. It just formalizes things."

"Such as?" Karl asked.

"Taxes for one. A minister can't raise the tax rate for his district unless the whole group agrees that it's necessary, so he has to present his case during the conference and let all of the ministers vote on it. That way a minister can't set himself up to get rich riding on the backs of the people in the district."

"Wouldn't it be better if the tax rate was the same in all of the districts?" Kevin asked.

"Ideally, yes, but look at a mountain district for a moment. They need a district sorcerer to help clear farm lands of boulders and trees, and there are always landslides in the spring. In addition, people traveling through often get themselves in a mess and have to be rescued. The people who live in the district have to chip in to help pay for a sorcerer, but since there are fewer people, they have to chip in a little extra, so they have a slightly higher tax rate," Tyree said.

"That makes sense, I guess. It just seems to me that everyone should contribute the same amount, no matter where they live," Kevin said.

"Then you would have to take the surplus from one district to pay the bills in another, and I don't think the people would like that very much," Tyree said. "Of course, you could suggest it if you wish."

Kevin nodded, but he knew that he was in over his head. He didn't understand economics and politics well enough to make suggestions about changing a system that had worked for years. Maybe Steve would have some ideas.

"What types of bills do they have to pay as a district?" Steve asked.

Tyree explained that in addition to the district minister, each district had to support a sorcerer, an army captain, and five or six lieutenants. The sergeants were local townsmen, and were given only a token pay, just like the town director. The individual members of the local army unit were not paid anything. It was their duty to serve.

"What if a town wants its own sorcerer rather than have to wait for the district sorcerer to get around to them?" Chris asked.

"Then the town has to come up with the money to pay him," Tyree answered.

"So, if I've kept up with things right, there are eighty ministers, eighty sorcerers, eighty captains, and over four hundred lieutenants being supported through taxes, right?" Steve asked.

Tyree nodded.

"Who decides how much these people get paid?" Karl asked.

"The assembly of ministers determines the base pay, but some districts offer a bit more, especially for a good sorcerer. If the official has a wife and a couple of children, they'll be able to manage, but if the family's large, they're either going to have to have a second income or work in a district that can afford to pay a little more."

"What about their staff?" Darrell asked.

"Ministers are allowed a secretary and each district captain has an aide, but no one else on the district level has any provisions for staff in their pay."

"Is anyone else supported by taxes?" Steve asked.

Tyree nodded again. "The governor, the army general, the three court judges, the seated sorcerer, and their staffs. The general has a small military staff and several companies of soldiers at his disposal. The governor has a secretary, the judges share a secretary, and the sorcerer has an assistant and office pages. And then there are the servants for the governor's house and the sorcerer's castle, as well as the guards."

"How many people does that involve?" Joan asked.

"I'm not sure. There are several cooks and kitchen aides at the castle but usually only one at the governor's house. Then there are the men and women who clean the castle and the governor's house, the stable men, the yardmen, and the personal servants for the families. And then of course, there are all of the men who make up the castle guard," Tyree answered.

"That's a lot," Kevin said.

"And sometimes you have to hire extra help for special events," Tyree added. "Remember, the castle isn't just your home. It's the residence of the Seated Sorcerer of Camden, as well as the Master Sorcerer of Terah."

"Sort of like 1600 Pennsylvania Avenue," Chris said. "Not your house, your fishbowl."

Tyree frowned, but he didn't ask any questions.

"How does the Master Sorcerer get any privacy?" Kevin asked.

"In general, he doesn't," Tyree answered. "I guess if you really needed to, you could find a quiet place somewhere away from the castle, but you'd have to let your assistant know where you are because your staff has to be able to get in touch with you at all times. There's no real privacy at the top, Myron."

"What about the judicial organization?" Steve asked. "You mentioned a court? Do you have trials?"

"I'm not sure exactly what you mean, but in most non-criminal cases the local director handles the matter. If the dispute is not settled in an agreeable manner, the disgruntled party can take it to the minister. If that's still not satisfactory, he can take it to the governor's office, where it's heard by a three-member court. The chairman is appointed by the governor, the seated sorcerer appoints a sorcerer, and the general chooses one of his captains to represent the army. Their decision is final."

"What about criminal cases?" Darrell asked.

"The criminal is turned over to the local lieutenant, who takes the prisoner to the district captain. The captain is responsible for holding the prisoner until the minister decides the case. Murderers, slavers, and highway bandits automatically go to jail, but not too many others are imprisoned," Tyree explained.

270

"Is there a jail in every district?" Darrell asked.

Tyree shook his head no. "There are four in Camden." He leaned over the map to point them out. One was in the middle of what would have been eastern New York on Earth, one was in Wisconsin, one was in southern Georgia, and the fourth was near the middle of Tennessee.

"Who's responsible for guarding the prisoners?" Darrell asked.

"The army," Tyree answered.

"Do you have many escapes?" Darrell asked.

"No, none that I can recall," Tyree replied. "The army is good at guarding its prisoners, not just in Camden, but everywhere. It's a matter of honor that no one escapes, so they take great care to protect that record."

"Is there any appeal for criminal cases?" Joan asked.

"Appeal?" Tyree questioned.

"Can a defendant ask that his case be heard by a higher court, especially the court at the governor's office?" Joan asked.

"Yes. In fact, a written report is always sent to the governor's court for review any time anyone is sentenced to jail time. And the court has the option of requesting that the prisoner be escorted to Milhaven for questioning," Tyree explained.

"What about cases where the sentence does not involve jail time? What if the defendant thinks that the punishment is too severe? Can he ask to be heard by the court?" Theresa asked.

"If he wishes, but he would have to take the time and effort to travel there, and it would cost him to stay there until his case could be heard and a decision rendered. It happens occasionally, but not often. Usually the defendant just accepts the minister's ruling," Tyree said.

"How does the district minister get his job? Is he appointed or do the people elect him?" Karl asked.

"He's appointed. As soon as a district minister takes office, he makes a list of about ten people who would be good candidates for the position should anything happen to him. Then, if he dies in office, his secretary forwards the list to the governor. The governor checks them out and announces the new appointment," Tyree said.

"Who's in charge in the meantime?" Steve asked. "The secretary?"

"No, the district captain would take over the basic duties of the minister until a new one could be named," Tyree answered.

"What about the local directors? How do they get their jobs?" Karl asked.

"They're appointed, too, but by the minister."

"And I imagine that the general hires his captains, and the captains hire their lieutenants, right?" Steve asked. Tyree nodded, so Steve continued, "What about the local sergeant? Is he appointed by the lieutenant?"

"No, they're elected by the local unit."

"Are they the only elected officials?" Karl asked.

"Yes, at least in Camden."

"Strange, I would have thought that the sergeant would be appointed and the town director would be elected," Chris commented.

"The town director isn't elected because he has to collect taxes. If he were elected, he might be swayed to look the other way sometimes," Tyree explained.

"Good point. This way, he isn't dependent on the good will of the town for his position," Steve said. "Does he make a lot of money?"

"No, he only gets a token amount, just a few coins a year," Tyree answered. "No one would agree to accept the position for the money involved. There's an honor in being asked to serve, that's all."

"Not a bad arrangement," Steve said, nodding his head. "Should cut down on corruption."

"It might cut it down, but unfortunately, nothing can cut it out," Tyree agreed.

"I don't know about the rest of you, but I've had enough politics for one night," Joan said as she stood up. "What do you say we call it a day and adjourn to the sitting room for some scog and non-political conversation?"

As the others made themselves comfortable in the sitting room, Steve asked Tyree if he would like to join him for a walk outdoors before heading off to Blalick's house.

After they had gone, Joan asked "So, what do you think of Tyree?"

"I'm not sure," Karl said. "He seems to know what he's talking about, but I'm a little surprised that he hasn't asked us any questions about where we're from."

"Maybe he's figured out that he shouldn't," Darrell said.

"Could be," Karl agreed. "In the meantime, Blalick and I have about figured out what furniture we're going to make and how we're going to pack everything in three wagons. If there's anything special you want to take with us, now's the time to let us know."

"And Ashni and I are drying a lot of fruits and vegetables so that we'll have a good supply of food for the trip. I'm also making jerky. That's a new one for Ashni. I have to admit it was nice to find something I could teach her after all the stuff she's taught me. Anyway, is there anything else that we need to prepare as far as food is concerned?"

"I don't know if we can take them, but some of those strawberry preserves would really taste good," Kevin said with a grin.

"And a big batch of chocolate chip cookies would hit the spot with me," Chris agreed.

Joan laughed. "I'll see if we can manage to take a few jars of preserves with us. And Chris, I'll pack as many cookies as I can, but no matter how many we take, they probably won't last more than a week the way you eat them. Is there anything else?" When no one had any other suggestions, she said, "Well, if you think of anything, let me know."

"I'll have more herbs this time, Karl," Theresa said. "A lot of the herbs that grow up here are rare at lower elevations, so I'll gather a lot of them."

"No problem. The only things we're planning to put in your wagon are the sleeping blankets and tarps. Maybe a few of the pots and pans, but we can pile all of that stuff in the middle. Don't worry about it; we'll pack around your herbs."

"Well, unless there's something else, I think it's about time for bed. We're going to need all the sleep we can get before the 'enemy' army gets here," Chris said.

Chapter 41

War Games

The elves and dwarves began to arrive on Thursday. Glendymere wanted to give them a couple of days to get their camp set up and organized, so he announced that the first of the mock battles would take place Monday morning.

Right before the first battle, Glendymere told Kevin to concentrate on defense and to leave any offensive action to the others, but Kevin soon found that trying to protect seven people from fifteen armed and experienced warriors was more than he could handle. Too many things were happening at once. While he was holding back a squad of dwarves with swords, the elves let loose a barrage of arrows. As soon as he focused on returning the arrows, some of the dwarves slipped in behind him and began throwing knives. And to make matters even worse, the other Tellurians wouldn't stay put. They kept darting off to engage in sword fights or to return fire with their bows.

Kevin was worn out before the battle was an hour old, and the longer it dragged on, the more frazzled he became. If Glendymere had not been there to back him up, the Tellurians would have been slaughtered a dozen times over.

Later, after everyone else had gone for the day, Glendymere and Kevin analyzed the day's battle, detail by detail. By the time they were done, Kevin felt that although he had done almost nothing right during the first battle, he was a little more prepared for the second.

Over the next week, as Kevin became more adept at defending them, the Tellurians began to try a few small assaults. Every afternoon, after the dwarves and elves had returned to their camp, the Tellurians rehashed the battle, figured out what worked, what didn't, and made plans for the next battle.

By the end of the second week, they were functioning as a team and Glendymere seldom had to intervene to protect them, so he asked them to come up with a plan to overrun the enemy forces, without involving Kevin in any offensive action. Kevin was restricted to protecting the others from injury and defending their territory.

Their first few attempts were complete disasters, but as the days went by, they penetrated deeper and deeper into enemy territory before they were driven back.

After a particularly tough day towards the middle of the third week, Darrell said, "This is really discouraging. Do you realize that they could take us out in an instant if they wanted to? We're going up against them with everything we've got, and they're walking all over us without even trying."

Karl nodded. "I know. Makes you feel sort of inept, doesn't it?"

Joan shook her head and said, "I think you're looking at this the wrong way. Glendymere didn't just invite some elves and dwarves to come fight us. He invited warriors, people he associates with battles and wars. After all, Duane's a warrior elf, and he's obviously a friend of Glendymere's, but he wasn't invited to participate. Why?"

"You may have a point there," Karl said slowly.

"I think Glendymere assembled the toughest group he could for us to go up against," Joan continued. "After all, you don't get better by playing against a weaker team. Frankly, I'm amazed that we've made any progress at all against them. I think we're a lot better now than we were a month ago."

"I won't argue that," Darrell said, still depressed. "We're just not good enough."

"Good enough for what?" Chris asked. "Chances are if we have to fight for real, it'll be against other humans, and don't forget, Kevin's had his hands tied during these games."

"I know. I guess it's just the old pride kicking in," Darrell acknowledged. "I don't like losing, period."

~ ~ ~ ~

The final battle took place on the last Wednesday of November. Glendymere gave each side a short flagpole with a small flag attached to the top, and the battle was to last until one side had captured the other side's flag. By sundown, the battle was still going strong, with neither side able to claim victory. Kevin was beginning to tire, but he still managed to thwart every attempt that the elves and dwarves made to invade his defensive perimeter. Darrell had spearheaded the attack all day, and was running out of ideas. Chris finally suggested that they needed some kind of a distraction to get the other team's attention so that they could sneak in and grab the flag.

"Kevin, can you make a tornado yet?" Darrell asked.

"Yes, but I can't control it all that well yet," Kevin answered. "And there are elves over there. They could take control of it and turn it against us."

After a few minutes, Chris said, "What would scare them?"

"Dwarves are afraid of heights and water. As for elves, I don't know of anything that scares them," Kevin answered.

"Good thing we won't usually have to fight them," Darrell mumbled.

"Maybe what we need is not something to scare them, but something that will draw their attention somewhere else," Joan said.

"Such as?" Chris asked.

"Let me think for a few minutes," Joan said.

"It's going to be nightfall soon. Dwarves can see as well at night as they can during the day," Steve said. "If we don't come up with something soon, they're going to have even more of an advantage than they already do."

"Okay, exactly what are the rules that we're fighting under? Kevin, what are you allowed to do at this point?" Karl asked.

"Well, according to what Glendymere said this morning, I can do pretty much anything except actively attack them."

"Exactly what does that mean?" Karl asked.

"I'm not sure what you're asking."

"What I'm getting at is could you simply lift that flag out of there?" Karl asked.

Kevin grinned and said, "I don't see why not. I hadn't even thought of that!"

"So, are you willing to do it?" Chris asked.

"You bet, and right now." Kevin looked towards the other camp and focused on the flag. Then he reached out and gently lifted the flagpole out of the ground. None of the dwarves and elves guarding the flag was actually looking at it, so no one noticed that the pole was suspended a few inches above the ground. "All right, I've got it. Now how do we want to handle this? Do you want me to just grab it? Or can we finesse this?" Kevin asked quietly.

"Let's try for finesse, with just grabbing it as Plan B," Darrell said. "How about if the rest of us sneak along the river and attack them from the rear? If we can get there, we could probably distract them long enough for Kevin to get the flag out of there without any of them realizing it."

"Teri, stay here and keep your eyes open. If Kevin's going to protect us, slip the flag out of their camp without attracting any attention, and try to hold our defensive line, he needs someone to watch his back and to keep an eye on our flag," Chris said.

"Okay," Theresa agreed.

274

"How are you going to let us know when you have the flag?" Karl asked Kevin.

"We'll probably be able to tell," Darrell said. "I imagine there'll be a bit of yelling from the other side."

"If not, I'll drop something on Chris," Kevin said as he began to look around for something to drop.

"What about this?" Joan asked as she took off her headband and handed it to Kevin.

"That'll work," Kevin said.

The rest of the Tellurians slipped off through the woods and quietly crept along the river banks. To cover any noise that they might make, Kevin stirred up a nice thunderstorm several miles away with plenty of whistling wind and crashing thunder.

Once the Tellurians were in place, they opened fire on the other camp. When the elves and dwarves turned to face the attack, Kevin slowly floated the flagpole towards the woods that encircled the enemy camp. As soon as the flagpole was safely camouflaged by trees, Kevin floated it more quickly towards his own camp.

Theresa grabbed Kevin's arm just as the flag was about to float out of the woods and into their campsite. "Look, over there." Theresa pointed towards the woods on the other side of the camp. "I saw a shape move. Is that a dwarf?"

Kevin set the flag down on the ground and turned some of his attention to the shadow that Theresa had seen. Several dwarves were sneaking up on their camp. Kevin reached out mentally and gave the dwarves a shove backwards and kept shoving them every time they tried to stand up until they gave up and turned back. Then Kevin floated the enemy flag over to Theresa.

Glendymere and Duane had watched the action from a vantage point high up on top of a ridge.

"He finally figured out that he's more than just a shield," Glendymere chuckled.

"I would never have bet that that little group could actually defeat a band of elf and dwarf warriors," Duane said. "I doubt if there is another squad on Terah that could have done any better."

"Of course, the elves and dwarves were hindered by the 'no kill' rules, and most sorcerers would have used magic to win at the beginning, but under the same set of rules, I agree. I've asked them to return in January to fight again, and I've also asked Jonquin to join in the fun. Want to join us for those games?"

"I might. I'll let you know."

They continued to watch as the dwarves and elves realized that their flag was gone and signaled surrender to the Tellurians. After the two "armies" congratulated each other on a well-fought battle, the combatants began to gather their arms and head for their respective quarters.

As the playing field cleared, Duane said "I want to talk to you about something else." Glendymere nodded, so Duane told him about Landis, how she came to be with Hayden, how Rolan had killed Tsareth, and why they feared for her life should Rolan find her. "The problem now is to find a tutor for her. Her power will be strong, and she'll probably learn quickly, but any sorcerer who agrees to accept her as an apprentice will run afoul of Rolan."

"What exactly are you asking me?"

"Do you think Kevin would make a good tutor for Landis? She's twenty-four now, and she could begin studying as early as next summer, but she doesn't have to. We could wait a while and let him get settled. Once Rolan finds out how strong Kevin's magic is, he'll leave him alone, and if she's Kevin's apprentice …"

"There are a couple of problems with that plan. For one thing, from what you've said, Rolan would not hesitate to resort to treachery. No matter how strong Kevin's power is, magic provides little defense against that, so they'll both be in danger should he agree to accept her as an apprentice, but I doubt that that would deter him. The second thing, and the bigger obstacle, is that Kevin cannot teach what he does not know."

"What do you mean? From everything I've seen, Kevin is a powerful sorcerer. What doesn't he know?"

"You're forgetting that Kevin is part elf. His power flows through him. He doesn't have to gather magic from external sources, he doesn't have to store it, and he doesn't have to replenish it. That's what he cannot teach."

"I completely forgot about that," Duane said quietly. "Maybe we could find someone who could quietly teach her how to do that and then Kevin could take her on as an apprentice later."

"Why do you want Kevin to teach her?"

"Mainly because he'll teach her, just like you've taught him. Human sorcerers hold their apprentices back, parceling out little bits of information while using their apprentices almost as slaves." Duane sighed. "I don't think she has years and years to learn to protect herself, not with Rolan out there."

"I see," Glendymere nodded. "Well, how about this? Suppose we wait and see how Kevin manages as Master Sorcerer. Then, if he agrees to handle the rest, I'll handle the first part of her training. Would that be suitable?"

"Are you serious?" Duane asked. He couldn't believe what he was hearing. When Glendymere nodded, Duane said, "I don't know what to say, Glendymere. That's a very generous offer! Are you sure you don't mind?"

"If I minded, I wouldn't have offered. Actually, my sympathies are with the girl. I've heard of Rolan's cruelty through various grapevines, and I wouldn't want her to fall into his hands. Tell Hayden that if things go well for Kevin, and if Kevin agrees to take her on as a student, he can bring her here next fall and I'll work with her until she can gather and store her magical energies."

"I don't know how to thank you, Glendymere."

"Well, keep in mind that this is dependent upon Kevin surviving his first few months as Master Sorcerer."

"I understand. But if he fails, we'll have much bigger problems than finding a tutor for Landis."

"Agreed," Glendymere said. Then he added, "I wouldn't mention any of this to Kevin at this point. He has enough to worry about for a while."

"I wasn't going to. It isn't my place to talk to him anyway. When I mentioned the idea to my father, he asked me to see what you thought about it. Then, if Kevin survives the first couple of months, he'll travel to Camden himself and talk with him about it."

"You know, we're going to have to find out who he's going to be, Kevin or Myron. Everyone on Terah is expecting Myron, but everyone who knows him calls him Kevin. Could get confusing."

"I think that's why he's using Kevin right now. The way he explained it to us was that if all of Terah was looking for Myron, he was going to be Kevin. Let them look somewhere else. But he did say that he would be Myron once he got to Camden. I imagine his friends from Earth will always call him Kevin though," Duane said.

"Like I said, could get confusing. That may be good, may be bad. We'll just have to see how it goes," Glendymere said as he stood up and stretched his wings. "Well, looks like everyone has gone home now. Shall we head back?"

~ ~ ~ ~

Thursday morning, Kevin, Karl, and Darrell rode over to the valley where the elves and dwarves had set up their camp to thank them for coming and wish them a safe journey home. Meanwhile Chris had gone over to Willow Canyon to straighten up the little room that he and Kevin had been using since June. The Tellurians had held their battle post-mortems in that room and it was a wreck. The extra chairs they had brought in took up most of the floor space, and there were papers, maps, broken arrows, new arrows, and spare bows scattered all over the place. It took him until mid-morning to clear out the extra furniture, dispose of the trash, and store the things they wanted to keep. By the time he had finished, Kevin had returned.

"I'm tired. What about you?" Chris asked Kevin.

"Yeah, I'm sort of tired, too," Kevin answered with a yawn. "Probably because we're finally relaxing after weeks of tension."

"Well, whatever the cause, I could use a nice long nap."

"So could I. Why don't we all take a couple of days off, say until Saturday morning? We haven't taken a break since you got here," Glendymere suggested.

"That's a great idea!" Chris agreed.

"Are you sure we have the time?" Kevin asked. "I mean, don't we have to start preparing for the magic duels?"

"Yes, but Saturday will be time enough. We're going to work on defense against energy bolts for a couple of days first, but you don't have a duel scheduled until Tuesday."

"Tuesday?! That soon?" Kevin asked in near panic. "Are you sure I'll be ready?"

"Actually, I'm quite sure you won't be, but I don't want you worrying about that right now. I want you to relax. Don't do any magic at all, just rest. I don't want you to burn out any more than I want you to burn up. Remember, I'll be at the duels. I won't let anything happen to you. Now, go. I want some sleep. After all, you don't want me to fall asleep in the middle of one of your duels with a dragon, do you?" Glendymere said as he turned around, settled down, and promptly fell asleep.

Chapter 42

The First Chills of Winter

Duane and Xantha arrived in North Amden along with the season's first blast of artic air. As they flew into Crinsor Run around daybreak, Duane spotted his father walking in the fields, so he asked Xantha to land there.

"Good morning," Duane said as he dismounted. The frost was so heavy that it crunched under his feet.

"Did you have a good trip?" Hayden asked. "Can you believe how cold it is this morning? Feels like the middle of January."

"I know. It was warm when we left Willow Canyon. How long has it been this cool?"

"Oh, just for the past couple of mornings. It won't last. We'll warm up again before winter settles in for good. Now, how were things at Glendymere's? Has Myron progressed as well as you had hoped?"

"Better than I had hoped. He's already one of the most powerful sorcerers I've ever seen, and he still has a couple more months with Glendymere. For the first time since he returned to Terah, I really think he'll be able to survive, and if he makes it, the others from Earth should, too. You should have seen them fight. You'd have thought that they'd been doing this type of thing all of their lives."

"So Pallor chose the companions well." Hayden's pride in his nephew's success crept into his voice. "So, what's next?"

"Glendymere has arranged for Myron to duel with a few dragons this month, and then in January, they're going to fight the elves and dwarves again, but this time backed up by Jonquin. Glendymere asked me if I wanted to return to watch the skirmishes."

"Are you going?"

"I don't know yet. I told Glendymere that I'd let him know."

"Did you have a chance to ask him what he thought about asking Myron to tutor Landis?" Hayden asked.

"Yes, and he brought up a point that I hadn't considered. Myron didn't have to learn how to gather magical energy, so there's no way he can teach Landis how to do it."

"His elven blood. I hadn't thought about that either. Oh well, we'll find someone. Don't worry about it."

"Well, Glendymere had a suggestion. He said that if Myron agrees to tutor Landis once she's mastered gathering and storing her energy, he would teach her that part himself," Duane said hesitantly. He wasn't sure how his father would react to Landis studying with Glendymere.

"Are you serious? He volunteered?"

Duane nodded. "He's the one who brought it up. I didn't know what to say. I just said that that was a very generous offer and asked if he was sure he didn't mind. He said that if he'd minded he wouldn't have offered in the first place. He's heard about Rolan, so he knows that Landis really is in danger."

"She'll be at her most vulnerable at the beginning of her training and there's no one who could protect her better than Glendymere. I'll need to think about what I can offer him for his efforts, but I think it's a terrific idea."

"Are you going to tell Landis? It might take her a little while to get used to the idea that she'll be studying with Glendymere. His legend is even bigger than he is."

"That may be, but I don't want to tell her that everything is settled until I know for sure that it is, until after I talk to Myron. After all, we don't really know that he'll be able to take care of himself, much less an apprentice. I think I'll tell her that I've started looking, and hope to have something arranged by next fall. That should suffice for now, don't you think?" Hayden asked. When Duane nodded, he added, "After all, what difference does it make whether she finds out now or later? The test will come when she faces him for the first time. If she freezes, she'll just have to get over it. I'm sure he's used to that reaction from humans."

"True, and they do seem to get over it. None of the Earth people seemed to mind being around him at all," Duane said. As they approached the courtyard he added, "I'm starved. Do you think Shelandra would mind if I stopped by your house for breakfast on the way in? Mother always cooks enough for an army."

"You're welcome to eat at our house any time, but as to whether or not Shelandra would mind, she's your wife. Why are you asking me?" Hayden chuckled.

"I wasn't really. I was asking myself. And I know the answer. Yes, she would mind if I went to your house before I went to ours. So, guess I'll catch up with you later. Give Mother a kiss for me, and tell her to save me some of her pastries. I'll be over later."

When Hayden reached his house, he asked Gwynn if Taelor, Landis and Rhianna were up yet. She told him that they had already eaten and gone out. After he recounted his conversation with Duane, she asked if he was satisfied with the plan as it stood.

"Yes, I think it's perfect, provided, of course, that Myron survives his first few months as Master Sorcerer."

"When do you plan to tell her that she might be leaving next fall?" Gwynn asked. "This is going to be tough on Rhianna, too. They're so close."

"I know. Maybe we should go ahead and tell her that tentative plans are set up for next fall, but not go into any details. That way they can both start getting used to the idea. What do you think?"

"I think it would be best. Oh, here they come now. No time like the present. Shall I stay, or should I go warn Duane? You know they'll try to get details out of him. They always do."

"Stay. Then we'll both go warn Duane,"

"Coward," Gwynn whispered as the girls walked in ahead of Taelor.

Hayden briefly told Landis that arrangements were being made for her to begin her training as a sorcerer next fall but he wouldn't have any details for her until everything was finalized next summer. Then he stood up, took his wife's hand, and said that they were expected at Shelandra's house for breakfast.

After Hayden and Gwynn left, Taelor felt that Landis and Rhianna wanted to talk, so he excused himself, saying that he wanted to do some target practice with the bow that Hayden had given him.

Landis collapsed in one of the chairs. "I knew I'd have to leave here one day, but it never seemed real until this very moment."

Rhianna reached for Landis's hand and said, "I know."

"I'm going to miss you so much," Landis said as she squeezed Rhianna's hand.

"No you won't. I'm going with you."

"They'll never permit that," Landis moaned.

"I don't imagine that they'll have a whole lot to say about it," Rhianna insisted. "You're going to need an assistant, right? Are you going to tell me that I'm not good enough for the job?"

"Of course not, but Rhee, be serious for a moment. You don't want to leave this valley any more than I do. This is home."

"Yes, this is home, and one day I'll come back. So will you. But when you leave here next fall, I'm going with you. You're going to need me and you know it."

"I'll be all right," Landis assured Rhianna, as her eyes began to tear up. "You don't have to worry. I'm sure Taelor will go with me,"

"I'm sure he will too, but he's your brother, not your best friend," Rhianna said through her own tears. "And another thing, once you leave here, you're going to be in danger. Taelor's not a warrior, no matter how hard he tries. I'm a much better archer than he is. I can hold my own against Duane with a sword, and my aim is true with the knives. You know I'm right. And I'm going. That's all there is to it."

~ ~ ~ ~

It was snowing in Trendon as Captain Yardner crossed the courtyard from his quarters to the main castle just before daybreak. He stomped the snow off his boots as he entered the great hall and shrugged out of his cloak as he approached Rolan's office. As he handed it to one of the pages, he asked, "Is he in yet?" tilting his head towards Rolan's closed door.

"Not yet, sir. Shall I go get you a mug of coffee?"

"Yes, thank you," Captain Yardner said as he walked down the hall towards his own office. "And let me know when Rolan gets in."

Captain Yardner walked into his office, sat down at his desk, and began to go through the messages that had arrived during the night. The first message was from the bounty hunters charged with finding the minstrels. Once again, they had nothing to report. The minstrels seemed to have vanished from the face of Terah. No one had seen them since the end of May.

The second message was from the squad charged with finding Myron. Captain Garen had sent a couple of his men into Milhaven posing as free-lance soldiers looking for work to see if they could pick up any gossip from the castle guards. No one there seemed to have any idea where Myron was or when he would be putting in an appearance, but no one that they had talked to seemed to be concerned about his absence.

"All in all, a strange situation," Captain Yardner mumbled to himself. "You'd think that the castle guard would be anxious to know where their sorcerer was, what his travel arrangements were, and who was with him. If they knew, they'd talk about it; they couldn't help themselves. And if they didn't know, they'd talk about the fact that they didn't know. But no one's saying anything. Strange." Captain Yardner glanced through the other messages. The only other message that would be of interest to Rolan was from the bounty hunters who'd tried to pick up Taelor's trail. They, too, had only failure to report. Captain Yardner shook his head. Then he gathered up the three messages and took them down the hall to Rolan's office. Rolan reached his office at the same time that Captain Yardner did.

"News then?" Rolan asked as he looked at the messages in Captain Yardner's hand.

"Let's talk about it inside," Captain Yardner said.

Rolan opened the door to his office and led the way inside. "Let's have the bad news." He held his hand out for the messages.

"It's more like no news rather than bad news, sir," Captain Yardner said as he handed them to Rolan.

Rolan sat down behind his desk and read the three messages. Then he just sat there for a few minutes staring at the desktop. "You know, I can't help but wonder why no one seems to be able to find any sign of the minstrels. You'd think that they'd be easy to locate, wouldn't you? It's been six months now. Do you have any ideas about what could have happened to them?"

"No, but I agree that it's strange. And I think it's also strange that no one in Milhaven has any idea where Myron is, and yet no one's worried about him," Captain Yardner said. "The only message that doesn't surprise me is the one about Taelor. If they didn't catch him when he first escaped, I doubt that they will now. He knows people are after him. He's probably long gone, in a province on the other side of the sea. Do you want me to tell the bounty hunters to keep looking?"

"I think so, at least for another month or two, but tell them to keep an eye out for Landis, too. She has to be somewhere, and there has to be someone who knows where she is. I really should have tried to find her earlier," Rolan said.

"What about the minstrels?"

"I think we might as well call that search off. Leave the reward in place though. You never know. They may show up again next spring. Enough people know about the reward that if they do show up, we'll hear about it."

"What do you want me to tell Captain Garen?" Captain Yardner asked.

"Tell him to keep looking. Myron has to be at the council meeting in April. I would think that he'd go to Milhaven first, but he doesn't have to. He could just meet Laryn at the meeting. I bet she knows where he is," Rolan said thoughtfully.

"Sir, I hope you're not thinking of trying to get the information out of her."

"It's a nice thought, but no, that would be entirely too risky." Rolan sighed.

"I'll send the messages out this morning. Is there anything else you want me to pass along?" Captain Yardner asked.

"You might remind Garen that he and his squad should not plan to return to Brendolanth if Myron is still alive by the April council meeting," Rolan said.

"Are you serious about that?"

"Very, and if Myron makes that meeting, I will have their families sold into slavery. You can remind them about that, too," Rolan said. "Just be sure that they understand that I'm holding them responsible for his death. Period."

Chapter 43

Magic Duels

Saturday morning Glendymere was waiting out in the canyon when Kevin and Chris arrived. *"Good morning! Did you enjoy your time off? I did. I slept the whole time."* As he was talking, Glendymere knelt on the ground and extended his foreleg for them to climb up on his back. *"I thought we would head off to an island I know to practice with energy bolts. I don't really want to destroy my front yard."*

Kevin and Chris buckled themselves to Glendymere's chain and braced for flight. As soon as they were settled, Glendymere soared into the clear, blue sky. About an hour later, they reached the ocean and soon afterwards the coastline dipped below the horizon. All they could see in any direction was water, lots and lots of water.

"You know, I don't think I like this. It's eerie," Chris whispered.

"I know what you mean, but it'll be okay. Glendymere won't let anything happen to us," Kevin said to reassure Chris.

"If he can help it," Chris mumbled. After a few minutes, he continued, "I got over my fear of flying by looking towards the horizon. It makes you feel like you're close to the ground. Well, the horizon isn't a whole lot of help here."

"No, it isn't, is it? I'd hate to try to fly over the ocean. I keep looking at those waves and wondering how I could manage to keep myself in the air. I don't know if I could do it."

"You could, and you could support Chris, too. Want to give it a try?" Glendymere asked.

"No. Maybe some other time," Kevin answered. And then, as he continued looking down at the waves, he mumbled, "Some other life."

They had been over the ocean for about an hour when Kevin spotted a tiny black spot in the water. At first he thought it was a whale, but as they got closer, he saw that it was basically a big rock sticking up out of the water.

When Glendymere landed, Kevin had the feeling that they were on the top of a mountain that was mostly underwater. The top of the rock was about half a mile long, a hundred yards wide, and fairly level, running north to south. The east side sloped gently down to the sea, about a hundred feet below, but there was no beach. The west side was steeper, with a few sheer drops. There was no sign of any kind of life.

Glendymere nodded towards the other end of the island and said, *"Kevin, I want you to go down to that end. Chris and I are going to stay up here."* Once Kevin had reached the other end of the island, Glendymere said, *"I'm going to throw an energy bolt in your direction and I want you to make an energy net to catch it. Let your net touch the ground, and it will direct the energy flow into the ground."*

A couple of seconds later, a bolt of energy streaked through the air across the island. Kevin shook his head and said, "I don't think I can do this. By the time I saw the thing, it was already gone. I'm just not that quick."

"You didn't think you were quick enough to defend against arrows at first either. Same idea, only energy travels faster than arrows. You'll get it," Glendymere said. *"Now here comes another one. Get ready."*

By lunchtime, Glendymere had thrown over a hundred energy bolts. Kevin had figured out how to make the net, but he hadn't been able to get it cast in time to catch any of the bolts. Although Chris couldn't see the net, he had kept up with what was going on by listening to Glendymere's comments.

While they were eating lunch he said, "Kevin, I don't know anything about this, but it seems to me that the best way to catch those bolts would be to keep the net up all the time instead of waiting until he throws one."

That afternoon, Kevin tried Chris's suggestion and stopped almost all of Glendymere's bolts. Right before they stopped for the day, Glendymere told Kevin to try to throw a bolt back at him after he stopped the next one. Kevin stopped Glendymere's bolt easily enough, but when he threw one back, his net caught his bolt and directed it to the ground, too.

"That's the problem with maintaining the net all the time. It's an excellent defense, but you can't attack, and sometimes you have to if you want to end the assault."

"I guess that's how one guy loses, by lowering his net at the wrong time," Kevin said.

"That's one way to look at it. The key is to know when it's safe to lower your net. Timing is crucial."

"So maybe the smart thing would be not to rush to attack, but to concentrate on defense while you watch how your opponent fights," Kevin said, more to himself than to Glendymere.

"That's a good strategy, when you can use it, especially since you don't have to worry about running out of energy. However nothing says that two sorcerers have to stand out in the open to fight."

"I thought there were a lot of rules governing magic duels," Kevin said.

"There are, provided it's a sanctioned duel, but the only duels that are sanctioned are for the seats on the council."

"How does that work anyway?" Chris asked.

"The challenger formally petitions for the seat by notifying the Master Sorcerer that he wishes to duel for it. Then the Master Sorcerer sets it up by naming a time and place. By the way, be sure you pick a really desolate place. You don't want to create any new wastelands. Some place like this would be fine.

"On the day of the duel, the Master Sorcerer, the seated sorcerer, and the challenger meet at the designated spot, along with their seconds or assistants. The Master Sorcerer protects the non-magicals, but other than that he just observes. When it's over, whoever's left claims the chair. It's all quite civilized really."

"Yeah, provided you aren't the loser," Chris mumbled.

"But you can't count on all sorcerers playing by the rules. You could be the victim of a sneak attack and not know who's attacking you until you defeat them, and if you score a direct hit before you find out who it is, you might not ever know."

"How can you protect yourself from a bolt out of the blue?" Kevin asked.

"By always being ready. Tomorrow when we come out here, I want both of you to listen to the sound of a bolt being thrown, watch the change in the light, feel the charge in the air. There are a lot of clues, if you know what to watch out for. Almost every sorcerer can throw energy bolts, and there are a lot of sorcerers out there."

Kevin thought about that for a few minutes. Then he asked, "Do sorcerers ever sign on with bandits or slavers?"

"Not often, but it happens. Just like some soldiers hire out for the money, some sorcerers go where the money is, too. They usually don't have to kill anyone though. All they have to do is fire off a couple of warning bolts. No one would keep fighting after that."

"If they get caught are they put in jail?" Chris asked. "Would a jail hold a sorcerer?"

"Not if he's any good. But no one tries to arrest a sorcerer anyway. All they'd get for their trouble is an energy bolt. Unless they hang around in a particular province long enough for the seated sorcerer to go after them, they usually either retire or end up being the Master Sorcerer's problem."

"The Master Sorcerer's?" Kevin asked.

Glendymere nodded. *"Taking care of rogue sorcerers is another one of your responsibilities, but don't worry about it. Most retire long before they make anyone angry enough to report them. Of course, you'll have to deal with any rogue sorcerers who show up in Camden, but since everyone knows that that's the Master Sorcerer's province, they'll probably avoid that area. Now, if you two are ready to call it a day, climb on board and let's go."*

After they set down in Willow Canyon, Kevin said, "I've got a question. When two sorcerers face each other in battle, do they do anything other than throw energy bolts at each other? So far, it seems like it's just a contest to see who drops the net at the wrong time."

"In a way that's true, but there's usually more to it than that. Most of the time there are other things around to work with."

"Such as?" Kevin asked.

"They might throw boulders at each other, set some trees or grasses on fire, sweep some sand up into a blinding storm, or coax a heavy downpour out of the clouds."

"Why?"

"The more things a sorcerer has to handle, the more likely he is to drop his net at the wrong moment. About the only thing that is considered off limits during a duel is attacking the sorcerer's second. Of course, that doesn't mean that it never happens. That's why one of your responsibilities as the Master Sorcerer will be to protect the seconds during a duel."

"Just the second? What about the assistant?" Chris asked.

"Same thing as far as the sorcerers are concerned."

"So, someone could attack Chris to try to distract me, and then get me while I'm busy defending him, right?" Kevin asked.

"That's about the size of it."

"So, the winner would probably end up being the sorcerer who can juggle the most stuff, who can remained focused, no matter what," Kevin concluded.

"I'd say that's about right."

Chris thought a moment and then said, "Then it seems to me that the way you convince everyone that you're good enough to defeat any and all challengers is to show that you can handle a lot of tasks at one time."

"That's not a bad plan. Even the most powerful sorcerer would be hesitant to go up against a sorcerer who could spread his attention over several things at one time without letting any of them slip. You might want to add some juggling to your exercises over the next couple of months."

~ ~ ~ ~

Kevin, Chris, and Glendymere spent all day Sunday and Monday out at the rock island with Glendymere throwing bolts and Kevin trying to deflect them. Kevin's skill with his net slowly improved, and by Monday afternoon, he managed not only to defend against all of Glendymere's bolts but to counterattack with some of his own. Meanwhile, Chris sat off to the side the whole time, watching little flashes of light and feeling completely useless.

Towards the evening of the third day, Glendymere asked Kevin and Chris to turn their backs towards him and watch the sea. Then he fired an energy bolt.

"What happened?" Kevin said as he jumped up and spun around.

"What do you mean?"

"You fired a bolt. Why?"

"What makes you think I threw an energy bolt?"

"I don't know," Kevin said slowly, "but you did."

"Sit down and look at the sea again, only this time, concentrate. You too, Chris." Glendymere waited a few minutes, and then tossed another bolt.

"Now!" Chris exclaimed. "You fired one just now, didn't you?" Then he frowned and asked, "But how did I know? I didn't hear anything. I don't understand."

"That's what I was talking about the other day, about picking up on the clues. You sense it. You don't hear it or see it, but the clues register, and you know. Chris, that's why I insisted that you come along. I was hoping you'd develop a sensitivity to the disturbances. Now, what do you do when you sense that a bolt has been fired?"

"Jump for cover?" Chris answered.

"You could, but you'd probably be too late. Although it would be better than doing nothing."

"Cast a net," Kevin said. Then he frowned a little and asked, "But where would you cast it? You don't know which direction the bolt's coming from?" Kevin stopped and thought for a minute. "How about a dome-shaped net? One that would cover both of us."

"That would work. Just be sure to make it high enough. You wouldn't want that much energy disbursing too close."

"How big should I make it?"

"Big enough to cover anyone with you, as well as the horses, wagons, everything you want to protect. You need to always be aware of where everyone and everything is because once the net is thrown, it's too late to make changes. Energy bolts travel fast."

"Let's try it," Kevin said. "Come on Chris. Face the ocean again. Glendymere, this time throw it at us."

"Are you sure about that??" Chris asked. "You haven't tried this before. Are you sure it's going to work?"

"Look at it this way, Chris. If it doesn't work, you'll never know it," Glendymere teased.

"Ha, Ha. Very funny," Chris said as he turned his back on Glendymere and sat down facing the ocean again. "Don't be surprised if I jump when that thing is thrown," he grumbled.

"Just don't jump too far," Kevin said. "I haven't thrown this type of net before. I don't know how to do it yet."

Glendymere flew down to the other end of the island and threw a bolt. To be on the safe side, he aimed over their heads, but just before the bolt reached them, Glendymere saw a huge hemisphere of shimmering light encase them. His bolt reached the net and followed the lines of the net until it was absorbed harmlessly into the ground.

"Not bad for a first attempt. Not bad at all."

"Hey, as long as it worked," Kevin said with a grin. Then he turned to Chris and said, "See, you're still here."

"Yeah, this time." Chris shook his head. "I don't like having one of those bolts headed in my direction. I know we've joked about not growing old, but sometimes the reality of that statement hits home."

"Which is why you never ever want to forget what it feels like when a bolt is thrown," Glendymere said. *"But don't worry about it too much, Chris. Chances are you won't ever have one aimed at you. They'll be aimed at Kevin. You'll be in danger only if you're close to him, but then, if*

you're close to him, he can protect you. So, are you two ready to go home or do you want to practice with the net some more?"

"Let's try a few more," Kevin said. "Then we'll call it a day."

A little while later Chris said, "It could just be my imagination, but the air seems to shimmer and sparkle when you throw that net over us, and things outside the net look blurred."

"I don't think it's your imagination," Kevin said. "I see it, too."

"A dome is more powerful than a net. It sort of seals you inside a bubble," Glendymere explained as he flew back towards them. *"When you're inside, you can't be seen by anyone on the outside, and you can't be heard, either your voice or your thoughts."*

"So we could use the dome to hide in, to have conversations that no one could overhear," Chris said. "Just like the spies in those old TV shows. We have our own 'cone of silence.'"

"That could come in handy," Kevin agreed.

"It might, but there are some drawbacks, too. You can't be seen, but anyone who sees the dome would know a sorcerer's involved, and the shimmers can be seen for quite a distance. Another problem is that you can't hear what's going on outside the dome. An entire army could ride up and surround you without you hearing a thing, and Kevin's seeing eye can't be projected outside the net if he's under it. You're completely shut off while you're inside the dome."

"How about at night? Would anyone see it then?" Chris asked.

Glendymere nodded and said, *"It wouldn't exactly glow, but there would be an area of faint light in the vicinity of the dome."*

"Oh well, at least it protects us from energy bolts," Chris said with a sigh.

"And that's the important thing," Glendymere said as he knelt down and extended his leg. *"Come on. Climb on board. We need to get back. Kevin needs a good night's sleep. He's sparring with his first dragon in the morning."*

~ ~ ~ ~

For the next few weeks, Kevin's time was spent sparring with dragons, analyzing his actions after each match to figure out what worked and what didn't, and coming up with new strategies. Any spare time that he could eke out was spent refining his skills, especially in the area of self-defense.

During the sparring matches, the dragons used whatever they had available to distract Kevin from tending to his shield. Glendymere controlled the level of difficulty for each match with his choice of battlefield. The first couple of matches were held on desolate rocks in the middle of the ocean where the dragons did not have a lot to work with, but as Kevin's skill in handling several things at one time improved, the natural options available to the dragons increased.

Kevin had boulders thrown at him that could have crushed an elephant, was peppered by stones large enough to break bones, and sprayed with gravel small enough to put out an eye. Large trees were uprooted and dropped on him, and smaller trees were thrown like spears. One dragon grabbed a shark out of the ocean and dangled its hungry jaws over Kevin's head. Another threw a hornets' nest at him, complete with angry hornets.

Mud was a frequent weapon, not handfuls or even bucketfuls, but huge scoopfuls, enough to bury him. Rivers were redirected from their course and aimed straight at him. A couple of dragons set fire to nearby grasslands, using the smoke to blind and disorient him. One made a small bonfire, then picked it up, and dropped the whole burning mess on him.

One thing that the dragons had in common was their fondness for playing with the weather. Some would drop the temperature so fast that icicles would form in Glendymere's goatee, and then shoot it up so high that Kevin could hardly breathe. At one point when they were sparring in the artic, one dragon melted the ice under Kevin's feet deep enough for the water to cover his boots, and then refroze it so fast that Kevin's feet were caught in the ice. He was pummeled by hail stones, stung by sleet, and blinded by fog, white-outs, and sandstorms. One sandstorm was so fierce that Kevin felt like the grit was sanding the skin right off his body.

Tornadoes were a favorite ploy of the dragons. The first time one was used against him, it caught him so off guard that the funnel picked Chris up before he could react. Glendymere stepped in to save the day that time. But after that, Kevin was ready for them and managed to either redirect the funnel or calm the storm, depending on what else was going on. One dragon used a waterspout to suck up a school of fish and dump them on Kevin in the middle of a barrage of energy bolts. Another dragon made good use of a local volcano, sending smoke and fire shooting up into the air. When that didn't rattle Kevin, the dragon sent lava spewing over the side of the volcano, heading straight for him. That one did the trick. Kevin froze. Again, Glendymere rode to the rescue.

Kevin and Chris had both assumed that the dragons would all look like Glendymere, but that was not the case. They were as different as their sparring tactics. One of the dragons had a long thin body, almost like a snake, while another looked like a giant ball with a little round head stuck on stubby little neck. The rest of the dragons fell somewhere in between. They all had scales but the colors were as varied as their shapes, with various shades of maroon and green topping the list. One was completely silver, and one was so blue that he faded into the sky. All of them had diamond-shaped eyes, but the colors were as varied as the scales. About the only thing that they all had in common, other than sharp teeth and smoking nostrils, was their goatees, but none of them had one as long and white as Glendymere's. He really did look like the grandfather of the whole group.

None of the dragons communicated directly with Kevin, and when he thanked them after a day of sparring, they acknowledged his thanks with a slight nod, but that was all.

Late one afternoon, after two and a half weeks of sparring with them, Kevin asked Glendymere why the other dragons never spoke to him or to Chris.

"Humans were the ones who made it impossible for magical creatures to live on Earth, and then a lot of them emigrated to Terah, bringing all their prejudices with them," Glendymere explained. *"Most magical beings prefer not to have anything to do with humans, so they basically ignore them, and dragons are no exception. The only reason any of them consented to these sparring matches is that you're part elf."*

Chris raised his eyebrows and looked at Glendymere. "And because you asked them to."

Glendymere shrugged. *"Well, yes, there is that."*

"I've got a question, too," Chris said a moment later. "Why are the dragons using weather against Kevin? Is it just so he can practice juggling things? I mean he isn't going to have to worry about that if he's fighting another sorcerer. They can't play with the weather."

"Kevin's a sorcerer and he can manipulate the weather, even form a tornado," Glendymere pointed out. *"Granted he's not as good as my friends are, but he hasn't had as much practice as they've had either."*

"But he can do it only because he's part elf," Chris argued.

"And who's to say that he's the only sorcerer out there who is?"

Chris hesitated. "Good point. Hadn't thought of that."

"Do you know of someone else who's part elf," Kevin asked.

"No, but that doesn't mean there isn't one. Besides, it's always possible that a human sorcerer might enlist the aid of an elf."

"Really?" Chris asked. "I didn't think they got involved in things like that."

"Not normally, but if the money's good enough, an elf might. After all, he could easily justify it by reasoning that since Kevin's part elf, all he was doing was leveling the playing field."

"How likely is that to happen?" Kevin asked.

"Not likely at all, but it is possible, so it's best to be prepared, and speaking of prepared, you need to get some rest before your match tomorrow, and so do I. See you in the morning," Glendymere said as he settled his massive head on his front leg and promptly fell asleep.

~ ~ ~ ~

During dinner a couple of days later, Joan asked Kevin how things were going.

"I guess they're going okay. At least, I'm still here," Kevin said with a shrug. "And there have been a couple of times when I wasn't sure I would be."

"He's being modest," Chris said. "He's doing great. You should have seen him against that blue dragon last Friday. I think he even surprised Glendymere."

"Really?" Darrell asked. "What happened?"

"The dragon sent an enormous tidal wave at Kevin. It rose up out of the ocean about five hundred yards off shore. I'd say it was well over a hundred feet high, wouldn't you?" Chris asked Kevin.

"Probably," Kevin answered, but he didn't pick up the story like Chris had hoped he would.

"I thought that thing was going to wash over the whole island, but as it approached, Kevin made a 'V' shaped wedge of compressed air, and when the wave hit the point of the 'V', it split, sheared off, and rolled around the island without so much as one drop hitting land. Meanwhile, the dragon threw a barrage of energy bolts at Kevin while he was busy heading off the wave. When the bolts hit Kevin's net, the dragon roared and stirred up a sand storm so thick you could hardly breathe, but Kevin came right back with a swipe of wind that blew the sand out to sea. During the sand storm, the dragon had picked up a huge rock and thrown it at Kevin, and when the wind swept the sand away, the rock was maybe eight feet from Kevin's head and moving fast. If he'd ducked, which would have been what any sane person would have done, he'd probably have dropped his net, but Kevin didn't even flinch. The rock hit the net and burst into a hundred pieces. The dragon actually bowed his head towards Kevin before resuming the attack. According to Glendymere, that's the highest compliment a dragon ever pays to an opponent. But was Kevin here satisfied? No. His only comment when Glendymere told him that he'd done a good job handling that attack was that he wished he'd been able to get off a couple of energy bolts of his own during that little scuffle."

"It sounds to me like you did pretty well," Darrell said to Kevin.

"I guess so, but I would have felt better if I could have fired a few bolts of my own. I was so busy defending that I didn't have a chance to attack."

"Yeah, well, don't push it too far," Chris said seriously. "The net comes first. Always." Then he added in a half-teasing manner, "Especially if I'm under it."

A few minutes later, Tyree joined them and the conversation turned to other topics. Joan mentioned that Christmas was only a week away. "I was thinking that maybe we should do something special on Christmas Eve. What do you think?"

Karl turned to Tyree and asked, "Do people observe Christmas in Camden?"

"As far as I know, all of Terah observes Christmas," Tyree answered. "How was it observed where you came from?"

"It was a really big deal," Darrell answered. "Most stores decorated for Christmas around the beginning of November, but some decorated even earlier than that."

"The only decorations here are in the homes, but no one decorates more than a week before Christmas," Tyree said with a puzzled expression on his face. "I don't understand why stores would decorate anyway."

"Because, where we came from, people gave gifts to everyone they knew," Karl explained. "It could get rather expensive."

"What do they do in Camden?" Theresa asked.

"Sometimes parents or older children make a few small toys for the younger ones, but those are the only gifts. Mainly it's a day of family, good food, and leisure."

"Do they do anything along the lines of religion?" Theresa asked.

"That's left up to the individual family. They can include as much or as little as they like, same as with all our religious observations here."

Theresa nodded.

"Would you like to have a party the night before, with songs, refreshments, and a few decorations?" Joan asked. "Maybe invite Blalick, Ashni, and the kids?"

"Sounds like fun," Darrell said, "but maybe we should have it at their house. Every time they're here, they have to stand."

Joan nodded and said, "I'll talk to Ashni tomorrow." Then she asked Tyree, "Do people in Camden put up Christmas trees?"

"Christmas trees?" Tyree wasn't sure what she was talking about.

"Do you cut down a small evergreen tree, bring it in the house, and hang decorations on its branches?" Karl explained.

"No, not that I've ever heard of," Tyree said, his frown deepening.

"Joan, do you want a tree for the sitting room?" Karl asked.

"No, not unless someone else particularly wants one." Joan looked around the table, but everyone was shaking their head no. "All right, that's settled. I'll bake some sugar cookies and maybe some gingerbread, but other than that, we aren't going to go all out for Christmas this year."

"And no one's going to do the presents thing, okay?" Chris said. "I don't want to feel bad because one of you talented souls came up with gifts for all of us and I didn't."

"Agreed," Darrell said and looked around to make sure that everyone agreed to forgo exchanging gifts. Everyone nodded. "That includes you, Joan," Darrell said as he looked directly at her.

"I agreed, didn't I?" Joan said defensively. "I have to admit I had thought about giving you the sweaters that Ashni and I just finished crocheting, but they aren't really Christmas gifts. They're survival gear for the winter."

"And what about you, Karl?" Chris asked, seeing a twinkle in Karl's eye.

"Blalick and I made each one of you a wooden box. They will be anchored around the sides of the new wagon when we leave. They aren't big, but at least it'll give you somewhere to store your extra clothes. If we had decided to exchange gifts, those would have been mine, but they aren't really Christmas gifts either. They're your suitcases."

"Speaking of the trip, are we about ready?" Kevin asked. "We're going to be rather busy for the first couple of weeks in January with war games, and we need to leave around the twentieth. Is there anything that we need to do? And by 'we' I mean Chris and me. I know we haven't been much help with the preparations."

"Everything's going fine, right on schedule," Karl said. "Don't worry about things here. You have other things you need to worry about."

Theresa sighed. "I don't want to even think about leaving here. This cave is home."

"I know," Joan agreed. "And it makes it even worse since we don't have any idea what we're heading into."

"Well, we may be able to help out a little bit there," Steve said. "Tyree and I have been working on a small model of the castle at Milhaven. It's in my room if you'd like to see it."

"Are you serious? You've built a model of the castle?" Joan stood up and began gathering dishes. "Give us a minute to clear the table."

"It's fairly accurate as of about ten years ago," Tyree said while they were taking dishes out to Joan in the kitchen, "but I haven't been back since then, and Badec may have changed some of it around."

"How much could he have changed things like walls?" Darrell asked.

"You don't really want an answer to that one, Darrell," Chris said with a chuckle. "He's the Master Sorcerer. If he wanted to get rid of a wall, BAM! It's gone!"

"Oh, yeah," Darrell said.

Tyree smiled. "Actually, it's more likely that something may have been added."

"Well, some idea is better than none, right?" Karl said.

"That's sort of what we thought," Steve said. "Besides, Badec probably hasn't made a lot of changes in the past ten years."

Once the dishes were done, they all gathered around Steve's desk in his room to look at the model. Steve and Tyree had spent a lot of hours putting the model together. They had made each floor a separate unit and fixed them so that they could be stacked. Looking down on the model from above, it resembled a blocked "U" with a wide base.

Tyree pointed to the open area inside the "U". "This courtyard is basically a big flower garden. There's a stone roadway around the inside, but the only people who use it are visiting dignitaries. They're the only ones who use the front entrance." He pointed to an arched doorway with double doors had been drawn in on the middle of the base. "Everyone else uses one of the back entrances."

"How do they reach them?" Darrell asked. "Is there some kind of driveway or something?"

Tyree nodded. "There's another roadway that curves around the southern end of the castle between the kitchen area and the vegetable gardens. It goes to the stable area out back. There's a river that loops around the back of the castle grounds, and there's a small meadow on the other side of the river, between the river and the forest. They turn the horses out over there for grazing."

"What's on the other side of the forest?" Karl asked. "Farms?"

"There are a few, but mainly it's mountains. The castle is at the foot of the chain."

"So the back of the castle faces east?" Kevin asked.

Tyree nodded. "And the front faces west, towards Milhaven."

"What are these?" Theresa asked, pointing to two boxes sitting on the front half of each of the two legs.

"Those are towers," Tyree answered. "When the castle was first built, guards were stationed in them. Now the guards patrol the roof of the castle, but no one's stationed in the towers themselves."

"Is one of those towers where Freddy has his roost?" Chris asked.

Tyree pointed to the tower on the northern leg. "This is the one Freddy stays in. It's over the sorcerer's family's living quarters."

Then he took the towers and roof off of the model to show them the layout of the second floor. He pointed to the two-story entrance hall that blocked the second floor off into two distinct and separate areas. "You could put a hundred people in that hall and still have room left over. It's so big that it echoes, and there are a couple of places where you can stand and hear every word spoken in there. Be sure you keep that in mind whenever you're in that room."

"Could come in handy," Darrell said quietly.

Tyree nodded and said, "I've often wondered if it was designed that way."

Then he pointed to the rooms on the northern side of the entrance hall. "This entire wing is the family quarters and is off limits to everyone else." He pointed to the largest room. It was in the back corner of the building, with two outside walls. "This is the sorcerer's room." Then he pointed to a slightly smaller room that was located between the sorcerer's room and the entrance hall. "This one belongs to his assistant or second. I've never been up there, but it seems like I heard that there's a connecting door between them, and I know that both rooms open onto a balcony that runs the length of the two rooms."

"And you said there was a river and mountains out back?" Joan asked. When Tyree nodded, she added, "Nice view."

Then Tyree pointed to four smaller rooms that were located in the leg, "The rooms along here are for the sorcerer's children. If Badec's still alive when you reach Camden, Laryn will give you one of these."

"But I thought all of the sorcerer's children were sent to foster parents," Kevin said, frowning.

Tyree smiled and said, "Only the ones born with magic in their blood are fostered, and that's only until they reach their twenty-fifth birthday."

Then he pointed to the rooms on the south side of the entrance hall. There were eight rooms about the same size as the children's rooms on the family wing. "These rooms are for guests."

"There are rooms for only eight guests?" Kevin asked. "I would have thought there'd be a lot more than that."

"Those rooms are only for family and close friends, like your advisors. I'm sure you'll want them to stay there, at least for a while." He looked around at Steve and the rest of Kevin's companions and then turned back towards Kevin. "Also, Badec and Laryn have several brothers and sisters, your aunts and uncles. They always stay in the guest quarters whenever they're at the castle. And you'll probably want to invite close friends to stay there whenever they come for a visit, but other than that, I wouldn't worry about it. I'd let official visitors, such as district officers or dignitaries from other provinces, stay at one of the inns in town. After all, this is your home, and you should be able to relax there."

Then Tyree lifted the second floor section of the castle off and placed it on Steve's bed with the roof and towers. "This is the main floor, and again the entrance hall separates it into two sections."

Tyree pointed to the southern side of the model and said, "The business of running the castle is handled on this side." Then he pointed to northern section and said, "And Camden is run from over here."

Kevin pointed to the northern side and said, "Let's take this side first. Who works out of here?"

Tyree pointed to the large room on the front side of the main hall. "The Governor of Camden works out of this office. He has a private office on one side and his assistant mans the reception area on the other."

"I thought the governor had his office in town," Karl said.

"He does have an office at his house in town, but it makes things simpler if he does most of his work at the castle."

"What about this one?" Chris asked, pointing to the largest room in the wing. It was on the back side of the castle and extended from the entrance hall all the way to the corner of the building.

"That's the sorcerer's office," Tyree answered. Then he looked at Kevin and said, "How you arrange it is up to you. Nolan liked to have his desk in front of the door so that he dealt directly with any and all who entered his office, but Badec preferred to work undisturbed, so he partitioned off a small office in the back for himself and left the front section as a reception area. Laryn has her desk out there and handles that area."

Then Tyree pointed to the wall that separated the sorcerer's office from the entrance hall. "There's a staircase here. We didn't try to put it in the model, but it's the only access to the family wing. The way the room is set up now, it's behind Badec's office. There's a guard stationed at the foot of the stairs twenty-four hours a day, seven days a week. Not many people would dare try to go up those stairs uninvited."

"What about these offices over here? Who works there?" Kevin asked, pointing to some smaller rooms in the leg of the "U".

"This office," Tyree said, pointing to the one next to the Sorcerer's office, "belongs to the Captain of the Guard. There's always a guard on duty at a desk directly in front of that door, and if the door is open, which it always is, he has a clear view of the hall in front of your office, the Governor's office and the doorway to the Entrance Hall. That hall is monitored twenty-four hours a day."

Continuing down the leg, there were two more rooms, one on each side of the hall. Tyree pointed first to the one along the outer wall and said, "This was the provincial courtroom when I was there, and the other was the general's office. Both of those rooms were divided into private offices and reception areas, but I'm not sure how they're organized now."

Kevin nodded.

Tyree moved over to the southern side of the model, which only contained four rooms: two small ones, and two huge ones. The small rooms were located next to the entrance hall, one on each side of a short hallway that led to the first large room. Tyree pointed to the small room that was on the back side of the castle and said, "This is the head groundskeeper's office. There's a door that leads from that office out to the stable area."

"Convenient," Karl said with a nod.

"The groundskeeper is in charge of the grounds, the gardens, the livestock, all the outside buildings, the walkways, the patios, and the driveways. Anything that's connected with the outside is his responsibility."

Tyree pointed to the small room on the front side of the castle. "The head of housekeeping works out of here. She assigns duties to all the housekeeping staff, makes sure the kitchen staff has enough groceries for however many people are at the castle, handles all the storerooms, arranges for the clothes to be made for the sorcerer's family as well as all the servants, sets up repairs, directs preparations for any of the special feasts or social events, and tends to anything else that comes up that involves either the castle or the people staying there."

"Quite a job," Joan said quietly.

Tyree nodded. "Just about anything that deals with the castle, its grounds, or its people is handled out of those two rooms."

Then he moved on to the large room that filled the rest of that side of the base of the "U". "This is the dining room, but most of the time it's set up as a combination dining room and sitting room. There's usually one large table that seats about twenty people, and the rest of the room has couches and easy chairs scattered about. If you have more than twenty people invited for dinner, some of the sitting room furniture is removed and extra dining tables and chairs are brought in. You can seat a couple of hundred people in there if you have to but if you need to feed more than that, tables of food are set up out on the grounds."

"Does that happen often?" Kevin asked.

"No. I only remember four times that the crowd was large enough to set tables up outside. The first time was when your parents got married, the second was for Nolan's funeral, the third was for your birth, and the fourth time was for Yvonne's funeral."

"Big social gatherings are not exactly my cup of tea," Kevin said, frowning.

"You won't have to worry about it. The housekeeping staff will take care of everything. The only thing you have to do is approve their plans, and if I were you, I'd go along with whatever they want to do. They know what they're doing, and if anything should come up that they don't already know how to handle, they'll make it up as they go. After all, who's going to tell the Master Sorcerer's staff that they're doing it wrong?" Tyree said with a grin.

"Is this other big room the kitchen?" Joan asked.

"Yes, but most of the time, they only use a small section of it," Tyree answered.

Then he lifted the ground floor off and set it on Steve's bed. The basement area consisted mainly of a series of small rooms on each side of a hall that extended the length of the main building and down one leg of the "U". The other leg was one large room.

"Most of the rooms in the basement are servant's quarters. I'm not sure how many rooms there are, but when I was there, two of the small rooms were used for general supplies, the large room was for furniture and kitchen supplies, and the rest of the rooms were used by servants. Once in a while, a married couple with children might stay at the castle until they can get their own place, so a few of the rooms are set up as two adjoining rooms, one for the parents, one for the children.

"Are they servants, or are they slaves?" Darrell asked.

"Most were brought to the castle as slaves, but both Nolan and Badec always freed them as soon as they arrived and gave them the option of striking out on their own as free citizens of Camden, or remaining and working at the castle. The ones who work at the castle are there by choice."

Kevin nodded. "That's one tradition that won't change. Now, I have a question. The sorcerer has an office, and his assistant has an office. What type of business do they handle?"

"First of all, you're responsible for supervising the district sorcerers and handling any complaints that come in against them."

"What kind of complaints? Incompetence?" Chris asked.

"Yes, and ethical complaints."

"Ethical complaints?" Kevin asked.

Tyree nodded. "Suppose a sorcerer's contract includes clearing farm lands in his district. The district is paying him to do it, so he shouldn't charge any of the farmers extra when they ask for his help, and he also shouldn't do a lousy job just because the farmer didn't offer him something under the table. Or maybe the sorcerer figures that he's entitled to the best of the crop since he helped clear the land, so after the farmer gets his harvest in, the sorcerer literally lifts what he wants. Most of the complaints will be that type of thing, but sometimes it's a little more serious. Once in a while you might have a sorcerer who's extorting money by threatening to harm someone or something. But no matter what the complaint's about, you'll have to investigate it and try to work out an agreeable settlement. Right now, with Badec out of commission, I imagine a few of the district sorcerers are taking advantage of the situation. You'll probably find a few letters waiting for you."

"And what happens if an agreeable settlement can't be reached?" Kevin asked.

"Then it's up to you to remove the sorcerer from that district. Most of the time, they'll leave rather than challenge you, but every once in a while …" Tyree shook his head slowly. When Kevin nodded, he continued, "And if for some reason a vacancy opens up in one of the districts, the district minister will ask you to interview the applicants and assist in selecting a new sorcerer. On one hand, it's like a professional courtesy. On the other hand, it's politics. Since you'll be responsible for supervising the sorcerer and tending to any complaints that the minister or captain lodge against him, you can't blame them for making a bad choice if you had a part in the decision."

"The minister's covering himself," Steve mumbled.

"Exactly," Tyree nodded. "And the sorcerers will want you to be there when they get hired so that you can witness the contract. That way the minister can't go back and add things later. Most of the sorcerers will consider you their advocate in dealing with the district government. By the way, I'd take detailed notes on every contract I witnessed if I were you."

"Sort of like a negotiator and mediator," Karl commented.

Tyree nodded again. "And you'll also be responsible for hunting down and stopping any rogue sorcerers in the province."

"Sounds like your main duties are going to be as a policeman," Chris said.

"I'm not sure what a policeman is, but if it's someone who goes after troublemakers, that's right," Tyree said. "And how often you have to go after them will depend on your reputation. If you're known as powerful and relentless, the greedy sorcerers will steer clear of Camden, and the ones who do work there will be more likely to behave, and so will the ones on the council."

"What do you mean, 'on the council'?" Chris asked. "Are you talking about seated sorcerers challenging him for the Master's Chair?"

"I wasn't really thinking about that, but there's always that possibility. What I was thinking about is the fact that as Master Sorcerer he's responsible for investigating ethical complaints against seated sorcerers, too. Some of them can get really arrogant and start thinking they can do whatever they want, whenever they want." Tyree turned to Kevin and continued. "You're the only defense the citizens of a province have against an unscrupulous seated sorcerer. Once you're seated, the other sorcerers on the council will have to decide whether they're willing to risk facing you in battle. The stronger your reputation, the less likely they'll be to cause you trouble."

"I understand what you're saying," Kevin said, "but I don't like it."

"I don't blame you. It's not an easy life that you're headed for," Tyree sighed.

"No, and probably not a very long one either," Kevin mumbled.

"We all hope you're wrong on that count. We would like to see you live a nice long life and have plenty of heirs. For one thing, Camden has been lucky with the House of Nordin. The sorcerers in your family have all been very honorable people, and we have been spared the horrors that a lot of the other provinces have gone through. For one thing, none of Badec's brothers or sisters tried to kill him before Nolan died just so that they could become the new heir. How could you trust someone like that to be fair?"

"Does that type of thing really happen?" Chris asked.

"Yes, I'm afraid it does. A lot of sorcerers dream of a council seat. If you're a seated sorcerer, you have to watch your back."

"But killing your own brother or sister?" Joan asked. "Why not just challenge a sorcerer from another province?"

"That happens sometimes and then we end up with two siblings on the same council, but some sorcerers would rather not risk death when a little treachery will accomplish the same result. That's when it becomes the Master Sorcerer's headache," Tyree said as he looked over at Kevin. "You'll also have to investigate any unexplained deaths among the council members, possibly beginning with Badec's."

"Does anyone know what's wrong yet?" Kevin asked.

"No, but in her last letter, Laryn said that she has little hope that her brother will ever recover. He must be near death for her to make that statement. Sorry."

"Thanks." Kevin nodded and then said, "Well, if there's nothing else, I'm going to get some sleep. I have a dragon to fight in the morning."

Chapter 44

Final Preparations

The Christmas Eve party was fun, but Christmas Day was depressing. Memories of families and friends left behind resurrected the guilt they felt for the pain and anguish their supposed deaths must have caused. The melancholy mood was made even worse by the fact that it would soon be time to move on, time to leave their valley, their cave, Glendymere, and the giants. The only bright spot in the day was the snow that was quietly falling outside in the valley.

Between Christmas and New Year's Eve, the temperature didn't climb above freezing and more than two feet of snow fell over the area. Joan handed out the heavy sweaters and Karl showed Blalick how to make snowshoes. Soon they all had a pair, even the giants.

During the night on New Year's Eve, the wind blew the clouds out of the area and New Year's Day dawned crisp and clear. When Kevin and Chris reached Willow Canyon that morning, Glendymere was nowhere to be found, so Kevin began to practice. Over the past few months, he and Chris had developed a "magical workout." It started out as a way for Kevin to quickly run through his basic skills everyday, but Chris soon found ways to add grace and flair to the simple magical feats, turning Kevin's practice routine into a major performance.

Glendymere returned while Kevin was practicing and watched in silence until he was finished. *"Not bad. And more impressive if someone just happens by."*

"Thank you, but how do I arrange for someone to just 'happen by' while I'm going through my routine?" Kevin asked.

"Leave that to me," Chris said. "I'll take care of it."

"The elves and dwarves are setting up their camp today, and will be joining us for a little while on Thursday to set out the ground rules. I thought we'd have our first battle Friday. Is that going to be all right with your friends?"

"As far as I know. The only one who's concerned about adding a dragon to the opposing army is Darrell. He's afraid he'll freeze up again," Kevin answered.

"Ask him to come over Thursday afternoon then. I'll arrange for Jonquin to join us for a few minutes and we'll see how Darrell reacts. I imagine he'll be fine," Glendymere said. *"Now, do you have any questions?"*

"Should we try to map out some kind of battle plan in advance?" Kevin asked.

"The whole point of these mock battles is for you and your companions to learn how to defend against an attack. Your battle plan is simple: do whatever it takes to survive." Glendymere paused for a minute and then said, *"If this were real, your first step would be to take out the sorcerer, and by take out, I mean kill. All sorcerers are dangerous. Even the less skilled ones can get lucky, and any sorcerer involved in an unprovoked attack is willing to kill. It doesn't matter how old or young the sorcerer is, or whether it's a male or female, take the sorcerer out first. You may not get a second chance."*

Kevin didn't say anything for a bit. Once again he was trying to come to terms with the idea of having to kill someone.

"Hesitation will get you killed, Kevin. If a sorcerer comes after you, only one of you will walk away. You have to see to it that it's you. Period. That's what this has all been about."

"I don't know if I can do that," Kevin answered quietly.

"Unfortunately, there's no way to practice that. You'll just have to see when the time comes, and it will come. Not today, but it will come. Think it through; prepare yourself. Your survival is important. You'll be good for Terah, but only if you're alive."

Glendymere hoped that some of what he was saying would sink in, but it was time to change the subject. *"Now, let's run through your routine again. I think I saw a few places where we can spice it up a bit with a little more showmanship and a little more challenge. Start at the beginning."*

~ ~ ~ ~

They spent the rest of the day practicing, and by the time Kevin and Chris left Willow Canyon, they were worn out. At dinner, Kevin told the others about the war games on Friday and asked if any of them would like to meet Jonquin Thursday afternoon.

"I don't want to meet him, but I guess I need to," Darrell said.

Chris grinned. "The second dragon's a piece of cake. It isn't anywhere near as frightening as the first. You know the old saying, if you've met one dragon, you've met them all."

"Right," Darrell said, totally unconvinced by Chris's banter.

"I'd really like to see Jonquin again. I haven't seen him in years," Tyree said. "Do you think Glendymere would mind if I tagged along?"

"No," Kevin answered. "I'm sure that would be fine."

"The rest of us will probably be there, too," Karl said.

"Okay. I'll let Glendymere know," Kevin said.

"I want to bring up something Tyree and I have been talking about," Steve said. "Anyone who works at the castle now is there by choice, but they're basically working for room and board, not for pay. Everything they need is provided out of the castle storerooms, but they don't actually get to buy anything. They have no money or anything else to exchange for goods in town. They have no feeling of independence, of being self-supporting. Tyree said that most of the servants were women and children. Young men who have grown up in the castle work there for a while, but few stay past their seventeenth or eighteenth birthdays. We've been trying to come up with some way to set up something like the company towns that grew up around the mines."

"I thought they were basically abusive," Joan said.

"A lot were, but not all of them. The original idea was to give the people who worked for the company access to goods because there weren't any other towns around," Steve explained. "They built houses for the people and rented them out, with the rent coming directly out of their pay. The company operated a dry goods store, a farmer's market, a tavern, maybe even a restaurant, things that would make life more attractive for the workers. The workers were usually paid in company script, and they could use the script to buy goods in any of the company stores. And, in the better company towns, there was a bank of sorts where the workers could exchange their script for legal tender. The abuse came when some of the companies started charging exorbitant prices for supplies and refused to exchange the script for currency. Some of the companies also refused to allow any businesses that weren't company owned to set up in their 'town'. If you avoid the abuses, the idea might be a workable one for us."

"You mean set up stores in the castle?" Kevin asked.

"Sort of. We don't have the coins you would need to pay a living wage to all the people who are needed to run a castle. That's one reason why slavery is so attractive," Tyree answered.

"We haven't worked it all out," Steve said. "In fact, we have more questions than we have answers. As it is now, all of the regular staff lives at the castle and eats at the castle. If you built extra houses near the castle, how would you decide who was going to be able to live in them? And how much rent would you charge? Would both parents have to work at the castle to qualify? If the families lived in town, would they get their food from the castle? Also, if you have any young married women working for you, what do you do when they get pregnant? Stop paying them? Suppose a man works at the castle, but his wife stays home to take care of the children. What if he gets hurt or dies? Do you take on the responsibility of his family? There are a lot of details that need to be worked out, but it has possibilities."

Kevin looked at Tyree and asked, "If we decide to attempt something like that, would you be willing to help set it up?"

"If you wish. I don't know that I'd be much help, but I'll be glad to offer whatever assistance I can," Tyree answered.

"I won't even think about starting anything like this until we get settled and see if I can survive the first few months as Master Sorcerer, but if I'm still there, would you be able to join us, maybe next fall? I think that would be soon enough, don't you?" Kevin asked and looked around to see if the others agreed.

Steve nodded and said, "It would take a lot of planning. We'd have to decide the relative pay for the different positions, the cost of things in our 'stores', how much to charge for rent and food, and so on. And then we'd have to convince the staff to give it a try. It's not going to be an overnight thing. It would probably take several years at least."

~ ~ ~ ~

Later, after everyone else had gone to bed, Chris asked Kevin if he had given any thought as to whom he was going to ask to be Governor of Camden.

"I hadn't really thought about it. I was sort of hoping that whoever is governor right now would be willing to continue for a little while after I get to Milhaven," Kevin answered.

"If he or she can," Chris replied.

"What do you mean?" Kevin asked.

"From what you said, the first question Tyree asked you was whether or not you had chosen your governor. I got the feeling that he expected you to say yes. Maybe a new governor has to be installed as soon as you take over."

"You may be right," Kevin said with a sigh. "We need to find out how much time we'll have. Can you find a way to ask him how soon a new governor has to be in place? I'm not sure I want him to realize that I have no idea. He's not too far from figuring out that we're not from Terah, and I don't want to add to his suspicions."

"And it would be more likely for me to have no idea? I'll ask, but I don't think it'll make much difference. If he's going to be around us in Camden, he's going to figure it out, if Steve hasn't already told him."

"I wonder when he's leaving here," Kevin said, more to himself than to Chris. "If he leaves when we do …"

"I know where you're headed. I asked Glendymere about it one day while you were fighting dragons," Chris said. "Glendymere's going to insist that he stay here until we're in Milhaven. I think he's doing that so we'll know that if anyone does find us, it isn't because Tyree talked. Glendymere trusts the man, and wants to be sure that you do, too. I think he thinks that Tyree might be a good advisor later on."

"I was thinking about asking him to travel with us so I could keep an eye on him." Then Kevin laughed and said, "Chris, I think your paranoia's contagious. That sounded more like you than me."

"A little paranoia is a good thing," Chris said. "Now, you want to know how long you have before you have to name a governor. Anything else while I'm at it?"

"No, I think that'll do for now. Oh, find out about this assistant thing. Is it an actual position, or does it just refer to an aide? Xantha said that I don't have to name a second until I have a child. Find out if that's right, too," Kevin added.

"And you want me to find out all of this without alerting him with my ignorance. Right!"

"You'll manage. You always come through," Kevin remarked.

Chris didn't say anything. He didn't know what to say. He could tell from the way Kevin said it that the comment wasn't intended to flatter or persuade, it was just Kevin's opinion, but it was the first time in his life anyone had ever seemed to rely on him. He found the idea a little intimidating.

~ ~ ~ ~

The battle Friday would have ended quickly if it had been real, and not in the Tellurians' favor. Kevin concentrated so hard on fighting Jonquin that he was not very effective in protecting the others. Glendymere became their primary shield instead of backup.

After Glendymere called a halt to the day's battle, Kevin and Chris joined him in his chambers while the others gathered their weapons and headed back to Rainbow Valley.

"That was horrible! I thought I could handle it, but I can't. There's no way I can deal with the ground barrage and handle Jonquin's attack at the same time. It's just too much," Kevin groaned in frustration.

"Which is another good reason for you to always neutralize the sorcerer immediately. That would give you one less thing to worry about."

"I understand, I really do, but what am I supposed to do now? Against Jonquin? I can't defeat him. He's too strong," Kevin moaned.

"He's a dragon! And he's a lot stronger than any sorcerer you'll ever face in battle. If you can manage to counter his attacks and still protect your friends, you can feel confident that as long as you're awake, you can defend your little group against any type of human attack on the way to Camden, with or without sorcerer assistance."

"Well, I wouldn't call today a rousing success."

"No, but neither was your first battle against the elves and dwarves, or your first battle against a dragon. You'll get better, you always do."

"I hope you're right, but right now I don't have a lot of hope."

"We'll work on it tomorrow morning. Our next battle won't be until Monday. Chris, bring your bow and a lot of arrows. I'll get Jonquin to join us. You can shoot at Kevin while he and Jonquin fight."

"And what are you going to be doing?" Chris asked. "Protecting me from magical fallout, or making sure that Kevin doesn't end up looking like a pin cushion?"

"With a little luck, we might just be able to manage both between us, right Kevin?" Glendymere chuckled.

"If you say so," Kevin mumbled. He felt like all of the self-confidence that he had gained over the last couple of months was more self-delusion than anything else.

"Just stop it! Don't start that again!" Glendymere roared.

Kevin and Chris both jumped back, almost as if the force of Glendymere's thoughts had physically assaulted them.

"What do you mean?" Kevin stammered. "What did I do?"

"Every time things get tough, you waste time complaining that you're not good enough, that you can't do it. You give up and decide that you're a failure at the first sign of trouble. You're constantly doubting your ability, whining that you're not sure you can handle this, don't know how to handle that, and I'm sick of it. I'm tired of propping you up! Instead of sitting on your backside feeling sorry for yourself, come up with a way to deal with it!" Glendymere snapped. *"It might be beyond you, but how do you know? Have you given it any real thought? Have you tried to come up with a way to survive? Or are you just sitting around waiting for someone else to point the way? Well, I've got news for you! It's time for you to grow up and act like the Master Sorcerer of Terah, the best of the best, because that's what you are!"* And with that, Glendymere turned away from them and stormed out of the chamber.

For a few moments, they were both too stunned to speak. Then finally Chris said, "I think your apprenticeship just ended. School is out."

Kevin nodded slowly. "Let's go home. I want something to eat. Then I'm going to figure out some way to defend us."

~ ~ ~ ~

The next morning, as Kevin and Chris were walking over to Willow Canyon, Chris asked Kevin if he had come up with a plan.

"Yes and no," Kevin said. "I think the object of the game this time is to protect us, not to try to 'win'. If we were up against a human sorcerer, I might be able to take him out of action, but there's no way I can take Jonquin out, so I'm going to quit trying. All I'm aiming for is survival."

"Okay. Sounds good to me, but what would we do if this were real?" Chris asked. "Would we have any hope of surviving?"

"Not if a dragon joined the other side, but that's not likely. And if it should happen, it happens. I'm not going to worry about that when we have so many other things to worry about that are a lot more likely to happen."

"Speaking of which, you might want to give some thought as to whom you are going to name Governor of Camden," Chris said. "While you were in your room thinking about all of this last night, I talked to Tyree. You have to have a new governor in place by the time you go to the council meeting in April."

"I was hoping to have a little more time."

"Yeah, well, you don't. And about the assistant thing, it's an actual position. You're supposed to name an assistant as soon as you become the Seated Sorcerer of Camden. Your assistant is like the Chief of Staff at the White House. He manages your schedule, meets with people for you when you don't have time, brings you up-to-date on things, and so on. The assistant is the same thing as a second, only he isn't called a second until there's a child involved. I got the feeling that Tyree sort of expects that you'll name someone from our little group for both positions."

"I'd prefer to," Kevin said thoughtfully. "But none of us know much about Terah. It'll be like the blind leading the blind."

"From what Tyree said, it always is at the beginning. You can ask the current governor to stay on as an advisor for a little while if you want to, and he said that he felt sure that Laryn wouldn't just pack up and leave the castle as soon as you take over. She'll be there for you to turn to, but you'll have to name your own people," Chris explained. "I asked him why. He said that he didn't know, that that's just the way it's done."

"Probably to keep the people who hold the positions of power loyal to the current sorcerer. It would be really awkward if a new sorcerer defeated a seated sorcerer and then had to try to get along with the old staff."

"Oh, and one more thing, you have the final word on the positions that you appoint. If you want to replace anyone, it's your prerogative. No one else is involved. And if any of your people want to resign or retire, it's up to you to grant the request."

"How does that saying go? 'I serve at the pleasure of the President'? Isn't that what the people who work in the White House always say? I guess this is 'I serve at the pleasure of the Sorcerer'," Kevin replied.

"Tyree didn't mention the general's post. I wonder if you're going to have to name a new general, too."

"I have no idea."

"I guess that's the next thing I need to find out, huh?"

"Yes, but there's no hurry. I'd just like to know before we leave here."

"In a little over two weeks."

"I know. It feels strange to think of leaving," Kevin said. "This place has been home more than any place I've ever lived. I hate to leave."

"Me, too. It's like leaving my mother's house all over again. Except that then I was excited about being out on my own. Now …"

"I didn't feel one way or the other about leaving my parents, but the thought of leaving Rainbow Valley makes me feel almost physically sick. I really like it here. And it isn't just because we're safe, tucked away inside our mountain. I don't think the idea of danger is entering into the dread I feel."

"No, it's the good-byes," Chris agreed as they stepped out into the canyon. "Well, time to concentrate on the present. Looks like Glendymere and Jonquin are waiting for us."

"Here goes nothing," Kevin mumbled.

~ ~ ~ ~

For the rest of the day, Kevin fended off attacks of arrows and magical bolts. By the time Glendymere called a halt to the practice, Kevin felt a lot more confident about defending himself and his friends, even if he couldn't manage attacking at the same time.

"I see you figured out what's most important," Glendymere said after Jonquin had left.

"I just decided that since there was no way that I could defeat Jonquin, maybe I should quit trying and concentrate on defense," Kevin answered.

"Wise decision. But keep in mind that the sorcerers you're going to face are not that good, not like a dragon. You'll have to attack them or the battle will go on indefinitely."

"Do two or more sorcerers ever gang up against one?"

"It happens, but not in a power struggle for a chair. After all, which one would become the new seated sorcerer? Usually when two or more sorcerers join forces, it's to fend off an invasion, whether it's slavers, renegades or whatever."

"Would a band of slavers or bandits ever employ two sorcerers?" Chris asked.

"The only way I can see that happening is if the sorcerer they hired had an apprentice," Glendymere answered. *"But if you happen to run across that situation, don't hesitate to take them both out, Kevin. Even an apprentice can get in a lucky shot. Go for the kill. They certainly wouldn't have any qualms about killing you or they never would have signed on with a band of cutthroats in the first place."*

"I guess that's one way of looking at it."

"It's the only way."

~ ~ ~ ~

During the next two weeks, Kevin's skill at defending himself and his friends improved to the point that he could provide some backup for their offensive actions. He was still not able to do too much about Jonquin other than defend against his attacks, but he did manage to get in a few strikes.

The rest of the Tellurians became accustomed to having strange things happen in the middle of battle, such as being pummeled by golf ball sized hailstones, blinded by swirling dirt or snow, threatened by flood waters, or chased by an approaching tornado. Their confidence in Kevin's ability to handle such emergencies grew to the point that by the end of the two weeks, they didn't pay any attention to them.

About the only weather disaster that Jonquin didn't conjure up during the war games was ground tremors. One afternoon, towards the end of the second week, Kevin asked Glendymere about that. Glendymere said that no one ever intentionally started tremors because they were impossible to control. A tremor in Nandelia could cause tidal waves out in the ocean, or cause a volcano to erupt several thousand miles away. Glendymere told him that since even the dragons were powerless to stop the tremors, no one was willing to take the responsibility of triggering such a chain reaction.

The final practice battle was on Friday, the eighteenth of January. The clouds were so thick and heavy with snow that it was completely dark by mid-afternoon, so Glendymere called off the games a little early. The giants had spent the afternoon setting out food and drink in the main reception area of Glendymere's caves, and after the elves and dwarves had eaten their fill, they bid the Tellurians good-bye and good luck and headed off for their own camp. The Tellurians sat around talking with Tyree, Blalick, Ashni, and the kids while Jonquin and Glendymere rested nearby and listened to the conversations floating around.

"*Looks like your boy will make it,*" Jonquin said privately to Glendymere.

"*I hope so, but you never know. A stray energy bolt can be as deadly as a full-scale assault. More so if you aren't expecting it.*"

"*True, but you've done all you can. And he seems to be smart enough.*"

"*That he is. I just hope I don't have to go to his funeral for a long, long time.*"

Jonquin sighed and said, "*That's the biggest problem with caring about any of the humans. They don't live long even if no one kills them. They're gone almost before you get to know them.*"

"*Too true. But he has enough elven blood running through his veins to keep him alive longer than most.*"

"*So did Badec.*"

Glendymere sighed. "*I wonder how young Myron is going to handle it when Laryn tells him that Badec's illness isn't natural.*"

"*Oh? You hadn't mentioned that,*" Jonquin's interest picked up.

"*I know. She hasn't said anything yet, to anyone. But it's one of those things that I just know.*"

"*I don't suppose you also just happen to know which human is responsible, do you?*"

"*No, or that human just might wake up dead one morning.*"

"*You can't do that,*" Jonquin said quietly.

"*Actually I can,*" Glendymere grumbled.

"*No, you can't. I'd worry if I didn't know you better. Leave it to the boy. It's his battle,*" Jonquin said as he nodded in Kevin's direction.

Much later, long after night had fallen over the canyon, Joan said, "I guess we need to get this mess cleaned up and head home. Karl, if you and the guys will take care of putting all the tables and chairs back in the store room, we'll take care of packing up the dishes and left-over food."

The guys all stood up, stretched, groaned over aching muscles, and began clearing up. Soon, all evidence of the feast was gone, and Glendymere's reception area once again looked like a barren cavern.

Jonquin and Glendymere magically transported all of the food containers to Blalick's house and then Glendymere offered to provide air transportation to Rainbow Valley for anyone who wanted a ride home. The storm clouds had moved out and left a clear moonless night full of stars.

Darrell surprised everyone by quickly accepting the offer. "I've never flown, and from the way Kevin and Chris talk about it, it's terrific. I'll probably never get the chance again, so yes, I'd like a lift. And don't feel like you have to go straight there either," he said with a grin.

"You've got a point," Steve said. "It might be fun."

Glendymere chuckled and said that if they would all like to come, he was sure that Jonquin would be happy to help out. When Jonquin agreed and knelt so that the humans could climb aboard, everyone except Tyree, Chris and Kevin quickly scrambled for a seat on one of the two dragons.

Kevin made sure that all of the Tellurians were buckled to the chains that the dragons wore and then he settled back down on the ground beside Chris and Tyree. "I guess we should head back now. I imagine they'll get there long before we do, even if Glendymere takes what we would call the scenic route."

While they were walking back through the tunnels, Tyree asked Kevin if he had any more questions that he wanted to ask. Kevin hesitated, so Chris said, "I have one. Who names the general? Is that up to the sorcerer, the governor, or do the two of them decide together?"

"The general is not exactly an appointed position. I imagine he could be replaced if you really had problems with him, but on the whole, the sorcerer and governor sort of leave him alone. When the general feels like it's time to step aside, he usually meets with the sorcerer and governor and tells them which one of his captains he plans to name to his position. His loyalty is to Camden, to its army, and to protecting the people of the province."

"But what if the general didn't like the current sorcerer? Would he be likely to try to help get rid of him?" Chris asked.

"No. If he really just couldn't stand the sorcerer, he'd probably resign and leave the province. There's no way a general would risk scheming against a sorcerer. It would be suicide. A non-magical human doesn't stand a chance against a sorcerer."

"What about treachery?" Kevin asked, thinking in part of Badec.

"How could a general command respect among his officers if he stooped to anything as dishonorable as treachery? That's not a problem," Tyree assured him.

"So my father's general will remain in control of the army, no matter what happens when I return?" Kevin asked.

"Yes. He's a good man. I knew him before I left Milhaven. His name is Crandal, and you couldn't ask for a man with a more commendable character. As long as you do not use your magic to harm the inhabitants of Camden, he'll support and defend you to his last breath. But I will warn you of one thing, he will be completely truthful. If you ask his opinion, and sometimes even if you don't, he'll tell you what he really thinks, whether it's what you want to hear or not."

"I guess that's about the best I can ask of anyone that I have to depend on," Kevin said.

Tyree nodded.

"Is he in charge of the castle guard?" Chris asked.

"No, the guard is separate from the army, at least in most provinces. Often the sorcerer chooses someone from the army for the position, but he doesn't have to. And how the guard is organized is up to the captain and the sorcerer. You'll have to name a new captain who will be completely loyal to you, not loyal to you just because you're Badec's son. You might want to give that a little thought while you're traveling. Just like the governor, you'll need to name a Captain of the Guard as soon as you assume the duties of the Sorcerer of Camden," Tyree explained.

When they came to the area Kevin thought of as the compass room, Tyree took the tunnel that led up to Blalick's house.

Kevin and Chris walked the rest of the way to Rainbow Valley in relative silence. When they got there, the others had not arrived so they decided to go outside and wait for them near the cave entrance.

About an hour later, Kevin spotted two dark shadows in the sky, slowly circling above the valley. He pointed them out to Chris and they watched as the shadows spiraled down towards the ground. Once both dragons were settled on the ground, Kevin and Chris approached.

"That was wonderful," Joan exclaimed as she slid off of Glendymere's neck. "The whole area is covered in a blanket of snow and it's beautiful. I don't know when I've enjoyed anything as much."

"It really was fun," Karl said, "once I got over the shakes at being so far above ground."

"If there is nothing else, I think I'll take my leave," Jonquin said. *"Glendymere, thank you for the invitation to the war games. I've had more fun over the past couple of weeks than I've had in centuries. Myron, have a safe journey home. You will do well for Camden and for Terah."* Then Jonquin stepped away, spread his massive wings, and soared off into the night.

"Well, time for me to say good night as well. You need some sleep. You have a big day ahead of you tomorrow," Glendymere said, referring to the fact that they had to get everything packed up and loaded the next day. *"I'll come over tomorrow evening for a few minutes. See you then."* Then Glendymere followed Jonquin into the black sky.

Theresa turned away from the others for a moment to wipe away the tears that had gathered in her eyes as she thought of leaving. Joan put her arm through her husband's and said, "Let's go inside. I need to get busy or I'm going to cry. Anyone interested in some coffee and pie?"

While Joan and Theresa busied themselves in the kitchen, the men gathered around the table. A somber air settled over them.

"I feel almost as depressed as I did when I found out about my knee," Darrell said quietly.

"You know, you could all stay here," Kevin said. "It might even be safer that way. I could easily travel from here to Milhaven by myself using magic."

"If you really think it would be safer to travel by yourself, we'd understand," Steve said, "but I plan to go to Milhaven regardless. For one thing, I'm curious about how our plans to turn the castle into a mill town will work out."

"We need to stick together," Darrell said. "We're the outsiders on this world. Either we all stay or we all go, and staying here really isn't an option."

"I agree. It's tempting, but it really isn't possible," Karl said.

"What isn't possible?" Joan asked as she brought in a tray loaded with the pie, coffee, and cups and set it on the dining room table.

"Staying here," Karl said as he took her hand.

"Makes a nice dream though, doesn't it?" Joan said with a smile. "Our own little corner of the world."

"I don't want to leave, but there's a part of me that is ready to get back to work," Theresa said. "I'm probably going to cry like a baby when I have to tell Sari good-bye. I'd take her with me if I thought Ashni would let me."

"I wouldn't mind taking Macin either," Darrell agreed. "Maybe one day I'll have a son of my own. If I do, I hope he's as decent a kid as Macin."

"I don't know how to say good-bye to Ashni. She's become such a dear friend," Joan said with a sigh. Then she put her hand on Karl's shoulder and said, "And old tough guy here is going to have a hard time leaving Blalick."

Neither Kevin nor Chris said anything, but they were both thinking about having to leave Glendymere. He had become so much more than a mentor to both of them.

The Tellurians sat around the table, drinking coffee in silence, each lost in memories. Finally, Joan gathered the cups, took them out to the kitchen, and set them in the sink. Karl stretched and said, "I think I'll head towards bed. After all, we'd better enjoy our last couple of nights on mattresses. It's back to the cold hard ground starting Sunday. And I do mean cold. That snow pack is going to be tough to deal with."

"Well, at least this time we don't have to worry about one of the wagons getting stuck," Darrell said as he nodded towards Kevin.

"Maybe there's something to be said for traveling with a world-class sorcerer after all," Karl teased as he and Joan left for their room. "See all of you in the morning."

Chris and Kevin were the last two to leave the dining room. While they were walking down the hall towards their rooms, Chris asked," How serious were you about heading for Milhaven on your own?"

"I wasn't really, unless everyone else wanted to stay here. I just don't want anyone to feel obligated to go with me, not even you. You can bail out any time you want to. I'd understand," he answered.

"Thanks, but no thanks. I signed on for the long haul. Count me in."

"In that case, I want to ask you something," Kevin said.

"Shoot."

"Would you be willing to be my assistant when we get to Milhaven, at least for a while?"

"I don't know how much help I'll be, and I'll understand if you want to find someone else who knows a bit more about how things are done once we get there, but I'll do what I can," Chris answered. "Let's say I'll serve as your assistant until after the first council meeting. Then we'll take another look at it. You might decide that you need someone else in that spot by then."

"I think the main thing I need is someone I can trust and that I can work with, but let me know if you decide you want out," Kevin said. Then he added, "Let's keep this between us for right now, okay? I have a few things I want to talk over with you, but they'll wait until we're on our way. We'll have plenty of time to talk while we're standing guard."

"Okay. I have to admit that standing guard is one aspect of the trip that I definitely am not looking forward to. I've gotten spoiled sleeping in a nice warm bed all night long. It's going to be hard to go back to sleeping in shifts."

"If the ground is as hard and cold as I think it's going to be, getting up for a while to sit next to a hot fire might not be as bad as it sounds," Kevin said with a grin. "See you in the morning."

Chapter 45

Time for Good-Byes

The next morning, Blalick and Macin were in the dining room when everyone showed up for breakfast.

"Glendymere and I discussed your journey last night," Blalick said. "Karl told me that you are planning to pick up a road somewhere north of here so that you will not have to go back into Abernon. The road that runs along the Pooley River might be your best bet."

"The Pooley River?" Theresa asked.

"It is one of two rivers that form the boundary between Nandelia and Brendolanth," Blalick answered. "There are roads on both sides of the two rivers. If you were really coming from the north, the most sensible route would be along the Pooley River to the Sandover River and then on to the Kivee River. Here, let me show you what I am talking about." Blalick pulled out a map of Calandra. "See this river? It is the Pooley. And the one it joins here is the Sandover."

"We could follow those rivers to this one," Steve said quietly as he pointed at the Mississippi River.

"The Kivee," Blalick nodded. "You could cross the Kivee at Glenarbour, there is a big ferry crossing there, and then follow this road to Milhaven."

"Which province is Glenarbour in?" Karl asked. "It looks like it straddles the Sandover River."

"It does, but it is considered part of Brendolanth," Blalick answered. "One of the advantages of this route is that you will not pass through any of the towns that you came through on the way here. You will cross the road you took to Abernon, but you will not even travel on any of the same roads."

Karl nodded and studied the map. "How long will it take us to reach the Pooley River if we head due north?"

"If you have to use paths wide enough for the wagons, it is going to take five to seven days," Blalick said.

"Ouch! We can't spend that long heading north. Do you have any other ideas?" Karl asked.

Blalick nodded. "I could head out this morning with the horses and be there by tomorrow afternoon. Kevin can move the loaded wagons out to the front of the cave tomorrow night, and then he and Glendymere can carry them up to the camp where I will be waiting with the horses. After everything is ready there, Glendymere can fly the rest of you up to join us. If it is done under the cover of darkness, no one will know. There are not many people living in these mountains, and no one would be out just wandering around in the middle of a cold January night."

"Sounds good to me," Karl agreed. "As long as we can do it without attracting undue attention."

"While they are transporting the wagons, and then all of you, Kevin and Glendymere will be on the lookout for spies as well as local farmers checking their barns. Do not worry. If necessary, Glendymere can erase all memory of the night from someone's mind."

"I keep forgetting just how powerful he is," Karl said, shaking his head. "When do you want to leave with the horses? And can you handle all of them by yourself?"

"Macin is going with me," Blalick said. "We thought we would leave as soon as we can get the horses ready to travel. If you do not have any objections, we will get started while you are eating your breakfast. Is there anything you need us to do before we leave?"

"Not that I know of. Joan?" Karl asked.

"No, not that I can think of. Blalick, I don't know how to thank you for everything you've done for us while we've been here. You and your whole family have been so terrific. I feel like I'm leaving my best friends," Joan said while tears glittered in her eyes.

"We have been enriched by your visit here," Blalick said with a slight nod of his head. "We shall definitely miss you. Come along, Macin. We have a lot of miles to cover."

While they were eating breakfast the Tellurians talked about what they needed to pack in each of the three wagons, and just as they finished eating, Sari and Ashni came in to help with the packing. It took them most of the day to pack Theresa's wagon. Then after dinner, the men packed most of the furniture and farming tools in the wagon that Kevin had driven down. Although Blalick and Karl had altered the wagon so that it now resembled a farmer's hay wagon, they had kept all of Palladin's little hidden cabinets so they could store the extra weapons in them.

They left packing Karl's new wagon until Sunday morning. After breakfast, Karl and Darrell anchored the individual cases around the sides of the new wagon, and then loaded the rest of the furniture, farming tools, and kitchen supplies. Bales of hay and bags of oats were stuffed in every spare corner and piled on top of furniture and tools. Finally, by the middle of Sunday afternoon, everything was ready. Joan and Ashni fixed some sandwiches and everyone gathered in the dining room for a snack.

"I've got something in my room that I want to show you. Be back in a few minutes," Steve said as soon as he finished eating.

By the time Steve returned, the table had been cleared. He laid a stack of paper on the table and said, "Ashni, I've drawn a few sketches over the past couple of months that I'd like to give you and your family so you'll have something to remember us by." Steve spread the pictures out on the table. There were sketches of Joan and Ashni seated at their spinning wheels, in the kitchen, and out in the meadow with the llamas. He had sketched Theresa and Sari in the forest, by the herb garden, and in the workroom. There were sketches of Darrell and Macin practicing hand-to-hand combat, sparring with swords, and doing target practice with long bows. He had sketched Karl and Blalick surrounded by wood and tools, with the horses, and walking along the crest of Wildcat Mountain. There were sketches of Tyree in the sitting room with some of the Tellurians, outside with Blalick and Ashni, and in Steve's room working on the model of the castle. Steve also had several sketches of Glendymere, one by himself, one in flight over the canyon, one with Kevin and Chris, and even one as he slept in his chamber.

While everyone was looking at those sketches, Steve walked over to Sari and handed her three sketches of Luci. One showed the condor perched on her rock in her cave, a second was of Luci perched outside on the edge of the cliff, and the third was of her in flight against a background of mountains and sky.

"Thank you for letting me go up to Luci's cave with you, "Steve said quietly.

Sari's face lit up as she looked at the pictures. She turned to Steve, hugged him, and said, "This is the best present ever. Thank you."

As Sari turned to show Theresa the pictures, Steve stepped over to Ashni and handed his last sketch to her. Sari was in the foreground seated on her rock in Luci's cave, playing her flute. Off to the side, Luci was perched on her rock with her beak extended in song. Ashni's eyes filled with tears as she looked at the sketch.

"It is beautiful," she whispered. Then in a slightly stronger voice she added, "Steve, I can not tell you how much this sketch means to me. I do not know what to say."

"I enjoyed doing it and this is my way of saying thank you for everything you and your family have done for us," Steve replied.

"Steve, I want copies of some of these. Did you make any for us?" Joan asked as she kept going through the sketches.

Steve nodded. "I've got about that many sketches, maybe a few more, in my room for Tyree to bring when he comes. I've already packed them up with my journal."

"Why are you giving them to Tyree to bring to Milhaven?" Theresa asked. "I'm sure we can find room for them."

"I thought it might be best not to have anything with us that connects us to this area," Steve answered.

Karl nodded. "We don't know who or what we may run into."

"Just as long as Tyree doesn't forget them," Joan said. "I'd hate for one of you to have to ride all the way back out here to pick them up."

~ ~ ~ ~

A little while later, while the men were checking the wagons to make sure that everything was tied down and ready for travel, Ashni and Sari helped Joan and Theresa finish up dinner. After Joan set the table and dished up the food, Ashni asked Sari if she was ready to go. When Joan objected, Ashni pointed out that Glendymere wasn't expected until after midnight, so the Tellurians had time to eat and get about six hours of sleep if they didn't waste any time sitting around putting off saying good-bye.

"I don't know how to say good-bye," Joan said through her tears.

"Then do not. We will see each other again. I am sure of it," Ashni said as she clasped the human woman's hand. She had never developed so much affection for a human before, and she was sure that her life was going to feel quite empty for a while.

Meanwhile, Sari couldn't say a thing to Theresa. All she could do was hold her and cry. Finally Theresa gently pushed Sari back, wiped her eyes, and said, "Go on now. This isn't going to get any easier. Here, I fixed some tea for you and your mother. Take this with you and think of us when you drink it."

"Teri is right, Sari. Come along. It is time to go. They need to get some rest." Ashni picked up the pictures, put her arm around her daughter, and gently led her out of the dining room.

A few minutes later, the men came back in. Seeing his wife in tears, Karl put his arm around her and said, "Come on. Let's eat dinner and get some rest. There's no telling when we'll get the chance to sleep in a comfortable bed again."

After dinner, everyone headed off to the bedrooms to try to get a nap before leaving. Kevin got up a little earlier than the others so that he could float the wagons down to the cave entrance without anyone else around. When he reached the wagons, he found that Ashni and Sari had loaded the wagon seats with bags of sandwiches, a wide variety of cookies, and a couple of cakes. Some of Kevin's favorite strawberry preserves were sitting on Theresa's wagon seat, right next to a big bag of chocolate chip cookies that were obviously intended for Chris. Draped over each of the wagon seats were heavy wool lap blankets for the wagon drivers.

By midnight Kevin had the wagons moved out to the clearing in front of the cave, ready to carry north to Blalick's camp. He was standing in front of the wagons looking at the heavy black sky when he felt rather than saw a shadow move across the clouds. A couple of minutes later, Glendymere settled in the snow beside him.

"Are you ready to go?"

"If you mean have we packed, the answer is yes. If you're asking if we're really ready to leave this valley, the answer's a resounding no."

"Ah, but this is what it's all been about, getting you ready to move on. Now that the time is here, I have to admit I'll hate to see all of you go. I've come to rather enjoy having you around," Glendymere said. *"Are the others about ready?"*

Kevin nodded. "They're all up. They're having coffee in the kitchen."

"Good. Then shall we take the wagons?"

"I guess so."

"I'll take two. You bring the third. Then just follow me."

"Maybe I should let them know that we're going."

"I already have. I also asked if anyone had any last minute things to throw on board. No one did, so I guess the wagons are ready. Let's go," Glendymere said as he and two of the wagons lifted straight up. Kevin took the last wagon and followed.

It took them about an hour to get to Blalick's camp with the wagons. When they got there Blalick was standing next to the campfire and Macin was with the horses in a small clearing about a quarter of a mile away. After the wagons were spread out in a circle around the campfire, Kevin and Glendymere headed back to Rainbow Valley.

When they were about fifteen minutes out, Glendymere let Chris know that they would be landing in a few minutes and as soon as Glendymere and Kevin touched down, the others came out of the cave entrance, ready to go. Although Kevin had gotten used to seeing them in long hair and beards, seeing them in their padded sweaters and long cloaks gave him a quick chuckle. They all seemed to have gained about thirty pounds since last night.

While the others climbed on Glendymere's back, Chris joined Kevin and handed him his sweater and cloak so that he could put them on before they headed north. "Are you sure you can support me for that long a flight?" Chris asked Kevin quietly. "I could squeeze up there with the others."

"There's no need to crowd them any more than they're already crowded. Relax. I just carried a loaded wagon up there without any problems. I won't let you fall," Kevin whispered back.

"Of course he won't let you fall, and if he does, I'll catch you," Glendymere answered Chris privately. *"It's good for the others to see that you have faith in his abilities, so, like he said, relax."*

When they landed near the campsite, Blalick and Macin greeted them with hot coffee. While they were drinking their coffee, Kevin mentioned that Ashni had left surprises on the wagon seats. After everyone inspected the blankets and the bags of goodies, they asked Blalick to tell Ashni that she had their undying gratitude.

Blalick laughed and said, "From what she told me, she is planning to send out some supplies every couple of weeks while you are on the road."

"How?" Joan asked.

"Well, I do not think she has mentioned it to Glendymere yet, but she is planning to use him as a delivery man," Blalick said, grinning.

"Humph! We'll have to see about that. Every couple of weeks you said? What does the woman think I am? I have better things to do than run fresh bread out to this crew!"

"He will do it," Blalick laughed, "or else he can live with her."

Glendymere addressed Kevin privately, *"I had planned to drop in on you once in a while during your journey just to make sure things were going all right. I don't guess it would harm anything for me to bring you a package or two while I'm at it. Any special requests?"*

"No," Kevin answered mentally. *"But I'm glad to hear you say that you'll be around some. I was afraid I wouldn't see you again for a really long time. I don't know how to thank you for all you've done for me."*

"The only thanks I want is for you to survive," Glendymere said. Then after a couple of minutes he added, *"And I think I'm going to need your help next year. Something Duane and I talked about. But there's plenty of time to think about that later."*

"You can't say that and then drop it. What are you talking about?"

"Nothing right now. I just might have to ask you for a favor next fall. Don't know yet. Have to see how things play out."

"Yeah, like seeing if I survive."

"That, and other things," Glendymere said. Then Glendymere addressed Blalick privately. *"The time has come for us to take off, Blalick. I'd like to be back home before daybreak. Would you get those medallions please?"*

"Before we leave, I have something for each of you," Glendymere said to the whole group. Then Blalick handed each of the Tellurians a medallion on a gold chain.

Glendymere explained that most crystals on Terah had the power to enhance certain character traits if those traits were already present. Then he spoke to each person privately, explaining the significance of the stones in his or her medallion.

"Kevin, each master presents a medallion to his apprentice when he's ready to strike out on his own. The red opal is the sorcerer's stone. It enhances your magical energies and helps you focus. Every practicing sorcerer wears one, but not always where it can be seen. I would suggest that you wear it inside your tunic until you take your place in Milhaven. The blue sodalite is to keep you balanced and ease your fears. It will help you look to the heart of the problems you will face and find solutions." As Kevin hung the medallion around his neck, the red opal began to glow with an inner fire. *"That light reflects your own fire. It will burn brightly as long as there is breath in your body, and will fade out when the life force within you is extinguished."*

"Chris, you are a loyal and sensible companion. The sapphire will protect you against evil, especially evil magic, and will enhance your ability to think through situations and see the broader picture. The topaz will help you find your path in life and handle life's headaches with creativity and humor without losing sight of your goals."

"Steve, you have the wisdom to guide and the experience to know that guidance is not always appreciated. The lapis lazuli enhances your clarity of vision and serves as an aid in presenting your views. The amethyst will heal your heart and let you open yourself to new friendships and love."

"Karl, the bloodstone is the soldier's stone. It enhances your endurance and vitality in defending what's right. The blue lace agate is the stone of the diplomat. It will help you hear what isn't said, to distinguish fact from conjecture, to make wise decisions, and to present clear arguments."

"Darrell, the tiger's eye is a warrior's stone. It fosters the courage to face your fears, the energy to carry on the good fight, and it will bring you luck on the battlefield. The citrine provides protection against the influences of evil, both on and off the battlefield, and will help you maintain a tight control over your emotions when you're up against an enemy."

"Theresa, my dear, you already wear the medallion of the Sisterhood. But the medallion that I present to you now has no connection with your role as a healer. The rose quartz is a mother's stone. It enhances your fertility and aligns your emotional, mental, and spiritual energies. The pink moonstone will help you conquer your anxieties and will increase your confidence and creativity in handling the different forces in your life."

"Joan, you wear many hats, and you wear them well. The green jasper will settle your mind, ease your worries, and bring you joy and happiness, while the red jasper will help you develop a high sensitivity to good and evil, as well as honesty and deception, and to recognize each, no matter how well it is disguised."

After each of the Tellurians had thanked Glendymere and hung the medallions around their necks, Glendymere nodded to Blalick and Macin. Blalick shook hands with all of the Tellurians and

309

bid them a safe and fruitful journey. Then he grasped Karl's hand again, held it for a few moments, and without saying anything else, took his place on Glendymere's back.

Macin shook hands with everyone except Darrell. When he came to Darrell, he reached for his hand, but ended in a bear hug. As the two men slapped each other on the back, each of them felt the sting of tears. Darrell stepped back, shook Macin's hand, and nodded towards Glendymere. As soon as Macin was settled on Glendymere's back, the dragon soared into the black sky.

No one stood around watching the dark shadow disappear into the night for more than a couple of minutes; too many things had to be done. Kevin, Karl, and Steve hitched the horses to the wagons, Joan tied the spare team behind her wagon, Darrell and Chris saddled the others, and Theresa packed the coffee pot and mugs and doused the fire. By daybreak, the wagons were ready to roll.

Chapter 46

Back on the Road

Although it was quite cold, they were lucky with the weather for the first few days. They had bright sunshine with very little wind during the day, and while the inns and stables that they stayed in at night were not exactly warm, they were bearable.

The Tellurians quickly stepped into their roles as rugged self-sufficient loners who were accustomed to hardships. Their attitude while they were in town was totally different from the friendly enthusiasm of the minstrels they had portrayed nine months earlier. Karl and Darrell handled the business for the group while the others hung back, almost shyly. When they went into the taverns for dinner, they found a couple of tables off in a corner and stayed to themselves. After dinner, the men usually sat in the tavern, drinking scog and talking amongst themselves, while Theresa and Joan went to their room. Kevin and Chris slept in a room next to theirs, and the others rented a section of the loft in the stables.

Early Thursday morning, clouds began to move in, accompanied by a cold north wind. They stopped for a quick lunch soon after they crossed the southbound road that had taken them to Abernon the previous May.

"We were at this point only a couple of days after the bandits attacked us," Karl said.

"I was just thinking about that," Darrell said. "It seems like it was years ago in one way, and like yesterday in another."

Theresa nodded. "Sometimes it's almost like the last eight months didn't even happen."

"Well, some things have changed," Joan said as she held her hand out to catch a snowflake slowly meandering its way towards the ground. "It wasn't snowing the last time we were here."

"No, it wasn't," Karl said as he looked at the sky. "Let's get ready to move on. I want to reach the next town before those clouds decide to really let loose."

As Theresa climbed back up on her wagon seat, she sighed, and said, "I'm glad we're finally on our way to Milhaven. I can't stop thinking about how nice it's going to be to have my own chapel one day, and then the next minute, I feel guilty about being excited. I feel like I should be miserable that we had to leave the giants and Glendymere."

"Don't feel guilty for being who you are," Darrell said. "I had a sociology professor who said that the world is made up of two types of people, those who embrace change and move on, and those who fight it tooth and nail. I think all of us must be the first type. It may seem a little cold at times, but if you weren't the type who could move on, Paul wouldn't have chosen you for this little adventure in the first place, and you'd be back on Earth, married to your banker."

"Ugh! You're probably right." Theresa grimaced as she flicked the reins and pulled her wagon out behind Steve's. "But I still feel like a heel for being happy."

~ ~ ~ ~

The snow covered the ground with a thin blanket of white, but it wasn't enough to cause any travel problems, and by the weekend, the weather had warmed up enough to melt it all away. By Tuesday morning, the ground was dry again. When they stopped for lunch, Karl suggested stocking up on a few supplies, finding a good campsite, and staying put for a couple of nights.

Shortly after lunch, they rode into a town that had a large livery stable, so Karl dismounted in front of it and went inside to see if he could buy some extra feed for the horses. The stable master offered to sell him several bales of hay and four bags of oats.

While the men were loading the hay and oats, Joan sat on her wagon seat, daydreaming. After a bit, she felt someone's eyes on her, so she slowly looked towards the inn. A man was standing beside the door, staring at her. The second their eyes met, a shock of recognition flashed through her. That man was the bandit that they had captured the night of the raid.

He sauntered over towards her wagon and just as he drew close enough to pose a threat, he reached out and stroked one of her horses. "She's a beauty. Reminds me of a mare I had last year. Gentle with my children but she had a strong heart. Had to put her down after she broke her leg running through a field outside of Billows. Tore my heart out," he said as he continued to rub her horse's head. "Ever been to Billows, ma'am?"

Joan's heart was beating so hard and fast that she felt sure that he could hear the thuds and see her pulse jumping. "No, not to my knowledge. But we've been through so many towns along the Pooley River that I really don't know."

"Oh, Billows isn't on the Pooley River, ma'am. It's several days north, in Brendolanth. Are you sure you've never been there? You sure do look familiar."

With that special bond that some married couples develop, Karl sensed his wife's distress and walked around the end of the wagon towards the front. As soon as he saw the bandit, he knew what had upset her. "Can I help you, sir?" he asked as he continued towards the front of the wagon.

"No, that's all right. I was just admiring your horse here," the man said. "Well, guess I'll be on my way. Have a nice day, ma'am." Then he nodded towards Joan, turned, and entered the stable.

"You recognized him, didn't you?" Joan whispered to Karl.

Karl nodded. "We're going to finish loading and then we'll ride out of town as if nothing happened," he said quietly. "I don't think he's sure about us. Remember, it was dark."

"Not when he saw us in the dry goods store," Joan mumbled. "What's he doing down here? You don't think he's looking for us, do you?"

"No. That would be too much of a coincidence," Karl whispered. "I can't see him setting out to track us down. He didn't strike me as a much of a thief, much less a bounty hunter."

"And since you've known so many of them …" Joan argued.

Karl laughed and told her she had a point. Then he walked towards the back of the wagons to see if everything had been loaded.

"All loaded. Want to grab some scog before we head out?" Chris asked as he nodded towards a nearby tavern.

"Not this time. Let's mount up," Karl said quietly. "I'll explain later."

Darrell raised his eyebrows and asked, "Trouble?"

"Could be," Karl answered.

Within a couple of minutes, the Tellurians were headed out of town on the eastbound road and they didn't stop until they had put about ten miles between themselves and the town. Then Karl pulled up and signaled for everyone to stop and gather around.

"While we were loading the hay and oats, Joan had an interesting encounter," Karl said as he nodded towards her.

Joan explained about the bandit, the flash of recognition that she was sure she saw in his eyes, her brief conversation with him, and the creepy feeling that he knew about the bounty. "I can't point to anything that makes me so sure he knows, but he does. Sounds crazy, I know."

"No it doesn't," Steve said. "Flashes like that are often right. So the question is what do we do now?"

"I think we should plan to put as many miles between us and him as we can, and as fast as we can," Karl answered. "I had hoped to take tomorrow off and rest the horses, but I don't think that's a good idea now. Maybe in a couple of days."

"Right," Darrell agreed. "Well, we have a couple more hours before dark. I say we move on and set up camp at sunset."

By the time they set up camp that night, it was dark. They dug a fire pit so that the flame wouldn't be quite so visible, and tethered the horses close by. After dinner, they quickly settled down for the night, hoping to be back on the road by daybreak.

The next morning was windy, with clouds blowing in and out, but no rain or snow. By lunchtime, the clouds had settled into a thick overcast. Late that afternoon they came across an evergreen forest that bordered the river for several miles. According to the map, their road headed south for about a mile, circled around the forest, and then rejoined the river.

About halfway along the forest, Karl rode into the woods to see if he could find a good spot for a campsite. He found two adjoining circular clearings close to the river bank. They could tether the horses in one and set up their camp in the other.

After everyone had followed Karl into the clearing, Darrell said, "I think this would be a good place to take a day off. If that bandit did recognize us and was going to try to collect on the reward, don't you think he would have done something about it by now?"

"Probably. I sort of expected him to make a move last night," Karl agreed. "Let's set up for two nights, and then if we feel uneasy tomorrow, we can move on. I'll string up a small corral for the horses while the rest of you set up camp."

The strain of expecting an attack at any moment had taken its toll. No one had slept well the night before and they were all exhausted. Shortly after dinner, everyone headed towards bed except Theresa, Steve, and Darrell. They had the first watch. All three of them spent the hours of their watch strolling around the campsite, afraid that they would fall asleep if they sat down. Finally, it was midnight and time to change shifts.

As soon as Chris and Kevin got up, they settled down near the fire to get over the shock of leaving their warm bedrolls for the icy cold wind sweeping down from the north. The sky was still overcast. The clouds completely blocked out the moon and stars, making the night even darker.

Around 1:00, Chris said, "I'm going to walk over and check on the horses. How about sending up your seeing eye and having a good look around while I'm gone, okay?"

"Okay. Am I looking for anything in particular?"

"I don't know. Just look."

"This is the first time you've suggested that I do that since we left Rainbow Valley. Are you sensing something?"

"I'm not sure. The feeling's there, but it isn't very strong. Maybe it's just reaction to the last couple of days. It's probably nothing," Chris said as he stood up and shook his head. "Forget I even mentioned it."

"Why don't you wait a minute and let me take a look around?"

Chris shrugged and sat back down to wait for Kevin to finish checking out the area.

"Whoa, what have we here?" Kevin mumbled to himself. "Chris, I think you're right on target. Let me see. We have three camps strung out along the road. One is west of us near the edge of the woods, where the road and river are fairly close together. One is east of us, about a mile up, where a rather large stream cuts through the woods, and the third is south of us, about where we entered the woods from the road. In other words, we're surrounded. They must have been following us most of the day and spotted the smoke from our campfire this evening."

"What are they doing?" Chris whispered.

"Nothing right now. There are about six or seven men in each camp, as close as I can tell. A few appear to be sleeping in bedrolls, so I may have missed one or two, but mostly, they're just huddled around their fires, waiting."

"Waiting for what?"

"I don't know. Maybe daybreak. Maybe for a break in the clouds so that they'll have a little more light when they attack us. Our friend from Billows probably isn't too anxious to charge in blind, but they're definitely ready for a fight. I see swords, bows and arrows, and a few clubs," Kevin said as he continued to look through his seeing eye. Then he looked at Chris and said, "If they were hunters, they wouldn't be traveling in that large a group, and they wouldn't be camping on the road. I think we can safely assume that they're after us."

"Next question. What are we going to do?"

"Well, I could take them out right now, but I really don't want to do that."

"I'm not sure it would be a good idea anyway," Chris said. "Rolan's already after us because of Taelor. If he finds out that one of us is a sorcerer, he's going to be even more interested in us. Maybe we can 'sneak away' in the night."

"I'm all for that, but how? We're boxed in to the east, west, and south, with a river on the north. Wait a minute. Let me check out the other side of the river." Then Kevin focused his seeing eye on the north side of the river. Not only were there no bounty hunters, there was a nice thick evergreen forest bordering the north bank, with a road running parallel to the river on the other side of the woods.

"If we could get to the road on the other side of the river, we could do it. We could actually sneak away into the night," Kevin mumbled. "Now, how can I get us from here to there? The wagons won't be a problem, but what about the horses? How can I get them across the river quietly?"

"Could we try tying something over their eyes? I don't know that it'll work, but that's what they always did in the movies," Chris said with a shrug.

"Let's get Karl. He knows more about horses than we do."

"We might as well get everyone up. We're either going to have to vanish or fight. This is a royal pain," Chris muttered angrily as he began walking towards the sleeping tarps. "Everyone's beat. We really could have used a day off,"

As Chris explained the situation, adrenaline started flowing, and all signs of exhaustion disappeared. Within minutes, everyone was up, dressed, and armed.

As they gathered around the fire, Karl said, "Chris said something about moving us to the other side of the river. How are you going to do this?"

"I'm not sure. I can move the wagons, no problem. It's the horses I'm worried about. We need to get them to the other side of the river without the bounty hunters hearing anything," Kevin explained. "Chris suggested covering their eyes. We can do that, but how are they going to react if I pick them up?"

"Not well. They're going to fight you. It won't be quiet and it won't be easy. Are you sure you can handle a fighting horse?"

"No, I'm not sure of anything except that we're going to have to fight if we stay here. We could defeat them easily enough, but I'd rather not advertise the fact that one of us is a sorcerer."

"Wait a minute. There's a way we might be able to do it," Karl said. "It'll take a little longer, but I think it'll be safer all the way around. I have a couple of platforms that Blalick and I built. One is anchored under the old minstrel wagon, and the other one's under the new wagon. I was thinking along the lines of using them to roll the wagons across washed out areas or deep mud, but I think we might be able to use them with the horses. They're about six feet long and three feet wide. I could stand on the platform with the horse and hold his head while you 'float us' across. They're used to crossing rivers on ferries, and a lot of the time they end up standing right at the edge. As long as they're standing on something solid, they should be able to handle it."

"It won't bother them to see the water passing by?" Chris asked.

"We'll have a scarf ready to use as a blinder in case one of them starts getting jittery. Let's try it with mine first. The water won't bother him and I know he's a strong swimmer, so if anything goes wrong, he should be able to make it out of the river okay."

Darrell and Steve helped Karl unfasten the platform that he had stored under the bottom of the old minstrel wagon. Once they had that one free, Darrell, Steve, and Chris said that they'd get the other one so that Karl could get his horse and see if his idea was going to work.

While Karl was bringing his horse down to the river bank, Kevin floated the heavy platform over to the edge of the bank and held it steady so that Karl could lead his horse straight onto it. Once Karl and his horse were standing on the platform, Kevin eased it out over the water. He held it about a foot above the water and slowly moved it across the river. When it reached the other side, he held it snug against the opposite bank so that Karl could walk his horse off the platform and onto solid ground.

Then Kevin quickly floated the platform back to his side of the river where Joan was waiting with the mare that she usually rode. After she and her horse were standing on the platform, she covered her horse's eyes with a dishtowel. As the platform began to move, Joan whispered, "When we reach the other side, wait for Karl. I'll stay with the horses over there. He can come back and help you."

By the time Kevin had floated Joan across the river, Darrell and Chris had the other platform ready, and Steve had another horse ready to cross. Within thirty minutes, all of the horses were on the north side of the river with Joan.

While the others were busy with the horses, Theresa cleaned out the coffee pot, rinsed out the mugs, gathered up the bedrolls and sleeping tarps, and stored everything in the wagons. Then Kevin told her to climb up on her wagon seat and get ready to cross the river.

"Kevin, have you given any thought as to where you're going to land the wagons?" Karl asked. "The woods are pretty thick over there. We had trouble getting the horses through."

Kevin nodded and said, "The wagons are going over the tops of the trees and landing on the road. I thought you might want to go over first so that you could help Joan handle the horses when the wagons start floating in."

"Good idea," Karl agreed and closed his eyes. Kevin lifted him over the woods and set him down about three feet from Joan. She didn't see him until he was almost close enough to touch.

Joan laughed quietly. "I think this is going to work. It's dark enough out here that no one can see what we're doing."

"If we can keep the horses quiet," Karl whispered.

A couple of minutes later, a black shadow began to descend towards the road. The wagon settled so gently and quietly that the horses barely noticed. A few minutes later, the old minstrel wagon drifted down with Steve on the seat, followed shortly by Darrell and the new wagon.

While they were busy hitching the horses to the wagons and getting ready to move out, the two wooden platforms floated down with Chris standing on top of them. Kevin still hadn't joined them by the time they had the platforms secured under the wagons, and Chris was beginning to get concerned.

"I wonder what's keeping him," Chris mumbled. "I thought he was coming right behind me,"

"He'll be all right, Chris," Joan said. "He can take care of himself. He's a sorcerer now."

"I know. That's part of the problem. I know he's got something up his sleeve, and I don't like it when I don't know what's going on."

After a couple of minutes, Kevin drifted down beside Chris. "I have an idea," he said quietly. "Get the others over here while I do a quick check on the bounty hunters."

When Chris had everyone together, Kevin said, "The bounty hunters are still at their camps. I don't think they noticed anything, but when they storm our camp tomorrow morning, it isn't going to take them long to figure out that we must have crossed the river, and then they'll be right back on our trail. I've been trying to come up with some way to convince them that we're dead so they'll give up and go home."

"Sounds good, but how are you going to do that?" Darrell asked.

"How about having a tornado hit right about daybreak and sweep through our camp? You know, one of those really ferocious ones that clears everything out of its path. If I brought it down the road, scattering them as it approaches, and then swept it through the middle of our camp before letting it break off, it would look like it got us, the wagons, the horses, everything, but to make it look real, I'll need to scatter a little debris around the campsite. What have we got that we don't need? Any pots or dishes? Does anyone have a shirt or maybe a pair of boots that they don't want anymore?"

"Sort of like what the submarines used to send up to make the destroyers think they'd been sunk," Darrell said with a nod. "I like it. I bet we can find a few odds and ends that we could live without, especially if it gets those guys off our trail. Let's see what we can come up with."

Within a few minutes, Kevin had a fairly large assortment of everyday items to use as debris. He was about to head back to the south side of the river when Chris stopped him and said, "Look, I know you're thinking of doing this on your own, but I know how you are when you're working with storms. If the bounty hunters attack while you're stirring things up, you'll never even know it. I'm going to go with you to keep an eye on your back while you're off in the clouds."

"It's too risky," Kevin whispered. "I've never tried maneuvering one this close before. I could get us both killed."

"I know that, but your chances of pulling this off are better if I'm there, and you know it. You need my eyes and ears," Chris whispered back.

"All right, but let's get everyone else out of the way," Kevin sighed. Then he spoke up loud enough for the others to hear him. "Chris is going to have to stay here and help me, but I want the rest of you out of harm's way so that I don't have to try to cover you, too. Karl, how far do you think you can travel by daybreak? Can you get ten miles?"

"I don't know. It's pretty dark out here, but the road seems to be fairly decent. If we don't drop a wheel in a hole we should be able to get about eight anyway," Karl answered. "At any rate, we'll do the best we can, and we'll stay on this road, wherever it's heading."

"As long as it's going away from those bounty hunters, it's heading in the right direction," Steve mumbled as he climbed up to the seat of the old minstrel wagon and picked up the reins.

Kevin and Chris watched as the wagons started moving down the road, led by Karl and shadowed by Darrell. As Darrell rode by, he saluted Kevin and whispered, "We'll be expecting you shortly after sunrise. If you don't show, we'll be back for you."

"No," Kevin whispered back. "If we don't join you, it's because we're dead. Keep going. Get to Milhaven. Let them know what happened."

Darrell shook his head and whispered back over his shoulder as he rode on down the road, "If you don't show, we'll be back."

After the wagons faded into the night, Kevin lifted himself, Chris, and the debris, and floated them back to the south side of the river to their campsite. Chris scattered the various bits that would serve as evidence of their destruction around the campsite. He wasn't sure why he was doing that, since Kevin's tornado would probably scatter them even farther, but it was something to do while he waited for dawn.

Kevin kept his seeing eye trained on the bounty hunters, watching for any signs of an early morning attack. About the time that the sky began to lighten in the east, the bounty hunters began to move around and pack up. Kevin scanned the overcast sky for a heavy cloud that would be easy to stir up, and found one not too far away to the west. He and Chris ducked behind a small grove of trees and he began to stir up the wind and lightening. Before long, he had a nice thunderhead growing.

The approaching storm spurred the bounty hunters into action, so Kevin took one last quick look around, warned Chris that the bounty hunters were on the move, and gave himself over to creating the tornado.

Chris unsheathed his sword and circled around so that he was within an arm's reach of Kevin but between him and the old campsite. He stared at the woods, watching for anything that moved as he listened to the distinctive roar of the approaching storm. He didn't have to look up at the sky to know that the funnel was forming; he could hear all about it from the screams of the bounty hunters as they tried to mount their frightened horses and ride out of the path of the tornado. After a few minutes, the only sound Chris could hear was the roar of the storm.

Chris knew that Kevin was in the middle of it mentally, and he couldn't help but wonder just how close they were to being in the middle of it physically. As he listened, the roar seemed to level off for a couple of minutes and a dark wind, thick with dirt and forest debris, swept through their old campsite, but it was only a wind, not a tornado.

After the noise from the tornado died out and the wind passed, Kevin grinned and said, "You should have seen them run. They'll be miles from here before they even slow down."

"What happened? Where's the tornado," Chris asked with a frown. "I thought you were going to hit the camp site so that it would look destroyed."

"Take a look. See what you think."

Chris stepped out from behind the bushes where they had been standing and looked around. Trees along a path about a hundred yards long had been uprooted and tossed around like kindling. Most of the debris Chris had scattered was pinned under fallen trees and half covered by dirt and leaves.

Kevin asked, "Do you think it looks like a tornado hit it?"

"What do you mean, 'looks like'?"

"Well, I sort of danced the funnel around and then sent it back up right before it got here. I didn't want to take the chance of a tree coming down on top of us while I was off in the clouds. After I had the funnel back up in the cloud, I stirred up a good dirty wind down here so no one could see me uproot the trees and set the scene."

"You did all of this?"

"Yeah, do you think it looks all right?"

Chris looked around again and nodded. "It really does look like the tornado went through here." Then he looked at Kevin and asked, "Are you about ready to get out of here? I'm not as sure as you are that those guys are miles away. Now that the storm is gone, they'll start heading back."

"Okay, but what are we going to use as a diversion so that I can lift us up over those trees without being seen?" After a moment, Kevin said, "I know what I'll do," and snow flakes began to fall.

"You're making history with this weather you know. A tornado in January? Followed by a snowstorm?"

"Not just a snow storm, Chris. There's a lot of moisture up there, and the temperature's cold enough. Let me see if I can't stir up a little blizzard out of this," Kevin said as he focused on the clouds again. A few minutes later, the snow was coming down so heavy and fast that it created a whiteout. Kevin lifted himself and Chris and quickly floated them across the river, over the trees on the other side, and down the road after the wagons. The snowstorm followed them until Kevin had the wagons in sight. Then he let the wind slack off and the snow settled down to a gentle flurry.

As they joined the others, Karl nodded and said, "There won't be any sign that we were on the road on the north side of the river now that it's covered in snow. Nice touch."

After Steve handed the old minstrel wagon back over to Kevin and he and Chris mounted their horses, Karl said, "Okay, let's see how much distance we can put between ourselves and those bounty hunters by nightfall," and turned his horse to head on down the road.

~ ~ ~ ~

Over the next few hours, while the Tellurians headed east on the north side of Pooley River, the bounty hunters, led by the bandit from Billows, returned to search along the tornado's path. After a grueling morning of digging through the snow that had been dumped on the area behind the tornado, they gathered in the middle of what had been the Tellurians' campsite with the debris that they had found. Even though none of them had found a body, they all agreed that there was no way any of the people in that campsite could have survived.

As he rode back to town with the rest of the posse, the bandit from Billows cursed the deaths of the minstrels and the loss of the bounty money. Fate was definitely against him where those minstrels were concerned. Both times that he'd tangled with them, he'd lost. His only consolation was that fate had dealt them a far worse hand.

While he was brushing down his horse, he realized that he might still be able to turn a profit off the adventure, so he decided to pack up that afternoon and head out. If he was the first person to reach an officer in Brendolanth and report the death of the minstrels, Rolan might reward him for the news.

When he reached Billows late Saturday afternoon, he went straight to the town director's inn and told him that he had spotted the minstrels while he was in Nandelia. "They didn't look like minstrels anymore though. They looked more like farmers than anything else. Even their wagon had been disguised, but they weren't smart enough to fool me, no, sir. You've got to get up pretty early in the morning to pull the wool over my eyes."

"Where are they now?" the director asked.

"I knew you'd want to know where they were headed, so I got a couple of guys to help me follow them. After all, it was just me, and they're all armed to the teeth."

"And they're in …" the director prompted.

"We didn't catch up with them the first night. It took us a while to get things together and get out of town, and we didn't want to get ahead of them, so we pulled up when it got dark and made camp. The next afternoon, we found where they pulled their wagons off the road and headed into the woods. Now the woods right there weren't all that big, so we set up three camps. Between us and the river, we had them trapped, so we settled down for the night, planning to attack at first light."

The director nodded. "Reasonable. So, did you turn them over to the district captain down there or did you bring them back here?"

"Well, the weirdest thing happened. Right as we were breaking camp at daybreak, a big storm blew up and the next thing we knew, this huge tornado dropped down out of the sky headed straight for us. We had to get out of there fast. Then, after the storm had passed, we rode into the woods to see what had happened to them. We found their campsite. Looked like they took a direct hit. The whole area was leveled, trees down, everything just plain gone. We did find a few things, some clothes, kitchen stuff, things like that, but all the people, horses, and wagons had been swept away. That big ol' tornado just scooped them up and swallowed them."

"Are you telling me that the minstrels are dead?" the director asked.

"Yes, sir, that's exactly what I'm telling you. Thought you might want to let Rolan know so he can call off the hunt."

The director's face paled a little, but he nodded and said, "Yes, I'll do that, and I'll see that you get all the credit you deserve for your efforts."

"Thank you, sir. Well, I guess I'd best be getting on home now," the bandit said.

When the bandit got home, he told his wife about the minstrels, the chase, the tornado, and his meeting with the director. "I wouldn't be surprised if I got some kind of reward from Rolan when he hears about this," he bragged to his wife.

Instead of the praise he was expecting, she glared at him and yelled, "I don't believe this! How could you be so stupid?"

"What?" he asked dumbfounded.

"Rolan's going to blame you!"

"For what?!" he asked with a deep frown.

"If you hadn't decided to wait around until daylight to attack, you'd have had them. Soldiers would be escorting them to Trendon right now, but no, you waited because you didn't want to risk attacking at night, and now they're dead. He'll never get to question them and he's going to blame you!" The whole time she was ranting she was pulling things out of the kitchen cabinets. "Bring the wagon around to the back door. Hurry!"

"Why?" he asked as he slowly got up from his chair.

"We're leaving."

"Leaving? What are you talking about?"

"Leaving here. At least the children and I are. You can do whatever you want, but I want to be out of here before Rolan decides to take it out on us that you lost those minstrels. You mark my words. When he hears about this, he's going to send someone out here to get us, and I plan to be long gone before then, long gone, hopefully out of Brendolanth. Now move!"

Chapter 47

More Surprises

Before daybreak Saturday morning, Kevin floated the wagons and horses back across the Pooley River. According to their map, there was a small road that headed east when the main road followed the river as it turned north. By taking the small road, they could cut across the plains, and reach the Sandover River by Wednesday, saving themselves a couple of days.

Around mid-afternoon they came to the eastbound road and left the river for the first time in nearly two weeks. After a couple of miles, the road became little more than a narrow track through the prairie. There was no sign of any farmhouses or towns for as far as they could see, and since the only thing around them was prairie grass, they could see for quite a distance. By the time they set up camp Sunday evening, they were beginning to feel like they were the only people on the whole planet. They hadn't seen another living soul for well over twenty-four hours. It was getting a little spooky.

Kevin and Chris had the third watch Sunday night, and shortly after they got up at 3:00, they heard Glendymere's voice in their heads. *"You've made good time. Where do you want your supplies? Next to the fire or closer to the wagons?"*

"Close to the wagons. We won't sort them until after daybreak," Kevin said.

Glendymere lowered the supplies to the ground slowly, more slowly than the contents of the bundles warranted. *"Any particular reason you decided to cut through Davenglen? Most humans tend to avoid the gnomes."*

"Gnomes?" Chris asked. "What are you talking about?"

"You know, short little people, maybe come up to your knees. The ones who live in this area. Didn't you know you were traveling through their lands?"

"No, we had no idea. Are they dangerous?" Kevin asked as he nervously looked around to see if he could see anyone in the tall grasses surrounding their campsite.

Glendymere snorted a laugh and said, *"Only to your supplies. Gnomes are basically thieves, although they don't mean any harm. They take whatever appeals to them, but usually just small things, pretty things. Are any of you missing anything?"*

"Well, now that you mention it, I couldn't find the belt that Ashni made for me when I got dressed this morning, and I know I had it on yesterday. And I heard Joan say something about losing her headband and a big potholder. Is that the type of stuff they would take?" Kevin asked.

"Sounds just like them. Cute little things actually. I didn't land because I was afraid I'd hurt one of them. You can't see them unless they want to be seen."

"Are there any around us?" Chris asked.

"Count on it. They live underground and travel from one section of Davenglen to another through tunnels. They could come into your camp and steal half of what you've got without you ever knowing that they're there. They're good at that."

"They must be if they took my belt. It was in our tent, and we had someone on watch all night long," Kevin said, still looking around to see if he could spot a gnome.

"Well, if I were you, I'd get through Davenglen as quickly as possible," Glendymere said with a laugh.

"How far does Davenglen go? When will we be out?" Chris asked.

"You'll be out by the time you reach the Sandover River. People who live around here could show you exactly where Davenglen ends. A small stream marks the boundary, but I doubt you'll notice it, so assume you're still in Davenglen until you cross the river," Glendymere answered. *"Now, tell me about your trip. Anything exciting happen?"*

While Kevin told Glendymere about the bandit from Billows, Chris walked around the campsite, looking for any sign that anything had been disturbed. He climbed up in the back of each of the wagons, checking every place where a gnome might hide. When he had satisfied himself that there were no gnomes in the wagons, he circled around the tarps, looking for anything unusual. He finished his inspection about the same time that Kevin finished telling Glendymere about their trip.

"Don't give up, Chris. I guarantee you that you're being watched and studied as we speak, and I would be willing to bet that before daybreak, something will be lifted from your campsite, if it hasn't already. It's just a game to them so don't do anything rash, like hurt one of the little fellows. They can get mean if they feel threatened."

"I thought you said we weren't in any danger from them," Kevin said.

"You aren't, as long as you don't hurt one of them. Well, I'd better head back. See you in a couple of weeks."

The next morning, Kevin and Chris told the others about the gnomes while they were eating breakfast. Theresa and Joan made a quick inventory of the kitchen supplies and herbs, Karl and Steve checked the furniture and tack for the horses, and Darrell checked the spare weapons. They found a few things missing, but the missing items were all small and relatively unimportant as far as their survival was concerned.

"The best thing we can do at this point is load up and try to get to the Sandover River as quickly as possible," Karl said after they finished the search.

"I wonder if there was something on the map that we missed," Steve said. He took out the map, spread it out on the ground, and looked at it carefully. There was no area called Davenglen, but there was a black dot where the eastbound road began. "I wonder if this dot here means anything. See? Here's another dot near the Sandover River, about where our road should end. I wish I knew what the dots mean. They could mean gnomes, proceed at your own risk, danger ahead, or stay out of here at all costs. Next time it could be a lot worse," Steve said as he pointed out the little marks.

"I saw those marks, but I thought they were specks of dirt, so I didn't worry about them," Karl said. "Why didn't Kalen warn us about things like that?"

"Probably because it never crossed his mind that we wouldn't know," Steve said with a sigh. Then he folded the map up and put it back in his cloak pocket.

"You're probably right," Joan said. "This isn't one of those things that he neglected to mention because he thought it would make us revolt, like slavery or dragons. This is relatively minor, all things considered."

"Well, if nothing else, it's a good reminder that we're in a strange place, surrounded by strange things," Chris said.

"It's easy to forget how different this world is," Joan commented.

"We just spent eight months living with giants and a dragon. I wouldn't call that exactly normal," Karl said with a snort of laughter as he put his arm around his wife and hugged her. "But you're right, Chris. We really don't know what else might be out there. We need to be careful." Then he mounted his horse and said, "Let's get moving."

~ ~ ~ ~

Monday and Tuesday nights the gnomes grabbed a few more incidentals, but none of the Tellurians caught a glimpse of them, although they were all even more vigilant than usual. It was a relief to reach the Sandover River Wednesday morning.

They crossed the river on a ferry, and traveled south along the river until late afternoon. Although they were still in grasslands, there were a few patches of woods scattered along the riverbanks, and they found an oval-shaped clearing surrounded by pine trees that looked like it had frequently been used as a campsite. There was enough room to set up a small corral for the horses in the north end of the oval, park the wagons around the fire pit in the south end, and set up their sleeping tarps in the middle. They finally managed to spend two nights in one campsite, giving the horses a much needed break.

The weather had been fairly good for the middle of the winter. They had run into a few snow showers, but the only significant snow was the one that Kevin had stirred up to cover their tracks. But a week after they crossed the Sandover River, the weather took a turn for the worse. That Wednesday a blast of frigid air out of the north plummeted temperatures. The harsh northwest wind buffeted them all day and shook the walls of the inn and stable they stayed in that night.

Thursday morning a mass of humid air from the south overrode the cold, giving them dark overcast skies, and around lunchtime the snow started to fall. By mid-afternoon it was so heavy that the wagons were beginning to bog down in the drifts. They needed to find shelter and wait out the storm, but the best the prairie had to offer was a small grove of leafless hardwood trees. They stopped on the edge of the grove to figure out what they were going to do.

"Kevin, can't you do anything about this storm?" Theresa asked.

"Not really. The system's too big. The best I could do is warm it up a little right around us, but a cold rain might be worse than the snow."

"Then our primary concern has to be shelter, and not just for us. I don't know how much more of this weather the horses can stand," Karl said. "I wish we could find some kind of cave, anything to get us out of this wind!"

"People in the prairies used to build their homes below ground." Steve said. "It kept them warm in the winter and cool in the summer."

"You could dig out a hole, couldn't you?" Chris asked Kevin.

"We could give it a try. I don't think I want to try digging a big hole right here under the trees though. Let me try it a little farther out," Kevin said as he wandered away from the others.

After a few minutes, he found an area that he thought might be pretty good. There was already a small dip in the ground, so it gave him a starting point. He made his outstretched hand as large as the shovel on a bulldozer. Then he decided that it was too small for the job and made it even bigger. He dug down into the ground, lifted out the dirt and piled it off to the side. After he had a hole about twelve feet deep, fifty feet long and six feet wide, he scooped dirt out along the side, leaving a three-foot thick overhang at the top. Every ten feet or so, he stopped, leaving a column of dirt to support the roof. When he was done, he'd made four separate rooms about 10 feet long, 10 feet wide, and nine feet high. Then he went back and packed the dirt in the roof, checking for weak spots. Next, he firmed up the sides of the hole by packing the dirt around the walls. Then he used the dirt he'd scooped out of the hole to build a windbreak around the sides. It reminded him of playing in a sandbox when he was a child.

When he had the hole finished he stood back and looked at it. There was no way to get down into it, so he scooped out a ramp at one end of the hole. While he had been working, the others had gathered around to watch.

"That should do the trick," Karl said. "Good work, Kevin"

"Having a sorcerer along definitely helps," Darrell said with a nod. "Now, let's get the horses out of this wind."

322

Karl, Steve and Darrell unhitched the horses and led them down the ramp and into three of the rooms. While Karl set out fresh hay and filled some feed buckets with oats, Steve and Darrell tied heavy blankets around the horses, and Kevin filled some buckets with snow, melted it down to water, and set them around the sides of the makeshift barn. Meanwhile, Chris unpacked the bedrolls and tarps while Joan and Theresa grabbed some food and kitchen supplies.

By the time the horses were settled, the tarps were set up in the fourth room, and dinner was ready. Kevin heated the air in the hole to a more tolerable temperature and everyone sat down on the ground to eat.

"These sandwiches are good, but I sure would love a cup of coffee," Steve said.

"I'm sorry, I didn't even think of that," Kevin said as he stood up and gathered a few rocks from the floor of the hole. "Joan if you would get the pot ready, I'll have a stove for you in just a minute."

Joan had the coffee pot ready by the time Kevin had the stones stacked into a small cube. Then Kevin heated the rocks and soon coffee was bubbling away inside the pot.

The next morning, they woke up to sunshine. The wind had died down during the night and the temperature was a little warmer. They loaded the wagons, hitched the horses, and then Kevin swept the dirt back into the hole and packed it down. The dip in the ground was more pronounced than it had been before, and there was a bare spot in the prairie, but those were the only signs of their shelter.

They continued following the Sandover River, and around the middle of the morning on the last Saturday in February they pulled into Glenarbour. Their road followed the Sandover River as it wound its way through the center of Glenarbour to the eastern edge of town, where the Sandover flowed into the Kivee River. All along the Sandover, ferries carried people, horses, and carriages from one side of town to the other.

At the bend where their road turned south to follow the Kivee River, there was a large livery stable that rented horses, wagons, and carriages, as well as boarded horses and wagons for the many travelers who passed through the town. As they headed south, they saw four inns, several dry goods stores, a cobbler's shop, a tailor's shop, a couple of farmers markets, five or six restaurants, and half a dozen taverns. All of the taverns advertised evening entertainment as well as cheap rooms. The sidewalks were crowded with humans, elves, dwarves, and a lot of other people who didn't seem to fall into any of the three racial categories that the Tellurians had met so far.

Houses lined all of the side streets. Streets that led off to the west seemed to end shortly after the last house, but the streets that led to the east dead-ended on an alley that ran beside the Kivee River. The alley looked like it was mainly for the oxen that pulled barges up and down the river.

Every once in a while the Tellurians caught a glimpse of the docks. Some of them were fairly small with fishing boats tied up to them while others were large enough for loading and unloading barges, but no matter how large or small the dock, water troughs and bales of hay were stacked on shore near the edge of the dock for the oxen.

The main road curved towards the east at the end of town, passed a second livery stable, and dead-ended at the ferry park. The Tellurians considered spending the night in Glenarbour, just for the novelty of staying there, but they decided that since it was so early in the day, it would be better to continue on their way. They pulled the wagons and horses in line for the next ferry, and two hours later, shortly after noon, they crossed the Kivee River into Camden.

Chapter 48

Milhaven

After they crossed the Kivee River, grasslands and gentle slopes gave way to forests and rolling hills. At first, especially while they were in the towns, Kevin was concerned that someone might notice his resemblance to Yvonne and figure out who he was, but no one seemed to give him a second glance.

The days got longer and the temperatures gradually rose, but most of the nights were still near freezing. As the days went by, the rolling hills got steeper, and by the second week of March, the hills had become small mountains. Friday morning, as they crested one of the mountains, they saw a squad of soldiers waiting by the roadside.

Karl pulled back beside Darrell and asked, "What do you think?"

"I don't know. Do you think they're Rolan's men?"

"They shouldn't be. We're getting close to Milhaven," Karl said, as he loosened his sword in its sheath. Then he and Darrell rode back to the front.

One of the soldiers rode towards Karl while the others waited. When he was about ten feet away, he stopped and said, "Good morning. My name is Captain Lawrence. I'm Captain of the Guard. I'd like to welcome you to Camden, and to Milhaven. Laryn sends her greetings and regrets that she could not be here personally to greet you."

Karl introduced himself, and then began introducing the others. When he came to Kevin, he wasn't sure whether he should call him Kevin or Myron, so he hesitated for a second.

Kevin sensed the problem and took over. "Captain Lawrence, I'm Myron, of the House of Nordin. Thank you for meeting us."

"My privilege, sir," Captain Lawrence said as he saluted Kevin. "Sir, I need to know how you want to do this."

"How I want to do what?" Kevin asked.

"The people of Milhaven and all of Camden have been anxiously awaiting your arrival. They know that you should be arriving within the next couple of weeks, but they have no idea that you're here. Do you want to ride through Milhaven quietly, go on to the castle, and get settled before making your presence known, or would you like for us to announce your arrival and let the people of Milhaven cheer you through town."

"I'd like to arrive at the castle as quietly as possible. I want to talk with Laryn and see my father before doing anything else."

"Very well, sir. I'll send my men on ahead to let Laryn know that we'll be arriving shortly." Captain Lawrence rode back to his men, gave them their orders, sent them on their way, and returned to lead the Tellurians through Milhaven.

As they approached the town, they passed a few houses and then reached a crossroad that ran north and south. Just like a lot of the other towns that they had ridden through, the little crossroad was lined with houses and seemed to end at the last house. After the crossroad came the business section. An inn, a tavern, a large farmer's market, and a dry goods store were on the northern side of the village square while a stable, a Chapel of Light, and a second inn lined the southern side. After the village square, there was a second crossroad with several houses on the northern end, but the southern end led through trees and gardens to a beautiful mansion. Kevin would have known that it was the governor's house even if Tyree hadn't told them about it.

After the crossroad, there were a few houses scattered along the road for about a quarter of a mile and then the forest closed back in. A half-mile farther down the road there was a long barracks on the left and a large house on the right. Although the general's house was not as large as the governor's, it was impressive.

The forest closed back in on the road for a little ways, and then opened up on the left for the guard headquarters and barracks. Shortly after they passed the guards' quarters, they saw the castle and courtyard. The gray stone castle looked cold and formidable, but the colorful gardens in the courtyard softened the overall appearance and added a warm and hospitable touch.

Captain Lawrence dropped back beside Kevin and asked," Would you like to stop at the front entrance, sir? We could hand the horses and wagons over to the staff and let them take care of them. Or, if you prefer, we can ride on to the stables around back."

"We'd rather ride on to the stables."

Captain Lawrence nodded and rode back up to the front next to Karl. He led the group around the kitchen, beside the dining room, and on to the stables in the back. As soon as they entered the stable yard, several young men walked up to take the horses and drive the wagons into the barns.

Captain Lawrence spoke for a few minutes with an older man and then returned to Kevin's wagon. "Sir, I told them not to unload any of the wagons, but to wait for your specific instructions. I assume that you want all of the horses brushed down and settled in stalls. Is there anything else?"

"No, that's fine. Thank you," Kevin said as he climbed down from the wagon seat. "Now, I'd like to see Laryn, if that's possible."

"Of course, sir. Will your companions be joining you or would you like for them to be shown to their rooms?" Captain Lawrence asked. "We have their rooms ready."

"They'll be coming with me," Kevin answered as he signaled for the rest of the Tellurians to follow him.

Captain Lawrence led them across a wide patio and through a large double door that opened into the dining room. Although they were familiar with the layout of the castle, they were not ready for the simple elegance of the furnishings. The tables and chairs were made of polished oak, as were the cabinets that lined the walls between the windows and doors.

The main dining table was at least twenty-five feet long and four feet wide with ten chairs on each side and one at each end, and all of the chairs had embroidered seat cushions and wide arm rests. There were three separate sitting areas, each furnished with a couple of couches, several large armchairs, a long coffee table, and a few small lamp tables. Several square tables with four chairs around them were scattered between the sitting areas.

Two sets of double doors opened onto the large patio area at the back of the castle, and a door in the south wall opened onto a smaller patio facing the vegetable gardens. Large windows gave the room an airy and spacious look, and Kevin could easily picture a couple of hundred people eating in there.

They left the dining room and went down the hall between the groundskeeper's and the housekeeper's offices. When they stepped into the entrance hall, the first thing they noticed were the two guards stationed at each of the three doors leading into the hall, including the one they had just come through. Although the guards acknowledged Captain Lawrence with brief nods, they eyed his guests with caution.

The floor of the entrance hall was so highly polished that it reflected the beams that supported the ceiling. There were a few clusters of two armchairs on either side of a small lamp table scattered about the room, but other than those, and a few paintings on the walls, the vast foyer was empty, and the echo of their footsteps made the entrance hall seem even more imposing.

As they approached the door that led to the government offices, one of the guards stepped up to open it. Captain Lawrence led them down the hall to the first door on the right, a wide double door of heavy oak. He knocked three times and waited. The guard standing beside the door saluted him but did not acknowledge his companions or make any move to open the door.

When one of Laryn's pages opened the door, Captain Lawrence stepped inside and said, "Would you please inform Laryn that I have returned with our guests?"

As Captain Lawrence led the Tellurians into the reception area, the page turned to go get Laryn, but before he could knock on the door to the inner office, Laryn opened it and walked through. At first glance, the Tellurians thought she was one of the pages. She was shorter than Kevin, slim, and had shoulder length brown hair that fell around her face in a pageboy style. There were no signs of age around her mouth or eyes, but she carried herself with a confidence far beyond the teenage years.

"I thought I heard your voice," Laryn said as she smiled at Captain Lawrence. "Thank you for escorting them, Captain." Then she turned to the pages and said, "I'm going to be busy for a little while. Why don't all of you take a break?"

She waited until Captain Lawrence and the pages had left the room, and then she walked straight towards Kevin. "Welcome home, Myron. I wish I could have been at Kalen's to welcome you and your companions to Terah, but circumstances didn't permit it. I hope you've had a pleasant journey."

Kevin thanked her and then introduced the rest of the Tellurians. After a few minutes of polite conversation about the weather, the onset of spring, and the lovely countryside around Milhaven, Laryn suggested that they go back to the dining room for some refreshments. "I'm sure someone's alerted the kitchen staff that you've arrived. They'll have some refreshments ready for you by now."

On the way to the dining room, Laryn turned to Kevin and said, "There's a lot we need to discuss, but first I'd like to get all of you settled in your rooms." Then she told Kevin that the staff had prepared two rooms in the family quarters and five rooms in the guest quarters.

"We won't need quite that many," Kevin said. "Karl and Joan are married."

"I know. Kalen sent me a little information about each of your companions. I asked housekeeping to prepare five rooms in case you needed a couple of days to select your assistant," Laryn explained.

"Oh. I've asked Chris to be my assistant. He was my assistant while I worked with Glendymere. I don't know how long he'll be willing to do it, but he's agreed to do it at least until after the first council meeting."

"That's fine," Laryn said as she stopped by the door of the housekeeping office. "Why don't you and your companions go on to the dining room? I need to stop in here for just a minute and then I'll join you."

When they reached the dining room, the large table was spread with sandwiches, fruit, small cakes, tarts, cookies, cheese, bread, a pot of coffee, and pitchers of milk, water, and scog. While the Tellurians ate, they quietly talked about Milhaven, the castle, the guards, Captain Lawrence, Laryn, and how out of place they felt.

As soon as they set down their silverware and leaned back from the table, everything except the mugs and drinks were quickly whisked away by the kitchen staff. Then, a few minutes later, Captain Lawrence and Laryn entered the dining room together.

"I hope you enjoyed your lunch," Laryn began. "Now, if you're ready, we'd like to show you to your rooms."

"If it wouldn't be too much trouble, could we please get some hot water?" Joan asked. "I'd really like to wash some of the dust off."

"And I would like to shave," Karl added as the other men nodded.

"That would be no problem at all," Laryn said with a smile.

"I'll ask housekeeping to prepare baths for all of you," Captain Lawrence said, and then he left the dining room.

While he was gone, Laryn said, "Please let us know if there is anything we can do to make your rooms more comfortable. If you need anything, anything at all, just ask someone from housekeeping. And if there are any problems, please let me know. We want you to be comfortable here and to consider this your home."

When Captain Lawrence returned, Laryn said, "Now, we'll show you to your rooms. Myron, if you and Chris would come with me, please."

Kevin nodded and he and Chris stood up to follow Laryn. Then she turned to the others and said, "Captain Lawrence will show you to your rooms as soon as you're ready to go up. I'll see you at dinner."

When they reached the family quarters, Laryn pointed out her room and Badec's room and then she led them around the corner to the rooms that had been prepared for them.

As soon as Chris saw which rooms were theirs, he said, "If you don't need me for anything right now, I'll go down and get some of our things." Kevin nodded, so Chris headed back towards the stairs.

"I'd like to ask you a question," Kevin said as soon as he and Laryn were alone.

Laryn nodded.

"How did you know when we'd get here? We didn't know for sure ourselves."

"About ten days ago, Glendymere sent me a message telling me where you were, so I was fairly sure that you'd arrive either today or tomorrow. This morning I asked Freddy to fly down the road and see if he could find out where you were. When he told me how close you were, I sent Captain Lawrence out to meet you," Laryn replied. Then she added, "Why? Was there a problem?"

"No, nothing like that. I just wondered how you knew," Kevin said. "I didn't think anyone had recognized me, but when Captain Lawrence was there to meet us, and obviously knew who we were …"

Laryn shook her head no. "The only reason he knew who you were is that I told him. He doesn't know anything about the others except that they're your companions."

Kevin nodded and said, "I'd like to see my father now if that's possible."

Laryn led the way to Badec's room. As Kevin entered the room, he saw a man lying on a large bed in the center of the room and a middle-aged woman standing by his bedside.

"Myron, this is Sister Agnes. She's been tending to your father since he became ill a year ago," Laryn said.

Sister Agnes nodded and whispered, "We've kept him alive, but it's a losing battle. We'll feed him and care for him as long as there's a breath in his body, but I really don't know how he's hanging on."

"Have you figured out what happened?" Kevin asked quietly.

Sister Agnes looked at Laryn, who was standing behind Kevin. Laryn shook her head, so Sister Agnes shrugged and said, "No, not really. We know that he wasn't injured, wasn't sick, didn't have a heart attack or a stroke, but as to exactly what happened …" Sister Agnes shrugged again.

"I'd like to sit with him for a bit," Kevin said as he reached out and touched his father's hand. He knew that coma patients tended to waste away, but he was surprised at just how frail and fragile the man looked. Then he turned to Laryn and asked, "Is there anything I need to do right now?"

"No. General Crandal, Governor Wrenn, and his wife, Jana, will join us for dinner tonight. I might as well tell you that Governor Wrenn was planning to retire last year. He'd already asked Badec to find a new governor and Badec had agreed, but he got sick before he could do it. Wrenn probably won't bring it up this evening, but he'll want you to name someone as quickly as you can, so you might want to think about it. You can't actually do anything until you become the Sorcerer of Camden, but that will happen on the sixth of April if not before."

"What's happening on the sixth of April?"

"The day of the next council meeting. You'll have to assume your father's chair at that time, and that will make it official," Laryn answered. Then she and Sister Agnes quietly left the room.

~ ~ ~ ~

After dinner that night, when Kevin and Chris went up to Kevin's room, he told Chris what Laryn had said about naming a governor as soon as possible.

"Have you made up your mind between Karl and Steve?" Chris asked.

"I really want Steve concentrating on the slavery thing with Tyree, and I want him free to give me crash courses in economics, politics, and everything else I never thought I'd need to know."

Chris nodded. "Karl will make a good governor. He's down to earth and practical, and he's a natural leader."

"Do you think he'll agree to do it?"

"I don't know. When are you going to ask him?"

"I don't know when the appropriate time will be, but soon. I need to talk to Laryn about that," Kevin answered. "What do you think of Captain Lawrence?"

"I like him. Are you sure we can't keep him on as Captain of the Guard?"

"Yes. After dinner, General Crandal asked when I was going to name someone else to that position. I told him that it wasn't my guard and I don't have the authority to name a captain. He agreed, but then he said that I'd have to take over soon."

"Any particular reason he's interested in whom you name as captain?" Chris asked.

"His aide has requested a position as a district captain and one of his captains wants to retire. So General Crandal is hoping that Captain Lawrence will agree to be his new aide. Then he can let his aide take over for the captain that wants to retire."

"Are you thinking about Darrell for that position?"

Kevin nodded. "What do you think?"

"I think he could do it, but he's going to need some help getting set up and organized," Chris answered.

"I was thinking I might ask General Crandal to hold off making any changes for a couple of months so Captain Lawrence could help Darrell get started."

"If Captain Lawrence is in the guard office, he'll be the captain, no matter who has the title, and that would undermine Darrell's authority. You don't want to do that."

"You're right," Kevin said.

"Maybe Captain Lawrence would agree to be available for advice for a while."

Kevin nodded. "I'll talk to Laryn tomorrow and see what the proper protocol is for all of this. I don't want to say anything to Karl or Darrell until I know it's okay. We don't want to seem over-anxious."

~ ~ ~ ~

Sometime during the night, a soft light that slowly grew in intensity woke Kevin out of a sound sleep. When he finally shook off the last remnants of sleep, he realized that Yvonne was standing near his bed.

"Mother?"

Yvonne nodded. "I'm so glad you're finally here, Myron. It's been a long journey. One that began many years ago."

"I feel like it's just beginning," Kevin answered, yawning.

"Yes, in a way, you're right. This is a beginning. That's what I wanted to speak with you about. Before you can begin, Badec must end, and you need to help him."

328

"What do you mean?"

"For the past year, the only thing that has kept him alive has been his determination to live until you arrived."

"Is he hoping to wake up, to see me, talk to me?" Kevin asked.

"No, he knows he'll never wake up again. He's hung on to life this long trying to give you as much time to get ready as he could, but it's time for him to let go now."

"Exactly what are you asking me to do?"

"You have to let him know that you're here and that you're ready to take over, that he's held on long enough, that he can let go of life."

"You mean you want me to tell him to die?" Kevin was aghast at the idea.

"I want you to let him know that it's all right for him to die, that he can stop fighting so very hard to cling to life," Yvonne said quietly.

"Wouldn't you stand a better chance of talking to him? I mean, he doesn't even know my voice or anything."

"He's so far gone that no one else can reach him. Laryn sits by his side talking to him every night. She has told him every day for the past month that you're ready, that Glendymere says that your power is strong, that you're on your way here, and that he can let go. But he can't hear her anymore. I've tried to reach him, but he resists me. He senses that if he reaches out to me, he'll lose his last hold on life. You're going to have to let your power reach out to the power in him. He'll know your essence. He'll know it's you, he'll feel your strength, and then when you release him, he'll be able to let go."

"I'll try. That's all I can promise," Kevin said slowly.

"That's all I ask." Yvonne began to fade away. "I must go now but I'll return soon. Be well, my son."

"Good-bye, Mother," Kevin whispered as the room became dark again.

~ ~ ~ ~

Before daybreak Saturday morning, Kevin went to Badec's room. He pulled up a chair and sat down beside his father's bed, took his hand, and talked to him. He talked of his childhood on Earth, his foster parents, his Uncle Paul with the funny ears, his college years, and the jobs he had held. Then he told his father about the tornado that Paul had created, the other passengers on the bus, the time at the Gate House, the journey to Rainbow Valley, Blalick and his family, meeting Yvonne, and his training with Glendymere.

Since Kevin was with his father when Sister Agnes arrived that morning, she asked the guard to have one of the household staff find her a comfortable chair and put it outside Badec's door. Normally, she sat with Badec during the day. She handled his bath, worked with his joints, exercised his muscles, and fed him through a hollow reed, but all of her herbs and care had not been able to halt the inevitable. Now, she prayed for his release.

Sister Agnes came in several times that day to check on her patient, to wipe his forehead and arms, and to add some wood to the fire in the fireplace. Laryn came in for a few moments around lunchtime, stroked her brother's forehead, kissed his cheek, and left. After Laryn left, Sister Agnes opened the door to ask Kevin if he would like some lunch. Kevin thanked her, but declined the offer, so she told Kevin that she'd be right outside the door if he needed anything.

Kevin talked to his father most of the afternoon. He thanked him for making arrangements for him to learn how to use his magical powers, and he spoke of his plans to carry on with Badec's work. He told his father that his only regret was that he had not arrived in time to get to know him, that he would have liked that, but he understood the constant struggle that Badec was engaged in just to survive another day, and that the need to rest must be overpowering. Kevin told his father that he was home now, ready to carry on, and he told Badec that it was time for him to get some well-deserved rest.

Then he just sat quietly by Badec's bed, holding his father's frail hand between his strong ones, watching Badec's chest rise and fall as the breaths became shallow and slow. He noticed that the fire in the red opal that rested on Badec's chest was growing dimmer.

As the sunlight faded from the mountaintops and darkness settled over the valley, Kevin saw an orb of blue-white light slowly take form on the other side of Badec's bed. As it floated near Badec's shoulder, the light grew stronger and stronger. A few minutes later, Kevin saw a second orb of light take form over Badec's chest.

As the light in the orb grew stronger, Badec's breaths slowed and became weaker, and the light in the red opal began to flicker. With a final sigh, Badec surrendered his hold on life and both orbs began to slowly rise and drift towards the balcony as the light in the red opal died. Right before the orbs disappeared Kevin felt more than heard his mother say, "Thank you, my son."

Kevin opened the bedroom door and told Sister Agnes that Badec was gone. As she entered the room to tend to Badec's body, Kevin asked the guard who had been waiting with Sister Agnes to find Laryn, let her know that it was over, and tell her that he would be in his room if she needed him.

When Kevin reached his room, he washed his face and stretched out on the bed. A couple of minutes later, there was a knock on his door. When he opened it, Chris was standing in the hall with a large tray in his hands. Chris walked into Kevin's room and set the tray down on a table between the two armchairs. There was a sandwich, a bowl of soup, a fruit plate, and two large mugs of scog.

"Thanks Chris, but I'm really not hungry," Kevin said as he looked at the food.

"I know you don't want to eat, but you have to anyway. You didn't eat breakfast or lunch. You can't afford to get run down or sick right now, so you're going to have to eat dinner. Remember, your health and well-being are my responsibility now."

"It's only one day. I can go without food for one day."

"True, but you'll be weak tomorrow, and tomorrow is going to be a rather busy day." Chris sat down in one of the chairs and picked up one of the mugs of scog. "This food's good by the way. Your cook is almost as good as Joan." Kevin sat down in the other chair and began to eat a little of the soup. "They all said to tell you that they're really sorry that this happened so soon after we got here. They didn't come up with me for two reasons. First of all, we knew you'd be tired and the second reason is that the guard wouldn't have let them."

"We'll have to do something about that. I'll talk to the guard in the morning and explain that they all have free run of the castle."

"I don't know if you should do that, Kevin."

"Why not?"

"The more people that the guards are told to let pass, the less protected the family quarters become. We all feel that the area where you sleep needs to be secure, or at least as secure as we can make it. The grounds under the balcony are patrolled around the clock, a guard is stationed on the roof, and right now, only Laryn, Sister Agnes, and the two of us can get past the guard on the stairs. Maybe it would be best to leave it like that, at least for a while."

Kevin nodded as he continued eating. He was surprised to find that the food did taste good and that he was hungrier than he had thought. After a few minutes, he asked, "What have all of you been doing today?"

"We unpacked the wagons this morning, getting out the things we wanted to keep in our rooms and putting everything else in the castle storerooms. I brought your case up here and put it in the closet. Your clothes are in the chest over there, and your sword is on the floor right under the edge of your bed. I know you don't need it, but I thought you'd like to keep it, and I didn't know where else to put it," Chris said as he got up, picked up the edge of the bed cover and showed Kevin the sword. Then he sat back down and continued, "You wouldn't believe this place, Kevin. It's so well-organized. There are a lot of people on staff, but not as many as you might think considering all the work involved. Everything seems to go like clockwork." Chris reached over and picked up a piece of fruit from Kevin's tray. "Then this afternoon we helped Laryn get the messages ready."

"What messages?" Kevin asked between bites of his sandwich.

"The ones announcing Badec's death. Laryn wasn't sure it would be today, but she felt sure it would be soon. She said that the only reason her brother was still holding on to life was that he was waiting for you to arrive, and that now that you're here, he could go in peace."

"It was peaceful," Kevin said softly. Then he told Chris about Yvonne's visit the night before, the way his father had relaxed during the day as Kevin talked to him, and the two orbs of light at the end. "I'm sure the first orb that appeared was my mother. I wish I could have known them."

"Maybe you'll get to now."

"What do you mean?"

"Your mother's already visited you twice. I bet it won't be that long before your father does, too."

"I hope you're right," Kevin said. Then he turned to the plate of fruit and quickly emptied it.

Just as he finished the last of the fruit, there was another knock at the door and when Chris opened it, Laryn stepped in.

"I just wanted to check on you. Are you all right?" she asked.

"I'm fine, just a bit tired."

"I'm sure you are. We just released the falcons with messages for the district sorcerers, our brothers and sisters, Kalen, Duane, and a few other close friends. I'll take care of the official notifications later."

"What about Glendymere?" Kevin asked.

"Freddy left as soon as Badec died, so Glendymere, Tyree, and Blalick's family will know soon, if they don't already. Now, you need to get some sleep. Do you want Agnes to prepare a sleeping draught for you?"

"No, I'm sure I'll sleep just fine, but aren't there some things that I need to do?"

"Yes, but nothing that can't wait until morning. Sleep now. We'll talk tomorrow," Laryn said as she walked over to the door and opened it. Then she turned back towards Kevin and said, "And thank you, Myron. It was time."

Chapter 49

Duty Calls

Kevin woke up shortly after daybreak Sunday morning. He was dressed and staring out the window, wondering what the day would bring, when he heard a light tap on his door. He opened it to find Chris standing in the hall with a large mug of coffee in each hand.

Chris handed one of the mugs to Kevin as he stepped inside and said, "I thought you'd probably be up by now."

"Thanks," Kevin said as he sipped the hot coffee. "I was thinking about venturing out, but I was putting it off. I have a feeling that this is going to be a busy day once it gets started."

"You're right about that. Laryn and I talked a little after you went to bed," Chris said. "She's asked all of the housekeeping and grounds staff to meet in the dining room at 8:00 this morning. She's going to announce that Badec has passed away, thank them for their services while he was the Sorcerer of Camden, and then introduce you."

"Thank them for their services?" Kevin asked in near panic. "Are they leaving?"

Chris shook his head no. "After she introduces you, you'll thank them for serving your father and say something like 'and I hope you'll be able to stay and help us just as you helped my father.' It's more a formality than anything else, but Laryn says it's important to let them know that you see them as people of free will, not as slaves."

"Of course. I keep forgetting about that."

Chris nodded and continued, "Then you'll need to ask Cryslyn, the Head of Housekeeping, and Neiven, the Head of Grounds, to join us for breakfast."

"All right. You wouldn't happen to know if these people are male or female would you? I can't tell by their names."

"Actually I do. I asked Laryn about Cryslyn. She's a woman about forty-five years old who has lived at the castle most of her life. Her mother was one of the cooks until she married a local farmer and moved away. Cryslyn has worked as a housekeeper, a cook, and the manager of the storeroom. She was named Head of Housekeeping about ten years ago.

"Neiven has lived here off and on since he was in his teens. He first worked as a stable boy. Then he left to apprentice with a dwarf blacksmith somewhere up north. When he came back, he asked Badec to hire him as the castle blacksmith. There never had been one before, but Badec liked the idea, so he set Neiven up in a shop near the stable. One thing led to another, and eventually Badec asked him to supervise all the stable, livestock, and grounds work. He's been doing that for about seven or eight years now."

Kevin shook his head and asked, "You got all of that from Laryn last night?"

"No, she told me about Cryslyn, but I met Neiven while we were unpacking. He told me most of what I just told you, but Laryn was the one who told me that he was in charge of the grounds. Nice guy, easy to talk to. Seems sort of laid-back and easygoing," Chris paused to sip his coffee. "I haven't met Cryslyn, so I can't tell you any more about her."

"Is there any particular reason that I'm inviting them to join us?"

"So that you can tell them that you realize the next week is going to be rough, that you know it will play havoc with their schedules and routines, and that they should feel free to ask for extra help whenever they need it. Again, this is mostly formality." Chris paused and then added, "I imagine a lot of the things that you're going to be doing for a while are going to be 'formality' types of things."

"Also known as politics," Kevin agreed. "What comes after breakfast?"

"Laryn wants to talk to you. From what she said, I think the two of you are going to discuss what will be happening over the next few days and what you'll need to do. That should take most of the morning."

"I want you to be at that meeting too, Chris. And take good notes."

Chris nodded as he picked up the two empty coffee mugs and headed for the door. "It's about time to head down. We don't want to be late for your first speech."

"Have I ever mentioned that I hate public speaking?"

"No, I don't think so," Chris replied with a chuckle. "But something tells me that you're going to get plenty of practice. Come on, let's go."

~ ~ ~ ~

After breakfast, Kevin, Chris, and Laryn went to what was now going to be Kevin's office. As soon as they walked through the door, both of the pages who were there that morning stood up as if awaiting instructions. Laryn shook her head and the two young men sat back down at the table where they had several sheets of paper with lists on them spread out between them.

Laryn opened the door to the inner office, turned back to the pages and said, "We're not to be disturbed unless there is a dire emergency, and by that I mean lots of blood or smoke."

The two pages grinned and the tension that had been in the air seemed to ease. The older one nodded at Laryn and said, "Understood."

The inner office was smaller than the reception area, but it was still larger than any office Kevin had ever worked in. Across the room from the door was a large executive-style desk, with a high back captain's chair behind it and three armchairs in front of it. Off to the side were two small secretarial desks with straight back chairs. One large table and several small tables were scattered around the walls.

Laryn motioned for Kevin to sit in the captain's chair behind the large desk. Chris sat at one of the small desks and Laryn collapsed into one of the armchairs.

"I suggest, for a while at least, you conduct business from this office and let Chris and the pages handle the outer office. It's quieter in here," Laryn said.

"But isn't this your office?" Kevin asked.

Laryn shook her head. "Not anymore. I cleared my stuff out last night."

"You didn't have to do that," Kevin protested.

"Yes, I did," Laryn answered. "You'll want to go through the letters in the top right-hand drawer soon, but they'll keep until after the funeral. Some of those letters have been in there for a year. Another week won't make any difference."

Kevin nodded. "When will the funeral be held?"

Laryn sat up a little straighter in her chair. "Next Saturday, the twenty-third of March. It's customary to have funerals within three or four days, but since Badec was the Master Sorcerer, we have to give people about a week's notice. I added the date of the funeral to the messages as I got them ready to go out last night."

"Where will the funeral be held?" Chris asked. "And what's involved?"

"The funeral itself is more like a procession than anything else. Sister Agnes has taken Badec's body to the chapel to prepare it for burial, and the body will remain there until Saturday. Neiven made a coffin for him a couple of months ago and it's already down there. Sometime around 10:00 next Saturday morning, the family will go down to Milhaven. By the way, Chris, as Myron's assistant, you'll go with us. At noon the coffin will be placed on the back of a wagon and we'll escort it to the family burial site, which is in the forest, about three miles from here. Mourners will be lined up on both sides of the road to watch the procession pass, but the only people allowed in the procession will be family, close friends, provincial sorcerers, Federation representatives, and district emissaries. When we get to the burial site, only family members will go in. I'll take you there sometime this week to make sure everything is ready."

Kevin nodded again. "How many people do you think will attend?"

"I don't know, but it wouldn't surprise me if there were a couple of thousand," Laryn said with a shrug.

"Do we need to do anything about housing or food for all those people?" Chris asked.

"No. The people of Milhaven will play host to the emissaries from the districts. The council sorcerers and Federation representatives will arrive that morning and leave shortly after the burial. The only ones we're going to play host to are family and close friends, and Housekeeping already has a list of those," Laryn explained. Then she took a deep breath and said, "I don't really know of any way to break this to you gently, so I'm just going to say it. By the day of the funeral, your people have to be ready to take over. While we're escorting Badec's body to the burial site, Governor Wrenn's personal belongings will be moved out of the governor's house and the new governor's belongings will be moved in. Captain Lawrence's things will be moved out of the guard barracks and the new captain's belongings will be moved in."

"So, I need to name a new governor and captain during the next week, right?" Kevin asked.

"No, you need to name them today."

"Today?! Why so soon?" Kevin felt panic begin to take hold.

"Because you only have seven days to make the transition, counting today. Governor Wrenn will need as much time as possible to bring the new governor up-to-date on matters that have not been settled. He'll need to discuss each of the eighty districts, the ministers, their concerns and problems, records of taxes collected, taxes due, who gets how much, finances for everyone on the government payroll, and probably a dozen more things that I don't even know about. And I imagine that Jana will want to meet with the new governor's assistant, too. She's been Governor Wrenn's secretary for the last ten years, and probably knows more about the mechanics of running his office than he does."

"Do you mean that as of next Saturday the new governor will be on his own?" Chris asked.

"Yes and no. The responsibility will be his and he'll have to make the decisions, but Wrenn's new house is right outside Milhaven. I imagine if you and your governor ask him to serve as an advisor for a year or so, he'll agree, but you need to make it a paid position, maybe pay him a certain amount for the entire year, or for each month, or maybe even for each consultation. I don't know how he'll want to set it up, but he's an honest man. He'll be fair."

"Okay," Kevin said slowly. "Should I approach him with that idea today, or should I wait and let him get to know the new governor first?"

"I'd wait until after the funeral. If your governor and Governor Wrenn hit it off, he might even volunteer his services, you never know. You might be able to make a similar arrangement with Captain Lawrence, but that will depend on where he ends up. I'm sure he'll have quite a few offers over the next few days."

"I know that General Crandal wants Captain Lawrence to take over as his aide. If he does that, he should be in the area."

"If he takes that position," Laryn replied. "He'll probably decide what he's going to do within the week,"

"What about you? I'm going to need a lot of help."

"I'll be around. I'll move into one of the family rooms for a month or so, and then I'll probably move into the guest wing, but I have no plans to leave the castle."

"Thank you," Kevin said, relief washing over him. "Now I've got another question. A few minutes ago you mentioned a Federation. What's that?"

"I wasn't going to say too much about that until you got past the April meeting of the Council of Sorcerers, but you represent the human race on the Federation. The Federation of Terah meets twice a year, usually on the first day of spring and the first day of fall. I filled in last spring and last fall, but they voted to wait until the humans had a functioning Master Sorcerer for this year's spring meeting. Since everything had to be settled one way or the other by the April meeting of the Council of Sorcerers, the Federation meeting was postponed one month, until the twentieth of April."

"Who's on the Federation and what's it for?"

"I'll go over all of the names and tell you a little about each one later, but each race and all magical animals have representatives. The main concern of the Federation is to preserve harmony and peace among the various groups. Humans can fight amongst themselves and the Federation won't interfere, but if it threatens to involve anyone else, or to destroy any of the lands, the Federation will take action. It was an informal group until the great magic war. After that, they took on the role of watchdog."

"I guess that makes me responsible for making sure the humans behave, all over Terah." Kevin was daunted by the enormity of the idea.

"More or less, but the other sorcerers on the council will help along that line. No one wants a war with the dragons, and the dragons see themselves as the final line of defense against destruction. They've agreed not to meddle in human affairs only as long as the actions of humans do not threaten anyone else. Even the slavers aren't willing to risk the ire of the dragons by trying to capture other races," Laryn explained.

"I guess you'll brief me on the council sorcerers before I go to that meeting, right?"

Laryn nodded. "And at some point I'll fill you in about each of the eighty sorcerers that you're supposed to supervise and help. Some of the ones from nearby districts will probably come to the funeral. We'll need to start going over all of that soon, probably tomorrow, but right now …"

"Yes, I know. A governor and a captain."

Laryn nodded. "The directors of Milhaven and a few of the other nearby towns will probably drop by sometime today to offer you condolences, as well as their help with housing and feeding the funeral guests. And don't be surprised if a couple of the local sorcerers come by to talk about Badec and welcome you to Camden. It's going to be that type of week." Then she stood up, stretched, and said, "I think I'll go get some sleep. You don't need me for what you have to do right now, and I haven't been to bed yet."

"Thanks, Laryn." Kevin nodded.

"See you at dinner, when I hope you can introduce me to the new Governor of Camden and the new Captain of the Guard. Good luck."

After Laryn had closed the door behind her, Kevin stood up and walked around his office to stretch his legs. "Do we ask Karl first and then tell Steve what we're doing, or should we talk to Steve first?" he asked Chris.

"You're afraid that Steve will be insulted, aren't you?"

"Yeah, I guess I am."

"I don't think you have anything to worry about there, but if it would make you feel better, let's find Steve and tell him what you have in mind."

"Would you go find him? I hate to send one of the pages."

"Be back in a few minutes," Chris said as he headed out of the office.

While Chris was gone, Kevin sat back down at his desk and began looking through the various drawers. In the small center desk drawer, he found paper, pens, ink, envelopes, and a wax seal that must have belonged to his father. It had a crest of some kind on it, probably the crest of the House of Nordin. He'd have to ask Laryn about that later.

A second drawer, the top right-hand drawer, held correspondence addressed either to the Sorcerer of Camden or to the Master Sorcerer of Terah. The ones that were in envelopes had not been opened. He felt sure that those were the letters that Laryn said he'd have to handle soon, but not immediately.

A third drawer held a stack of papers, covered in writing. As he looked through them, he decided that these were notes from the council meetings for the past few years. He decided to give them to Chris, let him read through them, and then Chris could tell him what he needed to know.

A fourth drawer held a bound book. When Kevin opened it, he realized that it was his father's diary for the past couple of years. He put it back in the drawer, but planned to take it to his room that night to read.

After he finished checking out the desk, he decided to look around the outer office. When he opened the door, there was only one young man left in the office and he quickly stepped forward to see what Kevin needed. He looked to be about seventeen years old. His blond hair was shoulder length with bangs that nearly hid his eyes and his facial skin looked so smooth that Kevin wondered if he'd started shaving yet. He wore a dark green tunic, black leggings, and black boots, just like most of the household staff that Kevin had seen so far. Kevin shook his head, and the young man walked back over towards the table where he had been working.

"I'm sorry, but I don't remember your name," Kevin said.

"Ariel, sir," the page answered.

"How long have you worked here?"

"Pretty much all of my life, sir. I started out helping my mother clean the guest bedrooms. Then when I reached ten, Badec let me start working in the stables. He asked me if I wanted to be a page when I turned thirteen, and I've been doing that ever since. He even let me go with him on a couple of trips," Ariel said proudly. Then, in a more subdued tone, he said, "I really liked him, sir. I hate that he's gone."

Kevin was quiet for a few minutes, not sure what to say. "I'd like for you to continue working in the office as one of my pages. Would you like to do that?"

"Yes, sir."

Kevin nodded and stepped back inside his office. Then he turned back towards Ariel and asked, "How many pages do I have?"

"Four, sir. Elin, Isak, Cameryn, and me."

"Are all of the pages boys?"

Ariel laughed nervously and said, "No, sir. Isak and I are the only boys."

"Do the four of you work here everyday, or is there some kind of shift rotation?"

"During the week, all four of us work everyday, but over the weekend there usually isn't as much going on, so only two of us work. We alternate weekends. I work with Elin, and Isak works with Cameryn."

"Where are the others today?"

"Earlier this morning Laryn asked the girls to go over to the aviary and help out with the falcons. We sent them out last night so they'll be returning this morning. Isak left a few minutes ago to go get the messages that have come in so far," Ariel answered. "I stayed here in case you need something, like coffee or food."

Kevin nodded. "I'm going to have a couple of conferences this morning, and I'd like to have something available for people to drink. Maybe they have some coffee left in the kitchen."

"Certainly, sir. Is there anything else you'd like? Maybe some pastries?"

"If they have some already made, but I don't want to put anyone to any extra trouble. If you don't see any, don't ask."

Ariel grinned and nodded.

Kevin hadn't been back in his seat for more than a couple of minutes when Chris and Steve walked in. Steve sat down in one of the armchairs while Chris took his seat at the small secretarial desk again.

"Kevin, I'm sorry about your father," Steve said. "From everything we've heard, he was a fine man."

"Thank you," Kevin said as he nodded. "Steve, there's something I want to ask you to do."

Steve held up his hand for Kevin to stop. "Kevin, before you go any farther, I need to say something. Tyree told me that you'll have to name a new Governor of Camden. I don't mean to sound presumptuous, but I really do hope you aren't considering me for that position."

"I'll admit that I've thought about it, a lot. You're better qualified to put a government together than any of us. You understand politics, economics, legal systems, all that stuff. You could definitely handle the job, but I'm going to be selfish here. I need you as my personal tutor, and I don't want you so tied up with your own duties that you don't have time to help me with things I don't understand." Kevin paused and then said, "Later today I'm going to ask Karl to serve as governor. I don't know whether he'll be willing to do that or not, but if he does accept the position, I'd like for you to serve as his advisor, too. We could inadvertently do some real damage here out of ignorance. Right now, I've got a lot of bits of information in my head, like pieces of a puzzle, but there are so many missing pieces that I can't get the big picture. Would you be willing to help us get a handle on things?"

Steve's relief was almost tangible. "I'd be happy to. Is there anything in particular that you want me to do?"

Kevin folded his arms on his desk and said, "Well, for one thing, I need a firm grasp of the laws here, of what's actually illegal."

Steve nodded. "Probably the best place to start would be with the decisions that the Provincial Court has handed down over the past few years. Tyree said that they have a secretary who records the facts of the cases and the decisions. Do you think I could get access to those records?"

"I'm pretty sure that I can arrange that. Let me talk to Laryn about it this evening and I'll try to set up a meeting with the chairman sometime tomorrow."

"That'll be fine," Steve said as he stood up. "You know, it might be a good idea to invite Tyree to join us now rather than have him wait until next fall."

Kevin nodded. "I hate that I didn't suggest that he accompany us. If he comes to the funeral with Glendymere we'll ask him then. If he doesn't, I'll send an invitation back with Glendymere."

"Then for now, I'll get out of your way. I think I'll take a walk around the gardens and maybe through the woods on the other side of the river."

"Want me to get someone to go with you?"

"No, I'll be fine. See you at dinner," Steve said as he headed for the door.

After the door had closed behind Steve, Chris said, "That went well, don't you think? Hope the others go as well."

"So do I. You want to see if you can find Karl and Joan now?"

"I told them that you'd need to see them after Steve. They should be here by now." Chris walked over to the door and opened it.

Karl and Joan were seated at the conference table, each with a plate of goodies in front of them. Ariel had two trays set out, one with coffee and scog, the other with pastries and fruit.

Chris grabbed a plate and started filling it up. "I could get used to this kind of service," he said with a smile.

"And gain twenty pounds," Joan moaned as she ate one of the pastries.

Kevin laughed. "Why don't you bring your plates with you and we'll go ahead and get started."

As soon as they were settled in Kevin's office, Joan said, "I don't know what you told Steve, but he was grinning like a Cheshire cat when he left your office."

"I asked him to do something for me that he's looking forward to tackling," Kevin answered.

"So, what do you want us to do?" Karl asked.

"I don't know how to ask, Karl. It's major." Kevin paused. This was even harder than he'd expected it to be. He felt that he already owed them more than he could every repay. What he wanted to do was give them a house, some land, and everything that went with it. Instead, he was going to ask them to put their lives on hold again and do even more for him. "I know you want to have your own farm again, and what I'm getting ready to ask you to do would mean putting it off for a while."

"I sort of figured that much," Karl said. "Go ahead. What's up?"

Kevin forced himself to look Karl squarely in the eyes as he said, "I'd like for you to be the Governor of Camden, at least for the next year or so, hopefully longer."

Karl frowned. "Kevin, I don't know a thing about politics."

"You know as much about being a governor as I do about being the Master Sorcerer," Kevin answered with a shrug. "Laryn said that Governor Wrenn would help you. He'll go over what you need to know, what you need to do, and so on. The job will be twenty-four hours a day, seven days a week, and that's an awful lot to ask, but I need someone I can count on, someone I trust. I really want you in that position."

"I'm guessing that there's some reason you either didn't ask Steve or that he turned it down. You know that he's the only one of us who's the least bit qualified to hold a position like that."

"I considered asking him, but I'd rather have him as an advisor for both of us than tie him down with the duties of one office, and although Steve is knowledgeable about government, you're a natural leader," Kevin replied. He waited a few minutes and then shifted his gaze to Joan. "Joan, if Karl accepts the position, would you be willing to be his assistant? It would be a full-time job, but I imagine Karl would be a lot more comfortable working with you than with a stranger."

Joan smiled. "I've been his secretary for years. That's a role I'm used to."

Kevin looked back at Karl. "You'll have to deal with problems from all over Camden, so there won't be much time left for all of the things you love to do. I know it isn't fair, and if either of you say no, I'll understand, but I really do hope you'll agree to do it. I wish I could give you days to consider this and discuss it, but I can't. I have to know your answer today." Kevin watched as Karl and Joan looked at each other with questioning eyes. "Actually, I need it now, so Chris and I will step outside and let the two of you talk about it."

As Kevin and Chris stood up to leave, Karl motioned for them to sit back down. "Are you sure you want us, Kevin? I'm just a simple farmer. I wouldn't know where to start."

"I'm sure, Karl. You're the one I want in that office."

"What do you say?" Karl asked as he turned to Joan and took her hand.

"Sounds interesting anyway. Sure, let's give it a try." Then she turned to Kevin and said, "On one condition."

"Name it."

"If you find someone that you think would be better at it, someone who could do a better job, you replace us. Right then. No guilt feelings, no loyalty issues, nothing. You just do it. Okay?"

"I agree. On that condition, we accept," Karl said with a quick nod.

"Deal," Kevin said. He stood up and reached across the desk for Karl's hand, shook it, and then shook Joan's hand. Then he sat back down in his seat and said, "Now for the bad news. You have to take over on the day of Badec's funeral, next Saturday."

"Next Saturday?!" Karl gasped. "That's too soon. We have no idea what to do!"

"I know. Same here. Anyway, let's go over to Governor Wrenn's office. Don't be surprised if he's already cleared his personal things out of the office. Laryn had all of hers out of here by this morning. From what she said, tradition calls for his stuff to be moved out of the governor's house during the funeral, and for yours to be moved in. They don't waste much time in transition here."

"Sort of like the Presidential Inauguration," Chris said. "Out with the old, in with the new."

"But there is one good thing about all of this, at least for Governor Wrenn. Yesterday Laryn told me that he asked Badec to let him retire a year ago, but Badec got sick before he could appoint a new governor, so it's not going to be like we're kicking him out," Kevin said as he stood up again. "After the funeral, we'll ask him to be available as a consultant for a year or so. Laryn seems to think he'll be willing to do that, but let's not mention it yet. If we're lucky, he might volunteer his services before we have to ask, but we'll work out some kind of payment either way."

Then Kevin, Karl, and Joan went across the hall to Governor Wrenn's office while Chris went off in search of Darrell. Governor Wrenn and Jana had finished packing up their personal belongings earlier that morning, so the office had a rather austere look. Governor Wrenn welcomed Karl enthusiastically and quickly took him into the inner office, while Jana took charge of Joan in the reception area. Before Kevin could get out of the office, Jana and Joan were huddled over a note pad.

While everyone was out of the office, Ariel had replaced the pastries with cheeses, raw vegetables, small meat sandwiches, and cookies. While Kevin was waiting for Chris to return, he fixed a plate and ate his lunch.

When Chris and Darrell entered the reception area, Chris eyed the tray hungrily, but since Darrell said that he'd already eaten, Chris opted to wait until after Kevin had talked to Darrell to fill his plate.

Kevin quickly filled Darrell in on the morning's activities and explained that a new Captain of the Guard would have to take charge as of Saturday. When he asked Darrell to take over that position, Darrell frowned, but he didn't say anything.

After a couple of moments, Kevin quietly asked, "Is there a problem, Darrell?"

Darrell's frown deepened. "I'm not at all sure I'm the right one for that job, Kevin. I don't know anything about protecting a castle or heading up a regiment of trained guards. Wouldn't it be better to get one of Captain Lawrence's men to take over? At least he would know the other guards, how they're organized, and their training routines. I feel like I'd be in over my head."

"You've handled security for us ever since we left the Gate House. I think you're the perfect choice to head up security here. And you won't be in over your head any more than the rest of us." When Darrell still didn't look convinced, Kevin added, "Darrell, more than anything else, I need people I know and trust around me. I'm not all that sure about what I'm doing either. If you agree to do it, I feel sure that Captain Lawrence will work with you and show you how he has the guard set up. And you know a lot about training. In fact, I feel sure there are a lot of things you could teach them."

Darrell sat quietly for a few minutes. Then he said, "How about if I agree to do it for now, until you have time to get to know some of the guards. Then, if we decide that I am in over my head, you can name one of them as Captain."

"Okay, but I bet you find that this is right up your alley. I really do think you'll make a good Captain. Now, let's go over to the guard office." Kevin stood up and led the way out of his office.

The guard who was stationed at the front desk in Captain Lawrence's office watched as Kevin and Darrell left the sorcerer's office and started down the hall. When he realized where they were headed, he immediately stood up and snapped to attention.

Captain Lawrence was sitting at his desk in the back of the room going over the week's schedule when his guard's reaction caught his attention. When he looked up and saw Kevin, he immediately stood up and walked around the desk to greet his visitors. After Kevin introduced Darrell, Captain Lawrence stepped forward to shake Darrell's hand, and at that point, Kevin backed out of the room, saying, "I'll let the two of you get started. Let me know if there's anything I can do."

Chris was sitting in one of the armchairs with a plate of sandwiches on his lap when Kevin got back to his office.

"What's next?" Chris asked as he picked up one of the sandwiches.

"I don't know. Maybe we should see what Theresa's doing and let her in on what's been going on."

"Oh, I meant to tell you. Theresa's not here right now. She and Sister Agnes took charge of Badec's body last night and General Crandal escorted them and the body to the Chapel of Light in Milhaven. She's still down there."

"From what I've gathered, Sister Agnes has spent a lot of time at the castle over the past year. Is there another sister who's been handling things in Milhaven?"

"According to Laryn, Sister Agnes handled both for several months but it became too much for one person, so the Sisterhood found someone to help out at the chapel. It was supposed to be a temporary thing. No one expected it to last this long. The relief sister came out of retirement and she is more than ready to go back home," Chris explained.

"Well, she should be able to now," Kevin said quietly. "Maybe I should go down there and thank her personally for giving up her retirement to help out. Do you know when she's leaving?"

"If Theresa has her way, not for a month or so."

Kevin frowned. "Why? What's Theresa got to do with it?"

"She and Laryn talked for quite a while yesterday afternoon. Laryn feels that Sister Agnes really needs to take a vacation before she takes over the chapel again, so Theresa said that she would handle the patients and staff at the chapel if the older sister would agree to stay on as a consultant for one more month. Theresa's not sure she's quite ready for the full responsibility of a chapel yet, but at least this way, Sister Agnes could take a break. She's going to talk to both the older sister and Sister Agnes about it today while she's in Milhaven."

"Good. At least one of us will be doing what she wants to do."

"Yeah. She really loves it, and she's good at it."

"It won't be long before the Sisterhood gives her an assignment," Kevin said with a sigh. "I just hope it's nearby. I'm not ready to split up our little group yet."

At that point, Ariel knocked on the door and gently opened it. "Sorry to disturb you, sir, but you have a couple of visitors who would like to offer you their condolences. Would you like to see them in your office, or out here?"

"And so it begins," Kevin said quietly. Then, a little louder, he added, "Thanks. We'll be right out."

~ ~ ~ ~

During dinner that night, General Crandal came by to tell Kevin that Badec's body had been prepared for burial. Kevin spent a few minutes talking with him and thanking him for his service to Camden while Badec was alive. Then he asked him to continue to serve as General. Although his position wasn't tied in to any particular sorcerer, Kevin sensed that General Crandal was pleased to have been asked to stay.

Later, while they were all relaxing after dinner, Laryn sat back and observed the way Myron and his companions interacted with each other and listened to their energetic conversations about the future. She felt that Pallor had done an excellent job in choosing Myron's companions, and doubted that he could have done any better if he'd had all the time in the world. She couldn't help but wonder if the elf had had any idea how things would turn out when he arranged for this mixed group to cross through the Gate.

After one last mug of scog, Kevin told everyone good night and said that he had some things that he needed to do. Before heading up the stairs, he made a quick detour into his office to pick up Badec's diary.

When he got to his bedroom, he opened the door only to find that none of his clothes were there, the bed had been stripped, and the washbasin and pitcher were gone. He backed out into the hall and stood there for a moment, wondering what was going on.

Chris, who had all the notes from several years of council meetings to read through, had followed him upstairs. He walked up while Kevin was standing in the hall, looking at the empty room.

"What's wrong?" Chris asked. Kevin stepped aside and pointed at the room. After Chris saw that Kevin's room was empty, he opened his door. His room was just as barren as Kevin's. "Where do you think our stuff is?"

"I have no idea. Think someone's trying to tell us something?"

"Wait a minute. Let me check on something." Chris headed back up the hall towards Laryn's room and opened her door. He saw his cloak hanging beside the door. The washbasin and pitcher that had been in his room that morning were now on the dresser in what had been Laryn's room. He opened the top drawer in the massive chest of drawers and found his clothes neatly folded. He walked over to the connecting door that led from the assistant's room into the sorcerer's room. When he opened it, he saw Kevin's cloak hanging beside the hall door.

Chris walked back out into the hall and said, "I think I know what's going on. Come on." Then he led Kevin to the door of what had been Badec's bedroom.

When Chris opened it, Kevin looked in. The room had been totally redone. Badec's bed was gone from the center of the room, and there was a completely different bed with its head against the north wall. Next to the bed was a massive chest of drawers, with his sword lying on the top. A new couch was on the east wall next to the door that led out onto the balcony. There were two armchairs facing the couch and between the couch and chairs, there was a long coffee table. Lamp tables were scattered around the room within easy reach of every piece of furniture. Along the south wall of his bedroom, next to the door that joined Kevin's room with Chris's room, was a large desk and captain's chair, just like the one in his office downstairs.

Chris sighed and said, "Well, I guess you're the Sorcerer of Camden now."

"Sort of scary, isn't it?" Kevin answered quietly.

Chris nodded. "They don't waste much time around here, do they? It's hardly been twenty-four hours since your father died."

"I know."

"What's that old saying? 'The king is dead; long live the king'? I guess this is 'The sorcerer is dead; long live the sorcerer'."

Chapter 50

The First Week

Monday morning, Kevin woke up before daybreak. He'd been in Milhaven less than seventy-two hours and already he felt like the weight of the world was on his shoulders. He had hoped that he'd have time to at least familiarize himself with the routines in his office before he had to jump in, but that was not to be. And after the funeral, he, Chris, and Steve would be the only Tellurians staying at the castle. All of the others would be scattered around, beginning their new lives. It was just too much, too fast.

He felt the need to do something that was comfortable, something familiar. As the sun started to rise, he made his way down the stairs and out the back door. None of the guards he passed spoke to him, they all granted him a respectful distance, but he could feel their watchful eyes following his every move as he crossed the backyard. Once he reached the river, he floated across to the other side and walked a couple of hundred feet downstream to a small grove of willow trees. Near the center of the grove was a small clearing, just large enough for him to be able to practice his magic without causing any damage. He felt completely secluded in the little clearing, free from the eyes of his guards as well as the castle staff.

It was the first time he'd had a chance to work out since leaving Willow Canyon, and although it took a few minutes to get into the routine, soon the familiar moves settled him down and he was able to close his mind to other things and focus on his magic. By the time he finished, he felt more relaxed and in control than he had since entering Milhaven.

When he returned to his room, he found Chris waiting for him. "Did you enjoy your workout?" Chris asked.

Kevin frowned. "Actually, yes, but how did you know?"

"I had a good view of the whole thing, as did anyone else who happened to be looking in that direction."

"What?! I thought I was hidden behind those willows."

"You were. I couldn't see you, but I could see most of what you were doing, and it looked good. No one who was looking towards the east this morning will have any doubt that there's a sorcerer in residence in the castle at Milhaven."

"I'm not sure if that's good or bad," Kevin said as he got dressed for the day. "Did you get a chance to ask Laryn about the court records yet?"

"During dinner last night. The chairman and the court secretary are supposed to come in this morning to meet with Steve and set up a place for him to review the cases. Laryn's going to handle the introductions."

"I'd like for you to go with them and sort of see what he's like. No one's said anything about replacing the members of the court and I'd like to leave it alone for a while if I can."

"What exactly am I looking for?"

"I don't know. Just check him out. I'm sure Steve will form an opinion, especially after reading the court decisions, but see what you think," Kevin answered as they headed down to breakfast.

Theresa joined them in the dining room, and after the others left, she asked Kevin if she could speak with him privately for a moment. When they got to his office, Theresa sat in one of the armchairs and Kevin sat down next to her.

"When I got to the chapel Saturday night, one of the aides handed me a letter that arrived a couple of weeks ago. I thought you might like to read it." Theresa reached into one of the deep pockets in her smock, pulled out the letter, and handed it to Kevin.

Theresa,

I hope this letter finds all of you safely settled in Milhaven.

When Macin came to Abernon in February, he lingered for quite a while in one of the taverns. After a few mugs of scog, he told those around him about a young sorcerer who had spent the last eight months in Willow Canyon, studying magic with Glendymere.

One of my aides was in the tavern and quickly came to get me. By the time I got there, Macin's audience had bought the lad more scog, hoping to loosen his tongue, and he obliged them. He told them tales of remarkable feats of magic, and said that the sorcerer must have some elven blood in him because he could create and stop the worst of nature's storms. He told of mock battles against bands of elves, dwarves, and dragons who came to Willow Canyon to help him train.

The longer Macin talked, the larger his audience grew. Finally one of the men asked who the sorcerer was and where he was from. Macin said that he had never heard anyone say where he was from, but he knew that the sorcerer was going to Camden and that both Blalick and Glendymere referred to him as Myron.

One of the men in the crowd asked if he meant Badec's son. Macin said that he didn't know, but that he had overheard his father say that Glendymere had said that Myron's power was even stronger than Badec's. Then another man said that Glendymere should know, since he had trained Badec. The men began to talk amongst themselves, telling newcomers the news, and repeating the stories to anyone who would listen. Soon the stories picked up a momentum of their own, and Macin slipped out of the tavern, hitched up his team, and quietly left town.

I feel certain that the evening was a well-planned performance, probably orchestrated by Glendymere. I'm not sure which of the young men traveling with you was Myron, but I felt that he should know that his reputation is growing throughout Terah as tales of his exploits spread from tavern to tavern. Before long, only the most foolhardy would consider challenging him.

According to the latest news from Trendon, Rolan has been told that the minstrels perished in a freak tornado along the Pooley River and has called off the bounty hunters and cancelled the reward. I imagine Myron had something to do with that, so I feel sure that all of you are safe.

My best wishes,
Evelyne

After Kevin read through the letter, he folded it back up and started to hand it back to Theresa. Just before she took it, he said, "I'd like for Chris and Laryn to read this if you don't mind. I'd like to get their reaction. I think it's good news, but I may be missing something."

"I know what you mean. I felt the same way," Theresa said with a nod.

"I'll get it back to you later."

"That's fine. I'm going back to Milhaven this morning to help out at the chapel. I'll probably stay there for a while if you don't need me here."

"As far as I know, everything here is as under control as it can be considering that none of us has any idea what we're doing, but if anything comes up, I'll send one of the pages to let you know," Kevin said as he walked Theresa to the door of his office.

A few minutes later, Laryn and Chris came back from the courtroom. Once they were all settled in Kevin's office, he looked at Chris and raised his eyebrows in an unspoken question. Chris grinned and gave him a thumb's up.

Laryn laughed and said, "Chairman Tremayne is one of the most levelheaded men I've ever met, and he and Steve hit it off right away. They'll work well together."

Kevin nodded, but he didn't say anything.

"I thought this morning might be a good time to go out to the family burial site," Laryn said, changing the subject. "Everything's fairly settled at the moment and no one who will be staying here has arrived yet, so neither of us are particularly needed right now."

"Okay. How are we going to get there? Shall I fly us out? Or should we walk?"

"Let's go by horseback. That's the way we'll go Saturday."

Kevin walked over to his door and opened it. Ariel stepped up to see what he needed.

"Would you go out to the stable and ask them to saddle three horses?" Kevin asked. Then he turned back to Laryn. "Do you have a particular horse that you want?"

"Ariel, ask if Corin's around. If he's not there, it doesn't matter. Oh, and we're going out to the burial site. Ask Miranda to fix up a basket for me to take."

Ariel nodded. "Shall I tell them to bring the horses to the front entrance?"

Kevin looked back at Laryn. She nodded, so he told Ariel that would be fine. "Let me know when they're ready."

"Yes, sir. Anything else?"

"No, that will be all," Kevin said as he shut the door. "I have something I'd like for the two of you to read while we're waiting. I'd like your reaction to it." Kevin returned to his desk, took Evelyne's letter out of the bottom drawer, and handed it to Laryn.

After she finished reading it she handed it to Chris. "I think it's good news. Anything that enhances your image is good."

Chris read the note quickly. "Looks like Macin took care of the problem of your reputation for us." Then he turned to Laryn and added, "We were wondering how to build up Kevin's reputation so that the other sorcerers would think twice before challenging him."

"Is there something I should know?" There was a twinge of alarm in Laryn's voice.

"Kevin's more worried about killing someone else than he is about getting killed himself, and that's the wrong attitude for battle. I keep hoping he'll get over it."

Laryn nodded. "Some of the other sorcerers may help on that score. A few of them are not exactly nice people. He'll probably get over it before too long. Badec did."

"I'm still here, you know. You don't have to refer to me in the third person," Kevin spoke up.

Laryn chuckled and said, "There's something I've been meaning to ask you. What name do you want to use? I know Kevin was your name on Earth and that's what your friends call you, but everyone here is expecting you to be Myron."

"Well, since half of Terah was out there trying to collect the bounty on Myron's head, it seemed like a good idea to be Kevin while we were traveling, but it really doesn't make any difference to me now."

"I would suggest that you introduce yourself to other sorcerers as Myron. They all know that Badec's successor is Myron, of the House of Nordin," Laryn suggested. Then she frowned and added, "Pallor was supposed to insist that your foster parents call you Myron."

"He might have tried, but they could get stubborn sometimes. My foster father's boss was named Kevin, and he gave my father a raise when he found out that I was named in his honor, or at least that's the story I heard. Anyway, I'll go with Myron officially, but I doubt if any of the Tellurians will switch to Myron."

"Tellurians. What does that mean?"

"It's just another name for people from Earth. We liked it better than Earthlings," Chris answered. "We came up with it when we needed a name for our minstrel group."

"Minstrel group?"

"Didn't Kalen tell you? We traveled to Sheridan as minstrels. You might say we sang for our supper." Chris grinned. "Actually, it was a lot of fun until we found out that Rolan had a bounty on our heads."

"Rolan? You mean the Sorcerer of Brendolanth?" Laryn said with a deep frown. "Is that what Evelyne was talking about? You were the ones all those bounty hunters were looking for?"

"In the flesh," Kevin said with a nod. "But Rolan thinks we're dead now, and I don't plan to tell him any different. Here's hoping no one recognizes any of us."

"Don't count on it," Laryn said, still frowning. "Things like that have a habit of coming back to haunt you."

Ariel knocked on Kevin's door and told them that Corin and the horses were ready and waiting out front.

"Who's Corin?" Chris asked after Ariel had gone back to his desk.

"He's a unicorn. We've been friends since I was a young girl. Don't let his gentleness around me fool you though. He can be quite ferocious if anyone makes him angry."

"Does he communicate telepathically like Xantha does?" Kevin asked.

"Yes, but unicorns seldom communicate with more than one human at a time."

"By legends on Earth, unicorns bond with maidens and stay true to one until she marries. Is that the case here?" Kevin asked.

"Not quite. Unicorns do bond with women, but the bond is for life."

When they went out the front door, Corin walked over to Laryn and nuzzled her cheek. Once they were all mounted, Laryn pulled Corin out in front and led the way down the road.

After they left the castle grounds, they rode through a countryside that was full of rolling hills backed by mountains blanketed with forests. Some of the hills had been plowed in preparation for spring planting and the smell of freshly turned soil lingered in the air. Other hillsides were dotted with cattle, horses, goats, and sheep. After a couple of miles, Corin turned off the main road onto a side road that quickly led into the forest and started up the side of a mountain.

About a mile later, the road opened into a small semi-circular glade that surrounded a gentle waterfall and splash pool. There were several small flower gardens and half a dozen stone benches scattered around the clearing, but the waterfall was clearly the focal point of the glade.

Laryn dismounted and stretched. "It is a lovely place, isn't it?"

"It certainly is," Kevin agreed. "How much farther do we have to go?"

"We're here."

After Kevin and Chris dismounted, Laryn pointed to a small shelf behind the waterfall and explained that there was a large boulder sitting on the ledge, covering the entrance to the cave that had served as the burial chamber for several generations of the House of Nordin.

"Today, you'll need to move the boulder so that we can go in and make sure everything is ready for the burial. Then on Saturday, once you remove the boulder, you'll lift Badec's coffin and float it into the cave. The only people who will be allowed to escort the coffin inside are his brothers, sisters, and you. Sorry, Chris."

"That's quite all right with me," Chris answered with a slight shudder.

"Myron, you'll have to stop the water long enough for everyone to climb up the steps behind the falls. Is that going to be a problem?"

"I don't think so. Here, let's try it now," Kevin said as he stopped the water and let the steps dry for a minute. Then he moved the boulder out of the way and held it beside the cave entrance. "Why don't you go on up and I'll join you after you get inside."

Laryn climbed the steps and disappeared into the cave. Kevin turned to Chris and said, "Keep a good eye out. I don't see anyone near here right now, but I don't know if another sorcerer might be able to block my eye. That's another one of those pesky details I forgot to ask Glendymere about."

Chris nodded and began to walk around the gardens while Kevin floated up to the ledge to join Laryn in the burial chamber.

There were quite a few heavy iron coffins lying on rock platforms along the sides of the cave, mostly in pairs. Laryn walked towards one pair of coffins near the back of the cave. "These are my parents, your grandparents," she said quietly. On the next platform there was only one coffin. "And this is Yvonne, your mother. Badec will lie beside her. We need to make sure that the platform is level and that the sides haven't eroded." Laryn ran her hand over the platform and looked along the sides to see if she saw any signs of weakness. "I don't see any problems, do you?"

"No, but then, I'm not all that sure what I'm looking for."

"Just look for loose rocks, cracks in the foundation, things like that. We don't want the coffin to fall off the platform. Wouldn't be very dignified." Then Laryn grinned and added, "Although Badec would probably get a kick out of it."

"Let me put a little pressure on it and make sure it's okay." Kevin concentrated on the air above the platform. He increased the pressure on the platform to several times the weight of a coffin just to be on the safe side. "Seems sturdy to me."

"When we get here, you'll be responsible for floating the coffin back here to its place beside Yvonne. Then, after he's settled, the rest of the family will leave. You'll be the last one out, and once you're back on the ground, move the boulder back into place and let the waterfall start up again. Just be careful when you release the water. Remember, there are going to be a lot of very good sorcerers in the crowd, including all of the seated sorcerers. You won't notice them, but they'll all be watching you. First impressions are always the strongest ones. You don't want to mess this up."

"I understand. I'll be careful," Kevin said. Then he looked around the cave at all of the coffins. "Sometime we need to come back so that you can tell me about all of these people. I really would like to know something about them."

"I'll be glad to," Laryn said with a nod. "But for now, let's get out of here and head back. We've got work to do."

After Laryn had joined Chris in the glade, Kevin floated down from the ledge, rolled the boulder back into position, and slowly released his hold on the waterfall. His release was so natural that neither Chris nor Laryn noticed that he'd let it start up again until he asked them if they were ready to go.

"We have one more thing to do. The local brownies tend to these gardens and make sure that the glade is kept up year round. I try to come out at least once a month and leave them a little something for their efforts. Over the last year though, I've had to depend on the pages to do it." Laryn retrieved the bags that had been tied to the saddle on Kevin's horse, walked over to what looked like a large tree trunk, and tipped it backwards. Under the tree trunk was a good size hole, lined with rocks. "Brownies leave holes at all their little gardens in the forest. People who visit are expected to contribute something to the colony of brownies that lives nearby. It doesn't have to be much, just a little gift to recognize the work that they do."

Laryn placed her gifts of breads, fruits, vegetables, and a few trinkets in the hole and replaced the tree trunk. Then the three of them quietly left the glade.

~ ~ ~ ~

By the time they returned to the castle, it was lunchtime. After they ate, Laryn, Kevin, and Chris secluded themselves in Kevin's office to begin going over the particulars about the different provinces and the seated sorcerer for each one. By dinnertime, they had only covered four of the twelve provinces.

Chris made careful notes while Laryn and Kevin talked, and after dinner he and Kevin went upstairs to Kevin's room to review them. They outlined the information for each province on one sheet of paper and information about the sorcerer on another.

After they had that day's information organized, Chris said "If you don't need me right now, I'm going outside for a while. I need to stretch my legs."

Kevin nodded. "I'm going to go over these sheets one more time. See you later."

After Chris left, Kevin sat down in one of the large armchairs with all four sets of outlines and started going through the first set. As he read through the notes on Jardin, the province that covered the lower third of what was known as South American on Earth, he fervently wished he'd paid more attention to Mr. Craven, his high school geography teacher. If he'd had any idea that one day he was going to need to know the location of mountain ranges, deserts, flood plains, volcanoes, and other geographical features, he'd have learned them then. As it was, all he'd ever done was memorize the information the night before the test and forget it by the time he left school the next day.

Kevin studied the outline for each of the provinces that they'd covered that day and then went back to the beginning to review them again to make sure he had it all straight in his head. At some point he became aware that his head was aching and his eyes were burning, but he kept on going. Later that night, sometime after midnight, he woke up, still holding the papers in his hand.

~ ~ ~ ~

For the next couple of days, Kevin rose early, ran through his practice routine, spent the day in his office listening to Laryn while Chris took notes, outlined the new material after dinner, and then studied the sheets until he couldn't keep his eyes open any longer.

Late Wednesday afternoon, right before dinner, Laryn finished going over the last province. She said that they'd spend Thursday and Friday going over the district sorcerers who lived close enough to attend the funeral.

"I have a question that I've wanted to ask you for a couple of days, but I didn't want to interrupt you to ask it," Kevin said.

"Go ahead," Laryn answered, raising her eyebrows.

"You talk about these far away provinces as if you've been there. Have you actually visited all of them?"

"Sure, most of them several times."

"How? Some of them are on the other side of Terah."

"With the key."

"The key?"

"Oh, that's right. You wouldn't know anything about the keys," Laryn said as she fingered a chain that she wore around her neck under her tunic. When she pulled it out, Kevin saw two keys that looked like old-fashioned door keys, one dark, the other silver. They were about four inches long, had a loop at one end, and teeth at the other.

"This one is the key to Terah," Laryn said as she fingered the dark key. "And this one is the key to the Gate Between the Worlds. They belong to you now." Laryn took the chain off of her neck and handed it to Kevin. "All you have to do is think of where you want to go on Terah, hold the key out as if you were going to unlock a door, turn it, and within a blink, you're there."

"What if I've never been to the place that I need to go?"

"Find it on a map and concentrate on its location. If you're not familiar with the place, the key won't take you to the center of town, or put you on someone's doorstep, but it'll take you to a clear area nearby, usually within a mile." Kevin nodded, so Laryn continued. "The key to the Gate works pretty much the same way. Just think of the place you want to go on Earth, turn the key, and you're there. Just be careful. Remember, no one on Earth knows about these keys."

"I don't understand how they work," Kevin said as he studied the keys in his hand. "Nothing Glendymere taught me would explain them. They're more in line with the tales of potions and spells on Earth."

"Actually, the basic idea is relatively simple. There's an energy flow around Terah, another around Earth, and one that flows between the two worlds. The keys let you into the flow. The trick was finding a way for the keys to open the door at the right time to let you back out where you wanted to go," Laryn explained. "A long time ago, a group of dragons, elves, dwarves, and sorcerers worked together to make four keys to the Gate, and each group kept one of them. Pallor has the elves' key, Palladin has the dwarves' key, Glendymere has the dragons' key, and the Master Sorcerer has the humans' key. Then, years later, the Federation used a similar method to make keys to Terah for all of their members and for the sorcerers on the council."

"So, if I wanted to, I could hold this key in front of me, concentrate on Willow Canyon, and go there?" Kevin asked.

Laryn nodded.

"Does Glendymere have a key to Terah?"

"Sure. He's the dragon's representative to the Federation."

"Then why did we spend hours flying to different places? We could have gotten there a lot faster with the key."

"True, but I doubt if you were really in that much of a hurry. It was better for you to get used to the idea of flying and to see a bit of Terah."

"Okay. I've got another question. I'll use the key to get to the council meeting, right?"

Laryn nodded.

"And Chris goes with me?"

She nodded again.

"Then doesn't he need a key, too?"

"No, you'll both use yours. You can take someone with you as long as they have physical contact with you."

"We need to try this out before we use it to go to the council meeting," Kevin said, glancing over towards Chris, who was nodding vigorously.

"We'll have time for you to experiment between the funeral and the meeting," Laryn said. "Now, let's go to dinner."

~ ~ ~ ~

During the day Wednesday, Badec's other brothers and sisters and their families had arrived at the castle, as well as some of Badec's close personal friends. Although some of them were staying with friends in Milhaven, they had all been invited to have dinner at the castle, so the evening meal took on a more formal atmosphere and Kevin wasn't able to slip away afterwards. He had to stay and play host.

Chris took the notes upstairs, outlined the information, and left it all on Kevin's desk in the bedroom. Kevin didn't get upstairs until close to midnight and by the time he skimmed through all of the notes, he felt like his eyelids were made of sandpaper. He covered his glowstones, and was asleep as soon as his head hit the pillow.

While he slept, he saw a young girl off in the distance standing near the edge of an empty field. As he drew closer he saw that she was older than he had first thought, probably in her late twenties. She had bright red hair that hung to her waist and eyes that flashed with hot anger.

Then Kevin noticed an older man standing on the other side of the field. He had red hair too, but it was darker than hers, almost auburn, and his eyes were as cold as those of a corpse. His features were harsh, like they had been carved out of stone. He was not handsome, but he had a powerful aura. His face was contorted with hate, and it was all leveled at the woman.

As Kevin watched, the two began to fight, and the magical energy was so intense that Kevin couldn't see what was happening. He awoke with a start before he could see which one survived.

Kevin sat straight up in bed, dripping wet with sweat. His head ached, his heart was pounding, and adrenaline was pulsing through his veins. He knew that sleep would be impossible, so he got up, dressed, left his room, and walked around in the back garden, waiting for dawn. He couldn't shake the image of the woman standing alone against such a man.

After Kevin channeled his pent-up energy into several vigorous magical workouts, he managed to convince himself that what he'd seen had just been a particularly vivid nightmare.

His day began as soon as he stepped into his office on his way to breakfast and remained hectic all day long as he played host to a lot of people who had known his father but who were perfect strangers to him. By dinnertime, all thoughts of the dream had faded. That evening he didn't manage to get to his room until well after midnight, and by that time he was so exhausted that he slept without any dreams at all.

~ ~ ~ ~

Kevin, Chris, and Laryn were working in Kevin's office shortly after lunch on Friday when Ariel knocked on the door to tell him that he had visitors, and to ask if he wanted to receive them in his office, in the entrance hall, or in the dining room. Before Kevin could answer, he heard Kalen's booming voice in the outer office.

Kevin and Chris jumped up from their desks to go greet the dwarf, but as soon as they stepped into the reception area, they both stopped dead in their tracks. Duane was standing in the reception area, too, with an older elf on one side of him, and one of the most beautiful women either of them had ever seen on the other.

Laryn stepped out of Kevin's office behind them and grinned at the stunned reaction they had to Duane's wife. Duane was the first person to speak. He stepped forward to introduce first his father, Hayden, and then his wife, Shelandra. Chris spoke to Duane and Kalen, and then told both Hayden and Shelandra that he was pleased to meet them, all without taking his eyes off Shelandra.

Kevin's fixation wasn't quite so obvious. He managed to tear his eyes away from her and look at each of the men as he said, "I'm so glad to see you. Are you going to come to dinner tonight? I know everyone else would like to see you, too."

"We'll come by to say hello, but we won't stay for dinner," Duane answered. "We'll be staying near Milhaven for a few days. We'll have time to catch up after the funeral."

Kalen nodded and said, "We just wanted to stop by for a moment, say hello, and offer our condolences. Laryn, I am so very sorry. I really don't know what else to say to you."

"Thank you, Kalen. It's hard, but it was time."

Kalen nodded. "Well, we know how much work you have to do, so we'll be on our way. See you tonight."

~ ~ ~ ~

After dinner that night, Kevin slipped out the back door and wandered down towards the river. *"Xantha, are you around?"*

"Of course."

"Where are you?"

"Look up," Xantha said. *"Come on up. We'll roam around the sky for a bit."*

Kevin flew up to Xantha and floated beside the pegasus, stroking his neck. *"You have no idea how much I've missed you."*

"I've been around, if not physically, mentally. I couldn't help but notice that you had a nice reaction to Shelandra. Unfortunately she's taken, but I'll be happy to be on the look out for someone for you."

"Don't start that again! I'm not ready yet," Kevin said with a chuckle and a shake of his head.

"Why don't you climb on board and let me do the work? You could use a bit of relaxation tonight."

Kevin climbed on Xantha's back, settled in, and enjoyed the feeling of soaring through the night sky. He hadn't had a chance to fly just for pleasure since he'd left Willow Canyon.

After about an hour, Xantha landed gently in the garden behind the castle.

"You seem more comfortable with your role on Terah now," Xantha said after Kevin dismounted.

"I guess I am. I still don't know what I'm doing, but I'm about to get used to that. I just hope I can do some good and don't end up a grease spot too soon," Kevin answered mentally.

"You'll be fine. Glendymere wouldn't have let you leave when you did otherwise."

"He didn't have much choice. I had to be here before the April meeting," Kevin pointed out.

Xantha shook his head. *"When we were there in November, he told me that if he decided that you needed more time, he'd keep you there and fly you out here right before the April meeting, so, since he let you leave in January, he must have decided that you were ready."*

"He didn't tell me that," Kevin answered slowly. *"All along, right up to the time that we left, he kept telling me that I wasn't ready for a challenge, that my only hope was to be just that bit more ready than the other guy."*

"Well, in a way, that'll always be true. I doubt if any sorcerer is ever really ready for a duel to the death, but with the reputation you've got, I doubt you'll have to worry about challenges for a while. Was that Glendymere's idea?"

"I don't know whether Glendymere had anything to do with it or not, but I know none of us did," Kevin answered. Then after a minute, he added, *"Or at least, I know I didn't. Do you think Chris might have been behind that one?"*

"I can find out for you if you really want to know."

"No, let it go for now. Maybe later. I guess I should go back inside. I have some more work to do tonight. Will I see you later?"

"Sure. We'll be here for a while yet. I'll be around, especially in the evening. Any time you want to take some time off, just call. See you later," Xantha said as he leapt up into the night sky.

~ ~ ~ ~

Saturday morning, Kevin woke up an hour before daybreak. Today would be his first public appearance as the Sorcerer of Camden and he was nervous. After he finished his exercise routine, he dressed in the dark green tunic with the red sash that signified his position. For the first time, he pulled his red opal pendant out from under his tunic.

While he was getting dressed, he heard a knock on the door. When he answered it, one of his guards told him that Freddy had a message for him, one that could not wait until the day was over. Kevin finished dressing and followed the guard up the steps to Freddy's tower. After they reached Freddy's roost, the guard quietly withdrew, leaving Kevin alone with the phoenix.

"Myron, I feel the presence of an evil heart nearby."

"How close by? In the castle?"

"It's not on the castle grounds, but it's close by, watching, waiting,' Freddy said, ruffling his feathers. *"I felt this same presence once before, the day before Badec was stricken ill."*

"Did you mention it to anyone?"

"No. By the time I realized that the evil presence might be responsible, it was long gone. There was no point."

"Do you have any idea who it is?"

"Today I opened my mind to his just enough to get a name. He calls himself Rolan. Beware of him, Myron. He means you harm."

"Thank you, Freddy," Kevin said quietly. "If you ever feel him close by again, please find a way to let me know."

Freddy gave one slow, deep nod in answer.

Kevin went back to his room. He wasn't sure what to make of it. No one had ever actually said that Badec was poisoned, not even his mother, but it was the only thing that made sense if Rolan was involved, and why else would he be slinking around the castle?

Kevin decided that he would have to think about it later, after he had gotten through the day. He didn't think he was in any immediate danger, and he felt fairly sure that no one would try anything during the procession, especially not with Glendymere around.

Another knock on the door interrupted his thoughts, but before he could answer, the door opened and Chris walked in with a mug of coffee in each hand.

"Today's going to be a long one," Chris said as he handed one to Kevin.

Kevin nodded as he took a sip.

"Kevin, today's going to be the first time the other sorcerers actually see you." Chris paused and sipped his own drink. "Actually, you're pretty much going to be the center of attention."

"I know," Kevin answered.

"They'll be watching your every move, especially at the waterfall."

Kevin frowned. "I know, Chris."

"I guess what I'm trying to say is, well, this is important Kevin. Don't screw it up."

Kevin rolled his eyes. "You and Laryn. She's already given me the 'don't mess it up' speech, the other day while we were in the burial cave. Believe me, I do realize how important today is."

Chris nodded. "Good. Just remember to make it look easy. And stay loose. As long as you're relaxed, I'm sure you'll do fine"

"Yeah, relax. No pressure at all. Right."

~ ~ ~ ~

After a solemn breakfast, everyone at the castle began preparing for the trip into Milhaven. The senior castle staff would attend the procession as it passed by the castle, and then they would move Karl and Joan's belongings to the governor's house and Darrell's things to the guard house. The staff at the Governor's house would take care of moving Wrenn and Jana's things to their new home, and Captain Lawrence had asked one of the guards to move his few possessions to the guest room that Darrell had been using in the castle.

By the time the procession returned from the burial site, tables of refreshments would line the road between the castle and Milhaven. The castle staff would handle the area around the castle, but the people of Milhaven would take care of the rest.

Kevin knew he wouldn't get a chance to meet any of the council members or Federation representatives that day, but before they left for Milhaven, he asked Laryn to point out Rolan. When they reached the Chapel of Light, Laryn saw Rolan standing off to the side, watching them as they rode up to the front door. She waited until they dismounted to tell Kevin where he was.

Kevin managed to look back at him without being obvious, turning as if to speak to Chris, but Rolan could hardly miss the look of shock on Kevin's face as their eyes met. Rolan was the man who had faced the young woman in Kevin's dream.

Chris saw Kevin's eyes open a little wider and his jaw drop a touch. Then a light flush crept up Kevin's neck and his cheeks reddened as he clenched his teeth and turned back towards the chapel.

Chris stepped up to walk beside him and whispered, "Are you all right?"

"I'm fine. Just thought I recognized someone in the crowd, that's all."

Chris looked at him with raised eyebrows, but he let it go.

A little before noon, the coffin was placed on the wagon, and one of Laryn's brothers climbed up on the wagon seat. Then Laryn and Corin moved to the front to lead the procession while Kevin and Chris moved their horses behind the wagon. The rest of Badec's family lined up behind them, followed by the council sorcerers and Federation representatives, with the local officials and emissaries from the various districts of Camden bringing up the rear.

After everyone was in place, a shadow fell over the wagon and coffin. Kevin looked up to see Glendymere slowly lowering his massive body until he floated about fifty feet above the wagon. Some of the horses pranced nervously, and a few of the mourners standing along the side of the road froze at the sight of the gold dragon, but for the most part, people took his appearance in stride. At precisely noon, Laryn began the slow ride out to the burial site.

Once they reached the glade, the family members dismounted and gathered around the wagon. Kevin stopped the waterfall, moved the boulder, and lifted the coffin. He floated the coffin to the entrance of the cave and held it there until Laryn climbed the steps and joined her brother's body on the ledge. Then Kevin slowly rose up to the ledge and stood on the other side of the coffin. Laryn and Kevin entered the cave, with the coffin floating between them, while the rest of their relatives followed.

Once they were all gathered around the platform where Yvonne's body had been laid to rest twenty-four years earlier, Kevin floated his father's body over to its final resting place. The family stood around the platform silently for a few moments, and then began to head back down to the glade.

Laryn and Kevin were the last to leave. While she walked down the steps, Kevin floated to a point over the center of the splash pool. As soon as she was down, he rolled the boulder back into place across the cave entrance and gently released the water, letting the waterfall cover all signs of the steps and cave entrance. During the entire time that the waterfall had been stopped, no one in the glade had spoken.

As the procession left the forest and approached the road that led to the castle, Glendymere spoke privately with Kevin. *"Sorry you had to step in so quickly, but you knew you wouldn't have a lot of time to spare. How are things going?"*

"All right, I guess, thanks to Laryn. I do have a question though. Can another sorcerer block my seeing eye? I hadn't thought about that until we rode out to the burial site earlier this week I didn't see anyone around, but I had the feeling that we were being watched."

"I imagine there were some brownies in the area and those were the eyes you felt. I've never heard of any way to block the seeing eye other than to cast a net, and you would have seen that," Glendymere answered. *"Now, unless you need me to hang around here, I'm going to head back towards Willow Canyon."*

"Wish I could go with you," Kevin said wistfully. Then he added, *"Would you ask Tyree if he would mind joining us as soon as possible? I know he said he'd come next fall, but we could use his expertise now."*

"I thought you might feel that way. I dropped him off at his home on my way here. He should be here in a couple of weeks."

"Thanks, and have a good trip home," Kevin said as the dragon began to climb into the sky.

Right before he vanished into the clouds, Glendymere said, *"Myron, the power flows strong within you, probably stronger than you realize, and the stronger the power, the greater the danger of treachery. Be careful. Watch your back."*

Chapter 51

Saturday Night, March 23

Earlier that morning, while Rolan was waiting for the funeral procession to begin, he observed the other seated sorcerers' reactions as they watched the young man who was to be the next Master Sorcerer take his place behind his father's coffin. Damien looked intensely relieved, Gwendolyn looked apoplectic, and the others fell somewhere in between. Rolan wondered what their reactions would have been had they seen what he saw earlier that morning.

Around daybreak, Rolan had made his way through the woods to a vantage point across the river from the back of the castle. His intention had been to find his source and pump him for details about Myron, but he'd ended up having a ringside seat for the sorcerer's morning exercises. At first Rolan laughed to himself that the Master Sorcerer of Terah was such a novice that he was still doing drills, but the laughter died in his throat when he realized that Myron was every bit as powerful as the stories claimed, if not more so.

Later, on the way back from the burial site, Rolan lingered around the refreshment tables near the castle and eavesdropped as the castle staff answered questions about the new Seated Sorcerer of Camden. He sneered when he heard the obstacle to his plans described as considerate, polite, and kind. Hardly the qualities needed by a ruler.

After a few minutes, Rolan figured he'd heard all he was going to hear, so he used his key to return to his office in Trendon.

He was annoyed to find Captain Yardner waiting for him.

"Sir, I hate to bother you, but you had a visitor a few minutes ago and I promised her that I would deliver her message at the earliest possible moment," Captain Yardner said.

"Oh? And who was this visitor?"

"Gwendolyn of Landoryn."

"Gwendolyn came here? Why?!" Rolan's frown was so deep that his eyebrows met.

"I'm not sure, sir, but she definitely wasn't happy. She wants to see you, today."

"Who does that woman think she is?!" Rolan said, sitting down behind his desk. He drummed his fingers on the desk for a few moments. "She didn't give you any idea what she wants?"

"None, sir. All she said was, and I quote, 'Tell him I want to see him, and I mean today,' and she was gone."

Rolan frowned. "Strange. I'd ignore it except that I am rather curious. Well, you've delivered the message. Was there anything else you wanted?"

"No, sir."

"Then you may go," Rolan said as he settled back in his chair to think. "And tell my pages that I want my dinner brought here, and I do not want to be disturbed until it arrives."

"Very good, sir," Captain Yardner said as he let himself out the door.

As soon as he was alone, Rolan got up and started pacing. He knew exactly what Gwendolyn wanted and he needed to figure out how to handle her before he went to Landoryn. He had all but guaranteed her that Myron would not show up at the April council meeting, and now that she'd actually seen him, she was furious that he was still alive, and for that she blamed Rolan.

It wasn't that she particularly wanted Damien to become the new Master Sorcerer, or even the five slaves a month that Rolan had promised to deliver once Damien did. She was angry because she hated Badec and everything connected with the House of Nordin. Rolan wasn't sure what was behind the animosity; it was possible that it went back several generations and was simply passed from one sorcerer of the House of Cornet to the next, along with Landoryn's seat, but no matter what its source, it was a powerful hatred. And one that he didn't want channeled in his direction.

He was going to have to convince Gwendolyn that this did not mean that he had failed; it was just a minor setback. There were other options, and he'd be quick to point those out to her, as soon as he could figure out what they were.

He was still pacing and trying to come up with a way to pacify her when his page knocked on the door to let him know his dinner had arrived. While he was eating, it hit him that the situation hadn't really changed. Whether Myron took his seat at the April meeting or not, his death would still leave the chair vacant. There was no other heir. Everything could proceed as planned.

All Gwendolyn had to do was be patient and give him time to arrange Myron's death. That should be simple enough to accomplish now that he knew where Myron was, especially with Captain Garen already in the area.

After he finished eating, he wrote a quick note to Captain Garen reminding him that he and his men were still responsible for Myron's death and emphasizing the price of failure. Then he sent for Captain Yardner.

"Send this to Captain Garen at once. At least now he can't tell me that he doesn't know where Myron is. He should be able to take care of his assignment within the next two weeks," Rolan said as he handed the note to Captain Yardner.

"Yes, sir. Anything else?"

"I'm going to Landoryn now. It's been a long day, and when I get back I want company waiting for me in my chambers. See to it."

"Any particular company? Or would you like someone new?"

"Someone new, I think," Rolan said with a smirk. "And pick her out yourself. The last one was a little hard on the eyes, if you know what I mean."

"Yes, sir," Captain Yardner said as he walked out and shut the door.

~ ~ ~ ~

Five minutes later Rolan was standing in Gwendolyn's office, listening to her rant and rave about Myron. Finally, after she'd pretty much exhausted her anger, he said, "You know, nothing's changed, Gwendolyn. He hasn't taken the seat yet."

"What do you mean, nothing's changed? Of course it's changed! He's the heir!"

"But if anything happens to him, the chair will still be vacant. He has no heirs."

Gwendolyn paused and thought about that for a moment. "You're right. All we have to do is get rid of him."

Rolan nodded. "And I have some men in Milhaven right now ready to do just that. They've been waiting until after the funeral to make their move."

"Good," she said as she sat down and motioned him to a seat. "When do you expect to hear that it's been done? Before the next council meeting, I hope."

Rolan nodded.

"And just how sure are you that these men you have in place are going to be able to kill him? Are they sorcerers?"

"No," Rolan answered, "but he's at home now. His guard is down. And I know that he goes outside by himself every morning to practice his magic. They can get him there, when he's alone. All the magic in the world won't stop an arrow if you don't see it coming."

Gwendolyn nodded. "That's true." Then she smiled a wicked smile. "Practicing his magic you say. Like drills?"

Rolan grinned. "Just like the novice he is. But at the same time, his power really is strong, stronger than I'd expected at this point."

"That elven blood!" she spit out. "He should not be allowed on the council, and he wouldn't be if it were up to the sorcerers today, but those fools hundreds of years ago decided to mark race by the father."

Rolan nodded and wondered if her hatred of everything that wasn't human might be behind her feelings for the House of Nordin, or possibly it was the other way around. Her hatred for Badec's family had led to her prejudices. Never mind. It didn't really matter.

"So, what's your backup plan?"

Rolan frowned. "What do you mean?"

"Well, there's no guarantee that your men will succeed. What are you going to do if they don't? If Myron makes it to the next meeting?"

Rolan hesitated. He hadn't thought that far.

"Oh, I see. You don't have one," Gwendolyn said with a frown. "I guess I could challenge him."

Rolan considered letting her do that. He'd seen Myron's magic. Unless he balked at the idea of killing, there was no way Gwendolyn or any of the other seated sorcerers could defeat him. But if Myron did freeze, and if Gwendolyn did become the Master Sorcerer, she'd find out about Earth and the key to the Gate would be in her hands. There would be no way he'd ever get his hands on it. No, that wouldn't do at all.

He shook his head and said, "You could, and I feel sure you'd win, but I thought you didn't want to have to deal with the hassle of being Master Sorcerer."

"I don't," she admitted. "I just don't want the House of Nordin to keep that chair." She drummed her fingers on her desk and then broke into a wide grin. "I've got it. I won't challenge him. I'll trick him into attacking me!" She stood up and started pacing around her office. "Yes, that would do the trick."

"What?"

"He's Badec's son. I bet he has all those same soppy notions about slavery that his father does. And I bet he's got a soft spot for the sisters, too, and if I went after their pendants, I imagine he'd jump to their defense. After all, it's Glendymere's flame that burns inside them, and everyone knows how the House of Nordin feels towards that dragon. I'll use that, too."

"To do what?" Rolan asked, frustrated that he didn't know what was going on in her head.

"Make him lose his temper, of course."

"What good will that do?"

Gwendolyn sat down and folded her hands on top of her desk. "If I can make him angry enough, I bet he'll throw an energy bolt in the council chamber."

Rolan narrowed his eyes and thought for a moment. Then he slowly smiled. "And before he even realized what he'd done, half a dozen energy bolts would be back flying at him. Do you really think you could do it?"

"No problem. I've had a lot of experience with young men and their tempers. My sons couldn't stand to be yelled at or ordered around when they were that age, and they hadn't been under anywhere near the pressure he's been under. It'll be easy to push him over the edge, and that'll be the end of the House of Nordin. Even if he does manage to defend himself, he'll be finished. No one could possibly object when we demand that he resign." Gwendolyn leaned back in her chair and smiled. "That would be even better than his death. The House of Nordin forced out of the council in disgrace. I love it!"

"Of course, he might not lose his temper," Rolan cautioned. "I think I'll still have my men kill him before the meeting."

Gwendolyn considered for a moment and then agreed. "But if he shows up at the meeting, he's mine."

Chapter 52

A Brief Respite

By the time everyone who was not spending the night at the castle had gone, it was well after sunset. Kevin and Chris dragged themselves upstairs and collapsed on the couch in Kevin's room, exhausted by the week as well as by the day.

A few minutes later, Laryn knocked on the open door and said, "I don't know about you, but I'm worn out. Let's take tomorrow off."

"I'm all for that," Kevin agreed, "and let's give the staff the day off, too. We can set the leftover food out in the dining room and let everyone fend for themselves tomorrow."

"That's a good idea. I'll go tell Miranda to let her staff know that they don't have to report tomorrow. What about the pages?"

"They need a day off, too," Kevin answered. "Housekeeping and grounds, too. The animals have to be cared for, but everything else can wait until Monday. Do you need any help letting everyone know?"

"No. I'll tell Neiven and Cryslyn on my way to the kitchen. They'll take care of letting their staffs know, and I'll tell the pages myself," Laryn said as she shut Kevin's door and headed back downstairs.

"What happened when we got to the chapel today?" Chris asked once he and Kevin were alone again.

Kevin told Chris about the dream he'd had Wednesday night and the conversation he'd had with Freddy that morning. "After Freddy said that Rolan meant me harm, I felt like I needed to know what he looked like, so I asked Laryn to point him out. While we were walking up to the chapel door, she told me where he was standing, and as I turned towards you, I spotted him. Our eyes locked and it was like the breath was knocked right out of me. He's the man I saw fighting that woman in my dream. I just wish I could talk to Yvonne and find out if what I had was a vision."

"I knew a girl in New York who had visions. She said that most of the time she didn't know the people involved. Sounds just like what happened to you. She thought they were just dreams, too, until she started paying attention to the newspaper."

"Do you think I saw something that's already happened or something from the future?"

"I have no idea, but if I were you, I'd assume it's from the future," Chris said with a shrug. "How old did you say the woman looked?"

"Late twenties or so. Other than that, all I can say about her was that she had long red hair, but I'd recognize her if I saw her."

Chris thought for a moment and then he asked, "Do you remember the girl Taelor told Karl about? Tsareth's youngest daughter. Rolan's sister. What was her name?"

"Landis," Kevin said quietly.

"Didn't he say that she would be twenty-five next year?"

Kevin nodded thoughtfully. After a couple of minutes he stood up, stretched, and said that he was going outside for a bit.

As soon as Kevin reached the gardens behind the castle he called Xantha mentally. Finally he heard Xantha's voice in his head. *"Why don't you come on up and meet me?"*

"I need to talk to you about something and that's easier on the ground."

After a couple of minutes Xantha landed beside him. *"Where are my oats? Don't tell me you called me all the way over here just to talk and didn't even bother to set out some food!"*

"Sorry. I didn't think about it. Next time. Look, I've got a question. You told me that we have a mind link. Does that mean that you see everything I see?"

"No."

"Well, if I have a picture of someone in my head, can you see it?"

"If you visualize it, I'll get an image."

"Okay. I want you to find someone for me. Taelor."

"Taelor?" Xantha asked. *"Who's Taelor?"*

"The guy who traveled with us for a couple of weeks last year. I'm sure I thought about him some, especially after he left in the middle of the night."

"You might have, but I don't remember every little thing that flows into my head from yours. Unless there's some kind of major emotion attached to it, it's in one ear and out the other, as you used to say."

"Oh. Well, he was an escaped slave, from Rolan's castle. I need to get a message to him."

"All right. Where is he?"

"I have no idea."

Xantha looked at Kevin for a couple of minutes, and then he said, *"Now, let me see if I have this straight. You're asking me to search for some guy that you knew a year ago, and all you know about him is that he's an ex-slave named Taelor?"*

"Well, I can show you what he looks like. Of course, he was half-starved at the time, and his hair was a bit scraggly, but it should help," Kevin said as he tried to bring up his memories of Taelor.

"You're trying too hard. Relax. Let the memory surface on its own." A couple of minutes later, Xantha said, *"So now I know what this guy looked like ten months ago, when he was in pretty bad shape. And you have no idea where he was headed, what he's doing, or anything else about him, right?"*

"I think he was going to look for Tsareth's youngest daughter, Landis. I don't know for sure whether or not he's found her, and to be honest, if he hasn't found her, then none of this matters anyway, but I want you to tell him something for me – if you can find him and if he has Landis with him."

"So I'm looking for the girl, too? And all you know about her is her name?"

"I know it sounds crazy, but Xantha, please! This is important."

Xantha lifted his head and stared straight into Kevin's eyes without saying a word.

After a minute Kevin said, *"Once you've found someone that you think might be Taelor, you can scan his mind. If it's Taelor he'll have memories of us, especially of Theresa."*

"You want me to search through the chaotic mess cluttering up his mind for some sign that he knew Theresa a year ago, and he only knew her for two weeks out of his whole life? Do you know how buried that memory will be?"

"You need to be sure you've got the right person, and that's the only way I can think of to check."

Xantha stared at Kevin. *"And you want this message delivered how soon?"*

"Well, as soon as possible."

Xantha snorted and tossed his head. *"What's the message?"*

"Tell him that I want to offer both of them whatever protection I can. Ask them to come here, to the castle. Please, Xantha. It really is important."

358

Xantha nodded once, stood there for a minute, and then leapt into the sky and soared towards the moon.

~ ~ ~ ~

Sunday morning, Laryn woke up as soon as the sun's rays penetrated her room. She decided to go down to the family gardens to see if the early spring flowers would lighten her mood. She'd been so busy since Badec's death that she'd had no time to mourn, and this morning his absence weighed heavy on her heart.

She followed the gravel path to the inner court, the circle where Badec had first announced his intention to foster his son on Earth. She thought back to before that, to the days after Yvonne had agreed to marry her brother, when happiness had settled over the castle, and then she remembered the shroud of sorrow that followed her death.

Badec had been very slow to recover, and for years did not seem to care whether he lived or died. A dark cloud had hung over the castle, dampening the spirits of everyone inside, until about five years ago, when he had begun to look forward to the future, to his son's return. His eyes had begun to sparkle with life again and there had been a new spring in his step.

To have his life cut down now, before he had a chance to get to know the son who had become his reason for living, was so unfair. Laryn sank to the ground beside the bench where her brother had always sat, folded her arms on the bench, laid her head on her arms, and let her grief engulf her. She cried until there were no more tears, and then she cried some more. Finally she was so exhausted that she fell into a light sleep.

Steve had taken his sketchpad down to the river around daybreak. After a couple of hours of walking and sketching, he headed back towards the castle. As he passed the gardens, he heard a light sigh, so he followed the path to the inner court, where he saw Laryn sitting on the ground with her legs curled under her and her head resting on her arms on a bench. She looked so vulnerable in her sleep. He wasn't sure if he should stay with her or leave her to her grief. He knew the desolation she must be feeling now that the ceremony of death was over.

While he was trying to decide what to do, Laryn woke up. She was embarrassed to find that she was no longer alone and she knew her puffy red eyes would make it obvious that she'd been crying.

"Don't get up," Steve said. "You look too comfortable there. I'll sit over here." He sat down on the opposite bench and took out his pen and ink. "I was just going to sketch a few of these flowers. Do you mind?"

"No, not at all," Laryn said as she stood up and stretched. "I used to do a little sketching myself, but it's been so long I doubt if I could do it now."

"Like a lot of others things in life, you never forget how; you just get rusty. Here, why don't you give it a shot?" Steve handed Laryn the sketchpad and pen. "I've already been sketching out by the river for a couple of hours this morning. I was actually on my way to get something to drink when I noticed that some of the flowers in here were in bloom, so I made a slight detour. Why don't I go get both of us something to drink? Would you like some scog? Or would you prefer something else?"

"Scog sounds nice," Laryn agreed.

While Steve was gone, Laryn looked through some of his sketches. She was surprised to see how good they were. She picked up the pen and started sketching the small clearing where she was sitting. Before she realized what she was doing, she had sketched her brother and Yvonne sitting on the bench on the north side of the circle. She was so absorbed in her sketch that she didn't hear Steve's footsteps on the gravel.

He walked up behind her and looked over her shoulder. "You're good," he said as he handed her a mug of scog.

"Thanks, so are you. I took the liberty of looking at some of your sketches while you were gone. I hope you don't mind. Have you ever tried painting?"

"Some. Not since Cathy died though."

"Cathy?"

Steve told Laryn about his wife. "You never get over losing someone you love, but you do move on eventually. It just took me a long time, and a tornado."

"A tornado?" Laryn asked with a light laugh. "What are you talking about?"

Steve told her about Paul and how he had managed to get all of the Tellurians on the same bus and then hit it with a tornado. As he told the story, Steve made the whole episode sound like a comedy of errors, including their first impression of Kalen as a mad hermit. Laryn was soon laughing over their first introduction to Terah.

"I'm surprised any of you stayed," Laryn said between chuckles.

"According to Kalen, going back was not an option, but none of us had anything to go back to anyway, except Kevin. It's ironic that he was the only one who was happy with his life on Earth, and he was also the only one who absolutely had to come to Terah. The rest of us were searching for a way out of the life we seemed to be trapped in," Steve explained. "After Cathy died, all I did was exist. I got up in the morning with the goal of getting through the day, and then I went to bed each night so that I could wake up and try to get through another one. Nothing was fun; nothing was interesting. I was ready to join her, and I probably would have before too much longer at the rate things were going. I have to admit that I've had a good time here and I have absolutely no regrets about coming to Terah."

"Tell me about Myron. What kind of man is he? How did he react to Terah? Most of our time together has been spent with me telling him about the people he's going to have to deal with. I don't feel as though I know him at all."

"I'm not sure where to begin," Steve said slowly. "At the beginning, at Kalen's, I think he was stunned. Finding out who he was, what was expected of him, was quite a jolt. But after the initial shock, I think he felt sort of betrayed, like he had been lied to all of his life, and then the guilt set in."

"Guilt? I don't understand."

"Everything that Kalen told us about Terah made this place sound really dangerous, and none of us figured we had much chance of surviving. Kevin felt that it was all his fault that we were even here, his fault that we were in danger. He tried to force Kalen and Duane to send the rest of us back to Earth by refusing to go along with their plans, but that didn't work because none of us wanted to go back. Once he realized that, he worked harder than anyone else. It really bothered him that he couldn't fight as well as the rest of us. He tried so hard to learn how to fight that we were all afraid he'd end up hurting himself, but you don't need to tell him that."

"I won't mention a word," Laryn agreed. "Go on."

"We decided to get a minstrel act together so that we would have a good excuse for traveling from town to town, and as it happened, we were pretty good, all except Kevin. He couldn't play any of the instruments, and he really is tone deaf, so he volunteered to work as our stagehand. When we were in towns, everyone thought he was our servant, so no one looked at him twice. All in all, it worked out pretty well, until Rolan put a bounty on our heads, but that's another story.

"Once we reached Rainbow Valley, Kevin worked on magic seven days a week. I don't know enough about sorcery to say how good he is, but I doubt if anyone has ever worked any harder at it, and it wasn't because he wanted to be the Master Sorcerer. He didn't, and probably still doesn't. He's not interested in power, and he's more than a little scared of the responsibility that goes along with it. No, I think he worked so hard to sort of hold up his end of the deal, like he owed it to us for some reason, or at least that's the impression I got."

"The seven of you seem to have worked really well together. Pallor did a good job choosing Myron's companions," Laryn said, more to herself than to Steve.

"Now, tell me a bit about yourself," Steve said. "I've been doing all the talking."

"There's not much to tell. I've worked with Badec since I was eighteen. My life has been defined by my role first as his assistant and then as his second. I don't know who I am without him," Laryn said as tears began to well up in her eyes again.

Steve nodded.

"His death just makes me so angry," Laryn said as she swiped at the tears flowing down her cheeks "I've kept the anger inside for almost a year now, but it hasn't gone away. It's getting worse, especially now that he's gone."

"It's all right to be angry with someone for dying and leaving you here to handle things alone. I was angry with Cathy for a while, too."

"No, that's not …," Laryn began, but immediately stopped herself. What was she doing? She'd almost told this complete stranger her deepest and darkest thoughts. But the longer they sat there in a silence that was more comfortable than it had any right to be, the more she felt that talking to him was the right thing to do. Finally she said, "What I was starting to say is that I'm not angry with Badec. I'm angry with the one who killed him." When Steve didn't immediately say anything, Laryn continued. "Sister Agnes and I have known that he was poisoned since a few days after he became ill, but we didn't dare tell anyone."

"Why not?"

"Because we can't prove it. And because we don't know who was responsible. There are a lot of people who would have been so ready to find someone to blame, some outlet for their anger, that innocent people could have gotten hurt. We couldn't say anything to anyone," Laryn said quietly.

"Do you have any idea what it was?"

"We think the poison was made from a rare mushroom called Sleeping Angel. It causes the mind to more or less shut down. The victim usually dies within a matter of days, or weeks at the most, but Sister Agnes came up with a way to feed him and give him water, and that kept his body alive. We moved him around a lot to keep him from getting sores and she spent hours every day moving his arms and legs around so that the muscles wouldn't draw up, but we've known the whole time that he'd never come out of the coma. No one has ever survived Sleeping Angel."

"And you're sure that it was deliberate? It couldn't have been an accident?"

"No, there's no way it could have been an accident," Laryn said forcefully. "Sleeping Angel doesn't grow anywhere near here. It doesn't even grow anywhere in Camden." Laryn sighed and stared out into the distance for a minute. "There was a mug of tea by his chair the next morning with only a couple of swallows gone. I think the poison was in the tea. It acts quickly, but it isn't immediate. He wouldn't have started feeling bad for a couple of hours."

"Does everyone know about Sleeping Angel?"

"No. I'd never heard of it, but Sister Agnes had. The valley where she trained is one of the few places on Terah where it grows wild. She nursed a few people who had eaten some of the mushrooms without realizing they were poisonous. That's why she recognized the symptoms."

"And no one else at the castle or in Milhaven got sick?"

Laryn shook her head. "There must have been just enough for one cup of tea."

"Is there any way to find out where it came from?"

Laryn shook her head again. "Local farmers bring us fruits, vegetables, and baked goods almost every day. Our cooks carry things to them, too. It's all part of being good neighbors. Someone could have given something to one of the kitchen workers and said that it added a lovely flavor to tea and suggested that they let Badec try it. Or some traveler could have traded it for a plate of food at the kitchen door." Laryn shrugged and then continued, "I don't even know for sure what form the poison would have been in. It might have been boiled down to a thin broth, ground into a powder, or possibly even dried and mixed with some tea leaves."

"And there's no way to find out who might have known about this poison?" Steve said as if he were thinking out loud.

"Not really. And besides, just because a person knows about the mushroom doesn't mean he's the one who poisoned my brother." Laryn shook her head slowly and looked at the ground. "Steve, no one intentionally poisons someone else here. It's unheard of. When someone on Terah wants to kill someone, it's either with a knife, his fists, a sword, or an energy bolt. Whoever this person is, he's really dangerous."

"You have to tell Kevin. He could be next."

"I know. I just hate to tell him something like this and not be able to point my finger at someone. I can't even say for certain that it was another sorcerer. It could have been planned by anyone, from anywhere." Laryn sighed. "Let him have today. I'll tell him tomorrow morning."

Chapter 53

The Sorcerer of Camden

After breakfast Monday morning, Laryn asked Kevin if she could speak with him privately, so they went into Kevin's office while Chris stayed in the outer office to help the pages get started on the task of answering all the notes that Kevin had received after Badec's death.

Once she was seated, Laryn said, "I have something that I need to tell you about Badec's coma." Kevin slowly sat in his chair and leaned back to hear what she had to say. When she finished explaining what she and Sister Agnes suspected, she said, "I have the feeling that nothing I've said surprises you."

Kevin leaned forward in his chair and said, "I don't know if you'll believe what I'm about to tell you or not, but Yvonne's spirit came to see me while I was in Rainbow Valley. She didn't much think the coma was due to natural causes either. She didn't have any theories as to what had happened, but poison makes sense."

"Did she have any idea who might have been responsible?"

"I'm not sure. I asked her, but she said that she wouldn't speculate about who might have been involved until we knew for sure what had happened. I got the feeling that she had some definite thoughts on the subject though."

"Do the others know about her visit?"

"Chris does. I kept meaning to tell the others, but it just didn't seem to come up." Kevin paused, trying to decide how much to tell Laryn about Rolan. "Saturday morning, before we went to Milhaven, Freddy told me that he sensed a heart of pure evil close by, and that he had sensed the same heart once before, the day before Badec became ill. When I asked him if he knew who it was, he said that it was Rolan."

"I wonder why he never told me."

"He didn't know who it was until this past Saturday."

"It's not proof, but it is interesting, isn't it?"

Kevin nodded. "We can't move against him without something concrete, but at least we have an idea where to look now."

"Is that why you asked me to point Rolan out to you in Milhaven?"

Kevin nodded again.

"I thought it was because he had put out a bounty on the minstrels."

"I would have waited for the council meeting had it not been for Freddy's warning. When I turned to look at him, our eyes met, and it was like two dogs sizing each other up, heading for an inevitable fight. I know that sounds melodramatic, but that's the way I felt. It was eerie."

"Don't underestimate him, Myron."

"I don't plan to. He's a dangerous man," Kevin agreed.

Laryn nodded and then said, "Shall we move on to the requests and complaints in the top right desk drawer?"

"Let me get Chris."

After Chris came in, Kevin took the letters out of the drawer and spread them out on top of his desk. "Maybe the first thing we should do is sort them."

"Not all of them have dates on them, but I did keep them in order. The most recent ones are on top," Laryn said as she stepped up to the desk to help.

"I was thinking more like easy to handle, need more information, need some thought, and then, in the last stack, those that we have no idea how to address," Kevin said. "That way we can get the easy ones out of the way."

Laryn nodded and said, "At least you'll be able to make a dent in the stack that way," as she began sorting through the letters.

A lot of the letters were complaints against district sorcerers who had overcharged for their services. Some of the complaints were made by individuals, but some were documented by district ministers. One sorcerer in particular had ten separate letters dealing with a variety of complaints resulting from his arrogance and greed.

There were also some letters from district sorcerers requesting transfers. Most of them were looking for higher paying positions, but a few were looking for less strenuous posts. Several letters were from young sorcerers asking for an interview, and one was from an older sorcerer asking that a new sorcerer be found for his district, as he and his wife would like to retire.

At the bottom of the drawer, there was a letter that was different from the others. It was written on high quality paper and had been sealed with a wax impression. When Kevin opened it, he found that it had been written by Robyn, one of Rolan's brothers. Robyn wrote that he believed that Rolan was directly responsible for his father's death and suggested that it would be helpful to interview one of the castle slaves, a man named Taelor.

After Kevin had read through the letter, he read it aloud to Laryn and Chris. "I wonder when this came. Is there any way to tell?" he asked Laryn.

"No, not unless the letter itself has a date on it. Was it opened when you took it out of the drawer?"

"I'm not sure. The wax impression was loose, but it hadn't been broken. There's no date anywhere that I can see," Kevin answered, handing her the letter.

"If Badec opened it before he got sick, he didn't mention it to me," Laryn said as she handed it to Chris. Then she looked at Kevin and asked, "What are you going to do about it?"

"Nothing yet. I'm not the Master Sorcerer until the sixth of April. We'll put it to the side for now, but I'm not going to forget about it."

By dinner, they had sorted all of the letters into stacks, tied them up into bundles, and stored them back in the drawer, ready to be tackled first thing Tuesday morning.

Most of the extra tables and chairs had been removed from the dining room so that one side was once again organized into informal sitting areas, and after dinner most of the residents and guests moved over to the couches and chairs to relax before heading upstairs to bed.

No one noticed that Steve drifted out one door a few minutes before Laryn slipped out another.

~ ~ ~ ~

Late Wednesday evening, Kevin was in his room reviewing the notes that he and Chris had made about the various provinces and their seated sorcerers when he heard Xantha's voice in his head. *"I'm back. Meet me outside the stable in ten minutes."*

Kevin rushed down to the stable, filled a bucket with oats, and set it beside a water trough. When Xantha landed, he headed straight for the oats. *"Ah, you remembered. We'll talk in just a minute."* A few minutes later, Xantha raised his head. *"Much better. Conversation always goes best with a full stomach."*

"I didn't expect to see you so soon. Did you find Taelor?" Kevin asked mentally.

"Of course."

"So quickly? I can't believe it!"

"What can I say? I'm good."

"So ..."

"Oh. Taelor found Landis last fall. The two of them are staying with her foster parents in a small valley along the west coast of Brendolanth. I asked if he remembered the minstrels he met last May. He didn't answer, but his thoughts were full of worry and fear that Rolan was trying to connect all of you with him. I told him to relax, that I was bringing a message from the one he knew as Kevin," Xantha paused while he drank some water. *"Somehow he had the idea that Karl and Darrell were in charge of the group, and that you were a servant. When I told him who you really were, he didn't believe me. I explained that you were on your way to Willow Canyon to train with Glendymere when he met you, but I don't think he ever did believe me."*

"What did he say about coming here?"

"He said to tell you thank you and that he would like to accept your hospitality, but that he needed to talk with Landis and her foster parents before making any plans. I think he wants to check all of this out. Anyway, I'll get back in touch with him in a couple of weeks and see what he says then."

"Good. And if they decide to come?"

"I'll bring them. Wouldn't do to have the two of them traveling across Brendolanth with a price on his head. Now, I'm going over to Duane's camp and get some sleep. Anything else before I go?"

"No, and thanks," Kevin said as Xantha took off.

~ ~ ~ ~

Badec's brothers, sisters, and their families packed up and left on Thursday. At breakfast Friday morning, Duane asked Kevin if he and his father could have a few minutes of Kevin's time. "We're going to pack up and head out later today, but there's something that we'd like to discuss with you before we go."

"Sure, just come by the office whenever you're ready. I'll tell Ariel to let me know as soon as you get there."

While the others told the elves good-bye and wished them a safe trip, Kevin and Chris left the dining room.

"Wonder what that's about," Chris said. "Should I stay or go when they get there?"

"Maybe you should hang around the outer office while I'm talking to them. That way you'll be close by if I decide I want you in there," Kevin answered. "While I'm busy with Duane, why don't you get the pages started on the letters we drafted yesterday?"

Chris nodded.

Kevin had just settled down behind his desk when Ariel knocked on his door to let him know that the elves had arrived.

After Duane and Hayden were seated, Hayden said, "I would like to ask you to consider accepting an apprentice. She's twenty-four now, but she'll turn twenty-five this summer."

"An elf?" Kevin asked in surprise.

"No, she's human. She's Tsareth's youngest daughter, Landis. My wife and I are her foster parents. I don't know how much you know about her half-brother Rolan, but he's a dangerous and evil man. If he finds Landis before she learns to protect herself, I fear her life would be forfeit. I hate to ask you to do this. I know how busy you're going to be, especially for the first few years, and I have to warn you that anyone who accepts her will be risking Rolan's wrath."

Kevin's jaw had dropped while Hayden was talking. He couldn't believe what he was hearing.

Hayden paused for a second because of the look on Kevin's face. He waited to see if Kevin had something he wanted to say. When he didn't, Hayden continued, "Duane and I have discussed this at length, and he feels strongly that you're powerful enough to protect yourself, Landis, and her other half-brother, Taelor, who will probably accompany her. I wasn't going to talk to you about this yet, but I was afraid to wait. As word of your exploits in Willow Canyon spread, I'm sure you'll have quite a few fathers approach you about accepting their sons or daughters as apprentices."

Finally Kevin spoke. "Tell me about Taelor. I think you said he is her half-brother? Does he have magical power, too?"

"No, he's not Tsareth's son. He and Landis share the same mother. When she died last winter, Taelor decided to try to find Landis. He's been with us in Crinsor Run since late last summer."

Kevin nodded. "Back to your request, I'll be happy to accept Landis as an apprentice when she's ready, but there is one problem. As you know, I'm part elf."

Duane held up his hand as a signal for Kevin to stop. "We know. I've already talked to Glendymere. He said that if you'd agree to let her apprentice with you afterwards, he'll take her next fall and teach her to gather and store energy."

Kevin nodded. Then he looked at Hayden and asked, "Have you discussed any of this with her?"

"Not really. I've told her that we were in the process of making arrangements for her to begin her studies next fall but we haven't given her any details."

"Do you think this is going to be acceptable to her?"

"Which part?" Hayden asked with a twinkle in his eye. "Studying magic with the most respected dragon on Terah, or serving as apprentice to the Master Sorcerer? I really don't think she could ask for any better tutors."

"I just hope I can live up to the title," Kevin said. "Fine then. Unless I hear something different, I'll expect Landis, Taelor, and anyone else she wants to bring in about a year or so."

"Probably not that soon. I imagine she'll be with Glendymere at least a year before she comes here. Anyway, we'll keep you informed," Hayden said as he stood up to go. Then he shook Kevin's hand and left the office.

Duane hung back for a couple of minutes. "Is everything all right? You looked almost in shock when he first told you about Landis. Are you sure you want to do this?"

"I was just taken by surprise. That's all. Tell me, do you know both Landis and Taelor?"

"Of course," Duane answered. "I watched Landis grow up with my baby sister, Rhianna, but I didn't realize she was Tsareth's daughter until Taelor showed up. I always thought of her simply as Rhee's friend."

"And Xantha knows them, too?"

Duane nodded and asked, "What is it?" puzzled by Kevin's questions.

"Nothing. It just explains a few things," Kevin said as he shook his head. "It's a long story, but last Saturday night I asked Xantha to try to find Taelor and offer him and Landis my protection. Anyway, Xantha never let on that he already knew them, or that he had any idea where they were, but when he got back Wednesday night he told me that he had talked to Taelor. I imagine you'll hear of my offer when you get home. Maybe you should warn your father. I guess I should have mentioned it to him myself."

"So that's where Xantha disappeared to. He told me that he was off on a secret mission for you," Duane grinned. Then he got serious again. "How do you know Taelor?"

"Have you heard about the reward that Rolan was offering for the group of minstrels? The ones that he thought had helped Taelor escape his bounty hunters?"

"Yes. He was determined to find them, but … you? The Tellurians were the ones who helped Taelor?"

Kevin nodded.

"But the minstrels were killed last winter, by a freak tornado."

"Let's just say that that's the second time a tornado has been used to imply that we were all dead," Kevin said with a grin.

Duane's eyebrows arched nearly up to his hairline. "You stirred up that storm?"

Kevin nodded again and said, "Ask Taelor about us when you get home, especially about Theresa. He's had some training as a chapel aide. They made quite a good team."

Duane left Kevin's office, shaking his head and grinning.

After Duane and Hayden left the main office, Chris went into Kevin's office, shut the door, and asked, "What was that all about?"

Kevin filled him in on Xantha's mission as well as Hayden's request.

"Are you going to tell the others that Taelor and Landis are coming?"

"Not yet. Maybe in a few months, provided we survive that long."

"Okay. Now, what do you want me to do about these?" Chris had a stack of letters in his hand.

"Which ones are those?"

"These are complaints of over-charging that were submitted by the district minister on behalf of the victims. I've pulled Laryn's notes on the individual contracts, and the minister's right in all of these."

"Send a letter to the sorcerer and a copy to the minister. Tell the sorcerer that he has one month to reimburse those people or else submit his resignation. Add a note to the minister's copy asking him to let us know one way or the other."

"You do realize that you're going to have some really angry sorcerers out there."

"I know, but do you see any way around it?"

"No, not really," Chris said. Then he pointed to another stack still on the desk. "What about these? These letters are complaints from individual citizens."

"Send a letter to the district minister asking him to try to find out what happened and mediate a settlement, but be sure you ask him to send us a complete report. Maybe, if we're lucky, we can stay out of those."

~ ~ ~ ~

By late Saturday afternoon, they were all tired from another long and busy week. Dinner was subdued, and soon after they finished eating, everyone drifted out of the dining room heading towards their bedrooms for a quiet evening.

Kevin decided to go to bed early and get a good night's sleep, but right after he stretched out on his bed, he noticed a faint glow near the balcony door. As he watched, the light grew stronger until he could make out Yvonne and a man standing beside her. The man was muscular and robust, and his hand rested on her waist in a proprietary manner. Kevin got up and sat on the edge of his bed, facing them.

"Myron. It's so nice to meet you at last," Badec said. "I've longed for this day ever since Duane took you away."

"You look much better than you did the last time I saw you," Kevin replied.

"I imagine I do," Badec said with a hint of a smile. "I remember you sitting with me and telling me all about your life on Earth and your adventures on Terah. I wish I could have been at the Gate House to welcome you, and that I could have been the one to introduce you to Glendymere."

"I do, too," Kevin agreed. When Badec didn't say anything else, Kevin said, "Mother, can I ask you something?"

"Certainly."

"I had a strange dream the other night," Kevin began. Then he told them about seeing Rolan and the woman fight each other. "What I need to know is … well … was that a vision?"

"From what you've told me, I'd say it was," Yvonne answered. "You're my son as much as you are your father's. You could have received the gift of sight from me."

"But nothing like that has ever happened to me before."

"A lot of seers don't begin having visions until they reach adulthood. I happened to start as a child, but there's no real pattern to it, and you may never have another one, or you may have them often. There's no way to predict the gift."

"What about the fact that I couldn't see what happened once the battle began?"

"That means that the end isn't written yet. As things stand now, the woman you saw in your vision will fight Rolan, but it remains to be seen as to which one will walk away. If the outcome had already been determined, you would have seen it, whether you wanted to or not."

"That's sort of what I thought," Kevin answered. "Shortly after I had the vision, I was asked to accept Rolan's half-sister, Landis, as an apprentice. I don't know for sure that she's the woman I saw, but I have a feeling that she is."

"I feel sure she must be. That's why you saw the battle. Her fate is basically in your hands," Yvonne said. "Teach her well."

"And beware of Rolan," Badec said. "He's the most treacherous of all the council sorcerers, although his magical abilities are not that great. He loves to stir up trouble and create tensions among the other members. He won't come at you directly, but watch your back whenever he's around. Gwendolyn is as bad as Rolan, but she's more direct, probably because her magic is a lot stronger. She'll come at you head on. And she has Malcolm in the palm of her hand. He'll go along with anything she wants. Damien is probably the strongest one as far as magical ability is concerned, and one of the most levelheaded, but you can't really look to him for much support. He'll do just about anything to avoid a confrontation. Overall, the best you can hope for out of any of the council sorcerers is respect, and you'll have to earn that, but don't expect loyalty or friendship from any of them, and do not ever drop your guard when any of them are around."

Kevin nodded and waited to see if his father had anything else to say. When he didn't, Kevin said, "There was a letter in your desk drawer from Rolan's brother, Robyn, asking you to look into Tsareth's death. Did you open it before you got sick?"

"Yes, I do remember something about that. I had some questions about Tsareth's death myself. Then, six years later, I received that letter from Robyn. I don't know if Robyn had just found out something that made him suspicious, or if he had questions all along. I didn't have a chance to talk to him before I got sick."

"Do you have any idea how you got sick?"

"Not for certain, and I had a long time to lie there and think about it. It had to be some kind of poison, but it wasn't one I'm familiar with. All I know for sure is that I felt fine when I went to sleep. Be very careful, Myron. Whoever murdered me will probably try for you, too."

Yvonne took Badec's hand as their images began to fade. "We must go now. We'll be back when we can. Take care, son, and good luck."

After they left, Kevin walked out on the balcony and looked at the stars for a while, replaying the conversation over in his head. Finally he went back inside, got into bed, and fell into a deep, dreamless sleep.

~ ~ ~ ~ ~

Tyree arrived Thursday afternoon, and after stopping by Kevin's office for a brief hello, went off to the guest quarters to get settled in. He joined the Tellurians for dinner and distributed the pictures Steve had left with him, as well as the presents Ashni had sent everyone, including some of her jams and preserves for Kevin, cookies for Chris, and the bedspread from their room in Rainbow Valley for Joan. Blalick had sent Karl some new woodworking tools, and Sari and Macin had sent letters to Theresa and Darrell.

After dinner, everyone lingered over scog for a bit, but then began to drift away. Steve clapped his hand on Tyree's shoulder, and said, "Let's go down to the court office and I'll show you what I've come up with so far."

Tyree gave Steve a questioning look, but followed him out of the dining room. Once they reached the court office, he said, "Steve, what are you doing? We aren't under any deadline here. There's plenty of time for us to review your notes. This isn't where you want to be, or what you want to be doing this evening."

"Of course it is. I've been looking forward to discussing these cases with you and getting your perspective."

"I don't doubt that old friend, but it still isn't what you want to do this evening. I saw the way you and Laryn were looking at each other. You need to spend the soft light of evening with her, not with me," Tyree said with a chuckle.

Steve sighed, sat down, and said, "Is it that obvious?"

"Oh, yeah. Only a blind man could spend five minutes around you two and not see that there's something happening there," Tyree said, "and that it goes both ways."

"You think so?"

"No doubt about it. I've known her most of her life and I've never seen her look at anyone the way she looks at you."

"I never expected to find someone else that I could care for like that. I thought after Cathy died …"

"I know," Tyree said. After a couple of minutes of companionable silence, he asked, "Have you told her how you feel?"

"No. I'm not sure it's a good idea."

"Why not? Aren't you sure how you feel?"

"That's not it. I know I'm falling in love with her; that's not the problem. I just feel like it's not fair to her." Steve sighed.

"Why? Has she implied that there's someone else? Well, I don't believe it. I saw the way she looked at you."

"No, nothing like that, but Tyree, I'm fifty-seven years old. What can I offer her? Maybe twenty, twenty-five years if I'm lucky? She's part elf. She'll probably live another hundred years. She needs to find someone who can be there for her to the end."

"You can't make that decision for her. Badec should have lived another hundred years, too. No one has any guarantees about tomorrow; all we have is today, right now."

Steve thought about that for a moment and then slowly nodded. "That's true."

"Look, it's your decision, but I think you should at least let her know how you feel. What have you got to lose? How many people get a second chance like this?"

Steve grinned. "Maybe I will."

"Good! Now get out of here. Find Laryn and walk in the moonlight," Tyree said as he stood up. "We'll tackle this tomorrow. I'm heading for bed. I've had a long day."

~ ~ ~ ~

A little while later, Steve found Laryn near the entrance to the gardens. "I was hoping to find you out here."

"I thought you were going to spend this evening with Tyree," Laryn said as she took his hand and turned to walk beside him.

"I had planned to."

"Then I don't understand. What happened?"

"Tyree saw us looking at each other at dinner this evening and pointed out that I didn't really want to spend my evening with him. He was right," Steve said as he turned Laryn around to face him. "I need to tell you something."

Laryn nodded.

Steve traced the side of her face with his finger, lifted her chin, and looked deep into her eyes. "I think I'm falling in love with you, Laryn. If you have any objections, you need to let me know now."

Laryn smiled up at Steve and said, "No objections at all. In fact, I find that idea rather intriguing."

~ ~ ~ ~

Friday morning, after Kevin, Chris, and Laryn were settled in Kevin's office, Laryn unfolded a large map of Terah and spread it out on Kevin's desk. She pointed to one of the smaller islands in the group that both Kevin and Chris recognized as the Hawaiian Islands and said, "This is Chamber Isle, where the council meetings take place. No one lives on the island except a colony of brownies and a few gnomes."

"Where do we meet?" Kevin asked.

"In one of the valleys near the center of the island."

"Where?" Chris asked. "I mean, in a building? Or out in the open?"

"In the Council Chamber. It's a pretty big building actually. It's round, maybe fifty feet across, and made out of stone. The roof is at least fifteen feet high in the center and made of thatch."

"Are there benches or something for us to sit on?" Kevin asked, still looking at the small dot on the map.

Laryn nodded. "You'll have a big stone chair. All of the seated sorcerers do."

"Do we just sit down anywhere? Or do we have an assigned seat?"

"They're assigned."

"How will I know which one is mine? Or do I just look for the empty one?"

Laryn shook her head. "Yours will be the largest one. You won't be able to miss it, and besides, I'll be with you the first time. I won't let you get lost." Then she pulled a sheet of paper out of her pocket and unfolded it. "Here's a chart of who sits where. I thought it might help if you knew where everyone sits before we get there."

"Thanks," Kevin said as he took it and studied it for a few minutes.

While Kevin was looking at the seating chart, Laryn turned towards Chris and said, "Each of the stone chairs has a desk and chair beside it for the sorcerer's second or assistant. One thing you'll both notice before long is that a few of the sorcerers will have a different person with them each time they come."

"From what Xantha said, I thought a sorcerer's assistant was supposed to be the person the sorcerer trusts above all others. How can that change all the time?" Kevin asked.

"It shouldn't, but they always come up with some reason why the current assistant can't continue to serve. Some of your colleagues have developed paranoia to an art form."

"Like I keep saying, paranoia could be the key to a long life on Terah," Chris said softly.

Laryn laughed and then turned back to Kevin, "After everyone's seated, I'll introduce you and you'll open the meeting by asking if there is any old business that needs to be revisited. If anyone has anything to say, they'll speak up. You don't have to worry that any of these characters are shy."

"What if I have no idea what they're talking about?" Kevin asked.

"Then listen. But if it really is old business it would be covered in my notes. Be sure you're familiar with them before tomorrow."

"Okay, I'll go over Chris's outlines and summaries again tonight, along with the notes on each of the seated sorcerers."

"After that, ask if anyone has anything new to bring before the council. You can count on something being brought up. Sometimes the things that are brought up are frivolous, sometimes downright foolish, but once in a while it's something important. Be sure you listen, and listen carefully. A lot of times you can prevent problems by hearing what isn't being said as well as what is. And keep in mind that your main role is that of facilitator, not critic, although at times you'll have to put a lid on things, just hopefully not at your first meeting."

"Agreed," Kevin said with a nod. "Anything else?"

"Not really. When no one has anything else to bring up, you thank everyone for coming and say that you'll see them next month, on the fourth of May. Then you stand up. No one is supposed to stand until after you do, so don't forget. I'd hate for all the sorcerers to be stuck sitting there, getting fidgety, just because you were so relieved to have it all over that you sat back in your chair to relax. Not a good beginning."

"No, that would be a bit embarrassing," Kevin agreed. "Chris, if I sit there too long, poke me."

"I doubt that that would go over too well either," Chris said.

"Pass me a note then," Kevin said and Laryn nodded. Then Kevin stood up, gathered up all the notes on his desk, and said, "If anyone needs me, I'll be in my room, studying for my debut as Master Sorcerer."

Chapter 54

The Master Sorcerer

Saturday morning, Kevin was out in the grassy meadow behind the castle before the sun came up, running through his magical workout. His nerves were raw from all the adrenaline pumping through his body, and his routine exploded with pent-up energy.

Chris was up early, too, dreading the day and excited about it at the same time. As he stood on the balcony watching the magical display across the river, he wished the other council sorcerers could witness what he was seeing. He wasn't positive that Kevin was the best sorcerer on Terah, but unless everyone around them was lying, he was one of the best, and this morning, he was better than ever.

Laryn was also up, standing near one of the back windows in the dining room watching Kevin's exercises. She, too, wished that all of the seated sorcerers could see her nephew in action. Then she would be able to relax. None of the others could come close to matching his power and control, and if they only knew that, no one would dare challenge him. Her only real worry was his reluctance to strike a fatal blow. That was the one thing that might defeat him.

When Kevin returned to the castle, he stopped by his office to look over the notes one last time. Afterwards he felt like he was about as prepared as he could get, so he went upstairs to get dressed.

Chris was sitting on the couch, waiting for him. "I noticed your exercises this morning. Quite a performance. You must have been feeling your oats today."

"I felt something, but I think it was nerves more than anything else," Kevin said with a laugh as he put on a new dark green tunic. "But it was a good workout. At least I feel better now than I did when I got up." He pulled the chain that held the pendant Glendymere had given him out from under his tunic and let the red opal fall to the center of his chest.

"I wish the other sorcerers could have seen it."

"I don't know about that. We don't know how good I really am. All we have to go on is what everyone around here is saying, and they could just be saying that to keep us from running for the hills."

"I was hoping you hadn't thought of that." Chris said with a grin. "But today doesn't have anything to do with sorcery. Today it's all about showmanship. All you have to do is radiate self-confidence."

"Too bad you can't pretend to be me. You've got enough moxie for both of us."

"Not really," Chris admitted. "It's easy to act that way when you know nothing is going to be aimed at you. If the situation were reversed, and I was the one front and center, I'd probably be hiding under the bed about now."

"Not a bad idea," Kevin said as he fastened the red sash around his waist.

"It's time for us to go down for breakfast," Chris said as he stood up. "You don't want to get a late start today."

"No, but I'm not at all sure that I want breakfast either. My stomach feels queasy," Kevin said, rubbing his hand over his stomach.

"Nerves. You need to eat something and give the stomach acid something to work on besides the walls of your stomach," Chris said. "Come on, let's go."

When they reached the dining room, everyone was waiting for them.

"We wanted to wish you good luck today," Karl said.

"And to let you know that we're all behind you," Joan added.

Steve nodded and said, "I just wish we could go with you."

"After all the hoop-la about this, it seems a shame not to see the big show," Darrell said with a twinkle in his eye. "Sure you can't take the Captain of the Guard with you?"

"No, he can't," Laryn said quickly.

"I was just kidding, Laryn," Darrell said.

"I'm sorry, Darrell. I'm just nervous. Don't take it personally. I know how volatile these meetings can get sometimes and I can just picture what would happen if the sorcerers brought guards with them. As soon as voices were raised, swords would be drawn, and then we'd have a lot of dead guards."

"Great," Chris mumbled under his breath. Then he looked at Laryn and said, "That's a detail you never mentioned before. Just how volatile are things likely to get?"

Laryn shook her head. "No one has ever gotten around to tossing energy bolts or anything like that, but there's a lot of arguments and yelling. I can't say that I'll miss going to those meetings."

Conversation eventually steered away from the impending council meeting and moved on to other topics while they ate breakfast. Finally, after everyone had finished, Laryn stood up, looked at Kevin, and said, "Well, I guess it's time for us to go. Are you ready?"

"I guess so. Chris, have you got something to take notes on?"

Chris nodded, pulled some paper and a couple of pens out of one of the large pockets on his tunic, showed them to Kevin, and put them away again.

"We never did get a chance to try this out," Kevin said as he took off the chain with the key to Terah and handed it to Laryn. "You know where we're going. I don't."

Laryn nodded and held the key in front of her. Kevin put his hand on one of her arms and Chris put his hand on the other. Laryn turned the key, and the three of them vanished from the dining room.

"What a way to travel!" Karl said. "Wish we all had those keys."

"I don't," Darrell said. "If we had them, so would everyone else on Terah, and I don't have any idea how we could make the castle secure if people could just pop in and out whenever they felt like it."

Tyree nodded and said, "And it's not really an easy way to travel either. It may be quick, but it rips your guts around and leaves you feeling like you've been torn apart. I hate it."

~ ~ ~ ~

By the time Tyree finished his comment, Kevin, Chris, and Laryn were on Chamber Isle. Laryn had taken them to a small clearing in the forest so that Kevin and Chris could recover in private. When they first emerged from the energy flow, they were all dizzy and disoriented, but since Laryn was used it, she recovered almost immediately. Kevin and Chris did manage to stay on their feet, but they stumbled around quite a bit as they tried to shake off the effects of traveling through a field of raw energy.

"That's why I wanted to arrive a little early," Laryn said quietly. "I didn't think you would want the more experienced travelers to witness your arrival the first time you zapped in."

"You're right about that. Man, I thought my stomach was upset before breakfast. Ohhh, it's no longer butterflies. There are vultures flying around in there now," Kevin said, as he rubbed his heaving insides.

"If you're going to get sick, do it now, before we get around the other sorcerers," Laryn warned.

"No, I'll be okay. Just give me a couple of minutes," Kevin said as he turned to Chris. "How are you doing?"

"All right, I think." Chris's face was pale and he had broken out in a sweat. "Did I forget to mention that I absolutely hate roller coasters?"

"I don't think that ever came up," Kevin answered with a faint grin.

"Roller coaster?" Laryn asked. "What are you talking about?"

"Where we used to live there were amusement parks with all kinds of rides. One of the worst was the giant roller coaster. You sat in little seats and were carried slowly way up in the air on a track, then the track swooped back towards the ground, twisting and turning as it went. They always made me nauseous," Kevin explained. "And apparently Chris didn't like them any more than I did."

"Well, get yourselves sorted out because we need to head over towards the Council Chamber. It's about half a mile from here."

After a few more minutes, Kevin and Chris were steady enough to walk, so Laryn led them down a narrow path that wound through the woods.

When they emerged from the forest, they were standing at the edge of the large circular clearing that surrounded the Council Chamber. They hadn't been standing there long before other sorcerers and their seconds began popping in. Laryn took Kevin around and informally introduced him to each sorcerer as he or she arrived, but not one of them had a welcoming smile or even a handshake. A few glared, but most seemed to look right through him, as if he were too insignificant to notice.

Precisely at noon, Camden time, a bell sounded and everyone began walking towards the chamber. Once inside, each sorcerer headed directly towards his or her chair and carefully took a seat on the hard gray granite. The name of the province was engraved on the top of each of the stone chairs except for Kevin's. His simply read "Master Sorcerer." Against the back wall, nearly hidden in shadows, was another chair that had "Camden" engraved on it.

Kevin took his seat and Chris sat down at the desk beside Kevin's chair. Laryn stepped up behind Chris and remained standing.

When everyone else was seated, Laryn stepped forward and said, "Presenting the Master Sorcerer, Myron, of the House of Nordin, Sorcerer of Camden." As soon as she finished speaking, she stepped back and took her place behind Chris. The council meeting was underway.

Kevin played his role flawlessly through the quick discussion of old business. When he asked if there was any new business, Gwendolyn flicked her hand to signal that she had something to say.

Kevin nodded towards her and she began to speak in a shrill and haughty voice. "I want a statement from the Council of Sorcerers condemning any and all assistance to escaped slaves, and I want this statement to specifically include Sisters of Healing who treat escaped slaves for either illness or injury."

Malcolm, the Sorcerer of Glyndal, quickly nodded in agreement but didn't say anything.

Kevin looked back at Gwendolyn to see if she was finished. She was looking at Malcolm like she expected him to add something, but when he didn't, she turned back to Kevin and stuck her chin out defiantly. He thought she looked just like the wicked witch from the Wizard of Oz, and it didn't help that her tunic was black.

"Yes, and we want you to tell Glendymere that he had no right to give them those pendants in the first place," Gwendolyn said indignantly. She might have been skinny and short, but her voice was piercing and there was no way anyone could ignore her. "You need to demand that he either confiscate them or give us something to neutralize them. We can't even arrest the sisters as long as they're wearing those things. They do whatever they want regardless of what we say, and I will no longer tolerate anyone living in my province who is not subject to my rules."

Several of the other sorcerers started nodding their heads in agreement with her statement, so Kevin stepped in and answered her in a quiet but sturdy voice. "The Sisters of Healing spend their lives helping others, and they wear the pendants only for protection, for self-defense. I can't understand why anyone would object to that, but I'll deliver your message to both Glendymere and Brena. Now, I need to know exactly who is registering the complaint." Kevin glanced over at Chris and said, "Please note that Gwendolyn of Landoryn and Malcolm of Glyndal are opposed to the sisters wearing pendants in their provinces." Then he looked back at the council members and asked, "Would anyone else like to join with them in their complaint?"

When no one spoke up, Kevin nodded and then directed his comments to Gwendolyn. "I feel sure we can reach a compromise and just not have those pendants in Glyndal and Landoryn. Would that help? Of course, that would also mean there wouldn't be any sisters in those provinces."

Gwendolyn shrieked, "You have to present our case to the Federation. Those pendants are in direct violation of the Federation agreement. You have no choice!"

Kevin waited a full minute, until once again, silence filled the chamber. "Actually, the pendants predate the agreement, so they fall under the grandfather clause. Therefore, there is no violation and no case to present. As far as your grievance is concerned, I told you that I would deliver your message just as soon as I return to Milhaven. Brena can notify the rest of the Sisterhood. Just be sure that you're willing to deal with the consequences. Now, once again, would anyone else like to join Gwendolyn and Malcolm in this complaint? No? Fine. Chris, make a note that the grievance is registered by the Sorcerers of Landoryn and Glyndal only, that no one else objects to the sisters' pendants."

Malcolm jumped to his feet and roared, "Now wait a minute. Wait just a minute here. What are you trying to do?"

Kevin kept a cool and steady gaze on Malcolm until he had taken his seat, and then he answered in an icy voice, "My job. I will not represent the view of two sorcerers as if it were the view of all humans, especially when it could have such disastrous repercussions. Anything else would be irresponsible."

Damien, the sorcerer of Nandelia, spoke up. "Maybe you should delay mentioning anything about the pendants until we've all had time to give this some more thought."

Kevin raised his eyebrows, looked at Gwendolyn, but said nothing. After a couple of minutes, Gwendolyn slowly nodded her head and then looked over at Malcolm. Following her lead, he nodded his head, too.

Then Gwendolyn looked around at the rest of the sorcerers and hissed, "Back to the issue of escaped slaves. We need to stand together on this."

Jason, the Sorcerer of Prosidian, spoke up. "Just what are you asking us to do?" Although his voice was loud, it was not belligerent.

Gwendolyn turned towards Jason. "Support the hunt for any escaped slaves who enter your province. Have your army and sorcerers assist the trackers. And help out in the search yourself if you can. We need to make a real commitment to returning escapees to their owners for execution. If we really go after runaways, we'll put an end to running."

Several of the sorcerers who had been uninvolved in the issue until now began nodding in agreement with Gwendolyn.

Kevin tensed as anger began to flow through him, and he addressed his remarks to Gwendolyn in a strained voice. "In Camden, we expect our citizens to fight all slavers who invade our shores, to resist capture, and if they are captured, to escape if at all possible. When slavers capture any of our citizens, our soldiers pursue them with two objectives in mind: first, to rescue the captives, and second, to apprehend the slavers. I feel sure that the citizens and armies of other provinces have similar orders." Kevin paused and looked around. Several of the sorcerers had frowned a little while he was speaking, but once he stopped, most slowly nodded in agreement.

375

After a moment, Kevin continued, "Now, if our citizens are encouraged to fight the slavers, and to try to escape if captured, how can we turn around and state that escape is a crime? Is it acceptable for a captive to try to escape from a slaver before he or she has been purchased, and only a crime after purchase? Exactly when does a captive become a slave?" He paused for a few moments and looked around the room as if he expected someone to answer him. "Does my saying that a person is my slave make him my slave?" Several of the sorcerers looked confused, so he added, "If so, then I could look at any of you and declare you to be my slave and there would be nothing you could do about it."

Gwendolyn visibly bristled, Malcolm's mouth dropped open, and several of the other sorcerers narrowed their eyes and shot him a look that dared him to try it, but no one spoke, so Kevin went on. "What reason can we give a man who lived, worked, and paid taxes in our province to explain why he must accept forced servitude in another province just because a band of slavers invaded his home? How can we tell him that he must accept losing his wife and children to slavers just because the army he's been supporting all of his adult life wasn't there to stop them? Do we not owe this man and his family our protection? Is that not what he paid taxes for?"

Once more Kevin looked around the room, taking the time to look into the eyes of every sorcerer who would meet his gaze. "Before we can say that escaping from slavery is a crime, we have a lot of questions to answer."

Then he leveled a cold glare at Gwendolyn and spoke with such a quiet authority that a hush fell over the chamber as the other sorcerers strained to hear his words. "I am speaking now as the Sorcerer of Camden, not as the Master Sorcerer. I cannot and will not honor any such agreement until I have satisfactory answers to all of those questions. In the meantime, anyone who tries to take anyone from Camden by force, or anyone who commissions someone else to take any of our citizens by force, will be considered a slaver, a criminal, and we will make every effort to rescue our citizens and return them to their homes, no matter where we have to go to find them, and if at all possible, we'll arrest the slavers and anyone else who is responsible for their capture. We owe our citizens that much."

A hush fell over the council chamber and the tension in the room intensified until the air seemed to crackle with it.

Then Trivera, the sorcerer of Wyndsor, cleared her throat and said, "We had an unusually dry summer this year, and when our crops came in, there was hardly enough to feed our farmers, much less all the townspeople. We need to barter with someone who has a surplus of food. Did any of you have a good harvest?"

Jason said, "We did. I'm sure we'll be able to work something out. Do you want to bring your governor to Wellbourne to meet with mine sometime next week? After we get the details worked out, you and I can transfer enough to hold your people until the boats reach Wyndsor."

Trivera nodded and said, "Thank you, Jason. I'll tell Governor Shardin the good news as soon as I return, and we'll see you in Wellbourne next Wednesday."

Geoffrey, Sorcerer of Havernia, added, "We have some surplus rice if you're interested. I'll check with my governor and let you know how much we can spare. Let me know how much you want and we'll see what we can work out." Trivera nodded to Geoffrey, thanked him, and then turned to her assistant to be sure that he had gotten it all written down.

Kevin asked if there was any more business that needed to be brought before the council. He waited a few moments to see if anyone else was going to speak, and then he thanked all the sorcerers for coming and adjourned the meeting.

Even if it had not been protocol, he would have stood up as soon as he closed the meeting. The stone chair was really uncomfortable. Kevin wondered if there was a reason for that, especially since all of the seconds had nice armchairs.

The sorcerers stood in front of their chairs, waiting while their assistants gathered their notes, and as soon as the assistants were ready to go, they followed their sorcerers out of the chamber. Kevin and Rolan were the last two sorcerers in the chamber and as Kevin passed Rolan on his way towards the door, Rolan placed his hand on Kevin's arm.

"You might want to reconsider your stand on returning runaway slaves," Rolan said in a pleasant tone.

"Oh? And why is that?" Kevin raised his eyebrows, lowered his eyes, and looked at Rolan's hand.

Rolan let go of Kevin's arm and said, "Out of deference to your father, I feel that I should warn you that you're making a big mistake by drawing a line in the sand and daring Gwendolyn and Malcolm to step over it. They would make formidable enemies. I'm just offering a word of advice out of friendship."

"Friendship?" Kevin asked. "Didn't you send out a couple of squads with orders to bring back my head?"

"There was nothing personal about that, but since you've been lucky enough to make it this far, you might want to be more careful about who you choose to go up against." It was all Rolan could do to keep the scorn out of his voice.

"I think I made my views clear enough. They're not going to change. But like you said, there's nothing personal about it." Kevin started to walk away, but then he turned back to Rolan as if he had just remembered something he wanted to tell him. "Oh, and while we're here, I guess I should tell you that I've agreed to accept Landis as an apprentice whenever she's ready to begin her studies."

"You what?!" Rolan sputtered. Then he tried to gain control again. "She's my sister, Myron. It's up to me to decide who she studies with."

"Your half-sister you mean, and actually I think it's her foster father's decision now that her father's dead. Anyway, we've reached an agreement and it's settled. Oh, and her other half-brother, Taelor, will be escorting her. I believe you've met him," Kevin said nonchalantly.

"Taelor?!" Rolan gasped as his face went red with rage. He snapped his jaws shut to keep from saying anything for a minute. Then he hissed through clenched teeth, "I'll have to insist that you return him to me. He's my property."

"Well, you see, this is one area where we disagree," Kevin said in a patronizing tone. "I don't believe that one person can own another, so that invalidates your request." An icy coldness crept into his voice as he added, "I've promised them my protection and I will perceive any move against them as an attack on me personally, so it might be a good idea for you to call off your bounty hunters and anyone else you've sent out looking for either one of them."

"You're making a big mistake here," Rolan growled.

"And you're saying that out of friendship, right?" Kevin asked sarcastically. He waited a heartbeat before he continued in a voice that was tinged with menace. "Is that the same friendship that had you skulking about near our castle the day before my father became ill?"

For a minute, Rolan stood there with his mouth hanging open, staring at Kevin. When he finally spoke, his voice was red hot, but there was a hint of fear under the anger. "Are you accusing me of something?"

"No, not yet. I'll be sure to let you know when I do though," Kevin answered evenly, turned away from Rolan, put his arm around Laryn's shoulders and walked through the chamber door.

Chris had been standing at his desk, a few feet behind Kevin, listening to the entire exchange. He acted like he was still gathering his papers while he watched Rolan out of the corner of his eye. He waited to follow Rolan out of the room rather than get in his way. He wasn't all that sure that Rolan wouldn't go after him out of spite.

Once Chris stepped outside, he found Kevin and Laryn waiting for him near the chamber entrance. Kevin turned to him, smiled pleasantly and asked, "Are you about ready to go?" while Rolan glared at the three of them from the other side of the clearing.

Chris didn't bother to answer; he just placed his hand on Kevin's arm and closed his eyes. When he opened them again, they were standing in Kevin's office. After his stomach settled, he said, "You really should warn me when you're going to do that."

"I'm sorry. When you put your hand on my arm, I thought you were ready to go," Kevin answered.

"I'm not talking about that. I meant that little conversation with Rolan."

"Oh, that. I couldn't warn you. I didn't know about it myself until it happened, but I have to admit it felt good."

"Well, you have definitely made an enemy out of him," Laryn said in a tight voice. "I wish you hadn't done that."

"He was my enemy before I ever heard of Terah, and we knew that going in. At least now it's all out in the open," Kevin said. "But I do have a question. What happens if I have an accident, or end up in a coma? Who takes over the Master's Chair then?"

Laryn sighed and said, "There is no one to take over. You're it. There's no one else who can step in. We'd all probably end up in the middle of another magic war."

"So all of this would have been for nothing?" Chris asked.

Laryn nodded. Then she looked at Kevin. "Myron, you need to find a wife, and soon. And you need to produce an heir. And until you do, you need to be really careful!"

~ ~ ~ ~

At dinner that night, Chris gave Tyree and the rest of the Tellurians a blow-by-blow account of the council meeting and the first part of the conversation with Rolan, but he left out everything about Landis and Taelor, as well as the bit about Rolan having been around the castle right before Badec became sick. They were pleased with the way Kevin had stood up to Gwendolyn, and since they were used to thinking of Rolan as an enemy, they weren't the least bit upset that Kevin had stood up to him, too. But Kevin couldn't help but wonder what their reaction would have been had Chris told them the whole story.

While they were drinking scog after dinner, Kevin heard Xantha's voice in his head. *"I'll be landing in about fifteen minutes. Want to meet me out at the stable?"*

"I'll try. If I'm late, don't leave. I'll get there," Kevin answered mentally. Then he said, "I think I'll go for a walk before heading to bed. It's been a rather long and exciting day. I need to relax."

Chris gave him a funny look, like he didn't really believe him, but he didn't offer to go with him.

By the time Xantha landed, Kevin was at the stable and had even managed to find a bucket of oats.

"You're learning," Xantha said as he began to eat.

"I'm surprised to see you. Is there any particular reason that you're here?" Kevin asked.

"As a matter of fact, yes. Hayden asked me to deliver a message," Xantha said as he continued to eat. *"He and Duane have discussed the plans with Landis, and she would be pleased to be your apprentice, provided you survive that long."*

"I don't think that last bit was part of the original message, was it?"

"No, that was from me. After all, I know what happened at the council meeting. Now Rolan will feel like he has to come after you. Congratulations. You went from being a minor irritation to being a major thorn in his side."

"I can always count on you to look on the bright side and make me feel better," Kevin said sarcastically.

"I do what I can."

"Everyone else thought things went well today."

"I bet Chris and Laryn weren't too pleased with that little exchange. Rolan is devious and clever, and as evil as they come. You need to be more careful around him. If he could get to Badec ..."

"Okay, Okay. Point taken."

"Now, on to more important matters," Xantha said. "You need to find a mate, and soon. We have no way of knowing how long you're going to last, making people mad like that, and you need to have an heir. And while you're at it, you need to give some serious thought to naming a second."

"You're a little premature there, aren't you? I don't have a wife, much less a child. And I don't need to name a second until I have a child, right?"

"That's true, but you don't want to wait until the last minute and let all the good people get away, do you?"

"Do you know something I don't?" Kevin asked with a frown.

"No. I just point out potential snags so that you can deal with them. Now, as far as a mate's concerned, the offer of assistance is still open. Just say the word and I'll have candidates lined up outside your door. You can take your pick!"

"Don't you dare!"

"Touchy, aren't you. Well, I'm off. See you soon," Xantha said as he took one last bite of oats and leapt into the sky.

Kevin wasn't ready to go inside yet, so he decided to walk through the gardens. While he was wandering around, he thought about what Xantha had said, about the people he trusted moving on with their lives.

Karl and Joan were already knee deep in the politics of Camden, but he doubted that they would be willing to devote more than a couple of years to it. Then they were going to want their own place, their own farm, and he couldn't blame them.

He had noticed that Steve and Laryn were spending quite a bit of time together lately. If anything developed there, would they be willing to stay at the castle? He doubted it. And Tyree had a home somewhere south of Milhaven that he would want to get back to before too long.

Darrell would probably stay at the castle for a while as Captain of the Guard, but he'd probably move on eventually, too. He was too restless to be tied down to one place for very long.

Theresa would stay in the chapel in Milhaven for a little while, but she was going to want her own chapel, and he had no doubt that the Sisterhood would find one for her.

Then he thought about Chris. When he had asked Chris to be his assistant, Chris had agreed to stay with him through the first council meeting. At the time, that had been enough. The April meeting had been their driving goal since the first day they had set foot on Terah and Kevin had never really thought about anything beyond it. He hadn't expected to survive to see that day, much less anything afterwards. But here he was. The first council meeting was over. They had made it. Now what? Did Chris think of this as a long-term position or did he have plans of his own?

As Kevin contemplated his uncertain future, his fingers found their way to the chain hanging around his neck. He chuckled as he thought about the key they'd used to get to the meeting, the key to Terah. What he really needed was a key to understanding Terah. Every time he thought he was finally getting a grip on this world and how to survive in it, something else popped up to point out just how little he actually knew.

Then his mind drifted to the other key, the silver one, the one that would open the Gate Between the Worlds, the key that could take him back to Earth.

Back to Earth. The thought whirled around in his mind. He could go home. They could all go home. He had a way to get them out of here, away from Terah, away from the dangers they faced every day just by being around him, and take them back home, back to electricity, cars, computers, microwaves, hot showers, television, telephones, and a thousand other conveniences that they'd taken for granted. They could leave the constant threat of magic wars and deadly energy bolts behind. They'd all be far away, away from Terah, away from Glendymere, and Xantha, and Blalick and his family, away from Duane, and Kalen, and Laryn.

The more he thought about it, the more uncertain he became. Did he even want to go back home? Would the others?

While he was pondering that, another, more disturbing thought crept into his mind. What if someone else got hold of that key? If he left, he'd have to give it back, and it would go to the next Master Sorcerer. Who would that be?

He thought back to the sorcerers he'd met that morning. If there were a magic war, which one of them would emerge the victor? Gwendolyn? His father had implied that her power was stronger than most of the others. What if she won? Or what if all the strong ones killed each other off and somehow Rolan managed to take the seat? What if Rolan had access to Earth?

Kevin shuddered as he pictured a sorcerer, any sorcerer, on Earth. A silent and invisible hand stealing anything, any time, from anywhere. Anyone who got in the way would vanish in a burst of light, and no police force or army would be able to do one thing about it. One quick turn of the key and the sorcerer would be gone in a flash, off to cause mayhem somewhere else.

No, he couldn't take the chance of unleashing anything like that on Earth. He'd have to stay on Terah, if for no other reason than to protect the key and see that it didn't fall into the wrong hands.

But what about the others? Should he offer them the chance to go back, or should he just keep quiet and see how things went? It was definitely something to think about, but it could wait until tomorrow. He'd had about enough for one day.

Kevin left the gardens and climbed the stairs to his room. He had just settled down on the couch when someone knocked at his door. As he started to get up, the door opened and Chris came in with a pitcher of scog, two mugs, and a few cookies. "I thought you might like a late night snack"

"Thanks," Kevin said, reaching for the tray to set it down on the coffee table. "What did you think of today, seriously?"

"I'm not sure. I think you handled the meeting just fine. And, like you said, we've known all along that Rolan was your enemy. My only concern is that now he knows that you are his enemy, and that makes him just that bit more dangerous. He would have found out before long anyway. I just wish we could have put it off for a little while."

"To be honest, I was sort of looking for a way to tell him about Landis and Taelor. I wanted him to hear it from me, not from someone else."

"I sort of figured that was behind the whole thing somewhere, but I still think we could have waited, a couple of months at least." Chris shrugged. "In the long run, I doubt it will make any difference, and you're right that it would have been a big mistake to let him hear about it from someone else." Chris handed Kevin a mug of scog and then fixed one for himself. They sat quietly for a few minutes, drinking their scog.

"Chris, I need to ask you something. When I first asked you to become my assistant, it was for while we were with Glendymere. Then, right before we left Rainbow Valley, I asked you to be my assistant here," Kevin began.

"And we said that I would until after the first council meeting."

"You said until after the first council meeting. What I said was to let me know if you ever wanted out. What I want to know is how do you feel about it now? Do you want out?" Kevin asked, almost afraid to hear the answer.

"Well, let's take a look at it. You've been the Sorcerer of Camden for right at three weeks. During that time, you've demanded that some corrupt sorcerers return money that they extorted from their neighbors and sicced district ministers onto some others. You've served notice to all of the seated sorcerers that from now on you intend to play havoc with the slave trade, at least as far as slaves from Camden go, even to the extent of marching into their homes to rescue any of our citizens who are being held there. You've infuriated one of the most dangerous sorcerers on Terah by granting asylum to two people he wants to see dead, and then you topped it off by letting him know that you suspect that he had something to do with your father's death. The way I see it, at the rate you're making enemies, someone needs to stick around to keep the knives out of your back," Chris said with a grin.

Then, after a couple of minutes, he looked at Kevin very seriously and said, "I've been truly scared more times in the past year than I have in the rest of my life put together. But I've also felt more alive, and I've had more fun than I've ever had before. I don't know what's waiting for us next month, or even next week, but I do know that I don't want to miss it. I'll be here until you kick me out to make room for someone who actually knows what he's doing. But even then, I'll be around if you need me. Like I said before, I'm in for the long haul."

~ ~ ~ ~

After Chris had gone to bed and the castle was quiet, Kevin stepped out on the balcony. He listened to the faint footsteps of the guards as they walked their rounds.

His thoughts strayed back to his life on Earth. He had been content going to the office during the day and playing on his computer in the evening, but in all fairness he had to admit that his life had been dull, even boring. No, even if he could, even if the key wasn't a factor, he didn't want to go back to Earth. There was no way he could go back to that now.

Chris was right. Life on Terah was scary, and it was often frustrating, but it was also exciting, and most of the time it really was fun. Kevin smiled as he thought back over everything that Chris had said, and although he had no more idea what the future held than Chris did, he was happy with his life. He gazed up at the same stars that he used to look at back on Earth while he was trying to figure out who he was and where he fit in. Now he had his answers. For the first time in his life, he really felt that he was where he belonged. He was home.

About the Author

Mackenzie grew up in a small town in the piedmont of North Carolina during the 60's, and after graduating from college, she returned to her hometown to teach high school. Thirty years later, after retiring from the classroom, she began to write.

Books have always played a large role in Mackenzie's life. She's been an avid reader since elementary school, and has always considered reading her favorite form of entertainment. Her goal in writing is to write books that she'd enjoy reading.

When she isn't working on one of her books, she likes to wander through the woods with her dogs. According to her, that's where some of her best ideas are born and begin to spin a life of their own.

For more information check out Mackenzie's World.

mcknzmorgan.com

Printed in Great Britain
by Amazon